— ALAN GOLD —
THE JERICHO FILES

HarperCollins*Publishers*

HarperCollins*Publishers*

25 Ryde Road, Pymble, Sydney, NSW 2073, Australia
31 View Road, Glenfield, Auckland 10, New Zealand

First published in Australia in 1993
Reprinted 1993 (twice)

National Library of Australia
Cataloguing-in-Publication data:

Gold, Alan, 1945– .
   The Jericho files.
   ISBN 0 7322 4994 5.
   I. Title.
A823.3

Cover design by Head Design
Typeset in Janson by Midland Typesetters, Maryborough
Printed in Australia by McPherson's Printing Group

9 8 7 6 5 4 3
97 96 95 94 93

'Joshua, son of Nun, sent two spies out from Shittim secretly with orders to reconnoitre the country. The two men came to Jericho and went to the house of a prostitute named Rahab, and spent the night there.'

The Book of Joshua
Chapter 2
Verse 1

The Jewish Community in Poland
Between the two World Wars

By the early 1920s, the Jewish community in Poland was already 10.5 per cent of the entire Polish population and numbered almost 3,000,000 people. The vast majority lived in major urban areas, but there were hundreds of small Jewish rural communities called *shtetls*.

The Polish Jewish community between the wars was far from unified, either politically or culturally. The population was composed of Communists, Zionists, Hasids, extreme right-wingers, centrists and revisionists.

In 1937, one of the leading Polish revisionist Zionists, Vladimir Jabotinsky, convinced that violence was the only way to create the Jewish State of Israel, planned to invade Palestine in 1939. Weapons for 10,000 men were provided for the invasion and the revisionists were preparing to smuggle guns into Palestine when the Second World War broke out.

MOSCOW, MARCH 1953

Josef Stalin's body lay stiff in its coffin, the skin blanched and waxen, the cheeks rouged like those of an ageing whore, the moustache carefully combed and held in place by pomade. A procession of mourners shuffled around the bier, held back from getting too close to the dead Father of All the Russias by tasselated crimson ropes draped around the dais. Four Kremlin guards stood at the corners of the catafalque, heads bowed low over their black and gold uniforms.

The mourners wore blank expressions, neither grief nor joy, as they prowled past. Only when a crew from the State Union of Cinema and Photographic Workers set up their camera and lights to record the grief of the nation, did the men and women bring out handkerchiefs to dry their tears.

The thin line stretched from the Hall of the Mourners out past Lenin's Mausoleum and deep into Red Square. Hundreds of thousands of people had queued all morning, and hundreds of thousands more would queue this afternoon to capture a glimpse of their father.

Deep below the State Chamber, in a dark and airless room, Lavrentii Pavlovich Beria sat with his feet up on Josef Stalin's desk. Plotting. His elbows rested on the worn wings of the armchair, his hands together, his fingers in a cathedral spire at his lips. Scheming. Before Stalin's festering body was even cold, he had to organise himself into the succession. First, he must amalgamate the MGB and the MVD, and increase the new body's powers. Appoint his men to positions of control. Then, when he was firmly in control of State Security, he could remove Krushchev, Molotov, Bulganin, Zhukov and the rest. And then there was the brat, Svetlana, disgusting fat little pig of a girl. A lifetime in Siberia should help her lose weight.

He smiled, and pushed the bell on Stalin's desk to summon

Petrovsky. Beria fancied a coffee. Petrovsky could fetch it, the jumped-up little … Petrovsky. Beria had forgotten him. Now there was another who would have to go. Hand in glove with Stalin. He pushed the button again, this time angrily. Where was he?

On the streets of Moscow, Andrej Krassovsky and Maxim Levchenko finished loading boxes and got into their car. All that morning, they had been heaving and carrying hundreds of files from shelves in the underground labyrinth. It was the first time that either had been allowed into Josef Stalin's personal file room. They drove speedily past the line of mourners, their car wheezing blue smoke as Andrej changed gear. Both men looked at the crowd with disinterest. They had been up since three this morning and spent four hours putting files into packing cases, sealing them, and leaving the Lubyanka by a rarely used back door. They were tired, dirty, and wanted to go home so they could get some sleep.

Two streets west of Red Square, the car pulled up outside an apartment block. The streets were empty. Everyone in Moscow seemed to be in Red Square, saying goodbye to the poisonous old bastard. A young man in the uniform of a colonel-general in the MGB came out onto the pavement, and waved them impatiently inside. It took them another fifteen minutes before they had carried all the crates upstairs.

Sweating and panting, they bade him goodbye.

'I have another job for you to do,' he said, locking the front door of the apartment block. Both men expressed their anger and frustration.

'But General,' said Maxim, 'we haven't slept all night.' The officer shrugged his shoulders.

'How long will this take, sir?' asked Andrej.

'An hour, two at the most. It's my dacha. There are papers there that I need urgently. We'll go in your car; then you can drop me back here. Take tomorrow off. I've already attended to all the details.'

They smiled in gratitude. A day off! Andrej drove out of the centre of Moscow on deserted roads until they came to woods to the east of the city. The general instructed him where to go. Left, left again, then right and finally left onto a narrow track. The trees grew denser, more menacing. The two men searched the vicinity for dachas. There were none.

'Stop!' said the General from the back. Andrej and Maxim looked around to question the instruction, but the young man had a pistol, pointing in their direction.

'Out!' he ordered.

'But …'

'*Out!*', he shouted, in anger.

'I don't understand,' said Maxim.

'Get out, and walk up that ridge,' said the General, waving the barrel of the pistol towards a hill to the right.

Both men were speechless, too terrified to argue. They climbed mechanically out of the car. As they did so, the General quickly got out of the back, keeping the gun trained on them. Both men slowly walked up the small incline until they reached the top. Andrej looked down the other side of the hill and saw a large, freshly dug grave. His eyes widened in horror, and he turned round to beg, but the bullet caught him in the chest, lifting him off the ground, and spinning him around. He toppled down the hill. Maxim gaped in shock, and the second bullet blew away his face and part of his skull. Both bodies rolled together down the decline.

Colonel-General Petrovsky casually walked over the crest of the hill, and grunted as he saw that the bodies had not fallen neatly into the graves as he had planned. He put the gun back into his pocket and walked down to where he had left the spade.

CHAPTER ONE

It was dawn, and it was dusk.

In the beginning there was Jerusalem. It always had been and it always would be. Jerusalem, the city of gold. The home of three ways to God. Judaism, Christianity and Islam. The Father, the Son, and the Spirit.

Dawn was rising over the city and the first horizontal rays lit the top of the minarets. Candles burning above the city. Elderly *muezzins* climbed the circular towers. With agony written on their faces, their mouths distended to create the sounds which had flowed over the rooftops for more than a thousand years, they called the faithful to prayer. Canticles made spectral by the loudspeakers, a legacy of the twentieth century. Boys from Jewish rabbinic academies struggled into their long white socks, black frockcoats and vestments before going to the Wailing Wall to pray. Greek, Russian, Roman and Armenian Orthodox priests led congregants in a swelling of prayer. And traffic spilled out of homes onto the streets as a cityful of residents began yet another midsummer day of work.

Jerusalem, where King David lusted for Bathsheba, where the first and second temples of the Jews were built, where Jesus the Messiah and his apostles brought new hope to humanity and where the Prophet Mohammed rested overnight before ascending to Heaven. Jerusalem was preparing to enter a new phase.

Soon, an expectant world would act as witness to the resolution of a conflict as old as human history. The ancient city at the crossroads of civilisation would at last find peace. The prophets, judges and kings of a hundred million people would gather in an arid wasteland of hate to begin a journey towards a new epiphany—Jerusalem belonged to all mankind, and not just to one nation.

A thousand miles away, on the island of Cyprus, men were gathering to decide the fate of Jerusalem of gold.

Even at 9 a.m. the temperature on Mount Olympia had soared and the tension was enervating. The air which usually surrounded the Hotel Akrotiri, which straddled the top of the Cypriot mountainside, was renowned for its clarity. Its quality had stimulated painters, sculptors and writers since the first flowerings of culture three thousand years earlier; but today the air was angry, tense, and full of electricity, the precursor to monumental events. The chirping of cicadas and the buzzing of flies prompted an eerie, surreal sensation—the foreboding which people experience moments before a disaster.

But even the noise of the insects ceased as silence descended upon the empty courtyard of the hotel. Outside, where Mercedes limousines, Jaguars and BMWs usually stood, not a car was to be seen. The only movement in the grounds was the patrolling of menacing teams of security guards, whose *de rigueur* black business suits, thin black ties and black wraparound sunglasses were in stark contrast to the blinding whiteness of the marble.

Everyone was awaiting the arrival of the motorcade.

The Hotel Akrotiri, a new development in an ancient land, had seen many important comings and goings since it was built five years earlier, but none quite like this. The site for the conference had been carefully selected because of its convenience to the Arab world, and because it could be hermetically isolated to protect those leaders whose lives were likely to be ended in a split second by a bullet from any one of a dozen assassination squads. In December 1975 the Venezuelan terrorist, Carlos the Jackal, had abducted thirty-five OPEC delegates from their meeting in Vienna, making the Austrian Chancellor a laughing-stock. The Cyprian President did not intend to make the same mistake.

For a week now, the hotel had lived an unnatural existence, empty of the usual influx of tourists. The Hotel Akrotiri was shrouded in a mood of claustrophobia at odds with the summer frenzy in other Cypriot resorts. The only noise which echoed through the empty dining areas, lounges, conference rooms and corridors was the menacing click from the heels of the security guards who examined and re-examined every hiding place of the hotel's eight floors.

There were guards and sniffer dogs everywhere. If the memory of Carlos' audacity in Vienna seemed distant in the mind of the Cypriot government, it was easier to recall the more recent horror that the Brighton bombing in England had caused for the organisers and security forces responsible to Mrs Thatcher and her Conservative Party conference.

The security guards were manic in their attention to detail, each country's delegations outdoing the others' for fanaticism. Anybody approaching within one hundred yards of the hotel's driveway was stopped and searched from head to toe. Guards equipped with telescopic and infra-red sights on their high-velocity AK 47, M-16 or Gallil assault rifles, and laser-guided shoulder rocket-launchers, manned every roof, ready to bring down unauthorised flights. All civilian air traffic had been banned from a twenty-five mile perimeter of the hotel. Mobile radar vans and missile systems were at the front and rear to give early warning of tree-top high helicopters making an un-authorised entry.

Commandos from elite Israeli, Syrian, Egyptian, Jordanian and American special units had joined the Cypriot guards to make regular sorties through the grounds of the hotel, spanning out to a four mile radius. It was unusual for so many security operatives to work together, and a good omen for the future of the talks.

As the important occupants of the eight gleaming limousines drove at various times during that morning along the winding road up to the Hotel Akrotiri, each knew with absolute certainty that it was entering a sanitised environment.

The cars and their escorts neared the blue and red canopy which stood before the hotel foyer and the delegates saw that the white flagpoles each flew the flag of an Arab country, while those of Cyprus and America, which hosted the conference, fluttered beside them. Central among the flags was the blue and white Star of David, the *Magen David* of Israel, the tiny land which was here to make a lasting peace for Jerusalem, the capital of a country which had seen more wars and bloodshed than any other country on Earth. Since the beginning of recorded history, Israel had been the prize of armies and conquerors from ancient times to modern; it was at the very heart of the fertile crescent; the epicentre of the trading routes between east and west. And Jerusalem was the treasure which every conqueror was seeking.

The delegates would be allowed to rest on the day of their arrival, although private, last-minute negotiations would doubtless take place in rooms and corridors as preparations were fine-tuned for the opening of the plenary session on the following morning. Speeches had been agreed months in advance. Now was the time for camel-trading in the *shuk*.

Later in the afternoon, the massive contingent of journalists from papers and news media around the world would file colourful background reports through their satellite and TV equipment, and build pyramids of scaffolding outside the hotel and in its foyer to record what promised to be an eventful three days.

Within the hotel, the activity became frenetic. It was the third week of June. It marked the culmination of years of subtle diplomacy by the American Secretary of State. Blood enemies sworn to kill each other had been tempted to sit down together for the first time to reconcile the most intractable of all problems, the question of who should own the sacred city. Arabs, Jews and Christians claimed the city as one of the pivots of their religion, yet only Israel claimed sovereign rights. Now, after experiencing the heights of success and the depths of frustration, the American Secretary of State had cajoled and bullied the countries in the region to begin the process of negotiation.

By late that night, all the last minute jockeying for position had come to an end. The deals had been cemented. The positions locked in. The concessions made. Only the Israeli delegation had kept to itself, except for an early meeting and drinks with the Americans.

Early the following morning, the delegates arrived in the hotel's ballroom, which had been converted into a secure conference venue. The atmosphere of tension in the foyer was at odds with the expectation inside the conference room itself. The delegates organised themselves in pre-negotiated positions. Behind them were their advisers, and behind the advisers were the senior administrative staff for each delegation, who acted as runners, note-takers, and supporters.

The centre of focus of the table was the man who had gathered the delegates together. The Secretary of State for the United States of America, John Dewhurst, a tall patrician New Englander, was already being tipped for the Nobel Peace Prize for his work in bringing together men who had been enemies for generations.

To the left of the American was the Saudi Arabian Prime Minister, Prince Rashid al Sirra. Next to him sat the delegation from Iraq headed by the Foreign Minister, Abbas Rahman, an Oxford-educated man whose ability to talk his country out of trouble had earned him the nickname 'The Teflon Diplomat'. The most difficult man to bring to the meeting, he had an uncompromising hatred of Israel and all it stood for.

To the left of the Iraqi sat the President of Syria, Abu Farawhi. His bloody climb to power had seen the extinction of 30,000 villages which had opposed the tribe of which he was now the most prominent member. Genocide, even on this scale, which had gone largely unnoticed by a world inured against massacres by nightly television. Abu spent much of his time looking like an elder statesman for the benefit of the journalists whose television cameras swept the room for the visual background which would be needed for that evening's news.

Then there was the Prime Minister of Jordan. King Idris had decided some weeks ago that he should not be present, as this was a meeting of Presidents and Prime Ministers, beings lower than a monarch. He had made it clear to Dewhurst that he would step in and be the signatory for an accord, but that his Prime Minister, the inconsequential Mohammed Quirri, would be his mouthpiece.

To Quirri's left sat the Prime Minister of Egypt, Lehum Kafkafi. Kafkafi hoped that his isolation as Israel's only official Arab ally would end with this peace conference.

Two important delegations, however, were noticeably absent. Lebanon's seat at the conference would remain empty. It was Syria's major client in the Arab world and despite intense diplomatic pressure, the Syrians had decided that the presence of the Lebanon would contribute little of substance to the talks. To John Dewhurst's disappointment, Syria had decreed that Lebanon would not send a delegation.

Also absent, despite frantic urgings by the USA, was the PLO delegation. From the very beginning, the PLO leaders refused to participate unless the leaders of Hamas, another Arab terrorist organisation, also participated. Even Dewhurst's diplomacy, in association with pressure from Syria, Saudi Arabia, and, latterly, Iraq, could not change the decision by the PLO to boycott the conference.

This decision had caused anger and frustration amongst the Arab delegates, as everybody assumed that, if there was to be a stumbling block to the peace process, it would be the hawkish Israelis' unwillingness to negotiate directly with the PLO. However, the Israelis had maintained their stance—hard-won by Dewhurst—that they would be willing to talk to anybody, even current terrorists.

Staring at his hands and refusing to meet the eyes of the other delegates at the conference table, was the Prime Minister of Israel, Raphael Ben Ari, who was sitting at the right hand of John Dewhurst. Raphael Ben Ari was an enigma, not only to the Arabs and to the Americans, but also to his own people. His position as Prime Minister had been consolidated by the unexplained resignation two years beforehand of Shlomo Ben

Dod, who for ten years had been a father-figure to the Israelis, a latter-day Moses leading his people through the hostile desert of Arab politics.

His place as Prime Minister had been taken by Raphael Ben Ari, a compromise candidate who, as a second lieutenant forced upon Ben Dod by Israel's system of proportional representation, had surfaced in the cauldron of aspiring candidates. When his name was announced as the country's new Prime Minister, a large section of the liberal Israeli population recoiled in horror, dreading their country being represented by a man who had alienated liberal governments throughout the world by his intemperance. Few people knew much about him even after two years as Prime Minister. He was thought to have been the genius behind the successes of Mossad, the Israeli Secret Service, and had come to politics late in life as a member of an extreme right-wing party. But two years as the country's leader showed him to be a skilled compromiser and pragmatist. He appeared to have settled into the job and had risen in stature to meet the demands made of him by his position. He had brought together rival factions and unified political enemies. Although a man who never shied away from his hawkish principles and whose philosophy was still to strike at any target before it could muster the strength to strike back, his vitriol was muted and he had resentfully agreed to the greatest act of pragmatism of his life, participation in the conference. But those closest to him knew that his newly acquired persona was skin-deep and were worried about his ability to conduct himself properly in a roomful of Arabs.

Ben Ari had few friends, even in his own Cabinet, but Israel's system of government forced him to adopt a consensus approach. And it had been his Cabinet's decision to negotiate the status of Jerusalem.

Only Yitzhak Stein, the Minister for Posts and Telecommunications, and Zalman Gershowitz, the Minister for Roads, supported Ben Ari's every move. Only they believed in private as well as in public that his actions were justified. His hawkish supporters were fervent in their promotion of many of his ideals. Concepts such as an Israel which spanned both sides of the Jordan, or which sought a Jewish homeland in the Sinai. But his supporters were dramatically outnumbered by the moderate Israelis and Jews throughout the world. And Ben Ari seemed to have realised that, although he was Prime Minister, he was not free to act unilaterally, but had to abide by the workings of his country's democracy.

Still, even under a more benign Ben Ari, the official Israeli Government policy of settlement on the West Bank and Gaza Strip had accelerated to the point where the entire Arab peoples and many Western countries condemned the building of the settlements as aggression, bordering on acts of war by conquest.

All John Dewhurst's training as a diplomat had been focused upon the need to bring the Israelis to the conference table. It would have been impossible when Ben Ari first became Prime Minister, but he had recently agreed to review the building of settlements on the West Bank and Gaza pending the outcome of the peace conference. This was the key which unlocked the conference. The American was relieved that the Israeli Foreign Minister, the calm, cool-headed Mordecai Avit, a visionary and man of integrity, was shadowing his Prime Minister and would act as a foil to Ben Ari's well-known irascibility. If any one thing was to earn Dewhurst the Nobel Prize, it would be securing Ben Ari's presence.

The delegates were seated. The past was a memory. The future was about to be shaped. The conference was beginning. One hundred journalists, all of whom had been bodily searched by security guards with metal detectors before being allowed into the room, and whose cameras and microphones had been pulled to pieces to ensure that they did not contain guns or explosives, were ushered to the well in front of the speakers' dais. Electronic flash-guns dazzled the delegates as they talked to each other, waiting for order to descend.

The President of Cyprus looked at the clock, cleared his throat and waited for the delegates to be silent before he walked to the podium. It was the signal for everyone in the room, both Arab and Jew, to put on their headphones for the translation which would begin the moment he started to speak. The room fell into an anticipatory silence, broken only by the electronic noises of the media.

'My dear friends, welcome to this conference, on behalf of the people of Cyprus and the people of the world. I am privileged to have been chosen to open this historic and eventful meeting of brothers …'

And so for ten minutes he talked about peace, harmony and reconciliation of differences. His words denied the history of his own country, where Greeks and Turks had been enemies for generations and where a full-scale battle could rage in the streets at the slightest provocation, as barely hidden hatreds erupted between neighbours.

Yet the Cypriot President's opening speech was more than merely a formality, a token of conformity. Until order had descended upon the conference, and delegates had settled down to listen, nobody, not even the most hopeful for peace, was certain that the conference would take place. There had been so many obstacles, difficulties and problems to overcome that, even as recently as a few days ago, the conference itself was in jeopardy.

The President's speech was the oil the Arabs needed to calm the waters and justify their sitting with the Israelis. The tension in the conference room subsided as the prospect of an international Jerusalem came closer to realisation. He had been asked not to talk for more than ten minutes, and at the end of his speech his remarks were greeted with warm applause.

The President walked from the podium to the place where the American Secretary of State was sitting, and in deference, shook his hand first. Then he walked over to each delegate, warmly shaking hands and grasping shoulders, wishing each man luck, fortune and strength in the coming days. The President then waved to everybody and walked out of the conference hall, to be followed by dozens of journalists—who would not be privy to the closed session which was about to begin.

As the door closed, delegates turned their gaze to John Dewhurst, the next man to speak. The *bonhomie* of the Cypriot President's good wishes soon evaporated. Reality brought a sense of coldness and caution to the room. Throats were cleared, papers shuffled, messages whispered. If there was going to be trouble, it would be now.

Each delegate had been meticulously briefed by his advisers and every other delegate knew precisely, to the word, what each would say. Formality was the key to the success of the conference, because, without a formal framework, the delegates could introduce topics which would open old wounds.

John Dewhurst had carefully scheduled every controversial subject for discussion at later meetings between lower-ranked officials. This conference was to act as a breaking down of barriers, an introduction to the peace process and to give the process an international imprimatur so that foreign ministers could later roll up their shirtsleeves and, where necessary, thump tables and hurl abuse at their opposite numbers. But at this meeting, everybody had recognised the need for decorum, which was the father of order.

The order of speeches had been one of the major stumbling blocks. Each delegate felt his country needed to speak first in order to set the scene. The front-line States at constant war with Israel wanted to show their amenability. The wealthy but unconnected nations like Saudi Arabia felt, as bankers, that they should call the shots. After the order of speeches had been agreed, it was necessary to settle upon the content so that no one nation would embarrass or offend any other.

As the conference organiser, John Dewhurst, representing an American president struggling with spiralling unemployment and needing a stunning foreign affairs victory to ensure himself of re-election, stood up, cleared his throat and walked to the podium.

In the cultivated, clipped tones of a fifth-generation East Coast American, modulated by twenty years as Harvard Professor of International Relations, John Dewhurst bade everyone good luck before mounting the podium. He took a sip of water and said:

'My dear friends. What an historic occasion. To have us all gathered around one table is in itself an achievement, not of any one man here, but a collective achievement of all peace-loving people in the Middle East. This meeting represents an end to isolation. In time it may represent an end to hostility and hatred. It was hatred that kept you all apart, an inability to perceive that enemies did, in fact, have a real and urgent viewpoint. But we have put that isolation behind us and we are now sitting down as brothers in the region to discuss how the millions of people you represent can best be served by the process of peace …'

Although his words were delivered in a casual, almost impromptu manner, every detail of Dewhurst's speech had been analysed in a four-stage process. Firstly it had been written by speechwriters expert in Middle East and international affairs. It had then been approved by the State Department to ensure that nothing in it could be taken as a slight or criticism of any one country or delegate. Then the President had approved it. Finally, it had been approved by the Arabs and the Israelis.

As he spoke, the aides behind their leaders carefully read the Arabic or Hebrew translations of his words to check that no syllable, no word, no phrase was in any way different from that which had been circulated to them beforehand. There were gratifying smiles and feelings of ease as he continued in his speech. The conference had begun exactly as everybody hoped it would and peace, it appeared, had a very real prospect of eventuating from this and subsequent conferences.

♜♜♜

'Look, Mr Prescott, can we please stop talking about your ill-health? That's not the issue here. I don't give a damn about your hernia, your heart, your falling hair, your diabetes, or your wife's sagging breasts … all I care about is that you forced my client to sell out. You made an undertaking to pay Mr Morwell $20,000 a month for the next twelve months to satisfy his claim for half of the business. Right now, you're in clear breach of that agreement. If you don't pay the full amount immediately, we'll seek orders enforcing the penalty clauses in the contract.'

Walter Prescott had never been spoken to like this before, especially by a young whip of a girl, lawyer or not. Her face was framed by cascades of raven hair. Prescott would never guess that as a feminist she objected to the use of make-up and never wore it at weekends, only abandoning her philosophy to the demands of her office with delicately applied make-up which accentuated her attractiveness. Prescott couldn't help but admire the result.

'Let me lay it on the line, so that it's crystal clear. If you don't pay the previous instalment immediately, and the next $20,000 instalment on time, I'll take you to court. I'll have the agreement nullified for failure to perform, and demand judgment in our favour for the balance of $140,000.'

She drew a breath. Until then, her emotionless thrust had been made without her seeming to breathe. Prescott was breathless listening to her. She continued: 'Which will have to be paid with interest and penalties, increasing the total sum to $175,000.'

Prescott's face turned puce with anger. His jaw clenched while he started to rise out of his chair to deal with the young, attractive and over-confident woman who sat coldly and calmly at the opposite end of the table. But his lawyer, David Franklin, placed a restraining hand on his arm to prevent him from doing anything which would make matters worse.

'Miss Davis,' Franklin said, 'the last thing that anybody in this room wants is to go to court. But you have to understand that Walter has been seriously ill recently, on top of which the economy was very buoyant when he made the agreement with your client. At the moment, the downturn in trade has affected my client's kitchen manufacturing business, and with his health problems he's having difficulty finding the $20,000 a month. It's placing too much of a strain upon his cash flow. If it continues, then the business will almost certainly be placed into receivership. Then, nobody will win. Look, can't we be reasonable and simply pay $10,000 a month until the economy begins to turn up?'

Miriam Davis smiled and shook her head without consulting her client to ask his approval for her negotiating stance.

'No way in the wide world,' she said. 'First, if the business goes into receivership, then our contract makes Mr Prescott liable against his personal assets of over three million dollars for the entire amount; and secondly, it was you, David, and you, Mr Prescott, who made the agreement. Now you've got to stick to it, or we'll see you in court. Oh, by the way Mr Prescott, if you're so sick how come you managed to play eighteen holes of golf with your accountant at Royal Sydney last Saturday?'

Prescott's jaw slackened. Whatever feelings he may have had towards the leonine beauty opposite him evaporated.

Miriam felt she had scored enough victories. Knowing how to leave the other party bleeding was as important in a negotiation as knowing what to say, so she decided to conclude the discussions, even though the meeting was only a few minutes old.

'Gentlemen, you have nothing of interest to offer, so I can see no value in continuing this conference. If you'll excuse me, Mr Morwell and I have other matters to discuss.'

Miriam Davis stood up, making it doubly clear that the meeting was over. Prescott and his lawyer didn't move, unable to believe that the negotiations had been brought to such a swift conclusion. She looked coolly down at Morwell and said to him, 'Come on Derek, let's go to my office.'

'Aren't you even going to discuss this further or look at our revised payment schedule?' Franklin asked.

But all he got for his effort to regain the initiative was a Parthian shot.

'We didn't make the terms,' Miriam said with impassive directness. 'You did! You forced my client to sell his share of the business for less than its market value, a business which he built up personally. Prescott's only contribution was money. My client put twenty years of his life into the place! Then you threatened to tie his money up in a three-year legal battle if he didn't settle for a paltry sum. Mr Prescott, you screwed my client. Now we're screwing you.'

Unable to restrain himself any longer, Prescott hissed: 'Jewish bitch!'

Miriam froze. She turned around and looked at Prescott. 'You stupid man. I won't even insult myself by getting angry at that. I've heard that sort of remark from schoolyard bullies and men with no balls. You're a bit of both, aren't you Mr Prescott? Well, you can treat your own staff like some feudal baron if you want, but try it with me and I'll use all the processes of law to destroy you. Now get out of my office. All future negotiations between you and my client will be through your lawyer.'

Prescott was an important client of Franklin's, one who should be courted, not offended, but as the door closed, the young lawyer turned to a chastened Walter Prescott and decided it was time to breach the normal client and lawyer relationship.

'You idiot!' he hissed. 'You moron! That was totally uncalled for. It was racist, vindictive and just plain stupid. Miriam Davis isn't the sort of woman to take that crap lying down. God knows what damage you've just done.'

Knowing he was so badly in the wrong, Prescott tried to justify himself. The whole trip had only been a fishing expedition to save money. He shrugged his large shoulders, his baggy suit rising and falling, an indictment of his excesses.

'Sometimes you say things in the heat of the moment which you regret later.'

Franklin stared at Prescott, fixing him like a cobra fixes a rat. 'Never make the mistake of saying anything to Miriam Davis that you're not prepared to back up with everything at your disposal. She's smart and fights with everything she's got.'

Prescott was tired of being lectured. It was one of the characteristics of a bully.

'Then maybe I'd better switch my business to her instead of you, David.'

David Franklin smiled. 'She wouldn't touch you with a barge-pole.'

Outside the conference room, Derek Morwell was trying to slow Miriam down by grabbing at her arm. She was marching along the corridors of the twenty-fifth level of the office block which housed the legal firm of Boyd, Royal and Trimmett. The junior commercial partner, she had been chosen above half a dozen equally qualified men because the firm wanted its clients to know how modern it was in its thinking. Miriam realised it was a sexist ploy on the part of the senior partners, but did not object—not when she was benefiting so handsomely.

'Miriam, slow down, will you.'

She stopped and turned towards him, smiling, 'Enjoy it?' she asked.

'Enjoy it? Are you crazy? You've just blown the whole thing. His offer wasn't unreasonable. Times are tough. Now he isn't going to pay and we really will have to go to court!'

'Don't be such a fuckwit, Derek. You don't think I'd drop you in it, do you? I checked him out with a contact at Westpac this morning. He's in the process of buying a new factory complex. He's just trying to squeeze you so he can fund it more easily.'

Derek's mouth gaped in surprise. 'Why didn't you tell me?' he asked.

'Because you would have become emotional and made accusations. *That* would have blown the negotiation. Anyway, I've got to go and prepare for another conference. Phone me tomorrow and I'll probably have some good news. Oh, and by the way, when they come back and tell us that they agree to our terms I'm going to tell them I'm invoking the penalty clause. That should put another $10,000 into your pocket.' Miriam smiled and gave him a cheeky wink. There were parts of this job she truly loved.

As she left him, Morwell's confidence swiftly returned. He watched her tall athletic body stride down the corridor. She was an attractive blend of femininity and athleticism. He had chosen her as a lawyer above another partner in another firm because she was so sexual. Not sexy. There were plenty of women sexier than Miriam Davis. But she was an exciting amalgam. She was a blend of dark, Semitic attractiveness and latent power, which she exuded in her manner of dress, her conversation and the way she peered through him.

Miriam had almost allowed Prescott to get through her skin. She had disliked him the first time they had met and now she detested him. Not that she was unused to the sort of anti-Semitic remark he had made. It was par for the course for a Jew in a foreign land.

Miriam smiled at her secretary as she entered her office to pack her briefcase. There was no conference. She wanted to get away early so she could have a birthday dinner with her *zeida*, her grandfather, who lived his life quietly and inconspicuously in the Rosenthal Elderly Persons Home where many of Sydney's Jews spent their final years.

Miriam's life was a subtle blend of the hard lawyer and the soft and dutiful grand-daughter. There was a boundary between the two. Although thirty-two and still unmarried, when she wasn't practising law Miriam liked to spend as much time as her social life allowed with her *zeida*, who was now eighty-two, but had lost none of his mental vigour. He was her moral code, her system of ethics, her history, her being. It had been her old *zeida* and *bubba* who had raised her while her mother and father were working hard to keep the family afloat. Her *bubba* had died fifteen years ago, and all Miriam's love had been trans-ferred to the old man. She loved her *zeida*, and he loved her.

Miriam bitterly opposed his move into the Rosenthal Home but he had signed the papers himself, much to her chagrin, when his rheumatoid arthritis had become so bad that he was incapable even of making himself a cup of tea.

It was already midwinter dark. Miriam told her secretary she was going for a meeting with a barrister and the secretary knew not to question her any further. It was a legal euphemism for going home early. But Miriam did not explain what she was doing. It was nobody's business but hers.

She had carefully chosen what she knew he would like for a present— a silver and gold *kippah* which he would put on his head every morning and night when he said his prayers. She opened her briefcase to ensure that it was there, and saw the parcel, wrapped in silver paper with a burgundy ribbon. She closed her briefcase again and checked her appearance in the mirror. Tall, olive-skinned, with a round attractive face, her eyes, she thought, were her best feature. They were the clear black limpid eyes of a young Jewess, the type of woman that David and Solomon had in their minds when composing their songs and psalms. But she and her generation were unlike their Jewish predecessors in the 5,000-year history of her race.

She was neither a matriarch nor a submissive housewife. Nor was she a mere extension of her family. Like many of her friends, she was thoroughly independent, able to guide her own destiny.

Not that she was universally admired. She had made a number of enemies in her dealings with opposition law firms and she knew that she was not liked by everyone within her own company. Some of the male lawyers found her intimidating and she had recently recommended the dismissal of a secretary who had become over-familiar, thinking Miriam would ignore her inefficiencies because she was another woman. One senior partner had even complained to the managing partner of Boyd, Royal and Trimmett about her aggressive stance, but her managing partner, who also happened to be a member of her synagogue, had defended her fully and told the lawyer that his own troops should toughen up their act.

She stepped into the lift when it arrived, and felt the familiar knot in the pit of her stomach, as though there was no floor and she would plummet 300 feet to her death. Or as though there was some dark malevolent force in the lift which would attack her the moment she left the security of her office.

The lift descended and she felt sick with vertigo. Miriam hated these lifts and held on tightly to the rail. A wave of anger swept over her. She was thirty-two! She should be able to control these ridiculous feelings. One day she would.

In the carpark, she gunned the motor of her BMW, slowly slid the car into first gear and began the helter-skelter climb towards street level. She loved the feel of the gear stick and that almost sensuous experience of sliding from first to second, then to third, and then to fourth gear as the car showed its true abilities on the expressway.

But the Rosenthal Home was nowhere near the expressway and Miriam had to manoeuvre in second gear through the clogging traffic of town, then into third on to the eastern arterial road before she turned off into the roads flanked by the large grandiose houses of Double Bay, where her *zeida* was watching the clock, waiting for his beautiful grandchild to arrive.

CHAPTER TWO

The Jerusalem Peace Conference in Cyprus was the clearest sign in more than a century that peace might finally come to the region. Since the moment of its creation in 1948 by the United Nations, Israel had been in a perpetual state of war. And even before the half century of official wars and ceasefires, the Jews of Palestine had fought for independence against the British occupation forces. With the exception of the elderly, who had once lived in relative harmony with Arabs and Druze under the Ottoman Empire before the First World War, no Israeli had known a time when the country was not surrounded by hostile neighbours.

Numerous countries attempted to reconcile the differences of Jew and Arab. Only America, and only in the wake of the disintegration of the USSR, managed to bring the former protagonists together at a conference table to resolve the seemingly irresolvable—the change in status of Jerusalem from being an Israeli capital to becoming an international city, home to the world's three great monotheistic religions.

And in Cyprus, the peace conference was just beginning.

John Dewhurst ended his speech. He sat and took a sip of water. He was gratified. The applause by those men around the table whom he had bullied, cajoled and coaxed into being present seemed both sincere and heartfelt.

It was now the turn of the Israeli Prime Minister. As most Arab nations were united against Israel, it seemed logical for Ben Ari to present its case for peaceful co-existence first of all. The Prime Minister's advisers had worked tirelessly on his speech. The more militant rhetoric had been removed on the advice of the Americans and the speech had become a passionate plea for reconciliation. What had originally been written as a statement of Israel's right to keep the government of Jerusalem in Israeli hands had been transformed by negotiation into a document of religious and ethnic brotherhood.

Once Raphael Ben Ari finished applauding his old friend, he cleared his throat, took a sip of water and stood up. If Dewhurst was met by a feeling of optimism and goodwill, the feeling in the room as Ben Ari stood and walked to the podium was still one of suspicion. Every Arab present knew exactly what the Israeli was going to say. But they would be listening to his tone, his bombast, the level of his arrogance, or any other indication of a cryptic meaning that might lurk behind his prepared statement. As he stood, the delegates again realised how physically small the man was. His size was one identifying factor. The other was the famous purple birthmark on his balding forehead.

A former terrorist, Ben Ari had been leader of one of the most violent gangs that the Hebrew nation had produced since the time of the Bible. Of all the militants that fought for their cause, Ben Ari had been the most vicious, leading his supporters to attack British civilians, Arabs and even Israeli Zionists who did not follow his brand of fanaticism. At the height of his murderous attacks, he was even disowned by his own people, sickened by the slaughter and repelled by his justification that it was done in the name of winning independence for the Jewish people. When the British Army occupied the mandated territory of Palestine, Ben Ari had a huge price tag on his head. Even the incipient Israeli defence forces would have nothing to do with him or the maniacs he led.

His small stature earned him the nickname 'The Rat'. International commentators, those writing from other far-off countries who supported the Jewish demand for nationhood, had been somewhat kinder to him and had compared Ben Ari's gang of thugs to an earlier group of freedom fighters, the biblical Maccabees. Only David Ben Gurion, Israel's first prime minister, had thought to harness Ben Ari's terrorist skills by placing him in the upper echelons of the newly created Mossad.

Raphael Ben Ari stood at the podium and looked at the other

delegates seated in the conference hall. His face remained impassive, hiding whatever deep feelings he held. The purple birthmark, in the shape of a small clenched fist, seemed to be more tightly clenched, more knotted, even more purple and angry than normal.

He picked up the printed speech and mouthed the first few words silently to himself: 'Fellow Semites, members of the brotherhood of one of the oldest and proudest nations on our Earth. Nations which have contributed morals, ethics, philosophy, mathematics and universal education to the pool of human experience ...'

He knew the words by heart. Yet they stuck in his throat. Ben Ari put the speech down and again surveyed the room, which was now so quiet the air-conditioning could be heard as a distinct hiss above all of their heads. He again read the first few words but stood silent. He refused to speak the rhetoric which his heart, which every fibre of his being, told him were words written by others and circumstances alone forced him to utter. They were not his words. They were not words he would have chosen to speak. His guts reacted against the instructions imposed upon him by his Cabinet colleagues. His silence had now lasted for close to a minute and the Arab delegates began to shift uncomfortably in their chairs.

Mordecai Avit, the Foreign Minister of Israel, was also beginning to worry. He had been the prime mover in forcing Ben Ari to the conference. He knew that Ben Ari hated every minute of this conference and was here because he had lost the vote in Cabinet. Avit knew Ben Ari wanted to unleash the venom of more than fifty years of hatred of the Arabs. An ominous feeling grew in the mind of the Israeli Foreign Minister. It transmitted itself to the aides sitting behind him. Finally, Raphael Ben Ari, born in Poland, who had grown to manhood in Israel, and who was his country's most hawkish voice, began to speak, softly at first, but then with increasing fervour.

'I ask myself, "Why am I here? Why is a Jew standing, talking peace to a roomful of Arab leaders?" '

Ben Ari's Foreign Minister looked up, his face draining of blood. His worst fears had materialised. Behind him, his support staff frantically searched through the text of the speech to find the words they knew were not there.

Around the table, Arab leaders sat motionless as the translation came through into their headphones. Those members of the Arab delegations who were reading the speech in Arabic looked up at this departure from the prepared script, knowing instantly that it was the beginning of the end.

Most surprised of all was John Dewhurst, who just minutes before had squeezed Ben Ari's hand and had assured him that, 'This meeting is the start of something historic, something which their children would talk about in years to come ... The start of a permanent peace. The start of Israel's rise to greatness.' Ben Ari had smiled, and held the arm of his friend. Now all Dewhurst could do was listen in horror as the Israeli Prime Minister continued.

'We have been at each other's throats as enemies, implacable and hated, for half a century. What have any of you done to make me believe that the situation today is different? Why should I trust a group of Arab leaders whose followers massacred *kibbutzniks* on our borders, who raised armies against a defenceless nation, who sent missiles against us, and who have created a nuclear capacity with only one intention ... to annihilate us? We are a nation which was created to save the brutalised remnants of its dispossessed people after centuries of pogroms, which culminated in the Nazi holocaust, the greatest inhumanity ever perpetrated by man on his fellow man.

'But you straddle your nations and suppress your people. You share none of your wealth, none of the billions of American dollars that have flooded into your coffers for your oil over the past half century. You keep it all for yourselves instead of building hospitals and schools and universities for your people. You are the people who have allowed a million Palestinians to rot in concentration camps while you beat your breasts, telling us it is all our fault ...'

Unable to contain his anger any longer, Mordecai Avit looked in horror at his Prime Minister. 'Raphael, shut up,' he shouted. 'What are you doing?' But the outburst didn't affect Ben Ari, who was now in full flight. Nor did Avit's palpable fear impress the Arab leaders, whose fingers held the headsets closer to their ears so they could listen to every word that was said. Showing the most violent response, the Syrian President banged the table and shouted in Arabic: 'Zionist dog! How dare you destroy the peace process? May your tongue cleave to the roof of your mouth and may you never speak again!'

But the Israeli Prime Minister continued speaking, shouting above the commotion which began to fill the room.

'You think you're so wonderful because you're sitting at the table with us. What makes you so wonderful? You've been defeated by us four times. You're all failures! Cowards! Losers! Why should we have to grovel and ask you to forgive us? What the hell kind of a peace process is this that the Israeli nation should have to come grovelling to the Arabs and beg to give away Jerusalem, our jewel, our finest possession? What gives you the right to grant peace to us? *We've* earned the right to peace in our land. Earned it four times in forty years with the blood of our soldiers and civilians! In 1948, six nations attacked us when we didn't even have an army. We lost six thousand people. One per cent of our people. And they died just three years after six million of their brothers and sisters were slaughtered by the Nazis. Were their lives in vain that we should freely give away what they died for?'

By now the room had erupted into bedlam, with arms and hands gesticulating everywhere with anger. If Raphael Ben Ari wanted to apologise or amend his outburst, or even continue in the same manner, it would have been impossible. He couldn't be heard above the din. The Iraqi delegate stood and stormed around the table, where he cuffed John Dewhurst's shoulder with the back of his hand.

'You see what a kind of a man this is that you tell us to sit down and talk with,' he shouted at the American in faltering

English. 'I say to you, there would be no peace. You make a fool of me and the Iraqis when you bring us here!'

Dewhurst stood to face his accuser. 'But Abbas, I had no idea …'

He was unable to finish his sentence. The Iraqi pivoted on his heels, walked back to his delegation and ordered them to leave the room. They marched towards the door and flung it open violently. The journalists and security men sitting around the lobby, waiting like eunuchs outside the doors of a harem, were caught unawares. No one was supposed to leave the room for at least two hours. But a group of irate Iraqis were storming away. By reflex, TV camera crews hit buttons and photographers from AP, Reuters, the *Washington Post*, the *New York Times* and a dozen other papers shot picture after picture of angry Arabs, hatred burning in their eyes, as they stormed past.

Following the Iraqi delegation, the Egyptian Prime Minister, already on his feet, shouted abuse at the Israeli Prime Minister that needed no translation and ordered his delegation to follow. Like actors leaving a stage, the other leaders and their delegations walked out.

Only the Syrian, smiling his cold and knowing smile, sat and watched the disintegration of the conference with any semblance of amusement. He had done his job. The world would see him as a peacemaker and the Israelis as fascists. He reckoned that this should be worth at least another billion dollars in foreign aid from the United States administration. But to show solidarity with his Arab brothers, he stood and walked purposefully over to where John Dewhurst sat, his head buried in his hands. He looked down with sympathy at Dewhurst. 'I'm so sorry, my friend,' he said. 'After all our work.'

John Dewhurst looked up into the face of the Syrian. His anger, frustration and fear of the future stopped him from speaking. He stood, and the two men shook hands. The Syrian turned slowly and apparently unemotionally, and was followed out of the room by his delegation. The only foreign leader to speak to the press who gathered around him like acolytes, he told them that the Israelis had ruined the conference by a vicious, unprovoked, premeditated and racist attack.

The scene in the foyer was at odds with the interior of the conference room. The melee after the Israeli's outburst had transferred outside to be recorded by the assembled journalists. But within the conference room, those few who remained sat quiet and numbed. There were only two delegations left, the Americans and the Israelis. The American support staff looked at their Israeli counterparts in anger and hostility. No one wanted to speak first. It was a time for underlings to remain quiet.

Realising that he no longer had an audience, Raphael Ben Ari gathered his redundant speech from the podium, walked back to his place, sat down, licked his lips and turned to face John Dewhurst. The delegates from America and the delegates of Israel, sitting behind their leaders, were slumped in their chairs, incapable of moving, transfixed by the moment. The only movement among the two delegations came from Mordecai Avit, who silently, mechanically, shook his head from side to side in disbelief. All his years of effort to secure a peace had been destroyed in a moment by the intemperance of his leader. He was in despair.

Unwilling to look Mordecai Avit in the eye, John Dewhurst forced himself to stand and face the Israeli Prime Minister. But he found the words would not come easily. His emotions were controlling his intellect.

'You bastard!'

Ben Ari looked up at the tall New Englander, and smiled apologetically. He shrugged his shoulders.

'You disgusting man!' Dewhurst said. 'Oh God, I don't know how you can live with yourself. You're a liar. You're a …' Dewhurst breathed deeply, wrestling to control his emotional state. 'We had the world at our fingertips, you and I. We could have brought peace to your rotten little country.' He turned to the Israeli delegation and shouted. 'You people don't deserve to be led by a man like this.' He turned back to Ben Ari: 'How could you betray them like this? How could you?'

He sat down again, took another deep breath and gathered up his documents. Slowly he put them into his document case, stood up and walked around the table towards the door. But before he opened it, emotion again took over from reason.

'There'll be no peace in your damned region for fifty years because of you. You're a small man in a small country. You're going to go the way of all mean little men. You'll be a footnote in the scrapbook of history.'

Before he left the room, he glanced at Mordecai Avit in whom he had deposited his trust. Avit stared at the ground, unable to look at Dewhurst.

The Secretary of State pulled open the door of the conference room and was met by an explosion of flashlights and a screaming rabble of journalists. He slammed the door shut behind him, and again the room descended into silence.

Stunned out of his torpor, Mordecai Avit caught the eye of his Prime Minister and said one word in Hebrew. '*Lama?*'

Ben Ari didn't answer for some time. Then he simply said, 'It seemed like the right thing to say at the time.'

♜♜♜

Within an hour of the Prime Minister's outburst, radio and television stations throughout the world were broadcasting the details of the break-up. All the world was hoping for peace. Suddenly there was a return to uncertainty and tension.

None were more stunned than the Americans. For a month, President Jack Harrison had spoken of a new world order, of a dawning of peace, of a new brotherhood of man. Now all the old ghosts between protagonists were about to be resurrected.

Harrison announced to a hastily gathered press corps in the briefing room of the White House that he would make a statement to his people as soon as he had spoken by telephone to Secretary Dewhurst. And this statement, he assured journalists as an off-the-record remark, would contain no carefully worded diplomatic niceties composed after consultation with other countries. This would be straight-shooting and straight-talking from an American President who had been insulted by those damned Israelis, who had been armed, fed and aided by every President since the Second World War. This time Israel had gone too damned far, he said. 'I don't give a fuck about the New York Jewish lobby. Or them in Los Angeles. I'll bet you a cent for a dollar that most American Jews will be as deeply horrified by what this maniac has done as will most other Americans.'

In Tel Aviv, Jerusalem, Haifa and other towns, the people of Israel listened in shock as *Kol Yisroel* announced the news of Ben Ari's outburst. On buses, which played the news on the hour to a people hungry for information, in factories, in offices, schools—everywhere through the tiny land of five million people—the new dawning of old hostilities was again the currency of conversation.

And in Sydney, Australia, every television and radio station announced in their news bulletin that the peace process had broken down, perhaps irretrievably. Nowhere was this listened to with greater keenness than in the newsroom of the weekly newspaper, *The National.*

One of *The National*'s most senior reporters, Paul Sinclair, was neither Jew nor Arab, but he was a sceptic. He had doubted the outcome of the talks from the start, though he had been called naive when he told colleagues that a leopard like Ben Ari couldn't change its spots. They called him a latter-day Cassandra. Unlike most Australian journalists, Paul had a good knowledge of Middle Eastern affairs, and his interest in the area was deepened by his relationship with Miriam Davis.

Paul was working late that night, to be close to the fax and to his newsroom's TV, which picked up CNN and NBC coverage of the conference. He knew from the start that Raphael Ben Ari would pull some sort of a stunt. Other leaders were predictable, their actions could be forecast to some extent from what they had done in the past. But Ben Ari was the least known, most private and most underestimated leader in the world today.

Before the conference, he had checked the biographies of all the participants in case he was asked to write a story. All the Arab delegates, as well as John Dewhurst, had pages devoted to their lives and careers in the newspaper library. But Raphael Ben Ari was different. There were hundreds of stories about him, but only since he had become Prime Minister. Before that, the newspaper library had failed to collect anything of substance. It was as though he had not existed.

Paul had made a bet with his editor when the delegates first arrived in Cyprus. Confidently he asserted that Ben Ari would do something at the conference to show his dominance. But as he stared at the television screen and the incoming faxes, he wasn't particularly happy to have won the bet.

He read the updated news reports and began to compose a story. If anyone would be asked to write a feature on the breakdown for next Sunday's paper it would be him. Jack Muir, his editor, knew all about Paul's interest in the area.

As he was composing a suitable introduction, the telephone rang. Paul decided to let it ring. It was not the time to be interrupted by technology. In the normal course of his working life, Paul had no problem with telephones. They were the lifeblood of today's journalists. But as it continued to ring, a nasty thought imposed itself on his mind. Today was not like any other day in *The National*. Today was different. Max Mandle, the newspaper's proprietor, was in town. He was upstairs in 'The Mausoleum'. From the beginning of the day, everyone in the building had become gripped by a fear of making errors and Paul reflected on how oddly everyone reacted. It was a building full of sophisticated people. Yet when the headmaster turned up, desks were put into order, suits were dry-cleaned and men and women walked around sporting fresh haircuts.

Paul was embarrassed to admit it, but he was as bad as everybody else. In case Mandle made a flying visit to the editorial floor, Paul had earlier gone to the toilet to comb his hair and freshen up. The cracked mirror in the bathroom made him look more swarthy than usual. He needed a brush to manage his tightly packed black wavy hair, combs breaking too easily, and it always took a while to make the hairs of his crown agree to sit flat. His hair had been his mother's favourite feature, although he would have preferred it to be straight rather than curly. It had not diminished his ability to attract women with his strong, yet gentle features.

The phone rang again. Paul still hesitated to pick it up. It was probably Muir, his manic Scottish editor, whose earthy expletives, complaints and condemnations were made in short, pithy sentences and followed by an invitation for a drink. Or it could have been one of a dozen contacts from stories he was working on that day. Yet something inside him told Paul that it was Max Mandle phoning. Why, he didn't know.

Max Mandle's phone calls were very different from Muir's. The moment a member of *The National*'s staff heard that heavy, thick, European accent politely inquiring whether it was speaking to the author of a particular article, he knew that doom was upon him.

Today, it could easily be Paul Sinclair's turn. *The National* had carried a story the previous week about ministerial expenses. It had been the lead story under the headline 'Parliamentary Travel Rorts—The Best Holidays that Public Money Can Buy?'. A photographer had set up a shot at an airport ticketing counter on which a photo of pigs around a trough had been carefully superimposed.

Paul had written the story from information leaked from a forthcoming Auditor-General's report, which revealed that members of the state parliament claimed official travel allowances for taking their families on Pacific holidays, or to skiing centres. One had even claimed for a trip to the sex parlours of Bangkok. He told Paul ingenuously that it was for research.

It was a good story and Paul had worked hard on it. He had scooped all other media, even the dailies in the same building. It deserved the lead.

Paul was confident but still felt a feeling of foreboding as he picked up the phone. As he feared, he heard the thick, throaty, Polish accent.

'Mr Sinclair, Mandle here!'

His neck muscles tensed, but Paul began the conversation affably. The two men had spoken to each other on three or four occasions, the most recent being a cocktail party for the Lord Mayor of Sydney, in the boardroom of the Mausoleum; a party designed to improve relationships between the newspaper and the city in which it operated. Mandle had been cordiality itself, introducing Paul as one of his brightest young boys.

'So, Mr Sinclair, tell me, this story on page one. You sure about the facts?'

Mandle never asked a question which was not rhetorical. Paul delayed his answer, and quickly thought through the details.

'Yes, I'm certain of them. Absolutely.'

'So, you're certain, are you? Good! Very good.'

There was a long pause. Paul wondered what was coming next.

'So, I'm glad you're certain. I'd hate any of my reporters not to be certain. I mean, for you not to be certain, means the story might be wrong, doesn't it?'

Paul was being baited. 'The story isn't wrong, Mr Mandle.'

'So who told you about the travel rorts?'

'I've got very good contacts in State government, and they told me …'

'Contacts, eh?' Mandle's accent made the word sound dirty. 'Vell, let me ask you something. I've just had the Premier on the phone, and he tells me that the story is bullshit. He says we're gonna be the fucking laughing stock of the country. He says that the story you ran was based on a draft fucking report, and that the Auditor-General has been given new fucking information. And that the real report on Wednesday won't say a fucking thing about fucking rorts and he wants a retraction and an apology.'

Paul interrupted. 'I know all about what the Premier's saying, Mr Mandle, but the Auditor-General's sticking by his report. The Premier is just …'

'Are you aware, you smartarse, that I'm currently negotiating with the State government to print their fucking lottery tickets, and to carry over 70 per cent of their advertising, which on its own will pay your fucking wages into the twenty-fifth century?'

Paul drew breath to answer but didn't get the chance.

'You know, Mr Smartarsed Reporter. This story of yours had better be good. You'd better have every fact right. I'm not going to back you up if you're wrong. I swear to God, if this story blows up in our faces you'll never work in newspapers again, anywhere. From now on, you'll not write a single word without me seeing it first. You got that, Mr Fucking Smartarse?'

Mandle slammed down the phone.

For the small band of senior reporters on Mandle's newspapers who had been on the receiving end of one of his harangues, it was a sort of a privilege, a rite of passage. They were called the Condors, these journalists, because they were fierce, proud and soared high alone, but most of all because they were an endangered species. Paul was now a Condor, and could apply for the club tie and certificate from the Condor Captain on the London *Daily News* once Jack Muir had verified the bollocking.

But he was angry. Paul didn't like being abused, especially when he was in the right. He looked up from the phone to see half a dozen colleagues staring at him and felt he owed them an explanation. All they had heard was the muffled roaring from the phone's earpiece.

'Max Mandle,' Paul said. Everyone nodded in sympathy.

A female colleague walked over to find out what had transpired. In short order, others arrived. In less than thirty seconds, he had a dozen colleagues standing around his desk.

Paul shrugged his shoulders and tried to smile bravely through their queries, although he was still stung by the humiliation. 'Usual crap. Told me that last week's lead was going to lose him advertising revenue.'

There was a chorus of comments.

'You're kidding'; 'No shit? Really?'; 'Bloody typical, isn't it?'; 'Jesus, you'd think the man would have more sense than to try to interfere'.

Paul dismissed it all with a wave of his hand. 'The guy's an asshole. But it goes with the territory of working here.'

'Are you going to apply to become a Condor?' asked one of the women.

The group burst out laughing.

'Bloody oath. Wouldn't miss it for the world. I'm even thinking of starting a Condor Convention Club. I'll call it the CCC. We'll meet once a year at Brampton Island or maybe somewhere in the Caribbean.' He scanned his assembled colleagues. 'Sorry, guys. You're not qualified yet.'

The impromptu meeting began to dissolve and people wandered back to their desks to resume their work.

But membership of the Condors did not make Paul any less angry. He knew that as soon as Mandle left the building on his way to some dinner, reception or other event, he would most likely have forgotten all about the incident. But the memory of it would stay with Paul for weeks. When eventually he edited a newspaper, if that would be his career route, Paul would exercise a benign power. If Mandle was still alive, he would show him how to be tough but fair towards his staff.

The back of Paul's head had throbbed with anger. Even the *bonhomie* of his colleagues had not calmed down his feeling of embarrassment and resentment. He opened his desk drawer to see what was there and closed it again. He picked up his telephone to call somebody but couldn't think of anybody he wanted to speak to. He decided to go to the toilet and wash his face. He hadn't been since early morning when he had prepared himself in case Mandle made an unexpected visit. What a mistake that had been! As he stood, he glanced at his diary, open on his desk, and sat down again. His mood began to change as he remembered that he was to have dinner with Miriam.

He and Miriam had been a serious item for five years now, but she still wouldn't agree to marriage. Something was holding her back and Paul knew exactly what it was. The fact that she was Jewish and he was nominally a Christian didn't matter a damn to him, but it mattered a lot to Miriam … more than she would acknowledge. But the fact remained that after a five year relationship she still hadn't assimilated him fully into her life. Assimilation would only come when, and if, he was allowed to meet her grandfather on Paul's terms, not as a cowering apologist for the crime of being Christian.

The first and only time they had met had been unpleasant. Before he had even spoken, Paul felt an emptiness between himself and old Yossi Samuelson … even some hostility.

As he was preparing to leave, his phone rang again. Thinking it might be Mandle coming back for a second round, he felt his anger rising. The man was acting like a schoolyard bully. Paul snatched up the receiver. He didn't give a damn about feigning courtesy. 'Yes! What is it now?' he snapped.

There was a drawn-out silence on the telephone, and a soft voice asked: 'Paul? Is that you?'

'Oh! Miriam. Sorry, you caught the tail end of a bad conversation with Max Mandle.'

The static from her carphone didn't allow the compassion she felt to be transmitted.

'Does that make you a Condor?' she asked.

'Yep, for what good that'll do me. That man's such a prat. Anyway, I'll tell you about it tonight.'

Another silence.

'Paul, you're going to be really pissed off with me.'

She was going to cancel their dinner.

'What is it this time?' he asked.

'Remember I told you it was Zeida's birthday? Well, he phoned and asked if I could have dinner with him. I was just going to pop around and see him for an hour or so but he said he had something to discuss with me. Something he didn't want to talk about in the home. I'm so sorry. I should have

36

let you know earlier, but I've been so busy this is honestly my first opportunity to tell you. Maybe we could meet afterwards … for dessert.'

Paul smiled and remembered the lunchtime sex at the Hilton Hotel the previous day when a half-hour bite in the downstairs bistro had turned into a two-hour dessert in the upstairs bedroom.

'So what time will you be finished at the Rosenthal?'

'Nine or 10 o'clock. Is that too late for you? I'm so sorry. It's very special for him. He's turning eighty-two, Paul. Please don't be angry with me. I'm all he's got.'

But Paul was angry. Sex with Miriam was a sharing, a relief, a voiding of tensions. And after Mandle, he needed his tensions to be voided.

'What time do you have to be at the home?'

'I said I'd be there sometime before dinner. I didn't give a time. I just thought to get there early to spend more time with him.'

'Meet me at my place at six. You can still be with him by seven. Please.'

Miriam smiled. She loved his impetuousness, his desire for her.

'Six. But I've gotta be out of there by six-thirty at the latest.'

Paul agreed. No matter how many times he made love to her, she always surprised him. Odd, really! In every liaison before Miriam, Paul had acted as the decisive partner. But not with her. Her hard-edged legalistic confidence was softened by the Talmudic wisdom gained from her grandfather, and it made her a mixture of the ancient and modern. She fascinated him. Some times, she would go along with his needs and desires; at others, he would meet a wall of resistance and would have to acquiesce if the relationship was to stay intact.

During the five years of their friendship he had tried to monitor the peaks and troughs—to see if they were predictable. Whether they were caused by tense times at work, or whether it was an aspect of her social life that caused the pendulum to swing. But whenever he came up with an answer, it was always simplistic, and invariably wrong. Miriam was … Miriam.

Although not happy about it, he was forced to subsume much of his own personality within the needs of their relationship. Usually, but not always. Sometimes they had flaming rows and broke up with a passion. But at the moment, their relationship was as close and tender as it had ever been.

Paul leaned back in his chair and put his feet up on the desk. Some journalists are compulsively neat, every paperclip, pen and notepad exactly in position like troops on a battlefield. Paul was messy, as his desk reflected. Notes here, books with broken spines and thumbed down pages there. Underneath the desk an old broken portable typewriter which should have been thrown away years ago prevented him from sitting properly. There were plastic coffee cups everywhere, along with a coffee cup holder with the name 'Paul Sinclair' Dymotaped to its side. Paul had a word processor on his desk as did every other journalist in the building, but his training had been on the ancient typewriter; he kept it in memory of the days when he was still thrilled to see his name in print.

And it wasn't just his desk which was a mess. His flat and his car were as much an extension of his desk as they were the opposite of Miriam's. As he was messy, she was obsessional. He had seen her office. It was a tribute to minimalism. Only her telephone had a permanent place on the empty surface; Paul's was wherever he had finished his last conversation. Often it could only be found when he heard it ringing. Thinking of his flat, he recoiled in horror at the thought of meeting Miriam there. He should have arranged to meet at her place. His still bore the residue of crockery and scattered clothes from the previous day.

But there were more immediate issues to be dealt with before he could leave the office. There was the Middle East, and the major news story of the day. Staring at the ceiling, he considered once again the shattering events in Cyprus. By the time *The National* came out the story would already have been covered to death by the dailies, so Jack Muir would have to find a whole new approach.

Tomorrow morning every paper would editorialise about why Ben Ari had destroyed the peace initiative. Given that he was hawkish, why agree to sit down and talk peace in the first place? Could he have been influenced by Mordecai Avit? Maybe the pressure from the Americans had been overwhelming. Dewhurst could be very persuasive and forceful. And just when everybody's objectives have been achieved, especially getting the Iraqis to the conference table, why had he pulled the plug and put the prospect of peace back for at least a generation?

To work out the tortuous pathways of Middle Eastern politics took unremitting concentration, but every time Paul turned his mind to what potentially could have gone wrong in Cyprus, he was drawn to the clock which was slowly edging towards five-thirty. In five minutes he would need to leave for the short drive to his home in Chippendale to meet with Miriam.

Paul loved Miriam both for her mind and for her body. He had no trouble with her body. It was lithe, sensuous and willing. It was her mind that he was incapable of defining.

He had read books written by Jews and about Jews. Miriam had explained the subtleties of her religion, its family values, history, ethics and moral stature. It was she who pointed out that three of the great belief systems of modern life—capitalism, Communism and Christianity—all owed their origin to Judaism. She glowed with pride when she told him of the number of scientists, philosophers, artists and intellectuals who had been produced by the Jewish race, quite out of proportion to its numbers.

Paul had become interested in the Middle East when he and Miriam had first started to go out together. It was unusual for an Australian reporter to take an interest in Arab–Israeli affairs. Most of his colleagues who dealt in foreign affairs concentrated on South-East Asia. The competition for articles to be published about Europe or Japan was intense. So Paul found it easier to have his feature articles published than did his colleagues, and publication was the stepping stone to success.

But for all his reading and research, the Jewish mind was still a mystery to Paul. Every time he thought he understood it, every time he came close to anticipating a reaction, Miriam or one of her friends would do something which surprised him. He didn't think he would ever understand them.

A copy girl put another fax on his desk. Paul scanned it. The PLO had issued a statement decrying the racism of the Israeli Prime Minister, citing it as the reason they had boycotted the conference. More propaganda! But why had Ben Ari given them the opportunity to use it?

When the story broke earlier, Jack Muir had sought his input. 'Do you follow this laddie?' he had asked in his clipped Scottish accent. 'I can't make head nor tail of what's going on over there. You've got an interest in this sort of thing. Write me something about it, will you?'

He and Muir talked around all the various possibilities but hadn't come up with an angle, other than the obvious … interviews with rabbis or politicians. But as he stared at the ceiling, Paul realised that although the enormous political forces were important, Ben Ari had dashed the hopes of ordinary people. And it was these that he would interview. Only a few months earlier he had attended a *Seder* service, the beginning of the Jewish Passover. Miriam and he had been guests at the home of one of the partners in Boyd, Royal & Trimmett. Although Paul had not understood any of the Hebrew, they had translated much for him. The *Seder* service was all about the exodus of the Jewish people from slavery in Egypt at the time of Moses. The last few words of the service were 'next year in Jerusalem'. For two thousand years, Jews in the diaspora prayed that the whole Jewish nation would be brought together as one in the holy city.

While other papers were interviewing foreign ministers and community leaders to get the official point of view, Paul would interview a few ordinary Jews and show how Ben Ari's arrogant and unilateral action had reversed the hopes of the Jewish nation.

Before he left, Paul phoned up Muir to give him the idea.

'I don't know, laddie. Its smart and I'd like to but I've got another problem. Mandle's told me to go a bit soft on the story. I said it might be a good idea to bring in local opinion, but he told me not to bother. Said the story would be pretty well dead and buried by the time we come out.'

Paul was surprised. Muir wasn't the sort of man to cave in like this, even when Mandle was sitting at his desk in the Mausoleum, waiting for someone, anyone, to make a mistake.

His mind lingered on the Middle East. There was still the lingering question … the unexplained rationale. Why had Ben Ari done it? Why scuttle the peace talks before the Arabs had put any of their cards on the table? It just didn't make sense.

That question would have to be answered tomorrow. Now he was off to meet Miriam. He left the office and within twenty minutes was at the door of his inner-city flat, a two-bedroom, 1950s utility with splintered floors covered by faded carpets. Miriam was waiting for him and they began to kiss as he put the key in the lock, but Miriam pushed him away. Paul was surprised.

'Let's get in first, shall we?' she said. 'We've only got half an hour. Let's make this a quickie. Short, sharp and sweet.'

Paul smiled in appreciation of her directness. He opened the door and felt embarrassed at the state of the apartment. Dishes still at the table, underclothes on his bedroom floor, CDs strewn all over the dining-room area. Miriam appeared not to notice, or if she did decided not to make any comment.

Miriam had only been to Paul's apartment a dozen or so times in the five years they had been going together. She felt much more comfortable in the antiseptic cleanliness of her Elizabeth Bay unit.

She turned and stood on tiptoe to put her arms around his neck. He smelt her perfume. It was one that he had bought her—Gucci No. 3. Its heady sensuousness made him feel dizzy as his lips pressed hard against hers and he felt her reach under his jacket and stroke his back. She began to pull his shirt out of his trousers, kissing him harder and harder. Paul put his hands on her shoulders. This time, it was he who pushed her away.

'I know we've only got thirty minutes but haven't you ever heard of foreplay?' he asked.

'We haven't got time for foreplay. You asked for this. Not me. Come on, let's get into the bedroom and get our gear off.'

Paul's face dropped. 'Oh, for Christ's sake, Miriam, put some romance into it, will you?' She laughed at his show of sensitivity.

'Paul, I love you. You know I love you. You'll always be my man. I'll love you in the morning and I'll love you at night. Now, can we cut the crap and go to bed?'

Paul burst out laughing and they walked into the bedroom. Miriam looked at the bed which obviously hadn't been made for several days. She felt like a whore in a sleazy hotel and her sexuality evaporated. Paul sensed her unease.

'Sorry honey, I was in a hell of a rush this morning. I was late last night because we got sidetracked at the Hilton.'

'Don't use me as an excuse, you slovenly bastard. I didn't get home until nine last night and I was working on a contract until one this morning. But if you go to my home you'll find it doesn't look half bad.'

Paul smacked her hard on the bottom. 'Don't be so bloody arrogant, little miss precious,' he said, and pulled her down on to the bed. He kissed her firmly on the lips and she began to undo his tie and his collar as he stroked her hair and moved his arm to feel the firm outline of her breasts.

He ran his hands down the curvature of her back and massaged her buttocks.

Miriam crossed her legs over his, hitching her skirt so that her body was directly in contact with his thigh, and began rubbing herself.

Within seconds, they had undressed and she mounted him, his hands joined casually behind his head on the pillow, enjoying the beauty of her wave-like motions as her breasts seemed to float up and down in one rhythmic surge after another.

She quickly came to orgasm, a heady, gusty orgasm, more of a deep exhalation than the cry of completion. But Paul was not yet ready. He still had further down the road to travel. He gently manoeuvred her body off his, until she lay on her side, and he entered her vagina from the rear.

Breathlessly, she said: 'Hurry up, darling. I've got another gentleman coming at half past six.'

Paul burst out laughing. 'Well, I'm coming now,' he said and cried out loud as his essence pumped into her body.

They lay together briefly, resting, his head on her shoulder. When Miriam had the strength to get up, she walked into the bathroom. Paul's knees were still too watery for him to contemplate moving.

He heard a 'yuk' from the bathroom. Miriam had discovered the ring around his bathtub. He really must do something about cleaning up the place. He looked at his bedside table out of the corner of his eye and realised with shame that he had forgotten to put on his gold ring. It had been a present from Miriam, created out of the melted-down gold from her mother's and father's wedding rings. Paul only wore it when he was seeing Miriam. He didn't enjoy wearing jewellery. Miriam had spent many hours trying to convert him. He reached out, picked up the ring and put it on his finger. He picked up his watch and looked at it. It was nearly six-thirty. Soon Miriam would be leaving to visit her grandfather. How oddly different Mr Samuelson's world of quiet, contemplative Judaism was from the political intrigues of the nation of the Jews, and their leader.

For the first time since leaving the office, Paul wondered what was happening on the other side of the world.

CHAPTER THREE

They stood at the threshold of a kosher restaurant in Sydney's eastern suburbs—a large room filled with noise and the smells of food from a polyglot of cultures. German, Russian, Polish, Hungarian and other culinary odours blended together in a heady cosmopolitan aroma. A waiter beckoned them to their table and Miriam grasped her grandfather's skeletal arm, gently but firmly guiding him through the maze of tables and chairs, past families eating or in conversation.

They sat and Miriam looked at her elderly *zeida* with pity. Even the short walk from her car to the restaurant had exhausted him. When he was seated, he asked the waiter for a glass of water. Before drinking, he put the silver *kippah* on his head and muttered a silent prayer. The waiter returned and thrust menus into their hands, reciting the specials of the day in a robotic voice. Her *zeida* ordered chicken soup. She ordered the same. When it came, it provided a further confirmation of his growing frailty. She watched in dismay as cascades of the golden liquid sprayed out from his spoon, into a pattern of stains, creating a mosaic on the tablecloth.

He looked up at her and met the consternation in her face. He felt what she was thinking. He felt shamed.

He continued to drink. He wouldn't give in, even though the yellow stains on the tablecloth at the edge of his soup bowl were beginning to join together. He struggled to hide the fact, even from her, that he was incapable of holding the spoon. The rheumatism in his joints was ravaging his body. The grasp which he held on to life was ebbing away. Every movement, from dish to spoon to mouth, was his embarrassment.

She reached over and cut up his matzo balls into small pieces. He had done it for Miriam when she was a child. While her parents had spent fifteen hours a day working to build up their

44

business, Miriam's parenting had been shared between the old world and the new, between her grandparents' traditions, customs, fears and memories of Europe and her parents' fierce pride in the materialistic opportunities of the new world of Australia. She was like a shuttlecock, bounced this way and that between the security of history and the attractions of modernism.

In those days, Miriam's father always seemed to be angry at the way his daughter was indoctrinated by her grandparents. When Miriam came home after an evening with *zeida* and *bubba*, and regaled her parents with stories of the past her father would phone *zeida* and say to him: 'You shouldn't be filling her mind with that stuff about the old times. Telling her about how you used to swing chickens around your head to cast out all the dybbuks and demons and evil.' Miriam would listen and feel confused. She knew her *zeida*. He would meekly shrug his shoulders, scared that his grand-daughter would be taken away from him. Miriam wondered why he was scared. To her, he had the power of knowledge, links with the Almighty, answers to all her questions. Yet her parents, always working and not a part of her day-to-day life, seemed to be able to hold sway.

It wasn't until her mid-teens that the sophistication of family dynamics began to give her the answers.

Over the hubbub in the restaurant, Miriam remembered the early days. They were good days. Warm days. Days of optimism. And days filled with wonder at the way in which her *zeida*'s Almighty organised everything. Miriam asked, 'Zeida, do you remember in the old days what you used to tell me about sins?'

The old man didn't flinch from his efforts to eat his meal, but merely responded, 'I told you many things. What in particular?'

'You used to say that wherever I walked, directly underneath me was a devil, a dybbuk, and that I could see the dybbuk in my shadow.'

He looked at her with a wry smile. 'And now you're a smart lawyer, you're going to tell me I'm wrong?'

Miriam smiled. 'No, it's just that I always used to be frightened of things underneath me in case the dybbuk was there. Walking in the streets, I'd always be the one in my class who'd be looking at the ground. I'd be frightened to walk over puddles in case I saw the dybbuk's face, or walk over cracks in the pavement in case he put his hand up and grabbed my ankles.'

The old man stopped eating. '*Nu?* So I was wrong. I was only telling you what my father told me. It didn't do me any harm, so I thought maybe it would be good for you.'

He was becoming defensive. It wasn't her intention to attack or accuse. She reached over and put her hand on his thin arm.

'That's not what I mean. It's just that with all my education, working in law, reading all the right papers and books and so on, I've never lost that fear of there being some malevolent world hidden below the ground. Like some vast, avenging army waiting there to reach out and grab the unsuspecting and the unwary.'

He smiled. '*Nu! Mazeltov.* So some of my teaching has stayed. Remember, *bubeleh*, a flower is beautiful but it grows from manure. Just because it's an old man's superstition doesn't mean that there isn't something rotten, waiting to trap you.'

Zeida looked at her with fondness. She was so grown up. So sophisticated. Now so comfortable with words he struggled to understand. All he could muster were simple thoughts and age-less homilies. It was all so different from when he was growing up in Poland. His life was a blend of piety and superstition. The piety of the Bible, the superstition to deal with ancient fears. It was a world full of demons and dybbuks, where children were protected by age-old prayers and offerings, where mothers wore amulets to ward off evil and fathers performed rituals to ensure safety. And all the while the real dybbuks were rising like an army from hell, wearing black shirts and swastikas. There was no amulet that could protect him or his family from that enormity of evil. But he had escaped the evil with his wife and son and come to live in a new land, free of the horrors of Europe. A Europe he was destined never to see again in the lifetime he had lived in Australia.

Miriam's *zeida* had only recently become frail. It was an undignified way to end up. Of all her fears, the fear of growing old and incapable was the most terrifying. Yet although his body was shrinking and he was losing his dominion, his mind was as vivid and alert as it had ever been.

That night in the kosher restaurant, he had held forth like a biblical patriarch, about the Australian government, anti-Semitism and the stupidity of the old people at the Rosenthal. But the main topic of conversation was the failed peace conference in Cyprus, and the possible consequences for Jews around the world.

'You know what they've done?' her *zeida* asked her. 'Dr Tauber, the *ganzer macher* at the Rosenthal, says because of Ben Ari we should have a security guard at the door. Can you believe it? What Arab terrorist is interested in killing a bunch of old *Yidden*?' He laughed and coughed at the same time.

Miriam had listened in fascination all evening to the way he spoke. His simple words were like soldiers, sometimes attacking and sometimes defending, but always marching. She was enthralled by his knowledge of world affairs and his grasp of current events.

He smiled at her. Beautiful, clever, and not yet married. Still, with these modern young people, there was time. And this talk about dybbuks? A real devil was in Israel, at the top of the government. 'So, tell me, *bubeleh*,' he asked her, 'What do you think about Mr Raphael Ben Ari? Bastard or saint?'

He was goading her, like a prosecution barrister about to pounce on a victim in the witness box.

'Neither one nor the other. I only know what I've heard on the radio this evening, but you know these commentators. They're all partisan. What's your view?'

He continued to eat his soup, balancing the sectioned matzo balls on to his spoon. He relished the taste. So different, so much more flavoursome than the pap they served in the home. Just because a person grew old, did his enjoyment of flavours and spices suddenly cease?

'My view? Tell me your view. Tell me the Zionist approach.'

Miriam broke a crust of bread. 'I don't think I'm particularly upset,' she said. 'You know what happens when a country like Israel makes concessions. Look at the Balkans and what happened with the Serbian minority. Look at Northern Ireland even. I'm not saying they're right. Don't think that. But if you give an oppressed people an inch, it's only natural for them to see it as a sign of weakness and to want to take a mile.'

The old man simply nodded, absorbing her comments to see whether they were in accord with his.

'And what about Ben Ari himself? What do you think of him?' her grandfather asked. His thick, Polish accent was incapable of dealing with the inflections of the Hebrew name. When he said it, it sounded more like '*Bin Uri*'.

'Look,' Miriam said, 'when he went in to this conference, everyone knew he was a hawk and wasn't going to sell Israel short. I'm disappointed that he didn't give peace a try but we have no idea what deals the Arabs were negotiating in the corridors. Come on, Zeida, you know as well as I do how staged those conferences are. Most of the real work is done behind the scenes.'

Again the old man nodded. He had that ability to sum up a situation in a few well chosen words. Miriam wondered what he was going to say.

'The man's crazy. All the way to Cyprus, just to kick people in the guts. It isn't just the Arabs he insulted, but the Americans. Who feeds him, if not American *Yidden*? What's going to happen now? Donations will dry up. You'll see if they don't. All through that *farshtinkener* madman.'

Miriam was surprised by his vehemence. When he started to speak about the conference, she thought he was being mischievous. Now his demeanour was different. The skin which was stretched like parchment over his scalp tightened and a tiny blood vessel throbbed in his temple. He wasn't playing games any more. Something was making him angry.

Growing up in his care, Miriam quickly learned the ability

to change from being a lively and impertinent child into a cautious and respectful grand-daughter. Her grandfather and to a lesser extent her grandmother gave clear signals. They would joke and she would respond. But when she went beyond their tolerance, a change came over them and they became stern and authoritarian. She saw now that her *zeida* wanted her to play the role of a respecful grand-daughter. He was getting serious and he expected her to become an adversary. It was the way they debated. Both enjoyed the exercise. It kept her *zeida*'s mind alert, and it was a pleasant change from the civil law she practised every day. Her grandfather was trained in the Talmud, that vast repository of laws, stories and morality that was the treasury of the Jewish religion. He was a skilled debater and he had passed on his love of discourse to her.

'I'm sure Ben Ari was partly to blame, but surely the whole peace process was just a sham. These things always are.'

'Sham? *Vus iz deiz "sham"?*'

'Sham. A sort of a falsehood, a pretence. It was all done for public relations. There was never meant to be anything serious coming out of it.'

'Oh, so my grand-daughter knows what's going on in the minds of prime ministers and presidents, does she?'

'Look, Zeida, Syria and Iraq are terrorist nations. They're not going to change overnight, just for Israel, unless there's a change of government. The whole conference was just …' she lowered her voice, 'just bullshit. Ben Ari probably realised it and rather than show himself as weak, he thought he'd make a stand for principle.'

But the old man dismissed it with a wave of his crooked fingers. 'I knew it would happen.'

Miriam nodded. 'Oh, I think many people were sceptical when Ben Ari …'

'No! I'm saying I knew it would happen. Not I thought it would happen. Ben Ari only ever thinks about himself. He doesn't have the good of the Jews in his heart. It's the sort of thing he's done all his life. The *mamzer* should never have gone if he was going to do what he did.'

'But Zeida, that's a bit harsh,' said Miriam 'Sure, he's right-wing, and xenophobic! But you couldn't call him selfish. Everything he does is for his people.'

'People! Ha! What are you talking? I've known him since he was a child and never once has he done anything for anybody but himself.'

Miriam stared at the old man in surprise. 'You know Raphael Ben Ari?'

'Sure.' Again the old man dismissed his grand-daughter with a wave of his hand. 'I taught him at Hebrew school when he was a boy. I was years older than him. He was a swine then, and he's a swine now!'

'I didn't know you knew somebody important like Ben Ari. Why did you keep it to yourself? Why haven't you said anything before? God, you're a man of surprises.' She frowned and said, 'In fact, I know nothing about your home. Why have you never told me anything about your village? Every time I ask you, you keep quiet about it. We've discussed Warsaw and Poland and Europe but you've never told me about your village. Why? Is it because of Ben Ari?'

The old man shrugged his shoulders. 'So now I'm telling you something. Wasn't it King Solomon who said, "To everything there is a season and a time to every purpose under heaven"? Well, now is the time.'

It was from Ecclesiastes, but Miriam didn't want to contradict him.

The old man looked at her with bemusement. He answered her question with more questions. It was a particularly Jewish trait, something which even Paul Sinclair had started to do.

'Ben Ari? Sure I knew him. What don't I know about him? Wasn't I born in the same village? Didn't I know his parents? What? You think you're the only one with a history. Do you know the struggles we had to go through in the old country?'

A waiter came over to their table and picked up the old man's bowl. He looked at the mess and smiled ingratiatingly at Miriam, as though sharing a common disgust with old people.

Miriam gave him the same withering look she gave a hostile client and he shrank from her view. She reached over and put her hand on to her *zeida*'s arm. The blue material of his suit collapsed as though she had grasped a deflating balloon. It was as if his arm was nothing more than bone.

'Zeida, please don't upset yourself. I know how hard it was in the old country.'

'Sure, life was tough. For me and for the others. Living on a *shtetl* wasn't like living in Vaucluse or Double Bay or Toorak. That's not Jewish life … that's not *Yidden*, living in a community together. You should have seen our village. Everybody knew everybody else. If a *Yid* was in trouble, the first thing he would do was to go to the rabbi. Today rabbis are just *schlemiels*.'

He waved his hand through the air again, this time to dismiss the current crop of university-educated rabbis. 'When I was a boy, a rabbi was a rabbi. He was a judge, a jury, an adviser. A man who knew God. You'd ask him questions about business, or the Communists, or whether the price you were paying for a new plough was too much. Rabbis knew everything in those days. Today, what's a rabbi? What do they know these days? They come out of *yeshivas* with degrees and they know how to pray and sing, but what do they know about God or life?'

Miriam had heard her grandfather's diatribe against the rabbinate in the past. 'But Zeida, what about Ben Ari? Don't just leave it there. You said you knew him. The Prime Minister of Israel! Tell me about him.'

'He was one of the children in Chelmnitz. That was our *shtetl* on the outskirts of Rawicz. I knew his parents. They were friends of my parents. Together, the two families started a small business carrying coal from Leszno to Rawicz.'

The other Jews and the restaurant faded from view. Miriam and her grandfather were alone in Europe. A time when there were no computers or televisions or filofaxes. A simple time. The smell was of the earth—a rich, generous, fertile smell. A smell of fresh *challas* on Friday night and barley soup and lentils. Of milk delivered in churns and meat hanging in the butcher's window. Of old women in scarves and young boys in caps with frockcoats and *payot* behind their ears walking quickly to the synagogue. A time of certainty, of questions with answers, and answers found in the Torah and the Talmud. A time when old men with long grey beards and *tallit* over their heads sat around long tables and endlessly debated whether an apple that had fallen to the ground could be picked up and eaten on the Sabbath. And if not, why not.

The old man drank a sip of water to clear his emotions.

'Every Monday, his father and I would go to Leszno and buy the coal and bring it back the same day. But we had so many problems along the road, it was too dangerous. The *goyim* sometimes used to tip the cart over and steal the coal. So, we gave it up.'

Miriam was astonished. 'I never knew you used to deliver coal in the old country.'

'Sure. What do you think? The Jews in the *shtetl* had to buy it from the *goyim* merchants and they were being charged two, sometimes three times what the Poles had to pay. So Moishe Mikolajczyk, that's his father, and my father decided to pick some up ourselves every week from the depot in Leszno. My dad made me go as his helper. But they stopped us, the *mumzers*.'

Miriam loved hearing stories about Jewish life in the past. She knew much about the Jews of Europe. Every time her *zeida* spoke she listened in rapt attention. For Miriam, it was living history. She and her grandparents had often discussed life in Europe, but never life on their *shtetl*. And her father had been a young boy when the family had fled to escape the pogroms and the rise of Nazi Germany just before the war. Her father, she knew, had come to Australia at a very young age and had spent his formative and adult years trying to hide his Polishness. He had no memory of life in the early days. Family history had rarely been discussed in her youth.

In her early years, Miriam had reflected her parents' embarrassment at being of Jewish-Polish extraction, until a revelation had made her come to terms with her origins and her ancestry. Happy to be Jewish at home, she was crushed by embarrassment at being different in school. She was a *reffo*, even though she had been born in Australia. During her school days she had painfully tried to hide her Judaism until she was given an essay to write about the anti-semitism of Adolf Hitler. She researched the details in her school library, asked friends and their parents and eventually came to her own parents to seek knowledge. They rebuffed her. So she asked her grandparents. Over the period of a week, she learnt in detail the awful truth of Nazism and its decimation of European Jewry. It was a seminal experience, one that changed her life. By the time she handed in her essay she had become proudly, fiercely, militantly Jewish.

She blamed her parents for trying to protect her and hiding the details of Jewish suffering, resenting the way they asked her grandparents not to discuss their life in pre-war Poland. But when she began her research, her grandfather opened up the world of Eastern European culture to her. And as she began to know its depth, she embraced her history with the vehemence of the convert.

Miriam had become a Zionist. Her first mission was to make her parents feel wrong about their self-consciousness. She went to Zionist Camp, learned the songs and wrote impassioned articles for youth magazines. But she still knew little about her religion. Her parents had rarely taken her to synagogue. She and her *zeida* would talk for hours about the books of Moses, the philosophies and ecstasies of the writings of the prophets and the judges. As she grew into womanhood, he introduced her to that most esoteric of Jewish religious writings, the Cabbala. He had warned her not to discuss its writings with anyone else, as custom forbade people under forty from reading the books of mysticism.

Her parents were forced to accept her change in attitude towards her ancestry. They realised that she was a woman, and no longer needed to be protected from the truth, but Miriam still found it hard to forgive her parents for their dissembling and they became increasingly estranged, as though they were divorcing, daughter and parents. For weeks at a time she failed to contact them. It distressed her grandfather, who acted as mediator. 'Miriam,' he would say to her, 'they're still your parents. Remember the fifth commandment.' He was the guardian of her moral values and when he chastised her, she would contact them, but it was always out of duty, rarely out of love. How could she love people, even her mother and father, who had tried to deny her, her past? And without the past, what was her present and her future?

The greatest regret of her life was that they had died without the rift having healed.

It had been one of those fruitless turning points in life. A momentary distraction, the sort of thing that happens to everybody several times a day. But this distraction had taken place at 90 kilometres an hour, and within a fraction of a second both her father and her mother had been killed on the road between Alice Springs and Darwin, when a truck driver had momentarily gone to sleep at the wheel. His truck veered over to the opposite side of the road and crashed head-on into the car, crushing it beyond recognition. The truck driver escaped with minor injuries.

Immediately Miriam began to pursue greater retribution from him than the fine and disqualification the court had imposed. She started a private prosecution but the senior partner in her firm took her into his office shortly after, put his arm around her and told her about the dangers of using legal process to expiate private grief. She returned to her office and sobbed for over an hour.

Her life was a jumble of confused imperatives. She had dropped her charges against the truck driver because she was being vindictive. But she was still expected to perform above average in the aggressive, male-dominated world of law. She also had to be a responsible and acquiescent grand-daughter.

And most difficult of all, she had to be a mother to her grandfather, helping him in his remaining years. Her social life fell to pieces. At first her friends were supportive, but as her mourning became a compulsion, the sympathy evaporated. Her work didn't suffer but her relationship with Paul became difficult for them both. He stuck by her, hanging around the periphery, waiting for things to improve.

Judaism only allowed a short period of intensive mourning but demanded that prayers be said regularly for a period of a year. She accompanied her *zeida* to synagogue every Saturday to hear him recite the mourner's *kaddish*. Miriam found it a period of extended pain and she determined to return to the world of normality as quickly as possible. Yossi Samuelson took a different path. Having been raised in religion, he found a comfort in mourning for his dead son and daughter-in-law.

Miriam seemed to pull life together when her parents' death was no longer so fresh and painful. Her friends marvelled at her strength. Her grandfather worried. One night, many months after the accident, she drove her car to the cliffs at Harbord, overlooking the Pacific Ocean to the north of Sydney. She looked at the black ocean and the white phosphorescence of the waves. She spent the night crying. It was cathartic. She began to repair herself. As she drove home in the early hours of the morning, dawn turning black streets into grey, she realised that she had a mission in life. But for her *zeida*, she was alone in the world. She had no brothers or sisters. Her mother had not been able to have other children, so all she had was her *zeida*. She would ensure that he was never alone.

Miriam employed a woman to clean the house. But he refused to employ a housekeeper to look after him … 'What am I, a Rothschild, that I need a maid?' he would say. Often he talked about putting himself into the Rosenthal Home to be looked after, but Miriam resisted the idea.

Late one Thursday afternoon, eight months after she had buried her parents, Miriam walked down the gentle sloping pathway of her *zeida's* Bellevue Hill home. The house was a small three-bedroom Federation cottage, which Miriam remembered with joy as images of her early childhood flooded into her mind. She carried two parcels of groceries to him on her way back from work. Miriam let herself into the house and called out: 'Zeida!'

She knew at once that he wasn't there. The house was cold. The furniture was still there, but his presence, his spirit, had gone. She hoped he was out for a walk. She put the groceries down in the kitchen and there she saw a note, the writing distressingly shaky:

Darling,

    I know you will be angry so this is my little trick. I have gone to the Rosenthal. I signed the papers last week. Come and see me if you have time. It is best for both of us.

    P.S. Could you sell the house and keep something for yourself, and transfer the rest to the Home.

The note wasn't even signed. Miriam was devastated, as she thought of the confusion that must have been in her grandfather's mind. He had an intrinsic dislike of associating with old people. Yet his path was clear. He had thought through all the contingencies and decided to institutionalise himself.

Miriam sat on one of the torn green kitchen chairs which she had always promised that she would replace. Now it was too late. She looked at the groceries and the note, and the empty kitchen, and the emptiness of her life. For months she hadn't cried. Not since she was alone at the beach. She had held herself together. She thought she was repaired. But his note was the final expiation for her parents. She sobbed. Like people throughout history wailing in loneliness, this time she cried for herself. She was alone in the outside world, totally and utterly alone.

In fact, her grandfather had made an easy transition into the nursing home. He had settled down and found more friends than he had expected to. Strangely, perhaps, it was not so easy for Miriam, but as the months went by she came to terms with her freedom.

She began to invite Paul to stay all night with her, something she had never done while her grandfather lived in his own home and there was the odd chance that he might come by in the morning. She began to go away for weekends with Paul without feeling a need to lie or excuse herself.

The noise of plates clattering in the restaurant brought her back to the present. She looked at her *zeida*. So often these days, her mind wandered from the task at hand. In practising law, her mind was focused, but outside of its confines she frequently vacillated. A passing waiter jolted her out of the daydream. Perhaps it was over-work, perhaps a boredom with life. She was only ever fully aware of what she was doing when she was involved with the strategies of a lawsuit.

'Somehow I can't see you behind a horse and cart. I've always thought of you as a sparkling urbanite.'

'Don't be so silly. Miriam, you of all people should know. Jews don't belong in a coffee house. We're people of the land. We're farmers as well as philosophers. That's the wonderful thing about Jews and Israel. Albert Einstein pulling a plough, thinking of relativity.'

She laughed, and nodded in apology.

'So what was it like on your *shtetl*?' she asked. 'Did you have streets and lighting, or were they tracks with goats and cows wandering? Did you have a matchmaker? How did you and Bubba meet?'

The old man's eyes were already clouding through age and cataracts, but he looked back through more than sixty years to another place, another life, another history.

The place … the plains of central Poland, flat, grassy, arid, freezing in winter, balmy in summer. There were distant hills, with clear springs and vast roaring rivers, a place where he and his parents and his family had lived for longer than their collective memory.

The time … before the war, before the madness, before his life was turned upside down by pogroms and Nazis. By nations fighting nations. By races being exterminated.

The history … a history where everybody spoke *Yiddish*. Where Hebrew was the language of holy prayer. Where the lives of Moses, Joshua, David, Saul, Deborah, Isaiah and the other towering figures of the Jewish faith had been the currency of the day. Where horses and donkeys and carts had walked the earthen streets of Chelmnitz. Where the edge of the village was the edge of his world. Where his simple innocent life had been made hell by marauding gangs of fanatics. Masked men who were intent upon killing him and everybody whom he loved.

'When did we meet? *Yoi!* You're asking me to think! We met at the beginning of the 1930s, I think it was. She was the daughter of the man who taught me Talmud. She wasn't strong, your *bubba*. Like your mother, she could only bear one child. I wanted a large family, but …'

The old man sighed. He looked at his grand-daughter with affection and said, 'We left Poland in 1937. After the pogroms started.'

Miriam interrupted. 'It's sad, Zeida, that in all the times we've talked about the past, you've never given me any details about your village. The times I've asked you and you've evaded the questions. Why didn't you want to talk about it?'

'What's to say?' asked the old man, shrugging his shoulders. 'A village is a village. You've seen one *shtetl*, you've seen them all.'

Miriam shook her head. 'You've taught me so much about Judaism and ancient times. It was your life I wanted to know about. Your history.'

'Who am I that I'm so important all of a sudden? *Moishe Rabbenu?* So now I'm telling you. What do you want to know?'

'Tell me about the village and the people. I've never known what you did for a living. After all these years I suddenly find out you used to drive a horse and cart, delivering coal …'

'So how do you deliver coal?' the old man laughed. 'In a Rolls-Royce?'

Miriam continued to ask questions of her *zeida* until he held up his bony hand. 'Wait. Wait. What is this, an inquisition? Who are you, Torquemada? Where's a rack to torture me so that I'll tell you the answers? You know, God rest their souls, your mother and father didn't like me to talk about the old days. Maybe you need to know. Maybe everyone needs to know. Shall I tell you when being a Jew was really being a Jew. When you lived on a *shtetl*. For a thousand years, the Jews in Poland, or in the Pale of Russia, or in Germany built a civilisation like you can't understand. Not like an Australian or English or American civilisation, with buildings and monuments and bridges. Our civilisation was the civilisation of the mind.'

He looked at the other customers in the restaurant.

'We had rabbis with their own courts of justice, when the rest of Europe was burning witches. We had our own theatres. Our own newspapers. Philosophers, musicians, artists. If you were a Jew in Russia and you went on business somewhere, you could travel from *shtetl* to *shtetl* and always you could find a friend or somewhere to stay. Or a family to look after you. Jews were never alone in those days.'

By now he had begun to speak in such an animated way that people at other tables looked around. He hadn't noticed but Miriam put her hand on his and said, 'Shh, Zeida, people are listening.'

'So maybe they'll learn something,' he said, raising his voice.

A father tapped his daughter on the arm and whispered in her ear. The girl turned around and stared with curiosity at the old man.

'Jews protected each other from the outside world. From the madmen in Russia or Germany or Poland who were out to kill them. But inside the *shtetl*, there was such a feeling of warmth and comfort. Such a feeling of belonging, like you children today don't understand.'

The old man continued. His pride in what he was saying became pain in what was to come. 'And with one man, it all went. Adolf Hitler put an end to a thousand years of Jewish culture. Do you know, darling, that half the Jews killed in the holocaust were from Poland? Three million Jews! Not just names. Not just families, but a thousand years of history. Tradition. Knowledge. Culture. All up in the smoke of those gas chambers. Even today, I can't believe it.'

Miriam turned and saw men and women at adjacent tables nodding their heads. Her *zeida* was speaking for everybody in the restaurant.

She was lost in silence. The old man fought to control his emotions. Even though Miriam's immediate family had been saved from destruction in the gas chambers because her grandparents had been clever enough to leave Poland early, she knew that most of his family and friends had been wiped out by the obscenity of Nazism.

'But Zeida, tell me more about Ben Ari. This is fascinating.'

He lowered his voice to a conspiratorial whisper. 'I knew him before he changed his name when he went to live in Israel. Then his name was Wladyslaw Mikolajczyk. He was Moishe's only son. All the others were daughters. But his parents were too weak with him. They spoilt him rotten. They used to worship him, the little *gonif*. But boy, did he grow up to spite them. He was so bad in *cheda* sometimes, I had to kick him out of class. Rude, silly, aggressive. Always questions. Questions, questions, questions. Never would he let me finish a sentence before he shot his hand up and said, "But *Melamud* ..." and then he would ask some stupid question about the Bible.'

'But Zeida, that doesn't sound so bad. Every child asks questions.'

'Hah! You don't understand. You don't follow. These weren't questions. The boy was trying to make a fool of me. Of his other teachers. He wasn't just showing off his knowledge. Oh, he was clever. Sure, very clever. He knew a lot. But it was like he was tormenting us. Trying to make us look silly.'

Miriam shook her head. 'But half the kids in school are like that, Zeida.'

The old man took a sip of water. 'Some people become rotten. This kid was born rotten. In all these years I've never forgotten the look on his face when he stood with his back to the class, challenging me. Telling me I was a fool. That's not a naughty schoolboy, *bubeleh*. That's a kid who's going to grow up to be a criminal. Sixty years and I remember his face like it was yesterday.'

Miriam could scarcely believe he harboured such hatred. 'He doesn't ask questions these days,' she said. 'He gives orders.'

'The other boys hated him,' Yossi Samuelson continued. 'He was always getting beaten. Every day I had to separate him from other kids beating him. But every day, there he was, keen to learn. If only he hadn't been so rotten. Then he grew to be a young man. That's when he went real bad. The *mumzer*! You know what he did. He joined the Radical Workers Party, which was just another outlet for Communism.'

'A Communist! What are you talking about?'

The old man held up his hand for silence. 'Listen, don't talk. Learn. It was Stalin's way of trying to get control of Poland in the early days. Boy! Did he ever work for them. Night and day he wrote pamphlets. Or he'd go to some training camp. He even organised marches against the Fascists. He was always busy organising, organising, like a little machine. He went to Warsaw once, handing out leaflets on street corners, trying to get the *Yidden* to let Communists from Moscow talk in the Great Synagogue.'

Miriam looked stunned. She shook her head. 'But he's a rabid anti-Communist, Zeida.'

Her *zeida* smiled. 'All I know …'

Before he could continue, the waiter brought the second course. Instinctively, Miriam urged her grandfather to remain silent until the waiter had left.

'We warned him about this Communism thing he was getting into. "Are you stupid?" we said to him, "Don't be so public. You'll get yourself and you'll get us into trouble." But he never paid any attention. He was so busy you never knew from one day to the next where he would spring up. One day, he just seemed to disappear from the village, and then a week or so later he would come back and try to get the young people to join the Party. But he didn't get any support.'

'Zeida, eat your *kreplach* before they get cold,' Miriam said, but the old man was too absorbed in what he was telling her.

'I remember he used to get very angry with us. He warned us about the danger we were in from the Fascists. Well, at least he was right in that. Unless we supported the Communists, bad things would happen. We laughed at him. He would get furious and scream and shout. That made us laugh more. Then gangs came and took away village leaders. Rabbi, *shammus*, the important people from the *shule*. They were never seen again. Nobody believed Mikolajczyk was behind it. It was just too horrible for us to think about. We didn't know who was doing it. Mikolajczyk went around the village saying, "I told you so." He said, "Join the Communists or more people will disappear." People were scared of him, despite his size. Then he moved out of his home and district. I think he went to Moscow. Already it was too late to do anything. It was the middle of the 1930s. Germany was making noises. The whole world seemed go *meshuggeh*!'

'Zeida, you're surely not saying that Ben Ari did these things against the Jews in your village? Ben Ari? The Prime Minister of Israel?'

Again, he dismissed her with a wave. 'You think he's a swine now? You should've seen him then.'

The emotion had made him tired. He stared down at his plate, picked up a spoon and tried to scoop one of the slippery parcels into his mouth. Miriam felt an agony of compassion for him. She reached over and helped him eat a few. He nodded with appreciation.

'Is this why you haven't told me before about life on your

shtetl? Is this what you were hiding from me? Why didn't you tell me about Ben Ari? Why have you kept this to yourself?'

'What's to keep to myself? Who's interested in a crazy Pole who's now Prime Minister of a crazy country? What's so unusual about that? Most of the Israeli Prime Ministers weren't born there. Ben Gurion. He was Polish. Meir, she was Russian. Begin, he was Polish. Shamir, he was Polish. What's another crazy Pole?'

'But Zeida. The fact that he was a Communist. That's a fantastic piece of information. The fact that he worked to make your village Communist. That he made people disappear, like in a pogrom. All his life, in Israel, he's been fanatically anti-Communist. Why doesn't anybody know anything about this? Just about every speech he's made has talked about the menace of the Soviets. Why haven't you told anybody this before?'

The old man struggled with another *kreplach* and looked warmly at his beloved grandchild.

He shrugged his shoulders in a gesture of five thousand years of Jewish resignation.

'Nobody asked.'

CHAPTER FOUR

Mikhail Alexandrovich Bukharin sat in the stuffy cabin, sweating in his thick uniform, and seethed with anger and frustration. He snatched the plastic tumbler of vodka from the tray proffered by the dour Aeroflot hostess and threw the contents to the back of his throat with one gulp. The cheap vodka was thick and oily and his lips curled in disgust. It offended the taste buds on the back of his tongue. High in alcohol, low in flavour and fit only for peasants. It would at least calm his nerves.

Along with 108 other passengers Bukharin had been cooped up in the Tupelov 154 at the beginning of the runway of Moscow's Vnukovo Airport for the past hour and a half, quietly going crazy.

Years earlier, when he was a Colonel-General in the KGB, he would simply have got out of his seat, marched to the cockpit, taken command of the plane's communication system and ordered the cretins in the control tower to clear the flight to leave immediately, or risk being retrained in Siberia.

But that was years ago. Today, Mikhail Alexandrovich Bukharin was still a Colonel-General, but not in the KGB. There was no KGB. It had been disbanded following the collapse of the USSR

Today he was ineffectual. He was an officer in an administrative division of a minor battalion of the Army of the Russian Republic, one of a dozen new national armies which had been created since the eruptions of the post-Gorbachev era. He was forty-five years old and his career had come to a full stop.

The Russian Army was the mightiest of the new nationalist forces, and carried the majority of what remained of the nuclear stockpile, but even that had diminished to the point where America could annihilate the country without serious fear of reprisal. Nothing was being spent to modernise or re-equip the Motherland's first-strike capacity, or to train and maintain the rest of the decimated defence forces.

Not that Gorbachev was solely responsible. At least in his early days, Gorbachev had respected the invaluable role that the KGB played in securing the integrity of the USSR. No. It was that white-haired, drunken, womanising fool Boris Yeltsin, the man who stole power from the people, declaring himself President, like the Tsar, who had humiliated the Service and disbanded it. And following its emasculation, he had encouraged witch-hunts of senior personnel, reminiscent of the American trials in the 1950s of so-called Communists and fellow-travellers, and had hounded hundreds of KGB patriots from their public offices. Many militant Communists, the more senior KGB officers and some of its army of informants had been exposed before the ignominy of public trials. The ruling elite of the commonwealth of former Communist states had certainly learnt a lot from the McCarthyist era in America. They had even come close to collaring Bukharin himself, who felt the wind of their anger. Some of his close colleagues, especially those who had publicly flaunted the privilege of being in the KGB to the detriment of ordinary Soviet citizens—those powerless little people who queued for hours for meat, milk and bread—had been placed on trial and were now serving long prison sentences in the Lubyanka. But Bukharin had escaped because he had always kept a low profile. He didn't enjoy power or privilege for itself. He didn't enjoy striding like some latter-day Tsar over the common people. He just enjoyed his job of protecting Mother Russia from the decadent West.

Those were the old days. Today, with the KGB inoperative, those colleagues of Mikhail Alexandrovich's who had escaped persecution were either officers within the various national armies or had left the security service in disgust. Others with good connections in the new Russian government had been absorbed into the newly created Russian Intelligence Service, which was currently cooperating with the CIA, the French

DGSE, Germany's HVA and Britain's SIS to halt the illegal flow of nuclear technology and weapons-grade plutonium from disgruntled former Soviet scientists to Third World maniacs.

Bukharin had refused to join this new intelligence service, finding the idea of cooperating with foreign intelligence forces he had spent his life fighting too much for him to bear.

That was only half the story. Once the boundaries which divided East from West had been dismantled, a number of former KGB officers had set up new lives for themselves in places such as Germany, Austria and Italy, using American dollars which they had salted away during the lucrative years of the Cold War. But Bukharin, who like his father before him had been scrupulous in his financial dealings with the former elite, was now suffering both professionally and financially.

Bukharin's transition into an administrative position within the Russian Army had not been difficult. As a trained KGB operative, he had spent half a lifetime adopting different personas, living underground in America, France and the United Kingdom. Or he had played the role of a junior diplomat, or chauffeur in some embassy, while recruiting local agents. So for him, playing the role of an unambitious clerk, living with his head down, was outwardly easy. Inwardly it was a daily agony, a crucifixion.

Despite the years which had passed since the witch-hunts, the people of the Russian Republic still bore a deep-seated resentment towards the former security service. If he had let any person on the plane know that he was once in the KGB, he would have been ridiculed and the journey would have been made intolerable. So he sat quietly, fuming along with all the other powerless passengers as he waited for the hold-up in air-traffic to be sorted out.

The boredom of the delay was broken as Bukharin listened to an angry confrontation three rows ahead between a drunken passenger and the unsmiling hostess. The drunk had demanded to know when the plane would take off, and was told curtly that it would only do so when permission was given. That didn't satisfy him, as it would have in the old days. He ridiculed her, stood up and began to sing an old Russian folk song about an old woman servant, a *babushka*, who was so stupid she drank the health of the Tsar every morning. The man, weaving around from the vodka, walked unsteadily up and down the aisle to the anger of the hostess and the amusement of the other passengers. He waved his arms for everybody to join in his song, but they all turned and avoided his face. He was alone. The other passengers simply listened to the entertainment.

Bukharin grudgingly admired the idiot. At least he had the balls to stand up to the petty authority she was exercising. Not like the rest of them. They would never dare to ask provocative questions, such as why there was a hold-up, whether it was due to inefficiency, or whether the huge salaries paid to over-pampered state officials running air-traffic around Moscow was just money down the drain.

The free-market economy ravaging Russia had not managed to change some things around the place. Most of its citizens were still cowed by officialdom. And the singer? In the old days, he would have found himself in a psychiatric hospital. Today, he would go home with a hangover.

Another twenty minutes went by, the only sop to the frayed nerves of the passengers being the free vodka given away by cabin crew. Then suddenly, the whine of the engines increased in pitch and the captain's voice sounded over the intercom: 'Please return to your seats. We've been given permission to take off.'

That was it! No 'sorry' … no 'I regret' … no 'please accept the apologies of the management and staff of Aeroflot for wasting two precious hours of your time and completely screwing up any plans you might have had.'

No! there was nothing like that from these petty little martinets … these jumped-up bureaucrats revelling in their newly won autonomy … just a curt and officious instruction to return to your seats.

There was a time, thought Bukharin, but that time was in another world.

The Tupelov slowly gathered speed and the atmosphere in the plane calmed down. Not only the vodka, but the air-conditioning began to work. It had been hot out there on the end of the runway. Most strangers in Moscow didn't appreciate that while the winters were bitterly cold, the summers could be divine, with blue skies, scudding white clouds and balmy nights. When they were airborne, Bukharin looked down towards the city in which he had been born, where he had grown to manhood, and where his position of prominence had once made him a silent member of the ruling establishment.

When he was a child he had not lived in Moscow itself, but just outside, in a compound in the woods built especially for MGB officers. Sometimes at night, when his father came home early enough, he would regale him with stories about Moscow life. About its gaiety, the lights which illuminated the fairytale buildings, the noise and warmth of the cafes, the shops with undreamed-of toys. It was a wonderland and every night Mikhail Alexandrovich would go to sleep dreaming about how one day he would be a man and he would go to Moscow and see the wonders for himself rather than through his father's eyes.

When Mikhail had graduated with first-class honours from university and joined the army, he began his first tentative footsteps along the path towards the privilege which would take him inside those buildings. When he was invited to sit for the KGB examinations and his fidelity to the Party was tested, he was one step further along the path. But it was not until he was a junior officer that he realised it was only the centre of Moscow which held the glory of Russia. The outskirts of the city, the drear, drab battleship-grey barrack blocks in which the powerless lived was the real Moscow, where millions of Muscovites lived a monotonous day-to-day and hand-to-mouth existence. It was the legacy of Stalin, and Lenin before him. And before them, the legacy of Tsarist privilege that a nation had rebelled against.

In the KGB he was in the centre of power, one of the privileged elite, but he deliberately avoided exercising and even enjoying that very power. He still lived the purity of his dreams. It was when he was awake that he felt angry.

As the plane climbed higher, the sunlight reflected off rivers and lakes. He still loved Moscow, despite its current state of chaos, despite the free market economy which had allowed people of no background, no breeding, to become the new Russian powermongers overnight. Like the barrow boys of the financial sector of London, or the yuppies of Wall Street, they were men and women whose street-smart entrepreneurial abilities had earned them wealth and prestige. In Bukharin's day, such accolades had come through hard work and dedication to the Party through a lifetime of patriotism.

The plane climbed rapidly to 10,000 feet and began a slow left-hand roll towards the south. Far below, luxuriating in the sunshine, Moscow looked beautiful as the sun flared on lakes and windows. On the ground, Bukharin's Moscow had become cold and indifferent. From the air, it still looked like a dream. The Moskva River, from which the ancient city took its name, glistened like a snake as it wound its sinuous path through the centre of the Russian capital. First it flowed north, past what used to be called Lenin's Train of Mourning; then it passed the Museum of Russian Culture; then under the Krasnokholmsky Bridge until it travelled westwards towards the Kremlin; then south through Luzhniki Stadium into the gentle Lenin Hills.

Bukharin stared down the aisle of the plane and had another mouthful of vodka. Moscow had once been his home, his pride, and his security, but in the past few hideous years, it had become a web of intrigue and danger. Odd! In the old days, the days of Stalin and Brezhnev, it was the ordinary Muscovite whose life was in constant danger. Now, the hunter was the hunted. He knew that if he were to make too much of a fuss like some of his colleagues, he would attract attention to himself and allow the monstrous spiders silently lying in wait in the Kremlin to trap another victim in their web.

The vodka was beginning to have the desired effect, not only on Bukharin, but also on the rest of the passengers. Heavy eyes began to droop, and interest in the countryside south-east of Moscow waned. Bukharin himself drifted into a dreamless sleep. He could never stay awake for more than a short time on a plane, which was both a blessing and a curse. In his former life it had been necessary for him to be totally aware of his surroundings at all times, especially on the long flights from Oslo to New York, the traditional route by which KGB operatives flew undetected into the United States.

After what seemed like a moment, Bukharin was awakened by a change in the aircraft's engine pitch as it slowed down and began its descent towards the Crimea. Bukharin realised with gratitude that he had not been awakened by the hostess during the flight to eat what Aeroflot advertised as food.

He looked out of the window and saw the vast expanse of the Black Sea, the gigantic body of water washing the soft underbelly of Russia. Through the heat haze, Bukharin could make out little settlements on the shores. They were not fishing villages, but the dachas of the new powermongers—dachas which had been sequestered from their Soviet owners when the new capitalist regime had taken over.

The plane swung for its final descent into Odessa airport. The effect of the vodka had worn off during his sleep and, as was his habit of a lifetime, Bukharin reviewed all the facts he would need for the forthcoming meeting. It was a meeting he had not ever expected to take place. The KGB was dead. Dead and buried! Yet a surreptitious message had been placed under the door of his flat asking him to take lunch with a man once considered to be the third most powerful person in the USSR. A man who was his one-time boss, but to whom he had only spoken on a handful of occasions. When Bukharin had followed the instructions of the note and signalled his agreement to meet, a messenger had delivered a wad of papers marked 'Ultra Secret'. The thrill of the old days had revitalised him. The papers were astounding. They told a story which was scarcely believable. And now he would have to give his opinion. For years he had been in a state of limbo, as once-powerful Russia, a mother with a multitude of children, floundered alone in the world. Forced ignominiously to watch as the United States, like an imperious landlord, strode across the globe bullying its tenants into order.

Bukharin had never been one to believe in monumental events, in turning points of history. He believed that events were the results of a progression, sometimes controlled, sometimes random. Perhaps this meeting would be the beginning of a train of events which could restore order and pride to the Russian people and give them a government they deserved.

'So, Mikhail Alexandrovich, you received my note!'

It was a statement, not a question. Seated in a wicker chair on the verandah of his dacha overlooking the Black Sea—just south of Yalta where the post-war world had been divided by old men seated on wicker chairs—Genardy Arkyovich Petrovsky had aged dramatically in the four years since the two men had last met.

Dressed in an open-neck white cotton shirt and baggy blue canvas trousers, his grey skin sagging and mottled with liver spots, he displayed none of the health that people who lived in resort areas were supposed to exhibit. Only the veins on and around his nose showed any colour, a florid red, tiny capillaries ruptured by years of vodka and brandy. And his eyebrows, bushy and overgrown, made him look like a medieval demon.

In comparison to Petrovsky, Mikhail Bukharin had not deteriorated physically. At 6 feet 1 inch, with a broad chest and greying black hair, he wore his health visibly, although in recent years his regimen of exercise had suffered at the hands of boredom. He stood at attention before the old man.

'Thank you, Genardy Arkyovich. Yes, I received your letter, and was proud that you should remember me.'

The old man gazed at the younger. His ability to see beneath the skin of subterfuge, the reason for his survival in the perilous world of the Kremlin, had not left him. It was an unnerving skill that had enabled Petrovsky to navigate in safety through the regimes of Stalin, Krushchev, Brezhnev and the others, even Gorbachev and Yeltsin. A smile slowly spread across his lips. 'Cut the bullshit, and pour me a drink ... lemonade! The woman put some out for us. Then go and get changed. You must be baking in that clerk's uniform.'

Mikhail Alexandrovich poured the old man a drink and went to his room. As he walked through the dacha he saw that, although small, it was exquisitely furnished. The cheap chairs, curtains, carpets and other furniture of apartments such as his own in Moscow were not present. Here was quality, the type of wealth assembled over a lifetime of comfort and success.

He peeked into the loungeroom. It was like entering a Tolstoy novel. Deep carpet, walls ceiling to floor with bookshelves, astrakhan rugs around the stovepipe fire, a velvet ottoman worn in the centre from decades of feet resting after a hard day, and a nest of carved cedar tables. Bukharin thought they might be Persian or Lebanese. On them rested a leather-bound book open face down. Pushkin? Gogol? He picked it up. It was a volume of Turgenev, but underneath, hidden from view, Bukharin saw *Collected Articles from Crocodil*, the Russian satirical magazine. He smiled and returned the Turgenev cover so the old man's secret would be safe.

He walked into one of the bedrooms and changed into cooler clothes. Bukharin's thoughts on the plane had concerned the document he was sent. Now it was necessary to think more about Petrovsky. Know thine enemy. Genardy Arkyovich Petrovsky! A man to be wary of. He had climbed inexorably to the heights of power within the USSR, yet it was a power wielded in secret. Only those at the top felt the brunt of his authority. Those below made assumptions and guesses as once-important men and women mysteriously disappeared forever or were last heard of in Siberia.

Petrovsky had been Stalin's right-hand man and had served

as adviser and confidant to every government since. His power, his contacts, once put him at the very epicentre of Russian strength. In retirement he had retained his power. No one had dared to attempt to remove him from his dacha.

Ten minutes later, the two men were seated opposite each other on the patio, the small table between them full of black bread, herrings, a plate of onions, red and black caviar, a dish of sour cream, a plate of cold boiled potatoes and a huge pitcher of lemonade. Both men were ready to discuss the reason for Bukharin's visit.

'Well!' said Petrovsky. 'You've seen the details of the plan.'

Again, the question was purely rhetorical. In fact, Bukharin had only been shown sketchy details of the plan. Petrovsky would show him more at the right time. Bukharin knew that Petrovsky held him in respect as a former strategic specialist in Middle East affairs attached to both the 8th, as well as the 18th, Departments of the First Chief Directorate (Foreign Intelligence) of the KGB. He was confident his opinion would count very highly.

'I've seen the plan. Yes. It's bold, dramatic and, I must say, unbelievably risky. If the decision were mine, I would have to advise against attempting it in its present form.'

The old man sat back in his chair and nodded his head. It was the answer he wanted to hear. If Bukharin had gushed with enthusiasm just to impress him, or if he had been unctuous in praise of its strategic genius, then Petrovsky would have worried about his value to the group. If Petrovsky decided not to invite the younger man to join the group, Bukharin would not have returned alive to Moscow.

'Why do you think it's risky?' asked Petrovsky.

Bukharin sat back in his chair and stared out across the pine trees towards the Black Sea, reflecting for a moment before answering. Instant answers were for the lower ranks.

'We have no assets in place today to carry out such a plan. We have no access to men and matériel. The KGB is destroyed, its men all over the place. I'm not saying it's impossible. But concepts of this magnitude fall apart because of poor planning. To make it work, there needs to be a small army of the sort of specialists who used to work with us. And we need men and women on the ground to feed us with intelligence. We need access to electronic, microwave and satellite communication systems. We need surveillance systems. We need to know what's going on in the White House, the Knesset and Downing Street.'

Petrovsky smiled and nodded. 'Is that *all* we need, Mikhail Alexandrovich?'

Bukharin knew the old man was toying with him, but he refused to rise to the bait. 'No, Excellency, that's not all! We also need to know what's going on in the Kremlin. This plan involves massive shifts of geopolitical manipulation. Without the support of those Tsarists in Moscow, it'll fall flat on its arse.'

Petrovsky frowned sternly at the younger man's flippancy. But after a moment, he smiled slowly. Then the old man threw his head back and roared a laugh. 'Tsarists! That's good. I like that.'

Bukharin had never heard the old man laughing and smiled in return. 'Enough,' Petrovsky said, 'back to the plan.'

Bukharin cleared his throat and continued. 'We need a huge amount of other matériel and equipment as well. They were available once and easily so, but all these have been squandered since Gorbachev.'

The old man nodded dismissively. 'Yes, yes, I know all this. If I can supply it, what do you think of the plan? What's your real opinion?'

Bukharin stared briefly at the wooden slats on the floor of the patio before he looked back at Petrovsky.

'In Stalin's day, it would have been considered clever, even brilliant. But since then, our relationship with the Middle East has changed dramatically. Our stakes there are at an all-time low, especially since we sided with America against Iraq.'

Both men reflected on how far Russia had sunk in its international standing. Its influence had waned because no money was being spent on external alliances. The government was pre-occupied with events at home. The Middle East was of secondary strategic importance to cabbages, potatoes and a need to industrialise the economy. Russia no longer trained freedom fighters or terrorists. Nor did it supply them with funds and equipment. The Arabs now looked towards the West, rather than Russia, for support and leadership. Even when Raphael Ben Ari overthrew the peace process, the Arabs had failed to involve Russia. Instead, they continued to hound America for action against the Zionists. Bukharin was disgusted with the way the Russian leaders had allowed the opportunity to pass and the day after Ben Ari's extraordinary outburst, he had written a memorandum which outlined the potential for Russian involvement in the aftermath of the conference debacle. It had been a well argued, closely reasoned memo. Bukharin read it a dozen times, then put it through his office shredder. Advising his commanders on a course of action would merely remind them of his role in the KGB. Now he read that Ben Ari's hold on the leadership of Israel was weakening and the stature of Arab nations had risen in American eyes. What a *volte face*!

Bukharin sat back in his chair to address Petrovsky. 'This plan that I was asked to review is brilliant in theory, but wholly impractical. The people who prepared it seem to have forgotten many things. As I have said, we have no assets in place. There may be a way of doing it but everybody involved risks death. Death at the hands of foreigners or more especially from our own government.'

The old man nodded.

Bukharin was concerned by Petrovsky's silence. He felt the need to modify his criticisms. 'It's going to need a lot of thought. We're going to have to build computer models to predict Israeli, American and Arabic reactions. I haven't got any programs which could help me. They'll have to be written from scratch and that will take months. You see, Genardy Arkyovich, as with so many things in our field, much depends on the time and resources devoted to them.'

'But if it works?' insisted Petrovsky.

Again, Bukharin allowed a silence to intervene between question and answer. He wasn't going to say anything glib. He knew his life could depend on it. 'If it works, the results for Mother Russia could be … positive.'

Petrovsky looked up in surprise. 'Only "positive"?' The gruff tone surprised Bukharin. 'You're a very conservative man, Mikhail Alexandrovich.'

Bukharin shrugged. The next few moments could make or break his relationship with Petrovsky. No one doubted the power of a man *Time* magazine had once dubbed 'The J. Edgar Hoover of Moscow'. The phrase, however, was not wholly accurate. For the many years J. Edgar Hoover was head of the FBI, his power had come from the tapes and photographs he held in his private collection, blackmail opportunities to be held over the heads of most American congressmen and senators. And he had still ended life as a discredited and ineffectual figure. Not so Petrovsky. No one knew for certain what his source of power was over the leaders of the USSR and many of the leaders of the CIS today. Still, nobody was brave or stupid enough to oppose him.

But this didn't concern Bukharin. His future lay in restoring Russia to its former power and prestige in the world. If there was a game plan being organised by this wily old powermonger, he wanted to be a part of it. But part of what? A hare-brained scheme dreamt up by a foolish old man, or a brilliant way of reversing the disasters of the past few years?

'Please don't mistake my caution for lack of enthusiasm. Modified, this plan could be the light which will ignite the hearts of those of us who are totally committed to the rescue of Mother Russia.' It sounded like Turgenev. Or *Crocodil*!

The old man listened and nodded. He settled back in his cane chair, apparently considering Bukharin's analysis.

'My major concern is that there are not enough of us,' Bukharin continued. 'And those of us who are left may not have the ability any more. Marshal, we will need to build an infrastructure but to do that we have to be able to trust people. Our society is so riddled by informers that details of the plan will surely be leaked.'

Mikhail Alexandrovich waited for the old man to answer. But still no answer came. Instead, Petrovsky closed his eyes and breathed in so gentle and regular manner that he seemed to be asleep. But his mind was far from sleep. Genardy Arkyovich Petrovsky was actively planning Bukharin's involvement in the next phase in the plan. The phase which would see its success, or its promoters shot in the back of the head by an executioner.

Abruptly he stood up and gestured to the younger man to follow him. 'Come. You must be tired. Go wash, then we'll have a late lunch. I assume you didn't eat the shit they serve on planes? Then I'll show you some more details of the plan that may interest you, and may answer some of the questions troubling your mind.'

As the old man retreated into the dacha and Mikhail Alexandrovich turned to follow, he realised that he had been accepted into the cabal. But that acceptance brought him questionable joy. The next few months would be difficult and dangerous. But the risks were worth it. He had been a time-server for too long. Now he had the chance once again to reverse the direction of the past few years. The weight of power had been above him, pressing him down. At last he could again be in charge of his own destiny.

Three hours later, Genardy Arkyovich sat on his verandah and thought he caught a glimpse of the Tupelov which had just taken off from Simferopol airport, flying Bukharin to Odessa, then north to Moscow. Bukharin now carried the next stage of the plan in his mind. He had instructions on who to contact in Moscow, who held up-to-the-minute computer programs for strategic models of the geo-politics and who would give him access to the information he would need. On the flight, he would formulate the letter that would enable him to resign his commission from his unit. What would he say? That he was taking a better paid clerical job with an import-export firm? No! He wouldn't offer them a reason. Merely a resignation.

As darkness descended on the Black Sea, Petrovsky settled back. He felt the joy of the warm evening breeze on his skin. Life had been lonely since the death of his wife. He had played around with some young women but he had become bored, even with that. The need for female company had evaporated years earlier. Life today was different. He had status and money, and still some power. But he was alone. When he was rocketing through the ranks of the NKVD there had been friends and women galore. Women, parties, the good life, excitement. Revisionist historians wrote of the Stalin years as being dark, drear, black with despair. What did they know? Petrovsky was an insider. One of the chosen few. He was the centre of a universe others scarcely knew existed.

Like Stalin, Petrovsky had been born in Georgia of Ukrainian descent. But he came from a wealthier family with stronger social links. Unlike Stalin, he had not gone to a religious seminary but had acquired his education through schools and by winning a scholarship to Moscow University. That was where he first met Stalin. The year was 1932 and Stalin had gone there to talk about political theory to young party members. He was then in his mid-fifties and was a difficult and diffident speaker, but he was at the very apex of his strength and had a magnetism which was beyond anything Petrovsky had ever known. It was a kind of animal power which drew people to him. Stalin had power. And Petrovsky realised that he wanted power more than anything.

After leaving university, Petrovsky used his party membership and social connections to join the NKVD, the forerunner of the KGB. He had quickly shown himself to be a master at strategic manipulation and had risen rapidly through the ranks, partly he realised because the sycophants surrounding Stalin favoured anybody who came from Georgia. Petrovsky had quickly made a reputation for himself with accurate insights and predictions into the cancerous growth and anti-Communist rhetoric of Germany's Nazi Party, as it peered greedily and venomously into Eastern Europe.

One day, while still a young officer sitting in the Stalingrad office of the NKVD, a courier had delivered a message to him. When he opened the envelope, he was amazed to see the Kremlin letterhead. Nervously, he read the letter, which asked him for an assessment of the value of a Soviet Union pact with Adolf Hitler. It was signed 'Stalin' and he still had the letter in his files in his flat in Moscow.

Petrovsky was at once ecstatic but terrified that he had received such a note. Stalin was not the only person in the Kremlin that the people of Russia feared. There was also Lavrentii Beria, the hideous sexual pervert and sadist who was Stalin's right-hand man. If Petrovsky was to report to Stalin he would also be reporting to Beria.

The situation Russia found itself in at the beginning of the war was complex and difficult. Until 1939, Moscow had been courted by the Western powers to sign an anti-German pact, but Stalin favoured a pro-German detente for reasons which were both strategic and military—buying him time to build up munitions and military preparedness.

It was in light of Stalin's distrust of the military information he was getting that he wrote to Petrovsky and a number of others, who were independent of his immediate advisers.

The question was whether Russia would be fighting war on one front against Hitler, or on two fronts against both Hitler and the Japanese. Since he had no European allies, Stalin thought it prudent to abandon his anti-Nazi stance and sign a non-aggression treaty with Hitler.

The report which Petrovsky wrote was different from the others Stalin received. Petrovsky urged Stalin not to sign the treaty and at the same time to move troops from the Japanese front. He was convinced Japan wouldn't be the enemy, that it would turn its aggression towards America. His report recommended transferring the battle-hardened men to guard the Western flank of Russia, to repel a Germany which was invading Russia's neighbours. But Petrovsky was more than merely technical in his recommendations. Since any pact with Hitler would severely damage Russia's credibility with America and England, he told Stalin that efforts should be made to bring America into the war earlier rather than later. He counselled Stalin not to buy time by befriending the hideous little Austrian housepainter.

This was one report which Petrovsky did not believe would be ignored. It had been requested by Stalin himself. Yet Stalin signed the pact.

Eventually, and inevitably as Petrovsky saw it, Hitler reneged on the agreement. In June 1941, accompanied by Luftwaffe dive-bombers, 150 divisions of more than three million men and over 3,500 armoured fighting vehicles began Operation Barbarossa, crashing through Russia's western border, bringing the Soviet Union to its knees. It was the start of the Great Patriotic War.

At the beginning of Russia's entry into the war, Petrovsky was a duty officer in the War Room of the Red Army, on secondment from the NKVD. But within a few days of the German offensive, a messenger arrived and told him to report immediately to Department TK4 of the Kremlin. Petrovsky, who had never heard of Department TK4, immediately called for transport to take him to the Russian Palace.

There, a young cadet dressed in a gold-braided navy blue uniform escorted him through a series of corridors, deeper and deeper into the centre of the web of the Kremlin. Petrovsky became disoriented. He had walked down stairs, along corridors, through vast resounding chambers and passed armies of clerks and civil servants. Normally only the most senior of men were allowed admission to the inner sanctum. The clerks looked on the young colonel with disdain.

Walking deeper and deeper into the centre of the Kremlin made him feel trapped. It was disarming how completely the outside world was excluded. As though the inner sanctum was working to a different rhythm. Outside the walls of the Kremlin, Russia lived and breathed, laughed and cried. As he walked down the carpeted corridors he looked in awe at the rows of black doors which receded into the distance. Behind these anonymous doors worked men known to him only through the pages of *Izvestia*. These were the most powerful men in his world. Petrovsky's muffled footsteps were engulfed by an unnerving silence, devoid of voices, telephones and the commerce of typewriters. The cadet knocked on a huge black oak door at the end of a windowless corridor lit by ineffective bare globes. The door was opened by a man whom Petrovsky recognised as Marshal Georgi Zhukov, Stalin's army head. The young man was overwhelmed. Zhukov introduced himself and shook the young colonel's hand. Petrovsky had no idea what it was all about, but knew better than to ask.

He was shown through another series of rooms until he stood in a darkened office, unimaginably deep in the Palace, in front of a huge mahogany desk. Behind the desk sat Josef Stalin.

Petrovsky was so frightened, so taken aback, that he could hardly speak.

Stalin said: 'You were the only one that advised me against the pact with Hitler. You were brave to do so. Brave or stupid. Only time will tell. You will be my secretary. You will have the office outside and will admit no one without first investigating the reason for the visit. That includes my generals. It will make you a hated man, but that is your problem. I need advice I can rely on and I expect to be told the truth when I ask for information or advice. If I don't like the answer, I may be very angry, but you will not suffer. You will only suffer if you try to flatter me. Today isn't the day for flattery. We have a war to win and Hitler is no fool. After the war, I may return you to the provinces. That depends on your performance. Now go.'

That was all. The job specification and the acceptance.

For the next four years, Petrovsky acted as a filter, distilling all the information he felt should reach one of the most powerful men in the world. Stalin had been right. He was soon hated by those whom Stalin had once allowed easier access, but Petrovsky performed his duties with dedication and an eye towards his own future. He quickly learned how to deal with Stalin's famous tempers and mood swings. But always, Petrovsky told Stalin the absolute facts, simply and succinctly, without the slightest embroidery or embellishment.

By the end of the war Petrovsky had organised his world so he would not be returned to the provinces. He had engineered himself into a position as one of Stalin's most trusted confidants. It did not suit either himself or Stalin for Petrovsky to be a public figure. Others could shine in the limelight. Petrovsky was quite happy to hold the power behind the scenes. When Roosevelt and Churchill were negotiating the distribution of the world during the Yalta conference, neither man knew that it was a thirty-three-year-old NKVD colonel who had formulated the strategy which Stalin used so effectively. Stalin's gratitude was expressed in a private ceremony attended by only a handful of inner staff, at which Petrovsky was made a Member of the Order of Lenin and a general in the NKVD.

Petrovsky continued to work closely with Stalin until the dictator's death, after which he developed similarly close relationships with subsequent leaders of Russia, until ultimately he rose to become a Marshal in the KGB ... never a public figure, but always a power behind the throne. Now he was apparently whiling his time away, feeding ducks by the shore of the Black Sea. But there were two things about him which were still active. One was his mind, which could still outpace the thinking of any Young Turk in today's Nationalist Army; and the second was the Jericho Plan, which he had proposed to Stalin in 1946.

As a strategist after the war, planning Russia's positioning against the capitalist West, Petrovsky quickly realised that oil and nuclear fission were the keys to the gates of heaven. Oil was in the Middle East, though there were encouraging signs of rich fields within the Russian sub-Arctic; and nuclear fission, so potently used against the Japanese, would need billions of roubles for its development. To afford the type of industrial-military complex which had made America so powerful while Russia remained essentially a rural economy, new trade relationships must be created. New influences must be developed. Stalin must embark upon a massive industrialisation program, which would require oil. And lying in bed one afternoon with a young redheaded secretary, Petrovsky had seen the light—a flash of inspiration which was at once so daring, so simple and so devastatingly obvious, he wondered why nobody else had thought of it. After all, they already had Communist assets in place in Palestine!

When the Father of all the Russias first read the outline of the Jericho Plan, then re-read it, his face showed no hint of emotion, no sign of approval. Petrovsky was concerned.

But then Stalin stood up, walked around the desk and threw his arms around the surprised man. He kissed him on the cheeks and said to him: 'Genardy Arkyovich, there are times when you amaze and delight me. This plan of yours will turn into reality what Russia has been trying to achieve for five hundred years. My faith in you has never wavered. You are a true patriot. You are a genius.'

Genardy Arkyovich Petrovsky took a final sip of lemonade. The sun was setting over the Black Sea and the sky had turned to indigo. It was fifty years since he had given the plan to Stalin. He and Stalin had worked privately on it, excluding everyone else except those who had to know individual elements to make it work. But only the two of them knew the complete plan. On Stalin's death, Petrovsky had taken back the files from the Lubyanka and hidden them—first in his flat, then in a disused warehouse in the southern suburbs of Moscow. Over the following decades, as the geopolitical mood of the world swung like a pendulum, he had maintained the integrity of the Jericho Plan. He, and he alone. When Stalin was no more than a memory, and the Cold War was nearly over, the Jericho files themselves became too dangerous for him to hold in his private warehouse. Late one night, Petrovsky organised their replacement, scattered in the millions of files and archives of Stalin's papers. Petrovsky could not bear to destroy them. Why should he, when they could be hidden in so public a place, yet lost and meaningless to anybody except himself. He was confident that the archives would not be opened for many more decades. They held too many dark secrets about too many people still powerful in Russia.

He smiled as he thought of the seeds that he had planted just after the Great Patriotic War. All those years of careful nurturing, as though hibernating beneath the ground. Now they had abruptly grown and flowered. His finest asset had matured into a man of power. And now the Jericho Plan could at last proceed.

Petrovsky always believed that everything in life has its own momentum. Men like Stalin, Ben Ari, even the young Bukharin, can only influence the speed of the momentum. He had never given up his hope of seeing his plan realised. And the momentum of events had ground on inexorably until now he was poised at the brink.

When he was a young man in the NKVD, he thought that it would be a part of his future. Today, Petrovsky wondered how much future he had left to see the plan in operation.

CHAPTER FIVE

The question hung in the air creating a chasm between them. It was impossible to bridge. They looked gloomily at each other, wondering how they had allowed their relationship to devolve so far. She, a Russian. He an American. She, a scientist, one of the new technocrats in the Kremlin hierarchy. He, a vestige of the Cold War, a man whose memories were of covert meetings on dirty railway platforms. He was lost in the new openness of hotel foyers and public places. In the old days, when it was 'them' against 'us' she would have been a conquest, both personal and professional. But now she came willingly and the information she was giving him wouldn't even be glorified with a 'top secret' classification when Langley read it in the morning.

Paul scanned the last couple of sentences. 'Shit!' He turned in his chair, and shouted into the bathroom, over the noise of the shower: 'I want to put in something about the German Secret Police. Do you remember what their initials are?'

From the bathroom the answer was a muffled 'What?'

Paul stood, straightened his back and stretched. He had been working since five that morning and was already drained before the day had begun.

Whenever he spent the night at Miriam's, he took his laptop PC with him. He enjoyed the flexibility it gave him, even though at times his large fingers failed to accommodate the delicacy of the keyboard. His day was spent in observation of people and events as participants for his book and he recorded his view of people or his impression of events for later incorporation. His cynicism as a reporter, a carapace of self-protection common to police, doctors and others who deal with the public, translated itself to his fiction. He was able to observe and report incidents, even those involving friends, without feeling borne down by guilt. *Ars gratia artis*. His writing was more important than friendships.

He walked over to the bathroom, and inside saw the indistinct body of Miriam through the steam haze and the frosted glass of the shower. She had a wonderful figure.

'I asked if you knew what were the initials of the German Secret Police?'

'How the hell should I know?'

'I just thought you might have come across them. Rescuing some poor sod from their clutches, or something.'

'You don't do that sort of thing in commercial law. Why do you want to know?'

'My novel.'

His novel! No further explanation was necessary. For the past couple of years, Paul's growing antipathy towards the world of journalism had been contained by his belief in his novel. Every time he had been on the verge of storming out over the destruction of one of his articles, Miriam had been able to lure him back with the simple question, 'Where else will you find characters and events?' It never failed.

Journalism, not patriotism, was the last refuge of the cynic. Its practitioners were eventually weighed down by the lies and distortions of politicians, or the carnage of society, or the self-serving waffle of businessmen and public relations people. Although it was probably more true of the tabloid press than of quality media such as *The National*, journalism was still a vindictive mistress. For most people working in journalism, every grieving parent, every battered soul, every victim was dehumanised to become a story. Victims became news, crimes became headlines, tragedies became page-one leads. In the beginning it was an adventure for Paul but any sensitivity, any regard for humanity, had been knocked out of him when he worked on the tabloids by the need to protect himself from the realities of life. It was why drink and journalism were lover and mistress.

Some of Paul's colleagues had grown indifferent to the practice of face-to-face interviewing. They preferred to phone people up or write considered opinionated articles. They detested the parochial humdrum world of the politician and the flag-waver. And they particularly disliked it when one of the impoverished appeared in the office, complaining about injustice. Their pet hate was for the vapid television personalities and their publicists, always preening themselves like jungle parrots; but for Paul, journalism was a library for his literary aspirations. He kept a notebook full of useful characters, plots and even phrases overheard in pubs. One day all would grace the pages of one of his bestsellers.

Paul considered himself more fortunate than his colleagues. His goal was to leave journalism and be a full-time novelist. Never once was one day the same as another. And now he had begun to write fiction, the interviews he did and characters he met were the seeds from which his novel would grow. He was like a fisherman, with the newspaper as bait.

Miriam finished her shower. As she emerged, her skin glistened with water droplets and steam rose in wispy clouds from her body; she looked fresh and lovely, redolent with life and potential.

She caught him staring at her and smiled. At the beginning of their relationship she would flush in embarrassment, and even after five years she had still not developed any ease in sharing the bathroom or walking around the room naked. It was the legacy of living alone for so long. She knew that when they were married, the bathrobe would be left in the bathroom. Until then, some ill-defined part of her upbringing kept it clinging modestly to her.

Her little quirks, though, did not affect the passion each felt for the other. They were physical lovers and relished every moment of their time together. But there was sometimes an invisible barrier between them, an unspoken, irresolvable gulf. Normally hidden by the care and affection each showed to the other, it only seemed to surface at times of stress. When one or the other was under particular pressure, the unmentionable would rise up and would hang between them like the Sword of Damocles, suspended by a delicate thread, threatening to break and rupture their unity. It was the sword of religion, the difference between them, and the reason that Miriam was incapable of committing herself fully to their relationship.

For Paul the tension was often more acute than for Miriam. He was keen for them to be married. He had reached a stage in his life and their relationship where marriage was the only future he could envisage. Yet … there was always a yet. Her Jewishness came between them. It was an obstacle to their future. She wanted love and companionship. He wanted a family.

They had much in common. Paul's father had died when he was thirteen and his mother, who became a professional widow, died when he was in his late twenties. Miriam was the closest Paul had to a family despite distant cousins whom he saw as little as possible. His insecurity in their relationship irritated Miriam. He spent many nights alone projecting his fears of the relationship ending. He wondered what she was thinking about in the loneliness of her apartment.

Miriam, though, didn't feel the same depth of insecurity. She loved Paul, and felt there was a good chance that she would ultimately end up marrying him. She was used to him and his ways. He was her comfort. But she wasn't naive, and knew that there was a void between them, impossible to ignore, possibly unbridgeable. And at the bottom of the void was her grandfather's dybbuk, that ancient demon which belonged to the world of fairy tales but had stayed with her way past her childhood.

When she was being honest with herself, she admitted that there was a fundamental reason for her not committing to marriage. It was in case her future could lie in marrying a Jew, someone whom she could comfortably introduce to her grandfather, the last remaining member of her family. Paul, for all his attention and goodness, his perception and gentleness, wasn't Jewish.

Her upbringing was in conflict with her intellect. She hated herself, but for all her feminist and liberal views, an ancient set of superstitions still held her back.

One other thing occasionally disrupted the harmony of their relationship. Paul found it hard to accept her occasional need for abstinence from sex. Often, when she was working particularly hard on an emotionally draining court case, with its attendant late night meetings with barristers, or early morning post-mortems with clients to discuss the previous day's pleadings, the last thing she wanted was to make love. At the beginning of their relationship, Paul reacted angrily and became surly. This caused Miriam to become more distant. But Paul had learned how to react to a rejection. Now, he simply groaned, rolled over and went to sleep. On these occasions, she preferred the cathartic effect of a cold shower, followed by a rich red wine and a long night's sleep, to having Paul grope her body. He still found it difficult to cope with these times of coldness. In these tense moments, she knew that he was consumed by doubts. Especially when he asked her whether she was seeing another man—as though that would explain her lack of sexual desire.

These were the times when she became angry with men in general, and Paul in particular. Why was it that men never allowed a woman the luxury of fluctuating sexual demand? Why did they assume that a woman's sexuality was as constant as a man's? Why could men not appreciate the privilege of celibacy, and the heightened awareness that it gave to one's perceptions—of people, places, emotions, friendships, relationships …

It wasn't a constant threat. When she was in the full blush of sexual need, there was an animalism within her which held him in thrall. But Paul had to realise that she was not an animal who could turn on and off her sexuality when her partner was on heat.

The telephone rang. Miriam frowned and pulled the towel tighter around her. She picked up the phone: 'Hello.'

'*Bubeleh*, how are you?'

She beamed a smile. 'Zeida, you're calling early.'

'I wanted to catch Paul before he left for work.'

Miriam froze. 'Paul?'

'Darling, I've been thinking about our conversation last night. I'd like to talk to Paul. You know, for years I think I should have said something. Now, I know I should.'

'Paul? He's not here, Zeida.' She was a little girl again, trapped in the web of a lie. The dybbuk rose up from beneath her feet and prepared to grab her ankles.

The old man waited a moment. 'Well darling, if he should happen to drop by within the next minute or two, perhaps he wouldn't be too busy to call me.'

Paul looked at Miriam and she blushed. She felt stupid. A grown woman prevaricating because of the fear of being caught out by her grandfather. It was stupid. She didn't bother apologising.

'I'll put him on, Zeida.'

He came to the phone, still frowning. Miriam held her hand over the mouthpiece, and whispered: 'It's Zeida. He told me something last night which he thinks will interest you.'

'He wants to talk to me?' Paul whispered back in surprise.

Miriam nodded and handed him the phone.

'Mr Samuelson. It's Paul. How are you?'

Miriam looked on anxiously, but Paul's expression gave nothing away. All he did was nod, say 'ah-ha' several times, and make an arrangement to meet the old man at the Rosenthal the following day.

When he got off the phone, Miriam asked: 'Well?'

'He says he's got information that he wants to share with me about Ben Ari. Says he talked to you last night. You could fill me in on the facts.'

'He used to teach Raphael Ben Ari … in the old days, when they lived in a little village in Poland.'

He listened with interest, thinking of his newspaper, and of a potential character for his book. It could solve his problem of a story about the failed peace conference for this Sunday.

'Could be newsworthy. What else did he say?'

'That he was a little swine as a student, always causing problems; that the other kids hated him; that he was constantly asking questions instead of listening to the teacher …'

Paul laughed, despite Miriam's serious tone. 'Doesn't seem to have changed much in sixty years!'

'Then wait for this! When he grew into a young man, he joined the Peoples' Workers Revolutionary, or some such party in his village, and became a rabid Communist.'

'A Communist?' Paul was stunned. 'I think your *zeida*'s memory is slipping. Ben Ari's a virulent anti-Communist. You know that! Even the Yanks told him to tone down the rhetoric.'

'I'm telling you,' Miriam insisted. 'Zeida said he joined this extreme left wing Stalinist group in the mid-1930s, and left the *shtetl*.'

'*Shtetl*?'

'Oh! Sorry,' said Miriam. Mixing with Jews in her social life and with much of her law firm being Jewish, she sometimes forgot that Paul couldn't speak Yiddish. 'A *shtetl* is a small Jewish village. He told me the most incredible things. I didn't believe it at first but now I'm not so sure. I know he's an old man but he was so certain and he's rarely ever wrong.'

'What did he say?'

'He said that Ben Ari left the *shtetl* for two years before the war and when he came back he was an idealogue for the Party. He happily informed on the rabbis and village leaders. Apparently he went right up against anybody who came out with anti-Communist or anti-Stalin remarks. A real Torquemada type. Pretty bloody frightening. Suddenly, top people in the village began disappearing and in the meantime Ben Ari lived like a lord. It seems as if he was a real shit in those days.'

Paul shook his head. 'Darling, your *zeida*'s got the wrong guy. Look, he's over eighty, and this was sixty years ago. Think about it. Can you remember in detail what happened last month? I know about interviewing old people. They often have these flashes of insight, but their facts are nearly always confused. Sorry, but of all the men in the world, Ben Ari is the least likely to have started his career as a Communist.'

Miriam indignantly defended her grandfather's mind. 'You reckon? Tomorrow, you'll find out. Then you can write to Ben Ari and ask him yourself. I'm not saying I necessarily believe Zeida, but I'll tell you one thing, I've never known him to be wrong.'

'That doesn't speak volumes for your training. What about the burden of proof?'

The moment he had said it, he wished he could bite the words back. He had just offended the two principal edifices on which Miriam's life was built. But to Paul's surprise, Miriam's anger did not flare. Deep down, she felt that he could be right. She was, after all, dealing with a statement made by an old man in a convalescent home about events a lifetime ago.

'Look. I know he's an old man, but his mind … It's so clear. He doesn't know English as well as you and me and he isn't trained in anything we might consider important. But you have no idea of his intelligence or his intellect. He's the closest thing I know to a thoroughly decent man. Without pretensions, without deceits or falsehoods. You'll find out tomorrow. Then you'll see whether you believe him or not.'

'Okay—but I wouldn't put too much store in what he says.'

She wanted to defend her grandfather, but she knew Paul could be right.

Paul went into the bathroom while Miriam prepared breakfast. She made bacon, eggs, toast and coffee for him, and a fruit and diet cheese platter for herself. It had taken her two years before she could allow herself to keep bacon in her kitchen. And despite its erotic aroma, she still could not bring herself to eat it.

After breakfast, she tidied the flat, while Paul made the bed and put away the breakfast things. Her cleaning lady was coming today. Miriam took a dollar coin, and decided on a new hiding place for the week. Each time her cleaning woman came, Miriam hid a coin in a different place. If the woman found it, she received a ten dollar bonus as well as the dollar coin. The flat was always immaculate.

'What's on today?' he asked.

'I've got an appeal with Doug Scotland against a decision by a real arsehole of a judge in the Supreme Court. Took the best part of a year to make a decision on a case, then completely ignored the central issue. You know, some of these judges should be kicked off the bench, the way they decide cases. I'm sure he didn't even read the papers. Some of the morons must flip a coin.'

Paul poured a final cup of coffee to empty the pot.

'What about you?' she asked.

'Mandle's in town. The management hierarchy's running around on tiptoe like someone's laid down hot coals. Everyone's too scared to make decisions. It's going to be another heads-down day at the salt mine.'

CHAPTER SIX

The attention of the world had been riveted by the behaviour of Prime Minister Raphael Ben Ari at the Akrotiri peace conference. Furious manoeuvrings by the Israeli Foreign Minister to bring Ben Ari back to the negotiating table had come to nothing. An urgency debate to remove him from office was defeated on party lines, the Knesset preferring to maintain the status quo in the face of an increasingly hostile world. Moves by Great Britain to act as mediator between Jews and Arabs had been rebuffed after Ben Ari's pointed reminder to the British Prime Minister that it was his country fifty years ago which had created much of the problem in the first place.

The world watched the spectacle of shuttle diplomacy by a bevy of foreign ministers who tried to rescue the hopes of a new order from the quicksand of the old. But the old world had extraordinary tenacity. The Balkans, Germany, Central Europe and even Iraq were on the march again. Old men wearing heavy medals on their chests inflamed young disenfranchised followers with dreams of the greater glories of the past.

Major events were beginning to happen around the globe as the ripples from Cyprus grew into tidal waves. And only a week after Ben Ari had wrested chaos out of the jaws of harmony, two separate events occurred which carried the drama further. One event was widely recorded throughout the world; the other remained a tightly guarded secret.

The incidents took place in Jerusalem at various times of the same day, both of them against a backdrop of a country riven with internal dissent. The first meeting was between George P. Kennett, an American journalist now resident in Israel and working for the newspaper *Ha'am*, and an Arab contact he had recently been developing. The second meeting occurred later that same night, under the cover of darkness in a black Mercedes travelling between Jerusalem and Tel Aviv.

George P. Kennett was a man whose life had taken a dramatic turn for the better since he went on *aliyah* to Israel. Unlike other American Jews, whose Zionistic commitment was confined to donations in their home country and the mandatory two week fact-finding visit every couple of years, fanatical Zionists who went to Israel on *aliyah* transferred their goods, chattels and worldly possessions to establish their lives in the country of the Bible and the Jewish peoples.

Journalists tend to have sceptical natures, but when George set foot on *Eretz Yisroel* at Lod airport, it was as though a current had passed through the ground into his body. He fell to his knees and kissed the ground in a Papal gesture. George arrived as an American, but stepped off the plane as such a fanatical Zionist his tour guide hadn't been able to cope with his proselytising. The other members of the group of Jewish American journalists voted him off the bus two days after the tour had started.

It was a seminal time for George. For a man who had been brought up in a Jewish home in Brooklyn, and for whom life was a constant apologia for being Jewish in an alien world, his arrival at Lod airport was as momentous for him as the revelation to Paul on the road to Damascus. It was a turning point for self-confidence. For the first time in his life, his body seethed with the ability to reach the potential for which it had been born.

When he returned to America, George told his colleagues on the New York *Daily Sun* that, for the first time, he felt 'safe', or 'at home', or whatever homily surfaced while he was extolling the virtues of his new land to anyone who would continue to listen. What he really meant was that he belonged; that he did not feel a stranger in his land; no longer was there the need to excuse, apologise for, or justify his existence as a Jew.

George was a tall, rotund man with a florid face, thinning brown hair and veins by the side of his nose. In the thirty-four years of his life before he arrived in Israel, he had made few female friendships, and the men whom he counted as friends were almost exclusively working colleagues. Disliking the loneliness of being a bachelor, he sublimated it by being a hard-working and efficient journalist. After a year in Israel, a rabbi had introduced him to a widow from Tel Aviv, an easy-going, good-natured woman with two young children and a mortgage. George married her, moved her to Jerusalem and had a ready-made family. Life was fulfilled.

Some of his colleagues on *Ha'am*, especially the Israelis, resented foreign reporters taking their jobs. Behind his back they called him an American buffoon. He lacked the stoicism of the Sabra, a native-born Israeli. His emotions were open to everyone, leaving no thoughts left unspoken; unlike them he wasn't diffident or taciturn at first meeting. Within the space of the first two minutes, he told strangers about his Zionistic conversion at the airport and his dream of uniting the Jews of the diaspora under the flag of Israel. It was a short road from pilgrim to missionary to messiah. But in their deprecation, his colleagues on *Ha'am* had to admit grudgingly that his hard work and wide net of newly-won contacts brought in scoops more frequently than luck would allow.

And today, George smelt a good story. It was all due to Ben Ari's extraordinary outburst in Cyprus the previous week, and the aftermath of civil disquiet and demonstrations which had followed. The currency of talk in the *Ha'am* newsroom, and every other journalistic meeting place, had to do with why Ben Ari had unilaterally defied the government line and scuttled the talks. No one had a ready explanation. Ben Ari had gone to Cyprus in a mood approaching compromise. He was a different man to the one who had been elevated to the prime ministership following Ben Dod's surprising resignation. When Ben Ari first became his country's leader he was militant and hawkish. But the two years seemed to have softened his stance and even the most sceptical of Israeli journalists thought that he had gone to Cyprus ready to negotiate. But George Kennett looked beyond the new Ben Ari now that the old hawk had risen again.

Having been brought up to believe that J.F.K. had been the victim of a Mafia/CIA/Cuban and KGB plot sponsored by a military/industrial complex, as well as numerous other conspiracy theories, George was certain that there was much more to Ben Ari's actions than met the eye. His views were at odds with those of his editors and colleagues, who considered Ben Ari to be an ultra-right-wing maverick whose mouth was bigger than his brain. But George was convinced that there was more and he was determined to prove it.

George had been more surprised than most sceptical Israelis when Raphael Ben Ari had pulled the plug on the peace conference and had been shocked beyond belief at the deterioration in the state of affairs in his new, beautiful liberal homeland. Demonstrations were taking place on every street corner.

He vividly remembered what had happened in America when the people took control of the streets; L.A.'s Watts district, where blacks had rioted against white police; riots in Chicago and in New York in the 1960s and '70s; and the more recent Los Angeles conflagration which had left nearly fifty people dead when law had favoured a white policeman and order had broken down. He feared the rule of the public in his newly adopted country.

What George couldn't come to grips with was why Ben Ari had sabotaged the conference. George had interviewed him just days earlier. The Prime Minister had still been moderately hawkish but had told him confidently that the situation of Israel in the Arab world would improve as a result of the Akrotiri meeting. There was no hint that he was contemplating any outburst. George realised that it could have been on-the-spot emotion taking over, but he had a nagging suspicion, based on years of governments lying to cover their asses, that it may have been pre-arranged. Since his arrival in Israel before the Second World War, Raphael Ben Ari had been militant in espousing Israel's right to exist within peaceful borders and the supremacy of Jerusalem as its capital. In the years when he was out of the spotlight, when he was a senior official in Mossad, it was always assumed that he was working for the security of Israel.

Since becoming Prime Minister his stance had softened and the Cyprus peace conference was an opportunity to show himself as a statesman. Now he had unilaterally given away the chance. It was contrary to his recent public sentiments, and all Israel was wondering why.

Being a conspiracy theorist, there was an ache in George's journalistic bones. Something was amiss.

Dwelling on the problem for a couple of days, George had worked out a scenario which he was in the process of testing. Being a one-time senior operative in Mossad, and a devious and consummate deal-maker, Ben Ari could very well have done a deal with the more moderate Arab nations to separate them from the radical ones. Why? Simply because his actions would further polarise the Middle East and isolate the radical leaders. Being shaky at the best of times, now they were without Russian support, they could be toppled by their disaffected peoples. Syria, Iraq, Iran, and the other militant states no longer had support as cubs of the Soviet bear and so their people would feel deeply isolated.

Or it could have been an even more subtle and devious plan to isolate Hamas and the PLO, then slowly form individual peace treaties with the more moderate Arab nations such as Jordan and Saudi Arabia? George didn't know, but he was determined to find out.

He had to get closer to the Prime Minister. But this was something which no Israeli journalist had ever done. Ben Ari detested journalists, didn't trust them and only grudgingly gave interviews. His recent conversation with George had taken a month to arrange. No! That would be too slow and wouldn't get to the heart of the matter. Ben Ari would never reveal to George what was really going on … wouldn't even hint at it. And besides that, every journalist in Israel was currently speculating and bombarding Ben Ari's office with questions.

To get to the truth George had to know everything there

was to know about the Prime Minister. First, he read his biography in the newspaper library. There was nothing about his early life, so George faxed a request for information to Ben Ari's office asking for details about his youth. Rule One in Journalism. Know thine enemy!

The next step was to find out whether Ben Ari had recently undertaken any negotiations with the moderate Arabs. Mossad, of course, was constantly in touch with moderate Arab governments, exchanging information about terrorists, and arms build-ups in the militant states. But such information was a lot trickier to unearth. Despite his contacts from the early days, Ben Ari would not have initiated contact. It would most likely have been Mordecai Avit. To determine what contacts had been made George would need to speak to somebody in Israel who was close to the moderate Arab governments.

When he was working on American newspapers he would simply have phoned a stringer or a correspondent in the Arab country, but working in Israel was much more confining. So he would have to use his Arab contacts in Jerusalem to source someone who could help him.

Then he would need to fly to the moderate Arab capital to talk to some high government official to determine the nature of any deal that existed to isolate the radical Arabic nations from the peace process. He would need to go to Egypt. No agreement could be made without Egypt being party to it, so it was vital to confirm the plan with Cairo. When he got to this stage, he would call for assistance from his former colleagues in New York. By pooling knowledge, he could get close to the conspiracy. But to do so, he must have some information to exchange … and that was why he was pulling in his contacts in Arab Jerusalem.

George called in a favour owed to him by the brother of the Mayor of Jamuel, a small village on the Jordanian border. The insignificant little man had proved cooperative in the past. George had met him two days earlier in a small hole-in-the-wall cafe in the Old City of Jerusalem, near to the Kotel Ha

Maravi, the famous Wailing Wall of the Temple of Herod. Unknown to George, the Arab was a local sympathiser of a radical Moslem fundamentalist group, who saw a chance to report an important matter back to headquarters and earn himself credit in the eyes of those for whom he hoped to work. The contact had listened sympathetically to George's requests, assured him he knew people who could help and took $US 500 for his expenses. The man contacted the Iran-backed Hezbollah, the infamous Party of God, the most militant of the Shi'ite Moslem sects.

George's request was referred back to the religious city of Isfahan, deep in the heart of Iran, and one of the centres of operation of Hezbollah. There, Said ibn Montezawhi, the mullah responsible for terrorist attacks within Israel, read the report with amazement.

Why was this Israeli Jewish infidel seeking a meeting with a person to find information about the Israelis? It didn't make sense. What was he after, Ibn Montezawhi wondered. Was it some crude attempt to recruit a spy? He threw the information sheet aside in anger but picked it up again and re-read it. He mouthed the words slowly to himself, then began to conceive a plan. Ibn Montezawhi loved plotting. He thought of a method of using a meeting with this Israeli to coincide with something which had been going through his mind since the fascist imperialist Jewish running dog Ben Ari had ruined the peace conference. It was based on a recent conversation he had had with the holy one in Iraq. Ibn Montezawhi revered the Imam, who voiced the righteous anger of Moslems around the world.

He smiled to himself as he saw a way of obeying the Imam's instructions of capturing world headlines and decided on a plan of action. Said ibn Montezawhi issued a fatwa—a decree of the death penalty—against this Jewish journalist. It was brilliant. It would ferment more tensions between Jews and Moslems. It would further isolate the Israelis. Ben Ari's recent actions in Cyprus had underscored the lack of moral fibre of the Jews, and the assassination of the journalist would aid destabilisation in the region, which was already split between those who backed the Prime Minister's actions and those who opposed them.

Said ibn Montezawhi, the mullah once described by the *Washington Post* as 'Hitlerian', felt no qualms about issuing the fatwa. The Islamic fundamentalist preacher had founded the Hezbollah Party of God in the Lebanon in the mid-1970s before moving to Qom. He ran it in such an autocratic manner that a simple instruction which he issued could lead to the deaths of hundreds. He was feared overseas, and also in Tehran. Ibn Montezawhi was a member of the *Maflis*, elected by the people to protect the sanctity of the Revolution. Those who opposed him in the Iranian parliament, and there were many, had disappeared, to be found rotting in the desert with a bullet hole in the back of the head.

His views were stark and simple. Iran was not an Arab nation. It was doing no deals with America, the Great Satan. The Arabs might put political expediency ahead of religious purity but not the fundamentalist Iranians. Iran's and the Islamic legal point of view was quite clear. The Americans and Israelis were waging a war against the true state of Palestine, against Islam, and against Muslims in general. They were *moharabeen*—people with no value—and he could strike them down with impunity. Their lives held no meaning and it was the duty of every Moslem to execute Islamic law. There was no escaping a fatwa. George Kennett would die just as surely as the five who had died, and the hundreds who had been injured, when his men bombed the World Trade Center in New York in 1993.

The instruction would be sent to the Palestinian and the Jewish dog would be killed. A fatwa was a death sentence which carried an imperative. It was every Moslem's duty to carry it out. For Ibn Montezawhi, the man's death was as important as swatting a fly. He had as much value.

Ibn Montezawhi wrote the order and gave it to his secretary, who transmitted it in code to the Hezbollah office in the Lebanon. It was delivered across the Israeli border late that night and carried to Nablus on the West Bank. Instructions were given to the brother of the Mayor of Jamuel, along with payment for his loyalty. Another bonus!

George was telephoned by his contact, who suggested they meet in the same cafe as previously, following which they would visit a friend of his uncle. The friend had indicated that he would be prepared to offer assistance, provided George could defray the cost of an operation which the man's elderly wife needed in order to save her life. By now George was familiar with Arabic customs. Arabs would often speak of an acquaintance as though he was a relative. There was no 'uncle'. There was no operation.

At 9.30 a.m., George walked from the taxi station outside the Jaffa Gate of the ancient walls surrounding the Old City of Jerusalem. The air reeked of petrol fumes. It had a heady, anaesthetising feeling. But as he walked through the ancient structure of massive stones towering above his head, all traffic noises were excluded, replaced by more ancient noises—the sounds of the Arab *shuk*.

Shouts, yells, calls, and a cacophony of human voices filled the air as George walked under the cool archway and into the narrow lanes of the Old City. As though walking through the gates of time, the twentieth century became a distant memory, replaced by ancient sights and smells, with which Abraham, Isaac and Jacob would have been familiar. George was transported into the past and became one with an ancient people, haggling, bartering and scurrying as they had done on this very spot for two thousand years.

And the perfume in the air was different. Outside the walls, in the twentieth century, were the refined aromas of petrol, or cleaning fluid, or ladies' perfumes. Here, in the land and the time of the Bible, just a few metres from new Jerusalem, were the smells of dust, donkeys and dogs, of filthy cloaks and shawls. Unwashed, unperfumed smells, smells of *humus* and *t'china* and *kebbe* and lamb marinated in spices which wafted from the *shukris*, small restaurants using recipes thousands of years old. Smells of uncleaned cellars and rotting meats, and flies which buzzed from one smell to the other.

This was the real, the essence of Jerusalem and the nursery of his own people—the origin of his species. What caused disgust to his colleagues and American tourists gave him the heady private delights of belonging. But this was no time for George to pause and savour. He had a meeting and who knew where it would end?

Walking swiftly down Jaffa Street, George turned into a small dark laneway where the sun never visited—permanently dank-smelling, despite the heat of the sun elsewhere in the early summer morning. He walked until he came to the low doorway, the entrance to the cafe; to enter, visitors had to walk down three steps, stooping to avoid the lintel.

Strangers were a curiosity at best, a threat at worst. They could be the Israeli police, Shin Bet, Mossad agents or nosy reporters; from his previous visit three days earlier, George was known to belong to the latter variety. Inside the cafe the mumble of conversation came to an abrupt halt. After his eyes and nose had adjusted to the dusty, airless room, he sat at one of the wooden tables, and waited for service. At his table was an open *sheshbesh* board, waiting for Jamal or Abdul or Ibrahim or one of the regulars to enter, take his usual place and while away the hours.

Without asking, the owner, dressed in a filthy striped *galabaya* walked over and aggressively placed a small demitasse of thick sweet coffee in front of him.

Minutes ticked by. The only the noise was that of urchins playing in the street. The other customers looked at him out of the corner of their eyes in suspicion and hostility. He was not cowed. This was his land. He looked back at them. He knew what they were thinking. He had made it his business to understand the Arabic mind. They were silently wishing on him one of a hundred Arab curses: may he be trampled by a wild camel; may his testicles be squeezed between rocks; may his mother be seduced by a he-wolf; may his wife be dry and barren and fruitless; or perhaps the worst curse of all, may the first child his wife bears be a girl.

George viewed the Arab customers with a mixture of pity and curiosity. These were a backward and defeated people. George could understand their hostility. He was a twentieth-century man, a man who daily bathed in the waters of western literature and whose thoughts could be traced lineally to Moses, Joshua, Solomon and David. And being American by birth, he had an additional advantage, because his thoughts were also tempered by his study of Aristotle, Plato and Socrates. How could he be expected to feel any empathy with men such as these; men whose intellectual and cultural heights had been reached a thousand years earlier, and who had been on an intellectual and social decline ever since.

George had lived in Israel long enough to know the danger of wearing a supercilious look. He averted his eyes to the table, fiddled with the *sheshbesh* board and waited for his contact to arrive. The sooner the better.

A few minutes later, the dim dusty slant of light from the door-way was obliterated by a silhouetted figure. The brother of the Mayor of Jamuel walked up to George's table, and bowed slightly.

'*Salaam Alekum,*' he said, kissing his hand.

'*Alechem Shalom,*' George responded in Hebrew, instantly re-gretting his lapse in courtesy. The other patrons sneered in disgust.

The Arab sat, and a cup of coffee was set before him. George eagerly began the conversation: 'You said you have a friend who may be able to assist me.'

The Arab frowned and put his finger to his lips, motioning to the other patrons. George nodded. The Arab did not touch his coffee but took out a coin, tossed it on the table and mo-tioned to George to follow him.

It had only been fifteen minutes since George had entered the cafe, but the air outside had become hotter and its dry dustiness burnt the back of his throat.

They walked quickly up the hills of the Moslem quarter until they reached the Sha'ar HaArayot and left the Old City via the Lions' Gate. They faced the Mount of Olives and continued to walk in silence down the dusty road, George several paces behind the Arab, until they caught sight of a 1963 black Ford covered in a thin white film of dust. As they neared the car, George heard its engine already running. He was keen to ask questions. He didn't. Perhaps the driver was not cleared for security. His mind dwelt upon who he was going to meet and what information he would be given about Ben Ari and his secret negotiations with the Arab world.

George already had the headline: 'Secret Arab/Israel Pact to Shaft Ba'ath Fanatics.'

No! the editors at *Ha'am* would never go for a word like 'shaft'.

He got into the car. The driver didn't say a word. They travelled left into Derekh Yeriho, left again into Suleiman, right into Salah ed Din and drove out of Jerusalem towards Ramallah. George looked back to ensure that they were not being followed. They passed new Jewish settlements, sitting cheek by jowl with ancient Arab villages, until the car turned right off the Ramallah road and followed a smaller, less well made road down into a dried-up wadi.

George turned to his contact. 'Before we continue this journey, I want to make it absolutely clear that you don't get a shekel unless I'm given information of use to me. Don't think you can bullshit me, my friend,' he said. 'Your uncle's friend had better come up with the goods or else I'm not parting with anything.'

The contact smiled. Despite the Western suit, striped Oxford business shirt and dark blue tie, his face was that of a Palestinian and his black beard shone with sweat.

'Would I waste the time of a man of your eminence?'

George nodded and said: 'Good. Then *In'sh'allah*, as Allah wills it. May this meeting be fruitful for us both.' His use of Arabic was a departure from his native English or Hebrew, but

George felt it appropriate in the circumstances. The Arab nodded and smiled, and looked out of the car's windows towards the white-grey rocks of the Judean landscape.

As the black bitumen of the unused road became ash-grey with dust, the driver turned onto a rough goat track which took them down towards the floor of the wadi.

When the car was out of sight of other cars, the driver stopped and opened his door. The dry wadi was devoid of life. They were alone, isolated. The air was silent.

George looked round. Where was the contact? he wondered. The Arab motioned for him to get out. As he stood on the dusty ground the air itself became hostile.

A fear seized George's body, gripping his mind with panic. His ears throbbed. Blood rushed to his forehead; his skin broke out into little beads of sweat, his neck muscles contracted, and his mouth dried up, as fear, naked, numbing fear, swamped bravado.

'What's going on here?' he asked, his voiced high-pitched as he fought for control.

'Jewish pig. Reporter,' said the driver. He spat at the ground between George's feet to show his contempt for both failings.

George's terror was palpable. His temples were throbbing. He desperately looked for a way out.

'What do you want? Money? You can have what I've got. Here,' he said, taking out his wallet, 'take all of it.'

The brother of the Mayor of Jamuel knocked the wallet out of George's hand to show his contempt for the money. He also spat at George.

'Keep your blood money, Israeli Jewish dog.'

'Just tell me what's going on. You said you would help me. I gave you money. What's going on here? Please, don't harm me. I'll do anything. I know things. I'll help you. I'll tell you anything you want to know. Only don't harm me. Please. Just tell me what you want. I have a wife now. And two children. I've only just started to live. Please.'

Tears were welling up in his eyes. How stupid he had been

in going off with two Arabs. Why had he been so arrogant and stupid?

What were they going to do? Torture him? God no! Sweet Jesus, no, not torture. He couldn't stand pain. He had a very low threshold to pain. He even needed injections at the dentist when he had a simple filling. He squeezed his eyes shut to obliterate the sight of his terror.

He heard movements, raised his head and opened his eyes. The driver had taken out a revolver. His companion was smiling cruelly.

They were going to shoot him! No! Oh God no!

George's body could no longer support itself in his terror. He slumped to his knees and fell forward until his head touched the wadi floor, his lips wet in the dust. His eyes closed tightly. His body lost control and warm slimy excrement leaked into his trousers. He moaned a high-pitched wail of uncontrollable nervousness. He shook his head in terror, but otherwise he was unable to move, fixed to the ground.

He screamed, and screamed again louder, as he heard the deafening explosion of the gun reverberating off the wadi walls. He screamed a third time … but then stopped as he realised things did not add up. He had heard the noise of the gunshot yet he was still alive. The hot stinking smell of his own excrement disgusted him. But how? If he were dead, he couldn't feel or smell his body.

He lifted his head and forced open his eyes. He saw the body of his contact lying on the ground nearby, eyes wide in the shock of being killed. But George was alive! Relief swept through his body. He struggled to his feet, kneeling first, then crouching, looking up smiling at the gunman. Thinking. Hoping.

A headline went through George's brain. It was his last thought before the hollow point bullet ripped through the bridge of his nose, and lifted the back portion of his skull off his head, carrying it and a large piece of his brain onto the white wall of the wadi, to be impaled by the sharp shards of rock, splintering George's matted scalp.

The solid bone of his skull fused itself into the rock as his brain splattered in a wide circumference. The grey-red jelly, which moments before had contained George's thought processes and controlled the sum total of his knowledge oozed slowly downwards to drip glutinously on to the dusty ground.

George's angry dead eyes stared blindly, like those of Tiresias, at the gunman who had just killed him. Blood still pumped onto the chalky white ground. The driver looked dispassionately at the way the rivulets of the Jew's blood mixed with the Arab's to form a pool. In the days of the Prophet, a literary man might have composed a poem. But he was not a literary man, and the image would pass unrecorded into history, like a million other deaths in this hostile land.

Satisfied by his efforts, the assassin checked that nobody was around to act as a witness against him. After a moment, the noise of the shots had dissipated to be replaced by a contemplative silence. Not even the insects returned to reclaim the wadi. He strolled over to the two bodies. He had been ordered to kill the Arab as well as the Jew. It seemed illogical, but those were his orders, and a fatwa has to be obeyed; it was a religious duty.

He prodded both bodies with his boot, then took out a note from his inside pocket and pinned it to the tie of the Jew.

Putting the gun back into his jacket pocket, he strolled unhurriedly over to the car, where he loosened his tie and adjusted his driving mirror to compensate for the absence of the two other passengers. When he gunned the engine, the car's rear tyres spun wildly and spat dust and gravel over the two dead men. He climbed the wadi to rejoin the main road. All he had to do now before crossing into Jordan was to telephone the Israeli police and tell them where to find the bodies.

The second event took place some fourteen hours after George P. Kennett had been shot. By now, George's body, still undiscovered despite a search of the area by Israeli anti-terrorist forces following a tip-off, had stiffened and bloated in the searing heat. Unable to escape, the gases in his gut had swelled his normally corpulent body into an obscenity, attractive only to flies and vultures. His skin had darkened in death and matched that of the Arab, who lay beside him on the wadi floor.

Nobody, Jewish or Moslem, had yet begun to mourn either man. And nobody had read the note pinned to the body of the Jew. Written in Arabic, it read:

These people, one Israeli and one PLO, were put to death to avenge the glorious martyrs of Islam. The Israeli was executed in condemnation of the Zionist Israeli government for rejecting the voices of moderation and for its aggression towards the Pan-Arab brotherhood. The other was executed for the arrogant refusal of the PLO to participate in the Cyprus Conference, and for rejecting an opportunity for peace in which peace-loving Arabic countries participated. Let this be learned by the Zionists, that Islam will prevail, and let this be learned by the PLO, that he who is stiff-necked will be harshly judged by Allah. In the Name of the Prophet, the All Merciful.

Both the note and the assassination of the Jew and the Arab would become headlines around the world when the bodies were discovered. The fanatical Moslems were not only blaming the Israelis for the breakdown of the peace initiatives but were also blaming the Palestinians.

The second event took place under the cover of darkness. By midnight, only one light shone brightly in the three-storey house in East Jerusalem. Its occupant moved cautiously from one room to the next, his shadow assuring the men on the gate who looked after his security that he was safe inside. Purposefully, he strode to the window and opened it. The guards, in the uniform of the elite Israeli Paratroop Regiment, looked up at the disturbance to the otherwise quiet night air. The only other noise was a cicada chirping in a nearby fig tree.

He looked down at the guards, smiled and nodded, and they smiled and nodded back at him. Quietly he lifted a glass of whisky to his lips to savour its aroma, so much in contrast to the perfumed air which was bursting with the scent of figs and jacarandas from his lush garden.

He drank a *schlug* of the whisky and, turning, closed the window. The guards turned back to the road to ensure that no cars or pedestrians stopped for longer than a second or two. Although they were slung indifferently at their hips, their Uzi submachineguns were capable to being fired within a fraction of a second if the circumstances demanded it. The guards were ready to take the top off any car which drove past and menaced the security of their client.

Inside the house, the Prime Minister of Israel, Raphael Ben Ari, turned off the lounge-room light and ensured that the one in his bedroom was turned on before he drew the curtains. This would eliminate the shadow of any movements from inside and give him the privacy he needed.

Keeping low to the floor, he half-walked, half-crouched towards the stairs and silently descended to the kitchen. There, he reached up into the broom closet and pressed his security code into the keypad which controlled the alarms attached to all windows, doors, pressure pads on balconies and microwave motion sensors in the garden. He picked up the phone and told the operator that he was retiring early with a sleeping pill, and wasn't to be disturbed for any reason. All calls were to go to the duty officer.

With the catlike stealth he had learned half a lifetime earlier, Ben Ari quietly opened the back door and minimised his already small body area by walking down the back garden path, legs and back bent, head bowed. Silently, he opened the gate and stood stock still to ensure that there were no pedestrians or cars in the vicinity. He closed it quietly and slipped from shadow to shadow until he was out of sight of his home and the guards in the front. There were no guards at the rear of his house. The alarms ensured his protection from intruders. He kept to the side of the path and walked slowly, inconspicuously, from shadow to shadow.

When he was convinced that he could proceed unnoticed like any other pedestrian, he straightened up, walking slowly and smoothly to avoid any second glances by onlookers. Ben Ari crossed Rechov Herzl and left the Rechavia district, walking north-west towards Rechov Ben Zevi.

At the junction of the Ruppin Way, a black Mercedes was parked, its engine running silently and effortlessly. Ben Ari stopped at the side of the road and looked left and right to ensure that any passing car was well out of the way, and that there were no late night pedestrians. Quickly, he crossed the pavement and as he did so, the back door of the car opened. He seated himself in the leather back seat and pulled the heavy door closed. Without any squeal of tyres, without any noise to attract attention, the Mercedes slid fluidly away from the pavement and entered the sparse evening traffic heading towards the main Tel Aviv to Jerusalem road. In the back of the car was a tall fair-headed man, wearing dark Western clothes and a look of amusement.

'How is my friend?' he asked.

In the old days, the long walk would not have affected him, but it took a couple of seconds before Ben Ari was able to answer: 'I've seen better days.'

'Haven't we all. Your friends from Moscow send you their regards.'

'And when next you contact them, you must send them mine.'

'I see that you haven't lost any of your skills. I didn't even notice you until you were halfway across the road.'

'Cunning and guile are the currency of a man who has lived his public life as a falsehood.'

'My dear friend, falsehood surely is a relative term. Many of us are forced to use cunning and guile because of the behaviour of our enemies. You above all should remember that from your time in Mossad.'

The Israeli smiled. He loved the games of verbal chess that he played with his control.

'But who are our enemies these days?' Ben Ari asked. 'Who was it who said, "I have seen the enemy, and it is us"?'

The control was amused. His education at Moscow University had stopped short of quotations of Western imperialists.

The Israeli felt free to speak openly. But he also knew that somewhere inside the car was a microphone, possibly no larger than a shirt button, and that strapped to the Russian's body would be a small tape recorder. Ben Ari was also aware that the back window of the car was criss-crossed with a filament of wires which acted like a large antenna and that the conversation was being picked up on a microwave frequency at a safe house, probably somewhere in Jerusalem. After scrambling, it would be sent by microwave and satellite link directly to Moscow.

The only thing that the Israeli did not know was precisely where in Moscow the conversation was being picked up. He didn't know, because he didn't need to know. That was the nature of the world of subterfuge. The less one knew about the activities of those above and below, the smaller were the risks of discovery. The Israeli had dealt with Russian controls for the past fifty years. He was content that his information eventually got to the right source.

In fact, their conversation was being sent from Israel to a small and inconspicuous three-storey import–export office in a southern industrial district of Moscow, where Marshal Petrovsky and his cabal of ex-KGB operatives had set up a SIGINT, or signals intelligence operation, that was currently monitoring information from listening posts and computers in America, Syria and Israel.

The Prime Minister continued. 'And what do my friends in Moscow say? Who is currently listening to this conversation? How are things now that the KGB is no more?'

The Russian smiled. 'It isn't finished. It is smaller now, and less visible. Some of it has gone underground, just as you, my friend, have been underground for these past fifty years. Let's just say that it has temporarily relocated itself in other premises, far from the current imperialist government. You have never before had to worry about the fidelity of the team which is ensuring your security. You still need have no concerns.'

But the Israeli would not be assuaged by gratuitous comments. 'The KGB has been purged. How do I know that those above you, whoever they may be, are not singing like larks? You're not dealing with some petty bureaucrat. You know who I am and what I have achieved.'

The Russian was stung by the Israeli's tone. 'Friend, a number of the noisier and perhaps less ideologically pure operatives of the KGB have been terminated by the new regime, but none have any connection with you.'

'And some of them have joined the new order.'

'I stress, none has ever been associated with your activities. Your work has been known to a very small number of people. I am privileged to be one of those few.'

Ben Ari looked out of the darkened window and saw the city of Jerusalem slowly retreating. His beautiful city. His city built on a hilltop, where King David had composed divine songs, and where Abraham had lifted up his eyes to God. Its white brick buildings and gold- and silver-domed mosques gleaming defiantly in the moonlight, shimmering in the haze as the rocks released their heat to the colder night air. They descended down the long winding road towards Tel Aviv.

'And what did my friends think of my performance? I know you advised me to be cold and hawkish, but those fat parasitic Arab pigs angered me, sitting there so smugly as though I should ask their permission. I got quite carried away.'

'The performance was masterful,' said the Russian.

'But the results? Are our Moscow friends happy with the aftermath? Has the current spate of diplomacy pleased or worried them?'

The Russian did not understand the question. Ben Ari's actions had been carried out by order of Marshal Petrovsky. He decided to play along, to see where the Jew was going.

'They were delighted, of course. Everything is going as we hoped it would, as we have discussed so often in the past. Your efforts have been nothing short of brilliant.'

'And do your planners still believe the chain of events will lead to our ultimate goal?'

The Russian turned to Ben Ari and placed a hand gently on his leg. He patted the man's knee and smiled enigmatically. *'In'sh'allah.'*

A silence settled on the two men, as the Russian waited patiently for the Israeli to get to the point. He, after all, had broken a dozen safety precautions by calling for a meeting, and meetings with Prime Ministers were difficult to arrange outside the spotlight of publicity.

While Ben Ari had been unknown to the general public, straight after the Great Patriotic War, he had used a standard signalling procedure several times a month. As a senior operative of Mossad, it was more difficult, but still possible, especially with the resources open to him. Between 1948 and 1958 he astounded those above him by uncovering extraordinary information about the Russians and the Arabs, which was dutifully passed on to the Israeli government. The information came to him indirectly from Marshal Petrovsky. And through his controls, he passed carefully selected information about the Americans and the Jewish nation back to the Russians. From time to time, he would receive information about the termination of some ordinary Israeli. It took Ben Ari years before he pieced together their backgrounds so that he finally understood the reason. The system worked well, and as Ben Ari grew in prominence within Israeli governmental circles, his requests for further assistance and financial help grew fewer and fewer. When he went into politics and became well known to the general public, the need for security became much greater. He rose through the ranks of Israel's right wing political process as a virulent campaigner against Communism and Russian interference in the area. It was what Moscow required of him.

Being a public figure, he tended to use the signalling procedure far less in the following decades. Meetings would be arranged in safe houses or after hours in darkened offices. During the 1960s, Marshal Petrovsky's operatives only sought his advice and input when there was a matter of urgency. He was too valuable an asset to risk. It was as though the Jericho Plan had been put on ice. Or shelved? And in all that time, only Petrovsky and a small number of insiders knew that he was a KGB asset; the Marshal's underlings never once suspected.

Every time Ben Ari had met with his control, he was assured that those in charge of the plan knew exactly what they were doing. In the 1970s Israel had taken a conservative direction and his brand of politics and xenophobia become popular once again. As he quickly rose to seniority within the Knesset, holding various ministerial ranks, he and Moscow saw little of each other. He thought that Moscow's relationship with the Arab nations had probably excluded him from future use, but with the advent of Gorbachev and the end of the Cold War he saw major potential for gains in the area. His meetings with his control had become increasingly frequent and it was unusual, to say the least, for him to request a same-day meeting. The Russian knew that there must be some problem. It would be wrong of him, though, to admit that he was worried, so he remained silent. At last, Ben Ari came to the point.

'The foxes are beginning to snap at my heels,' he said.

The Russian stayed silent. It was his way of retaining control.

'I'm not only talking about the political situation, though that may see me lose control of the country to my enemies. I'm talking about people who are keen to drag up my past.'

'But surely, it was to be expected. Foxes always snap at heels. That is their nature. But those who wonder why you changed your tune will find no answers. Your past has been sanitised. Anyway, what in particular is worrying you?'

'Nothing in particular,' the Israeli answered. 'Just an early prescience. An irritation here, a comment there. Some Israeli journalist asking questions, a Russian from Leningrad making enquiries to our Chargé d'Affaires about my early life.'

'Do you perhaps think you are over-reacting? Surely, it is natural for people to try to delve into your past.'

Ben Ari turned to his control. 'Did you accuse me of over-reacting when I warned you of how the Arabs would turn against Russia when the Soviet Union broke up, and would become clients of the United States?'

The Russian stayed silent and Ben Ari imagined with some delight how those words would irritate what was left of the KGB hierarchy when they were picked up in Moscow. The words delighted Marshal Petrovsky, when he read them.

'My dear friend,' the Russian answered cautiously, 'fifty years ago you embarked upon a course of action we believed could alter the destiny of the peoples of the world. Despite the radical changes which have taken place in the world, neither you nor your friends have deviated from that path. No asset has been more successful than you at rising to the top.'

Ben Ari snorted. After decades in Israeli politics, he had become used to short, clipped statements. He found the Russian's hyperbole unctuous.

The Russian control continued, more for Marshal Petrovsky than for Ben Ari: 'Despite the current mayhem in Russia, your friends know exactly what we should be doing to ensure our victory. Dear friend, we are coordinating a massive effort to ensure our goals are met. Critical to our efforts are that you succeed in those actions which we are currently ...' here, the Russian searched for the right turn of phrase ... 'advising you upon.'

'Well,' said Ben Ari, 'may I suggest that you advise me upon how you intend to keep the foxes from my heels.'

'Nothing is more important to any of us than to maintain the secrecy of our relationship. Be assured of that. If your current actions draw attention to your past, we will act.'

Later that night, Marshal Petrovsky read a transcript of the tape. He shrugged his old shoulders. Everything had been anticipated. Of course there would be a massive groundswell of anger against Ben Ari. What did the stupid Jew think? That he could destroy peoples' hopes and escape condemnation? Or enquiry?

Petrovsky thought back to the five decades of work which had gone into ensuring that his asset remained undiscovered. Five decades in which dozens of operatives had carried out orders to terminate a family here, an individual there, wherever they were in the world. Or to destroy records and files which could lead to the asset's discovery. And in all that time, like a juggler keeping a dozen balls in the air at the same time, Petrovsky had ensured that none of the operatives knew each other, that none knew the reason for the orders and especially that not one knew Genardy Arkyovich Petrovsky was the puppet master. And the cleverest of all was organising for Ben Ari to help create Mossad, back in the early 1950s. A stroke of inspiration. How better to hide an asset like Ben Ari while eliminating anyone who once knew him, than by keeping him out of the limelight as a spy! Pure genius.

He smiled to himself, and drank another mouthful of Courvoisier.

CHAPTER SEVEN

As Raphael Ben Ari left the darkened Mercedes which had stopped in a quiet laneway three streets from his Jerusalem house, Paul and Miriam were parking at the Rosenthal Home thousands of kilometres away. In one city, it was the middle of the night; in the other, the middle of the day.

The Israeli Prime Minister felt uneasy as he crept the last few metres to his back door. Miriam also felt a sense of disquiet, though for entirely different reasons.

The regard in which she held her *zeida* had governed her life since she was a little girl. She had rarely lied except where her relationships with non-Jewish men were concerned. This created a sense of guilt. And a fear for retribution in the afterlife which was at odds with her intellect. Both emotions were racially based and sat uncomfortably with her.

It was only when she had inadvertently mentioned Paul's name one day that he had learned of the truth. Shortly afterwards, she had introduced one to the other. Both men felt uncomfortable. The old man had wisely recognised that his grand-daughter was a grown woman and by now beyond his authority and his influence. He decided not to interfere with her decisions but prayed to himself that she would ultimately remember her racial responsibilities and marry a nice *Yiddisher* boy.

Even as a little girl, when she lied through her teeth to her parents to avoid getting into trouble, she had been meticulous in telling the absolute truth to her *zeida*. On one occasion when she was nine, she stole money from her parents to buy herself a new pencil case. She told them that all the children in her school were given one. They believed her. But when she took it out in front of her *zeida*, she felt a compulsion to tell him how she had acquired it, even though he hadn't asked. He looked at her sternly and told her about the Angel of Bad Dreams, who flies over peoples' houses every night, only entering those houses where children are bad. Miriam, he said, could expect a visit that night. She was terrified, but *zeida* offered relief. 'The Angel won't come if you tell your Mummy and Daddy what you've done.' Their punishment later that night was infinitely preferable to a visit from a malevolent spirit.

Her *zeida* held Miriam in thrall. Anybody who could invoke the wrath of a personal God and His band of Angels was not to be trifled with. And anybody who knew about the dybbuk beneath the ground was someone to be held in awe.

This sense of reverence stayed with Miriam through the effervescence of her teenage years and had lasted into the present, despite a secular education and the experiences of being an adult.

Paul parked the car and they walked slowly towards the home. Miriam was suffused with a sense of reservation. She felt a sense of inappropriateness that Paul was going to visit her grandfather in such a private and entirely Jewish environment. But her grandfather had asked for the meeting, which was disconcerting in itself. As though it was a natural outcome of Miriam's relationship with Paul. Now he knew they were lovers. Now she waited for the judgment, with a deep sense of apprehension that the meeting could injure her relationship with both men.

They climbed the ramp which led to the front door and Miriam was surprised to see a guard, standing just inside the glass entrance.

'Come to visit someone, have you?' he asked.

Both Paul and Miriam smiled at him and nodded. He allowed them through with a smile, not bothering to ask for further information or identification or whom they were visiting. Odd security, Miriam thought. As they entered the vestibule they were met by an officious nursing sister who viewed Miriam and Paul with suspicion. Normally, the home was an open house to the Jewish community, but because of the troubles in Israel, and the increased tension felt by Jews throughout the world, the fear of a backlash had put everyone on edge. Everyone, it seemed, except the security guard, who regarded the home as safe territory and his job as a waste of time.

When they reached her *zeida*'s room, Miriam knocked apprehensively and stood there, palms sweating, waiting to be admitted. Paul played with the ring Miriam had given him, feeling unaccountably uneasy.

'Come,' said a feeble voice. Miriam opened the door and saw her elderly grandfather sitting in his favourite chair beside the window. He was reading a copy of the *Sydney Morning Herald*. Again she saw with despair how his clothes tended to mask his body, hanging in folds around him like an ill-fitting bathrobe. The collar of his suit hardly touched his withered neck. Every day he seemed to grow frailer, as though he was slowly disappearing with age.

He turned and looked at the two young people as they stood in the doorway. It was a tense moment, which the old man recognised and handled with aplomb.

'Children, children. Come in. Come, sit down,' he said, attempting to put them at their ease.

Miriam walked over and kissed her grandfather.

'So. Paul, we meet again.'

Paul walked over and shook the old man's hand.

'It's nice to see you again, Mr Samuelson. I've been hoping that we could spend some time together.'

'What's this Mr Samuelson? To everyone, I'm Yossi. Who am I, the Prime Minister that you have to call me "mister?" Its nice to see you, Paul. You've been seeing Miriam long enough. I guess it's time you knew the grandfather.'

'Miriam's told me so much about you, I feel I know you well already.'

The old man smiled and shrugged his shoulders dismissively.

'My boy. For you to know me, you have to live five thousand years. Don't be too quick. You've got lots of time.'

Paul burst out laughing. He enjoyed this style of self-deprecating Jewish humour. The old man laughed as well. Finally Miriam unwound, caught up in the infectious moment. She smiled broadly as the two men settled down for their conversation.

'Miriam tells me you've got some information you'd like to share with me about Raphael Ben Ari.'

'Information? I don't know. Information? Maybe! Such a big word for such a little man. Facts, yes. I've got facts. In my head are some. On paper are some.'

Paul was no newcomer to Talmudic reasoning and thought he perceived where the old man was going. He wanted Paul to ask questions and to slowly extract the information from him. He would not volunteer the information freely. Giving it away, it would have less value to Paul.

'So when did you first meet Ben Ari?'

'I've already told Miriam. I assumed she would have told you. Miriam, darling! Is this how you brief barristers? I first knew him in the 1930s, his name was Wladyslaw Mikolajczyk. He was born on my *shtetl*. A swine he was then. A swine he is now. Always that boy, a swine.'

'And you taught him Hebrew?'

The old man shrugged his shoulders again. 'I taught *cheda* when I was a young man.'

Paul turned to face Miriam for an explanation. 'That's a Hebrew school where they learn the three Rs, and about Jewish customs.'

'And when did he join the Communist Party, Yossi?'

Miriam looked at Paul in surprise. She had only ever heard elderly people call her grandfather 'Yossi'. This would take some getting used to.

'This I don't know,' the old man replied. 'Was I there when he signed on a piece of paper? But one thing I'll tell you. From the day he was kicked out of *cheda* he went bad. He was kicked out because he was a *nogoodnik*. He was disruptive. He manipulated the other boys. He was bullying. I couldn't teach and the others were always ganging up and beating him. Sometimes

I even felt sorry ... So I said to the *shammus* ...'

Miriam interrupted: 'That's sort of a synagogue official or guard.' Paul nodded his thanks.

'I said to him. He's got to go. I can't teach here with him. For his sake and for mine. And the *shammus* agreed. His parents were ashamed. I said to his father, "Moishe, I have to kick your son out of *cheda*. I'm sorry, but he's a bad influence and I can't teach the other children." To this day, I remember Moishe's reaction. He just nodded. He didn't say anything.'

The old man cleared his throat with a cough and breathed in with some difficulty. He was enjoying talking to these youngsters. It was different from talking to the old people in the home. Usually he didn't talk this much. Conversation more often comprised clipped short sentences and angry grunts when somebody was sitting in somebody else's favourite chair. It was why he spent so much time in his room. Why should he spend time with people who sat in other people's chairs?

He continued: 'Moishe was hurt. Him and his wife would be shamed in the village, but I wasn't responsible for his son, and I had other children to teach. Moishe knew it. He was having terrible trouble with the boy at home. Next week, I kicked out the son. After that he went bad. I mean a bastard, such a *mumzer*.

'Wild, he went. He joined up with some rough *goyim* kids from our town and sometimes they would walk through, a whole gang of them, and stand outside the room where I was teaching the others. They'd laugh and throw stones, and disrupt the lesson.'

'How old was Ben Ari when this happened?' Paul asked.

'Ten maybe, twelve.' The old man thought back, frowning. 'Something like that. He wasn't a baby. I complained to the rabbi and he complained to his father, and the first few times we chased them away. But they kept on coming back. Time after time. In the end, there was nothing that could be done to stop him.'

'But didn't the police ...' Paul began to ask, but the mention of the word made the old man laugh.

'Police? Paul, you think this was Sydney we're talking about? The Poles hated us. They thought we were controlling the economy and business. Stupid. But police? We had to look after our own problems.'

'Carry on, Zeida,' said Miriam.

'After the attacks, he started to wear the badge showing he belonged to the Komsomol. It might as well have been a swastika.'

Paul was fascinated but still held severe doubts about the old man's ability to change Ben Ari from a wild youth into a rabid Communist. 'But why did he become a Communist, Yossi?'

'I've often wondered that. I mean, you could be a rotten kid, but lots of rotten kids come good, don't they? But this one! He turned so rotten I didn't recognise him. One minute, he's with a group of kids throwing stones at the window of the school … next minute he's leading a march of the Workers' Liberation Movement down the main street, and beating up old people. Like he was proud of it. Why Communist?' The old man shrugged his narrow shoulders. 'Maybe he was looking for something. We had the Bible. He had nothing. He got so bad with the violence against the *shtetl* that Moishe, his father, said *kaddish* over him …'

Miriam recoiled. Paul stared at her. 'He said *kaddish* for his *own son*?' She turned to Paul to explain her reaction. 'To say it when someone's still alive … it's the most terrible thing that a parent can do to a child. It's like saying the child is dead. Cutting him off from his family forever.'

'Moishe did. This boy was so rotten, so evil, that when he came back from where they taught him to be a Communist it would be better he was dead.'

Paul looked back at the old man whose eyes had closed, focusing upon the mists of the past.

'You see, it wasn't just that he was a *mumzer*. He was hurting our village and everyone in it. Rotten, we can put up with. We got rotten rabbis, rotten beggars, rotten criminals, all Jews. Them, we can absorb. We can hide them. But this one. Boy!

He was something special! Then, when he was about sixteen, he suddenly announces that he's going to Moscow to learn how to be a good Communist. By this time he was living away from our *shtetl.* I don't know for sure, but I think he was living in Warsaw.'

Paul shook his head and spoke to the grandfather as he would speak to a colleague. 'And this is Raphael Ben Ari we're talking about? The Prime Minister of Israel.'

The old man fixed him with a stare. 'Don't talk. Listen. Learn. When Hitler was making noises about Jews and about needing more room for the German people and turning towards Poland, that was when the Communists started to get serious. Paul, how much Polish history do you know?'

Paul shook his head. 'None, if you want me to be honest.'

'There were facists in Poland who wanted to join with Hitler, and they were anti-Semitic; and then there were Communists who wanted to fight Hitler, and they were anti-Semitic. Everybody blamed the Jews. One day we would have the Black Hand Fascists come to us with a pogrom and beat up half the town. Next day we would have the Workers' Liberation Party or some such do the same thing. Always we were the excuse for them to fight and kill. That's all they wanted, those people, just an excuse to fight the Jews and turn them into Poles.'

'And Ben Ari was a part of this?' asked Paul.

'He organised it! He organised the pogroms of the Communists. He told them who to get. Who to beat. He told them who was speaking out against the Communists. He used to inform on the village. None of what he said was true. But by the time Hitler was in power in Germany, saying all those lies about the Jews, we were so scared, you think we would have said things that would have got us into trouble? But Wladyslaw didn't need the truth. His enemies were taken away and we never saw them again. The rabbi, the *shammus*, the cantor, advisers to the *Sanhedrin* in Warsaw, teachers. Even ...' the old man choked back the words, in his disgust ... 'even his parents, can you imagine ... to have your parents and family arrested.'

'But why didn't you do something? Why did you just take it? Surely you could have done something!'

'You think so? So from where did we get the guns? We weren't fighters. We were farmers and tailors and *yeshiva buchers*. We were frightened for our families. You think you can fight back against these people who have guns and swords? Sometimes you've got to lie there and take it. We thought that if we didn't fight back they'd get bored and just go away. Boy, were we wrong!'

The old man felt defeated by the cruelty of the world, and stared down at his knees. The silence in the room was punctuated only by the noises of officiousness outside.

'But Yossi, I still don't understand,' Paul asked gently. 'If he was a Jew, and the Polish Communists were anti-Semitic, why did they allow him to join?'

'They weren't all anti-Semitic; but they didn't like the way in which the Jews kept to themselves in *shtetls* and villages, in Warsaw and other towns in ghettos. They thought we should go out into the community and become more Polish than the Poles. If a Jew became like the Poles, especially in the eyes of the Communists, that was all right. All he had to do was give up his Jewishness. That was good.'

'But why have you kept silent about this all these years? Why haven't you spoken out, for heaven's sake?'

'Mister, do you know what it's like to be a refugee in a strange country? I was lucky to get out of Poland with my wife and son. You think I wanted to remember a *mumzer* like Wladyslaw Mikolajczyk? All I wanted to do was to forget Poland and everything about it; and anyway, who in Australia had ever heard of this man? Nobody. He was nothing.'

The old man coughed up a bolus of phlegm and spat it into his handkerchief. Perspiration glowed on his forehead. Miriam looked at him, concerned that he was becoming too tired to continue. 'Would you like a drink, Zeida?' she asked.

He winked at her. She got up, opened the drawer of his bedside table and took out a small bottle of *Dio Likor*, his favourite nut brandy. She poured a measure into the cup the nurses used for his teeth and handed it to him. He reached into his pocket, took out a small skull cap which he placed on the back of his head, mumbled a blessing over the spirit and drank it.

The old man looked at Paul and grinned. Then he continued: 'A few years ago I see his face in the paper. For the first time in sixty years, I set eyes on him again. Then he was nothing. For sixty years, he was nothing. Now, he's something. He's on the front page. I see his eyes. I realise that he's changed his name and got a new identity. He's become the Prime Minister of Israel. But I recognised him. So I think "Should I say something?" And then I think, who is going to believe an old man? His name was never mentioned before. I thought he was dead *halevai*. I'd even forgotten about him. He was just a part of the past, of the nightmare. I came to this country, I left the nightmares behind. Before he becomes Prime Minister of Israel, you never heard about him in Australia. Maybe something about him in Israel, but never here.

'I'm reading the paper, the *Sydney Morning Herald*, and I see Israel's got a new Prime Minister, Raphael Ben Ari. I look and I think, *yoi* it's him! I say to some people here, "You recognise this man?" but they don't. I think to myself, I should say something. And then I ask, why. I'm over eighty. Sixty years is a long time. Maybe I'm wrong.'

'Do you think you're wrong?'

The old man looked out of the window at the changing colour of the trees. In the unseasonable warmth early yellow fronds had begun to appear on the wattle. He turned back to Paul.

'I could be wrong. And every time I think, you're talking like an old fool, I take out the picture and I look at that *mumzer*. I look at that bastard and I think to myself, he killed his own parents. He killed my parents. My family. The whole village. This man murdered a whole village of Jews!'

Paul and Miriam looked at each other. 'You have a picture?' Paul asked.

'Sure. Sure, I've got a photo. You think I'd ask you to trust an old man's mind? I said to you at the beginning, facts, you want facts. I've got facts on paper. A photograph is on paper isn't it?'

Paul held his breath. The old man got up and moved painfully, slowly to the bedroom cupboard, his twisted hands finding difficulty in turning the key which opened his closet. Miriam wanted to get up to help him but she knew his dignity was important and she remained seated. Ultimately it opened revealing a few suits, a few shirts and a small pile of underwear … one man's remnants of a lifetime. He carefully and reverentially carried over an old shoebox and, sitting back in his chair, opened it to reveal twenty to thirty, maybe forty photographs.

Some were modern colour prints showing scenes of families enjoying life in Australia in the 1950s, '60s and '70s. Others were grainy black-and-white photos with distant mountain views and long forgotten people smiling in the foreground. And in the deepest level of the box were sepia photographs of Miriam's grandfather as a young man, a wedding photo taken in the early part of the century, and others which Paul assumed were members of Miriam's ancestry. Paul looked at Miriam and saw the fascination in her face. Could it be possible that the old man had never shown Miriam this collection of his memories?

The old man fossicked with his bent and knobbly fingers until he came across a photo which he carefully extracted from the bottom of the pile. He put the shoebox down and held on to the photograph, not yet showing it to Paul.

'So, don't you want to know about the *shtetl*? Aren't you going to ask me questions about the way I lived and what it was like?'

Paul realised that his keenness to see the evidence was overriding his training. Rule Number Three, the need for background to the story. He smiled with self-consciousness. 'Forgive me. You're right. May I make some notes? What was the name of your *shtetl*? And can you please spell Ben Ari's Polish name. I won't even be able to pronounce it.'

The old man smiled, and carefully spelt it while Paul wrote it down, letter by letter.

'You would have enjoyed going to my village, Paul. It had a lot of names. The Poles called it Marowzitzki. It was on the outskirts of a small town called Rawicz. We called it Chelmnoz. But it depends on when you're talking about. So often, there were different people in control of the district. In the old old days, last century and before, it used to be called Chelmnitz.'

'And how many people were in the *shtetl*?'

'When I was there …' the old man rubbed his eyes and thought back. 'A thousand, fifteen hundred, maybe. I don't know. We had such a large *shul*.' The old man, now adopting Miriam's role as translator, said 'synagogue' and continued:

'And the rabbi was always deciding the outcome of disputes. He was judge and jury. But that didn't stop arguments from flaring up. The town was always divided on rabbinical matters. One group said this. Another said that. Some wanted to say a prayer standing. Some wanted to say the same prayer sitting. The rabbi decided. These were the sorts of problems that we had. It was a small centre but we had a very good *yeshiva*. A sort of a Jewish university, where Jews from smaller communities came to study. My father, God rest his soul, decided that the *yeshiva* in Chelmnitz was too small, so when I was a boy he sent me to Warsaw to the big *yeshiva* there.'

Paul was scribbling furiously, trying to keep up.

'Boy! Was that a place. Thousands of students they had, and in Warsaw, the Jewish life in the old quarter of the city … you wouldn't believe what it was like. Our own newspapers, our own theatres, kosher restaurants on every corner, the Jews even employed *goyim* to do the menial work. That was the middle of the world for Jews. Warsaw before Hitler.'

'When did you come back to your *shtetl*?'

'Times weren't easy. My father's business wasn't doing well. All the meat was taken by the authorities in Warsaw. People had to eat vegetables which they could grow themselves. So he brought me back when I was a boy of fifteen or sixteen to help him, and, please God, to study with the *rebbe* and learn as much as he knew about Torah and Talmud. In exchange, my father gave them free meat.' He looked at Miriam. 'That was when I met your grandmother. She was the daughter of the *shammus* who looked after the *shul*. The *rebbe* used to get angry because I wasn't paying attention to my lessons. I'd always be looking for a glimpse of your grandmother, God rest her soul.

'Your grandmother and me used to meet after lessons in the back of the *rebbe*'s house. The *shammus* knew something was going on, and sometimes he left us alone and we used to hold hands under the kitchen table. *Yoi!* Those were times! Touching your grandmother's hand was the highlight of my week.'

Miriam smiled. She couldn't imagine her elderly grandfather holding hands and kissing in the way that she and Paul loved each other.

'In fact, ours was one of the few marriages in the village that wasn't arranged by a *shatchan*. I told her father direct. I said to him, "I'm going to marry your daughter," and he smiled and said to me, "If God wills it, you will marry her. But first you have to show the *rebbe* how much Talmud you know." You know, Miriam, if I hadn't been a good student you might never have been born.'

Paul was amused but concerned to relate the incident back to Ben Ari. 'And how did Ben Ari figure in all of this?'

'You mean the picture?' He still held it close to his chest. 'Well, it was around the time when I was due to leave my *shtetl*. Hitler was on the warpath and I wanted to get my wife and son to safety. One day there had been a nasty incident. I'll never forget it. He comes into the village, driving in the back of an open car like some lord or other. He's dressed like a Hollywood film star, all five feet nothing of him. With a smart grey suit and a hat. He steps out of the car and looks around and tells the other people in the car to get out and look at "my village". That's what he says, "My village"! Like he was the landlord. Like he was proud of us. A couple of days later he comes back. This time, he's on a horse, and he rides around the town like he owns the place. Still nobody wanted to mess around with him. His manner, his confidence, were intimidating. Not his size. The two years in Moscow had obviously done a lot for him. Somehow made him grow …

'Me, I was ten years older than him, but even so, there was something about him that made me say "Don't cross him."

'Suddenly, there was a pogrom. This was …' The old man thought deeply for a moment, trying to capture the year … 'My memory. I can't remember when it was—'38, '37—*yoi*, I'm getting so old. Anyway, suddenly there's this pogrom, and these madmen come into the village at night, and they start to burn houses and drag people off. But it wasn't like any other pogrom. They went straight for our rabbi's house and dragged him and his wife and children away. He was the one who was the most critical of Wladyslaw. He should have kept his mouth shut, like the rest of us. We never saw them again.'

The old man fell into silence once more. A silence both of reminiscence and distress. Paul was bursting to ask another question but he knew by instinct to keep quiet. After many seconds, the old man cleared his throat. With misty eyes, he looked at his grand-daughter and her young man.

'It was just the beginning. Hitler was already making noises. The Communists in Russia were making noises. There was no peace or silence. I knew it was time to go. I begged my father. "We have to get out," I said to him. "The whole world is going mad." He argued with me. I shouted at him, the first time I had ever raised my voice to my father. I said, "We're all going to die if we don't get out. You have to come with me. You and Imma. I'm going to tell everybody it's time to go. Time to get out. If we don't, we'll all be killed."'

Paul had stopped writing and stared at the old man, sensing the horror of what he had gone through.

'I remember the look in my father's eyes. Like he was haunted. I remember him sitting, nodding his head, saying,

"You're right, it's time to go." I talked to other people but they just said, "Things will pass; things will get better." I argued. I cried. I begged. But they wouldn't listen. Just your *bubba* and our child and my parents.

'Next day, I said to your *bubba*, I said, "I'm going to take some photos so that when we're in our new land, our son will know what a life we led here." I went around the village taking photos. We went out into the fields so I could take photos of the hills in the distance, so he would know how beautiful the land was. And when we were there we heard these shouts and screams and I knew it had all started again. I went running to save my parents. Your *bubba* was holding our boy and she screamed at me not to go. But I had to go. And then I saw them in the distance.'

Painfully, he reached into his pocket and pulled out a hand-kerchief to blow his nose and wipe his eyes.

'Horsemen. And there right in the middle was Mikolajczyk. I hid on the ground, I was so scared, but I cursed at him. I wanted to kill him with my hands but I knew I would be killed, so I crawled behind a tree and waited, and he points to the village and tells the other horsemen to go down there. Then he's on his own and I take a photo of him. The swine. The *mumzer*. I lie flat on the grass and I think to myself "A Jew killing other Jews. It can't be!"'

'When it was over, your *bubba* and me tried to find my parents, but the shop was destroyed by fire and I couldn't go in. I should have, but I was too scared to see what had happened. My *abba*, my *imma*, my brothers and sisters. All dead. We tried to find your *bubba*'s family, but same thing. Burnt. Dead people were lying in the streets. We were in shock. We just turned around and started to walk towards the West.

'We walked for weeks. And all the while we had to hide from the Nazis. They weren't yet in command but they were making life hell for Jews. The only thing which kept us going was when we talked about what life would be like in America. With no money we had to walk half-way across Europe to get to a port so we could get a ship. To eat, we had to beg for food from other *Yidden*. Thank God we had a child. That made the begging easier. When at last we got to Holland, there was almost nothing left of us. We were like scarecrows. Like ragamuffins. We looked for a boat going to America, and we thought that you spell America like you spell Australia. How were we to know? We could only read Polish.

'We were given enough money for the voyage by Jews in Germany to help us get to America. Suddenly, we're in Australia.' The old man laughed.

The story was overwhelming, almost unimaginable. Journalism had hardened Paul against the evils that life had to offer, but listening to the living history of the struggle to escape the horrors of pre-war Europe made Paul realise how secure his own life had been.

'But I don't understand,' said the young man. 'Why should Ben Ari organise pogroms against Jews in your village? What could be the reason? Surely he couldn't have had that much hatred. I mean, it defies logic. He was a Jew himself … and now, he's the head of the Jewish nation? If what you say is right, there has to be some ulterior motive.' Before the old man could answer, Paul posed another question. 'And not only that. Surely, for God's sake, he would have been exposed before now. You've made him out to be a mass-murderer. Surely he would have been exposed by somebody. He's the Prime Minister of Israel!'

'Hoo ha, mister! All these questions! Answers, I haven't got. Did I say I knew the reasons why? I'm as much in the dark as you. That's the reason I'm talking to you. Who knows what he's up to now? There's an old saying, "The devil never sleeps." That's why I asked to talk to you. So the world would know that this man is a swine that killed a village, and his own parents. So, Mr Reporter. You're the intellectual. You and my darling grand-daughter. You find for me the answers.'

The room sank into silence, broken by Miriam saying: 'Maybe, after all these years, Zeida, your memory's not what it used to be. Maybe you think it was Ben Ari but it was somebody else. Maybe Ben Ari did come back to the village, but the man on the horse, maybe it wasn't him at all.'

'May I see the photo?' asked Paul.

Proudly, like a prosecuting barrister, Yossi Samuelson showed Paul the photo; it was remarkably well preserved, the sepia brown giving warmth to the detail.

Paul took it, handling it with the delicacy of a religious object. In the background, he could see a conflagration. There was brown-black smoke curling upwards towards an overcast sky; in the foreground, looking intently at the scene of terrified men and women running from horsemen in uniform, there was a man seated arrogantly on a horse. The horse was far too big for the rider. His face was the clean-shaven face of a young man. His clothes were those of a Russian peasant—breeches, a cotton shirt, and riding boots. As Paul peered closely at the face, his skin crawled in horror.

Staring at him through half a century were the steel-cold eyes, the thin smile, and the menacing expression which the world saw most nights on their television screens. It was the Prime Minister of Israel, today known as Raphael Ben Ari, taken when he was a young man.

Paul knew at once that it was Ben Ari, but had there been any doubts in his mind they would have been assuaged by one unmistakable piece of evidence. Above the rider's right eye was the trademark of the man himself—a vivid birthmark in the shape of a fist.

All Paul could manage was a whisper. 'I don't understand why nobody has said anything before now? Somebody from your village?'

The old man gave Paul a fatalistic stare.

'Who should speak out? Nobody was left. Gone. Everyone. Just me and my wife and son. Maybe a few others, I don't know. Before, some got out. Not many. But the rest; they just stayed, waiting for things to get better. But they never did.'

Miriam stood and poured herself a *Dio Likor*.

CHAPTER EIGHT

Miriam read the same paragraph in the contract of sale for a shopping centre complex for the third time. And for the third time the words swam before her eyes. The more senior she became as a lawyer, the more intolerant she was of jargon.

If she couldn't complete the contract today it would have to be done first thing the following morning, and her diary already read like a nightmare, beginning at seven-thirty and not ending until early evening.

The tortured phrases that the other side's lawyers had used in the document were in stark contrast to the word pictures her grandfather had painted on the previous day. In simple, elegant, unaffected prose he had drawn for her a portrait of the world from which he had stepped. In all their long life together he had avoided telling anything about the black side of Poland. Yesterday, she had been a witness in the gallery of his memories.

In a fit of anger at the preposterousness with which lawyers bamboozle ordinary people in order to keep the law within a tightly held clique, Miriam flung the lease aside, picked up her Philips micro-recorder and dictated a letter to the other side's lawyers. After the usual felicitations, she said:

> We are unable to advise our client to agree to the terms and conditions of the sale because in order to explain his obligations, we would first have to understand the document ourselves. As it was obviously written by a Medievalist in your firm who enjoys using arcane phraseology, it will require a team of our own lawyers skilled in such things to translate it into the language of the twentieth century. If you will defray our costs, we will be happy to comply. If not, please rewrite the document in more accessible language.

She chuckled as she pressed the stop button. Her letter would save her at least ten hours of grindingly boring work. Although it would lose her partnership $2,000 of income, it would cement her relationship with one of the firm's most important clients and Miriam knew her action would be supported by the senior partners.

Throughout the firm, and increasingly within legal circles in Sydney, Miriam Davis was known as a bit of a loose cannon. She enjoyed the practice of law, though not as much as when she had first graduated. She had seen too much law and not nearly enough justice, especially in the courts. She had a particular hatred of some senior judges, who tended to allow their personal likes and dislikes to affect the fairness of a decision. And too often, the small individual suffered the disadvantage of the cost of law against the morality of seeking redress.

Law was a peculiar thing. To the outsider, it was pitted with snares and traps, many introduced by lawyers to stop other lawyers from misinterpreting intentions. In the old days, two people would shake hands on a deal. Any dispute would be debated over a pint of ale. If it was irreconcilable, it would be taken to the local witch-doctor or priest or lord or squire to adjudicate. Sometimes you won, sometimes you lost. It all came out in the wash.

But then lawyers began to build their expertise, and people in dispute were shielded from each other by codes of practice and precedents and torts and contracts written in Victorian English sprinkled with Latin expressions never used anywhere outside the courtroom … anything to keep people from spitting on their hands and shaking over a deal. It was all so different from the law of the *shtetl*, where the rabbis worked hard to bring aggrieved parties together, and everyone abided by the decisions of compromise.

Why was she beginning to have doubts about the law at the present state of her career? She surveyed her large, opulent office and her chrome and glass desk, opened the bottom drawer of her filing cabinet and took out a mirror and brush. It was a question she could not answer.

Straightening her hair, Miriam thought back to the difference between her world and that of her *zeida*. She was a successful woman in every regard. She had a secretary, computers, faxes, databases, an apartment … anything she wanted. She was potent, a woman in command of her own destiny. In control of her career, her mind, her body. She could choose the sex of her baby. She could make choices about her sexuality, and not be condemned by society. For the first time in the history of humanity, a small number of women were now enjoying the capacity to be equal and not beholden to men.

Yet. Yet, what? Yet she looked at herself in the mirror and felt unworthy. Felt beholden to her grandparents and her parents for who she was, as though her success was attributable to their sacrifices rather than her abilities and hard work. Miriam closed her eyes as the vision of the gas chambers again invaded her daytime. It was happening with increasing frequency. It was not an uncommon occurrence for children of concentration camp survivors. But why was it happening to her? Her parents had not been interned in a concentration camp, and her grandparents had been clever in leaving before the evil took hold. But she mourned for everyone else. Maybe hers was a racial memory and she was a daughter of the Holocaust. Not directly. Not like so many of her own friends or their parents, who had lost whole families in the gas chambers of Poland and Germany, those expedient devices of racial purification. It was her grandparents who had lost, but not her parents. They were lucky. She grimaced at the word. Lucky? Lucky to have been deprived of their birthright, because *bubba* and *zeida* had been shrewd enough to get out when there was still time. By the skin of their teeth.

Why did she still feel resentful of her mother and father so long after their death? Was it because they hadn't atoned for the losses which her *bubba* and *zeida* had suffered. The old people had lost their entire world. Yet her parents had hardly been affected, especially her mother, who had been born in Australia. And worse, they had tried to shield Miriam from the awful truth. They had closed their eyes to the black swirling smoke from the tall towers above Auschwitz and Treblinka. They had pretended her *zeida* and *bubba*'s horror had not existed, just as the rest of the world had ignored the smoke of those human spirits, the dust of six million Jewish souls, as it spun and danced in the cold black skies over Europe and weaved a tracery in the firmament—and was then lost forever. She shook her head, hoping that the evil pictures would shatter and float away like pollen into a clean blue sky.

Miriam thought back to yesterday's meeting with Paul. Her grandfather had played the situation like a master, knowing just how much to tantalise the sceptical reporter. A bit of self-deprecation, reluctance and modesty, and Paul was hooked.

She smiled when she thought of Paul. The change in her face caught her eye in the mirror. He really was very special. Kind, attentive, sexy, yet riddled by insecurities, the same sorts of insecurities as were suffered by the callow boys whom she had spurned as a teenager. But his insecurities only surfaced when she resisted his requests to marry. She was woman. She was empowered. In her mother's day, to be single and over twenty-five was a death sentence. Yet … yet … most of her friends were married and didn't seem to have lost their grip, their careers, their hold on life. None had settled meekly into the role of *hausfrau*, fussily justifying her existence by being an extravagant hostess or an exclusive wife.

She could simply say yes and have done with it. Why not get married? Why not have children and see them grow up in an evolving world where the potential of the future was realised every day? She looked at her reflection in the mirror on her desk top. Her reflection didn't have the answer, either.

A knock on her door made her jump, grab hold of the mirror and sweep her vanity back into the dark recesses of the filing cabinet.

Richard Page, her assistant, swung in the door, and held his position with his hand high on the lintel. He looked and dressed like an ageing schoolboy, but had a good mind and an embryonic killer instinct that Miriam was trying to nurture.

'Sorry to break in on you, but …'

He closed the door and walked to her couch.

'Problem?' she asked.

He was not a tall man. She was taller, yet he seemed to shrink even as he sat down.

'It's Prescott *v.* Morwell …'

'Christ, Richard. Can't you speak in English? I've just given another firm a mouthful for using that type of phraseology …'

Richard flushed. Miriam regretted her outburst. He had entered her office at precisely the wrong time to talk about a case that she thought had been settled. Prescott had agreed to meet the original payment schedule and had promised to send a bank cheque made out to Derek Morwell for $20,000.

'So what's happened, all of a sudden?'

Richard cleared his throat. 'I'm afraid that our Mr Prescott's pulled a bit of a swiftie and is going to begin proceedings to have himself declared bankrupt. He's going to start the process this morning, which means Derek Morwell's cheque won't be coming.'

'You're kidding.'

'No. A friend of mine who works for his law firm phoned me just now and told me.'

'Morwell's lawyer told you that! Why? Bit unethical, isn't it?'

'I was at uni with him. He's disgusted at Prescott. Nobody in the firm can stand him. He's such a pig of a man and last week he was in there, boasting that he was going to …'

'Out with it,' demanded Miriam.

'He said he was going to screw you personally.'

Miriam burst out laughing. 'Not literally, I promise you. So what did this friend of yours tell you?'

Richard was diffident. 'Well, it was sort of in strict confidence. He was kind of giving me advance warning.'

'Oh! cut the crap, Richard. You've already broken the confidence. We're working for a thoroughly decent man whom Prescott tried to destroy. Just tell me what's going on.'

'Well, apparently he's been transferring all his assets into his wife's name for some time and he's got nothing left. The houses, the kitchen company, other properties, all transferred. Apparently he's used a few different law firms around the place, in case we heard about it. Anyway, now his wife owns everything, and she lent him ten thousand dollars six months ago, which he can't pay back. It's his wife that's seeking the bankruptcy orders.'

Miriam shook her head in surprise. 'But surely he's been advised that won't work. His lawyers must have told him that we can get the Bankruptcy Commissioner to look behind the transfers, and to rescind them if they were made to avoid debt.'

Richard shrugged his shoulders and didn't answer. Miriam began to realise what was going on.

'He must really hate me. You know what he's doing? He realises he'll have to pay in the end but he's decided to string it out for a couple of years to make Derek Morwell suffer … and to make me suffer professionally.'

Miriam stood up and paced the floor, considering her next action. She spun on her heel, pointed a finger at Richard and said: 'Right. Get on to the Clerk of the Bankruptcy Commissioner and find out the time of the appearance. Prepare an injunction against Prescott for something … anything. Child molestation, parking infringements, blasphemy. I don't care what it is, just find something which will let him know that we know what he's up to. It's going to take him some time before he can be declared a bankrupt. While you're doing that, I'll get onto his law firm, speak to David Franklin and tell him I know what's going on. You organise a conference with Doug Scotland. He knows a fair bit about bankruptcy. I'll make that bastard regret taking me on. Off you go and come back with at least five measures we can take to stop Prescott in his tracks.'

As he began to walk out of the office, she said, 'If he thinks he's going to screw me, he's going to get it right back where it hurts …'

♜♜♜

The only sound in the Mausoleum was the low hiss of the air-conditioner, which maintained an even temperature. No matter where Max Mandle was in the world, it was always a northern spring day. He worked in the same temperature in Sydney, London or Los Angeles, from where he ran his television empire. And it was perpetual spring on his yacht which was currently cruising the Mediterranean with his wife, two daughters and a small party of their friends. It was one of the idiosyncrasies that had made Max Mandle's personal and professional life a legend throughout the business world; that, and his volcanic temper. Once he had lifted an editor bodily out of a chair and carried him to the lift, where his career with the Mandle group plummeted. It had cost Mandle a fortune in compensation but every other editor in his empire had been cowed by the news.

Although Max was itching to join his wife on the islands where Mrs Mandle and company had recently enjoyed fame in the social pages, the financial problems which were causing the share price of his debt-ridden empire to fall forced him to stay close to his desk. Better stories meant more newspaper sales and that would see his share price return to the days when it had made lots of people fortunes. Then he would repay his debts and return his employees' superannuation funds.

His life was full of urgency. Urgent messages, urgent meetings ... yet he had to give this meeting serious attention because it involved an old friend of his, Raphael Ben Ari. The messages from government leaders and from timid bankers who wanted to discuss their exposure at a time of international recession and declining advertising revenue would have to wait.

Mandle had become involved in the meeting at the insistence of Jack Muir, who earlier that morning had listened with fascination and disbelief to Paul Sinclair's story. When Muir asked for proof, Paul said he had seen a photograph showing the Israeli Prime Minister as a young man leading a pogrom, but that the old man would not let it out of his possession. Paul didn't enjoy lying to his boss. He did it on the rare occasions when he had to protect a source, but he had placed the photo in a safe custody deposit box in a bank. And Jack Muir was confident enough in Paul to realise that the photo would be produced when necessary.

When Paul first told Muir about Yossi Samuelson's allegations, Muir had dismissed out of hand the notion that Ben Ari could be a closet Communist at best, and a mass murderer at worst. But Paul had insisted that the facts needed further investigation and had proposed an imaginative plan which required more authority than Muir could exercise. He needed the stamp of approval of the big boss—the guy in the sky—the man in the Mausoleum. Conversations with Max Mandle were invariably traumatic and Muir detested phoning him, but the circumstances demanded that he do so. Now the three men were seated in Mandle's private office where Paul Sinclair had just finished telling his story.

Paul resented Jack's decision to refer the matter upstairs. The owner of a newspaper was different from the editor. The editor should have the daily responsibility of deciding on newspaper content, not the owner. That wasn't, of course, to deny Mandle's ability as a journalist. His grandfather had owned and edited a Yiddish language newspaper in Poland at the turn of the century and in the 1920s his father had begun a similar one in London to cater to the huge number of refugees from Eastern Europe. Mandle had worked for newspapers before going into the family business and buying up half of Fleet Street, as well as much of New York's press and other newspapers around the globe. But while *The National* was a publication of world standing, it was very different from the 'tits and bums' newspapers that made Mandle's money, and Paul worried that a story of this sensitivity might not be treated with the respect and circumspection that it demanded.

When he had finished, Paul waited in trepidation for Mandle's reaction. The tycoon, whose florid face, jowls and puffy eyes revealed a lifetime of hard work and excess, sat back and put his feet on his huge teak desk. He stared up at the ceiling, head back, resting on the top of his leather armchair, as though examining the air-conditioning ducts, and breathed deeply. He gave no indication of what he thought. Ben Ari was Mandle's friend and confidant, and Paul feared that an on-the-spot judgment would be based on emotion rather than logic.

As it was only a matter of a few days since Mandle had told Paul what he thought of his journalistic abilities, he felt that he was out of favour before the conversation had begun. The truth was very different. Mandle didn't remember the conversation. His temper frequently flared and calmed within minutes and he had completely forgotten that he had given Paul one of the worst dressings-down of his professional career. Mandle had even forgotten the name of the editor he had carried to the lift.

Slowly Mandle corrected his chair into the upright position, took his feet off the desk and went over to the drinks cabinet, still without saying a word. He turned to the two men and said 'Whisky? Gin? Beer?' as though a drink was *de rigueur*. When the three men had glasses in their hands, Mandle walked around to the front of his desk and sat in one of the armchairs.

'Let me see if I have this correct. An eighty-something-year-old Jew is the sole survivor of some village in Poland, where he says that the current Prime Minister of Israel was born and where he turned from being a nice *Yiddisher* boy into some hideous Commie who killed his parents, a rabbi and all the other Jews. Then years later he turns up in Israel and becomes Prime Minister ... do I have this correct, Mr Sinclair?'

Paul was being baited and he knew it. Within minutes he and Muir would most likely be escorted from the building by security guards.

'Mr Mandle, these are allegations which we want to investigate.'

'Allegations,' he sneered. 'Oh! so now you're a detective, not a reporter.'

Muir reacted defensively. 'Paul's a damn good reporter. One of the best. It's his job to investigate.'

Mandle sipped his drink. 'Jack, please don't tell me what my reporters should be doing. I pay them to investigate facts, not stupid allegations. If I said the Queen of England was a Commie, would you spend a fortune investigating? No! So why …'

'Mr Mandle, Paul interrupted, 'all I'm asking …'

'Mr Sinclair, I know what you're asking. What I'm asking is whether I've got this crock of shit story correct. So far, have I summed up what you've told me accurately or not?'

Paul stared at the elderly owner. 'Pretty much.'

'You are aware, Mr Sinclair, and you, Mr Muir, that Raphael Ben Ari is a good friend of mine. That I've got newspaper interests in Israel. That I support a number of charities there. That I've never made any secret about the fact that my sympathies are Zionistic. You're aware of those facts?'

Paul looked at Jack. 'Yes, Mr Mandle. I'm aware of those facts.'

Mandle nodded and finished his whisky. 'I think I need another one of these.' He got up, walked to the bar and poured himself another drink, not offering his employees a refresher.

'So on the basis of what one old man tells you, I could destroy my friendship with the Prime Minister of Israel. You are aware of that, Mr Sinclair? And you, Jack, you're aware of that, too, are you?'

Like a congregation responding to a preacher, they said, 'Yes, Mr Mandle.'

But Paul continued, 'I must reiterate that we don't know one way or the other whether these allegations are true, but they deserve investigating. That's all we're asking. Just to follow up the story.'

'You're really asking a lot aren't you, Mr Sinclair? I mean, if this story is right, then so what? So somebody was a wild Communist in his day and is now an anti-Communist. Maybe committed some excesses before the war, when the world was going crazy. But if the story is wrong, then suddenly Max Mandle becomes one of the enemy. Somebody who could do incalculable harm to Israel and its Prime Minister. Somebody who could destroy a man whom my wife and I dined with not two months ago.'

Mandle's voice rose in pitch and anger. 'A man who asks my advice on how Israel can survive in a hostile world. Who asks me to facilitate certain deals and fundings and meetings with prominent people throughout the world ... people whom I know personally but whom you only know from the papers you read. You're saying I should trust you and an old man and that I should forget my years of friendship with Ben Ari and the Israeli government.'

Paul was tempted to answer, but felt that discretion was more important than justification. Jack Muir, on the other hand, was not going to let the matter drop.

'Max, please don't think we're unsympathetic to anything you've just said. We know what we're asking. That's why we're here. That's why I didn't send Paul off on the story without referring it to you.' He stood up, went to the bar and poured himself another whisky. 'But you can't just simply say it's a question of a wild youth turning into a responsible adult. If this old man is right, then Ben Ari was more than just a Stalinist in his younger days. He organised pogroms, he organised for the deaths of his fellow Jews. He was effectively instrumental in killing an entire village ...'

'And you think this isn't the case with the Arabs?' Mandle shouted 'You think that Saddam Hussein, Gaddafi or the others weren't like that? Do you know how those bloodthirsty bastards climbed to power? What do you think happened to the Kurds in northern Iraq? You think that Saddam became a dictator by some sort of parliamentary vote? The whole world's full of Commies or fascists who've killed or tortured and slaughtered. Why should Israel be any different? It's surrounded by a hundred million Arabs out to push five million refugees into the sea. Refugees from the Nazi holocaust! Don't be so fucking naive, for God's sake ...'

'Max,' Muir cut in, 'we're not talking about these dictatorships. We're talking about Israel. That's the point.'

Mandle suddenly became quiet. Paul and Jack stared at him, wondering what he was thinking.

He walked over to his desk and perched himself on its edge. He looked at the two men and continued in a lower, more moderate voice, 'You think Raphael Ben Ari is like those madmen? Well, you're wrong. But to stop you spreading rumours, I don't mind squandering this company's money on proving you wrong.

'I was there in 1948 when Israel was declared a state.' He stabbed the air with his finger towards the two men. 'I was there. You weren't. You don't know from nothing. I saw the look on the faces of men and women who had just escaped the death camps in Germany who suddenly had a country to call their own. You can't even begin to understand what they suffered, you two. But I'll tell you one thing. No matter what he might have suffered, Ben Ari isn't a cold-blooded murderer.' His voice changed and became low and serious. 'How sure are you of this story?' he asked Paul.

'I'm not sure,' Paul said. 'All we're sure of is that having seen the photograph, it's crying out for investigation.'

Mandle dismissed it with a wave of his hand. 'It could have been anybody. That picture was what … fifty, sixty years old!'

'I looked into those eyes,' Paul said. 'They were the eyes of Ben Ari. His birthmark was clear and the old man's story had such depth and clarity to it.'

'I want to see the photograph.'

Paul breathed in. 'I'm sorry but my informant won't let it out of his possession. And I've guaranteed to protect him. He's my source.'

'Don't come that fucking journalistic moralising crap with me. I remember you, now. You were the one with that story about the rorts that got me into trouble with the Premier …'

'Paul was right about that, Max. The Premier was bullshitting to you,' Jack Muir interrupted.

Mandle began to calm down and stared at Paul. Then at Jack

Muir. 'Will your contact make it available for publication?'

Paul nodded.

'And the consequences?'

Jack Muir looked at his boss. 'The consequences, Max, are not our problem. If we hurt somebody by telling the truth, then that's not our liability.'

Mandle walked around to the operations side of the desk, tipped himself back in his chair and placed his feet again on the latest copy of *The National*. 'What do you propose to do, Sinclair?'

'Well, I've got to be very careful none of this leaks out, but I need to get some more information about Ben Ari's early life. It's pretty much a mystery. Then I want to contact our stringer in Tel Aviv and get him to do some digging in preparation for my going over there.'

'You want to go to Israel?'

'Of course. You don't think I can do it by telephone, do you?'

Mandle nodded. 'And what will you do over there?'

'Ben Ari's early life may be a mystery, but I'm sure the people around him know things that haven't appeared in any biographies. I'll try and source somebody who's willing to talk to me. Probably one of his political enemies.' Paul looked at Mandle with a cheeky grin in his eye. 'Actually, Mr Mandle, why don't I start with you? You're a good friend. Why don't you tell me what you know about him?'

Mandle guffawed. 'If I knew anything that could be of help to you, young man, it would have appeared in my papers thirty years ago. I've already told you Ben Ari may have been involved as a freedom fighter in Israel, but the man is no mass murderer.'

'But do you know anything about his early life?' asked Paul.

Mandle walked over to the window with its panorama of Sydney, looking like a man standing before the Ark of the Covenant and praying to God to unburden him from his troubles.

'Me? Why should I know? We've never talked about the old

days. They were too painful. Anyway, I was born in England. Sure I went to Israel when I was a kid. I even thought of becoming a citizen and joining the army but my father wouldn't let me. No! You'll have to find your own sources, I'm afraid.' The thick Polish accent he had acquired from his parents had returned as it did when his emotions ran high.

'But that brings me to another problem. Israel's full of reporters. How're you going to keep this under wraps so that we keep it exclusive?'

'Believe me, I'll be careful,' replied Paul. 'A lot of the digging I do will be from records, not just interviews. I understand that the Museum of the Diaspora and the Holocaust Museum have fantastic resources. And I'll be interviewing Israelis of Polish descent …'

Mandle sat down again at his desk, calmer than he had been several minutes before. He was embarrassed that he had been using his Polish accent again. 'Sinclair. This story of yours. You follow it through. But keep it strictly to yourself, Jack and me, or we'll lose it. If another paper sniffs it, we're dead in the water. Now listen. I've got amazing resources behind me. Reporters in every country who can do some digging. If the request comes from me, they'll never put two and two together. So field everything about this directly through my office. I'll brief Jack. Understand?'

Paul nodded.

Mandle took a drink, a sip this time, and looked at Paul.

'But listen to me, Sinclair, and listen good. I'll back you up 100 per cent but I'm going to tell you one thing and I swear this to you by all that's holy. If you make a mistake I'll have your balls. I don't want anything at all to get out about the fact that Max Mandle is investigating Ben Ari. This is top secret. Firstly I don't want any other newspaper to publish before we do if the story's true. And secondly, if it's not true and word gets out, then God help you because I won't. I'm very serious, Sinclair. I'm not advising you, I'm telling you. If you fuck up on this one, it's the end of your career. I'm not

Rupert Murdoch publishing that bullshit about Hitler's diaries. Cover yourself, Sinclair, but mainly, cover me.'

Paul started to respond but a quick look from Muir told him to remain silent.

Mandle continued: 'If Ben Ari was a Communist, and did do what you've said he did, then he belongs behind bars. And that's where I'll put him. Like Eichmann. Like Barbie. Like Hess. But whatever you print, you make sure it's right. Do you get what I'm saying, Mr Sinclair?'

Paul nodded. The road he was about to travel was going to be long and lonely.

CHAPTER NINE

Paul and Jack walked out of Max Mandle's office like a boxer and his coach after a successful fight. Both were dizzy from the exercise of winning a match with one of the world's most pugilistic businessmen. Despite their concerns, they had managed to corner him. His only way of disproving their allegations without seeming partisan was to let them go ahead.

Now it was up to Paul. Muir turned to him as they walked down the stairs to the editorial office. 'You realise it's not only your job on the line if you fuck up. I'll get the flick too. Max Mandle isn't the sort of man to quietly forgive mistakes.'

'I don't know how you tolerate the way he deals with you,' said Paul. 'I'd tell him to piss off. I know you've got a wife and kids and all the baggage but it surprises me that you let him dictate what this paper says. I wouldn't if I was the editor.'

'My wife and kids have got nothing to do with it, Paul, and I don't need you to tell me about editorial interference. What he does to me is what I do to you. You don't like my interference with your stories any more than I like his interference with my paper. But I'm your boss and you've got to put up with it, and he's mine. Anyway, I don't know what you're crapping on about. We've just won a hell of a bloody victory.'

Paul shrugged and let it go. He was too excited and too concerned about the immediate future to bother with the morality of editorial independence. As the newspaper's unofficial Middle East specialist, he could now concentrate all his efforts on the story at hand.

Back at his desk, Paul considered his next action. He scanned the incoming news reports. Looking for the most recent news from the Middle East, he read with interest that overnight, Tel Aviv and Jerusalem had witnessed massive anti-government demonstrations. There was also an item about some Israeli journalist of American descent being abducted and murdered in a remote spot outside Jerusalem. The Arabs claimed responsibility. Paul shuddered. Journalists these days were no longer observers. They had become participants. In the last decade militant fundamentalists had begun to understand the value of news footage and learned how to create and stage instant demonstrations for the benefit of television news teams. He knew Miriam would be distressed now that he was no longer an observer. But that was inevitable. He continued to read the news reports.

Another story told of Iraqi Foreign Minister Abbas Rahman's denial of claims in the United Nations of genocide against the Shi'ites in the south of the country. Their traditional homeland in the salt marshes between the Tigris and the Euphrates was being drained by a huge new canal which would make capturing and eliminating them easier for the Iraqis. Claiming that the marshes were being drained only in order to provide additional agricultural land, Rahman said that the UN claim was a Zionist trick to divert attention from the Israelis' destruction of the peace process in flagrant violation of the rights of the people of the world to an international Jerusalem. Paul smiled at the self-righteous cant.

More menacing than the Iraqi sabre-rattling was the decision of the King of Jordan, reported to a press conference by the gentlemanly Prime Minister, Mohammed Quirri, that he was moving two additional regiments of the Royal Jordanian Army to the border with Israel because civil unrest in the Jewish state posed a threat to stability in the region.

There was quiet in the newsroom. He surveyed the vast space, sandwiched between the ethereal executive offices above and the throbbing press room below. Meat in a newspaper sandwich.

None of his colleagues were there. Monday was a holiday on a Sunday paper and he sat at his inconspicuous desk, nestled in a corner beneath the dominating bank of clocks which gave the time in New York, London, Tel Aviv, New Delhi and

Tokyo. Odd how bland the room was without jockeying staff. On working days, *The National* was like a college common room, full of wit and craft. And the people varied between the pompous and the popular. Paul? How did his colleagues find him, he wondered? And did he care? He'd been there long enough to feel secure, but security and working for Max Mandle were incompatible. He was liked by some, respected by others. But those who were not part of the inner clique on *The National* viewed him with suspicion because he had the editor's ear.

His secret project would deepen the rift. Not that he gave a damn. He was about to leave them far behind like a pony in a field of carthorses. He had relied on his novel to differentiate him from the herd, but that was nowhere near being finished. And two publishers had already rejected the story synopsis with phatic excuses like 'our list is full for the next year', or 'doesn't meet our publishing objectives'. Perhaps when they read his world scoop, they'd open their blinkered eyes.

The blank screen on his PC stared maliciously at him, taunting him to take the first step, tantalising with potential.

The first fax he would send seemed innocent enough. It read:

Please provide as much personal family detail as possible concerning H.E. Raphael Ben Ari, Prime Minister of Israel, for a biographical feature. Special reference to his early life, from birth to manhood prior to arriving in Palestine would be greatly appreciated.

It was addressed to the cultural attaché of the Israeli Embassy in Canberra and was received at 10.23 a.m. by Judith Abramovich, an Israeli native, or Sabra, who chose to go to Canberra when the Foreign Ministry in Jerusalem offered her a posting in the Far East area. She had chosen Canberra for two reasons. The first and most important was because of her grandparents, who lived in Melbourne. And the second was because of her pleasure in remembering the fling she had had four years earlier with a young man from Sydney who had been visiting Israel. They met in a cafe on Rechov Dizengoff, Tel Aviv's principal street, and within a couple of days were travelling all over Israel together. They had not kept in touch, despite desperate promises at Lod airport about undying love and loyalty. In her more flippant moments, Judith considered the effect of turning up on his doorstep. She took gleeful pleasure imagining the expression on his face, and the excuses he would make to his family.

Judith had known about Australia, its customs and its people for as long as she could remember. Her grandparents had left the Pale of Settlement in Russia during the pogroms at the end of the last century and, unlike millions of others who travelled to America or England, they had decided to settle in Australia—as far as possible from Europe.

But her father had felt alienated as a Jew in an Anglophile country and had migrated to Palestine, where Judith had been born. She joined the Foreign Ministry after completing her degree in English at Tel Aviv University. As with all young Israeli men and women, she had spent three years in the armed forces, where she became a lieutenant in the elite tank corps. Stationed all over Israel, she had fulfilled her share of border patrol responsibilities, along with the men.

What distinguished the Embassy of Israel from other embassies was its egalitarianism in staff composition. Judith was born in, and still lived on, a kibbutz. Her home was in the northern part of Israel, near the town of Zichron Ya'acov, in the Carmel Mountains. Most Israeli Embassy people were from the metropolitan areas, but, unlike London or Parisian diplomats whose views of their country cousins were coloured by their urban upbringing, Judith was fully accepted by her colleagues as part of the inner circle. Israel was too small to suffer the differential of urban sophistication pitted against rural simplicity.

She gave the fax to the cultural attaché who read it with interest and asked Judith to leave it with him. When she had gone, he entered his personal code into his PC and brought up his hidden files on the computer menu. Ben Ari's pre-1940 file was flagged as reportable to Jerusalem HQ. He encoded the information, downloaded it to Mossad in Israel, then passed the request back to Judith with an indifferent shrug and asked her to deal with it. This didn't surprise her. All the Embassy knew that his job was a sinecure, a reward for the work he had done against the PLO in Europe in the mid-1970s as a Mossad operative.

Routinely, Judith dug out the skimpy details of Ben Ari's life, photocopied them and wrote a covering 'with compliments' slip, which she put into an envelope. Then, just to cover herself, she re-read the request. She had missed the specific request for information concerning Ben Ari's early life, so she read the biographical details she usually sent out.

It started with hyperbolic descriptions of Ben Ari, the young freedom fighter in the Stern Gang, and later the Haganah, and went on to describe his achievements as an MP and now as Prime Minister. But nothing, not one word, had been written about his life before Israel.

So she looked up her Prime Minister's details in the Israeli *Who's Who;* again, the only reference was to his age, the fact that he had been born in Poland, and that, when he came to Israel after the war, he had joined … again, the same biographical details.

Intrigued, she went to half a dozen reference books in the library, but she could still find no records at all about Ben Ari's childhood. There was a condemnatory article published in the *New York Times* about his life in Israel as a terrorist, which mentioned him attending a gymnasium in Warsaw, but there were no further details.

Judith was increasingly surprised. Although she knew a lot about Israel and its politics she had never thought about the early life of the leaders. Most had come to Israel in the 1930s or '40s and their lives as teenagers had not seemed important. Yet when she looked up the references to the other leaders of Ben Ari's generation, there were full details. Where they had studied; who their parents were; what Zionist organisations they had joined. Judith was mystified.

So she asked her boss, who knew nothing; then she asked the head of diplomatic mission, who knew nothing; and she asked the Ambassador, Michael Dershowitz, who had known Ben Ari most of his adult life and had been in the Prime Minister's right-wing HaMadrichim Party in the Knesset before becoming a diplomat. He was forced to admit that he knew nothing. He even admitted to Judith that his ignorance made him feel embarrassed.

It was surprising to say the least. Almost as though there was a conspiracy of silence about him. Public figures, especially prime ministers, were not allowed to have gaps in their lives. Newspapers, the common man's denominator, ensured that a politician's private past became a readership's public property. How could her Prime Minister have evaded the reporters' web?

Judith walked to the fax room, passing through the Embassy reception area to get there. The normally tight security was even more pronounced since the murder of the journalist in Israel. The terrorists had been reawakened, like the kraken, out of their slumber. Everyone in the Embassy was concerned about security. The note pinned to the journalist's body was a precursor of hideous things which would inevitably happen.

Arriving at the communications room, she sent a fax to the Ministry of Foreign Affairs in Rechov Herzl, a busy thoroughfare in the north of Jerusalem, requesting assistance from the Chief Librarian.

Her fax was received by the duty officer who logged it, and saw that it was an enquiry from the Canberra station. He placed the fax on the desk of the secretary and kept a copy for the Head of the Ministry.

When morning came, the Chief Librarian's secretary, Malka Schuller, walked into her office and wiped the perspiration from her face with a handkerchief. She found Israeli summers increasingly oppressive as she grew older. Nobody knew her exact age. Nobody was close or interested enough to ask. She was an elderly woman, who had worked for six chief librarians in the Foreign Ministry in the forty-odd years she had been employed there. An émigrée from her native Germany which had sentenced her to spend five years interned in Bergen Belsen for the crime of being Jewish, she had entered Israel as a hollow shell. In the following years little had happened in Malka's life to bring back the young woman that Nazi Germany had destroyed.

During her internment, she had witnessed the slaughter of her parents, and the beatings, rape and destruction of her brothers and sisters. She had suffered as much as they, but her life had been spared. Being attractive, she spent the war as a plaything of the camp commandant, a woman whose creative sadism made her a legend in the Nazi leadership. Malka survived, if survival was the way to describe a woman whose body had been systematically brutalised and tortured for five years, and whose mind had become incapable of opening to the comfort of love and friendship. It was hate that had nourished her when most around had starved to death. Hate was her food and her oxygen. Hate kept her alive. Her only reason for living was to work to destroy the German race, to eradicate it from the face of the world forever. And when she watched the evening news and saw the same neo-Nazi youth disgorging their anti-Semitism again, her hate burned brighter.

So she was pleased to covertly assist the Committee For Retribution which had arranged a job for her in the Foreign Ministry soon after her arrival in Israel. The committee originally approached her in the mid-1950s and explained that its mission was to prevent the new and increasingly powerful Germany from rising like some Gothic phoenix from the ashes of its own destruction. Their only request of her was that, working in the library section of the ministry, she should assist them in their aims. The Germans, they told her, were still dominated by hidden Nazis, but now they were trying to bring down the fledgling Jewish state. They were constantly trying to gain access to Israeli intelligence services. If she could supply them with details of who was making requests about the lives of prominent Israelis, then they would know where the neo-Nazis were operating.

At the time, it had seemed logical. She didn't think to question why it should need to be a covert operation. In the early days, her work for the committee had been a mission, but for the last ten years her struggle for survival in the harsh economic climate had dulled her hatred of life, though not of the Germans. Being by birth Teutonic, she made sure that she continued to perform her tasks correctly. The older she grew, the more fastidious and set in her ways she became. Her desk was always tidy and efficient. As tidy as her life. And as empty of the personal items which gave life meaning.

She read the fax with irritation before giving it to her librarian. But she recognised it at once as a special request, and an unusual one at that. It concerned one of the people in whom the committee was particularly interested. It was yet another request for information about Ben Ari. Thank God she only had to give the committee information about who was asking after Ben Ari when he lived in Poland. Why did people ask questions all the time? It wasn't their right to know. And it wasn't as if what he had done was wrong. He was right to have put Israel first. She knew the Israeli people hated him, but he was right. Give the Arabs an inch and they'd take everything she'd worked so hard for. Give them Jerusalem and the next thing, they'd take Tel Aviv and Haifa. And where would the Jews be then? Where could they turn? Who would take care of them when the Arabs constructed concentration camps and led the Jews away for their final solution? Who would cry out against the grey smoke from the chimneys this time? Who would be left to wipe the tears from their eyes?

In the old days, when she was younger, she would have handled the situation with aplomb, but these days, as a woman in her early seventies, this sort of thing was becoming more and more difficult. But then she remembered the neo-Nazis and her fists tightened in anger.

She secreted the fax in a manila folder, walked to the photocopier and, ensuring that nobody saw what she was doing, she took a copy. She walked back to her desk, put it in her bag and placed the fax on her librarian's desk. Breathless from concern at possible discovery and the energy spent walking down the long, airless corridors, she picked up the phone and dialled the number she knew by heart.

A recorded voice simply said in Ivrit: 'Leave your message after the tone.'

Even after forty years, she still disliked the throaty cadences of modern Hebrew, so in German she said: 'This is Malka. Please contact me at home tonight concerning lunch tomorrow.'

She hung up immediately, and resumed her work. Telephone calls were sometimes monitored by Shin Bet, but she had been so quick she felt secure. And it was not as though she was acting against the interests of her people.

Later that night, her telephone rang. A gruff-voiced man enquired after her health and welfare and suggested that they meet the following day for coffee. But there was to be no coffee, and no meeting. Malka Schuller knew what she had to do, as she had done many times before. She had to buy a copy of the afternoon newspaper, *Ma'ariv*, put the photocopy inside it and leave it in a rubbish bin in the quiet laneway near the Israeli National Museum at precisely 5.30 p.m.

She had no idea who would pick it up. She didn't know who was on the other end of the phone. Her contact had only ever been by phone, except in the early days when a Polish refugee told her about the secret work of the committee and asked her if she would be interested in assisting.

The best news was that her meagre income from the Foreign Ministry would be augmented that month, allowing her to buy a few more of the luxuries of life. But nothing, not money, political philosophy, luxuries … nothing would quell the burning hatred. She had never asked herself how the seemingly innocuous information she occasionally gave would assist the committee in its work. She merely carried out her orders. But she hoped before God Almighty that the information would be of use to whoever it was on the other end of the phone, so that he could somehow make the Germans suffer as she had been made to suffer.

Her suffering would have increased, to the point of driving her further into madness, if she had ever known that for all these years the information which she had given so proudly to destroy the Germans had been used by the NKVD, and later the KGB, against the interests of Israel.

CHAPTER TEN

A wallful of cartoons of bleary-eyed patrons, as well as framed front pages with headlines trumpeting world-famous events, characterised The Pen and Ink. It was still the local watering hole of the seven newspapers that made up the Australian branch of Max Mandle's empire, but it no longer served the opposition newspapers whose building had moved from around the corner to the western suburbs of Sydney. Journalists employed by both empires once met there regularly. Opponents in working hours, they would use The Pen and Ink both to unwind after hours, and to boast if they had stolen a march on their adversaries. Those were the days that Paul Sinclair remembered best. The good days of camaraderie in the club-like atmosphere of Sydney journalism.

Until the advent of Rupert Murdoch and the destruction of Fleet Street, newspapers throughout the world had always seemed to be centralised. They sat virtually side by side in an area of their city, like grapes in a bunch. Now there was a world-wide trend towards decentralisation; newspaper offices and their printing presses setting up close to transportation routes. Modern electronics had made information-gathering a global phenomenon which had destroyed information-sharing in many cities. The intimacy was gone.

And today, much of the camaraderie was also gone. Only Mandle's men and women gathered in The Pen and Ink at the end of a working day, to unwind from the tension and frustrations of their profession. The rest of the pub's patrons were yuppies and wankers, eager to rub shoulders with those whose by-line was a daily feature.

At six o'clock, Paul and Jack found themselves the only two patrons from the newspaper in the crowded bar.

The two journalists sat at one of the round tables by the bay window of the mock-Dickensian building, waiting for news-paper colleagues to finish their work and come in for a drink.

'I've told you a lie,' Paul said.

Jack looked at him in surprise but remained silent.

'I said that the old man, my contact, had kept that photo of Ben Ari. That he wouldn't let it out of his possession.' Jack continued his silence. 'He gave it to me for safe-keeping.'

Jack winced. 'Why did you lie?'

'I don't know. I've asked myself that same question a dozen times. I guess I was covering my arse.'

'Against who?'

Paul took another swig of beer.

'Against me?' Jack asked.

''Course not.'

'Then against who? Mandle?'

'No, not even him. I don't know, Jack. The old man treated that photograph so tenderly, like it was a religious ornament, that I didn't want it … sullied. I can't really explain it. I know it's dumb, lying to your editor and your proprietor. But when I was carrying it in my pocket from the old peoples' home, it was like carrying a piece of history. I was so worried about it falling into the wrong hands, or getting lost or destroyed, that I took it to my bank and put it in a strongbox.'

'History?' Jack said in a tone bordering on contempt. 'It wasn't history you were carrying, laddie. It was evidence. Proof. If you had shown the bloody thing to Mandle, our job would have been much simpler. Don't go bleeding-heart on me, Paul. Just produce the sodding thing when you're ready to run the story.' He frowned and continued, 'Anyway, surely you've got to take the picture over to Israel to show it to Ben Ari when you confront him?'

Paul nodded. 'I've thought of that. Tomorrow, I'm going to have a copy made. In sepia, to keep that tone.'

Jack snorted. 'Well just be careful how much it costs to have it done.' Both men drank silently and surveyed the room. There were no familiar faces. Those at the bar looked around expectantly, watching the door for famous faces every time it opened, then turned back in mild disappointment to their drinks.

For the next two days, Paul was busy gleaning facts about Ben Ari from sources around the world. It was like walking a tightrope. As journalists were the most suspicious of all creatures, Paul could only request information without giving any hint of what he was doing, not even to his colleagues. Muir and Paul even constructed a dummy story about secret negotiations between the Australian Minister for Foreign Affairs and the Secretary General of the United Nations. The Secretary General, Ratu Sir Sidomante Bara, had asked the Australian ambassador to act as a Kissinger-style mediator to bring the conferees back to the Akrotiri peace table. It was a plausible enough story. Australia was a distant land and could act as a disinterested party. Paul let a few close colleagues into his story, then swore them to secrecy, which ensured it would spread like wildfire. But keeping up the subterfuge also slowed up the process of gathering information.

One of the first sources Paul approached was Mandle's offices in Israel. His request for background information took only moments to be faxed from Sydney to Jerusalem. Paul was annoyed when the response came back so quickly—within half a day—indicating that the researcher who was assisting with the information hadn't treated it properly. Obviously he wasn't impressed by the message's importance.

Paul's fax for information about Ben Ari and his pre-war past was sent to Yoram Garon, *The National*'s Israeli representative, whose desk was situated in the Jerusalem office of the *Tel Aviv Post*.

Garon was known amongst Israeli journalists as an overweight parasite, feeding second-hand information culled that day from the latest editions of the Jerusalem and Tel Aviv papers to his Australian employer. Taking no interest in Paul's request, he read it, categorised it as a research job and sent it straight down to the library of the *Post*, where it was given to a librarian. She punched the name 'Ben Ari' into her computer, and then further characterised the information which Paul requested by sub-branching the network into 'Pre-1939'. There was little there. General stories about waves of refugees into Palestine had been included, presumably as padding. Nothing about him in particular. She printed out copies and dumped them on Garon's desk. When he finished his mid-morning *felafel*, he faxed the stuff back to Paul.

But Garon and the librarian were not the only people to know about Paul's request for information. Within the librarian's program was a pathway to duplicate all requests for information from overseas to the central computer of Mossad. Secret services around the world regularly monitored overseas telephone calls, faxes, and computer data and had built flag-falls into their programs, so that whenever a particular number was dialled, or name was used, the scanners recorded the information. This same method, used by GCHQ in Cheltenham, England, had caught out members of the Royal Family in their adulterous liaisons. And Mossad was no less interested in what information was flowing into and out of Israel than their counterparts in other areas of the world. Mossad was listening keenly to information to and from the Occupied Territories, especially if the source was an Arab capital.

For its general eavesdropping, Mossad had links into most governmental, journalistic, legal, business, academic, and diplomatic computers. It operated one of the largest data-gathering networks outside of the United States' computer installations at Langley, the Pentagon and the National Security Agency.

But it also went beyond the intelligence service, unknown even to Mossad's computer operatives. Within their own giant Honeywell was an old, but well-trodden data pathway. Inflowing information concerning Ben Ari's pre-1939 history was further downloaded and sub-branched to a terminal operated by an uninspiring and inconspicuous clerk whose position in Mossad had been secured by the shadowy Committee For Retribution. Later that night, Paul's fax would find its way into the hands of a one-time KGB operative who owed his loyalty to those who worked for Marshal Petrovsky.

By early the following day, Marshal Petrovsky's operatives in Southern Moscow were briefed that a reporter called Sinclair in Australia was asking background questions about the young Ben Ari. In fact, it was one of over a dozen such requests that day from news organisations throughout the world. But it needed to be monitored.

Miriam Davis also sent a fax that day to Loeb and Loeb, her firm's correspondents in Jerusalem. Her contact there, Nathan Loeb, reminded her of her grandfather, especially his way of talking. Often they faxed each other when they had nothing in particular to talk about. She would write about Australia and her family; Nathan, a widower, would write back long avuncular letters to his bright young friend half a world away. It was his vicarious flirtation, distant enough to be safe.

They had never met in person, though Nathan had often threatened to come to Australia to marry Miriam. When her elderly grandfather had put himself into a home, her faxes to Nathan had become more intimate. She had asked his advice, using his worldly experience to help her cope with her new inner-loneliness. Since her dealings with other lawyers and colleagues was terse and legalistic and her life with Paul was frenetic, these faxes to Nathan were like a valve on a pressure-cooker. She would unburden herself, tell him anecdotes, ask his advice; and she would wait anxiously for his return fax, which she would read once at the office, and time and again in the privacy of her apartment.

She told Nathan about her grandfather's allegations and the photograph of Ben Ari. She told him how vivid were his memories, as though what happened half a lifetime ago was yesterday. She told him that her *zeida* and Paul had enjoyed a long and rich conversation about the old days and that Paul was fascinated—sufficiently fascinated to write a story from the information. But what Miriam had never told Nathan was that Paul was non-Jewish. She couldn't bring herself to tell him. Perhaps now her grandfather had accepted him, she would unburden herself fully to the Israeli.

She asked Nathan for his help in opening up areas where she could glean further information about Ben Ari. And as an afterthought, she asked him to treat the matter with complete confidence. He read the fax twice, and still the elderly lawyer shook his head in bemusement.

When a copy of Miriam's fax was read in Mossad's Tel Aviv headquarters, the Duty Officer filed it for further investigation. There had been so much wild speculation about Ben Ari's motives since the peace conference that at first he put the transcript of the fax into the *Meshuggeneh* file kept for such purposes.

Half an hour later, he took it out and re-read it. It was crazy. Some lawyer had evidence that the Prime Minister was a Communist, a murderer who had led pogroms. He laughed out loud. He was on the verge of putting the file back where it belonged with all the other crazies. But that would have been a dereliction of duty. No matter how stupid, it was not his decision alone to consign it to the rubbish bin. He put it into an envelope and stamped it 'confidential'. He marked it for the attention of his superior who would be in after lunch. It was his problem now.

But a covert link from Mossad's computer to a safe house in Jerusalem, which transmitted the details of Miriam's fax by microwave link to Moscow, caused a much more considered reaction.

When the SIGINT specialists working in an office block in the south of Moscow put Miriam's fax together with the fax from Paul Sinclair, Australia, unlikely as it was, became the subject of an urgent meeting between Colonel-General Bukharin and Colonel Anatoly Scherensky.

There were no such animals as coincidences in covert surveillance work, just a series of facts which, when fitted together, could build a picture. The facts made interesting reading. In Australia a reporter called Paul Sinclair was asking about Ben Ari's pre-Israeli life. This was not important on its own. There were hundreds of stories written around the world every week about Ben Ari—some commenting on how little there was known about his origins. Yet put together with another piece of evidence, it painted a more complete portrait. Also in Australia, a girl (presumably Jewish—the Israeli connection, the way she wrote to the Jewish lawyer in Jerusalem) was asking questions about Ben Ari's youth. She mentioned a grandfather in a home, who was known personally to Ben Ari. She also touched on his involvement in pogroms and said there was an incriminating photograph. A man called Paul, possibly her husband or lover, would write a story for his newspaper about the photo and the asset's part in pre-war events.

Colonel Anatoly Scherensky once headed the infamous 8th Directorate of the KGB—the so-called 'wet' division, responsible for the permanent dispatch of those people whom the Soviet government needed killed.

He had made the decision two years earlier to resign from active service in the Russian Republican Army, and was, to all intents and purposes, working as a clerk in a South Moscow import–export firm. However, his skill as a wet operative coordinator was currently being used by Marshal Petrovsky. With the money which the Marshal had squirrelled away in the Banque de Lausanne during his time as head of the KGB, Petrovsky had control of a sophisticated and highly effective covert operation. It was a testament both to Petrovsky's disgust with the current government and his ability to enthuse those in his cabal to follow his vision.

Colonel Scherensky was assigned by Bukharin to the task of retrieving the picture. Miriam's message to Nathan Loeb had only talked in the most general terms of her elderly grandfather in some Jewish old person's home in Sydney. For a man of Scherensky's abilities, finding him would prove relatively easy. The man was obviously not in hiding and in a country like Australia, where records and data were in abundance, it would be relatively easy to identify him. While he conducted investigations in Moscow, he dispatched his number one wet operative, a gentle looking, matronly Kazakh woman, to Sydney to retrieve the photograph and dispense with the old man as well as the reporter and the girl.

Katya Smolonov was one of those women of indeterminate age. She could have been a troubled forty or a jolly sixty. She looked like a *babushka* doll, fat and jolly, but beneath the matronly innocence resided a pit bull terrier. A senior operative in the KGB's wet division, she had personally dispatched over a hundred people in twenty countries in the past fifteen years.

Multilingual, Katya was an expert in hand-to-hand combat and with explosives, knives and guns. She was a specialist at killing using injections of ultra-sophisticated drugs inside the nasal cavity, as well as laser-guided poison darts which dissolved subcutaneously on impact, and nerve gas, through to the most ordinary of objects such as pencils, hair-clips and handkerchiefs. Katya willingly accepted Colonel Scherensky's offer to join his private offshoot of the KGB when Yeltsin disbanded the service. True, she needed the money, but she also loved her work, especially the travelling. Katya was an unreconstructed tourist, revelling in new sights and experiences which she would then selectively share with her family. She was particularly excited about visiting Australia, a continent she had never seen.

Katya steeped herself in the identity of Hilda Spurgin, an Austrian Jewess who had lived in Potts Point, Sydney, since 1953, emigrating to Australia at the age of ten with her parents, and spent time reading travel books picked up from her local library.

The real Hilda had been killed in a car accident at the age of twelve. The Russian Embassy in Australia had read the paragraph of Hilda's death in the Sydney *Daily Telegraph* in October 1955. They sent the details to Moscow and quietly, without fuss, began to build a history for her, for use in the future by agents needing a bona fide identity.

Because of the inadequate communication between departments and the way in which government records are usually kept in most countries, the Australian authorities who had processed the late Hilda's immigration and naturalisation papers were not made aware of her untimely demise. According to most Australian authorities, she was still alive and well.

This enabled an Australian Communist sympathiser to apply for a passport, health insurance card and driver's licence, open a bank account in her name, along with credit cards, shop accounts, magazine subscriptions, graduation certificates and all the hundreds of other official documents which such a person may have acquired. All of the official documents had been sent to the Marrickville home of the sympathiser, paid monthly for use of the accommodation address.

In its heyday, the KGB ran hundreds of living histories of dead citizens in dozens of countries, and Marshal Petrovsky had acquired the best of them when the KGB fell apart at the seams.

A couple of days after Katya had first been briefed, the metamorphosis was complete. Hilda flew into Sydney, supposedly returning from a short visit to Fiji. The customs officials noted the Australian exit stamp on her passport, as well as the Fiji immigration stamps, and she simply walked through the green 'nothing to declare' channel. Her Russian accent was replaced by clipped German-English cadences as she spoke a few words to the Australian officials. Nothing had shown against Hilda Spurgin's name as the passport officer tapped her details into his computer.

A taxi dropped her off at the Hotel Nikko in Kings Cross, where an unostentatious room had been booked for her by Eurotravel. After a long night's sleep, she awoke and had a light breakfast, still suffering the effects of jetlag. She opened her suitcase and took out a new packet of sanitary towels. Ripping it open, she searched for a computer floppy disk. She placed it into her Sony electronic notebook and called up the menu. Finding the item she wanted, Katya typed up and recalled the file concerning the little that was known about the old man, as well as Colonel Scherensky's research on Sydney's Jewish old people's homes. There was only one—the Rosenthal—which she looked up in the phonebook in her room. The further background on Australian Jews, their idiom, dialect, customs, geography and a plethora of other details she would read later.

At 9.00 a.m., she phoned through to the Rosenthal, using a deliberately accented voice which told the operator that she came from Eastern Europe, as did most of the residents.

'Hello, tell me please, I am visiting mine *bruder* from Sydney. I am *shvester* … how you say … sister from Germany. What time, please, I come to say hello?'

The operator spoke slowly and clearly, having dealt with elderly Europeans for many years.

'Visiting hours are from 10.30 a.m. onwards.'

'Unt do I sign? What? I must see somebody, yes? Doctor? What?'

'No, just come in and ask for your brother's room. Do you know his room number?'

Katya assured the operator that she would be arriving with her daughter, who knew those details, and hung up. She had found out that there was probably little security or formality at the home, which could be both a blessing and a curse. While it would make her entry simplicity itself, finding the identity of one old Jew amongst many might not prove so easy.

She was surprised by a knock on the door. Opening it cautiously, she found the porter standing there with a large suitcase, offering to carry it into the room. She was expecting it. Katya opened the case and saw that it contained everything she would need—a uniform identical to that used in the Rosenthal Home, as well as other nurses' accessories and disguises which she might need in the event of having to escape from the country. Colonel Scherensky was nothing if not thorough. He had arranged the purchase and delivery of the collateral material through local contacts, while she was en route.

Dressing, she timed her exploratory visit to the home to coincide with lunch, when all standard hospital security systems generally break down. She donned a simple disguise of a grey wig, arched her eyebrows with a make-up pencil and created a face which looked less heavily Russian. Then, she put on a grey coat to make her less conspicuous and took a taxi to the Rosenthal.

As she could not pretend to be a relative or a friend without knowing the name of the resident she was visiting, she had to rely on hospital records, which were kept in the administration office. Walking towards the front door, she saw a security guard, reading a copy of a local newspaper. Her training had shown her how to deal with security such as this. She walked directly up to him, and said, 'Has Dr Sakharov arrived yet?'

The guard put the paper down in surprise. 'Sorry, love, who?'

Testily, Katya repeated, 'Dr Sakharov. The geriatric specialist. Has he come in yet? I said I'd meet him on the first floor.'

'Haven't seen him,' said the guard, not wishing her to realise his incompetence.

Katya grunted in Teutonic annoyance. 'I'm going to see if he's arrived. If he comes in, tell him to wait for me upstairs, please,' and before the man could reply, she marched off as though she owned the place. The last thing the guard was going to do was to argue with a bossy German. He had only been here a couple of days and had already had his fill of them.

Katya smiled as she walked down the corridor, slowing her pace. How would an ignorant guard know the name of Russia's father of the hydrogen bomb? She had perhaps taken a small risk, fronting up to the guard like that, but it had worked. Little people confronted with an authoritarian always go to pieces.

She doubled back down a corridor which she judged to be behind the entrance foyer so she could get a better feel for the layout of the ground floor. Just off the foyer, she noticed a large visitors' book, but the area was too busy for her to look inside without attracting attention.

She considered returning in the evening, when there would be far fewer people about and she could see what the book had to offer. But this would increase the danger of discovery, and would be of questionable value; people these days didn't usually sign such books. She walked down one corridor after another, using the lift and the stairs, smiling at the people she passed. For now, she had done enough. She had spied out the Rosenthal Home and knew what she was going to do.

Returning to the Nikko, Katya put her feet up on the bed, ordered a light snack from room service and reviewed the events of the day. The Rosenthal would not present too many problems once she knew the old Jew's identity. Security was a joke. She could operate inside the home with impunity. No, her only problem was finding out the old man's name.

All she had to go on was the fact that an Australian reporter called Paul Sinclair knew about a photograph held by an old man in a home … and then it dawned on her. It was so obvious, she was angry she had wasted so much time. She would phone the young woman later, if the man proved unproductive.

She knew from Miriam's fax that she and a man called Paul had a relationship. A reporter called Paul Sinclair had faxed Israel asking questions about Ben Ari's youth. Both faxes had left Australia on the same day. It wasn't too much to assume that the 'Paul' in Miriam's fax was the reporter.

It was worth a try. If she was wrong, the phone call would be meaningless to him. Then she would phone the Jewess and ask about her grandfather.

She looked up the telephone number of *The National* and asked to be put through to him. A pleasant-sounding young man answered the phone.

'Mr Sinclair,' said Katya, donning her best Australian-European accent, 'this is Sister Weintraub from the Rosenthal Jewish people's home. When you were here recently visiting Mr Swerdlin, did you inadvertently take one of our library books, *A History of the Jewish People*, by Rabbi Joseph Semple?' She sounded officious but made up the details up as she went along.

Nobody likes to be accused of theft, and Paul sprang to his own defence.

'No, I didn't take any books. I'm sorry, I don't know what you're talking about.'

Wonderful, thought Katya. Wonder of wonders! The man and the woman are connected!

'Well, Mr Swerdlin is absolutely positive that you were reading the book ...' she continued, gaining in confidence.

'I didn't visit this Mr Swerdlin,' Paul interrupted. 'I was seeing Yossi Samuelson. I've never heard of Mr Swerdlin. Look, I'm sorry, but you've got the wrong man.'

'I'm so sorry. I must have confused you with another visitor. Mr Swerdlin is having a bad time at the moment with Alzheimer's. I don't even know where he got your name from. Sorry to have bothered you ...'

If Paul hadn't been so busy researching Ben Ari, he may have wondered about the conversation, such as how the sister had got his name and telephone number ... but he had too many urgent things to do, and put the incident out of his mind.

Satisfied with her performance on the phone, Katya treated herself to a Captain Cook tour of the beautiful harbour, had afternoon tea at Pepper's Hotel in Double Bay and spoiled herself with dinner at Doyle's in Watsons Bay. On Sunday morning Katya transformed herself once again in body and mind to become Hilda. She rose early and checked her equipment. The nurses' uniform of the Rosenthal also came with a pocket watch, thermometer, Bic pens and notepad, making her look like any other nurse.

In her hand was a bag containing her equipment, plus an identification badge which showed her to be a State Registered Nurse who had been sent by the New Era Nurses Employment Bureau of Chippendale to assist at the home for the week, beginning Sunday. Hilda surveyed the local man's forgery, and was pleased with its professionalism.

Because it was Sunday, there were lots of people coming and going. Nobody challenged her, not even the guard, and Hilda quickly found her way to the nurses' locker room. It was empty. Depositing her coat, she picked up a clipboard left there by another nurse. Out in the corridor, she saw a senior nurse, who looked as though she knew what she was doing, making the ward rounds, pushing before her a trolley full of pills, medicines and vials. Katya introduced herself, explained that she was a temp and asked whether the nurse knew the room number for Mr Swerdlin.

The nurse looked quizzically for a moment, until Hilda explained that she had been told to pass on a telephone message that his relatives would be delayed for an hour.

'I don't know any Mr Swerdlin,' the nurse said, and took out the patients' medicine list. As she looked up residents' names beginning with the letter 'S', Hilda carefully noted the name 'Samuelson' and his room number. 'No one here by that name. I think you'd better go back to the office, and check.' Hilda thanked her, apologised and retreated. Then walking up the long ramps to the second floor, she found her way to room B6, where the old man Samuelson was, she hoped, alone.

Had his relatives been there, she would have excused herself, tidied his room and left, to return later in the day. She knocked cautiously, and a weak voice said, 'Come.'

Hilda pushed open the door and saw a diminutive, white-haired man dressed in baggy blue trousers, a loose-fitting shirt and a jumper, sitting at a chair near the window reading the paper. 'Hello, Mr …' she looked at the clipboard with its chart ' … Samuelson, is it?'

Her accent was German or Austrian, and Yossi didn't particularly like Germans or Austrians. 'Yes,' he said curtly.

'Excuse me for interrupting, but I'm Nurse Spurgin. How are you feeling today?'

The old man grunted 'Fine' and resumed reading the paper. Always, they sent new nurses to him. Why, he wondered. Didn't they pay enough so that the good ones stayed?

'I've got a new medicine for you. For your blood pressure. Doctor thinks it's a bit high, and wants to bring it down a fraction.'

'What new medicine? I don't want no new medicine. And there's nothing wrong with my blood pressure.'

Hilda took out the small vial of Salbutamol, which she had carried with her from Moscow. Each dose contained 5,000 micrograms, fifty times the normal dose. So massive an over-

172

dose, even in a young, strong asthma sufferer, could lead to sudden illness from overstimulation of the heart, which rocked in the pericardial cavity. In a man over eighty with constricted arteries and ageing heart muscles such a dose would be positively dangerous and make him feel dreadful. Then it would be time for stage two.

'Come on, Mr Samuelson,' she said with irritation in her voice. 'I've got lots of people to see today. I can't waste time here. Look, do you want to do it yourself? You just place the little piece inside your mouth, push down here four times and breathe in and out deeply each time. Try to hold your breath each time you breathe in. You'll feel much better when you've taken the full dose. It'll reduce your blood pressure right away and take away any giddiness you've been feeling.'

'I'm not feeling giddy, and I don't want no new medicine,' snapped the old man.

Hilda knew it was time to be firm. 'Look, darling, just breathe this in and I'll go away. Come on, for me. Please don't make me have to get doctor ...'

She handed him the metal vial in its plastic outer sleeve, but Yossi suffered from arthritis and had difficulty gripping it. She took it back, placed it in his mouth and depressed the vial. He breathed in sharply, holding his breath, and exhaled. She repeated the procedure three more times. Hilda could see a distinct reddening in his cheeks.

As the Salbutamol filled Yossi Samuelson's lungs, his arteries carried the massive overdose to his heart. At first, his heart started to beat quickly, making him feel flushed and uncomfortable. His blood vessels strained with the increased load and his blood pressure rose beyond measurement. Within half a minute, the old man was sweating and clutching his heart. Hilda feigned concern: 'Don't worry,' she said. 'I'll give you a small shot to make you feel better.'

Being so sick, he didn't make a fuss. That was why she began with the inhaler. If she had given him the injection first, he could have cried out. Now, he was too ill. She took out a disposable hypodermic filled with potassium chloride, lifted the clothes on his arm and injected a bulging vein.

His eyes stared with incomprehension at the kindly face of nurse Hilda Spurgin, who smiled and said: 'Goodbye *Zhid*.'

The old man's face was turning blue and his lips contorted as he struggled to breathe; his pulse beat wildly through the parchment-like skin at his wrists. When the potassium chloride hit his heart, it was all over. And the best thing was that it was all but undetectable in an autopsy.

Yossi's feeble heart didn't last more than a minute. To assist him in dying, Katya gently placed her hand over his nose and mouth to restrict his breathing. When she could not even feel the feeblest breath under her hand, she took it away and saw his lips had turned death-blue.

Yossi died in a short, vicious agony of heart failure. Should there be an autopsy, his death would be seen as nothing other than a not-unexpected heart attack. The likelihood of an inquest being ordered by a coroner was negligible, taking into account the man's age and medical condition. And the puncture mark of the injection wouldn't be noticed amongst all his liver and ageing spots.

When he had stopped breathing, Hilda felt for vital signs but detected none. She locked the door, put on a pair of latex gloves and carefully searched his room. It didn't take her long to discover the shoebox with its collection of photos. She looked at them with complete disinterest. She had seen thousands of photos during her career and these were just the prosaic record of an unimportant little man. She flipped first through the more recent colour photos of the old man, an attractive young woman, two middle-aged people, outings at zoos, photos of houses, a birthday celebration, until she came to the deeper collection of black and white photos and deeper still, sepia photos of authoritarian men and women dressed in Eastern European peasant clothing, or more formally in winged collars and suffocating ties, or women in whaleboned bodices, their bodies constricted by the fashion of the day. And that was all she found.

Concerned, Katya searched through the photos once more, but there was no photo here of villages on fire or men on horseback. She put the box back carefully where it had been and searched other parts of the cupboards, opened drawers and rifled through clothes. She turned back to the old man. His lips were now a dark blue. His mouth was gaping in a death grin agony. She searched his clothes, careful not to disturb his posture.

All she found were handkerchiefs, a bottle of eye drops, a wallet containing Australian money and notes. No photos. She took off the old man's shoes and searched for a secret compartment. She returned to the closet and felt inside the linings of his clothes and along the seams. She could feel nothing. She took the risk of opening a small aperture in the stitching of the suits so she could see inside. Then she turned her attention to the mattress, the bedclothes, on top and behind the cupboard and every drawer in the room. Her movements were like oil, her gloved hands gliding delicately over the furniture and the fittings, her fingers searching every spot that could possibly hide what she was looking for.

In desperation, she began to examine the wallpaper to see whether he had been clever enough to create a little crevice for the photo, but it was nowhere. After twenty-five minutes of frantic searching, Katya left the room, having to report the failure of her mission.

She retrieved her coat and caught the bus back to the Nikko Hotel. In her room, Katya picked up her phone and dialled a telephone number in Canberra. It was answered instantly and a male voice asked: 'May I help you?'

The voice was Australian though she recognised Russian cadences. Presumably the man was a sleeper. Scherensky's meticulous approach to covert work had paid off. He had set up the line two days earlier in case of extreme emergency.

'I need assistance,' she said.

'What is the nature of the assistance you require?'

'I need urgently to speak to my friend.'

'There's a public phone box on the corner of Macleay Street and Noffs Avenue close to where you are. I'll phone you there in ten minutes.'

Instantly he hung up the phone. Katya grabbed her coat and ran downstairs. In the unlikely event of the Canberra phone being monitored, the authorities—be they Australian secret police or overseas intelligence services—would be physically unable to fix the location of the phone and intercept in time.

Katya stepped outside and saw the phone booth. As she walked towards it, so did a young man who got there just seconds before her, but Katya wasn't willing to discuss it. She put her hand on his arm and applied pressure to the artery at his wrist, twisting his arm down and back until he was in extreme pain. 'I have an urgent call to make. Would you mind using another phone?' she asked politely. She released her grip. 'No, you go ahead,' said the young man. He walked away as quickly as possible, terrified of the incredibly strong matron.

The phone didn't ring for another four minutes and Katya had to fend off three irritated passers-by who wanted to make a call. When it finally rang, she picked it up instantly.

'Yes,' she said.

'It's me. I'll patch your friend through.'

The phone line suddenly echoed and became hollow. 'This is your friend. I believe you have a problem.' It was the voice of Colonel Scherensky. They spoke in English to avoid attention from passers-by.

'The parcel has been dispatched without problems but I couldn't find the bill of lading. I searched everywhere for it, and it was impossible to find.'

There was a couple of seconds pause. 'You are no doubt aware of the name of the journalist I gave to you when we spoke last.'

'Yes,' Katya nodded.

'Well. It is possible that he has it in his possession. May I suggest that you retrieve it from him.'

'That will not be a problem. Your instructions were to dispatch two further parcels. We must hope that the bill of lading is with one or the other.'

'Under no circumstances are you to dispatch any further parcels. The potential for complications is too great and could be catastrophic if any more parcels are dispatched. Your orders are rescinded. Merely collect the bill of lading and return home immediately.'

Katya put the phone down and returned to her room. She felt a sense of relief that she would not have to dispatch Paul and Miriam. An old Jew was one thing. Katya was not a traditional Russian anti-Semite but had no problem in dispatching Jews. But she was less happy with assignments where innocent young people were terminated. Although she loved much of her work she found killing youngsters unaccountably distasteful.

Had she retrieved the photograph, the original plan would have enabled her to leave Australia the following day, catching Ansett's Flight 2 to Melbourne, then flying with MAS to Perth and on to Kuala Lumpur before catching a flight to Vienna. In Austria, she would have resumed the identity of Katya Smolonov, translator and assistant to the managing director of Inter-Ural agencies, a Moscow-based import–export company.

However, this would have to be delayed until she had retrieved the photo from Paul Sinclair. All of this would be no problem; it was part of her job. But although she was relieved, she still couldn't understand why Scherensky didn't want Sinclair or the Jewess dispatched. Killing Paul and Miriam, distasteful as it might be, would tidy up the loose ends.

Miriam was experiencing a greater depth of loneliness, a colder clarity, and a more uncontrollable seething against the world than she had felt a few years earlier when she had sat on the same bench in the *Chevra Kaddisha* after her parents had been killed. Then she had sat beside her grandfather, holding his cold hand as they lost themselves in the platitudes of the rabbi.

Today she was bitterly alone. A solitary figure isolated from friends and community, sitting on the bench listening to the banal comments, the same platitudes of the automaton who was eulogising her grandfather. The rabbi stood there reciting poems for a penny, his transparent affection insulting her memory of her grandfather's piety. A funeral service by numbers.

She knew that a hundred pairs of doleful eyes were resting on her back and desperately needed to hold Paul, to touch his hand, to lose herself in his comfort, to let him put his arms around her, stroke her hair as her grandfather had done after her parents had been killed, to assure her that, 'This nightmare will pass in time.' But she didn't want it to pass. She needed to suffer. For him. Because he was dead and she was alive.

It was the final agony. There was no more pain left for her to suffer. Within the space of three years, she had lost her parents and her grandfather. Her past. She had lost her history. She was nobody's little girl any more. Her life seemed to be composed of intervals of fantasy between the realities of death.

And all she could focus on was how little she had done for him, how much she owed him, how late was her regret. She couldn't remember his face. Try as she might, she couldn't visualise him. Her mind fluttered in anxiety, split between her need to show dignity, her desire to wail for comfort and a need to put an end to the wrench in her heart.

She could only remember the times she had done wrong by him, upset him, caused him to shout at her. Shakespeare's sonnet rang in her mind:

For sweetest things turn sourest by their deeds;
Lilies that fester smell far worse than weeds.

If only the dybbuk would reach up, grab her and pull her down to make her atone for the selfishness she had shown him towards the end.

In front of her was a marble and brass plinth, a catafalque covered in a heavy black cloth. On top was the coffin of her *zeida*, swathed in a black shroud as simple as death itself.

So little left of a man who had been her life. She felt tears well up when she thought of how selflessly he had committed himself to the Rosenthal to prevent her life from being burdened. His life for hers. Now, too late, she realised how wrong it was. He should have lived with her until his death. She should have looked after him. If only she could reach out and touch him and tell him. If only she could apologise.

Miriam's body ached in anguish. Vaguely, in the absence of reality, she heard people standing and realised that the rabbi had come to the end of his speech and was intoning the prayer for the dead, *El Malè Rachamim*. Miriam stood and mouthed the words. Minutes later she knew that the *kaddish* would be said in memory of her *zeida*. Being a woman, she wasn't able to say it. It could only be said by a man and she had asked a close friend if he would honour her grandfather's memory by saying it on her behalf. With no male relatives, it was the only expedient that she could think of.

Her *zeida*'s death revived all the memories of the horror of those few days after her parents had been killed. It had taken her ages to come out of her shell. Now she was in danger of erecting a barrier between her mind and reality to isolate and protect her sense of being.

The rabbi sang. During the ancient Hebrew prayer, she thought back to the days since his death. They were a tangle of confusion, suspicion and anger. When Dr Tauber had phoned and asked her to come to the Rosenthal, she knew that her grandfather was either ill or dead. Her worst fears were confirmed. She had seen him lying peacefully in the mortuary as if he was in a deep and restful sleep. A sleep from which he would never wake. She couldn't cry then, although grief was pouring into her body, taking it over.

Paul had joined her an hour earlier and together they had left the Rosenthal to return to her flat. They had spent that night together, embraced in each other's arms for comfort and warmth. The following morning Paul had been stoic in making arrangements on Miriam's behalf, phoning her company, friends and associates and letting everybody know what had happened.

On their way back to the Rosenthal to sign various papers, Paul and Miriam had stopped off at his flat so that he could pick up some fresh clothes. As Paul tried to push open the door he met an unaccustomed resistance. He forced the door open and there they were met by a scene of devastation. Books were pulled from their shelves, couches were ripped to pieces, cupboards had been opened and emptied. Miriam didn't have the strength to scream, she just stood there with her mouth open.

'Oh shit!' Paul shouted. 'Look at this! Can you believe it? Look at what they've done to the place.'

Miriam began to recover. 'I'll call the police.'

'Wait, let's see what damage the bastards have done first.'

Paul and Miriam walked through the flat, careful not to disturb anything, and were even more dismayed when they came to the bedroom. All of Paul's clothes, shoes and underwear had been pulled out of cupboards or wardrobes. When she looked at his clothes, she felt sick. Each of Paul's suits had been slashed and opened, as though by a manic tailor, razor-cut along the edges of the collar, and the stiffening had been pulled out. The bedclothes had been pulled back and his mattress had been sliced open, as though it were a tin of sardines.

After a few minutes of looking around, Paul shook his head. 'What the fuck is going on? There's nothing missing. They've even left $300 that I had in the top drawer … look, it's still here.'

Miriam was puzzled. She rifled through the mess, trying to find clues. She looked at his bedside cabinet and saw with joy that they had left the ring she had made him when her parents died.

'Paul,' she said excitedly. 'They've left the ring. Look! It's still there.'

Paul looked back distracted. 'Oh good,' he said, half-heartedly, as he searched his clothes to see if any were missing.

They walked into the loungeroom. 'They haven't touched the TV or video. My CDs are still here!'

Miriam was equally amazed. 'They must have been vandals. Not thieves. Just destroying for the sake of it. Or could it have been revenge for something ?'

Paul shook his head. 'God knows.'

'Could they have been looking for something?'

Paul was lost in anger and confusion. 'I've just got no idea.'

'Things don't add up here, Paul.' Miriam took on the persona of the prosecutor. In a way, it was a relief from the role of grieving grand-daughter. 'The place gets done over. Nothing's stolen. They slash open your clothes, your bed and your mattress. Paul, this has got something to do with Zeida's photograph.'

Paul shrugged his shoulders. 'I don't know, Miriam. I haven't got a clue. I work on lots of stories. It could be somebody to do with the state government. Some vendetta. I just don't know.'

He sat down heavily on a chair. He felt abused; it was as though someone had intruded into his most private thoughts. 'I suppose it could be something to do with that photo, but I've only told Mandle and Muir about that. Nobody else knows. We've all been so careful.'

'Paul, you stay here and call the police. I've got to go to the Rosenthal to sort things out.'

Paul nodded mechanically, but old Yossi Samuelson's death was far from his mind. Who could have done over his flat? And why? Mandle? No! Why would he organise this? And it certainly wasn't Muir. It couldn't be the photo. Maybe it had something to do with the story about the travel rorts. Some bastard from the Premier's Department getting even.

Later in the morning, after the police had taken statements, Miriam and Paul, both still shocked, sat as Dr Tauber ran through all the conventions of regret. The arm gently placed on her shoulder. The usual noises of consolation. The clipped platitudes which sounded disharmonious to Paul because of the doctor's German accent. He led them into his office.

'We've not been into your dear *zeida*'s room, of course, Miriam, since we removed his dear body. Our policy is that you should be the first person in there. Then when you have removed his personal effects, we will tidy the room up after you. You have the choice of donating the rest of his investment here, and his personal effects, to the home. Or you may remove them should you wish to. But we'll discuss the arrangements after a suitable time.'

Paul and Miriam left Tauber's office and walked up the long and lonely ramps and corridors to the room where her grandfather had lived the past few years of his life. She hesitated before the door. Recognising her distress, Paul gently opened it, put his arm around her shoulder and led her inside.

A prescience of evil told her instantly that something was wrong. Her grandfather's life had been meticulous in every detail, but the room was not as he had lived in it. Looking around on the surface, it was the same, but there was a presence in here that hadn't been here before. She felt the skin on her neck contract and her head tingled. She grabbed Paul's hand. 'Paul, something's wrong.'

'What do you mean?'

'I don't know. There's something wrong here. It's not as Zeida … it's not what it used to be.'

'Miriam, darling, naturally it feels different. Your *zeida* used to …'

'No, I don't mean that he isn't here. I don't know what it is.'

Paul put his arm around her and tried to lead her out of the room. 'Come on, let me get you out of here.'

'Stop it. Leave me alone,' she snapped angrily. 'There's something wrong here.'

'Miriam, sit down over there. You're still distressed. Your *zeida*. What happened in my flat. Let me tidy up. I'll put his clothes out on the bed and you can sort out what should go to charity and what you want to keep. Let me do everything.'

Miriam refused to sit in the chair by the window, her *zeida*'s chair, but stood in the middle of the room, trying to divine what was wrong. Paul went over and opened the old man's closet. As he did so, he felt the blood draining from his head and his fingers. His heart started to pound, as his eyes viewed the harsh reality. Miriam instantly sensed his disquiet.

'What's wrong?' she asked.

'I think you'd better have a look at this.'

Miriam walked over to the cupboard. There were inch-long nicks along the line of the collars and the lapels of her *zeida*'s suits. Exactly as Paul's had been discovered just hours earlier. Miriam said nothing. She felt faint and walked backwards to her grandfather's chair where she sat down with a bump.

'I don't believe it. What's going on? What's happening to me?'

'This is too much of a coincidence. I'm calling the police!'

Paul surveyed the room, trying to remember it as it was a few days previously. It looked the same, but Miriam had been right. Now he too preferred to trust her instincts. As he looked around, a thought struck him. He looked at Miriam, sitting white-faced and stunned in her grandfather's chair.

'I'd forgotten it in the confusion. A couple of days ago some sister from the home phoned me and talked to me about a Mister … I've forgotten his name … she accused me of having stolen a book. I told her I'd been visiting your *zeida*. I named him. But how would this sister have got my name and phone number, and who is this Mister … Swerdlin, I think? I don't know what's going on, Miriam, but we've obviously got to be unbelievably careful about what we say from now on. And who we say it to.'

He looked at Miriam. Her body had slumped further into the chair, as though her spirit had been transported elsewhere. She merely shook her head. 'What is going on, Paul? Who's doing this to us? What's happening?'

Paul sat back on the bed and faced Miriam, struggling to

think clearly and carefully. 'It must have something to do with that damned picture. I've only told Mandle and Jack Muir about it, and I didn't show either of them the photo. I didn't even tell them Yossi's name or where he lived. Nobody knows about the story except the four of us. Nobody! Even the bloody faxes didn't say a word about the things Yossi told us. I only asked for background information. I took a copy of the photo but that's in my wallet.'

Miriam's attention slowly began to return. She looked at Paul in shock, suddenly realising what he had said: 'You told Max Mandle about it?'

'Of course,' he said automatically, but a frown appeared on his forehead. 'Oh my God. I don't believe it. Mandle is a close friend of Ben Ari. Christ, Miriam. Mandle could have organised all this. And that means that Mossad could be involved.'

Miriam's already pallid face somehow drained of its last remnants of blood and warmth. 'You mean the Israelis could have done this to protect Ben Ari? That's stupid! That's absurd.'

'I'm not saying anything for sure. Jesus, Miriam, it could have been them. This is a typical Mossad operation, from everything I know about them. If they're involved in this, we've got serious problems.'

'Don't be stupid,' Miriam snorted in contempt. 'The Israelis wouldn't do this.'

'Why not? Ben Ari was some sort of senior official in Mossad when it was first formed.'

'Jews don't go around killing …' She stopped mid-sentence, remembering with awful clarity her grandfather just days earlier describing how a young Jewish Ben Ari had murdered other Jews in his village.

Paul nodded in silent understanding. 'We must call the police.' Miriam agreed.

'I've met a couple of Israeli diplomats who I'm pretty sure were Mossad. They were real heavies, and you know what Mossad did to the Palestinians who killed the Israeli athletes in Munich. They …'

'You're saying Mossad killed Zeida?' Miriam was still having trouble coming to terms with the possibility.

'But there's so much I don't understand about this,' Miriam said. 'Let's say that Mossad has got information about Zeida and the photo. Why would they kill him? If they knew that their Prime Minister had been involved in pogroms and had been anti-Semitic they would want to get rid of him … unless … unless somebody close to Ben Ari … Oh no, that's stupid. That's impossible. It just couldn't happen like that.'

Paul reached over and held Miriam's cold hand. It was like touching a mannequin in a shop window. She sat there, immobile, staring sightlessly into the distance.

'Then how do you explain what happened?' he asked.

Mechanically, she said: 'Paul, I want an autopsy on Zeida. I want to know how he died.'

Paul turned to Miriam and put his arm around her, but she rejected his approach. She stood and slowly began to pace the floor in the small room. 'I'm serious, Paul. I want an autopsy to be conducted.'

'Miriam, listen to me. Everything we've said is just supposition. It's pure guesswork. I don't know any more than you do, but I'll tell you one thing. If we go rushing into demands for autopsies, we could make ourselves look complete idiots.'

She turned towards him venomously. 'You listen to me. He's my grandfather and if he's been harmed by anyone, I'm going to get to the bottom of it. I've a right, as his next of kin, to find out how he died and I'm going to!'

Ten minutes later, Paul and Miriam sat in the office of the irate and distressed medical director of the Rosenthal Elderly Persons Home. Dr Tauber was white-faced, barely able to restrain his anger. 'My dear young woman. As physician in charge, I absolutely refuse to carry out an autopsy on your late grandfather. How dare you suggest that his death may not have been natural? Do you think I didn't examine him? He died of a myocardial infarction, which is absolutely natural for a man of his age. To perform an autopsy would be an obscenity.'

Firmly, stressing each syllable, he added: 'And not in the best interests of the Jewish religion, or your grandfather's blessed soul.'

Dr Tauber looked at Paul and shifted uncomfortably in his chair. 'Young lady, could I please speak to you alone?'

'No you may not. You may say anything to me in front of Paul.' She reached over to hold Paul's hand.

The doctor unhappily continued: 'By rabbinical law Jews are not permitted to perform autopsies unless the circumstances are demanded by the law of the land. A body must be returned to God untouched. You, of all people, should realise this.'

'As his next of kin, I am instructing you to carry out an autopsy, or I'll go to the coroner this afternoon and get a court order.'

Dr Tauber softened his approach. 'But why? Why do you want to interfere with your dear *zeida*'s body? What possible motive could you have? Are you claiming that we were negligent?'

'Not at all. But I believe that his death might not have been natural.'

Tauber's mouth gaped open in surprise.

'What? What is it that you are saying?'

'I'm not saying anything. I want to know the real cause of his death. I have a right in law to satisfy myself as to how my grandfather died. I also have the right to cross-examine you in a coronial enquiry and even to seek an injunction against this home by applying to the Supreme Court for a stay of burial. Not only that, Dr Tauber, but I would like to see the visitors' book and I also want to determine if anybody visited him yesterday. I want to talk to the nurses who attended him during the morning.'

Dr Tauber's patience was at an end. He couldn't remember the last time he had been spoken to like this. 'You stupid girl! How dare you make these allegations? If you think there's some impropriety, you call the police, but I'm not going to have you disrupt this home to satisfy your neurotic hysteria.'

'Dr Tauber,' Paul said, trying to sound as reasonable as he could, 'there are certain grounds which lead us to believe that an inquest is advisable. I know I'm not Jewish, but I respect your faith's injunction against autopsies. However somebody has entered Mr Samuelson's room and searched it. His suits have been cut open. Surely you can understand why we want to talk to the nurses to find out who was the last to see him alive.'

Tauber looked at Paul in distaste. 'Sir, you quite rightly say that you are not a Jew. You do not understand our customs or our ways. Yossi was a respected member of our community here. He had many friends. No enemies. To suggest that his room was searched …' He waved his hand in dismissal.

For the first time since entering the doctor's office, Paul became angry. 'Believe me, Doctor, we will go to the police unless we're satisfied, and I promise you that that will cause far more grief to this home than acquiescing to our wishes.'

Dr Tauber stood up and walked to the window and looked at the tall ghost gums which grew along the Rosenthal's perimeter. They had always given him a feeling of tranquillity when his mind was distracted. He knew Miriam's allegations were made out of the grief she felt and not out of any sense of reality. And that Miriam's passion would indeed take her to the authorities if he didn't agree to an autopsy.

'What is the value of this? You know your grandfather died of natural causes. If you go to the authorities, I'll go to the authorities. I've already given a death certificate and I stand by it. I'm not covering up for anything or anybody. I'm just trying to save you, me and this home the pain of a terrible mistake. I'm sorry, Miriam, but I'll fight you every inch of the way on this. You're suffering from the effects of grief and I'll not allow your distress to cause pain to the Rosenthal.'

Miriam stood up, her face ashen, consumed with hate. 'Now you listen to me. I'm going to go to the police and to the Supreme Court to get an injunction against you, and this home. My grandfather didn't die of natural causes, and I intend to find out what killed him.'

Miriam turned quickly and walked out the door. Paul followed her. Dr Tauber sat back in his chair and slumped against his desk. Never in his twenty years at the home had he encountered a situation like this. If Miriam was a woman scorned, then hell certainly had no fury like it.

Miriam sat alone in her apartment. Tomorrow she would bury her grandfather. Paul had wanted to stay the night but she had asked him to leave. She lowered her head and stared at the floor, angered by the way in which the powers she wielded as a lawyer had proved to be so inadequate. The Coroner, the Supreme Court, everybody had rejected her legal processes for the inadequacy of the facts she could bring to bear. She had made a fool of herself in front of people who had once thought her able.

She had always viewed herself as a woman who wielded the law, and not as its victim. Now she felt helpless and utterly victimised. The Supreme Court had refused to hear her injunction because of Dr Tauber's representations; the Coroner had been sympathetic, but refused her request for an autopsy, and it took the police inspector at Darlinghurst fifteen minutes to realise that she was not joking. He had then refused to investigate what to all intents and purposes was the peaceful death of a man in his eighties—a death made licit by a perfectly good certificate—in light of Miriam's flimsy evidence of disturbed clothes, or some such nonsense. He had even patronisingly suggested that the old man might have cut the clothes himself in an Alzheimer-type cloud of confusion just before his death. 'The mind,' he had told her, 'is a strange thing.'

Sitting on the tenth floor of her apartment block, she knew that somewhere beneath her feet was a dybbuk. It had reached up and she could feel its cold icy fingers trying to grasp her ankles. It had pulled down her grandfather and now it was after her. All her old fears and superstitions rose up. Her apartment had become a cold and heartless place. The memories of the deaths that had touched her young life, the deaths of those she loved most, were relived every time she looked at one of the dozens of photographs around her. But this was not a time for sharing. She was alone and was numb with incomprehension.

Before he left, Paul had tried to comfort her but had got nowhere. When her grandfather was buried all the evidence of foul play would be buried with him. Now she regretted sending Paul home. She needed his support. Earlier in the evening she had admitted: 'I don't know if I'm going to be able to cope. I'm just so hurt, so angry at the complete dismissal of what I've been saying.'

Paul had waited before answering. 'Look, you can understand the authorities' lack of sympathy. Telling me that whoever did over my place was just a vandal is pure bullshit, but that's the way they look at things. We've got no proof that Mossad or anyone was involved. All we've got are suspicions.'

Miriam nodded. At last she appeared to have given in.

'They're suspicions at the moment,' Paul added, 'but there's something very wrong going on here.'

CHAPTER ELEVEN

Diplomatic activity between the Middle East and the capitals of the West rapidly intensified from late June, after the Israelis packed their bags and left Cyprus. The Secretary General of the United Nations, Ratu Sir Sidomante Bara of Fiji, shuttled from Damascus to Jerusalem to Cairo, then back to Jerusalem in the hope of bringing the antagonists back to the peace table. Initially, his efforts were greeted with sympathy by the moderate Arabic nations, but he met resistance from the extremist Arab States and from Raphael Ben Ari. The Jewish nation itself was divided. Those in Ben Ari's party, and those in minority parties whose positions were vulnerable, rallied around the leader in a display of unity, especially in light of the vehemence of world reaction. Nothing consolidated governmental unity like an external threat. But the nation was split into opposing camps, buzzing so angrily, like hornets disturbed from their nest, that there was hope in other world capitals that Israeli public opinion could be galvanised to force Ben Ari to step down and to be replaced by a moderate. The CIA pumped a couple of million dollars into the opposition's coffers to speed up the process.

In one of his journeys, the Secretary General was given an uncomfortable insight into what the future held now that the American peace initiative had been rebuffed. Sitting in the private apartments of Abu Farawhi, the Syrian President, the Ratu sipped coffee and asked his host what he felt might happen in the Middle East over the next year or so.

The Syrian President listened to the translation of the diplomat's question and smiled before answering. When he did so, the Ratu didn't need a translation to understand the import. 'For many centuries, Jew and Arab coexisted in Palestine, working together on the land, praying to the same God, revering many of the same prophets. Then the cancer of Zionism grew in the Jewish heart, and these lands were invaded by millions of aliens, dispossessing the rightful heirs without compensation. My friend, we Arabs take a perspective of centuries, not months. We will deal with Ben Ari and any who might follow in his footsteps in our own way. We do not need outside help.'

The Ratu wondered what compensation had been made to the swarms of Jews dispossessed by militant Arab governments and taken in by the impoverished Jewish land, or why Arabs hadn't absorbed their Palestinian brethren instead of leaving them suppurating in the open scars of the refugee camps. Being a diplomat, he realised there was nothing to be gained by opening the old wounds any further.

♜♜♜

At the same time as the Syrian President spoke to the Secretary General, another meeting was about to take place in the Iraqi capital of Baghdad. This meeting was covert, known only to a handful of people.

The atmosphere in the cavernous mosque was tense, the air redolent of the intensity of Moslem devotion and politics, those organic halves of Islam which make it so alien to outsiders. A blue light slanted in dusty shafts from the windows of the high golden cupola down to the lavishly carpeted floor.

No one spoke. Eyes were averted, most looking down at the multi-coloured Arabesque patterns of the rugs which covered the floor of the interior. Some sneaked quick, surreptitious looks at the impassive face of the Imam, a face which was the authority of Islam. His face was as beloved by millions of Moslems through the world as it was hated by the infidels of the West. But he was the voice of the ordinary people of the Islamic faith, especially those in Iran, Syria and Palestine. And as much as he was loved by these, he was hated by the Sunni rulers of Iraq and the rulers in other Arabic nations, who viewed him with the same fear and detestation their forebears had felt for the Kurdish-born Saladin 800 years earlier, as he fought the invading Crusaders. It was a face carved in the granite of absolutism … the fire of conviction … the certainty of fundamentalism. The Imam, whose long grey beard and narrow black eyes were made more prominent by the simplicity of his cloak, acted in the divine knowledge that everything he did was preordained; that his actions were guided by Allah, and his hand was moved by the Prophet Mohammed.

He was in many respects an unpretentious man, despite his revered position. The militant rhetoric which he used to inflame his acolytes of the Arab world was condemned in the West. The Imam of Iraq had one burning, overriding passion. The most holy sites of Islam were controlled by dogs … the Saudi royal family of Sunni Moslems in Mecca and Medina, and the Jewish dogs in Jerusalem who had captured the glory of the Moslem world in the 1967 war. In 687 the Umayyad Caliph, Abd al-Malik, built a shrine to commemorate the last place on Earth where the Prophet Mohammed rested before beginning his night journey to Heaven to sit at the feet of Allah. He built it fifty years after Jerusalem fell to the Moslems, and intended it to rival the site in hostile Moslem hands where the great *Kaba* had come to rest in Mecca. But it was also the site where Abraham had been told by Allah to lift up his eyes and to stay his hand from slaying his son, Isaac.

It was there that the Imam of Iraq wanted to be … where he would preach the word of Allah and spread His glorious message around the world. And today, thanks to that dog, Ben Ari, the opportunity had at last presented itself … an opportunity for which he had been waiting since 1967.

The Imam had been sitting motionless for nearly half an hour. Waiting. His legs were tucked beneath the folds of his thick robes, enshrouding his body, which was perched precariously on a thick red cushion.

Beside him, two mullahs sat rocking gently backwards and forwards on their cushions, waiting for a sign from their Imam. They would wait until an eyebrow was raised or there was an imperceptible nod of the head; only then would they spring into action. Such patience was inbred. They had waited on the will of their Imam many times before and would not dare to initiate action without his consent. Maybe, with the grace of God and his servant Mohammed, the All Wise and the All Merciful, they would one day rise to be imams. In time, they too would grant audiences such as this … audiences which would determine the fate of the world.

But the spiritual devotion of the Imam's acolytes did not suffuse downwards to the others, who were impatiently seated on cushions in the northern corner of the Al Kasim mosque, one of the most beautiful and holy shrines in Baghdad, on that blisteringly hot July day. They were not so content to wait on the Imam's pleasure. Indeed, in their own countries, their status was such that others would wait on their decisions, or movements, or raised eyebrows. But in Baghdad they had to wait on the Imam, and the Imam would not begin the conference until the arrival of the last member of the group. Through his hooded eyes, the Imam slowly surveyed the dogs who were seated before him. These were not soldiers of Islam. These were whores who would sell their skills to whoever paid them the most money. Slowly he moved his eyes to a carpet hanging on a nearby wall.

Everyone was waiting for Hassan al Sayyid, the man who had the shortest distance to travel. The others had flown in to Baghdad's newly repaired international airport from Cairo, Tripoli, Damascus, Berlin and Beirut, whereas al Sayyid only had to travel from the modern Karradet Mariam district on the West Bank of the Tigris, over to the ancient centre of the city whose roots for two thousand years had been almost exclusively on the East Bank.

Although travel was still difficult because of the destruction of most of Iraq's bridges and transport infrastructure, Hassan could easily have been the first there. But his arrogance and his theatricality were such that he would force everyone else, including the Imam, to wait.

Outside, crowds milled around in the ruins of the once-glorious Baghdad, desperately seeking shops which might have food at a reasonable price. Or they were queueing for the daily ration of water from the tankers. But the inside of the mosque remained cool, quiet and calm.

All those gathered at the request of the Imam seethed with anger as they waited. A movement at the door of the mosque caught everybody's attention. One of the guards walked in, followed by a tall, lean man in Western dress. When Hassan had crossed the floor of the enormous mosque, there were no signs of apology. He walked proprietorially into the group, knelt and bowed before the Imam and took his place. If the fury of the others was palpable, it was not shared by the Imam. Beginning the meeting now or later was of no importance. Time on Earth was inconsequential. Actions were measured by results, not by when they happened.

Without reference to the delay, the Imam began to speak softly, in the monotone which was his hallmark in the Arab world. The other men strained to listen as he explained the reason for his asking them to come to him.

'Brothers in Allah. Recently the balance of forces in the Middle East was reversed. By the actions of the Zionist imperialist running dog, Ben Ari, the prospects for Islamic gain in our area have dramatically changed. We have seen the destruction of the Godless Soviet Union and the ascendancy in influence of the Great Satan of the United States during the past few years. And just when the people of the world assumed that peace was at hand and that our courageous Moslem freedom fighters could put away their weapons, the Zionist Ben Ari has handed us an unrivalled opportunity.

'An opportunity to pick, like vultures, on the carcass of the body that was the Cyprus peace conference and again assert our dominance as Moslems who oppose the Zionist imperialist filth infesting Palestine, and to re-assert Islamic supremacy once again over Jerusalem and the entire country now known as Israel.'

The men sat listening to his tortured phrases. Even his most militant devotees found his medieval phraseology difficult to understand. But these men, who were not devotees, grew restless at his rhetoric. One interrupted, asking: 'Are you saying that we should use the scuttling of the peace conference as a reason to resume terrorist activities against Israel and its supporters?'

The Imam merely smiled, while a mullah sitting beside him answered in his stead: 'What my master is saying is that an opportunity has arisen. How you should respond is the purpose of this council. But our brothers in Hezbollah have already begun the task which my master has outlined. A fatwa was recently issued and a Jew and a Palestinian have been killed.'

The Imam nodded. Although none of the men gathered held the burning religious principles which governed his own life, they were needed in furthering his purpose. The Imam and his colleagues had agreed that there was one overwhelming require-ment for Islam to prevail. This was to continue the Islamic crusade begun by the one true Prophet, Mohammed, in the seventh century after the birth of the Prophet Jesus, known to Christians as the Christ. The crusade would only be complete when the last of the Infidels had been crushed, or converted to the One True Way of the Prophet. And foremost in his mind was the freeing by Holy War, by Jihad, of the city of Jerusalem, that most sacred and beautiful of cities, so that the Imam could walk in the footsteps of the Prophet where he had last set foot on Earth.

All the men gathered around the Imam were representatives of terrorist organisations, or unofficial representatives of gov-ernments who supported terror tactics against imperialist op-pressors such as Israel, America, most European countries and, in the recent past, the Russian Republic. But they excused themselves, and were excused by Islam, because the crimes they committed were in the name of the Prophet.

Today the Imam hoped to persuade these recently discarded men to take up arms again. Since the creation of a state of tranquillity by America, they had been without function or purpose. Now they must take up their weapons, and again strike terror into the hearts of the unbelieving West. From a fundamentalist Islamic legal point of view, these unbelievers were in a state of war with Islam and Moslems. By recreating the state of terror which had existed between the Islamic and Western worlds in the 1970s and '80s, the Imam knew that his goal—domination of the world by Islam—would be easier to achieve.

It was a simple yet effective scenario. Already short-tempered with Israel for destroying the peace process, the West would fear for itself and become distant from Israel. The Imam reasoned that an increasingly isolated Israel would become paranoid and ultimately more belligerent. Given sufficient world-fear and po-litical isolation, Israel could be pushed over the edge into attacking neighbouring Arab countries. Alone, and deprived of America's aid and matériel, it would surely lose, as it had so nearly lost in 1973. Israel could not sustain a protracted war without resupply, and today's American President was in a very different mood from the lackeys of the past who had granted any request from Israel because of their fear of the New York Jewish lobby.

And on the blessed day when a lonely Israel at last lost a war, Jerusalem would be Islam's and the Imam would preach the word of God in the footsteps of the Prophet. He would walk along the walls of Suleiman the Magnificent in the Mosques of the Dome of the Rock and al Aksar. Over a period of cen-turies, nine vicious Pope-inspired Crusades had slaughtered Moslems to wrest back Jerusalem to Christian control. Since 1967, Jerusalem had been in Jewish control. Now, with the perspective and blessing of history, it would soon be time for the rightful owners of Jerusalem to reassert their control. But first, he had to persuade this assembly of terrorists that it was time for them again to take up their arms.

'Brothers in Allah; this opportunity will never again present itself. Now that Israel has cut itself adrift from America by its declaration of war upon all peace-loving peoples, it has exposed itself as friendless and alone. There will never be a better time to strike at the heart of the devil.'

The representative of the Black September movement raised his hand, like a schoolboy asking permission to speak: 'My colleagues and I have been trying to determine why the Israeli Prime Minister committed the extraordinary action in Cyprus. We cannot understand his actions, and since he destroyed the talks, Ben Ari has been remarkably silent.'

'And,' said the representative of the PDRP, backed by the Libyan People's Republic, 'the situation in Israel is that of a man teetering on the edge of a precipice. Today there was another massive demonstration in Tel Aviv against the action of Ben Ari. Four of his coalition partners threatened publicly to resign. Even though his Cabinet is behind him, he appears to have little public support. He may well be brought down by his own people.'

'I think I can explain his actions,' said the Syrian representative. The room became silent. 'My President was instrumental in bringing the Israelis to the conference table. We have spent the past two years working with the Americans to create the Cyprus talks. This has won us the respect of the world. However, there was a secret agenda. We knew that Ben Ari would ruin the talks and it was my President's ploy to expose his fascism to the world, thereby gaining public sympathy for the Arab cause ...'

The room erupted.

'Liar,' screamed the Libyan.'Your government is a whore. It lies down with whoever pays it the most. For two years, you have been acting like the harlots of the world. Don't think that we don't know about your clandestine trips to Jerusalem, or your meetings in Geneva with the Zionists. I feel insulted and dirtied by your presence.'

The Syrian stood to shout at the chorus of voices raised against him, but the Imam held up his skeletal hand and the room drained of noise.

'Brothers. Our fight is with the Israelis and the Americans. It is not against each other. Think now about how close we are to feasting in Jerusalem. Rather than shout at each other for past sins which you all have committed, let us work out how our abilities can be used against our enemies.'

During the next two hours, the representatives of the Revolutionary People's Party (backed by the Syrian government); Black September; the PFLP; the People's Democratic Revolutionary Party (backed by the Libyans); the Popular Front for Revolution and Democracy (backed by the Iraqis); the Revolutionary People's Party (based in the Lebanon); the People's Democratic Freedom Fighters (backed by the Iranians); and the PLO, all argued about how best to expose Israel's fanatical anti-democratic imperialism.

In the 1970s and '80s, the frustration of the Palestinian, German, Irish, Basque, Japanese and other young militants against an apathetic world had expressed itself through bloody orgies against civilians, involving bombings, hijackings and kidnappings. But with the gradual realigning of traditional allegiances, governments which had traditionally sponsored terrorism to strike at the heart of Anglo-American imperialism had become more cautious. When the Syrians, the Emirates, Libya and even Iran realised that terrorism was hurting their standing in the world, most international terrorist organisations became dormant. Funding for terrorist groups had all but dried up as their use as instruments by rogue governments became more questionable. Even American hostages held for five or more years by the Iranian-backed Hezbollah groups had been released back to their families.

It was because of this tranquil atmosphere of international reconciliation in the Middle East that Syria, Egypt and the other Arab governments looked towards the West rather than the East. This enabled the Americans to bring the former adversaries to the conference table in Cyprus to discuss the internationalisation of Jerusalem.

Ben Ari's impetuous move had presented the Moslem leadership with an extraordinary opportunity. Again, Jerusalem could be within their grasp. In order to make it into a reality the Imam of Baghdad had contacted the Ayatollah of Iran, as well as his religious colleagues in Syria, Libya, Morocco, Egypt and Indonesia, and had enlisted their support. The Imam had no money. Iraq was still penniless because of the huge war reparations it was forced to pay. His brothers had willingly sent vast amounts of money to help the cause of Islam. The other religious leaders had sent messages to the groups represented today, instructing them to attend the conference. Now they were gathered, it was the Imam's job to persuade them how best to make his plans work.

'You brothers in Islam have a particular and deadly expertise. Your ability to strike fear into the hearts of the world must be harnessed. The Zionist government of Israel has stupidly left itself exposed to world condemnation, by its unilateral decision to break off the peace initiative. This means that it is a pariah, friendless in a world desperate for international peace and harmony. Now that this sense of harmony is destroyed, Israel will be put under righteous pressure. Just look at how the hijackings and bombings in the 1970s benefited the cause of Islam. Never have we been stronger. Never have there been more devotees. It is not for me, a simple religious man, to tell you how to do your jobs. But give the world a shock from the very beginning and it will take notice.

'From then on, any further actions must be directed against Israel. The Zionists must be pushed over the edge. They will become paranoid and belligerent. Israel is the arch-militarist of the Middle East. It has proved so since it was spawned in 1948, when its bloodthirsty leaders attacked the peace-loving nations of Syria, Jordan, and Egypt.'

The Imam looked closely to see what type of a reaction he was getting. It was demeaning for his hands to be soiled by talking to men such as these, but he was forced to deal with them. It was his only way of getting the governments surrounding Israel to act in the way he desired. They had shown themselves to be more pacifist than he had predicted, except for the Syrians and the Iraqis. Still, terrorist groups could be enlisted in his aim, and alone they could force massive retaliation by

Israel against its Arab neighbours, who would be forced to defend themselves. When war did break out, as the Imam knew it inevitably would, Israel would stand alone and would surely lose.

For the next two hours, the terrorist leaders debated the most effective methods of bringing about the goal set by the Imam. Terror tactics were well known to these men, who discussed them as parents discuss fund-raising at schools. Ultimately a course of action was decided upon, and a communique was written. One after another the terrorists stood, kissed the Imam's hand, and departed.

He watched them disappear from the mosque, his contempt for them plainly apparent. Then turning to one of his mullahs he gave a curt nod and the mullah stood and walked towards a carpet hanging on a nearby wall. Pulling it aside revealed a tall heavily built man wearing the robes of a Palestinian. The Imam indicated for the man to come forward. He sat cross-legged on the left-hand side of the Imam and looked him directly in the eyes.

'You heard the conversation?'

The newcomer nodded. 'Yes, Holy One.'

'Am I wrong to trust these men?'

The man looked down at the carpet before answering. 'They are not like us. They are freedom fighters. The spirit of Islam does not burn in their hearts.'

The Imam nodded slowly. 'And Hamas? Does zeal burn in the hearts of members of Hamas?'

The newcomer smiled. 'Our beginnings were of the Moslem Brotherhood nearly sixty years ago. Our founder Hassan al Bana did not believe that Islam should be restricted to worship and that it should be confined to a few theologians …' The Imam looked at him with a flash of anger in his eyes. Undaunted, the newcomer continued: '… but called on all Moslems to renew their faith and to recognise that Islam is a religion of worship and struggle. After the beginning of the Intifada our movement grew and now combines our religion with our political beliefs. And that, Holy One, is the difference, for we have beliefs. The dogs you had here today merely have hatred.'

The mullahs looked at their elderly Imam. He remained silent for many moments, at last turning to the newcomer and saying, 'It is good. These dogs will work outside of Israel, putting pressure on its borders, sometimes committing acts of terrorism within the country. They will send a message to the world that Islam demands its vengeance against the Israelis. You and your brothers in Hamas will act for me from the inside. You will foment anger and disruption within the Occupied Territories and in Israel itself. You will organise yourselves to make Israel look inside as well as outside. You will weaken the body of the Jews.'

When the representative of Hamas had left, the Imam retired to prayer. In the meantime, the communique was sent from a secret transmitter in Baghdad to the foreign ministries of America, Britain, Canada, and all European capitals. It had been anticipated by security forces in the West, who had been monitoring the area for any increases in terrorist activity, but even so, when it finally arrived it still managed to strike fear into the hearts of the foreign ministers who read it, and who immediately sent it to their heads of state. It was a simple message, but its meaning could spell doom for many of their citizens. It read:

Because of the actions of the Zionist Imperialist, Raphael Ben Ari, the Combined Front of Arab Unity, comprising units of Arabic Freedom Fighters, the People's Democratic Revolutionary Party, Black September, Popular Front for the Liberation of Palestine, The People's Command for Revolution and Democracy, and the Revolutionary People's Party, now declare that unless the Governments of the World force the unlawful government in Jerusalem to resume Peace Talks by July 15th, a state of Jihad will be in force, and retaliatory action will be taken against any target deemed to support the unlawful Government.

After a blossoming of spring, the world was again bracing itself for an unseasonal winter of terror. Following the receipt of the communique, nothing more was heard from the Combined Front of Arab Unity, despite frantic efforts by several countries to contact a representative member of the group for negotiations. The terrorists meanwhile returned to their homelands by covert means and called together their operative cells. They had money; they had means; and they had a purpose. The adrenalin was beginning to flow in their blood.

And it was adrenalin also that kept the various anti-terrorist advisers awake during those long days from the beginning of July when the communique was received. A world-wide, ultrasecret series of coded messages was transmitted from capital cities to their embassies throughout the world.

The American State Department, responsible for the safety of all of its embassies, sent an 'M93' coded message. The 'M' was a sign that it was 'eyes only' for the ambassador, the only man in the diplomatic mission authorised to receive and subsequently decode the message.

Depending upon the local time, American ambassadors around the world who were dining, breakfasting, relaxing by their swimming pools, making speeches or receiving delegations suddenly found that a Marine corporal walked up to them and whispered into their ears, 'Mr Ambassador, your Head of Mission requests your immediate presence for discussion about tomorrow's agenda.' This was a coded indication that an 'M' message had arrived. Regardless of what he was doing, each ambassador had to cut it short as quickly as possible and return to the code room in his embassy. None treated it lightly.

On arriving in the code room, the cipher clerk stood aside, as the ambassador tapped his personal identification number into the computer. The printer instantly began to type out the coded message. The ambassador was then joined by his head of chancery. They went to the ambassador's safe in his private office and withdrew a squat titanium-reinforced steel box. Had anybody attempted to open it by force, the box would immediately discharge a small thermal explosive inside the lid, destroying the contents beyond recognition.

To further protect these most important of codes, the boxes also contained two separate wheels of cogs, each having separate combinations. The ambassador knew one combination; the head of chancery the other. Neither was permitted to use his combination within visual range of the other. A new code box containing a new combination was sent monthly to every embassy.

Once the office door was secured and detection devices put into operation, the box was opened and the 'M' code book was taken out and opened on the ambassador's desk. All the other embassy codes were kept in the cipher room under Marine guard.

The head of chancery slowly read the letters and numbers which comprised the message and the ambassador wrote them down on a 'once only' pad which was steel-backed so that no impression of the ambassador's pen would be left. It contained a unique jumble of letters and spaces, and by placing the decoded message within the spaces nominated by the instructions, the message became clear. Once the pad had been utilised for this exercise, the State Department would send out a new code book and a new decipher pad. As further insurance against code-breaking, the pad was made of chemically treated light-sensitive paper. If it were to be photocopied or flash-photographed, it would immediately become opaque and unreadable.

After two minutes the message had been decoded. It read:

Ultra top secret. Eyes only. Ambassador, Head of Chancery, and First Secretary. Message received at State Department, Eastern American Standard Time 0950 believed to be ex Baghdad but potentially from elsewhere in Mid-East, warns of imminent terrorist attacks beginning July 15, against American and European targets following breakdown of Mid-East peace talks. State Department advises Ambassadors to treat warning with extreme gravity and to take all precautions to protect US interests in your country. Anti-terrorist-trained personnel of Schwarzkopf Brigade and Navy SEALS currently training Fort Bragg to be transhipped to nominated countries soonest. Commander of Marines will debrief Ambassador and Head of Chancery only on arrival . Do not, repeat, do not warn, advise or discuss with American business or tourist interests your area. This action to be undertaken by State Department ex-Washington. Your responsibility to secure embassy, personnel, and to institute Condition Yellow immediately. Condition Red to be instituted July 12, unless negative command rescinding received ex-State Department.

One hundred and forty American ambassadors, and their Heads of Chancery, were suddenly thrust into the maelstrom of Middle Eastern politics.

CHAPTER TWELVE

Aristo Haggopian was an Armenian whose Greek mother had brought her son to live in Athens after her husband had deserted her in the Anatolian town of Smyrna. They had met in the aftermath of the Second World War, and while they were not romantic lovers swept by tenderness or passion, they enjoyed a comfortable relationship until the birth of Aristo. Although he had been known to like some children, the father didn't enjoy the disruption to the pleasures of his home which came with nappies and breast-feeding. One day he told his wife he was going to the nearby shops to buy some tobacco. He never returned.

Shamed and impoverished, she took baby Aristo back to the Plaka, the district of her birth in Athens, to live with her parents. The anger that she felt was transmitted to her son, who bore the scars of a family where the woman was both mother and father.

Aristo grew to manhood in the Plaka, and easily fitted into its colourful and cosmopolitan atmosphere. He belonged to its steep and narrow streets as surely as the exotic cafes and night-club life which made it the heart of Athens. His home was haunted by characters who trod both sides of the divide between right and wrong. He loved its confusions and contradictions. A chubby boy, he was pampered by the women who lived and worked there, a polyglot mixture of the matronly and the erotic. And although sworn to secrecy, he was used by its men. It was a way of life in the Plaka, but it took Aristo many years to come to terms with the fact that his homosexuality was unacceptable in the world outside.

Aristo knew how to survive in the Plaka, how to make it work for him. Even as a small boy, he was street smart. And he learned to be a survivor. But he wasn't school smart and his mediocre academic career meant that much of the exciting life he had planned for himself was not open to him.

He was useful with his hands and managed to obtain an apprenticeship as an aircraft mechanic. It was better than being a thief or a pickpocket. Every day, he thrilled as the huge planes took off from Athens airport and roared over the sea to climb into the sky and fly to exciting places. He fantasised about becoming a pilot, but without a university education, it would always remain a dream. Working close to aircraft on the ground was the best that he could manage.

Well paid, he could easily have purchased his own apartment when he reached his mid-twenties. But Aristo squandered his money on good living, expensive clothes and the erotica of homosexuality. By the time he was in his mid-forties he was still living in his mother's house in the Plaka. In earlier years he had been popular with Athens' homosexual community and remembered the joy of his many lovers, but he had grown fat and careless and now found it difficult to attract lovers. Until Raoul, Aristo had not enjoyed another man's body for months.

During the last few days his life had been transformed by his new Lebanese lover. His sensitive and virile lover seemed to be genuinely fond of him. Raoul had even suggested that they go away on holiday together; and after that, marriage might not be out of the question. He had given Aristo a few lovely presents and seemed to want nothing of him other than his comfort and his femininity. When Raoul asked him the best way to send a present quickly and securely to America, Aristo proudly suggested that he take charge of the matter. Raoul was excessively grateful and suggested that Aristo place the small parcel, addressed to his uncle in New York, on an aircraft. When Aristo explained how easy it was, Raoul paid special attention to him that made him squeal with delight. Both men enjoyed the idea of putting one over the authorities. It was a simple way of avoiding paying the exorbitant costs charged by the airfreight companies. Anyway, sending things by post wouldn't always guarantee they would arrive in safety.

When Aristo awoke on a blistering hot mid-July day after an aching night of sexual experiments, he was sore and uncomfortable. He smiled when he remembered the passion, the frequency and the strength of his orgasms. Over coffee, Raoul gave him the parcel. It was tied with string and simply addressed to an apartment block in the Bronx. All that Aristo had to do was to place it in the cargo hold of the Magnum Airlines flight MA120 to the USA and his cousin, who worked at Kennedy airport, would find it and give it to his uncle the following day. Simple, efficient and free of the intrusion of officialdom.

At quarter to eight, Aristo got into his car and drove to the airport which was situated close to the sea between Athens and its major seaport, Piraeus. The small parcel was placed in his workbag, which also contained his lunch and a pornographic book showing beautiful young men doing extraordinary things with each other. It was rampant eroticism which he had always dreamed about. Pure pleasure. With Raoul, fantasies had come true. At work, Aristo often daydreamed about taking beautiful young boys into his bed. Now, again, it was happening. Was this the beginning of a new life? The end of loneliness?

As he drove in his tiny Renault, he felt sick with the foul stench of petrol, diesel and human pollution which was so vicious it caused respiratory disease amongst the citizens and was killing the pure white delicate marble that had stood for two and a half millennia on the Acropolis, the greatest wonder and joy of the world.

Aristo was forced to drive slowly as he negotiated the tight corners and narrow laneways from his lover's apartment block near Syntagma Square, until he reached the larger, noisier, less claustrophobic streets east of the Plaka. When he descended from the area of the Parthenon, he continued to drive slowly through the dense traffic until he reached Thrassilou, then left onto Areopayitou until he joined with the highway directly south to Ellinikon airport.

The morning was busy and the monotony was only broken

when a 747 was wheeled in for service. Even after twenty years Aristo still felt a thrill as he stood on the ground and looked upwards at the vast silver underbellies. After being coddled and catalogued, they were wheeled out of the hot stinking hangar, beside the airport runways. At lunchtime when Aristo and his friends opened their satchels to take out their brown paper bags of food and bottles of retsina, he saw that he had not yet put his parcel on to the Magnum Airlines jet. He excused himself from his colleagues and took his workbag to the No. 3 hangar, 400 metres away, where the plane was being prepared for the evening flight from Athens to London, and then to New York. He knew most of the mechanics working on the airliner and waved to them as they sat around tables eating their lunches or playing cards. Suitcases are not placed directly into 747s. They are loaded into huge cages, and then the cages are loaded by hydraulic lifts into either side of the aircraft's tail. There would have been suspicion of Aristo climbing into the hold of an aircraft he was not working on, but there was no suspicion of him walking towards the baggage storage area beneath the vast underbelly of the plane.

A cage was already being loaded with suitcases. Aristo found a suitably inconspicuous place, trapped in between two pieces of canvas webbing which formed part of the mesh used to hold suitcases steady during take-offs and landings. Having secured the parcel for Raoul's uncle, Aristo walked away from the belly of the aircraft to rejoin his colleagues. He was happy he had assisted his lover and was sure it would earn him special attention that night.

In the early evening the huge Magnum Airlines 747, captained by John McGillis, ex-USAF, with over twenty years flying experience, climbed through 1,500 metres, heading out to sea before starting a gentle right-hand roll, skirting the Athenian coast south of Piraeus, heading north-north-west over the Saronic Gulf towards Brindisi in Italy. The aircraft would be at

10,000 metres when it crossed the Italian coast, and maintain a 12,000 metre ceiling until the French coast, when it would slowly descend to whatever runway Heathrow air traffic control allocated.

The 260 passengers on board by now had got used to the droning monotony in the aircraft cabin, and the children had already unbuckled their seatbelts and were running up and down the aisle. More experienced travellers in first and business classes were opening their briefcases to take out papers. Passengers travelling in the coach section smiled as hostesses placed small sachets of peanuts and plastic beakers on their trays.

It was 7.45 p.m. when Athens air traffic control notified Captain McGillis that he would shortly be leaving their area and they would be handing him over to Rome air traffic control. Captain McGillis had an easy relationship with the Athenians and enjoyed listening to their broken English. His co-pilot was Derek Franks, an Australian with an accent both incomprehensible to, and the delight of, Magnum's passengers. He had less flying experience than McGillis but was a cool and dispassionate No. 2. Derek noticed that they had already reached 10,000 metres and began to switch on the aircraft's auxiliary back-up systems so the captain could shortly go to autopilot.

Both men then settled back to enjoy the mind-numbing tedium of flying a 747 across vast tracts of the globe. The huge periods of uneventful time in which the only person working was the navigator meant that both men could read books and magazines, play a game of chess or stretch their legs by wandering back from the flight deck into the upper lounge of the plane to have a quiet soft drink with passengers.

Seventy feet below them in a back hold of the 747—dark, noisy, and by now freezing cold—the suitcases belonging to the passengers were straining against the canvas leashes in their cage. Also restrained was a small brown parcel addressed to a fictitious man at a false address in New York.

Inside the parcel was a small Sony portable radio. Within the radio was a pressure-sensitive mercury barometer which responded to the rapidly decreasing pressure in the aircraft hold. As the plane flew higher, the passengers in the pressurised cabin space were hardly aware of the changing altitude, but in the hold the decreasing pressure in the outer atmosphere altered the volume of the mercury in the barometric tube.

As it did so, the mercury, which is one of nature's best electrical conductors, was forced through a tiny capillary tube, causing it to bridge a small gap between two exposed wires and complete an electrical circuit. This electrical circuit activated the radio battery, which suddenly came alive to a high megahertz frequency. The frequency activated one kilogram of Semtex, recently manufactured in Czechoslovakia and smuggled into Beirut. The Semtex exploded with enough force to blow a hole ten feet in diameter in the underbelly of the plane. All the wires which enabled Captain McGillis to control the plane were severed and sucked through the gaping hole to flap outside the plane in the freezing night sky. But that was not the major problem. When the Semtex exploded, so did the plane's fuel tanks, and within milliseconds a huge explosion began to rip through the entire length of the fuselage, instantly killing all those passengers in the coach section who were directly above the cargo hold. They died by a combination of two agents. One was the expansion of the fireball itself, as it exploded from the cargo hold, crushing bodies against overhead cabin lockers. The other was the superheated flame of the aero fuel. Huge metal shards which were ripped from the floor skewered and amputated limbs and carried them like pieces of butcher's meat around the plane, or sucked them out of the widening hole in the plane's body.

Passengers in first class instantly knew something was terribly wrong when there was an enormous noise from the rear of the plane, and a rapid depressurisation which sucked papers, pens and briefcases through the flapping curtains towards the rear. Passengers who had foolishly taken off their seatbelts were sucked down aisles or over the tops of seats like puppets, banging and crashing against other passengers who were pulled by the massive force through the hole in the jet's body. The lights instantly went out, but before anybody had the chance to scream, a hideous amoeba of yellow and black fire and smoke flowed through the body of the plane, exploding in people's faces, entering their throats and cutting off any noise. The holocaust further opened the thin metal skin of the plane exposing the scene of madness to the evening sky.

Even if he had realised what was going on in the body of the plane during those milliseconds of the fireball, Captain McGillis wouldn't have had time to touch the radio to broadcast a Mayday message. Within a fraction of the time it took for him to turn around, he was dead, crushed beyond any recognisable human form against the 747's console.

The plane began its plummet 10,000 metres into the sea between Greece and Italy. When it finally hit the water, no one was alive.

Aristo Haggopian slammed the phone down in fear. It was the fourth time he had phoned. Raoul was never away from his apartment after 7 o'clock. They had an arrangement. He paced the floor of the tiny apartment. Why was he not there? Aristo got into his car and drove from the Plaka towards his lover's apartment. At first he was worried Raoul might be sick. Now he was frantic. It was a hot night and Aristo had the windows open. The car radio was repeating the news that a Magnum Airlines jet had disappeared off radar screens. Everyone in Athens listening to the announcement was riveted by the horror. A Greek tragedy. An airliner full of people had disappeared. Everyone, except Aristo. He listened, but he did not hear. The words from the announcer did not penetrate his consciousness. His only thought was of Raoul, and his whereabouts.

His car screamed to a halt outside the apartment, as the news reader talked about fears for the lives of 260 people. Magnum

Airlines? That was the plane in which he had placed Raoul's present for his uncle in America. He must find Raoul and tell him that the present would not arrive. Where was he? Aristo slammed the car door and ran up the stairs to Raoul's apartment. The door was ajar. Police sirens were screaming in the far distance. Aristo entered the apartment and knew at once that Raoul was no longer there. There were none of his personal effects any more. His perfumes, his silk pyjamas, his underwear. All gone. He searched the bedroom, the wardrobe and the bathroom. All Raoul's beautiful things had been taken away from him. Aristo sat down in the loungeroom and waited an hour, just in case.

But there was no sign of his lover. Until the advent of Raoul, Aristo's life had been empty. Raoul had been such a comfort. Such a love. Tears flowed down his cheeks as he looked into the future and saw a continuation of the emptiness. He stood up and tucked his shirt into his trousers, over his bulging stomach. He walked out of the flat in a state of numb shock, but when he saw his car he could not face getting into it. It would mean defeat. He sat on the stone steps leading up to the apartment block, in which so many of his recent nights had been spent in ecstasy, and tried to think. The night air was a cacophony of noises—the sound of radio and television broadcasts, the calls of mothers, the quarrels of husbands and wives, the music of the evening. And above the din, the question pounding in Aristo's head … Why?

He continued to cry as his lover's faithlessness began to dawn on him. His future was so bleak that all sense of the outside world left him as he sat on the steps trying to plan his next actions

Cut off from all sense of others, he didn't notice a black Mercedes slowly gliding past. Nor did he notice the back window roll down, or the slim, matt barrel of a silenced machine pistol poke out, and spit a lethal tongue of flame at his forehead.

CHAPTER THIRTEEN

The Greek Coastal Patrol was hopelessly inadequate and ill-equipped to deal with a disaster of the magnitude of the Magnum Airlines crash. Hundreds of bodies were floating bloated and broken in the sea and the Greek government was forced to request international help. The defence forces of Italy immediately sprang to action and supplied Augusta Sea King helicopters and two carriers to assist in the task of recovering the corpses. Egypt sent a warship speeding north. The offer of aid by Turkey was declined. Boats, from simple fishing trawlers to the fabulous yachts of millionaires, which sailed the Adriatic and the Mediterranean, also rushed to the scene of the disaster. Their owners were not ghoulish sightseers but were revolted by the enormity of the crime.

All the while, the bloated grey remains of men, women and children were picked up by rescuers, or slowly tossed back onto the coastline of Greece as the tide washed them back onto land.

The image which flashed through Paul Sinclair's mind as he re-read the story in *The National* was of the dead birds and fish which had buffeted the shores of the Persian Gulf when Saddam Hussein had opened up the oil wells and caused the biggest oil spill in history. But the photographic images were not of birds and fish. They were dead human beings. He shook his head in horror and disbelief. It was beyond his comprehension how people could blow up a plane, kill 240 innocent passengers and twenty crew, and then proudly boast that they were responsible.

The communique, carried in reversed white type on a black background next to an aerial photo of what remained of the wreckage floating in a dull sea, said it all. Paul re-read it:

The Central Command of the Combined Front of Arab Unity claims responsibility for the execution of suspected CIA agents aboard the Magnum Airlines flight MA 120 tonight.

The deaths of innocent civilians aboard this flight is the direct responsibility of the government of the United States, which refused to heed the righteous warnings given by the Combined Front of Arab Unity, and has failed to exert either pressure or force upon the Zionist Imperialist Government in Israel to alter its Fascist warmongering stance towards the peace-loving nations of the Arab World, and to return to the conference table.

He felt sickened by the self-righteousness of the words, the moral parody, but was shocked out of his mood when the telephone rang. He picked it up, but was unable to submerge his mood of depression.

'Yes,' he said, despondency in his voice.

'Paul, it's me. What's wrong?' said Miriam. 'You sound really down.'

'Oh hi. Sorry. I'm just in the middle of reading about this disaster in Greece.'

'Yes, I know. I saw the pictures on TV. Let's hope they catch the bastards that did it.'

'Why should they?' asked Paul. 'They hardly ever do. Then places like Italy and France cave in to the bastards and just let them go.' Paul felt an anger welling up inside him. 'They'll be treated like heroes in Tripoli or Beirut or Tehran, or somewhere. Anyway, you can forget about coming to Israel with me. I know I agreed last night, but after this, no way! I've got to go because of my job but I'm not going to have you risking your life just because of some missionary zeal.'

'Paul, let's discuss this tonight,' said Miriam biting her lip to stop herself from becoming angry.

'Miriam, I know that tone of voice. There's a hardarse Arab terrorist group blowing up planeloads of tourists. I don't know what you think we're going to discuss tonight because there's no way you're coming with me.'

Miriam's hackles had now fully risen. Paul was making decisions for her, as he had tried to do at the beginning of their relationship. Now, though, he was making his profession sound more important than her need to find out how her grandfather died.

Immediately after her *zeida*'s death, Miriam asked one of his friends at the Rosenthal if he would say *kaddish* for him during the year. The old man willingly agreed, telling her it was a privilege and a blessing for him to do so.

She had attended the first couple of services at the Rosenthal after his funeral, but excused herself after that, citing a desire to grieve privately at home. In truth, she felt hardly affected by his death. When the funeral was over, she was bathed by a profound sense of relief, the false euphoria in grief. Sometimes she felt like laughing, like going to a movie, like talking all night to friends. Her grief for her grandfather was in contrast to her feelings when her parents had died. Then she had welcomed the dozens of solicitous friends who came to pay their respects. Now her fears and confusion about his death made her lose sight of its awful reality, of the hideous potential which it created.

One of the ways her grief expressed itself was an anger with the world, a passionate yearning to learn why her grandfather had been killed. What modern-world dybbuk had reached up and pulled that gentle benign old man back into the agony of the past? Miriam intended to find out, Paul or no Paul. She couldn't make progress in Australia, so she was going to use every ounce of her abilities and the power which the twentieth century had vested in her to drag the answer from whatever Israeli Dr Jekyll had loosed his Mr Hyde on the world.

Whoever it was dictated that her grandfather had to die would soon feel the full weight of her vengeance! If he thought that he could end her grandfather's life at the stroke of a pen he had another think coming. If it was Mossad, she would shame them by exposure. If it was Ben Ari, then the world would soon find out.

Paul could hear Miriam breathing hard on the end of the line, trying to control her resentment. He had learned early not to challenge her head-on by telling her what she could and couldn't do. But this situation was different and in their five years together he had not been so dogmatic, so commanding, since their early days.

'Paul, I appreciate your concern. I know you've got your job to do. So have I. You don't own me. Please don't think I haven't thought this whole thing through. I know all about the terrorists and the plane that was bombed and the Israeli reporter that was killed a couple of days ago. But there's just as much danger for you as there is for me. I'm prepared to take the risk. I'm coming, and that's all there is to it.'

'Look Miriam, I just …'

'I'm going over to Israel for a very good reason. Something you should understand better than most. I'm going to expose whoever it was that did this, not just so they'll be brought to justice but for my own self-protection. Mine, as well as yours. Your place was vandalised and you could have been murdered if you'd been there. Then there was Zeida. And I'm next on the list. Well, I'm not going to sit back and just let it happen. I don't know much about the secret services, Paul, and I really don't want to. But Mossad, or whoever it was, are the type of people who duck for cover when they run the risk of exposure. They hide behind officialese, and D-notices, and military censorship.'

Paul realised that Miriam was still in shock from her grandfather's death, but her reaction was extraordinary even for someone in mourning. She was going to cause more problems.

No matter how it looked, speculation was their only certainty. And Miriam, trained at the altar of law in the eucharist of fact, was forgetting the very essence of her training—the burden of proof.

'Miriam, what do you think exposing them is going to do? Do you think they're going to come out into the open to contradict what you're saying? This is Mossad we're talking about. They're not going to meet you head on in the marketplace for a debate.'

'Well, I'm doing no good here.'

'Look,' said Paul, 'we've got no proof of what's going on. If we go around making allegations, we're going to look like fools. Was it Mossad? Or the CIA? Or MI6? I've given it a lot of thought, Miriam. All we know for certain is that your grandfather had something happen to his clothes. That's it! End of story! And now, you're going to let a conspiracy theory take control of your actions. We're both guilty of that but the test I use is whether I'm willing to go into print on the facts that I've got. So far, they just don't add up. We've jumped to the conclusion that telephones have been bugged, faxes intercepted and murderers have done away with Yossi … Do you see how it sounds?'

'There's something you seem to be forgetting.' Miriam's voice had changed. 'Raphael Ben Ari was once high up in Mossad. You told me that. If anybody could direct them to do something like this, it's him.'

'But there's no evidence …'

'Evidence! Listen. This isn't a fucking court of law. I don't need enough to convince a judge and jury. My grandfather had a picture of Ben Ari, that suggests he's a mass murderer. You've seen it, and you know that it's genuine. He died in mysterious circumstances, after your flat had been searched … You were phoned by some phoney sister purporting to be from the Rosenthal. And finally Paul, you seem to have ignored the fact that your clothes and his were slashed in exactly the same way, almost certainly by the same person!'

'But Miriam …'

'I'm not a conspiracy theorist, Paul, and I know a hell of a lot more about the burden of proof than you do. But I've got some pretty compelling circumstantial evidence that's going to take me to Israel to find out what in the name of God is going on.'

Paul sighed. 'Okay, Miriam. See you at the airport.'

He returned to his story about a young Austalian girl who had been de-programmed after her parents had rescued her from a fundamentalist church in America's Bible belt. Where was religious fundamentalism heading over the next decade or so? he wondered. What would it do to the world? Paul was interested in following its path as it continued to spread. But try as he might to concentrate on the screen, his mind kept wandering to the dangers that Miriam might encounter if she tried to expose Mossad in Israel. The thought of his own danger didn't enter his mind. Journalists often felt that working for newspapers gave them the same protection as a suit of armour. He finished the story.

Miriam put the phone down and was sorry she had vented her anger on Paul. She knew he was only acting in her best interests, patronising though he was. Her mood swings had recently become quite pronounced. It had only been a few days since she had buried her grandfather. Now she was feeling insecure, poised at the edge of a precipice. Once she had stood on firm ground, but now she was standing on quicksand.

Her *zeida* had been her rock, the link between her life in Australia and her origins in Europe, a concatenation that she was only just beginning to appreciate. He was gone and she teetered precipitously as dybbuks from the bottom of the black pit, the old world, the world of ancient superstitions and customs, of vast uncontrollable forces, threatened to buffet her like chaff from a thresher's flail.

She was determined to resist with all her might. To use every ounce of training and guile, every legal and moral device at her disposal, to prevent evil things happening to her.

Unlike the Jews of Europe who saw the ground cut from beneath their feet and who flailed about helplessly, prey to overwhelming forces, Miriam would be going in armed to the teeth, a lawbook in one hand and in the other a torch to shine light into the dark recesses of the pit.

Paul and Miriam sat back, comfortably ensconced in Business class on Qantas Flight 2 to London, en route to join an El Al flight to Tel Aviv.

'Mandle insisted that if there was any trouble in Israel I was to get out straight away. He was quite dismissive. He told me that I wasn't like a foreign correspondent. All I was doing was background research. I wasn't to risk my life.'

Miriam looked at him, and tenderly squeezed his arm. She knew he hated the way Mandle minimised people's importance. Demoralising and insulting, it was Mandle's way of controlling those beneath him. It showed the man's insecurity.

'Will you leave if I'm told to go?' he asked.

Miriam shrugged her shoulders and said that she would think about it. 'Don't worry, I'm not going to get myself killed. It would be a bit ironic, wouldn't it? After all, I'm here trying to find out what happened to Zeida and prevent it happening to you and me.'

In the few days it had taken to arrange the flight to Israel, Paul had been frantically busy. Using the resources of Max Mandle's empire, he had managed to arrange interviews on his arrival in Israel with many men and women who knew Raphael Ben Ari, had worked with him, fought with him in the old days, been in government with him or had opposed him.

Paul was particularly delighted that the editor of the *Tel Aviv News* had offered to make a private office available to him while he was working in Israel. It was a luxurious contrast to the conditions he usually worked under at *The National*. From his office, he would arrange interviews with leading journalists, broadcasters, writers, academics, historians, and numerous other sources. It sounded as if Paul was going to be offered royal treatment because *The National* in Australia was an important recipient of the external news service provided by the *Tel Aviv News*. So his visit was viewed as a way of showing courtesy to a valued client.

The flight itself was therapeutic, a necessary break. The speed with which events occurred was a nightmare for Paul, but the rush of events forced Miriam's grief and anger into the background. The death of her grandfather, the furious row with the authorities in the Rosenthal, the Coroner's Office and the police, all of whom treated her as though she were crazy, had also denied her from the therapy of mourning. Paul was concerned for her and hoped that sometime during their visit she would find time for tears. On the flight, they talked a lot about Israel. Paul had been there twice previously, both on Mandle-sponsored journalistic trips aimed to show reporters and editors Israel from the Zionistic point of view. No pressure was ever applied, but the subtlety of the PR job ensured that even the most sceptical journalist returned home with Israel occupying a more preferential share of mind.

It was Miriam's first time in Israel; her first time properly overseas—she refused to count her trip to Fiji as being overseas, where she had been with Australians all the while and hadn't experienced any of the indigenous culture.

Miriam clutched onto her seat as the 747 swooped low over the Mediterranean and crossed the coast just north of Haifa. Below her, she could clearly see the hills and the majestic sweep of the bay as it arched north towards the Crusader fortress of Akko, with blindingly white buildings hugging the side of Mount Carmel. Halfway up the mountain, flaming like a beacon welcoming visitors to the very end of the Mediterranean, was the Baha'i Temple. Its massive golden dome burned furiously in the brilliant sunlight. It was the Shrine of the Bāb, the Gate, and it stood at the entranceway to Israel.

The plane banked to the right over the hills. Miriam was stunned by the view of the coastline of Israel. To prevent herself suffering vertigo as the plane came nearer to the ground, she took the magazine out of the seat pocket, opened it to the map section and tried to identify the towns below her. She could clearly see all the way to Hadeira, just a few dozen miles north of Tel Aviv. Miriam realised how tiny the country was. It had taken the jet five hours to reach the northern coast of Australia. Five hours to leave the protection of her home. In Israel it took a couple of minutes flying time to be encircled by the hostility of neighbours. The precarious hold which the Israelis had on this crescent-shaped skin of land was reinforced when Paul pointed out that from the other side of the plane, the borders of Syria and Jordan could easily be seen east of the Jordan Valley.

Miriam's excitement grew as the plane came in low to land. As she was landing, she revelled in being in Israel. The land of her ancestors. Of her Bible. She thrilled to experience the new and the undiscovered.

From the right hand side of the plane, she looked down at the small perfect rectangles of cultivated land, bearing citrus fruits, cotton, avocados or grapes, interspersed with large pools of water. Paul explained that these were fish farms. Israel was a rural pauper and used every square centimetre to grow, nurture or create. Necessity was the mother of intensive agriculture in a tiny country surrounded by hatred, where self-sufficiency was the brother of survival.

As the plane's wheels dropped in preparation for touchdown, her mind flashed back to the last meal she and her grandfather had eaten, when he had told her of the Jews who had worked the fields of Poland. Then he had ridiculed the Jews of Australia, calling them urbanites, as though it was a term of abuse. These fields and fish farms made her wonder whether her grandfather's view of modern Jews was correct. Miriam had never thought of Jews as farmers. Yet below her was the living proof. On the Israeli side of the border was a verdant land, bursting with life and vigour, seducing what was once a malarial swamp to produce a cornucopia of life-sustaining goodness. On the Jordanian side, clearly visible from the plane, was a grey land, an uncompromising desert of lifelessness.

Below her, Jewish men and women were tilling the soil and getting dirt under their fingernails, just as they had done in the time of the Bible. *O tempora, o mores!* Were these a different type of Jew? Did they go to synagogue, read books, study Talmud and Torah? Or were they like the farmers of New South Wales, introverted, taciturn and self-sufficient?

The plane's wheels screeched on the hot tarmac and the airport slowly rolled to a standstill after its helter-skelter rush past the aircraft's windows.

Within half an hour, Paul and Miriam were inside the noisy and bustling customs hall. Miriam thrilled to every sight and sound and smell, so totally different to anything at Sydney airport. In Australia, porters, customs officials and the occasional Federal policeman inconspicuously propping up a pillar looked indifferently at the tired and confused passengers. Here, there were smiles. From everything she had been told, Miriam was prepared for military uniforms everywhere in the customs area, especially following the massacre of terrorists by the Japanese fanatics many years earlier. She expected to walk past dark-skinned Israelis staring suspiciously at her. She prepared herself for a feeling of disquiet at entering an armed encampment. But to her surprise all she could see were the blue uniforms of policemen and women and the traditional green and grey casual clothes of customs officials.

'I don't understand,' Miriam whispered to Paul as they stood in the long queue. 'I would have thought after terrorists blew up that plane the place would have been crawling with security. Look,' she nodded at the vast hall. 'It hardly looks like there's any security here.'

'See those cameras up there,' Paul said softly. 'We're under more surveillance than you think. The moment anybody makes a suspicious move, there'd be a dozen armed guards down on him like a ton of bricks. Just because it's unobtrusive doesn't mean to say that there's no security.'

Miriam looked more closely through the customs hall and saw that cameras were omnipresent on ceilings and on columns. The faces of incoming travellers were matched against computer images of terrorists to give early warning to officials. Israeli missions all over the world regularly filtered updates on terrorists into Mossad headquarters. Even before a terrorist had left his country, the Israeli customs and security operation at Tel Aviv airport was on full alert. The country dealt with millions of tourists every year and the security had to be both efficient and unobtrusive.

Paul and Miriam approached a customs officer and showed

their passports. He keyed the details into his computer and checked that their faces matched the passports. Looking at the screen, no red flags showed. Further security checks did not have to be made. He stamped their passports and waved them through.

Paul and Miriam entered the country without fuss. As they walked to the baggage check out, the customs computer, part of a giant IBM network, was noiselessly processing millions of bytes of information which it shared with another computer in the air-conditioned basement of Mossad's Tel Aviv headquarters, two blocks north of Kikar Jabotinsky, the city's busiest roundabout.

When Paul's name was flagged on the computer's central processing unit, it was instantly diverted to a sidebar file headed 'Journalists—Non-Israeli' and matched against the names of all working journalists throughout the world. It determined whether stories recently written or broadcast had been friendly or critical of Israeli interests.

Paul's name was diverted along the 'no threat posed' branch of the 'friendly' tree within the program, and stopped there. No further surveillance was deemed necessary. No Mossad or Shin Bet internal security operative would be delegated to check his hotel room, keep track of whom he met or detail his movements.

But when Miriam's name was keyed into the computer, something very different happened. Unknown to the customs official, when the information of Miriam's arrival was logged in Mossad's headquarters, a red flag appeared on the screen. The operator keyed in the lognumber against her name, which instructed him to report her arrival to the watch commander. Yonathan Davidovitch looked up the instructions to see why Miriam's name and arrival were of interest to the Mossad hierarchy. The message was cryptic. Aparently she had sent a fax to a lawyer which required further investigation. His instruction was to inform Mossad's Office of Internal Security that she had arrived.

But the information trail did not end there. Many years previously, when the IBM network had been installed and programmed, another branch of the network had been created under a hidden password into the customs computer. Something of which even Mossad was unaware, it had been installed covertly by a German Jewish immigrant named Konrad Baumbauer, who had died shortly afterwards in a car accident. He had been indoctrinated by the NKVD after the war and was one of the men the young Colonel Petrovsky had organised to emigrate to Israel. His NKVD control found him a job in the fledgling electronics industry and ultimately, in 1972, into Mossad's computer operations as a programmer. This was despite extensive checks into Konrad's background by the security organisation, who found him to be a fanatical Zionist and loyal Israeli. They failed to discover his deeply buried double life. While installing the network, Konrad entered his own program under instructions from his KGB control. It was invisible even to regular de-bugging, unless activated by key command words which led to a flag fall mechanism. As soon as certain information in which the KGB was interested became available to Shin Bet, the resident program instantly sent it by optical fibre and microwave link to the Russian Embassy in Tel Aviv.

Since the demise of the KGB, Marshal Petrovsky had made alternative arrangements through an employee at the Embassy who was now on the lookout for any messages concerning people interested in the early years of Raphael Ben Ari.

Colonel Scherensky had requested immediate information concerning Miriam Davis and Paul Sinclair to be flagged should they arrive in Israel. When their names were flashed to the Russian Embassy, Oleg Volkovsky recognised them. He had been advised by Scherensky and Colonel-General Bukharin to report the moment they arrived.

When the signal came through, he made a print-out and hid it in his jacket pocket. One telephone call from a pay phone in the restaurant where he ate lunch was all that was necessary to organise a pick up.

By nightfall, Marshal Petrovsky's operatives in Israel knew that Paul Sinclair and Miriam Davis were staying at the King David Hotel in Jerusalem. Colonel Scherensky and General Bukharin breathed a huge sigh of relief that they now had control of the young couple.

They had searched Paul's flat and failed to uncover the photograph. Katya had tried to search the Davis woman's apartment but it had proved to be almost impossible in the amount of time she had been given. After the termination of the old man, Katya was instructed not to kill either Paul or Miriam. It was an on-the-spot decision, made because of the risk of Katya being discovered. At first Scherensky thought to terminate the reporter, using local talent in Sydney, perhaps an electrocution in his bathroom; but he had second thoughts. Better to keep both Paul and Miriam alive until the photo was recovered. Then he would have them killed. He and General Bukharin decided to institute an observation program in Sydney, but before it could get under way, the couple had disappeared. Scherensky decided not to raise the matter with the Marshal. From Miriam's fax he knew that she was planning to go to Israel, so he was forced to wait. Scherensky alerted his Israel-based operative to let him know when Paul and Miriam arrived. He discussed his decision with Bukharin. 'Forty-eight hours. If they haven't reappeared by then, we tell the Marshal.'

Within an hour of establishing their location, Scherensky's men had taken a room on the fifth floor of the hotel, right below Paul and Miriam's. A complete control centre was established by 7 p.m., incorporating telecommunications, optical fibre, visual and microwave listening devices.

A bundle of fibres was installed in the air-conditioning units in the bedroom and living room for later implantation, and a microwave antenna erected on a building opposite, able to monitor any conversations which took place on the balcony. Powerful binoculars had been brought into the building opposite, and a lip-reading expert assigned, in case Paul and Miriam were astute enough to whisper information. It was not easy for Marshal Petrovsky's operatives to do all this. Firstly they had to set up a surveillance operation without Shin Bet realising what they were doing; and perhaps more difficult was avoiding questions from Russian colleagues in the Embassy who were not loyal to Petrovsky.

The Marshal's operatives would now be able to listen to every conversation Paul and Miriam held, wherever they were within the hotel suite. When they left their suite, they were monitored within the hotel's public areas and followed around Jerusalem by Petrovsky's men.

All of Petrovsky's surveillance was conducted without Mossad realising what was happening in its own backyard. Mossad's interest lay in uncovering the reason for the dramatic increase in activity between diplomats in Arab capitals and well-known terrorists around the world. In the old days the KGB and funding of terrorism had gone hand in glove. Today, Russia did not have the money to train or nurture international mercenaries, fanatics or fundamentalists. It had enough within its own borders. Russia was not even on Mossad's agenda.

The King David Hotel was no stranger to terrorism itself. The old hotel, which had been the headquarters of the British Forces during the Mandate from 1945 to 1947, had also been the site of a bomb outrage. The explosion killed eighty-two people, including forty Arabs and seventeen Jews. A week later the British responded by hanging three suspected terrorists. The future Prime Minister Menachim Begin, in reprisal, ordered the execution of two British sergeants held captive by his organisation. Their bodies were booby-trapped and left hanging upside down. Raphael Ben Ari had been instrumental in planning and carrying out the massacre.

Once they had entered their room, Paul threw open the glass doors of the balcony to look over the rooftops. The silver and gold domes of the mosques in the Old City shone above the grey-white buildings, like decorations on a cake. Paul held tightly onto Miriam as they stepped outside. Her fear of heights was still present but she was comforted and reassured by the way he held on to her. As she looked at the skyline, impatient to see the ancient city, Miriam realised properly for the first time that she was in Israel and nowhere else. As her eyes surveyed the wide horizon, she grew desperately tired, her body exhausted from the long trip.

The Russians listening on the floor below heard Miriam turn to Paul and say, 'This is the most beautiful city on earth. It's so …' but the words failed to come.

'Told you you'd love it,' said Paul.

'Are you exhausted?'

'Why?' asked Paul.

Miriam moved her body closer to his, and nuzzled her head into his neck. 'I don't suppose you'd fancy making love would you?'

Paul looked at her in shock. 'But what about your time of mourning? I thought Jews weren't allowed to make love for months or something.'

Miriam smiled and shook her head. 'I don't know of any prohibition about making love while you're mourning for your grandfather. I'm already breaking the rules doing it with a *goy*. Let's face it, you can only burn in hell once.'

Paul squeezed closer to her. He prayed that this adventure in Israel would not see the end of their relationship. He had never prayed in Australia. Which God, he wondered, was listening? Miriam was now in the land of the Jews. Perhaps being in her ancestral land would change things.

Paul gently swung Miriam back into the room. Despite his tiredness from the flight, they walked into the privacy of their bedroom and made love on the king-size bed. They were observed by an ex-KGB colonel, a lieutenant, and two sergeants, all of whom clustered around the fourteen-inch colour television monitor. They were impressed by Miriam's figure and her energetic approach to sex. Miriam and Paul made love for twenty-five minutes. The colonel and his associates spent the time comparing the Australian approach to sex with that practised by Russian men and women.

Two days later, the Russians recorded a conversation which took place on the balcony of the King David Hotel. Although she still tended to grasp the railings tightly when she stood at its edge, Miriam enjoyed eating breakfast or having a late night drink out there. They were sitting at the metal and glass table covered with half-finished pina coladas and a tray of sandwiches discussing their day as the sun was sinking in the west. Its horizontal rays lit the tops of the white stone buildings, the metal cupolas and minarets of the mosques as though they were candles, illuminating the indigo summer sky. The city had looked exactly like this for a millennium, and yet every time Miriam saw its harsh sculptured beauty, she felt she was the only person ever to have witnessed it—that she enjoyed a private relationship between herself and Jerusalem—her cultural, spiritual and emotional altar.

She took a sip of her drink and looked at Paul. He seemed to be tense. It had been another day of frustration for him. Miriam had spent the day sightseeing and shopping, losing herself in the new experience of being in Israel. She was committed to phoning Nathan Loeb but kept on putting it off. She knew that the moment she phoned him, all the pain and grief of her recent past would come flooding back. Now she enjoyed the simple delights of being a tourist.

'You never thought it was going to be easy,' she said.

'There's always the hope of a break-through,' Paul said softly. 'It's a bit like being a gambler. The next bet will be the big win. I've interviewed a dozen people in the last two days and it's the same story from everyone. But you always hope that the next interview is going to pay dividends.'

'Is it worth pursuing? Maybe you should try another angle.'

Paul shrugged his shoulders.

'Maybe tomorrow you'll be luckier,' said Miriam.

'Luck! I spoke to historians, journalists, even a couple of guys that have written biographies of him, but even they don't know anything before he arrived here. These guys work at the Hebrew University. I told them what I wanted to know and they both burst out laughing. Apparently nobody has any such knowledge of him before he came here. Bearing in mind what we think he might have been involved in, it's hardly surprising, is it?'

Miriam drank the remains of a pina colada. 'That's bloody stupid. The man's Prime Minister. He can't keep his early life a secret. Somebody must have investigated him before he became leader.'

'Wanna bet? He hasn't told anybody anything about himself. Not even his closest allies know where he was born, or what happened in his early life. He says that he was always a Zionist at heart and that his real life began when he set foot on *Eretz Yisroel* and that anything he did before has no importance. He wrote in an article in *Paris Match* ...'

Paul opened up his notebook, and flipped through several pages until he found the quote. ' "I began to live when I first allowed the soil of *Eretz Yisroel* to run freely through my fingers. When I was on the boat coming over, I was in a limbo. Like being in a state of suspended animation between gestation and birth. I was born the moment I set foot on our holy soil. I've forgotten my life before. I've forgotten my parents. I've forgotten my family and my background. I'm not a product of Europe. I'm a product of Israel, and every breath, every thought, every action is devoted to Israel and her needs." ' Paul looked up from his notebook.

'It's very hard for you to understand that kind of statement,' said Miriam. 'It's hard for me as well, being Australian. If you're not a Jew ...'

Paul shifted uncomfortably in his chair. 'Miriam, just because I'm not Jewish ...'

She reached over and held his hand. 'Paul, you know what I think about Ben Ari. He's a hypocrite and much worse, for all we know. But somehow I think I can understand what he means. It's odd, isn't it? If what we know is true, then everything you've just read out would be sickening ... a travesty ...'

'And yet?'

'And yet it's the way I feel. I hate to admit having something in common with him but it's not until you touch the stones and realise the history of this place that you realise how much it's a part of every Jew.'

'Miriam, this difference between us is reaching a head. I was terrified of both of us coming over here, not only because of the danger but because of something else.'

Miriam looked at him and frowned.

'Even back home, my not being a Jew has been a barrier. It's never meant anything to me but it's always meant a lot to you ...'

'Paul, that's not ...' He held up his hand to stop her from speaking.

'It has, Miriam. For five years, you kept me away from your grandfather. Oh! Sure, you've made me welcome among your friends. But where it really counts ... with your grandfather, well, that's different. I had to wait for him to break the ice with me. I was scared that when we came over here you'd see me in a new light. Sort of ... not part of your life. Now I'm afraid that's coming true.'

She wanted to reassure him but she sank back into her chair and stayed silent.

Paul squeezed her hand. 'I know you're having difficulty being here, but ...'

Miriam put her finger to his lips. 'Just listen. Let me try and explain. For the first time I'm with my people, where I belong. Sydney isn't home to me. It's just a place where I live and work. Here I'm alive. I feel a sense of identity, a sense of security. Every fibre in my being feels charged with a sort of energy. I'm not ashamed of my Jewishness while I'm here. I don't feel I have to defend or apologise for it. I feel I want to reach out and touch people and say to them "I'm a Jew like you."'

Paul nodded. 'Were you ashamed of being a Jew in Sydney?'

'I felt as if I had to be better than other people because I'm a Jew. Or as if I have to explain myself and my actions because

I'm a Jew. I'm not a part of the Australian culture or the community. Oh, don't misunderstand me. It's been a wonderful country and I've loved every minute of growing up there. I've enjoyed my education, my friendships, my work—but I didn't realise until these last few days how isolated I felt from myself. As though I was too concerned about expressing my feelings, in case somebody said "That's because she's Jewish."'

Paul stood and walked to the balcony railings. Miriam stayed behind, away from the edge.

'Do you know what it's like, Paul, to have to be cleverer and better than everybody else and then to be an apologist for material possessions in case somebody says "Rich Jew"? You know something? Just a few days before I came here, somebody called me a "Jewish bitch" in my office. Can you believe it? After we lost six million souls at the hands of Hitler, some people still feel racially superior. I didn't realise until coming here that I was so much of an outsider living in a strange land.'

Paul was angry. 'How can you say that? Don't you know that you're part of my life, that I want to marry you because you're you and not because you're a lawyer or you're Jewish? Do you think that everyone treats you like that in Sydney? You've got dozens of friends who love you because of who you are, not because of any label attached to you.'

Miriam shook her head. 'Paul, being Jewish isn't a label. It's part of my being. Most of my friends are Jewish. You're one of the very few that's not. Everybody else is an acquaintance.'

Paul sat back in his chair. 'There's no satisfying you, is there, Miriam? You're determined to feel abused by the world because of what's happened to you. Just because you're in Israel you think you've found the answer to all your problems. Well you're wrong! You're going to have as many problems here as you have in Australia. It's not where you are but who you are that makes the difference.'

Miriam looked at her lover with sorrow. He would never understand. He hadn't suffered. For once in her life, she wasn't the outsider; he was. She would never change him, nor could he ever see into her. Together they looked at the darkening domes of the Old City as the Mediterranean swallowed the sun.

Paul had never experienced difficulties in belonging; he was a part of Sydney ... of Australian life. His education, friendships, family, profession were all rooted firmly in the Anglo-Saxon cultural soil. Yet Miriam felt disconnected from her background. He felt helpless, as if there was some force acting within her, pulling her away from him. He grasped the rail tightly in anger. Why couldn't he make her see that religion was only a small part of her life? That he was the major part of it. Yet she wouldn't see. She wouldn't open her eyes. He knew it could spell the end of their relationship. It was his greatest fear. A rift had opened, a rift called Judaism had grown between them and Miriam was already too far from him to bridge the gap. He realised that by bringing her to Israel he had lost her to another lover. One infinitely ancient and all-pervasive. If she had vacillated about marrying him in Sydney, her trip to Israel, amongst the family of Jews, was the straw which would ultimately break the back of their relationship.

He tried to comprehend what she was feeling. He must allow her to experience her range of emotions. His only hope left was that she would come back to him of her own accord. That would only happen if he didn't fight for her. He must allow Israel to prosecute its own weaknesses, to expose itself for what it was. He decided not to mention it again, but to treat her as a lover on a working holiday.

Later that night, over dinner in a nearby restaurant, and unwittingly away from the prying ears of Marshal Petrovsky's KGB operatives, Paul and Miriam talked about their search for information.

Paul was despondent. 'I think this trip is useless. It's just a stone wall wherever I go.'

'Well, what did you expect? Sometimes it takes years to find information if it's deeply buried. Even in my own work it's not always easy, but I've got the advantage of being able to sub-poena people and documents. You've just got to rely on making instant contacts and hoping they'll come good.'

Paul nodded. 'If only I could find a way into Mossad.'

'Paul, there's no Freedom of Information Act in Israel. It's not like the States. You can't just walk into an organisation like Mossad and say "Show me your files."'

He looked and smiled wryly. 'You sound like a character in my book.'

'I hope I'm a bit more three-dimensional than that.' She lifted her face to the ceiling and laughed. It had been a put-down but she knew Paul would take it in good stead. He took another sip of wine. A semillon from Rishon le Zion, it was thin and bodiless compared with the robust wines he liked to drink in Australia.

'Well, what are you going to do?'

He stared down at his fish and poked around at the white flesh with his fork.

'I actually don't know. Everything was so rushed before we came here. When you come to think of it, we've been pretty naive. If there was something hidden about Ben Ari, the CIA or the KGB would have found out about it by now. Are we just being stupid, or what?'

'We might be dealing with a unique set of circumstances here,' said Miriam. 'If what Zeida said is true then Ben Ari got rid of everybody who may have known him from his village. That not only says a lot about the man, but it could explain why people like the CIA haven't exposed him. Or if they did know about it, maybe they thought it was better to do nothing. You know how they let Mengele go, and half the Nazi war criminals. People who work for the CIA and the rest of them aren't patriots. They're prostitutes. They'll sell themselves to the highest bidder. And they've never heard the word "morality". They don't give a damn about people and information just as long as it suits their purpose.' Miriam took a bite of her fish. 'Do you think it's impossible to get any information on Ben Ari?'

Paul shook his head. 'It's in the lap of the gods. So often these things depend on luck. At the moment, we're only starting out, and we haven't been particularly lucky. You've just got to keep following the trail. Making sure that every detail is investigated. It isn't easy at the best of times in a foreign country. On our own, it's going to be bloody near impossible.'

'One thing it's done, it's made me put what happened in Australia into the back of my mind. I don't know whether that's good or not but at the moment I feel as though I'm travelling on a cloud of non-reality.'

The waiter took their plates away and gave them a dessert menu.

'Don't you think it's about time we started to find out more about the area where Ben Ari was born?' Paul said. 'One of the academics I interviewed yesterday told me that there's screeds of information in museums. Maybe you could investigate that tomorrow and find out more about Rawicz while I'm doing some interviewing.'

'It'll cost you,' she said with a cheeky grin.

Immediately after breakfast next morning, Paul went by taxi to the office of the Prime Minister's Secretariat. He knew it would be another wasted meeting. Miriam decided to hit the phones. She had delayed her call to Nathan Loeb long enough. Now it was time to phone him. A partner in the firm of Loeb and Loeb, Nathan was one of two Czechoslovakian brothers who had come to Israel in 1956. Miriam had spoken to him many times from Australia, but as she dialled his number she realised she didn't even know what he looked like.

'My dear,' he said when she got through, 'shalom and welcome to Israel. How nice to hear from you. Tell me, how are you enjoying your visit? It's your first, yes?'

'Yes, and I must tell you I'm having the most wonderful time of my life. It's the greatest place I've ever been in.' She sounded like an over-enthusiastic school girl but if Nathan was amused he was too much of a gentleman to show it.

'So, how long are you staying?'

Miriam told him, and spent several minutes in conversation about what she had seen and experienced. Finally, after accepting his invitation to lunch in two days time, she got to the point.

'Nathan, I sent you a fax about my grandfather and …'

'Miriam,' he said interrupting her. 'That fax was not a good thing to send. I think we had better talk face to face before you say anything else.'

'But it's so important. Can I see you today?'

The old man laughed. 'I assume it's about that *mumzer*? I'm very busy today, my darling. I've got somebody in the office with me. From what you wrote to me, though, I think it would be a good idea. I'll fit you in.'

Nathan gave her directions to his office. One floor below Miriam, the Marshal's operative recorded the same details. He tore the piece of paper off the pad and gave it to an Embassy chauffeur with the clipped instruction: 'See to this.'

'Do I deal with him immediately?'

'No. Wait till we know what they tell each other.'

An hour later, Miriam was sitting in Nathan's office, which wore its heritage in the furniture and carpets. The walls were stucco rendered, interrupted by credenzas carrying decades of collected objets d'art, and private mementos and bookcases creaking under the weight of dusty law books in three languages.

High on his walls were photographs of Nathan and his brother meeting faded Israeli politicians and business leaders, and panoramic views over the Jerusalem skyline. The room was not big enough to accommodate a coffee table and easy chairs, so they sat formally, he behind his desk, she in a battered chair in front of him. Nathan wore a short-sleeved white shirt and a grey and red necktie. Nobody in Israel, not even politicans, wore ties and Miriam appreciated the way in which he had dressed for the occasion.

'So, tell me what's so imperative?'

She smiled. 'I shouldn't have sent you that fax.'

'No, you shouldn't,' he said, but he wasn't chiding her. 'You're dealing with a very dangerous man in Mr Ben Ari. If he's not careful, he's going to get us all killed. Never mind this rubbish in the last few years when he's been so friendly to the rest of the world. I remember how he was when he first started in politics. You should have heard what he said at rallies and in the Knesset. I've never heard anybody as right-wing, almost neo-fascist as him.'

'I think that fax might have caused some problems,' Miriam said. She looked down at the floor before she finished the sentence. 'It could even have led to my grandfather being murdered.'

Nathan was too old to react in surprise. He had seen too many horrors, too many lights extinguished. He took on a proprietorial air. 'Explain yourself.'

Miriam clasped her hands. 'In the fax I mentioned the information my grandfather gave me. A short time later he was dead … '

Miriam's voice caught on the last word and she struggled to maintain her composure. Grief was only thinly buried.

'I wish you a long life,' Nathan said. 'I had no idea your grandfather, God rest his soul, had died. But why do you link it to the fax?'

'When my boyfriend and I were putting away his things we noticed that his suits had been slashed down the seams and his room had been searched.'

'But that may have been …'

'The same thing happened to Paul. His apartment was ransacked and his clothes were slashed in the same way. They must have been looking for the photograph.'

'They?'

She lowered her voice as though 'they' were listening. 'Mossad.'

'Mossad killed your grandfather?' he piped in surprise. He looked at her as the information slowly filtered in. Nathan picked up a glass absentmindedly and drank the remaining droplets of water.

'It's the only thing I can think of. They're trying to protect Ben Ari.'

'Are you saying that they read the fax you sent?'

'Does it surprise you? They must have a link to all lawyers' offices. It wouldn't surprise me. Paul is an investigative journalist. He says these things are possible.'

'I have done a lot of work with the civil liberties organisations and with Amnesty International in Israel. I have no doubt that Mossad scrutinises incoming faxes when they arrive at the Israel Telecommunications centre in Hadera. I'm not denying it happens, but to me it's unlikely. Anyway, we all know that Ben Ari is one of Mossad's best friends. But even so …'

'So it could have been them.'

'My darling, who am I to say? During the Intifada, Mossad, Shin Bet and especially the army were guilty of some terrible acts against Arabs. They broke arms with rocks. They locked up people without trial. They fire-bombed houses in reprisal. Ben Ari and his crew said it was all justifiable. Because the Arabs were doing it to us, they said we should do it to them. They don't particularly like me because I spoke out against them, sometimes at public meetings. But it's like water off a duck's back. They just keep doing it. We've become a conqueror now and it gives us the right.'

'But what can I do about it?' asked Miriam. 'How can I find out if they were involved?'

'Miriam, you'll never find out. Who knows what Mossad did in Europe after terrorists killed the Olympic athletes? Suddenly a bunch of Arabs are murdered or die mysterious deaths. Am I going to question it? It's divine retribution as far as I'm concerned. But that is different from killing an old man like your grandfather. The one thing I'll tell you is that nothing will come of this quest.'

'Nathan, you're a dear friend but you're wrong. What my *zeida* told me about Ben Ari needs to be exposed.'

Miriam told him her *zeida's* story in more detail and when she had finished Nathan shook his head in amazement. 'It can't be. No Jew would do that. Don't waste your first visit to Israel chasing spectres. Enjoy the country. Enjoy your heritage. Don't pursue this thing. Your grandfather was a confused old man. Of course Jews were Communists and there were even a few Fascists. But no Jew ever led a pogrom or acted like a Nazi. It's not in our soul.'

Miriam took a sip of coffee. How could she argue with a man like Nathan? He was so much like her grandfather used to be when she was a little girl. That same quietness, his gentle approach, even the receding hairline and deep-set eyes.

'Nathan, please help me. Where can I go to investigate?'

He shook his head slowly and gave in. 'The best place is a museum called the Institute of the Diaspora. It's near the Hadassa Hospital. We act on their behalf. My brother is very interested in the Hasidic movement although, thank God, he isn't Hasidic himself. Anyway, the head of the Institute is well known to us. Shlomo Gur. He speaks good English, so you should have no trouble with him. Use my name and he'll see you.'

Excited that she had a lead to follow, Miriam took the details down, confirmed she would have lunch with Nathan in two days time and asked whether she could phone Shlomo Gur to see him immediately.

After speaking to several secretaries, she finally got through. '*Nu!* So what can I do for you? Just because you know that *gonif*, Nathan, doesn't mean I'm going to help you!'

Miriam immediately liked the old man. If Nathan was a gentleman of the old school, Shlomo was of a school even older, a school of Talmudic wit and self-deprecation. It had produced the brilliant Jewish comedians that had made generations of Americans laugh at themselves from the late nineteenth century onwards. Shlomo, from just the little she had heard of his voice, sounded like the role model on which Jack Benny, Milton Berle, George Burns and Mel Brooks had built their careers.

Miriam decided not to discuss Raphael Ben Ari with Shlomo. Explaining that she wanted to find information about her *zeida*'s village, she made an appointment to see him at 11 o'clock.

The Institute of the Diaspora was a large white marble building, topped by the eight-branch candelabra or *menorah*, the traditional symbol of Jewish freedom and enlightenment. It had been funded by the wealthy New York Hasidic community of ultra-orthodox Jews, the bearded, ancient-looking men, famous on television screens throughout the world for their fur hats, ringlets and seventeenth-century clothing. The movement owed its origin to fifteenth- and sixteenth-century Eastern European mystics. Through the study of the meaning of the Bible, these men sought to explain why Jews had suffered for millennia. Its adherents believed that, through study and a mystical approach to Judaism, their lives could be made joyous. Ultra-orthodox Hasidic sects were often disliked, sometimes hated by other orthodox Jews, who saw them as superstitious and backward-looking reactionaries. However, their place in Israeli life was secure.

Miriam went back to the hotel and changed into a long-sleeved blouse, a below-the-knee skirt and low-heeled shoes before going on to see Shlomo Gur. Arriving by taxi, she climbed the white, greying steps and entered the dark, cool interior.

Once she had been shown into Shlomo Gur's office, she was surprised by his appearance and manner. He was nothing like she had imagined. Shlomo was a small, almost tiny, wizened man with a white beard, whose peppery white hair fell in fussy ringlets behind his ears, the blue skullcap above them almost his only piece of colour. His bent body was racked by arthritis and his movements were slow and painful. He was so different from the man to whom she had spoken on the phone that she thought there had been a mistake.

He sat down, deliberately not shaking her by the hand. Orthodox Jewish men do not like to touch women other than their wives. Miriam wondered how the interview would progress. Like a comedian who suddenly tells a joke and puts his audience at ease, Shlomo fixed her with his magnetic cloudy eyes and said, 'So, what's a nice girl like you doing in a place like this?'

Miriam burst out laughing. She quickly told him the origin of her grandfather and asked whether he knew any details about the Polish *shtetl*, home to a thousand or more Jews, called Chelmnoz. She told him it was near a small town called Rawicz. Shlomo sat back in his chair. It was far too big for his small body. He peered at the ceiling. 'Chelmnoz.' He said it several times, rolling it around in his mouth to make it become real. 'Wasn't that called Marowzitzki? I think that was the name.' He pressed the intercom on his desk.

'Shoshannah, my love. Please would you be so kind as to bring in Volume 2, I think it's Book 12, Mazaritcz's *History of the Polish Jews*. You'll find it in the library under 1910-1939.'

Within seconds Shoshannah had entered. She was roughly the same age as Miriam, but her dress indicated that she was the daughter of a Hasidic family. She smiled at Miriam and deposited the large, faded blue book on the desk in front of Shlomo. 'Let me see,' the old man said, and opened up the book, flipping through the index and turning to various references. Miriam sat in anticipation, looking at his gnarled fingers trying to turn one page at a time. She felt desperately sorry for the old man. Did his grand-daughter, too, feed him his chicken soup?

'Here. Here it is. Chelmnoz. *Nneh!* Home of ... Lubavicher Rebbe ... Eastern border with ... one time large community ...' He looked up, having found something to excite his interest. 'I thought so. They had a *yeshiva* there.'

Miriam nodded, already knowing that from her grandfather. 'Rabbi Luzovski was the chief *rebbe* in '29, '30, up to 1937, when he was killed in the pogroms. They accepted students from all over Poland and some came from Russia, some from Hungary. They trained rabbis who went to other communities …' The old man continued to read and mumble and Miriam strained to pick up his words. He became absorbed in what he was reading and forgot that she was still in the room.

Miriam decided to interrupt his rumination. 'Does it say what happened to the village, or its inhabitants?'

The old man looked up at her, trying to peer behind her mask of innocence, to see whether what he was going to say would upset her.

'My darling. It's like many other Polish or German communities. Some were wiped out before the war by pogroms. Some were wiped out during the war. People in Chelmnoz suffered. All Jews suffered. Chelmnoz was destroyed before the German invasion. Polish anti-Semites. At least it saved them from Hitler's gas chambers.'

'Does it say anything about survivors?'

The old man didn't even bother to look at the book. He already knew the answer. 'Unless they managed to escape in the middle of the 1930s, even perhaps as late as 1936 or 1937, they wouldn't have got out at all. They would have been killed by one of half a dozen right-wing organisations, or the Communists, or the Stalinists, or when the German army moved in. In this case it looks as if the entire village was wiped out. Your grandfather sounds lucky. Lucky he got out before.'

'An entire village! It's beyond my understanding. I just can't imagine how it could have happened,' she said.

The old man looked at her with sad eyes. 'Thank God you can't imagine, my dear. You're lucky that you know so little about those days.'

'I pray they never come again,' she said.

The old man caught her eye. 'Never come again?' he asked quizzically. 'Miriam, with the whole world looking on, Saddam Hussein wiped out 4,500 out of 5,000 villages in northern Iraq where the Kurds live. Don't think that brutality was confined to what happened before the war.'

She lowered her eyes in deference, an apology for her naivety.

'Were there any other survivors apart from my *zeida* and *bubba*?'

'Oh sure. There's bound to be others. I can look up who we've got registered in the diaspora, or living in Israel, who came from the village, but I don't think you're going to find many. Usually only a handful of families were clever enough to get out.'

The old man coughed. 'I know it sounds madness to you, but believe me, people in those days didn't think that a whole village could be exterminated. That sort of thing happened in the Middle Ages. That's why they stayed. They were always waiting for things to get better. The memories of the pogroms weren't powerful enough. And they always happened to other people. Back then, people who left villages like Chelmnoz were considered to be cowards. If only they had known then what we know now.' The old man sighed.

Shlomo took Miriam to an antechamber along whose walls were cabinets full of small deep drawers in which there were tens, perhaps hundreds of thousands of individual index cards. Collected before the days of computerisation, these cards were his children. They were the lives of his racial family. Having spent his existence steeped in the history of the Jews in the diaspora, Shlomo knew exactly where to go. He opened a drawer in a filing cabinet halfway across the room, and under the heading Chelmnoz found just two cards. One contained the name of Miriam's grandfather and grandmother. She was surprised to see her *zeida*'s writing on the card. He had obviously filled it in many years before in response to some questionnaire or other when he was living in Australia.

The other index card was from Haifa. Miriam jotted down the name and address.

'It's almost impossible to believe that there were just two families left out of a whole village.'

'Maybe there were more. These records are not complete. Sometimes people turn their back on the past. They don't like what they see. Me? I must know where I've come from to know where I'm going.'

'A whole population …'

'Three million Poles were killed by Hitler, my darling. Most from Warsaw, but an awful lot from villages.' The old man looked at her with the wisdom of the Prophets. 'Today we know. Then, who knew?'

She remained silent. She hated herself for having to mention his name in this place, as though it would sully these walls.

Miriam looked at Shlomo Gur surreptitiously. 'Your Prime Minister, Raphael Ben Ari. He was Polish, wasn't he?'

The old man nodded. 'Sure!'

'Any idea where he was from?'

Shlomo smiled. 'What do they say in America? That's the sixty-four dollar question. Darling, for years I've been cataloguing our race and its fate at the hands of the Nazis. You'd think the one man in the world, the one *yid* out of all the *yidden* that we should know about is the *Rosh ha Memshallah*, the Prime Minister of this country of ours. You'd think so, wouldn't you? Yes? No! He won't tell us. Years ago, I wrote to him when he was a *nebish* already, a nothing. Nobody knew about him except me. He didn't write back. Then I wrote to him when he became the Speaker of the House. So important. But still he didn't write back. So I phoned him. Why shouldn't I phone him; what, I can't phone the Prime Minister? And still he doesn't tell me. So I gave up.'

Miriam left the building, and took a *sherute* back to the King David Hotel. As she got into the taxi, the door of a nearby car opened and a middle-aged woman hailed another passing cab. Two men who had been scrutinising the building got out of their car and approached it slowly. They were planning their break-in that night. They had broken into the Museum ten years beforehand and removed a small number of files which related to the village in which Raphael Ben Ari had been born. Now they were about to tidy up some loose ends. One of the loose ends was forcing the old white-haired man who had accompanied Miriam to the steps of the building to reveal what he had discussed with her. And there was still the matter of what to do about the lawyer, Nathan Loeb.

✦✦✦

The Imam's private office in the western wing of the Al Kassim mosque was totally different in atmosphere and feeling from the interior of the mosque itself. While the vast colonnaded hall was cool, and suffused with a quiet blue light, cutting out the viciousness of the Baghdad sun, the Imam's private office was a madhouse of bustling inefficiency.

Mullahs, secretaries and advisers walked in and out at all times of the day and night, regardless of whether the Imam wanted peace, quiet or privacy.

On his low table, where the Imam discussed religious and secular matters with his associates, was a collection of newspapers. Most prominent was *al Ahram*, which carried the banner headline: 'United States Set to Retaliate for Magnum Airlines Outrage.'

The Imam was pleased. His plans were beginning to go well. Naturally, as a deeply religious man who believed passionately in the sanctity of human life, he was saddened by the carnage which the terrorist animals had wreaked at his instigation; and it was especially distressing for the Imam that the man chosen to lead the terrorist assaults was an infidel, rather than a man of the faith. The Imam had argued, but the man selected by the committee had particularly appropriate qualifications as a leader around whom all the coalition forces would rally.

Glancing once more at the papers, the Imam thought about the way in which Islam believed in the divinity of martyrdom, and those unfortunates who had plunged out of the sky. They would be close to the heart of Allah, even though they were not true believers.

It was war. Casualties were inevitable. The reaction of the United States was predictable. They had accused the Libyans and the Iraqis, and after a few more bomb outrages, or hostage takings, or hijackings, the American people would turn against Israel for its intransigence. Israel would rally to its own protection. It would become defensive and militaristic. And on the day that Israeli forces marched against Jordan, Syria or Egypt, they would surely lose. Then the Imam would reclaim all Jerusalem and all Palestine for Mohammed.

♜♜♜

In a large, fussily decorated five-roomed flat, three storeys above the busy Wilhelmstrasse in central Berlin, overlooking the vast Brandenburg Square, an old man sat and worried.

Newspapers in French, German, English, Russian and Spanish were spread out in front of him, on the imitation Louis XV dining table which dominated his private study. His maid was busily vacuuming the floor. With that noise, and the din of traffic outside his window, he found it very hard to concentrate.

He re-read the story on the front page of *Berliner Zeitung* and shivered with horror at the stance taken by the US.

Was this going to be like the retaliatory raids against Libya or Iraq in the '80s and early '90s? The raid on Libya had targeted Gaddafi, but like a fox in the desert he had been secreted away from Tripoli two hours beforehand and had escaped the fate of dozens of his countrymen. And had not Saddam Hussein strutted like a schoolyard bully, taunting and cocky, before the Americans made him a target?

The Americans, unaware of the facts, were blaming Libya and Iraq, but all the old man's instincts and contacts told him that the governments of those two nations had nothing to do with the destruction of the plane. And he felt certain that his old adversary, Genardy Arkyovich Petrovsky, had nothing to do with it either. It was too crass, too crude, too public for the Marshal.

No, the only explanation was that a group of terrorist fronts had got together somehow to force Israel into a preemptive strike. That's why the old man felt certain that the next attack would be either inside Israel, or against some Jewish target. He considered passing on his ideas to a former adversary, Eliezer

Sharom, currently head of Mossad. No! Sharom would have worked that out himself.

He stood up from his chair and walked towards his study window. Down there on Wilhelmstrasse a band of neo-Nazis was openly defying the government. They were brandishing replica machine pistols and plastic handguns and wearing swastikas on their arms, and screaming like feral dogs into the night sky about 'one people, one Germany'. The guns, including the occasional real Kalashnikov (purchased illegally from the entrepreneurial Russians) indicated the desire of the young neo-Nazis to become a private and dangerous armed militia. Their hatred of Poles, Serbs, Croats, blacks, yellows, Jews, anybody who had sought asylum in the re-unified Germany, was demonstrated nightly by their attacks against refugee hostels or shops owned by foreigners.

Had these morons no memory? Had they no shame? Did they not feel a collective horror at the inhumanity of Nazism just half a century before? They had learned nothing from the lessons of history and were repeating the same obscenity. And what had Petrovsky learned, the old man wondered?

What was he up to? First, there was that series of meetings with junior officers in his dacha on the Black Sea; then a couple more in his flat in Moscow. And now, his goons were following some hapless reporter and his girlfriend around Jerusalem. Why? What was going on?

CHAPTER FOURTEEN

By 9.00 p.m. both Paul and Miriam were exhausted. But it was not that pleasant exhaustion which comes from a satisfying day's work. Jerusalem in summer was enervating. It was high, dry and dusty. For days now, Jerusalem and other cities in Israel had been frustrating and tiring for residents and visitors alike because of the *champseen*, the desert wind which frayed nerves and drove people to distraction with its electric intensity. The *champseen* matched the political process. Every Israeli city suffered a series of pro- and anti-government marches which put security forces, police and medical services on tenterhooks. Added to the city's normal bedlam of shoppers, taxis, cars, army vehicles and public transport, it was enough to frustrate anyone, to drive friend against friend, neighbour against neighbour.

In the short time Paul and Miriam had been in the city, Israel had reacted for and against the high-handedness of its elected officials. In contradiction to the reputation of their country in the outside world, the people of Israel were a liberal, egalitarian-minded community, who treasured their democracy and its institutions. Possibly because of their biblical experiment with kingship and their devotion to the judges and prophets, the people were not easily led by authoritarianism or dictatorial behaviour. One Israeli Prime Minister had even told an American President how lucky he was only to rule 250 million people. 'I,' said the Israeli, 'rule five million Prime Ministers.'

And so the unusual sight of tens of thousands of placard-waving Jewish demonstrators chanting the plainsong of their anger disrupted cities all over the country and caused grief in Jewish communities around the world. Israel was in dichotomy. While most Israelis were demonstrating against Ben Ari, many others were demonstrating for him.

Miriam had arrived back at the King David Hotel earlier than Paul. She had a bath so that, by the time he arrived, her nerves were calmed. Over gin slings on the balcony overlooking the silhouette outlines of the Old City, they were able to compare notes.

She told him of the Institute's lack of information concerning former residents of Chelmnitz. 'I was able to track down the name of only one man left alive who used to live in the *shtetl*. Now that Bubba and Zeida are dead, I guess he's all there is left of what used to be a medium-size Jewish community. He lives in Haifa. I'll call him tonight, and visit him tomorrow, if he'll see me.'

Paul told her he'd had no luck at all in his quest. Nobody, anywhere, had any information concerning the early life, history, upbringing or experiences of the current Prime Minister of Israel.

'It's inconceivable. A head of government in any other country you can think of is known about from birth to death. Every detail. Where they were educated, married, who they played with, their affairs ... the lot. But here, in this model of democracy you call home, nobody knows a damn thing about the guy who runs the place.'

Miriam was embarrassed by his description of Israel and agreed that it was an odd situation. She also felt frustrated and annoyed. In the few days after she arrived in Israel she had revelled in being a tourist. For the past several days, she had spent much of her time in a fruitless quest for information about Ben Ari.

She had searched libraries, museums and spoken to a wide cross-section of people in the academic and legal fields, but all she had managed to track down was the one lead from the Institute of the Diaspora.

Her real goal, the reason she was in Israel, was to determine whether Mossad had murdered her grandfather. She phoned the Ministry of Defence but was referred to the press office. They gave her the run around. When she asked whether she could speak to somebody in Mossad, she was given a telephone number to ring. The number belonged to an official in another press office. 'Yes,' he said, he was attached to Mossad. No, he would not give her the name of somebody senior she could talk to. He advised her to approach a member of the Knesset and communicate on an official level. Miriam knew that would be a waste of time. Mossad's facade was impossible to breach. It was impregnable. But that was not her only difficulty.

Her enquiries had been made while constantly looking over her shoulder, talking guardedly on telephones, using lines which could not have been bugged, never walking alone down empty streets or alleyways. The memories of her last week in Australia were always with her. The naivety she had shown in sending the fax to Nathan would not be repeated.

As best he could, Paul had given her a thumbnail sketch of ways in which to avoid being scrutinised by the forces of officialdom. Miriam still had that night of horror clearly in her mind when she came to the realisation that her grandfather had been murdered. The same killer had come close to touching Paul and possibly even herself. Sometimes she felt sick when she thought about how close they had been to death. It was a reality that she had to deal with. Everyone in the street, people following her … even a passerby who stared at her … anyone could be an assassin from Mossad, or whichever spy service it was that had killed her *zeida*. The only way she could cope was to be vigilant, to concentrate her mind on the next task. She had hoped that by now she would have spoken to a senior officer in Mossad. To put him on notice. To let him know that she knew, so that she too became impregnable.

'But surely,' she asked, 'someone, somewhere must know about Ben Ari. With your interviews and my investigations, we've got to come up with something … haven't we?'

A rhetorical question, it remained unanswered. Paul and Miriam spent the remainder of the evening indoors. For once, the balcony was unpleasant. The *champseen* had stripped the calmness from the air.

Twelve hours later, and thousands of miles away, her question could have been answered by Colonel-General Bukharin. Assisted by Colonel Scherensky, he was personally responsible for the security arrangements to protect the anonymity of the Israeli Prime Minister. The job would continue to last for at least the next six to twelve months, until the Jericho Plan could be put into operation. They had recently taken over the cleansing task from a succession of ex-KGB agents who had spent the past forty years ensuring that their asset's past remained a secret. Now that a series of unpredicted but fortuitous events meant the Jericho Plan was about to be put into operation, it was imperative that Ben Ari's past did not rise up to haunt him before the endplay.

In retrospect it had been a clumsy and dangerous mistake to search the Australian reporter's apartment when they failed to find the photograph with the old man. The decision had been reactive, rather than planned. It was a mistake Colonel Scherensky would not make again. When he was forced to admit he had failed to locate the photograph, Bukharin reacted with clinical dispassion. He did not scream and shout, as others might have done, but assessed the situation, worked out a contingency plan and put it into operation. Scherensky didn't even waste time apologising for the failure of his field personnel. He should have left the reporter and his mistress alone, and merely set up a surveillance operation. All the break-in to Paul Sinclair's flat had done was arouse their suspicions. Keeping the situation under control would now be more difficult.

Once the young couple believed they were targets, they had become far more careful and circumspect. For some extraordinary reason, they believed that Mossad was interested in them. Bukharin could not fathom their hypothesis, but continued the observation in case they came close to exposing the identity of the asset. And soon Bukharin's men would recover the photograph.

Killing the reporter and the girl in Israel, with its attendant publicity, could be more problematical than leaving them alive.

Better to let them scurry around like rats, trying to dig up some dirt and find nothing. Scherensky had assured Bukharin that Paul and Miriam's search would prove fruitless. Eventually they would return home to Australia, convinced that the old man had made a tragic mistake and that the photo was not that of a young Ben Ari. If they happened to come too close to the truth, they would not survive to tell the tale.

The bungle in Sydney could also have wider repercussions for Bukharin. Neither the reporter nor his lawyer girlfriend was a fool. Although the asset's past had been effectively sanitised, it was always possible that the Australians could discover some detail which had been overlooked in the five decades of careful cocooning of Ben Ari. Being new to the files, Bukharin did not have Petrovsky's confidence in the asset's security.

♛♛♛

The question of Ben Ari's true identity didn't matter to Hassan al Sayyid, the Chairman pro tem. of the Central Command of the Combined Front of Arab Unity. Nor did it matter to the Libyan or the Egyptian gathered in Hassan's home in Tehran to discuss the second stage in the war against the Zionist aggressor. None of the terrorists gave a second thought to the Russians, either. They considered Russian influence to be dead and buried, of no further use in the struggle against Israel and Zionist imperialism.

The antipathy between terrorist organisations and the USSR had grown long before the demise of the Soviet Union in 1991. There had been major disaffection since the death of Andropov. In the Krushchev and Brezhnev years, Russia's Patrice Lumumba University had been the training ground for some of the world's most fanatical terrorists, and the KGB had sponsored arms, information, explosives, transportation, matériel, training, construction … anything to aid any government or group which was willing to act against the interests of the USA, the United Kingdom, France, West Germany, Italy, the fascist dictators of South America or any anti-Soviet country.

But with the ailing Andropov and Chernenko both too sick to care about terrorism, and with the advent of Gorbachev, Shevardnadze, Yeltsin and now the new leaders of the Commonwealth of Independent States, sponsorship of terrorism had ended, technical assistance ceased and education and support was truncated. Suddenly the IRA, the PFLP, the PLO, Abu Nidal, Hamas, the IRA and a dozen others who had not managed to tap the West's publicity machines had found themselves friendless in a hostile world.

Libya, Iran, North Korea, Syria and other rogue nations had stepped into the breach at the beginning with some money, but with the United States as the world's only superpower, many governments decided that it was better to maintain a low profile. The easy cohesion and the ready international affiliations and facilities needed to plan and commit a major terrorist act had gone. And for that, the terrorists blamed Russia, adding it to the demonology of imperialistic, fascistic, anti-humanitarian nations of the West.

The destruction of the Magnum Airlines jet had not only horrified world governments and their peoples. It galvanised the underworld of terrorism. Men and women who espoused fanatical causes read newspaper articles with interest as the United States and other Western countries used the media to warn their citizens of the coming dangers. Militants who had been dormant for years came out of their quiescence and began to hone their skills yet again in preparation for a decade of activity.

When the Imam had breathed life into the decaying body of international terrorism, he began a trail of action which would escalate of its own accord. Rhetoric was a part of the terrorist currency of Hassan al Sayyid and of the Central Command of the Combined Front of Arab Unity, and when they met to plan the second stage of their activities, the phrases flowed like water.

The terrorists were meeting as the world was still absorbing the new reality of global insecurity ushered in by the airline disaster. Their task was to decide how to capitalise upon the shock. The world-wide publicity they earned had been gratifying, but they knew from long experience that the second and subsequent acts of aggression must build upon the first. It was not enough to bring down another airliner. The second attack must be cleverer, or the world would become immune to danger.

They met in a squat stucco building in north Tehran, to decide what orders were to be given to the French-Algerian mercenary who had been chosen to act as the leader when the band of terrorists went into action. With so many groups, it had been decided to select no more than two fighters from each, to band together as a tight-knit cadre, a unit of supremely skilled mercenaries brought together for the specific purpose of following the directions of the Central Command. And because of the internal faction fighting, it was decided to employ a professional mercenary to lead the cadre. The choice had been easy.

To make strategic planning simple, a steering committee had been formed of three terrorists who represented the other groups. Hassan, being the chairman, had a coordinating role. He could not act in isolation, but his advice as one of the world's leading terrorist intellectuals and prime-movers was held in high regard by his colleagues. He surveyed the faces of the men seated around the table in his kitchen. On the formica table were a dozen or so pages of scribbled notes, plans, flow charts and maps, each one a piece of a murderous jigsaw. When complete, the picture would spell death and destruction for many Israelis. For the past couple of hours, the three terrorist leaders had been reviewing options and discussing feasibilities, each aiming at the right combination of greatest disruption with maximum publicity.

It was now time to focus world consciousness upon the true and anti-humanitarian aggressors, the Zionists living in Israel. The men, women and children who plunged from the sky several days earlier had not been imperialist soldiers, but every citizen in Israel was a genuine fighter and a valid target. By its nature, Israel was an armed camp. Every person within its borders was trained to fight against Arab interests. So Israelis were a more legitimate quarry than American civilians.

Israel was a cancer in the Middle East and the committee would surgically remove it, even if it meant killing umpteen people to achieve their goal. Most of Israel's external defences were currently weakened because of the need to redeploy its forces to control the internal divisions and demonstrations against Raphael Ben Ari. They were further strained by moving strategic units close to the border areas in case of Arab militarism. Hamas had also suddenly become active again, with well-planned attacks on Israeli settlements and *kibbutzim*. Followers of Hamas were also rioting almost constantly in the Occupied Territories. The Israeli military forces and police were stretched to breaking point.

'Our operatives say that Jaffa is the best way in by sea,' said Mansor Yazdani of the Iran-backed PDF. 'Tel Aviv at this time is too crowded, even at night, but south of Jaffa is less patrolled.'

'Why should we risk a sea-borne invasion when the Syrian front is so open to us?' said Hassan, thumping a map which showed the Golan Heights area, with current defences marked in red. 'For God's sake, understand that we haven't got the money to mount an expensive exercise. All we want to do is capture some world headlines and to push the Israelis over the brink. Not to try to win the war. That is for another day.'

The others nodded in agreement, but Mansor knew that a raid over Mount Hermon or the Golan Heights would not capture as many headlines as a massacre on a beachfront, despite the number of terrorist martyrs who would be created. He knew, though, that his militancy could push the mood of the meeting in Hassan's favour and so he fought to retain his moderation.

'My dear brother,' he said passively, 'the border defences are not to be underestimated. While we must reap the benefit of world attention at the moment, we must also succeed in our plan and not look like fools or incompetents. Too often, our raids have made us seem like children tottering around the playground. We've lost the publicity benefit. What we need, my brothers, is something dramatic and spectacular …'

'More dramatic than the loss of an airliner with all its passengers?' asked Hassan.

'Little could be more dramatic than that, but the second incident has got to focus as much attention as the first. It's not the number that's important, but the target and the way in which it's done. I'm not saying that we have to be more bloodthirsty than we have in the past, we just have to be more clever, more direct.'

'What are you talking about?' asked Ibrahim Bulbek, an Egyptian now resident in Syria and the lieutenant to the head of the PFLP. Ibrahim was a man whose directness was both verbal and physical.

Mansor stared at him, trying to find words. It wasn't easy for a man of his intellect to deal with a bull like Ibrahim. It was essential that he maintain his moderation. 'Brothers, it's hard to explain, as all I have is a feeling. What I'm saying to you is that if we bring down another airliner we'll only earn half the publicity. If we bring another one down after that, we'll earn a quarter. We have somehow to get underneath the Israelis' skin. We have to maximise the horror of the attack, both within Israel and also without.'

Hassan interrupted: 'Do you mean attack children, old people, an orphanage, or a hospital? What are you saying?'

Mansor shook his head, unable to answer. 'I'm expressing a feeling, not a conclusion. Perhaps it's our choice of weapons. Perhaps we should use chemical weapons. Perhaps we should use rockets or biological weapons. I don't know. I'm just saying that more killing will have fewer results.'

Mansor was met with blank expressions. Philosophers, even those who deal in death, often find their ideas hard to communicate to lesser minds.

After another ten minutes the men decided to have a break. Hassan's servant carried in trays of coffee and sweet pastries. It was a strange scene. Three of the world's most wanted and feared international terrorists, each responsible for the murders of hundreds of human beings, were drinking coffee and eating pastries like elderly ladies in a church meeting.

As he raised the demitasse to his lips, Hassan's eyes glanced down at an article in the Egyptian newspaper, *al Ahram*, about the Pharaoh Tutankhamen. The beginning of the article concerned the magnificence of ancient Egypt. Hassan grinned as the thought took shape in his mind. He had been mulling over Mansor's idea for drama rather than mayhem, and believed that he had the kernel of an idea, something which could blend the need for publicity with the guarantee of Israeli retaliation.

'Why don't we obliterate their past?' he asked.

The other men stopped drinking and looked questioningly.

'The Israelis are a people who claim history as their own. Why don't we cut them off from their ancestors?'

Ibrahim put down his coffee. 'What in the name of the Prophet are you talking about? Speak clearly, will you.'

A smile began to spread slowly over Mansor's face as comprehension dawned. Ibrahim stared at both of them, losing patience.

'Brother,' said Hassan, 'the Jews say they are the people of the Book. But the Book is five thousand years old. They were the subject of genocide by Adolf Hitler yet still they survived. They are a people with a racial memory. They trace their present suffering directly to the past. If we destroy their past, we cut them off from their present and their future.'

But Ibrahim still did not understand what Hassan was talking about. The blank look on his face forced Hassan to continue.

'At the moment, the world is feeling a strong anti-Israel sentiment. But the feeling is tempered by the perception that the Jews have suffered more than others as a result of the Holocaust …'

'Historians say that six million weren't killed in the gas ovens, that they died of typhus,' interrupted Ibrahim. But Hassan waved the protest away with his hand.

'This is not the issue, my brother.'

'Then what the fuck are you talking about?'

Mansor came to Hassan's rescue. 'For half a century,' he told Ibrahim, 'Israelis have been trading on their misery at the hands of the Germans. What Hassan is saying is that we should blow away their memories by blowing up the Museum of the Holocaust … get rid of their records, cut them off from their past, force them to forget their suffering … make them deal with today, rather than justify their actions because of yesterday.'

Ibrahim understood, but couldn't appreciate the enormity of the idea. 'A fucking museum. What's so important about that? We could blow up the Smithsonian in Washington, or the Louvre, and have more effect.'

Mansor was irritated by the man's stupidity but maintained his composure. 'Brother, do you not understand? The present of the Israeli Zionist is his past. Without his past, he has no present. He has no future. If we blow up this museum, obliterate his records and cut him off from the past, it will have the effect of isolating him spiritually. It will cut off his race memory. It will destroy the man from the inside …'

Hassan took up the theme with zeal: 'And more, it will create a massive rift between Jew and non-Jew in the diaspora. Wherever Jews live, not just in Israel, they all look towards Israel as the repository of that memory. Take it away and it will create a despondency around the Jewish world. Ultimately, Israel will react like a blind and drunken fighter, flailing around in a boxing ring.

'Brothers, I believe we have a plan which can generate maximum publicity. It will create a massive Jewish retaliation, and it can be blamed on Syria or Iraq. Not only that, but it can be accomplished without serious loss of our brothers' lives.'

♖♖♖

The Israeli sat at his white metal desk and shifted uncomfortably in his chair. He hadn't moved for the best part of three hours, not even to go to the toilet despite an urgent desire to do so. Every time he tried to stand, another phone would ring or a clerk would put yet another file on his desk. Damn and blast the bloody government for this stupidity. It was getting like Stalin's Russia. Security files on everybody. The CIA, the KGB both had been fanatical in the days of the Cold War, keeping voluminous files on their citizens. But Mossad had never been involved in the internal control of the citizens of the country. Its sister organisation Shin Bet may have kept files on dissidents for all he knew, but Danny Navar never for one moment suspected that he would be in that position. Mossad looked after Israel's external security—not internal—sod Ben Ari and those fascist bastards. What the hell did they think they were doing? He picked up a memorandum which had recently arrived and read it.

Miriam Davis, Sydney, Australia, arrived Tel Aviv airport 0950 today. Subject allowed through. Subject staying at King David Hotel. See security file K2-598-417.

He put the memo aside and went to the toilet. Two hours later the memo surfaced again. He entered the code number on his computer and its reference flashed up onto the screen. Apparently this girl had sent a fax to some Jerusalem lawyer claiming that Raphael Ben Ari was implicated in pre-war pogroms in Poland and had been a member of some extreme left-wing group. Danny burst out laughing. Why wasn't this confined to the *meshuggeneh* basket? Why did they have to fuck around with crap like this when Israel was falling apart at the seams and when his time should be spent running his agents in Syria, Egypt and Lebanon.

Ben Ari a Communist? A mass murderer? Who in their right mind could have thought that one up?

CHAPTER FIFTEEN

The Israeli Cabinet met in room 4D on the second level of the Knesset building in central Jerusalem every Monday afternoon while the parliament was in session. When it was in recess for religious or national holidays, the Prime Minister's 'kitchen cabinet' met to discuss day-to-day governmental matters. Only on a few occasions were serious decisions taken in the absence of the full body of parliament. When the Knesset was not in session, the country was run on a care and maintenance basis. But today was different. With Israel approaching a state of civil insurrection in the aftermath of Raphael Ben Ari's actions in Akrotiri, the cabinet had been called together to deal with the looming crisis and the darkening mood of the people. It was a smaller cabinet than normal, several ministers recently having resigned in protest. Most of those remaining put on a public face of solidarity, very different from their private anger at the plummeting state of Israel's fortunes in the eyes of the international community.

However this day was unlike any other that room 4D had seen in its dramatic history. Since the Prime Minister's destruction of the peace process the Knesset had been full of furious politicians, people shouting in corridors, enemies accusing each other and politicians hatching schemes. It was as though the building itself was alive with anger and tension. When the cabinet, a loose alignment of various political parties, met to chart Israel's course through tormented waters, no one knew for certain how the day would end.

Israel's system of proportional representation makes it, perhaps, the most ungovernable nation on earth. The interests represented in room 4D on any normal occasion were incompatible. There were socialists, capitalists, ultra-religious, irreligious, *kibbutzniks*, Arabists, anti-Arabists, pro-West, pro-East …

the entire national opinion was represented by one or more of the men or women who composed the government. And on this particular July day, Israel was not being governed.

The day started at 7 a.m., after another night of public demonstrations, marches, Israeli flag burning, stones being thrown at police, Arab uprisings in the occupied territories, and Israelis in Tel Aviv, Jerusalem and Haifa marching against the Ben Ari government.

When the fifteen cabinet members filed anxiously into the room in the breakfast hours, every man and woman knew that it was a turning point for the nation.

The moderates were there, hoping to persuade Ben Ari to step down as Prime Minister and allow their candidate to become the national coalition leader. Then steps would be taken immediately to overcome the guarded hostility in which Israel was increasingly being held.

The religious party had met the previous night to formulate their approach. They decided to back the Prime Minister, provided he promised that no religious obligations were exchanged in the pursuit of reconciliation.

The conservatives of Ben Ari's own party decided after much acrimony to back their Prime Minister, even though they were concerned that all the collateral which the Israel nation held in the minds of the people in the Western world was being squandered by Ben Ari's intemperance.

All in all, it was going to be one hell of a day of battling between the factions. Only three people were confident of the outcome. For a few days now they had been planning how to play this act out. One of Raphael Ben Ari's colleagues had reservations before they walked into the meeting. He asked, why have a cabinet meeting? Ben Ari smiled before walking into the cabinet room, saying, 'Every dog should have his day.'

Ben Ari and his Defence Minister Zalman Freiman walked into the room. Ben Ari, small and wearing confidence like a badge of office, looked at the assembled faces to see who was present. A number of the cabinet had resigned, to be replaced by lesser luminaries. He saw Mordecai Avit, the former Foreign Minister, who had resigned days after the peace conference. The leader of the moderate Hapoalim faction, he looked coldly and antagonistically at his old boss. At best, their relationship had only ever been professional. Never friendly. Now they would always be enemies. Avit was determined to use the opportunity of the Cabinet meeting to force Ben Ari to resign. He almost had the numbers and would rely on his rhetoric to convert a couple of waverers. If he was elected Prime Minister, so much the better. If not, he would work closely with whoever was selected to re-build Israel's stocks.

Clearing his throat, the Prime Minister called the meeting to order and introduced the only item on the agenda—what should be the Cabinet's response to the current rioting within the country?

Within minutes of the competing factions making their views known the room erupted into a cacophony of claims, counter-claims and accusations. Men and women were quickly standing in their places around the table, shaking fists, making their frustrations visible. Ben Ari had anticipated exactly what would happen. He sat back and let his colleagues talk themselves hoarse. At ten-thirty, he ordered a recess, and stewards brought in trays of coffee, sweet pastries and cookies in an effort to let tempers subside. It was nothing more than a ploy on Ben Ari's part. He had allowed his colleagues to vent their anger. The time had arrived to put the next phase of the Jericho Plan into operation. It had all been determined between him and his control. He and Moscow had determined the actions. He alone chose the timing.

When the trays of food and drink had been cleared by the military stewards, he re-convened the meeting. It was now 11 o'clock and there were still people anxious to make their feelings known. When the room was empty of everyone except ministers, Ben Ari called for silence. Six people around the table anticipated it would now be their turn to talk. They were mistaken. The diminutive Prime Minister looked matter-of-factly at each of his colleagues in rapid succession.

'*Chaverim* ... colleagues ... I have listened with interest and concern to your competing views. I know that a number of you still have to speak but I can anticipate without too much difficulty the arguments that you'll be using ...'

The ministers bridled at the anticipation and began to rise in unison, but Ben Ari held up his hand for silence. Then he banged the table. 'I have listened to you all morning. Your words have made a great impression on my heart but I have now come to a conclusion. The time has come to stop talking. The time has come to start acting. When I went to Cyprus I carried your instructions to seek the first step of a negotiated peace agreement with our Arab neighbours over the future of Jerusalem. I know that you were shocked and disheartened by what the rest of the world has called my intemperate language. I'm aware of the damage it has caused to our reputation.'

Ben Ari lowered his voice and continued to speak in the monotone of quiet command. His voice, in muted contrast to the anger in the room, was the epitome of control. But everyone remained silent. With an inevitability based on years of experience of the Israeli political method, everyone knew that something monumental was going to happen. They sat back to listen to Ben Ari, like defendants in a court of a Third World dictatorship attentive to a corrupt judge.

'Many of you here have asked why I went against the dictates of the cabinet and truncated the peace conference. Until now, I have not answered your criticisms. Now I will tell you.' Those in the room held their breath. Even the air-conditioning seemed to be quieter. 'If you had been in my shoes and looked at the faces of our enemies, and seen the smugness of the Americans, and the way in which the world is heading towards total United States domination over the rights of every country in this and other regions, you may have understood my anger.'

People were shifting uncomfortably in their chairs. 'Arrogant bastard,' someone muttered. Ben Ari took no notice. 'Russia was always our enemy,' he continued, 'but it was a balancing force against the imperialism of a dominant America. The

Arabs hated us when we were created as a nation, and they hate us today. That shouldn't surprise us. But the United States, our active friend, is forcing us into a position of giving away our birthright. I'm not prepared to sell the heritage of the Jewish nation for a short-term accommodation with countries who've vowed to destroy us. I don't care about our reputation in the rest of the world. I don't care if money dries up and we have to live off milk and honey until we can be self-sufficient. All I care about is that the Israeli nation shouldn't be imperilled at the instigation of an American President who is out to cast himself in the role of a world peacemaker for the purpose of his own re-election, and is willing to make pawns of us, sacrifices at the altar of his ambition.'

Mordecai Avit had had enough. As the most outspoken critic of Ben Ari, he had addressed dozens of public rallies in the last few weeks. His views were well-known. But he couldn't contain his anger at the table.

'You two-bit bastard,' he yelled. 'How dare you sit there and tell us the way we should behave as a nation? Who do you think you are, God Almighty? That you can tell your colleagues, your cabinet, what we should be doing. This is a democracy, Raphael. A democracy! Who the hell gave you the right to talk to us like that? You've caused more damage and harm to this nation in the past two weeks than 100 million Arabs in the past half century. How dare you go against the decisions of your cabinet, or do make decisions without consulting with me or with my colleagues?'

Ben Ari shook his head in sadness, seeing the hatred in which he was now held by the man with whom he had worked for the last few years.

'Mordecai, don't talk, just listen. We're going through a short, hard realignment of loyalties. The world has changed. We can no longer count on America. We have to make new treaties, new arrangements; arrangements which we, which Israel, dictates; not those dictated to us by an American President, or an American Secretary of State.'

Ben Ari paused and took a deep breath before continuing. 'Democracy is a funny institution, isn't it? It's a wonderful form of government when everything's going right. But when things begin to unravel then it becomes too unwieldy. I think the time has now come for us, in the short term, to cease our democratic institutions and for a strong captain to take the helm of this ship of ours.'

Everyone in the room stared at Ben Ari as something previously incomprehensible became inevitable.

'In the end you'll see that I'm right, but now isn't the time for discussion or for democracy. The time has now arrived when we must quell public disquiet and calm our citizens.

'As Prime Minister, I am exercising my judicial prerogative under the Articles of War to order a cessation of civil liberties within the country. I am appointing Yitzak Davidovitch as Minister of Internal Security. Zalman Freiman will continue in his post as Minister for Defence. He will meet with the Chief of Staff of the Israeli Defence Forces and invoke the emergency provisions of the Public Order Act which is currently being drawn up by members of my department.'

He looked at the stunned faces around the room. 'This Act revokes the right of habeas corpus, prohibits demonstrations of more than ten people meeting in any public place at any time and revokes the patents of authority granted to each of you by the President of the State of Israel. Furthermore, it ...'

The constraints were released. The dormant volcano erupted. Everyone shouted in anger.

'Are you crazy? What have you done?'

'We're not in a state of war, you fool. What Articles of War?'

'That's martial law!'

'How dare you ...'

'You can't do that without our permission!'

'That's unconstitutional ...'

'In the name of God, Raphael ...'

All his former colleagues were standing and gesticulating at the same time. The only people to remain seated were those

Ben Ari had just appointed to become his co-rulers. They were the only men not surprised by the turn of events.

Ben Ari sat and listened to the protests. He held up his hand for quiet but the screaming continued. People were shouting and shaking their fists, people with whom he had worked for the last dozens of years and whom he knew as colleagues, if not his friends. They now held such a blind hatred towards him that he felt his own safety was in peril. He moved his finger close to the panic button under the table in case he should need to summon the twelve-man security force he had instructed to wait outside. With his other hand, he rapped the table for silence, but it took a few minutes for some semblance of order to be restored.

'As Prime Minister, I and my two colleagues will take control of the country's external relationships. The Knesset will still meet to decide and debate internal matters, but the Ruling Council has the right to overturn any decisions which we do not believe accord with the needs of the country …

'You are hereby all dismissed from your cabinet posts until further notice. The provisions of the Martial Law Act will be signed into force immediately by His Excellency the President of Israel and will come into effect straight away. Martial law will be repealed upon the satisfaction of the Ruling Council of the State of Israel that public order and confidence have been restored.'

The room became quiet as the reality sank in. Many Israelis had discussed the possibility of the imposition of martial law, but nobody for one minute believed it would happen. Mordecai Avit looked at the little man at the end of the table and in a low voice, full of sadness, said: 'What an interesting group you are. Nebuchadnezzar, Pontius Pilate, and Herod. Tell me, the Knesset? Why are you keeping it sitting if it's going to be nothing more than a puppet parliament? The sort we sneer at when we read what's going on in Baghdad, Tehran and Damascus.'

Ben Ari looked at his former Foreign Minister and decided

not to answer. It was a signal to all the others that the end had finally arrived.

'If you would leave this room please, you are no longer a member of this Council. The army will escort you to your homes. You have no further function in the running of this country except as members of the Knesset. May I remind you, ladies and gentlemen, that you don't have the right to meet in public if there are ten people or more present, so any rallies will be dealt with severely by the army or the police. Do be assured that I'm very serious. I intend to get Israel back into order.'

The elderly leader of the Religious Party held up his hand for peace and asked: 'Ten people cannot meet, Raphael? That is a *minyan*? Can ten Jews not get together to pray?'

As their unofficial spokesman, Mordecai Avit rose slowly to his feet. He gathered his papers, an act reminiscent of an occasion not quite three tumultuous weeks earlier in Cyprus. 'You'll never get away with it. The people will rise up. They'll never stand for this. They didn't live through two thousand years of persecution just to be persecuted by you. The army won't tolerate it. They'll revolt. So will the police. You'll have nobody to carry out your edicts. Then we Jews will confine you to the scrapheap of history, like Nebuchadnezzar, and Haman, and Tiberius, and all the other fascists who tried to take from us our freedoms.'

Mordecai Avit spat the last few words as he stormed out of the door.

Rabbi Menachem Scholem shook his head in pity, while under his breath he said a prayer for peace in the country. There would be no peace now. He knew that this could, and probably would, lead to a civil war.

Sirens on army jeeps, half tracks, police vehicles and motor cycles screamed through the streets, the first indication to the general public that something was seriously wrong. Police, army, air force and other security services rushed to take up strategic positions. The offices of *Kol Yisroel* and newspapers were entered by the security forces. Control was taken from the lawful owners or managers and put into the hands of experienced army or police censors.

Patrols and road-blocks were set up outside buildings or population areas designated as being potential troublespots for the new martial law government. At midday the offices of Israeli television and radio found themselves supervised by new management. Instead of the advertised programs, funereal music was played throughout the early afternoon, much to the surprise of the information-glutted public. At two o'clock Raphael Ben Ari went on television and announced the reasons he had been forced to introduce martial law at midday.

At first, the nation was stunned beyond belief. People laughed at the words, but their laughter soon evaporated as the increased army and police presence on the streets gave truth to the fiction. Several hundred people gathered spontaneously in Kikar Dizengoff in Tel Aviv to talk, to discuss, to show their disgust. But the Prime Minister had anticipated this would happen and showed his strength from the beginning.

A phalanx of police vehicles drew up, surrounding the gathering crowd. A police inspector stepped out of his vehicle carrying a bullhorn. When he shouted at the crowd to disperse, he was met with catcalls, ridicule and derision, the Israeli answer to officialdom. But when he turned and ordered his men to draw their guns the crowd was shocked into a stupor.

There was a hesitancy amongst some of the policemen. None had yet faced a hostile crowd of fellow Jews. Most obeyed, realising that they had to carry out any command. The crowd fell into the silence of disbelief. It was unprecedented. To use force against a peaceful demonstration. And of Jews! The guns were cocked and again the police inspector shouted over his bullhorn for everybody to disperse. In Ivrit, English and Arabic, he reminded them of his governor's command. Not more than ten people were allowed to meet in any public place.

An elderly man stepped up onto the plinth of a statue of the Russian freedom fighter Vladimir Jabotinsky. Looking diminutive below the massive Zionist, he addressed the crowd. 'Is this Israel?' he screamed, tears in his eyes. 'Is this what we died for in Nazi Germany? So that a bunch of fascists in Jerusalem can take away our rights and freedoms? Rights and freedoms which we died for, so that never again would we live under the yoke of tyranny. The ovens of Auschwitz and Treblinka are testament to the suffering of the Jews who died to protect the laws of God. Are our brothers and sisters to have died for nothing? Until today, Israel was respected by the whole world as a humanitarian ...' but he got no further.

Three heavily armed policemen, their Uzi submachineguns pushing people aside, moved towards him, slipped handcuffs over the speaker's wrists and pulled him down. It was a catalyst, and galvanised the rest of the crowd. They shouted, whistled and screamed abuse at the policemen. At the order of the inspector, police handguns were fired into the air to restore a semblance of quiet. People panicked and ran from the square. The police, on orders, chased one of the more voluble groups of men and women. Catching them, they were handcuffed and pulled into police wagons.

Having virtually no experience of civil unrest or armed confrontation against their own police and army, the Jews who were gathered in Kikar Dizengoff acted like lost sheep. They wandered around in small groups, talking, crying and moaning over their loss of freedoms as their forefathers had done two thousand years earlier. The scene was reminiscent of the riots by Arabs against Jewish control in the Occupied Territories and the Gaza Strip ... no one ever thought they would see it in central Tel Aviv, Jerusalem or Haifa.

Men and women who had fought for their country in five wars sat in the gutter, shaking their heads in disbelief, cold and friendless in the hot July day. They were the new outcasts in their own land.

While the international community reeled at the imposition of martial law in a country which had always seemed the model of a popular democracy, the people of Israel spent the next couple of days in a state of numbness. When small groups of friends gathered, nobody talked of anything but the current state of events. Shops were closed, offices were unattended, synagogues were empty.

It was not as though martial law was a concept new to the Israelis. It had been imposed by them for more than a decade on the Arabs in the Occupied Territories. Most Israelis were familiar with curfews and limitations to civil rights when they applied to others. Never in the history of Israel, indeed not since the time of the British occupation under the pre-1948 Mandate, had an Israeli citizen lived under a state of martial law in peacetime.

Within hours of the announcement being made public, the United States, Britain, Germany, France and many other nations began to advise their citizens visiting or working in Israel to leave the country and to return home as early as possible. Tour operators contacted clients to say that their State Department or Foreign Office had issued a circular. Travel to Israel was to be undertaken in emergency only, and was considered extremely dangerous.

Ambassadors were recalled and arrangements made for diplomatic missions and consulates to be scaled down, in the hope that this would prompt the Israeli government to come to its senses and remove the stigma of de facto military rule.

But not everyone was despondent. The Imam in Baghdad was pleased, as were the various terrorists with whom he had recently had dealings; the governments of Iran, Syria and Iraq were cautiously happy, despite their concern about the re-emergence of Israel as a belligerent; Marshal Petrovsky, and his senior aides were happy that their plans were going along so well, and that their friend in the Middle East was now effectively running the country as a dictatorship. Soon, the third stage of the Jericho Plan could be put into operation.

Even President Jack Harrison was looking on the bright side of things as he sat in the Oval Office with Dick Charlesworth, head of the National Security Agency; Secretary of State John Dewhurst; Brett Whiteman, head of the CIA; and General Colin Manners, Supreme Commander of US Forces.

'Well,' said the President. 'At least the Jewish lobby here will have lost some of its teeth. For Chrissake, you can't move in this town without someone from the Anti-Defamation League or the United Israel Appeal or the Friends of Israel wanting you to listen to their incessant promotion of the country. Let's see how they react, now that our little friend over there has gone over the top.'

Dewhurst marvelled again at how his President managed only to see the small picture in every major event. He tried to steer the President's thoughts in the right direction. It was a risk. In the past the President had reacted curtly when Dewhurst, whom Harrison called 'Old Ivy League', appeared to be lecturing.

'Mr President, I think that the imposition of martial law today could be somewhat more significant than you realise. It's going to isolate Israel even more from world opinion, and make the new military government over there …'

'So what?' the President cut in. 'What the fuck does it matter if Israel becomes more isolated? They've been a fucking drain on the American people for the last forty years. We've pumped billions into their economy, fed them, armed them, been their friend and ally … well, all that's not so important now. Since the Soviets self-destructed we've cut closer ties with Egypt, Jordan and Syria. The CIS ain't going to back the Arabs. Why should we help the Israelis just because half the lawyers and politicians in town are Jewish?'

Brett Whiteman of the CIA, himself a Jew, was used to the President's plain speaking. It seemed endemic to Texans and middle Americans, but he knew that the man was just stating things as he saw them and was no anti-Semite. So he decided to answer: 'Because, Mr President, if we allow the situation to continue, without forcing Israel to back down, it could lead to border conflicts and war. We've already had one major terrorist incident, and I've got reports about terrorist meetings in Iraq, Iran and Egypt. We're trying to get a fix on what's going on.'

General Manners continued: 'Sir, I can understand your anger at Israel, but any terrorist activity against Israel could lead to a full scale war. The whole area is tinder dry at the moment. It could catch fire at any time. Anything could lead to war …'

The President stood to stretch his legs. He walked over to the trolley which his steward left and poured himself another cup of decaffeinated coffee. All eyes in the room were on him, waiting for his next thoughts.

'So what?' he asked, simply.

John Dewhurst looked at him quizzically. He didn't understand the President's question.

'So what?' the Secretary of State repeated.

'Yes, so what? So what if there's a war? So what if the Israelis have to fight again. Whose fault is that? Why do we have to be the world's policeman any more? We created an international peace opportunity … You bust your balls, John, trying to bring all them hokey little countries around the table … and what thanks? Ten minutes after the start, Ben Ari gets his dander up, tells 'em all to whistle Dixie and ruins two solid years of work.'

The President looked with amusement at the amazed faces of his Cabinet.

'I say again, so what? So there's another war. We'll pick up the pieces, I'm sure, but with the Soviets out of the way and with no one caring a fuck, so what?'

The men sat in silence, trying to see if there was a way for their boss to perceive the danger of what he was saying. At last, Dick Charlesworth spoke up. He was the President's closest adviser on security matters and the two had an easy, informal relationship.

'Jack, let me paint a scenario for you. If we don't intervene and put pressure on Israel to reverse its anti-democratic stance, something a lot more serious could happen than I think you realise. This isn't Vietnam or Cambodia. This is the Middle East.'

'What's your point, Dick?'

'Jack, if Israel's action leads to armed confrontation with one or more of its neighbours, we will be forced to act. This situation is different from any that has been in operation in the region before.'

The President shook his head. 'Why? Every fifteen minutes there's something going on in the Mid East. Some war or other.'

'This is different,' Charlesworth said. 'In the past, there's been a balance between Soviet and American interests. That balance has now shifted.'

'That's because the Soviets aren't in the game any more,' said the President.

'And that's given us the opportunity to sign trade, cultural and defence agreements with the Arabs. But we also have long-term commitments with Israel. If Israel attacks one of our treaty partners, or if they attack Israel, we'll have to choose sides. And that, Jack, will be the most difficult decision you'll ever have to make.'

The President began to interrupt, but Charlesworth continued to speak.

'Mr President, don't you see where this is leading? Since the rundown of the Soviet nuclear stockpile, those warheads have found their way into the Arab world. The Russians deny it but they've been desperate for cash and have been quietly marketing their nuclear stockpile via France and Pakistan to whoever wants to buy them.'

'Hey, come on,' the President interrupted. 'We've been working with the Russian Intelligence Service to track those warheads.'

'Maybe. But we all know that the Russian government is behind the sales. They're blaming the Russian mafia and rogue members of the Army but most of the cash ends up in the Kremlin coffers. Our new treaty accords with Russia have prevented us from speaking out too strongly, but things have changed. The new equations mean we've gotta be much more careful about what we say in future than we had to be in the past.'

Jack Harrison snorted. He was being lectured again. Damn it, he was the President.

'The reality is, Mr President, that Iraq, Syria and Iran are in a position to launch a limited nuclear strike against Israel if this situation gets further out of hand. Israel's got a massive nuclear stockpile that can be hooked up to artillery, rockets or planes in less than an hour. Jack, in a couple of weeks time, we could have a full-scale nuclear war on our hands.'

♜♜♜

Paul and Miriam stared at their television set, frustrated in their attempts to decipher what the presenters were saying. The broadcaster was speaking in the calm and measured tones of an actor reciting his lines. Although they could not understand his Hebrew, it seemed from the impassive look on the newsreader's face that the message he was reciting had been heavily censored. The pictures behind him showed demonstrations, stone throwing, placards, and angry mobs who had turned out onto the streets to protest against the imposition of martial law. The newsreader read with professional detachment, much like newsreaders used to recite the propaganda of Soviet Russia, or in broadcasts from Eastern Europe. But in Israel, where television censorship was anathema, the expression on the newsreader's face made it apparent that he was delivering the government line. The only parts of the broadcast which they understood were when the interview was with an overseas official or politician who spoke in English, his words translated into Hebrew on pull-through captions.

The situation reported on the television was nothing new to Paul and Miriam. Trying to get back to the King David that evening, their taxi had been stopped four times in the streets by armed militia who had demanded their papers, identification and passports. They had sat rigidly since early evening, having returned to the hotel after a day of watching police and military personnel break up demonstrations, or drag furious Israeli citizens screaming into the backs of paddy wagons for the crime of meeting together openly on the streets.

When she first returned to the hotel Miriam had been in a fury, shouting about 'Hitlerian dictatorships'. She had calmed down after a cool bath and two gin slings but her perceptions towards the country had changed dramatically. She hated what was going on. She feared that the action of the lunatic at the head of the government would ruin Israeli relations with the rest of the world for decades to come. Paul reminded her that he had tried to stop her coming to Israel. He had already phoned *The National* with an eyewitness account and had promised Jack Muir to keep in touch daily. He had braved the middle of the demonstrations while leaving Miriam at the peripheries in order to get an insider's view. He had been terrified as the crowds surged from street corner to street corner, but he knew it was his job. In all his years as a reporter, he had never been close to a demonstration or a war. It was uglier and more frightening than he had imagined.

Miriam's attention was diverted from the television when the telephone rang. She reached over and picked it up. A trip switch on the Ericsson telephone motherboard on the ground floor of the hotel was activated, which turned on a Nagra tape recorder in the listening post of the Russian operatives situated in the floor below Miriam and Paul's room. Within four seconds, the seven-digit telephone number from where the call had originated was displayed on an LCD screen attached to the recorder. A reverse telephone book, giving numbers with names, told the Russian listeners who was calling.

'Hello,' said Miriam.

'Miriam darling, it's Nathan. How are you?'

When she heard the warm voice of her friend, she felt relief.

In all the alienating frenzy of the demonstrations in the streets and the anger of the public, Miriam had forgotten that it was men like Nathan Loeb who had created the state of Israel from the desert.

'Nathan, how are you?' she asked happily.

'I'm fine, but I'm very anxious about this political situation that our wonderful Prime Minister seems to have got us into. It's just like Nazi Germany, isn't it? You know, yesterday I was living in a democracy with problems. Today life is a problem without the security of democracy. I can't believe it's the same country.' It was a statement which did not require an answer. 'But that's not the reason I'm calling you. I'm afraid I'll have to break our lunch date tomorrow.'

Miriam had forgotten all about having lunch with Nathan.

'Don't think it's got anything to do with Ben Ari. I wouldn't let scum like him spoil our date.'

Miriam smiled involuntarily.

' Do you remember old Shlomo Gur?'

Miriam frowned. His tone made her anticipate bad news.

'It's very sad. His staff found him in his car in the garage. A massive heart attack. The funeral is tomorrow and naturally I must pay my respects to him and his family.'

She had only met Shlomo for a couple of hours, but in that time he had been so warm, so gentle, so caring … so like her grandfather. Now he too was gone.

'Oh Nathan, I'm so sorry.'

Paul had been interpreting the conversation somewhat one-sidedly. He came over and put his arm around Miriam, not knowing the bad news but appreciating that she was in some distress. She held his hand. 'It's odd, you know,' Nathan continued. 'I thought he'd live forever. He was such a survivor. But I have some news which may cheer you up. Do you remember I told you about my brother Morrie and his connections with the Hasidic community?'

'Yes' answered Miriam.

'Well, I was talking to him about your late grandfather, may

God rest his blessed soul, and he mentioned to me that he knew of a rabbi who came from the same town as your *zeida*. Chelmnitz, wasn't it?.'

Miriam was confused. 'But I don't understand. Shlomo Gur told me that there was only one other survivor apart from Zeida. Some old man who lived in Haifa. He didn't mention anything about a rabbi.'

Nathan laughed. 'Miriam, Shlomo was a wonderful man but as a record keeper … *nyeh*. He lived in the nineteenth century. From what Morrie told me, everything was on card files. Anyway, this rabbi comes from the same place. Do you want to talk to him?'

'Of course,' said Miriam. 'Desperately. I phoned the family of the other survivor but he's been dead for five years. Then this martial law business happened and I haven't thought about things since then.'

'Well, before I give you this rabbi's name, promise me one thing. This man is a Hasidic rabbi … ultra, ultra-orthodox, very conservative … very strange. He lives in Mea Shearim where they throw stones at cars which drive nearby on the Sabbath and where they spit at girls who wear short-sleeved clothes.'

'Nathan, I know a lot about the Hasidic movement.'

'Knowing about them, *bubeleh*, is different from being with them. On television, you think that they're cute and fascinating. But they're incredibly narrow-minded and they just wouldn't understand a modern woman like you who …'

'Who what?'

'Miriam, don't make me say these things.'

She smiled. 'Out with it. Come on. I can always tell when I'm going to be lectured.'

She felt Nathan smiling over the phone. 'I was going to say that you're a modern woman who lives with a young gentleman who isn't Jewish. And you wear short dresses and you wear make-up and that type of thing.'

'I'm surprised at you, Nathan. Do you think I'd be so gauche as to insult the Hasidic community by going into their homes like I was dressed for the beach?'

'Remember that the Hasids don't live in this day and age, darling. They live in the eighteenth century. Please just accept him as a curiosity. Deal?'

Miriam smiled at Nathan's concern. 'Deal,' she said.

'His name is Rabbi Haim Gartenbaum'. She took down the rabbi's name, address and telephone number, thanked Nathan sincerely and promised to get together with him the following week. As Miriam put the phone down and told Paul all about her mixed fortunes, ten feet below them, two Russians at their listening post, who knew all about the death of Shlomo Gur, assessed this new information but were unaware of its significance. Their job was to report. Not to analyse.

However, Colonel-General Bukharin and Colonel Anatoly Scherensky immediately recognised the significance of the rabbi. When they had read the transcription of the tape recording two hours later, they determined to do something about him.

CHAPTER SIXTEEN

Colonel-General Mikhail Alexandrovich Bukharin was the third man to arrive at Marshal Petrovsky's apartment on Tvezskaya Prospekt that warm July evening.

As he entered the spacious, airy reception hall, he smelled the perfumed air. The normal Russian signature, the acrid smell of boiled cabbage, was absent. The apartment was so totally unlike his family's claustrophobic two rooms that he was again struck by the tenacious way in which the Marshal had managed to stay in the centre of Soviet power for half a century, always enjoying the trappings of privilege. In many ways, he exercised the same staying power as other *éminences grises* like Richelieu, Mazarin or Talleyrand. Each, in their time, had been the powers behind the throne. Each had survived the vicissitudes of high office under trying circumstances.

Not only had Petrovsky served Stalin, and every leader since, but he had managed to retain his standing in the eyes of the new Russian Republicans. Yet he enjoyed more than prestige. On the walls of the apartment were sumptuous Afghan and Persian rugs, antique Russian icons, paintings by minor French Impressionists. Every room portrayed the man's lifetime of acquisitions. Only a few classes of people were wealthy in Russia these days. One was the new entrepreneurs. Above them were the men of old wealth, such as Petrovsky, who had spirited away fortunes while in the service of the Communist Party. But the new Russian peerage, the zenith of wealth and power, were the Russian mafia bosses who ruled commerce and crime in all the major cities. Independent of government, they rose above the geographical divisions into which the former USSR had separated. They were immune to censure.

Petrovsky's wealth had been acquired by diverting vast sums of money during his time as Russia's number-one spymaster.

As the head of finances of the KGB, he opened numbered accounts in various Swiss banks to finance operations. He was accountable to no one. Most of the money, of course, had been handed back when the KGB was disbanded, but Petrovsky had retained one substantial account which not only funded the old man's lifestyle, but also supported the massive operation which he was currently mounting.

Settling down with a Courvoisier—very different to the Stolichnaya Pertsovka, or pepper vodka which he traditionally drank—Mikhail Alexandrovich talked amiably to Petrovsky and the two other men in the room. All were former colleagues. All knew each other well. In short order, the two final plotters arrived, one an ex-lieutenant-general in the GRU, now a lieutenant-general in the Ukrainian army, the other a colonel in what used to be the Eighth Directorate—wet affairs—of the KGB.

To the outside world, each man appeared to be a remnant of the past, warriors meeting to discuss old battles. To this most inner of all cabals, each was pivotal in Petrovsky's future scheme.

The men gathered around the Louis XVI table in the dining room of Petrovsky's apartment, where they could talk in absolute security. The whole apartment had been swept earlier that day for bugs, and none had been found. Neither the foreign spy services nor the security forces of the new Russian Republic were active in central Moscow these days, but it still paid to be cautious. Petrovsky invited those directing the Jericho Plan to his apartment for a briefing and a review. Each knew enough of the plan to enable him to operate in his section. Now Petrovsky needed to explain the entire concept to everyone as the plan neared the endgame.

'Gentlemen, an overview. For the past five years I have been working towards the culmination of something I began many years ago. Some of you at this table were involved with me when the plan was resurrected after being virtually dormant for over a decade. Your work then appeared to be insignificant and little more than doing me an odd favour or two for which you were well rewarded. I have slowly involved you more and more in the day-to-day operation of the plan as it nears its conclusion. Others of you who have joined much more recently …' he looked and nodded towards Bukharin, 'have been involved in the modelling of the later stages of the plan. Although some of you at this table may wonder why it was necessary for me to involve General Bukharin, let me assure you that his services as a strategist are required now that the plan has reached its final stages. It may strike you as odd that I did not involve him before. Be assured that it is only in the latter part of the plan that Bukharin's abilities were required. Now you are all needed to work as a team for the implementation of the final stage and to assure its smooth running.

'The Jericho Plan was conceived by me a lifetime ago. It is now time for me to explain to you its ramifications and why it is only now that its full measure can be put into effect.'

For twenty minutes, Marshal Petrovsky explained his life's pet project to his colleagues. He told them of the days shortly after the war when Russia had been liable to attack by American forces in Europe, who even proposed to unite the dispirited remnants of the German army and set it against Moscow. He explained the way in which the plan had been placed in abeyance during the days of Brezhnev, when Russian interests in the area lay exclusively with the Arab nations and it had looked as though Israel would be destroyed on three separate occasions. And he explained how the careful nurturing of his asset in Israel had finally flowered. Everyone at the meeting listened in awe. When he ended his synopsis, the room remained in silence until Colonel-General Bukharin slowly applauded. It was a measure of admiration and respect, not of sycophancy, and the others all joined in. The Marshal smiled and nodded to each one. He had been decorated a dozen times by Russia's most powerful men, but had rarely felt this degree of satisfaction. Somehow, the approbation of peers was of more value than that of his masters.

When the applause was at an end, the Marshal asked others for their reports. Anybody around the table who anticipated praise or compliments on the current success of their planning was sadly disappointed. Petrovsky did not waste time or effort on praise; he just wanted results.

Petrovsky looked towards Bukharin and nodded.

'Phase One of the Jericho Plan is proceeding particularly well and Phase Two has just been put into effect. Ben Ari has consolidated his power. The country is now ruled by a Ruling Council of himself and two other assets. The Knesset has become a puppet of the state ...'

'A bit like the Russian parliament,' commented Petrovsky.

Bukharin smiled and continued, 'He has arrested 120 people whose activities were deemed by him to be against the interests of the state. Eight people have been killed in clashes with soldiers, and the Israeli public is now reluctant to demonstrate. Any thought of civil disobedience becomes increasingly unlikely as time goes on. The army and police are also less likely to revolt.'

He cleared his throat before he continued. He was about to broach a difficult matter.

'That is not to say that the situation is calm. There is massive public resentment towards the Ruling Council, and currently there are, according to our operatives in Jerusalem and Tel Aviv, ten dissident groups actively plotting armed coups d'état. I should perhaps remind you that virtually every Israeli man and woman has been trained in the armed forces. Most are skilled reservists. To say that Israel has a civilian population is to do the men and women a disservice.'

Petrovsky waved his hand at Bukharin, telling him to skip the background details.

'We have extremely limited access to Ben Ari to inform him of the plots, but we believe Shin Bet has already informed him of them. In effect, we can tell him nothing new. Another situation is the way in which mainstream opinion is divided. We have seen in our own area the former Yugoslavia split along geo-nationalist lines and internecine warfare develop. It is possible that Israel could split into different groupings. Three, four … perhaps even more.'

Petrovsky interrupted. 'And how do you read reaction?'

'Better than we expected. A computer model has indicated that world reaction would be aggressive but non-interventionary. However, it appears that we underestimated the anger of the world and the degree to which Israel's ruination of the peace conference in Cyprus has alienated world opinion.'

'Underestimated?' asked Petrovsky.

'The Arab governments have been highly critical, which was to be expected. To date, however, they have failed to mobilise, except for neighbouring states who have moved a few divisions closer to the border, but interestingly, American reaction has been to isolate Israel from the world community, both in the United Nations and in private meetings with other governments. As you know, American tolerance of Israel has become increasingly thin. Now Harrison seems to be driving along the road of peace at any price, and to hell with the New York Jewish lobby. Without a USSR, America has no real need of Israel as a Western outpost. Its concordats with Jordan, Egypt, Saudi and Syria seem to have secured its place in the area. It no longer has to play policeman, though it is still desperately worried about Islamic fundamentalism coming out of Iraq and Iran.'

'Iraq?' said the Marshal. 'They're Sunni, not Shi'ite.'

Bukharin nodded. 'True, but one of the Shi'ite leaders happens to be an Iraqi. He's an Imam. Very reminiscent of the Ayatollah Khomeini.'

The Marshal nodded. 'And what will the Americans do?'

'It is likely that within the next three days John Dewhurst will impose United Nations-organised sanctions against Israel, cutting off all aid—financial and military, medical and humanitarian, and all trade. All favoured-nation status arrangements will be revoked, and most credits and financial advantages will have been removed within seventy-two hours. Bank accounts in Switzerland, London and America will have been frozen. Canada has refused to freeze its accounts, but there we are only talking about several billion United States dollars. Israel will effectively be in a state of siege.'

Petrovsky nodded. He already knew most of the information, but as coordinator of the cabal it was important that everybody was up to date with such detail.

'And the Arabs?'

'Their governments are playing a waiting game, but there has been a dramatic upsurge in terrorist activity. Some of our former terrorist assets have been extremely active. We are fairly certain that there have been meetings with the Imam in Baghdad, one of which resulted in the destruction of the Magnum airliner. We understand from one of our agents that there is currently a plan to blow up the Museum of the Holocaust in Jerusalem.'

Petrovsky was surprised. 'A museum?'

'Yes,' replied Bukharin.

Petrovsky frowned and shook his head. He would never understand Jews, Moslems or conservationists. He motioned for Bukharin to continue.

'The inspiration of terrorism was not predicted but it's quite obvious why they are reacting. The frontline states have backed away from armed involvement because of the Israeli nuclear threat—instead, money has been flowing into the Imam's account in the Banque Nationale de Paris in Geneva. Mainly from Egypt and Syria. He is obviously financing this terrorist activity. I personally find this unusual. Up until recently the Imam was not connected with Hezbollah or any similar groups. Perhaps he feels he can gain some short-term advantage. We have been unable to get our man in place among the terrorists and have to rely on a somewhat dubious double for what it is worth.'

Petrovsky interrupted. 'Aren't these people for sale? One source alone is very dangerous, as you would know!'

'Sir, they are for sale but we haven't had time to identify

them closely enough and approach them. This double agent is a man that I ran some time ago. He still supplies me with information from time to time. It is fortuitous that he was chosen as one of the terrorists in this little group of theirs. Nonetheless, despite the highly secretive nature of these operations, we are confident of properly infiltrating the group or groups within the next few weeks.'

'Does the terrorist activity concern you?' asked Petrovsky.

Bukharin thought for several seconds and answered slowly. 'I've entered their activities into the computer model and have come to the conclusion that their muddying of the waters is an advantage. In the model we have taken into account a variety of contingencies, of which a terrorist upsurge was one. Others include a Jewish backlash altering American foreign policy and the intervention of the United Nations. However, the terrorist groups coming together will ultimately assist us, provided …'

'Yes?' asked Marshal Petrovsky.

'Sir, terrorists are unpredictable at best. We have control of all aspects of the Jericho Plan with the single exception of these maniacs.'

'Then stop them,' said Petrovsky.

'That's not possible, Marshal. Without knowing what's happening from the inside, we can't predict what they are going to do next. Our own agent is not yet in place and relying on the double is dangerous.'

'We are at the stage where nothing can be left to chance,' Petrovsky said to the younger man. 'A top priority is to place our own man in this cabal. If you're unable to do this for any reason within the next two weeks, we must review the situation and exterminate the terrorists. Invite them to Moscow en masse for some reason and drown the lot of them in the Caspian.'

Bukharin ended his address. He had not told Marshal Petrovsky about the Australians. He would let his colleague broach the subject.

Petrovsky turned his attention to Colonel Scherensky: 'And

how is the protection of our relationship with Ben Ari?'

'Naturally there has been an increase in interest in his ante-cedents. The only problem on the horizon, which we are currently dealing with, is some reporter from Australia, of all places, whose mistress is keen to expose the identity of our asset. Apparently, her grandfather and grandmother slipped through the net before the Great Patriotic War. The old man had given the girl information which she is currently following up. They are a long way from proving anything, of course, but they have recently turned up in Jerusalem, presumably to get closer to Ben Ari's past.'

'What precisely have they found so far?' asked Petrovsky.

'They have uncovered a photograph of Ben Ari that we did not know about. Apparently it was taken by the girl's grand-father in Poland in 1937, but the old man has been dealt with.'

'Photograph? What photograph?' demanded Petrovsky.

'It is, we believe, in the possession of the reporter and his mistress. We have been unable to recover it, despite extensive security surveillance. We have searched his apartment in Sydney, as well as the apartment of the woman when she left her home to travel to Israel. Prior to her leaving Australia, we were unable to search her home. We have of course searched their hotel in Jerusalem. There is still no sign of the photo, but we are continuing our investigations.'

Petrovsky banged the table. 'Why was I not informed about this photograph? Are you seriously telling me that some Jewess knows about our asset's background?'

Bukharin and Scherensky looked down. Bukharin then coughed and said: 'Marshal. I was made aware of the existence of the picture. I decided to retrieve it. To date we have failed. I am in the process of reversing our failure.'

The glass-faced grandfather clock in the room ticked slowly on as Bukharin waited for the axe to fall. It didn't. Petrovsky said: 'Continue with your report, colonel.'

'As I said, our operatives in Israel have made a thorough search of their room and we are monitoring their conversations and activities every moment of the day. As a result of the investigations of the man and woman, we also found out that the Institute of the Diaspora in Jerusalem had some records which previous operatives had not cleared up. They have now done so. Apart from that, the girl and her lover are currently scratching around in fallow ground.'

'You were not brought here to talk platitudes, colonel,' said Petrovsky, reacting angrily. 'You were brought here to give details. I want to know precisely what she has found out. I am extremely concerned about your failure to retrieve this photo. I have spent my lifetime ensuring Ben Ari's security. At the most critical time, you tell me his security may have been breached.'

Colonel Scherensky felt his face flush. 'The man and woman are currently planning a visit to an old rabbi in Jerusalem who may have known Ben Ari's family. Apart from that, they have absolutely no leads. The rabbi will be taken care of, as will a lawyer in Jerusalem who we know was the girl's confidant. As for the reporter, he is talking to everybody and finding nothing. We know this because of our listening post in their hotel.'

'Why are we not taking care of these two Australians?' Petrovsky shouted. 'Why are they being allowed to continue to investigate?'

'Sir, the photo is currently hidden. Until we have recovered it, it could be too dangerous to terminate these people. Our only chance of recovery lies with our monitoring them. We also don't know who in Sydney has been told about the grandfather's past. The girl may have told friends, as indeed may the journalist. His newspaper editor would certainly know about it. Frankly, we originally discovered the existence of the photograph from a fax which the girl sent to Jerusalem. It is probable ... no, it is certain ... that she and the reporter would have informed people of the old man's allegations about the Prime Minister. If we take action against them now, their vague allegations may seem to have some validity and we will not be able to contain the damage.'

Petrovsky snorted contemptuously: 'I think you underestimate the amount of danger we are in and the damage that could have been done. Not informing me about this before is a most serious breach. I also hold you responsible, Bukharin.'

'Marshal,' Bukharin said, 'I knew of the reporter and the existence of this photograph. The colonel is not at fault. He reported its existence to me and I acted on my own initiative. If anybody is to blame, it's me.'

Petrovsky looked at Bukharin and shook his head. 'I'm not interested in blame, general, I'm interested in clearing up this problem. Nobody is to blame for the existence of the photograph but you and Scherensky are entirely to blame for failure to recover it and to terminate the man and woman. I want them terminated straight away.'

'That would be a grave mistake, your excellency,' said Bukharin. 'An old man's allegation and a naive girl and her boyfriend are trying to prove that something happened fifty years ago. They will seem ridiculous if we leave them alone. If we terminate them, their deaths will add credence to their story.'

The room again fell into silence as everyone around the table held his breath. Nobody had contradicted Marshal Petrovsky in fifty years. Bukharin felt desperately alone. He looked directly at the Marshal, who slowly nodded.

'Very well, Mikhail Alexandrovich. I will follow your advice.' Fifty years earlier, Josef Stalin had exhibited the same respect for Petrovsky's forthright manner as he now showed to Bukharin. In a softer tone, he said, 'Is there anything else you haven't told me?'

Colonel Scherensky continued. 'For some completely unimaginable reason, the Australians have privately blamed Mossad for the old grandfather's death.'

'Mossad? Are they stupid?' asked Petrovsky.

'I think its a measure of their naivety, Marshal,' said Scherensky.

'Nonetheless, I want that photograph found. I will not tolerate any reason or excuse if you fail. Is that clear, gentlemen?'

Both nodded. Scherensky was relieved that his report was

concluded. Other men around the table then presented their reports concerning their areas of responsibility.

When everyone had spoken, Petrovsky concluded the meeting with an overview.

'Well,' he said, 'except for the Sydney incident, things appear to be going splendidly. I must congratulate you all. Within the next few days we will see Israel further isolated. As a natural consequence she will look throughout the world for friendships. South Africa can be discounted now it has a black government. So her only avenue will be the Eastern bloc. Ben Ari will then have to turn somewhere in order to create global friendships.'

The men around the table grinned.

'I can confidently assure you that he will look towards the Russian Republic and seek some form of *rapprochement*. Our government's reaction will be very important, as will be America's reaction to the decision to send key personnel from the Russian Army into Israel as advisers.

'I am, as you know, working in this area with certain old friends who are currently in the Republic's government. They are as keen as I am to re-establish a foothold in the area and regain our prestige. I will report back to you as soon as the approach has been made to our President. Gentlemen, shall we retire to the lounge for some more brandy?'

♜♜♜

In his five-room flat in West Berlin, full of ersatz treasures, an old man, Andrei Alexandrovich Yezhov, read the inbound reports from Israel, Russia and Syria with increasing concern. What was Petrovsky up to? Yezhov's friends close to the Russian government had told him of strange goings on. There were private late night meetings between Petrovsky and some of the old guard who were still clinging to power, running the Russian Republic. These meetings were confirmed by his operatives in Moscow. Now his operatives in Israel had reported strange activities by the Russian embassy ... They had set up a covert operation to listen in to the activity of an Australian reporter and his girlfriend, and the wet division had been active, both in Australia and in Israel.

Petrovsky was planning something. He felt in his old bones that it had something to do with the state of martial law which had been declared by Ben Ari.

But why was Israel behaving in this unprecedented way? Why was Ben Ari acting like the dictator of some banana republic? Petrovsky had to be behind it, but why would Ben Ari dance to Petrovsky's tune?

None of it made sense, but it was too big a problem for Yezhov, whose men and women were unable to scrutinise things as closely as was necessary. He had to find out what the hell was going on with Petrovsky. The only way was to get some of his old friends currently in the Russian government to do a bit of eavesdropping on the Marshal.

♜♜♜

While Yezhov, a former Russian spymaster, was wondering about his nemesis, Marshal Petrovsky, Paul and Miriam were walking towards the cobbled streets and twisting laneways of Jerusalem's orthodox ghetto of Mea Shearim.

Miriam had opposed Paul's demand to accompany her, not because she felt any proprietorial rights towards the rabbi they were about to meet, but because Paul was obviously a Christian. His presence could affect the rabbi's willingness to help. Still, his insistence had won her over when she admitted her fear of the dangers in the streets of Jerusalem, where the police and army personnel were edgy and nervous.

As they walked towards the narrow, twisted streets of the fanatically orthodox Jewish ghetto, Miriam's sense of unease increased. She felt she was being scrutinised by disapproving eyes hidden behind curtains in the claustrophobic environment. She was wearing an ultra-conservative below-the-knees dress. Her arms were covered to her wrists, but she still felt like an anachronism, a chic modern woman walking through the corridors of the eighteenth century, as out of place in the streets of Mea Shearim as a Western tourist in a rural village in China.

And her unease was compounded because she was walking into this centre of ancient Jewishness with a gentile. Miriam felt alienated from him, as though Paul was a stranger and she was about to parade her innermost thoughts and most private rituals in front him.

The type of mystical Judaism practised in Mea Shearim was totally different from her style of secular Judaism. Hers was a religion based on family, heritage, learning and tradition … but the Judaism of Mea Shearim was that of the superstitious denizens of medieval Europe, the religion of mysticism, of hidden rituals and whispered incantations. It was a world Miriam had never sought to get to know, as foreign to her life as voodoo or witchcraft. If she felt uncomfortable entering the enclave of this Hasidic rabbinical family, she hated to imagine how Paul would feel. Miriam flushed in embarrassment at the anticipation of his alienation.

Her dread was punctuated by Paul's voice. 'How are these Hasidic Jews different from the ones in Sydney? Are they more religious or something?'

'There are all sorts of Hasidic Jews,' Miriam answered.

'Are they the ones that believe that modern Israel shouldn't exist until the coming of the Messiah? The ones that don't use the currency or the postage stamps and things like that?'

'No. They're the way-out branch called the *Naturei-Karta*. It means "Watchmen of the Tower". They don't recognise the government. But not all Hasidic Jews are like them. Most of them are quite reasonable.'

'Is Rabbi Gartenbaum one of them?'

'No. If he was, he probably wouldn't talk to me.'

'So tell me more about Hasidism. What kind of things do they believe in?'

'They don't believe in things,' she said defensively. 'It's a mystic movement, which seems to be growing in popularity every day. I think it's a crock of shit, but there are hundreds of thousands of believers in America and Israel, even Australia, who are passionately devoted to it.'

'Are these the guys that go around dressed in strange clothes, looking like some Middle Ages throwback … the ones you see praying at the Wailing Wall?' he asked.

'That's them,' said Miriam. 'People like me, even Jews much more religious and orthodox than me, dislike them, sometimes hate them. I see them as a sort of antediluvian curio, people who have somehow taken a narrow branch of Judaism and diverted its purity from the mainstream.'

Paul was fascinated. He had always been amazed by the way otherwise worldly men and women, many with good educations, could submit themselves to the ritualistic dictates of ancient times. Since boyhood, he had watched in awe as his parents and their friends genuflected in heartfelt worship on a Sunday, only to lie, cheat and fall down drunk, swearing and cursing during the rest of the week.

He was interested in Catholicism, and mystified by Islam. And the Jews were, perhaps, the most difficult and fascinating people he knew.

The Western perception of Jews was so totally at odds with the earthy reality. Jews had contributed so much to Western thought, culture and progress, yet were exclusive about admitting any outsider into their ranks. They bred resentment, hostility and envy because of their exclusiveness, yet it was because of it that they had remained close and coherent over nearly four millennia.

When Paul got to know what was behind the closed-door facade of Miriam's Jewishness, what he found both baffled and pleased him. As a non-practising Christian, he could look at his own religion dispassionately and take the best that it had to offer. Its art, its history, its moral strength. And he rejected what he found silly, superstitious or simply inconvenient. It was like a friendly lapdog. But even though Miriam decried the Hasids, she would not disown them.

Somehow, she reminded him of Ruth the Moabitess, a

modern woman, yet one who refused to turn her back on the ways of the ancients, and said to her elderly mother-in-law Naomi: 'Whither thou goest, I will go; and where thou lodgest, I will lodge: thy people shall be my people and thy God, my God.'

He smiled when he compared Miriam to Ruth. It was a particularly apt analogy, as they walked towards the fanatically orthodox area of Judaism. Apt because the author of the Book of Ruth was quietly and subtly making a stand against the prohibition against marriages between Jews and Gentiles, which had been introduced five hundred years before Christ by Ezra and Nehemiah to retain the racial purity of the Jews.

'But what's Hasidism all about?' he asked. 'How does it differ from the type of Judaism you follow?'

Miriam hesitated before answering. She only knew of them in theory, and she didn't associate with them in Sydney. They were an exclusive and idiosyncratic group. But she knew a fair amount about them from general reading, enough to give Paul more than just a thumbnail sketch.

'Hundreds of years ago, Israel ben Eliezer—a lime digger in Poland, I think he was—was searching for an explanation of why the Jews were so mercilessly tortured throughout history. Because he was so pious and righteous, he soon became known as the Ba'al Shem Tov, or the Master of the Good Name. Anyway, what he believed was that traditional rabbinical scholarship and teachings needed something new, something more than the ascetic withdrawal from the world; it needed to face up to the fact that God was in everything and everybody, not just in books. That true, real worship is in every human activity.'

'Sounds pretty reasonable,' said Paul. By now, they were well into the ghetto. The dress of the people had changed to the more conservative, traditional dress of middle-aged Europeans … though the frockcoats, fur hats and leggings of the Hasidic sect were not yet in evidence.

'Yes, at first sight, it does sound reasonable. How they interpreted this need to come closer to God was what brought them into conflict with mainstream Judaism.'

'Why? What did they do?'

'Its a bit hard to explain,' said Miriam, again feeling defensive, remembering the way in which her grandfather had disparaged them for being superstitious, while at the same time invoking his own curses and dybbuks and other demons.

'Hard, or embarrassing?'

Miriam remained silent for some moments, while they walked deeper into the heart of Mea Shearim. They could see its streets narrowing, compounding their sense of unease and uncertainty. When they finally crossed the barrier—a psychological barrier which divided the eighteenth century from the twentieth century—they both felt more like voyeurs than travellers in time, as though they had stumbled on an esoteric world which they could easily taint by their presence.

The streets were full of little children, dressed in grey, loose-fitting clothes, leggings, breeches; the girls wearing headscarves, the boys wearing skull caps and sporting ringlets of long curly hair behind their ears or down the sides of their cheeks. Men and women who had been huddling on street corners, or talking together in doorways, stopped and looked at Paul and Miriam as they walked deeper and deeper into the ghetto.

Miriam felt a need to reach out and hold Paul's hand, to feel the comfort of a person who shared her world, her values. But she knew that touching him would be viewed with hostility by the residents and so she maintained a respectable distance.

Anticipating her unease, Paul tried to focus her mind back on their conversation.

'So what was the problem between the Hasidic community and the mainstream rabbis?'

Miriam glanced at the men and women who were looking at her with a mixture of curiosity and enmity. She struggled to remember the details of the Hasidic tradition which she had learned from her grandparents when she was a young teenager. What she most clearly remembered was her grandfather's disdain for the sect. 'Superstitious people who treat their *rebbe* like he was the Messiah. They worship the crumbs which fall from his plate. Disgusting!' he had said. That was many years ago. Recently, the Lubavitcher Rebbe, leader of one of the largest groups of Hasids, had been touted by his followers as the Messiah, something viewed with horror and embarrassment by mainstream Jews throughout the world.

She tried to put aside her prejudices and retain some objectivity. 'They tried to get closer to God through piety, which they thought was more important than scholarship. They thought they could get to know God in everything they did. They taught that everybody, however poor or ignorant, could get near to Him if they were enthusiastic and had an open, honest and trusting heart.'

People emerged from their houses to stare at the young couple. Miriam wondered how much trust there was among Hasids today. Paul stared back at them with equal curiosity, not cowed into embarrassment. Miriam stared at the ground.

'And they translated that enthusiasm into their daily lives, even to eating, drinking, dancing, walking, talking,' she continued.

'It sounds reasonable to me,' said Paul, impressed with the philosophy. 'I can't see why the orthodox Jews couldn't accept it.'

'Because Judaism has always been the religion of study and scholarship. Learn more about the Talmud and you'll be closer to piety, and therefore closer to God. Suddenly, there was this popular breakaway movement of poor, ignorant, pious people, dancing wildly, ecstatically, getting drunk, doing all sorts of oddball things and saying that they were getting closer to God. Middle European rabbis looked on with horror, and eventually excommunicated the entire movement.'

'Just for being happy?'

'No, not just for that. As the movement developed, they became more and more rowdy. They said that certain of their most holy leaders had the power to talk and intercede directly with God. That was blasphemy, and totally against the Jewish code.'

'Is that why the rabbi's followers in New York claim him to be the Messiah?' asked Paul.

Miriam turned quickly to Paul to shut him up: 'Don't mention that here. He never claimed he was the Messiah. It was his followers who did, and it caused terrible trouble. It's still a red hot issue'.

As they walked from the Street of the Prophets, they were greeted by a prominent sign on a post, written in English, Hebrew and Yiddish. Paul read it carefully.

JEWISH DAUGHTER!
The Torah obligates you to dress
with modesty. We do not tolerate
people passing through our streets
immodestly dressed.
signed: Committee for Guarding Modesty

Paul was amused, but sensed the embarrassment of Miriam who tried to ignore the sign. Without saying so, she knew that the next hour or so were going to be very difficult.

In retrospect, she could not have been more wrong.

Rabbi Haim Gartenbaum was a man surrounded by the entirety of his life. In his tiny five-roomed house were four generations of his family. There was his wife, plump, matronly, grey-haired and pallid-skinned, dressed in a floral-print frock and headscarf—looking as though she had just stepped out of a pre-war European village—daughters and sons, daughters-in-law and sons-in-law, grandchildren and great-grandchildren. All talked and gesticulated animatedly, clamouring for the attention of the rabbi, who looked on in benign amusement, stroking a head here, kissing a cheek there, whispering in an ear, or wagging a finger in reproof.

The elderly rabbi, whose bushy grey-white beard hid much

of the lower part of his face, neck and shoulders, sat in a decaying armchair beside a fireplace and acknowledged the two strangers who stood framed in his doorway.

Miriam had telephoned the rabbi the previous day to make an appointment. He had advised her to visit him between two and three in the afternoon, when, he said, things quietened down. Miriam knew about the lifestyle of Hasidic rabbis. All day, every day, dozens, sometimes hundreds of people came to their houses to talk, seek advice, ask counsel, settle disputes, argue, debate … an endless round of socio-religious intercourse. The most famous of all, the venerated, deified dynastic head of the Lubavitcher movement, who lived in the Williamsburg district of Brooklyn in New York, received dignitaries, other rabbis, general visitors, acolytes, and took telephone calls, all day and all night, pausing only to think, write, eat and catch a few brief moments of sleep.

It was the rule rather than the exception that strangers would turn up at the home of an Hasidic rabbi, and so without questioning, the rabbi's wife summoned them in, sat them at the dining table, and placed an unrequested poppyseed cake and a cup of coffee in front of each of them.

Miriam introduced herself and Paul to the rabbi, whose heavy, hooded eyes had retained their vitality.

He held up his hand: *'Sprechen sie Yiddish?'*

Miriam shook her head. 'My *zeida* spoke Yiddish,' she said, 'but I'm afraid I don't. Neither does my companion.'

'At medaberet Ivrit?'

Again, Miriam confessed that she didn't speak any Hebrew. The old man nodded.

'So, we will continue in English', he said, the hint of an American accent audible within the heavy Polish cadences.

Well, thought Miriam, the clever old bugger has just put me in a position of inferiority. This, she knew, was a typically Hasidic approach to life, the implication that they had some esoteric secret which non-Hasids didn't share, and so maintained a superiority, a sort of spiritual one-upmanship.

'So, daughter, why have you come to see me?'

Miriam spent the next few minutes explaining about her grandfather's and grandmother's early life together in the village of Chelmnitz. She didn't mention Ben Ari. She wondered whether the rabbi knew the name Samuelson.

'Your grandfather was Samuelson! So, you are married to this man?' he asked, pointing to Paul.

'No. We're not married. We're friends.'

The rabbi smiled: 'Your name is Davis; you're unmarried; so your father is Davis and yet your grandfather is a Samuelson.'

Miriam was beginning to get defensive.

'Yes, my father changed his name because "Davis" …'

'Sounds less Jewish,' interrupted the rabbi.

Miriam was starting to feel anger, but was forced to submerge her defensiveness out of respect for the old rabbi. His gentle smile showed that there was an absence of malice.

'No matter,' he said. 'Now, the Samuelson family from Chelmnitz … Samuelson … Samuelson …' the rabbi rolled the name around his tongue, searching his memory.

'You know, I left Chelmnitz in 1933 in order to go to Warsaw and study at *yeshiva*. As soon as war broke out, I couldn't get back to my village and I was interned in a concentration camp. By God's grace I was saved, and after the war travelled to America to study under Rabbi Fishman of blessed memory. Then I came to Israel, so I haven't thought about Chelmnitz for … what … fifty years. My family, God rest their souls, were wiped out. I have no connections there. But let me think.'

Paul interrupted his deliberations: 'Rabbi, may I ask a question?'

The rabbi looked at him curiously, then nodded.

'Miriam spent quite some time recently in the Museum of the Diaspora, searching the records of people who lived in your village. Yet your name was not included. Was that an error?'

The rabbi shrugged his shoulders. 'Maybe, maybe not. You know, many of us in this community don't have very much to do with the State of Israel. We accept it but we don't thank God for it. We believe that Israel will be properly reborn when the Messiah arrives, and so far He hasn't come, despite what the *meshuggeneh* Lubavs say. We don't bother the Israelis, and they don't bother us.'

The rabbi could see that Paul was confused. 'But Rabbi, the Institute is run by people like you, Hasidic people.'

'Hasids, maybe. But not like us. The Institute was set up by the Lubavs. We follow a different *rebbe*.'

Uninterested in the petty jealousies between one branch of the Hasids and another, Miriam interrupted, unable to restrain her curiosity any longer: 'Do you remember my family in the village?'

The rabbi's family scurried around the house as the old man stroked his beard, thinking back through more than half a century.

'Wasn't there some butcher called Smuelshon in Chelmnitz …?'

Miriam's heart raced. 'Yes, it was Anglicised to Samuelson when he came to Australia. His own father was a butcher. I don't know if he was the only one, or if there were many, but there couldn't have been more than one butcher called by that name.'

Suddenly, the emotions poured out … she had found a link to her *zeida*'s family.

'What do you remember of the family? Was it a large one? Were they religious? Who else was there? What part did they play in *shtetl* life?'

The rabbi smiled at her enthusiasm. So often, young people were fascinated by the lives of their European parents and grandparents. Yet just as often, the older generation closed off the horrors of life in the old country, trying to shut out the memories and protect their children from the past. But before he answered Miriam, Rabbi Gartenbaum inexplicably turned his attention to Paul.

'And you, mister. What do you say to all this?' he asked,

waving his arm proprietorially around the house. 'Must be very different from the life you lead in Australia.'

Paul knew the rabbi was trying to find out more about the couple before divulging any further information. Despite Miriam's reluctance, Paul decided to be totally open with him. He recognised him as a man who would easily identify dissembling.

'You may have gathered, Rabbi, that I'm not Jewish. But I'm fascinated by the lifestyle of the very religious Jews. It's so totally different to the lifestyles of people in my own religion.'

The rabbi smiled at Paul, glad that he had not prevaricated.

'Why different?' he asked. 'God is God, religion is religion, different people have different ways of reaching Him.'

'Yes, Rabbi, but the very religious in my faith usually lock themselves away in monasteries, or nunneries. Your religion seems to have found the balance between family and communal life and worship of God.'

The old rabbi looked at Paul and nodded his head slowly. Paul had obviously passed some small test—honesty, forthrightness, courage?—so the rabbi continued to address Miriam. She was interested in the way he was able to shift the focus of attention of the conversation from one subject to another. Barristers used similar techniques to undermine opposition witnesses. But solicitors tended to be far more direct. Orthodox Jews had a labyrinthine way of dealing with issues.

'*Nu!* So the butcher was Smuelshon, Samuelson. So does this help you? The family, I'm afraid I don't remember clearly. I was young when I left the village. Some years afterwards, it was destroyed by a pogrom, and my family and all the rest were killed by the barbarians. Your *zeida* and *bubba* were lucky to have got out alive.'

Miriam hesitated before answering: 'Luck certainly played a large part. My *zeida* and *bubba* tried to get the rest of their family out, but no one believed that the Holocaust would happen.'

The old rabbi slowly nodded: 'We knew. For years our *rebbe* had been predicting what would happen. No one listened until there was no one to listen.'

Miriam tried to drop the next question conversationally into the dialogue:

'So you would have been in the village at the same time as Raphael Ben Ari?'

She averted her eyes and looked at her poppyseed cake, in case her face betrayed the real purpose for her visit, and fumbled with her cup of coffee. She looked out of the corner of her eyes to see the reaction, but the rest of the family continued in their activities and the room did not come to a sudden stop at the mention of his name.

'Ben Ari? What does he have to do with Chelmnitz?' asked the rabbi.

'My *zeida* said that Ben Ari was born in the village. His name was Wladyslaw Mikolajczyk,' she said, trying to imitate the way in which her grandfather had pronounced the tongue-twisting name. Miriam looked up and searched the rabbi's face for a reaction.

The rabbi just shook his head: 'I don't remember him. Could have been. Maybe yes, maybe no. You sure he was from my village?'

'My grandfather was sure. He said he taught him at Hebrew school.'

'Ben Ari? Let me think. He could have been. Then, he might not. Of course, Ben Ari is younger than me. I may not have known him. Why do you want to know about him? I thought you wanted to know about your family?'

Paul jumped in to rescue the situation. Though he was hesitant about revealing details in the outside world, this world of the mystical and religious seemed secure and impregnable.

'Rabbi, Miriam's grandfather said that Ben Ari was instrumental in causing trouble for the Jews in the village, that he was some sort of turncoat, working with the Communists. We've tried all the official channels to find out more about him, but his early life is a closed book. We've come to Israel to try to find out whether Mr Samuelson's allegations are true.'

The old rabbi stared at Miriam and Paul. Their deceit, however minor, had been exposed.

'So at last we find the real purpose of your visit?'

'I really did want to find out about my grandfather,' Miriam replied. 'He's only just died and I didn't want his memory to die with him. I honestly want to know more about his earlier life. When I was a little girl, he wouldn't discuss what happened to him in any great detail, and now its too late. But the things which he told me about Ben Ari, they're very serious, and need to be investigated.'

Again, the old man resorted to a nodding silence. His initial reaction was to castigate them for lying, but they weren't Hasidim. They were the others. Their sense of propriety was questionable. Better to help them and hasten the end of the conversation, than to *schlep* it out, trying to teach them the path of righteousness.

'Children. The ways of *ha kodesh b'ruch hu* are strange. Ben Ari is not a religious man. If he was, your *zeida*'s claim would be unthinkable. Ben Ari is a man of the outside world. A world which holds no allegiance to Godliness. I don't know whether what your grandfather said was right or wrong. I don't remember. But there are people who have records. For years, these people have been working to document the murder of three million Polish Jews. They have been here to see me, and many of my *landsmen;* and they have been to New York to speak to many there. They have a vast repository of facts in Warsaw; like Simon Wiesenthal in Vienna.'

Miriam began to say something in gratitude, but the rabbi's manner stopped her. He took out a pen and called to his wife to bring him some paper. From the depths of his jacket pocket, he took out an ancient bottle-green address book, flipped through several pages and eventually wrote down the details of the Organisation for Polish Martyrs, which was based in Warsaw. Rabbi Gartenbaum said the man they should talk to was Rabbi Miklos Abrahams, assistant to the

Chief Rabbi of Warsaw. This man had come to Israel many years before and spoken to dozens of people in Mea Shearim who were of Polish origin, trying to chronicle pre-war, and wartime events.

'Normally, I don't correspond with people about the past, especially about the Holocaust. But with Rabbi Miklos, I became friendly and continued the correspondence. It was good to write to someone about Poland after all these years. Pity that he's not a Hasid. Such a fine Jew, wasted as an ordinary rabbi.'

Rabbi Gartenbaum also told them that the Polish rabbi had spent months in Tel Aviv, Jerusalem and Haifa, speaking to hundreds of Israelis of Polish descent, creating records to be used for the forthcoming publication of a massive treatise: *Three Million Martyrs—The Slaughter of Polish Jewry, 1900 to 1945*, to be published for the fiftieth anniversary of the end of the Second World War. The work had taken more than thirty years to research and was now reaching its conclusion.

While he could not be certain that Ben Ari had been in Chelmnitz, if there were any records in existence, copies would almost certainly be in the possession of the Rabbi Miklos' organisation.

Miriam and Paul thanked the Rabbi and before they departed he called them over. Under his breath, he mumbled a short prayer, then bade them goodbye. As they walked through the front door, Miriam glanced back—but the rabbi was not staring at their retreating backs. He was absorbed in playing with his tiny great-grand-daughter, who had already climbed onto his knee and into his lap. The old man was tickling her tummy and the child was squealing in delight. An eternal scene, it put the obscenities of Ben Ari, his past and what he was currently doing into an timeless perspective.

As they left the house and walked away from the neighbourhood, a middle-aged, heavy-set man looked into the window of a religious artefacts shop over the road from the rabbi's house. Neither Miriam nor Paul noticed the man ... but he noticed them. And he noticed that there was a small laneway beside the rabbi's house, which would give him access to it later that night.

CHAPTER SEVENTEEN

It was already dark by the time Paul and Miriam returned to their hotel. It was a humourless night, a night of warm wind, and angry cicadas chirping in trees, a night full of sirens and screams—the mirror image of the normal gaiety and fellowship of a Jerusalem midsummer evening.

After Paul and Miriam left Rabbi Gartenbaum, they decided to reward themselves with a treat. They became as much like tourists as the emergency situation would allow. During their short time in Israel, Paul had seen little of Jerusalem, and virtually nothing of the country. They had visited offices and secretariats, interviewed cautious men and women, fruitlessly telephoned one possible lead after another, only to be frustrated by officialdom or ignorance. It was like working behind the Iron Curtain in the worst days of the Cold War, where secrets were buried in dark crypts and conversations were whispered in corridors. Israel had become a whirlpool of secrecy and despondency, with Ben Ari and his phalanx of lieutenants at its vortex.

Paul and Miriam travelled to see the Knesset building, the Chagall windows in the Hadassah Hospital, then wandered through the narrow Via Dolorosa in the Old City, enjoying the city despite the random interruptions of officialdom. It had been a stimulating and satisfying day for them both. For once, the overwhelming sense of frustration which ran through their every action over the past few weeks was subsumed within feelings of relief.

♜♜♜

Thirty miles away on the outskirts of the Arab city of Nablus, darkness also descended. If Jerusalem was a city seething with barely restrained anger and hostility towards its governors, then

Bethlehem, Nablus, Hebron and the other cities of the West Bank were at fever pitch, like dogs straining against the leash of a cruel, unremitting master.

Deep within the narrow dusty alleys of the outskirts of the ancient town of Nablus stood an imposing blue-painted house, where eight people sat in an airless room, its curtains drawn tight, a ceiling fan lazily stirring the stale cocktail of grey and blue cigarette smoke which hung above their heads. They had arrived at various times during the day from different parts of Israel—two from the north, one from Tel Aviv, one from Haifa, three from Gaza and the last, the leader of the group, had flown in that day to Lod airport from Athens.

The house in which the eight men met was owned by Kemel Hadad, deputy mayor of Nablus and member of the West Bank Council of Arab Unity. Recently, Kemel had narrowly escaped being placed under house arrest for organising the Nablus uprising against Israeli authority as part of the Intifada. Although his home, office and private life were under constant scrutiny by Mossad, Shin Bet and police agencies, he managed to continue to be a thorn in Israel's side.

When Anwar Ibn Mazouni contacted him, using a coded fax message purporting to order goods from Kemel's fig and date export agency, the Palestinian was delighted. He desperately wanted to play a more active role in the struggle against the Israeli oppressors and would have done so willingly, provided he did not imperil the investments which he had built up over the past twenty years. Kemel had seen too many idealists lose everything—homes, businesses, even their liberty—by an ill-considered action. Nothing Kemel did was ever ill-considered. That was why he had not been expelled from the country like so many members of Hamas and the PLO. He kept two feet firmly planted on the ground of caution.

The fax asked Kemel for permission to use his house as a meeting place for a group of 'friends' to gather for a social event. Having weighed the benefits of associating with the struggle, against the danger of discovery by the authorities, he agreed. Kemel was an old-style Palestinian, a man whose family had been prominent in West Bank politics under Jordanian rule and whose prestige and fortunes had sunk significantly since the 1967 war. He bore a deep-seated resentment against Israel, though it did not stop him profiting from the sale of his produce to merchants in Tel Aviv and Jerusalem. Despite this, he still had a feeling of outrage at the occupation of his land.

To improve security for the gathering, Kemel ensured that the area around his house was free from observation. During the afternoon, the trusted residents in Nablus created minor disturbances outside the town—traffic squabbles or neighbours' arguments which kept the police and military authorities busy in the north.

With blinds drawn and the atmosphere becoming increasingly poisonous in the closed room, Kemel's wife, two daughters and servants spent the day offering refreshments to the visitors who sat taciturn, cleaning their newly-acquired guns and knives or muttering under their breath to each other.

Kemel had been garrulous, hospitable and welcoming to each man as he arrived. His friendliness was repaid by grunts and curt nods of the head. No one spoke openly. No one introduced himself. No one explained why he was there. Kemel soon became antipathetic towards the group, feeling that his hospitality was being abused by such lack of consideration by his guests.

On the other hand, he had been asked to make his home available. As was the way with these types of groups, he was not told the reason. So he contented himself merely to act as host to an uninspiring group of guests, while snapping orders at his wife, daughters and servants in the kitchen.

It was pitch black outside when the final man arrived. Kemel did not know the faces or names of the others who had appeared on his doorstep. They were probably Syrian or Egyptian flotsam, the scum which rises to the top of a cauldron. But the man who had flown in from Athens was well known to him.

His face would also have been known to Israeli and most European intelligence services had he not recently undergone extensive plastic surgery in the Fournier Clinique de la Médecine in Geneva. His supraorbital ridges, high forehead, cheekbones and square jaw line had been modified to make him look more European, less Arabic. He was a new creation. Yet his eyes were unchanged. As he stood on the doorstep in the half-light of the hallway, Kemel recognised the eyes the moment the man appeared. Plastic surgery could alter the physical appearance of anyone, but the inner being, the intrinsic essence of the subject, was beyond the reach of the scalpel. And the eyes of the man who stood on the doorstep were devoid of warmth and compassion. They were the eyes which Aristo Haggopian fell in love with. They were the eyes of Marcel Dupain, also known as Barrak Salaam, also known as Ibrahim Montazami. Aristo knew him as a beautiful Lebanese playboy when he called himself Raoul Montalban in Athens.

Kemel let out a gasp of surprise and bowed his head low. 'I did not know this operation was important enough to involve a man of your eminence,' he said.

Angry that the fool's obeisance was made so public, Marcel pushed past him into the hallway. 'It appears that my surgery has not been successful. You were able to recognise me.'

'I hardly knew it was you. Your surgery is a miracle of disguise, but I would sense your presence even in a blackened room. The rest of your men are here. When do you begin your activities?'

Kemel had first met Marcel during a secret visit to Damascus, introduced to him by the Syrian Minister of the Interior as a future contact. It was only after that meeting that Kemel was given snippets of Marcel's background—enough to make him wary about crossing his path in the future. From the little that the Syrian minister told him, he sounded like one of the gods in the terrorists' pantheon, a man to be admired from afar, but avoided near at hand.

Marcel walked past him without answering. He entered the

meeting room, where everyone stood up to greet their leader, each man bowing his head in respect. Kemel tried to follow but Marcel closed the door in his face. Kemel ordered his wife to bring him a pack of cigarettes and his daughter to make him a cup of tea.

Marcel was the most feared and hated of all terrorists—a freelance mercenary … a sadist without a cause … a man who hawked his expertise to the highest bidder. Whose mind thrilled at engineering the large-scale, merciless, hellish destruction of innocents.

The son of a French legionnaire and an Algerian mother, Marcel grew into manhood in one of the most inhumane environments that humanity has devised. His father was a sergeant in the French Foreign Legion. As a child Marcel only experienced the viciousness of dispossessed men. When his father left the Legion in disgust at de Gaulle's Algerian capitulation and travelled back to Paris, leaving his mother alone and ashamed, Marcel's life went from intermittent episodes of viciousness to one of unrelenting boredom. His father abandoned the boy to wander the streets of one of Paris's working class *arrondissements*, where he was brutalised by older boys for being an Arab, despite his protestations at being French. Marcel's father became a hopeless alcoholic, and daily beat his son in the frustration that he felt in his new life. And Marcel very quickly learned to defend himself. Isolated from control, he learned how to inflict grievous wounds on those who opposed him without either being caught or even recognised. He learnt to thrust from behind and escape into the comforting anonymity of alleys and passages.

The next ten years saw Marcel refine his skills as a petty criminal and knifeman in the Parisian underworld, and quickly gain notoriety as a vicious young killer. But crime did not pay enough for Marcel's tastes. With his second-hand Foreign Legion experience he was easily able to pass himself off as a young ex-Legionnaire mercenary looking for work … and the work came in abundance.

Marcel's reputation as an ingenious, independent agent of mass destruction spread throughout the terrorist cells of Europe and the Middle East. He quickly became the No. 1 public enemy of Interpol and all other secret services.

When the terrorist groups lost their funding in the late 1980s, Marcel went deeply underground, using his wealth to alter his appearance. His re-emergence had been at the behest of the committee of terrorist groups funded by the Imam of Baghdad. When some substantive acts of terrorism against the Jewish nation were considered necessary, Marcel was contacted by the head of the organising committee for whom he had once worked and asked to put its plans into effect.

How he did it was up to him. The first job had been the destruction of the Magnum 747. Athens was one of the least security-conscious airports in the Western world and Marcel had an easy opportunity in poor Aristo, who had been spotted by PFLP agents many years earlier for his potential use as a dummy carrier. The Greek's seduction had taken Marcel a mere two days. The total time period he had spent in Athens was no more than a week. Marcel enjoyed shooting the stupid fat Greek between the eyes.

The second job was the destruction of the Holocaust Museum, which the group was meeting to carry out. The third job was yet to be planned, but Marcel had his own ideas. He was awaiting the opportunity to discuss them with some of the fools on the committee.

Because his appearance had been changed so dramatically, Marcel determined that it was still safe for him to lead the attack that night. He sat down at the table, and grimaced at the stench of stale men and clogging smoke in the air. Each of the men had been briefed individually by their cell leaders. They in turn had been briefed by the head of their organisation. In this way, only a handful of people in each component or-ganisation were aware of the overall plan, keeping security tight.

Only Marcel had been commissioned directly by order of the Command Council to run the terrorist attack. He, in turn, had selected the people gathered today from different terrorist units. A few had worked with Marcel before, but each knew his reputation as a terrorist and as a leader of men. He had been known to shoot dead one of his soldiers at point blank range, when the man flinched in an execution.

Marcel sat down and poured himself a cup of coffee and a mineral water. His eyes stung from the smoke in the room. He must shower as soon as the operation was over. 'You have all been briefed about some parts of the plan. I will now brief you more fully about the specifics.

'Tonight at 8 o'clock, we leave by five separate vehicles and travel at five-minute intervals into Jerusalem, where we will assemble at the Cafe of the Prophets in Al Sayyid Street. There our agents have readied enough Semtex to level the building but not to damage any others in the surrounding area. I will now detail further plans for getting into the museum. Once there, each of you is aware of his task. Are there any questions before I begin?'

There were none and Marcel briefly outlined the details. When he had finished, there was a general murmuring of agreement. Marcel said, 'Good. Now we must rest. Those who wish to pray may do so. Those who do not wish to pray may play cards. No one leaves this house.'

Although Jerusalem was under a night-time curfew, it did not come into effect until 10.30 p.m. and the streets remained active until the last minute. Jerusalemites were fond of walking with arms linked through the streets, looking in shop windows and enjoying the cooling breezes of midsummer. Although there was little wind to speak of on that airless night, the streets were still thronged with people. All of them were aware that there were limitations on how many friends could meet together and there was only one topic of conversation—the mounting unrest with the Ruling Council and the prospect of the police or army revolting, handing back democracy to the people. Israel was seething with anger and frustration.

There were four dangers for the terrorists in planting their bomb in the Holocaust Museum. The first was discovery in the Cafe of the Prophets by the Israeli security services, which were trigger-happy and stretched to the limit. The second was being searched by Israeli police or army personnel when they left the comparative security of the Arabic Quarter in the Old City and moved into the New City of Jerusalem. The third was when, in groups of two, they approached the gardens surrounding the Holocaust Museum and met in the service area, which admitted trucks and delivery vehicles during the day but at night was guarded by only one elderly security guard occasional visits by a car patrol. The fourth was being discovered before they had a chance to place and explode the Semtex.

The risks were made greater on each of the four counts because the country was in a state of martial law. Where once the populace had gone about its business quite casually, now everybody—citizens, police, military—was nervous and agitated. Only Ben Ari and the two other members of the Ruling Council appeared relaxed and confident.

The eight men sat at four different tables in the crowded and noisy cafe. A nod from the owner assuring him that there were no unknown faces in the cafe at that time, Marcel stood and walked into the back of the cafe. He picked up a large suitcase containing 100 metres of wiring, a cadmium battery, a box of mercury detonators and a mains lead in case the battery failed, and the Semtex wrapped in wax paper. Marcel divided the bag's contents up amongst his men, with instructions to place them unobtrusively in pockets. A man carrying a suitcase would be more likely to be stopped and searched than citizens innocently strolling in the evening air, hands visible. Before he left the cafe, Marcel said to the owner: 'Have you got the sardines?' The man handed over a small package, wrapped in polythene.

Marcel and his companion were the first to leave the cafe. They walked along the Street of the Prophets towards the ancient Damascus Gate of Jerusalem, where a fifteen-year-old boy would act as their guide along the walls of the Old City, towards the Museum of the Holocaust.

Five minutes later, two other men, dressed in casual knit tops, slacks and sandals, left the cafe and walked in a different direction towards the Jaffa Gate, to be guided by another boy towards their destination. Within twenty minutes, all of the terrorists were in different parts of the Old City, slowly walking in pairs towards their destination. Marcel had instructed them to talk animatedly, even to argue in a good-natured fashion, or simply to chat in the manner of Arab men. He didn't want them to look furtive in any way.

The Holocaust Museum was built in 1974 with donations from American Jews. It was a four-storey building made of white concrete blocks, faced with travertine marble. On its wrought-iron doors was a sculpture by the brilliant young Israeli artist, Avram Mizrachi. He had portrayed a stylised scene from a concentration camp—men and women, boys and girls, whose bodies were sprawled like needles on a compass, pierced by barbed wire, as though they were pieces of chaff which had been thrown there by some obscene threshing machine.

The building was one of the central focuses of Israeli tourism. Yearly more than a million and a half people visited its horrific displays—vivid portrayals of ghetto life in Warsaw, pre-war German Jewry being humiliated or brutalised by SS units and Black Shirts, and scenes of unremitting despair from concentration camps such as Auschwitz, Treblinka, Bergen Belsen and Maidenek.

Central to the Holocaust Museum was a marble plinth, twenty feet high and fifty feet long, in which were etched the names of tens of thousands of Jews who had been exterminated by the Nazis. It did not pretend to be a complete record; no such record could exist. The Nazis had done a Germanically thorough job of obliterating entire families, congregations, communities, and populations from the face of the Earth. It had been created to give tangible evidence to visitors that the Holocaust was not merely history, but was the real and personal experience of millions of Jews in Nazi Europe.

At 10 p.m. the inside of the museum was in virtual darkness, except for security lights on each floor. The only sound from inside were the footfalls of the elderly security guard whose job it was to patrol the echoing corridors at two-hourly intervals. Outside the museum, the perimeter lighting cast elongated shadows, which the terrorists used to hide themselves from the two guards patrolling the grounds. As one came around a corner, he was silently garrotted by two of the Arabs, who held his body until it had stopped struggling. Three men cautiously went in search of the other guard.

Sitting in his booth at the service entrance, Chaim Katan knew that within the next fifteen minutes he would both have to go to the toilet and walk from the ground floor to the fourth, to ensure that everything within the building was in order. Even though he had a bank of television sets and the entire area was monitored by remote cameras, Chaim's job specification was to walk the floors—both to keep him from going to sleep on the job and also as a final insurance.

Not being a building which could conceivably be deemed as a terrorist or criminal target, the directors of the Holocaust Museum determined that this simple internal surveillance, plus a couple of guards outside, was all that was needed. Nobody in their right minds, they reasoned, would try to damage or steal anything from a museum whose only exhibits were photographs and the hideous memorabilia of the Nazi legacy. After all, this was Israel, not the new Germany with its strong growth of neo-fascism.

When the pressure on his bladder became annoying, Chaim stood and walked from his desk away from the service entrance on the ground floor, to where the employees' toilets were situated. Through the stillness of the night, he vaguely heard sirens wailing somewhere in a distant part of Jerusalem. He thought sadly how much things had changed in his country.

Outside the back door, Marcel took out the small plastic parcel which the cafe owner had given him. Opening it, he removed the fresh sardines, and laid them out on the grass. He hid behind a bush, indicating for the other men to hide as well. Their surveillance had told them that the elderly guard was a cat-lover, who every now and again opened the museum doors to feed the animals.

Within seconds, the first of a dozen strays which haunted the grounds came within view, ears pricked up, nose sniffing the air. Behind it were two others. Soon the reek of fish would attract every cat in the neighbourhood. As soon as one of the cats started to eat the sardines, Marcel threw his coat over the animal, and sprang towards it. Before it had a chance to bolt, Marcel had it gripped tightly in his arms. It spat and scratched, but the terrorist's grip was too firm for it to escape.

Marcel took out his knife, and nodded silently to the other men to position themselves at the door. Using a cat was a simple way of getting the old man to open the door. Using explosives to gain entry to the museum would attract every police car within ten miles.

Standing close to the doorframe, Marcel used the point of his knife to scratch the belly of the cat until its hair was matted with blood. The animal shrieked in pain. He waited, holding his breath, but there were no sounds from inside the door. Marcel scratched the animal again, this time near the groin where the skin was more tender. The animal howled, and struggled to get away, trying to rip Marcel's skin with its claws. All the other cats scampered away, terrified by the noise. The animal continued to screetch, but Marcel was listening for activity near the door. Finally, he heard footsteps. He nodded again, and two men stepped forward, one readying a silenced pistol.

Old Chaim Katan slowly unlocked the door, crouching to look on the ground for the cat. As he opened it wider, he said: 'Come on puss, time for …'

When he saw men's feet standing there instead of his cats he began to straighten up, but too late. One of the men kicked his old head hard under the chin. It snapped back and lifted him off the ground, carrying his body into the hall. Chaim looked up in shock, and started to ask who the men were, but before words could form one of the terrorists had shot him through his left eye, the bullet exploding inside his head. His body was propelled further into the room, carried backwards by the force of the bullet. It slammed against a marble pillar. Chaim's blood and brains poured out of the gaping holes in the front and back of his head. The pristine white travertine marble slowly began to absorb the red and grey stains.

The old man's limp body slid to the floor, where his bladder voided itself of urine. In seconds the four men had burst in through the doorway. They ran into the building and immediately began to place their deadly cargo of explosives around the supporting pillars. Marcel walked in leisurely, as his troops scurried around. He lifted the cat level with his eyes. The hair on its back bristled like a brush, and it tried to hunch its body to escape, but Marcel's grip was too firm. Marcel whispered: 'Good cat. Good pussy.' The animal relaxed slightly. Marcel raised the knife, and in one stroke severed its body from its head; the body dropped to the floor and twitched within the jacket. Marcel stepped quickly away so that no blood soiled his other clothes. Then he threw the head of the cat onto the body of old Chaim Katan. 'Here old man. You liked cats. Now you can rest in peace together.'

Marcel wiped his hands on a handkerchief and looked around to see that his troops were obeying their instructions. Each man had been meticulously briefed on his role, so it took them less than five minutes to place the Semtex around ten of the columns supporting the building. Marcel ran from column to column, placing a detonator and electrical wiring in each charge, and collating all the wiring of the Semtex together in parallel, finally joining the wires up to a mother board. From the obverse side of the board, he ran an insulated battery wire. Unrolling the cable, the four terrorists ran out the back door, crouching low, to join the four other men who were placed strategically in the garden to deal instantly with any prying eyes. He could have exploded the Semtex using more sophisticated electronics, but he wanted the Israeli authorities to think that this was a bit of an amateurish job.

Marcel carefully placed a sweet wrapper under a nearby bush—a wrapper identical with the ones he'd left inside the bloodied jacket. The sweets were made by a small Syrian company in the north of Damascus. Hopefully, they would point Shin Bet in the wrong direction.

He continued to unroll the full extent of the wire. When all of the men arrived at the far end of the gardens, they lay flat on the ground, thankful that no one had spotted them. Marcel joined the end of the wire to the battery terminals, muttered a small prayer under his breath and pressed the 'on' switch, which was connected to the battery.

Paul and Miriam were in bed when the explosion ripped through Jerusalem. It invaded the curfew peace and was heard all over the city. People living twenty miles away also swore they heard the noise.

'Shit! What was that?' said Paul, as he ran to the balcony to be joined a moment later by Miriam. The hotel balcony, however, looked over the Old City, and they were unable to see the plume of fire and smoke which rose furiously into the clear dark summer sky on the other side of the hotel. All they heard was the noise, the screams, the shouts and, within seconds, the wailing of police sirens.

One floor below, the Russian observers were equally surprised, but were too highly trained to run to their balcony window in case they were spotted.

In nearby East Jerusalem, Prime Minister Raphael Ben Ari, who was meeting in private session with his military commanders for central and north Israel, spilled his *schlug* of whisky at the noise of the explosion. 'God Almighty, what was that?' he exclaimed as he reached for the phone which was constantly connected to the headquarters of Israel's internal security force, Shin Bet. The phone was answered immediately by the Duty

Officer. Knowing it was the Prime Minister, he said, without being asked: 'Sir, we have heard the explosion but we have no idea what it was. We're investigating and I'll get back to you.'

Within a minute of the massive cloud of smoke disappearing into the night sky, and when the debris from the explosion had settled and landed in the streets surrounding the Holocaust Museum, a crowd gathered to look at the concrete and steel wreckage. People seemed to have come from every corner of Jerusalem, gathering to view the unimaginable.

In many ways it was a pity that shocked sightseers stood in groups looking at the wreckage. The large number of people enabled eight casually dressed men to strip off their tight rubber gloves, put them in their pockets, mingle with the crowd and slowly disappear back into the haunting confines of the Old City.

CHAPTER EIGHTEEN

The onion-shaped domes of the Kremlin stood silhouetted against the dark sky over Moscow. The queues of tourists visiting the palace's state rooms and exhibitions of Russia's exotic past had disappeared as night approached. Now, it stood alone, isolated, an island of brilliant light and colour in a sea of despondency. In the days of its former glory, Moscow had been wealthy and vibrant. That was before the advent of the Russian government and its inability to turn the country into a modern industrial nation. Then came the Russian mafia, darkening Moscow with standover tactics, murder and drugs. Food shortages completed the degradation of the once beautiful city.

Inured to deprivation, the grumbling public initially accepted the darkness. But as despondency grew and the Abayev Government failed to reverse the devastation brought on by the attempts of President Yeltsin to drag Russia into capitalism, the people became divided. The old-guard Stalinists confidently postured on the pavements, telling anyone willing to listen how secure life had been under Communism. President Abayev's troubles were compounded by the deterioration in relations with former Communist allies. Racial, religious and ethnic disharmony strained the borders between the new nations. Those with large standing armies posed a continuing threat of launching a retaliatory nuclear strike against one-time friends. President Harrison's mediations in the various border and internecine wars did little to calm the waters.

The disruption to life which Russia suffered had adversely affected the look of the City of Moscow. When the City Council had money to spend on such things as street lights, and illuminations, the familiar domes of the Kremlin were subtly lit from below by a hundred powerful klieg lights. They were an international symbol of the success of Communism over

Tsarism, freedom over repression, a beacon for tourists and residents alike. The centre of Moscow in those days had looked part medieval castle, part Arabian fantasy. Today, only a small part of the centre was alight. The rest was cold, dull and in the main dark, with people scurrying along pavements like rats in a sewer. And rats from the sewers scurried emboldened between the legs of citizens to eat the piles of refuse left by the thousands of free market food vendors. The only communal light of any note was the luminous wash around the Kremlin, which remained the Russian Republic's showplace to the world. It was an irony not lost on the Russian people. The Palace of the Tsars was once again illuminated while the rest of Russia remained dark.

As Andrei Alexandrovich Yezhov's taxi drove through the drear streets in the early evening, his heart sank. Moscow was the eternal survivor. Even during his lifetime, it had changed character many times. When he was a youth, it suffered the cold winters of repressive Bolshevism; as a young man, the leaden, poisonous air of suspicion created by Stalin and Beria; in his middle age, the isolationism of those warriors of the Cold War, Krushchev and Brezhnev; and in his old age, it briefly enjoyed the warm winds of cosmopolitanism ushered in by Gorbachev before being plunged back into winter by economic uncertainty. And always the Palace of the Kremlin was the centre of the Russian world, bathed in light and glory, a sentinel against the changes, its palaces, monuments and official buildings indifferent to the dramas which successive rulers wrought on its people. But during the years in which he had been living in Berlin, his city had changed, perhaps irreversibly. Today, Moscow was a crone, dispirited, haggard, a decaying body swathed in torn, rotting clothes, with only its heart beating strongly.

Yezhov had flown into Sheremetevo airport after a Lufthansa flight from Templehof. His German passport gave his name as Gunther Boeder, a retired mine worker whose place of birth seventy-two years earlier had been in the Ruhr. When he gave 'pleasure and holiday' as his purpose for visiting Moscow, the young customs officer had looked wryly at him. Nobody visited Moscow for pleasure these days. But a harmless old man was no threat to state security and he waved him through with a salutation.

Outside the airport, Yezhov stepped into the taxi line. He was used to travelling by cab. In Berlin, most taxis were meticulously clean and antiseptic Mercedes, maintained with a Teutonic attention to detail. He noted with distaste that the cabs of Moscow were at the oppposite end of the spectrum. The faded yellow and check insignias were covered by mud and grime, a residue of city snow which had turned to slush, and remained unwashed when the days became hot. Wipers had scraped their impression on each of the windscreens. The drivers sat idly and bored in their seats, most of them smoking, all waiting, uninterested in the Russian passengers emerging from the terminals. The only spark of interest came when a well-dressed foreigner emerged with expensive luggage. Then the race was on to take him into the centre of town. He would be worth a sizeable tip, sometimes a month's income.

Yezhov nodded at one taxi driver who looked him up and down and glanced at his elderly valise. Before starting the car to move towards him, the driver looked at the other passengers in case there was a richer one. He grudgingly started the car and Yezhov climbed into the back. He told the driver to take him to the Kremlin.

'So, how are things in Moscow?' he asked.

The driver shrugged laconically. 'If it wasn't for the government, the President, the Church, the mafia, the Communists, the capitalists and the economy, Russia would be a wonderful place to live.'

Yezhov let out a wheezy laugh. It was good to be back in Russia after nearly five years.

'How's the housing situation? Is it still as critical?'

'Everyone still lives either in *kommunalka* or *baraki*.'

Yezhov remembered the terms, newly introduced when Gorbochev's policy of every family having its own flat by the year 2000 became just another political promise from another politician. *Kommunalka* were the communal flats all over Moscow where people shared baths, toilets, kitchens, halls, phones, and doorways; *baraki* were slightly more private but would have been classed as prison accommodation had they been in the West.

The taxi driver continued: 'Yesterday, I picked up a man. He said to me "Drive me out of the city." I negotiated a huge fare which he paid up front. I didn't say a word as we drove south. I knew he was on the run. He wanted to talk. "I couldn't stand it any more," he said to me. "I've just beat the shit out of my neighbour and his wife. I've told them a thousand times when you finished a bath, clean the fucking ring of grime you always leave."'

The taxi driver chuckled. He half-turned to Yezhov who suddenly looked towards the floor, not wanting the driver to commit his face to memory.

'You know what he told me? He said that he was going for a job that day and he couldn't bear to bathe in a filthy bath. I dropped him off outside Moscow. He probably spent his last money just getting away from his home. Terrible, isn't it?'

The taxi driver flicked his cigarette out of the window as his car began to enter the centre of Moscow. Yezhov didn't answer but he nodded silently. The taxi approached the Kremlin along Tvezskaya Prospekt, and dropped Yezhov outside one of the gates, where he had been instructed to ask for Colonel Lubin of the Kremlin Guard.

Colonel Lubin was seated in his office when the soldier entered to tell him of his visitor. He was eating a kransky sandwich. He peered through the leaden, one-way glass to observe the man. Old, shabbily dressed. He could wait until Lubin had finished. When the kransky was washed down with a measure of vodka and the crumbs of bread wiped from his moustache, Lubin walked business-like from his office to observe the old man at close quarters. He had been told to expect him but had not been given details of who he was or why he should be there. Colonel Lubin had been a Kremlin Guard long enough to know that his job wasn't to ask questions. Merely to use the huge forces at his disposal to protect the Russian government from civil unrest. He had been one of the defenders of the White House when Boris Yeltsin was attacked by KGB and Red Army forces in those final, glorious days before the collapse of the Soviet Union. Then, and for the first time in his life, he had refused to carry out a direct order from his commander. The order had come from the traitor Ligachev. Lubin refused point-blank to march against the White House and the lawfully elected government of Russia. That refusal still troubled his conscience. Looking at the way Russia was today, with Abeyev ruling over a rabble of technocrats who couldn't work out which direction to follow, he wondered whether he should have carried out the original order. Maybe the coup conspirators were right in 1991. Maybe Gorbachev and Yeltsin should have been swept away by the reactionaries. Maybe then the country could have had stability, instead of years of chaos and the threat of civil war; or worse, the threat of unrecanted hard-line Communists, trying to wrest back control of the government from the people.

Still, that wasn't his concern at the moment. Walking towards the elderly man he saluted and without being introduced, he said, 'Follow me please'. The colonel led Yezhov into the east portico of the Kremlin and down a flight of stairs towards the basement elevators.

Yezhov didn't say a word. He didn't want to betray his Russian accent. The story given out was that he was a technical adviser on agriculture from United Germany. Although he tended to be unduly cautious in his work, this time it was probably necessary; five years earlier he had been a familiar sight in this building. He deliberately kept his head bowed low, so that neither Lubin nor any other curious passer-by should recognise him.

They took the elevator to the eighth floor of the Kremlin

executive office suites. It always amused Yezhov that in a country where everyone was supposed to be equal, the lifestyle enjoyed by the Kremlin masters was still very much more equal than that enjoyed by their fellow countrymen. The carpets along the corridor were of a deep green pile, the carved chairs beautifully ornate in the style of the Romanovs, and the walls hung with priceless Russian Orthodox works of art, a heritage that the Russian people would never get to see. Once confined by Lenin and Stalin to the Hermitage and the bowels of the Kremlin, they had been restored to their historical place by President Abayev. They had even been the subject of a photospread in *Paris Match*.

Colonel Lubin stopped outside a large oak door and gently knocked. Without waiting for an answer, he opened the door and said to the man behind the desk, 'Your visitor, sir.'

Yezhov walked passed him into the enormous state room which served as the office of the Minister for Agriculture of the Russian Republic. Colonel Lubin closed the door behind him and left the two men alone.

The minister, Ivan Yeszersky, stood to greet his friend of forty years, his booming voice taking no account of the fact that the room might be bugged.

'Andrei Alexandrovich.' He came around the side of the desk and threw his enormous arms around Yezhov's frail body and hugged him with the embrace of a bear. Ivan kissed the old man on both cheeks. 'What is it, four years, five, since we've seen each other? How are you, my dear old friend? How are things in Berlin? How's life in that wicked neo-fascist capitalist city?'

Yezhov grinned. It was good to hear Russian being spoken by a cultured literate after all this time. Yezhov sat down in the armchair in front of the desk.

'Ivan Semyonovich, of all the men I've missed in my retirement, you I have missed most of all. How's your Alexandra? And your children?'

'Good, you old bastard.'

'You have no idea what life is like for Russians living on the outside,' Yezhov continued. 'For all the problems which you have here, you're still in daily contact with the soil of Mother Russia. For me, and the thousands of exiles like me, it's as though our umbilicus has been severed.'

'Oh! come on, you old fraud. You're living the life of a Rockefeller. I'll bet you haven't missed the soil of Mother Russia once since you left.'

Yezhov shook his head. 'Remember Solzhenitsyn. The world's greatest writer when he lived in Russia; the minute he was exiled, he lost his voice. Same thing ...'

The two men laughed and the minister stood up and went over to his drinks cabinet. He took out a bottle of Stolichnaya vodka and poured a large measure for both of them. For the next twenty minutes Yezhov pumped the younger man about the new Russian Federation, its relationships with other independent nations and ex-Communist states; and about life in Moscow, its difficulties and its joys. The minister answered fully and freely, not guarding his words, knowing that in all his years of friendship with Yezhov, never once had a secret or confidence been betrayed. As Yezhov had never once betrayed a confidence given to him by Yeszersky's father before him.

When Yezhov had finished asking questions, the minister pumped him for information about Berlin and the attitude of the government towards Moscow. 'I see they're still treating Eastern Europeans and Jews badly. How long do you think they'll keep it up?'

'Dear friend, I'm just an old man living out his years in a cold and alien city. What do you expect me to know about the German government that you don't know from *Pravda* or your embassy?'

Ivan smiled and scrutinised Andrei Alexandrovich carefully for a moment or two. Then he leaned back in his chair and said: 'You old fox. Do you think I don't know what you've been up to these last years. You run the best network of agents in Europe. You supply information to the CIA, MI6, the GKO in the Ukraine, the Japanese security services and God knows how many others. You're a dissembling old bastard. You're making more money now than the Queen of England, and even she, unlike you, has to pay taxes. Don't come that bullshit with me. You're as active today as you were when you were our resident in America, or when you returned to head up the First Chief Directorate.'

Yezhov looked slyly at his friend, and smiled. 'Everybody has to have a hobby in retirement. Oh, and by the way,' he added as an afterthought, 'like the Queen of England, I also pay my taxes.'

The minister again roared with laughter, looking like a giant bear. Yet as a former professor of Russian literature at Moscow University, and as the author of two volumes of the most lyrical and beautiful poetry written since Boris Pasternak and Yevgeni Yevtushenko, he was probably the most cultured and intelligent man in the government. The *Times Literary Supplement* had called him 'the Mandelstam of the Computer Generation'.

'Andrei, tovarich, I've a file in my office kindly lent to me by my friend down the corridor, the Minister for Defence. It details the size and scope of your operation. You are currently running fifty agents in Europe, Latin America, North America and the Far East, and have excellent relations with twelve countries who are currently your clients.'

The Russian minister looked at the old man to gauge his reaction. Yezhov smiled broadly.

'Is there anything else you'd like to tell me about my life?'

'Yes, your clients buy information which you gather. You send it to them in the form of confidential bulletins. By the way, we've managed to gain access to every one of them so far,' said Yeszersky.

'Not every one,' the old man responded. 'Only the ones I wanted you to read.' Yeszersky again roared with laughter. 'But go on, tell me what else I do. It's fascinating to hear how my life is of such interest in the Kremlin.'

'You analyse all the information, and then your brilliant mind assembles it and draws parallels, makes assumptions and then prepares the reports which you sell at vastly inflated capitalist prices. On three occasions you've beaten the CIA by a couple of months in predicting situations in Eastern Europe, of which their giant computer prognosticator failed to warn them. You're at least a decade ahead of MI6 and the rest of us. Now why don't we cut the crap and you tell me why you've come to see me.'

In the days under Gorbachev the only intelligent people in government had been Foreign Minister Shevardnadze and the economists co-opted from Moscow University. Shevardnadze had tried to establish the new Russia as a major force in international affairs; the economists had tried to turn around the decaying body of Russian industry before it disappeared forever into the swamp. Both had failed in their missions.

Abayev was attempting to run his huge republic in the same way as the Americans ran their country—the President gathering in the most brilliant men from universities and industry to form an inner cabinet. Ivan Semyonovich was such a man.

'I'll tell you why I've come to see you. I'm getting disturbing reports from my people which may be of interest to you. Naturally, I'm here to sell the information, but this time it will be at a discount because the centre of the maelstrom isn't in the West, but is here in Russia … in Moscow, to be precise.'

Yezhov studied his younger friend's face, but the minister didn't react at all. Conspiracies were boringly frequent in Moscow. But unlike the old days, the new Russian approach was to allow them to happen. They would be reported in *Pravda* or through *Izvestia* and the Russian people would decide what to do. The days of repressing Russians were well and truly over now that there was no KGB or GRU.

Yezhov continued, 'I should point out though that this isn't a threat against the Russian Republic, but has implications for world peace.' The old man was relieved to note a look of surprise in the minister's eyes.

'World peace?' said Yeszersky. 'That sounds Machiavellian. What area of the world are we talking about?'

'The Middle East. I think that Marshal Petrovsky is doing something in Israel and I can't find out what. I need your help to set up surveillance on him.'

The minister was far too sophisticated to drop his glass of vodka in surprise. He simply clutched it more firmly. In a hushed tone, he said: 'Petrovsky? You have to be joking. He's been retired for five years. He's farming or fishing or something.' The minister said this totally without conviction. He knew that Yezhov's information would be more accurate than his own. He had a reputation for it.

'Dear friend, Petrovsky has had three meetings at his dacha on the Black Sea with senior Russian and Ukrainian Army officers. He has had four meetings in his Moscow apartment with members of the Russian government, and ex-KGB and GRU personnel. Do you want me to continue?'

Yeszersky nodded. Andrei Alexandrovich opened his briefcase and took out a notebook. 'He has sent an operative to terminate some old Jew in Sydney, Australia, and currently has a very extensive surveillance on an Australian reporter and a Jewess in Jerusalem. Something is going on in Israel which doesn't meet the eye. I know that Petrovsky is behind it. However, my operatives are incapable of breaching the security that he has built around his activities. But the fact of the matter is that he's planning something in the Middle East. I'm sure I can't get close enough to find out why, what or when. That's why I need your help. We need to set up a double blind so that we spy on the spymaster.'

The minister sat stock still in his armchair. His face had become noticeably paler.

'I'm only a simple English teacher who happens to be responsible for Russia's agricultural output. I don't know how to cope with this sort of a situation. If my colleagues are involved, who do I talk to? Do I go to the President? Do I drag Petrovsky in here screaming and shouting, and confront him directly?'

Yezhov shook his head vigorously: 'No, absolutely not. You mustn't confront him until we know what he's up to.'

Yeszersky nodded in agreement: 'Then what the hell do I do? Tell me.'

Yezhov smiled and again opened his briefcase. He took out a file and handed the minister a piece of paper. The minister read it carefully.

He looked up at his old friend, smiling, and said, 'You really are a clever old bastard, Andrei Alexandrovich.'

♜♜♜

Marcel Dupain had many different aliases. Because his mother's Algerian heritage was reflected in his swarthy looks, it suited him to be called by Arab names, although he viewed Arabs no more favourably than any other group. But he was also a South American, a German and a Swiss. At times, he thought he knew more about his aliases than he did about himself.

In all the years that he had lived with his father, he learned little about him. There was no intimacy in their relationship. Although as a small boy he craved it, he never shared the father and son experiences which enable young people to learn about life. Even in death there was still no closeness, no memory.

René Dupain had been a petty criminal in France just after the Second World War. A pompous magistrate had offered him time in the Foreign Legion or a prison sentence after he was caught beating a man close to death. René chose the Legion and never for a moment regretted his choice. Here was the company of men, tough men, dispossessed men, men who owed allegiance to themselves and to a fanatical camaraderie, which came from the isolation of manning forts in deserts or outposts in towns whose names sounded like a man spitting and hawking into the gutter.

The Legion was everything, and everything was the Legion. It fed him, clothed him, housed him, paid for his whores and enabled him to see himself with respect for the first time since his birth in the slums of Marseilles. Men survived by their fists in the Legion. Fists and cunning. René had an abundance of both. Authority was strength and his strength gave him authority. The Legion was a peculiar animal. A French military corps, it consisted chiefly of foreign volunteers, although the officers were nearly all French. In the ranks, René mixed with Germans, Swedes, Dutch, British and men from many other countries. Upon enlistment, René swore an oath, not to France, but to the Legion, and from that moment on, the Legion's unofficial motto 'Legio Patria Nostra'—the Legion is our Fatherland—told René and every other recruit where his loyalties lay.

The first and only tender moment of his adult life was when he fell in love with a lithe belly dancer in an Algiers cafe. He and his platoon had broken the place to pieces in a drunken orgy of fun. René rescued the terrified dancer. They spent that night in a cheap hotel, making love in a dozen different positions.

René was both in love and loved—an experience that questioned the very fibre of his being. Sex had never been a problem for him. If he wasn't visiting a brothel, he would while away his time by masturbating. He never felt the same depths of frustration that his colleagues spoke about. And now, at last, somebody cared for him. Somebody who put René first and herself second. Somebody who held her outstretched hands to him and said, 'Love me for myself alone, and I will love you.' A wellspring of tenderness opened up in René's heart. It was the first warmth he had experienced since childhood … the first weakness he had shown since manhood.

For a year, he and his wife loved and lived the life of normal people; she for the first time in the security of a man's love, he in the tenderness of endearment. But the Legion quickly ended the love of his life. Legionnaires can have sex with, rape and abuse any number of Arab men, women, children or animals, but there is no place for a French Legionnaire to marry one of them. René's marriage earned him the contempt and ridicule of his former friends. Despite the birth of Marcel within a year, René had to chose between his allegiance to his wife and his allegiance to the Legion. He allowed his love to be poisoned and his heart to be damned by the Legion.

Over the next two or three years, René treated his wife with a contempt exacerbated by alcohol. His tenderness turned to ridicule and violence. Ultimately, she was forced to leave him for her own protection and move into town with the little boy.

René visited his family infrequently. When Marcel was eight years old, René and his wife had a furious argument. She had dressed the boy in Arab clothes in defiance of René's instructions. Marcel hated Western clothes, which earned him the contempt of the other street kids. But René refused to allow his son to look like a 'stinking Arab'. He knocked her to the ground, breaking her jaw, and came close to killing her. René picked up his son and took him screaming back to the barracks where he refused to allow his wife to visit. The commandant was irate and insisted that the boy be moved out of the fort. René stood up to his commandant and called upon his Legionnaire colleagues to come to his aid. Terrified of a mutiny, the commandant backed down. René was promoted to drill sergeant.

For many years, father and son lived together in an unhappy alliance. The boy was adopted as the fort's mascot, marching around the parade ground, wearing a small Legionnaire's suit and joining in the training. When he was twelve, he was taken to brothels by the Legionnaires and was inducted into the sort of life normally led by soldiers.

Marcel's fledgling homosexuality was given full vent as the boy was sodomised by half the Legionnaires in the fort. The other half taught him other forms of sex in brothels. He learned to get drunk and fight in bars, and when René left the Legion in disgust after de Gaulle's backdown to the Algerian nationalists, both father and son tried to replicate the life of the Legion in the cheap streets of Paris. René became a hopeless gutter-crawling alcoholic, increasingly dependent on the teenage Marcel as a provider. One day, Marcel looked at the old diseased man with contempt, took all the money and weapons in the house and walked away, never once looking back. In the years that had passed, Marcel never wondered what had happened to his father, though occasionally he sent money to his ageing mother in Algiers.

Walking through the Al Kasim mosque in central Baghdad, Marcel's mind was thrown back to those early boyhood days when he was torn between the Moslem world of his mother and the godless world of the Legion. He followed the mullah towards the Imam's office and was admitted after a cursory knock on the door. The office was empty. Marcel assumed that the Imam was dealing with some matter of state or was at prayer. He sat on one of the low cushions and cast his eye over the newspapers scattered on the Imam's table. The headlines all told of the destruction on the previous day of the Museum of the Holocaust, and the dramatic increase in tension within Israel. The picture in the paper showed a crowd demonstrating. The placards demanded the removal of the Ruling Council and a resumption of the peace talks. Marcel smiled.

Al Ahram, the Egyptian newspaper, wrote of troop movements by the Israeli military dictatorship towards the Syrian border. In a separate news item surrounded by a double-edged border, the paper reported a press conference given by the military commander of Jerusalem in which he identified clear evidence that the Syrian government had been behind the outrage. The Syrian government denied it but had moved two divisions to the Golan Heights, to counter the divisions of Israeli troops which had moved north-east of the city of Kuneitra.

Marcel delighted at the ease with which the assault was carried out and the resultant escalation of tension. And the sweet wrapper! So simple, so elegant.

The Imam entered through a side door and glanced at Marcel. He was followed by a mullah and two lower order priests. The Imam sat at the table. Marcel was interested in why he had been summoned to Baghdad but, having nothing

to fear from the Imam, he assumed that he was to be congrat-
ulated for the skill with which he had carried out the two
terrorist operations. He was mistaken.

Without formality, the Imam said, 'You have within your
group a turncoat; a man who is running both with the dogs
and the sheep.'

Marcel looked at the impassive face of the Imam, tempted
to ask for proof. But he decided to wait and see what else the
old fox had to say.

'Information has come back to me from the Imam of Egypt
of a message sent from the Russian embassy in Cairo for transmission to Moscow. The interception of this message was
purely by chance. It is fortunate that one of the Imam's
staunchest followers is a devout Moslem who works for the
Russians as a translator within the Cairo embassy.'

'Message?' asked Marcel.

'The message told of the planned bomb attack against the
Jewish museum. We allowed it to go through, but we have no
idea who sent the message. It may have originated in Egypt or
elsewhere; it is your job to find out.'

'Holy one, this is just not possible …'

'I have spoken to the man who appointed you,' the Imam
interrupted. 'He swears his life by your loyalty. I have spoken
to the leaders of the other groups represented in the command
structure which you set up. They all assure me of the fidelity
of each of their men. You are the commander. You will find
out who the traitor is, and deal with him.'

The Imam finally looked at Marcel to judge his reaction.
Marcel had lived for twenty years as a terrorist. He was too
professional to allow his emotions to rule his reactions. But
behind the confidence he felt a hint of insecurity. He had
chosen men of the greatest experience and loyalty to their cause
to join with him in a combined cadre of terrorists. For one of
them to be a Russian agent was beyond his comprehension.

'Holy one, your information must be incorrect. It is not conceivable that one of my men is such an agent.'

The Imam looked at him through hooded, expressionless eyes. Moslem clerics, as they grew older and more holy, seemed to lose the passion which inflames the hearts of younger men.

'Denial without investigation is meaningless. You have been told there is a traitor in your ranks. Your job is to ensure that his evil work does not continue.'

The two mullahs who had accompanied the Imam stood as though by a pre-arranged signal, indicating that the conversation was at an end. They helped the Imam rise from his cushion. All three walked out of the door without the courtesy of a goodbye, leaving Marcel still seated, stunned at the news.

Of course there were traitors in terrorist organisations. There were double agents, moles, double dealers, mercenaries, men and women who would sell their children if it benefited their personal cause. But all the men Marcel had picked for the cadre were carefully chosen for their loyalty to the Command Council and its objectives … men who came with high credentials as experts in their field. Fearless in their exploits and merciless in dealing with whoever they perceived as their enemy.

All of them were known to counter-terrorist units in England, America and most European countries. Many of them had lain dormant for two or more years but reinvigorating them had proved simple. They had all, without exception, run to Marcel's side. To think that any one of these could be a traitor, giving information to Russia or America, was beyond his understanding. And why Russia? Like Syria, Russia refused to assist the terrorist groups. They had headed straight for the Western camp when Russian support and interest evaporated in the Middle East, leaving only Iran, Iraq and Libya as major sponsors. Iraq was bankrupt, Libya had been badly hurt in bombing raids by the USA following a number of terrorist incidents in New York, and Iran maintained its fanatical religious isolationism.

None of this answered the question of why one of his group would be selling information to Russia. Because the Russians no longer had any interest in the Middle East or terrorism, the only possible candidate to purchase such information would be America, the great Satan. The thought of one of his group lying in bed with the whores in the CIA was unimaginable.

How could he determine which of the men was a turncoat? Marcel rose from his cushion. Feeling like a schoolboy who has been punished by his headmaster, he walked out of the Imam's office into the cold blue light of the mosque.

♜♜♜

As Andrei Alexandrovich Yezhov left Minister Yeszersky's Kremlin office, he allowed himself the luxury of a smile. Years of espionage, of clandestine meetings, of secret rendezvous had given him the power to be impassive. Not even the flicker of an eyebrow would give away his innermost thoughts, the doubts and troubles which are inextricably woven into the fabric of an espionage agent's life.

Colonel Lubin walked two steps in front of Minister Yeszersky's visitor, down the corridors of the Kremlin. As they reached the door of the lift to take them down to street level, both men stopped and stood shoulder to shoulder, facing the doors of the iron cage. Lubin was thirty years younger, stocky, and muscular. He wore that unsmiling facade of introversion, by which the world recognised Kremlin leaders as they stood on the plinth of Lenin's tomb during parades. He faced the lift doors, waiting for it to arrive. Yezhov also stood in silence, lost in thought.

Without warning, Colonel Lubin broke the silence of the corridor. 'How are you enjoying Berlin, Andrei Alexandrovich?'

Yezhov turned in surprise to Colonel Lubin. 'So you recognise me?'

'I was a part of the Kremlin guard for many years while you were in Dzerzinsky Square. When the junta failed I was among the men who guarded Yeltsin in the White House. I've seen you many times.'

Yezhov smiled and shook his head. 'Russia is like one huge family, isn't it? Everybody knows everyone else. Anyway, colonel, I'm doing very well in Berlin, thank you. I miss my home, but when you reach my age you have to enjoy a few creature comforts. The deprivations since the collapse of the KGB would have been too great for me had I stayed here.'

The colonel nodded. 'Do you regret leaving your country?'

No matter where a Russian lived in exile, Russia was always 'your country'.

'Berlin is brash and bold and brassy—a little bit like a strumpet—but she is also warm and friendly and comforting in my few remaining years.'

Colonel Lubin continued to stare at the doors of the lift. He said not another word until he had escorted Yezhov to the gates of the Kremlin. As a gesture of respect, the colonel held out his hand and the two men shook hands, smiling warmly at each other. 'God go with you, Andrei Alexandrovich.'

'My dear colonel, don't tell me that the opium of the masses has reached the Kremlin walls.'

Lubin smiled. 'Not everything that has happened since the Communist Party collapsed has been bad.'

'Then may God go with you too, colonel. I hope that the better aspects of Mother Russia become for you what they were for me when I was your age. I hope that these days of torment are over soon.'

With that, Andrei Alexandrovich Yezhov turned and walked towards the Moskva River, once again to wander down the embankment beside the vital artery which ran through the heart of his beloved city.

Thousands of miles south, in the streets of Tel Aviv, Jerusalem and Haifa, the streets were choked to capacity with people and vehicles. There was anger in the air.

Paul and Miriam stared with concern out of the window of their taxi. For the best part of an hour it had tried to push its way through the crowds to link up to the Jerusalem-Tel Aviv road so that they could catch their flight to Poland. Surrounding their taxi were tens of thousands of Jerusalemites. Some had seeped onto the streets in the fury of a friendless people alone in battle against an unseen enemy, like boxers striking at shadows. Others marched boldly out in defiance of the martial law edicts to demand the removal of the junta which had brought Israel to such a parlous state. But regardless of their political views, each and every one was horrified by the terrorist action against the Museum of the Holocaust.

Attack the country's soldiers, sailors and airmen, yes, they were fair game. Attack border settlements, attack army posts and planes and ships, yes, these too were targets, however obscene the slaughter may be. But to attack the memory of the Jewish people ... to attack the symbol of Jewish suffering under Nazism ... to attack the symbol of a hideous holocaust. That was unforgivable! How could anybody, any government, any terrorist group, any individual have thought to blow up the Museum of the Holocaust? What value, what purpose, did it serve? What kind of a mind was it that would eradicate the living proof of the dead past? The tortured death of six million mothers and fathers and children, brothers and sisters, uncles and aunts.

In every civilisation there is a turning point in the national psyche when the whole of a people is transmogrified from one state to another overnight, as if by the wave of a magician's wand. In England, it had been Winston Churchill's speeches, which had raised the national consciousness against the spread of Nazism. In Russia it had been the sight of Yeltsin standing on a Red Army tank. From its turret he had declaimed to his people, as Lenin had declaimed seventy years earlier, that the time of the tyrants was at an end. And in Israel it was the destruction of the Museum of the Holocaust. Liberal voices opposed Ben Ari's unilateral declaration of isolationism; academics protested vigorously against the destruction of the peace conference; and Opposition parliamentarians used Ben Ari's stance for their own political gain; but every one of them screamed their outrage as the full force of the destruction hit home.

Israel had learned to deal with the massacre of innocents on *kibbutzim* or with bombs exploding in city bus terminals. These were part of the currency of being an Israeli. But the anger which welled up in every Israeli who heard the news of the destruction of the Holocaust Museum was channelled into a need for action. There was a crescendo of voices in the land calling for the Ruling Council, Ben Ari and his colleagues, to do something. Hundreds of thousands of people poured out into the streets when the news was flashed on television. They appeared from everywhere. They came to express their indignation, their horror and their unmitigated anger. Within hours of the bombing, a huge crowd had formed outside the American Embassy. By 1 a.m. the crowd had swelled to close to 200,000 people. A pitifully small number of armed US marines stood by every doorway and behind every locked gate. Some protesters waved placards. Others held hands and sang the *Ha-Tikvah* or the *Kaddish*. Other people shouted and gesticulated at the locked windows and doors, blaming the recent hardline American stance for inciting terrorists to new depths of obscenity. Still others demonstrated outside the Knesset, screaming that Ben Ari and his actions had brought destruction on the Jewish people, like the actions of King Herod two thousand years earlier.

A battalion of policemen was dispatched from Tel Aviv police headquarters to stand guard outside the American Embassy to ensure that nobody broke through. The crowd was ugly, but it behaved. It would not do any damage. The people just wanted to vent their anger.

A similar crowd, though half the number, gathered outside the Russian Embassy, shaking fists and rattling gates. But the dispatch of another battalion put paid to any attempt to break in. A rabble rouser could have led the crowd to do whatever damage it wanted. But Israelis were more disciplined than that. Every Israeli over the age of seventeen had been in the armed forces. Although it appeared on the surface to be a totally undisciplined army—sloppy uniforms and a general refusal to salute officers—it was the most highly self-disciplined and sophisticated force on Earth. This discipline seeped through to their expression of anger outside the embassies and the Israeli parliament.

In Jerusalem, the crowds eventually went home but emerged again the following morning, just as Paul and Miriam were leaving their hotel. They were booked on a Lot Airlines flight from Ben Gurion to Warsaw and left in plenty of time. But they were delayed by the crowds and were now running late.

Miriam had never experienced an angry crowd before, but Paul knew how easily one could turn hostile and aggressive at the slightest provocation. Like a swarm of angry bees. If the demonstration thought that the passengers in the taxi were Americans or Russians, the entire mob would have focused its hate. They could easily have overturned the taxi and killed Paul and Miriam. The situation was fragile.

Paul tapped the driver on the shoulder. 'I don't care where we go,' he said, 'but get us out of here. Take us by a back road out of Jerusalem, even if we have to go via Lebanon.'

The driver did not need to be told. He was as terrified as his passengers and already in the process of working out a way to detour around the mass of people. He turned right into Hayarkon to escape the main road and the surging crowd.

Following the bombing outrage the previous night, Israel had thrown its security machine into top gear. Within minutes the Masada Plan had come into operation. Road blocks were set up on all main Israeli roads, airports and seaports, and borders were sealed. Every passenger leaving the country was bodysearched. Arab activists in the occupied territories were rounded up and taken into central headquarters for interrogation.

Police and Shin Bet operatives flooded into known Arab enclaves and made their presence obvious to the terrified inhabitants. Israel began to change from a country polarised by internecine arguments between pro- and anti-Ben Ari forces, into one in which those favouring strong military action by the government grew into a majority. The minority, who felt Ben

Ari's removal would solve Israel's problems, were forced to keep a low profile.

Tanks, armoured personnel carriers, troop vehicles and police wagons poured out onto the streets of the major towns in a show of strength. F-18s, Harriers, Tornados and even elderly Mystères and Mirages ripped through the air above the main cities to reassure the public that the government was fully in control of the situation. Many Israelis looked up, saw the visible proof that their Ruling Council was taking action and felt re-assured by their country's strength. Others only wondered how quickly the country could be rid of the madman and be re-stored to its rightful place as the guardian of morality within the area. But one thought was common to all political points of view—Israel was alone.

Overnight almost the entire population came to realise that the prophetic words of Ben Ari—his prediction that Israel could only stand alone and could rely upon nobody—had come true. The Americans had dumped Israel because they had scut-tled the peace conference. Most European nations had frozen Israeli bank accounts. The United Nations had vigorously con-demned the tiny country for its policies towards the Arabs. But the greatest outrage which the population suffered, more ter-rible than the murder of innocents, was the eradication of the Jewish racial memory.

Eventually, the taxi left the confines of Jerusalem and Paul and Miriam arrived at the airport. As they entered they were faced with a phalanx of soldiers toting Uzi submachineguns. It was a totally different environment from the one they had en-countered when they first arrived. They carried their bags over to the Lot Airlines counter, where they were faced by ground crew surrounded by security officers.

'Put your bags under the X-ray machine,' they were in-structed by a guard.

Their passports were scrutinised.

'Go over to that cubicle. Men on the left, women on the right.' Miriam froze at the instruction and the way it was delivered. So reminiscent of dividing new entrants into the concentration camp, young and old, healthy and sick, men and women. Right and left.

Miriam entered the cubicle—nothing more than four screens with a small door. In there she met a sullen-faced Israeli policewoman. 'Open your handbag,' she demanded.

Miriam didn't argue. 'Why don't you allow me to put it through the X-ray machine?' she asked.

'Plastic explosive doesn't show up in X-ray, madam,' said the policewoman. She tipped the bag upside down onto a white plastic sheet on the table and picked through Miriam's private possessions. Miriam was forced to put everything back herself.

'Put your hands above your head,' Miriam was told. The policewoman ran her fingers expertly over Miriam's entire body. She felt everywhere that could possibly hide a weapon or an explosive device.

'Take off your shoes,' said the policewoman, who examined the heels thoroughly.

The policewoman then put on a pair of thick rubber gloves and dug her hands deeply into Miriam's coat and trouser pockets. 'Why on earth do you need gloves for that?' asked Miriam.

'In case you have a syringe in your pocket. I don't want to catch AIDS.'

Miriam was amazed by the speed and thoroughness of the search. Within a minute, her entire body and possessions had been expertly scrutinised. She had never been subjected to this sort of treatment but she couldn't find it in her to be annoyed. She felt just a little bit grateful for the security precautions that were being taken.

Miriam left the booth and met Paul. 'You were quick,' she said.

'I didn't have anything to declare.' In Sydney it would have been a joke. Here it had a cathartic effect. Together they walked through customs and into the transit area.

Four hours later, Paul and Miriam prepared to land at Warsaw's Okecie Airport.

Marshal Petrovsky listened with great interest to the report on Radio Moscow's foreign service. The commentator described the feeling of confusion and anger in Israel following the destruction of the Holocaust Museum. He said that the crowds, while furious, had been generally well-behaved and no incidents had taken place. Petrovsky thought to himself how brilliantly events had worked out. His group had not planned the bombing, but he had known about it in advance from Bukharin's agent within the Arab terrorist cadre, and had allowed it to proceed because he couldn't have done a better job had he tried. It was a brilliant device for fomenting anger in Israel and marshalling a majority of the population together behind Ben Ari. If things went well in the next few days, the rest of the plan could be brought forward by several months. What Bukharin now had to do was to ensure Ben Ari capitalised upon the new feeling in the country and didn't go overboard in repressing opposition. Strength with reason was the order of the day.

The model Bukharin had constructed in the early days of his involvement assumed that public hostility towards Ben Ari's martial law edicts would last at least three months. His hypothesis was that the people would slowly settle down and accept the status quo. After that, their finances in a dreadful state, Israelis would accept financial help and trade credits from whoever offered them.

The intervention of the Arab terrorists had contracted Bukharin's critical time span and things could now proceed at an accelerated pace. Petrovsky drank a glass of brandy and chuckled. He had always discounted the Arabs as a limited, short-sighted and barbaric people, somewhat akin to the Cossacks. This act had redeemed them in his eyes. They were obviously trying to create a pan-Arab unity and foment another war with Israel. They assumed, probably wrongly, that Israel would lose. The winner was Petrovsky. Their recent terrorist activities had helped his plans immeasurably.

Bukharin's computer model would need to be revised to compress his estimated time to completion of the Jericho Plan. His time scale for an extreme left-wing backlash among the Israelis was now wildly inaccurate.

Petrovsky now had a hostile, aggressive Israel, the majority of its citizens behind Ben Ari and a world which was recoiling in horror at the sudden aggression of the Middle Eastern combatants. Another few terrorist attacks and there would undoubtedly be war clouds gathering in the area.

And with Israel vulnerable and friendless, Russia would happily step in to fill the void.

♜♜♜

President Jack Harrison sat in his swivel chair with his feet on the *Resolute*. His desk, which had been used by every President from Rutherford Hayes, was made from the oak timbers of the British ship HMS *Resolute* and was a gift made in 1880 by Queen Victoria. George Bush had moved the desk to his private office but Jack Harrison, with a view to history, had insisted it be moved back. The men now gathered around the *Resolute* felt its presence. It was a barrier between their President and themselves.

He had listened to the advice of his most trusted colleagues, Brett Whiteman, Colin Manners and, of course, John Dewhurst, for most of the afternoon, but now the decision was his. He turned to look at each of the men in front of him.

'Fellas, what you're saying to me is that I've got to pull back from the brink. You're saying that I've got to show Israel a bit of support or else we could be facing another war.'

He clasped his hands behind his head and arched his back. An habitual floor-pacer, hour upon hour of sitting had given him a numb backside. He looked into each man's face and tried to predict their reaction to what he was going to say.

'Well frankly, guys, I don't give a tinker's shit. They're not going to use nuclear warheads, neither Israel nor the A-rabs. No one's that stupid. You can't set off a nuclear weapon in

342

Tel Aviv without ruining the air and water supply of Mecca.

'It ain't me that's got Israel into this situation. If I show support for Israel now, it would be contrary to the interests of the American people. I'm sworn by oath of office to serve and protect them … not the fucking Israelis.'

Dewhurst stared at the carpet and shook his head. He had been expecting this reaction. His colleagues at Harvard had advised him not to sully his hands in the service of a boor like Harrison, but he had put possible value to his country above personal interest. Now he realised his colleagues were right. 'Mr President, if you don't offer support to the Israeli nation as a result of this heinous crime, you will be derelict in your duty. You must soften your hard line policy towards Israel and issue a condemnation of those who destroyed the Holocaust Museum … and a message of sympathy to the Israeli people. If you don't then I'll have to tender my resignation.'

It would be such a simple thing to do. Yet supporting Israel and condemning the bombing would run the risk of alienating America from the Arab world. That was something which Harrison was loath to do. He had predicted that Dewhurst would offer his resignation. Ivy League wimps were all the same. But he didn't want any resignations—not at this stage anyway. Harrison got up and went around to sit on the arm of John Dewhurst's chair. He put his muscular arm around Dewhurst's shoulder.

'John, c'mon. That's a massive overreaction and you know it. I'll tell you what I'll do, son. I'll send a message of sympathy. I'll tell the people of Israel how angry we are at the destruction of this museum. I'll even go into the Beth Israel Temple in New York this Saturday and tell every Jew in America how outraged I am by this wanton, senseless act of destruction. But that's as far as I'm going to go, John boy. No way I'm going to soften my stance to the Israelis just because they've had a museum totalled. America's interests lie in forcing Israel back to the negotiating table. If I soften my stance now, it's going to cause a division between America and the Arabs. We've gotten a whole lot closer to the Arabs than we have to the

Israelis these last few years. You're not going to resign, John. I won't let you. You're too valuable.'

The President stood up and walked back to his desk, leaning against it and waiting for Dewhurst's reaction. The other two men in the room sat silent. Dewhurst stood and walked over to the credenza. He poured himself a Perrier water and cleared his throat. Life would be so much easier if he returned to Harvard, the sculptured colonnades, the elm trees, the manicured lawns. And the regard in which he was held by students and colleagues alike. He knew he was only tolerated by these two-term politicians and this one-term President. His sole reason for joining was to do something constructive for the country. But the days of Metternich and Kissinger diplomacy were at an end. Today was the day of the deal-maker, not the conciliator.

'Very well, Mr President, I won't resign. But I'm still cautioning you not to sever relationships with Israel. The results could be catastrophic.'

President Harrison nodded. 'Hey! Come on, John,' he said reassuringly. 'Things will brighten up soon. The Israelis ain't got money, ain't got no friends, ain't got no support. They'll come around. You'll see. Trust me on this one, John. You spent too many years in Harvard. Don't forget I've been in the real world this last quarter century. And I know how people react.'

CHAPTER NINETEEN

'Any regrets?' asked Paul

Miriam turned back from the window to look at him. 'Regrets?'

'Yes, at leaving Israel. I was wondering what you were thinking.'

She smiled, and nodded. 'Some. What about you?'

'It's a beautiful country,' Paul replied. 'But I found the time there totally frustrating and in the last couple of days I was shit-scared.' Miriam looked at him in surprise. 'Come on, Miriam, you can't deny that you were frightened.'

'Of course I was, but I'm not going to let a man like Ben Ari spoil my first memories of Israel.'

'I don't have the same emotional ties as you,' said Paul. 'I was working rather than visiting. It gives you a different perspective. In one way, I'm glad to be out of there; but in another, I saw you in an entirely new light, which was … interesting.'

Miriam's emotions were being pulled this way and that by competing forces within her. She had tried to remain dispassionate and level-headed on the outside, while dealing privately with the conflicts within her.

'What do you mean, "a new light"?'

'It's not easy to explain. In Sydney your Judaism didn't matter all that much to you, whereas here, you've discovered a whole new side to your being. A wider, deeper dimension.'

'And how does that make you feel?'

Paul shrugged his shoulders.

'Excluded?' she asked.

Paul grinned. 'Boot's a bit on the other foot, isn't it? In Australia, you think of me as the insider and yourself as the outsider. In Israel, it was vice-versa. Yes, I suppose I have felt excluded. We've drifted further apart than we were in Sydney.'

'But I've never tried to exclude you from that side of my life. You've been with me when friends have celebrated weddings and bar mitzvahs.'

'Yes, but they were very Australian affairs. They were like everyday events with a few blessings thrown in and people remembering they've got to wear skullcaps. But in Israel, I felt you didn't want me to be part of things. As though I was a threat to your enjoyment of the religious side of the place.'

'But it was a totally new experience for you,' Miriam protested. 'Even I felt alienated from some of it. I found it a bit like watching a foreign movie.'

Paul didn't answer immediately. He had felt Miriam slowly ebbing away from him for days now, as though pulled by some inexorable tide, a force older and stronger than him. His only method of defence was to wait for their return to Australia, where he hoped that her usual surroundings would reinvest her with the feelings she once held towards him.

'I guess what I'll remember most about Israel is how threatening it was. Not just the riots and the bombing, but the way you've reacted. I feel as if I'm battling some hidden enemy called tradition.'

She reached over and squeezed his arm. 'I know I've been difficult. It's been a bitch of a time for me. I feel vulnerable and exposed. If ever I needed somebody's shoulder to lean on, it's now …'

'Then why not mine?'

Why? The eternal question. Why waste yourself on a non-Jew? Why turn your back on God? It was what her grandfather had asked her when she was at university. Nothing much had changed in a decade.

Why indeed? What was going on inside her which prevented her from throwing her arms around Paul, sharing in his strength and inner resolve?

She had travelled way beyond the radical feminists who rejected any male intervention in their lives, so it wasn't that.

She had accepted Paul as lover and soulmate in all her day-to-day existence, so it wasn't that. And she was not a committed Jewess who saw anti-Semitism in off-hand remarks by gentiles, so that wasn't it.

She knew all the reasons for relying on Paul, for using his shoulder to rest her confused head on; but there was a barrier between them, which seemed to have grown thicker, taller, more substantial. Like the massive stone walls around Jerusalem.

Only when she knew how to overcome the barrier without making the rest of her life crash down around her, could she put her grandfather's dybbuk finally to rest.

Her eyes began to moisten. She turned back to the window so Paul would not see her tears. She hated being emotional. It was her tiredness, she told herself, and the strain. She would be all right by the time they arrived in Poland.

But her mood didn't improve. The nearer the plane flew to Poland, the more forlorn she became. During the journey the conversation came in snatches. They talked fitfully about Israel and Poland, the land of the Bible and the land of the Diaspora. Paul tried to cheer her up but she couldn't escape the sense of foreboding as she approached her *zeida*'s homeland. The place where the dybbuk lived.

She found it difficult, painful, to control her emotions as the 747 banked over the city of Lodz prior to its approach to Warsaw's airport. She buried her forehead against the perspex of the window, its coldness soothing the flush of her skin.

All her life she had struggled to understand her emotions. She had even learned to contain most of them, but since arriving in Israel she had felt as though she was a marionette, with her emotions pulled by some invisible puppeteer.

Paul also felt doubts but not towards Poland. Emotionally drained by the precariousness of their relationship, he felt as though he were looking down to the bottom of a steep valley and that one false move could make him plummet headlong into it. Not even his professionalism as a journalist could halt the despondency he felt.

He had come to Israel and Europe like Parsifal, in search of the Holy Grail. He sought knowledge of Ben Ari and whether the man was masquerading on the world stage as a munificent leader at the expense of truth. Yet he had found nothing. His only reports to *The National* had been about the riots. He had not been able to make any progress on his real quest. He hadn't even told them he was going to Warsaw. He was scared they would recall him.

But inwardly he feared that Poland would be another wild goose chase and that his time would not be well spent. He was visiting Warsaw more to indulge Miriam than to benefit his paper. Or was it to benefit himself? To acquiese to Miriam's inner needs in the hope of rescuing their former relationship?

Miriam looked ten thousand feet below her at the towns which she thought might be Leszno or Rawicz. Towns where her grandparents and others like them played and prayed half a century before she was born. Where her own father was born. Where he suckled at her grandmother's breast. Where he first learned to totter, and then walk into his uncertain future, a future in another land, a vast land full of strange sights and sounds. An alien land where her grandparents and her father were treated with suspicion and hostility. A land where they weren't people, but refugees, where their inability with the language was seen by Australians as a form of inferiority.

As the plane came closer to landing, a feeling of vertigo welled up inside her once again. She turned away from the window to Paul. She would not let her weakness affect her this time. Not here. Not in Poland. Not where her grandfather had grown to manhood. Poland was the umbilicus to her family. For all her life, she had called Australians 'her people'. Yet a brief visit to Israel had opened her eyes and shown her how wrong she had been. Israel was the land of her religion; below was the land of her roots. Every cell, every fibre, every thought had its origins in the black soil and green fields below. A strong feeling of dissociation began to grow inside her. Her home was no longer her home; her people no longer her people; her land no longer her land. Like her ancestors since the time of the Roman Emperor Vespasian two millennia before, she was a wandering Jew, condemned like Ahasuerus to tread forever in the footsteps of those who had gone before her. Her Australian upbringing and education were merely forerunners to her future. Like Jews of old, she was condemned by her religion to be a stranger in a strange land.

In Israel, and now flying over Poland surrounded by Europeans, with people on the plane speaking guttural Polish, German and other languages, Miriam experienced an unnerving dichotomy. In Israel she had felt herself to be a real Jew, a part of a society. Not merely an adherent of a religion. But landing in Poland, she began to feel that she was a product of Eastern Europe. She flushed with embarrassment. Was she shallow? Who was there who could help her? To whom could she turn and ask advice? Her roots in the past had been severed by the death of her grandfather. Without knowledge of her past, where was her future?

Most of the Polish she had learned as a child, as well as a smattering of Yiddish, had been forgotten years ago. When she spoke to her grandfather she had only used the occasional phrase. Now she bitterly regretted forgetting her vocabulary. How was she going to communicate with people? How did her ancestors communicate when they were expelled from one land to another for the crime of being Jews? They had managed. So would she.

As the plane sank lower on its final approach to Okecie Airport, the sun was reflected in the mighty Vistula River which fed the country's heartland. The plane turned in its final bank towards the city. Miriam turned towards Paul and held his arm tightly. 'It'll be all right. Don't worry. Just give me a bit more time.' He squeezed her arm tenderly and smiled.

Miriam turned back to the window to look out at the countryside and once more felt giddy looking down. She breathed deeply to recover her composure. She had a need to see Poland. She felt she could identify the very streets in which her grandfather had walked. Her eyes captured a small group of old buildings on the outskirts of the city. Miriam convinced herself that her grandfather had once been there. Her heart and mind played word and picture games, skittishly seeing women in crinoline skirts and black bodices, men in frockcoats meandering in the turn-of-the-century innocence of summer days, walking the streets and nodding to acquaintances as they drove past in open landaus.

She knew she was being ridiculous. The city was dealt a terrible blow by Hitler's forces in the Second World War. But she couldn't help imagining her grandfather as one of the doll-like people that she could only just identify far below her.

As the plane touched down, she was swept by the irony of her situation. She knew from the history of her own people that three million Polish Jews, virtually the entire population, were exterminated by Hitler. In fact, a fifth of the total Polish population—around six million human beings—had perished under the Nazi occupation. The Poles, as much as the Russians and the Jews, suffered as a result of Hitler's insanity.

The huge plane shuddered as the tyres screeched on the runway. Paul turned towards Miriam and tried to determine what emotions were going through her mind and how he should react. At times she was like gunpowder, one comment igniting her anger; at others she was soft and coy, gently accommodating his needs and emotions. It was a mystery to him how there could be so many shades of behaviour in the one person.

'You okay?' he asked.

She turned to face him. 'I'm all right. Why?'

'Just checking. Must be difficult for you, being here.'

She shrugged her shoulders. 'Not really,' she said non-committally, and turned back to face the window.

'Miriam, this must all be very hard for you. All the memories and confusions. I do understand …'

'You've been wonderful, Paul. Don't think I don't appreciate it. But you can't help me. Only I can.'

Paul nodded.

The plane slowed as it reached the end of the runway and pivoted on its massive axis. It slowly rolled towards the airport terminal. The name of the terminal was emblazoned on its roof in blue neon. Miriam couldn't even pronounce it.

Paul leaned over and kissed her gently on the ear. 'When I used to go back to visit my folks in Townsville, I'd be swamped with all sorts of emotions. Sometimes I'd have an overwhelming urge to stay there and live a small town life.' Miriam turned and looked at him. For the first time in days, her face seemed to have relaxed. 'But then I'd have this urge which would pull me back to Sydney, to where I was independent. I'm a different man there from the one I am in Townsville. Do you understand what I'm talking about?'

Miriam's mind was dealing with her own raft of emotions, but his intentions were clear and she nodded.

'Are you saying that I'm playing a role?' she asked.

Paul took a deep breath before continuing. 'Only in Sydney. You don't seem to be role-playing any more. I've met a new Miriam. She's a bit more abrupt, more independent and more distant. I feel I'm being cut off from the old one and I'm not sure I like it. Right now, I think we've got very real problems, you and me.'

Miriam held his hand tighter. She could have said things to relieve his mind, to ease his concerns, but she decided not to. 'Paul, I don't know where things will lead.' She saw a look of hope in his eyes but she didn't want to give him a false sense of security. 'I don't love you any less than I did in Sydney, Jewish or not, but who knows? By the time we get back to Sydney you mightn't want me any more.'

Paul continued to look at her. She turned back to the window. From their disembarkation, through Customs, to the time when they stepped into a taxi to take them to their hotel, they held hands and remained close to each other.

'You are England, yes?' said the taxi driver as they drove out of Okecie Airport's circuitous road system into a medley of cars and trucks. Emission control standards were obviously lacking, with cars, buses and trucks pouring out black cloying smoke.

'No,' replied Paul, 'we're from Australia.'

'Austrich. No! You don't have German accent. English, I think you are, yes. Why you say you are Austria?'

'Not Austria … Australia! Down south. Kangaroos, koalas … Australia.'

The driver banged the steering wheel and laughed. 'Ah! Australia. Yes. My wife, she has cousins there. In Sydney. Is beautiful. She says, "You come" but, um, how we come? Poland today. No money.'

Before they could say anything, the taxi driver half-turned towards them, indicating to the passing buildings, and asked: 'Tell me, you like my city Warsaw. Is old, no?'

Miriam agreed: 'It's charming. All these magnificent buildings … That's what you'll miss if you come to Australia. No building there is more that a couple of hundred years old.'

'No building here more than forty years old!' said the taxi driver.

'What?'

The taxi driver let out a belly laugh. He'd fooled yet another tourist.

'No, lady. Nothing here more older than Second World War. 1945! Germans destroy whole city after Warsaw uprising in 1944. Millions killed. All buildings gone. Like that!' He clicked his fingers. 'These buildings … what do you call it when you put up like was there before?'

'Replicas?' suggested Paul.

'Yes, replicas. All fake. But good. Like was used to be before. Is nice, but not very practical. Cold in winter, hot in summer. But Warsaw people like it like this. Is link to past, yes? No city ever suffer like we do. So we rebuild Warsaw. Tell me, lady, gentleman. What you think? Good, no?'

Paul admitted it was very good. Miriam stared silently out of the window at the buildings as they rushed past. She tried to distinguish one from another. But she couldn't master the words on their facades—all those z's and k's and w's—and allowed the false antiquity to envelop her. She was surrounded by her history, yet in a sense it was a false history. She sighed. Life was so complicated. The veil of time was obscuring her view.

But what did it matter if her grandparents had not visited these very buildings in the 1930s? They were exact copies. The ground was still the same. And she could always pretend.

The taxi travelled speedily up Ujazdowskie Avenue until it reached Zankowy Place and entered the maze of narrow cobbled streets which comprise the Old City. It was very different from Jerusalem's Old City. The river was just to their right and the taxi slowed as cars painfully tried to pass each other in the narrow confines. It took them fifteen minutes to reach the Hotel Victoria.

After the formalities of registration they were shown to their room. It was a functional chamber, unlike the ornate and grandiose entrance hall in the reception area, but they were too tired to care. They showered and lay down. The mania at Tel Aviv airport, the officiousness of the Lot cabin crew and the nightmare driving in central Warsaw made them both crave sleep, which came as a relief after their conversation in the plane. Perhaps tomorrow they would relax into the new city and life could begin afresh.

They slept until ten that night, when Paul's need to go to the bathroom woke Miriam. Rather than try to go back to sleep, they decided to dress and explore the Old City of Warsaw.

The contrast between Warsaw, Jerusalem and Tel Aviv could not have been greater. Tel Aviv was a brash, uninhibited cosmopolitan festival of a city, while Jerusalem retained much of the Ottoman and British Imperial conservatism, intermingled with ageless monuments of the Bible. Both were testaments to biblical timelessness; Israel as a polymorphic testament.

Warsaw, on the other hand, was independent of its buildings. Neither as old as Jerusalem, nor as young as Tel Aviv, it had its own feeling of excitement. It was one of the intellectual and artistic capitals of the world, and its reconstruction had been undertaken with a passion and sensivity.

Even late at night, the streets thronged with people. They walked arm-in-arm, gazing into the darkened recesses of nearly empty shops or sitting at sidewalk cafes, enjoying a brandy, a beer or a vodka. Unlike the cities of the Balkan states and other Eastern European nations which suffered internecine destruction following their freedom from Communism, Warsaw had not been affected.

Paul and Miriam found themselves in Swietojanska Street looking in awe at the Gothic Cathedral of St John, and the nearby Jesuit Church which dated from the early 1600s. For the first time she was exposed to Gothic arches, flying buttresses, colonnaded archways, gargoyles, carved lintels and the numerous other glories of Renaissance stonemasonry.

She clutched on to Paul's arm as they entered the Old Town Market Square, with its delicate and ornate seventeenth- and eighteenth-century architectural styles. Here, the mansion houses had been converted into dozens of boutiques, beautiful shops which portrayed their wares in subtly lit windows, as well as arts and craft shops and cafes and restaurants. A short walk brought them to the defence walls and Barbican whose architecture dated back to the fifteenth century. It spoke movingly to them of the medieval fortifications needed by this city which divided Western Europe from Russia. Miriam was lost in a world of which she had no prior experience and Paul instinctively understood how she felt. Not wanting to impose himself upon her thoughts, he remained silent.

While they were engrossed in the baroque splendour of the centre of Warsaw, Paul and Miriam failed to notice a sleek white Polish Fiat following them. Its three unsmiling inhabitants each focused his attention on where they had been, and to whom they might have spoken.

Miriam began to tire despite her long sleep. After the tensions of Israel, it would take days for her energy to be restored. They walked slowly back to their hotel and returned to the security of their bed. The Fiat parked outside the hotel. The men waited for their relief, who would show up the following morning.

Next day, Miriam telephoned the Director of the Organisation for Polish Martyrs, and was immediately put through to Rabbi Miklos Abrahams.

'*Dzien dobry.* Means good morning, my dear young lady. My Polish better than my English,' he said. 'Yes, I know of you already. My friend Rabbi Gartenbaum telephoned me and told me you would be coming. So how are you? How did you enjoy your flight? Where are you staying? Come see me this morning at 10 o'clock. We will talk.'

And having made the arrangement without allowing Miriam to answer any of his rhetorical questions, he put the phone down. Miriam was amused. She wondered whether his manner was typical of Polish Jews. It certainly didn't remind her of her grandfather or any of his friends. Maybe they had become Australianised.

Paul and Miriam dressed and took a taxi to Zbawiciela Plaza, near to the Technical University of Warsaw, where the Organisation for Polish Martyrs had its headquarters.

It was on the third floor of a seven-storey replica of a rococo building, standing in a phalanx with other, equally magnificent buildings in a wide tree-lined street. Miriam stood on the pavement for a moment while Paul walked towards the building's entry. She looked up and down the road. The buildings were all similar. Austere, authoritative and enduring. Like buildings in any city's financial or legal district. Yet according to the taxi driver, all the buildings were replicas, modern images of a former world, a bygone glory. Where, Miriam wondered, did falsehood end, and truth begin?

The two armed security guards who stood outside the main entrance brought the harsh reality of the current century into focus. Paul and Miriam were asked who they were visiting. When Rabbi Miklos confirmed their visit on the intercom they were shown upstairs, where there were more guards. The front door of the office was encased in thick bullet- and bomb-proof glass bricks within a steel cage. Entry was only possible after an electronic keypad was activated by someone inside the office.

After a short wait, a spectral image appeared on the opposite side of the glass bricks. As he came closer and activated the lock to admit the visitors, Miriam could see from his bushy beard and balding head that he was a rabbi.

Miklos Abrahams was a short, rotund man, Friar Tuck with a *yarmulka* instead of a tonsure. He wore a faded bottle-green cardigan, baggy trousers and his half-moon spectacles were falling off the end of his nose. He was every child's vision of the quintessential grandfather.

'Children, children, come. Come this way. Come over here and sit down. You are from Austria?'

'No, we're from Australia.'

Rabbi Miklos boomed a laugh. 'Yes, kangaroos, koalas, Opera House. Sorry I make mistake.'

'It happens quite a lot. Don't worry about it,' said Paul.

'So what can I help you with, my dears?'

Miriam explained to him that her grandfather was one of the last remaining survivors of a Jewish ghetto called Chelmnitz, attached to the small village of Rawicz. Since his recent death, she was desperate to learn more about his early life and the village. 'Ah!' said the old rabbi, who nodded, 'if only we could ask those questions before our loved ones are gathered to the bosom of *ha kodesh, b'ruch hu*. Rawicz? Yes, that's in west of country. Is near Poznan, I think. South from there, somewhere. Come, we see what we got in files, yes?'

Together they walked down a series of corridors into a brightly lit room containing bank after bank of filing cabinets. It was reminiscent of the Institute of the Diaspora. That brought a flood of sad memories for Miriam. Rabbi Miklos spent twenty, perhaps thirty minutes searching through file after file until eventually he came to the one that he sought. 'Here is the thing,' he said with a satisfied grunt. 'Come, we go back to my office, we see what it says.'

Like a couple of schoolchildren, they followed the rabbi back down the corridor until they came to his office, where he opened the file. It was disappointingly thin. There were only half a dozen yellowing pages of typed material.

Rabbi Miklos read and re-read and shook his head. 'Here she talks of Rawicz and the community goes back to 1280.' The rabbi scanned the information. In broken English, and even more broken sentences, he skipped over non-essential details. 'Fleeing from pogroms in Spain, Germany ... settled by 1265 Act of Prince Boleseaus the Pious ... guaranteed Jews full religious freedom and trade ... craft guild established by King Casimir the Great in 1364 ... legal protection so Jews flocked to Poland, with Rawicz a major entry route from West.'

The rabbi flicked through several pages of the typescript until he came to more immediate details. 'In 1918, 33 per cent of Poland was ethnic, most were Ukrainians, then Jews. This I know. All this is old. Ah ha, yes here. In Rawicz between 1918 and 1937 there were some fights between Nationalist Democratic Party which was anti-Semitic, and on the other hand the Communists and socialists, which had ties to the Jozef Pilsudski group. They came to blows many times, often centred in provincial towns like Rawicz where police presence wasn't strong; where there were many Jews. These people tried to cause problems. The socialists weren't anti-Jewish, but the others were.'

The rabbi stopped reading and looked up at them over his half-moon spectacles.

'This is typical of problems of Jews in Poland,' he said. 'Because there were many Jews, Poles think that they held too much of the economy in their hands. Everyone tried to Polanise the Jews, and Rawicz was sometimes in the firing line. But so was Poznan, Krakow, Lublin ... many places, not just Rawicz. Was small, Rawicz. Small village, not big ...'

'But I thought there was a *yeshiva* there,' Miriam interrupted.

Rabbi Miklos dismissed it with a wave of his hand. 'Sure, many towns had *yeshiva*. Some very small. Two rabbis, ten students. Some very big, like a university today. Is nothing to have a *yeshiva* in a small town.' He shook his head. 'Is all it says, I'm sorry, but no records. Don't know why. Should be more. Maybe before my time here there were more records. We been collecting records for forty years, maybe at the beginning there were more details but now, maybe someone has taken from the files and not put it back. I'm sorry I can't help you more.'

Miriam sunk back into her chair. Her body seemed weighed down by lead as she struck another dead-end. The old rabbi looked at her with sympathy.

'My dear, you are angry, yes?'

Miriam let out a deep sigh. 'No, rabbi, not angry, just terribly disappointed. We've come so far, and we've spoken to so many people. You were really our last hope. And now …'

The rabbi shrugged. 'Very sorry. Many people want to find details of relatives but Nazis kill almost all Poles. Very bad records.'

Miriam and Paul looked at each other.

'Tell me, rabbi,' asked Paul, 'do you have any details here of who may have been born in Rawicz?'

The rabbi frowned. 'Some yes, some no. Who you want to know?'

Miriam intervened. 'Say there was somebody very famous who was born in Poland, somebody like … Ben Gurion or Menachem Begin or Yitzhak Shamir? Would you have details of where they may have been born?'

The rabbi looked closely at Miriam. Then at Paul. He frowned again. It was as though a barrier had dropped between them. 'Why you ask?'

'Rabbi,' said Paul, 'we're interested in finding out who else was born in Rawicz, apart from Miriam's grandfather. We'd like any information you've got which may or may not be in the files. Are there any other sources of reference that we could go to?'

'This is all source of reference. Is no other. In Israel is

Museum of Diaspora with records. Maybe you try there? Yes?'

Miriam felt deflated. 'We already have. That's why we're here.'

The rabbi's mood had altered when they began asking questions about people other than Miriam's grandfather. He became surly, taciturn, unwilling to help further.

'You here to find out about *zeida*, yes? Why you talking about Ben Gurion and these others?'

Paul explained. 'There's a lot more that we need to know. You see, we have information from Miriam's late grandfather that the Prime Minister of Israel was born in Rawicz. His name was …'

Without any warning, the rabbi put his finger to his lips and stood abruptly. 'I'm sorry you have wasted your visit,' he said in an unnecessarily loud voice. 'Is shame, really, all this was without result. Let me buy you vodka, come, is nearly time for lunch … I go down with you and we drink together, yes …'

The rabbi grabbed Paul's arm and nearly lifted him out of the chair. He beckoned for Miriam to follow. In Polish he said something to the people in the general office area, indicating he was going out for a while.

Walking back through the security gate and descending the three flights of stairs, Paul was desparate to ask the rabbi what was going on but he remained silent. Miriam followed his lead.

On the street, the rabbi nodded to the two security men and walked across the wide and busy thoroughfare to a cafe on the other side of the road.

As they crossed the street the back door of a black 1972 Opel opened. A heavy-set man carrying a briefcase left the car and sauntered nonchalantly in the same direction.

The cafe was much larger than it appeared from the street. A waiter, dressed in a white shirt and black apron, showed them to a table. The rabbi indicated that he wanted to sit at one much deeper within the cafe and away from the window. Assuming that everyone in the world drank vodka in the middle of the day, the rabbi ordered three drinks without bothering to ask Paul and Miriam.

'Rabbi, what the hell's going on?' whispered Paul, looking around to see if anyone was listening. 'One minute you're giving us the impression that we're like pariahs and the next minute you drag us down here for a drink. Now what's happening?'

'Mister, some questions upstairs you do not ask. In Poland you must guard tongue all the while if you are Jew. Is not so easy, especially these days since neo-Nazis start again all over Europe. Just like before war.'

'Oh come on, rabbi. I know there's trouble in Germany, but you can't seriously expect me to believe that there's neo-Nazism in Poland. Not after what Hitler did to the Poles.'

The rabbi reacted angrily. 'And why not? Why shouldn't there be anti-Semites here? Not neo-Nazis, sure, but you think Poland is free of Jew-haters just because all Jews were killed? You're very naive man. You don't understand the way Jews are hated in Eastern Europe. You are non-Jew, I think. You won't tell me about how we live here, thank you!'

Miriam intervened. 'Rabbi, Paul is non-Jewish but that doesn't mean he doesn't have any understanding of what you have suffered. Don't think we're trying to cause problems for you. When we tell you why we're here, you'll understand how important it is that we find this information.'

The rabbi looked at them and calmed down. They were so young and had not been embittered by experience. He nodded. 'So, we will all start again, please. Now, you will eat?'

'You surprise me,' said Miriam. 'How can an orthodox rabbi eat and drink in a place like this?'

The Rabbi shrugged. 'I don't eat, but I think that the Holy One, *b'ruch hu*, will forgive me cheating a bit with the vodka. It helps me think.'

As they spoke the man carrying the briefcase entered the cafe and sat at a table two places from theirs.

'What happened upstairs?' Paul asked. 'What's all the secrecy?'

'All people I work with are not the same. The rabbis, the Jews, yes, them I trust like myself. But is Polish government gives us money for research. All money donated by Jews in America, Europe, Australia for our work is taken by Polish government, and they give only half back to us. Rest they say pays for their expenses.' He said the word in disgust. 'So we must employ some non-Jewish historians and librarians to equal balance in report. They are like spies. They tell government what we say, what we do. Papers become missing, files go. Maybe Rawicz file go, who knows?'

Miriam looked at Paul and nodded her head. Paul remained silent.

The rabbi continued. 'I say nothing upstairs, but when you talk to me about Israel and Prime Minister, then I think, this news not for Polish government to learn. I think, stay quiet upstairs. Now we are private, you tell me what you want ...'

Since her time in Israel, with the sudden and massive disruption to the country's reputation as a bastion of democracy, Miriam didn't think that anything could surprise her anymore. But for a little old rabbi to be acting like some character out of a spy novel was unexpected, to say the least.

Paul shared her surprise. 'I'm stunned that the Polish government is behaving like this,' he said. 'I thought things here had got better since Lech Walesa and the breakdown of Communism.'

The Rabbi smiled. 'For Poles is better. For Jews, no. Always Jews are reason for bad economy, bad relations with other countries, bad this, bad that. Poles is Poles. Jews is Jews. We are thorn in the side of Polish body. But enough. You tell me what you want to know.'

Paul explained the photographs, the odyssey to Israel, the constant frustrations with officialdom and the total lack of information concerning the Polish life of the Prime Minister. However, he omitted to tell Miklos how Miriam's grandfather died. And he said nothing about his apartment being ransacked, or their suspicions that Mossad was involved.

Throughout the monologue, the rabbi sat transfixed, listening to every word as though it were a biblical revelation. The thickset man in a baggy suit with a battered old leather briefcase scrutinised them. His vodka came and he threw it to the back of his throat. He ordered a beer, which he sipped more slowly.

When Paul had finished his story, the rabbi sat silently. He took a drink of vodka and nodded to the waiter for refills.

'Is amazing. Years ago, 1970, '72 maybe, I think about Ben Ari, when he join Israeli parliament but before he became well known. I read he is Polish, and I think, "Where he come from?" I write a few letters to government, to town councils; I say, "Have you records of Ben Ari when a boy in Poland?" I write to him, himself. I say, "Give me details of you as boy in Poland for book. What was your name when you were boy in Poland before you change to Israeli name." He write back and say "I am Israeli; my past is not important."'

'That's the attitude he's been taking ever since he arrived in Israel,' Miriam said. 'It's been impossible for us to discover his past.'

Rabbi Miklos continued: 'I think no more. Then a few weeks later, after I write to him, we have big burglary, many records stolen. No one knows what or why. Not like today with computers, and back-up disks stored in bank vault. Then, everything written by hand or typewriter. So who knows what we lost? Maybe big parts of Rawicz file stolen. Names from village. People who lived there. Who knows? Police come and they try to find thief, but no good. So we get security on downstairs, and upstairs. Now I think "Who organise robbery?" When it happened, I think it was vandals, anti-Semites. Now, I wonder.'

If their lives had been spent during the past month in trying to construct an obscure picture from an insane jigsaw puzzle, then a few more pieces suddenly fitted together.

No one at the rabbi's table had noticed the man with the briefcase walk into the cafe. No one saw him finish his glass of beer, pay the bill and walk out of the cafe, leaving his briefcase underneath the table. As the waiter bent down to clear the ashtray, glasses and coins, his foot hit an object hidden by the large white tablecloth. He lifted the cloth, saw the briefcase, and looked for its owner. The man was just about to reach the cafe door.

Over the noise in the room, the waiter called after the man. He appeared not to hear. The waiter held up the briefcase and called again, but the customer moved quickly through the door. The waiter walked hurriedly towards him.

By now, most customers were looking quizzically at the waiter trying to return a briefcase to a fast-disappearing customer. The waiter ran out of the door, calling all the while for the customer to stop. But the customer ran across the road to an old dark car. It looked like something out of a Marx Brothers movie. Miriam turned to Paul to say something. The words never left her mouth. A huge concussion of fire, smoke, noise, exploding window and searing heat knocked Paul, Miriam and the rabbi off their seats in a rag-doll heap on the floor. Miriam screamed in panic as the fireball leaped into the cafe towards her, carrying with it a million shards of razor-sharp glass which cut her clothes and stuck like needles into the side of her face, arms, neck and hair.

Tables and chairs which had been lifted like toys off the floor suddenly landed all around them, causing greater pain and devastation.

When the sound of the explosion had died down, it was replaced by a momentary silence, which was then broken by the sounds of people screaming. Men and women were crying and wailing at the shock, the hurt, the injuries which the explosion had caused.

The explosion would have been fatal for Paul, Miriam and Rabbi Miklos if the waiter hadn't carried the briefcase out of the cafe. Its impact blew a nearby table on its edge, which acted like a shield, warding off most of the larger shards of glass which would have severed their arteries.

Miriam lay on the ground, screaming hysterically until Paul pushed furniture, glass and cutlery aside and crawled over to her. He put his arm around her shoulder. She winced in agony as he inadvertently pushed the glass shards deeper into her back. Blood seeped through her blouse in a growing red mosaic. She looked into Paul's eyes and stopped screaming. Instead, she began to sob, her body in pain, her mind numb with shock. Paul knew that he was safe and well. His only concern was for Miriam.

Nearby, Rabbi Miklos was lying in a heap, moaning words in Yiddish and Polish, and saying prayers in Hebrew.

After a moment or two, the noise of screaming and wailing was drowned out by calmer but strident voices taking control of the situation. Voices of authority shouted orders and barked demands. But the three remained on the cafe floor, lying in a limbo of broken glass and the smell of burnt flesh. Their ears rang from the explosion, their skin throbbed from the tiny needles of glass and the heat of the fireball.

♖♖♖

The eight men were exhausted. For three nights since they had destroyed the Holocaust Museum they had travelled from town to town, country to country, to avoid being detected. Each had averaged only a few hours sleep, snatched in a truck here, or a car there. They had spent their time travelling on back roads, in and out of cheap hotels, or scurrying from one safe house to another. To avoid detection, they never stayed more than a few hours in any one place. A constantly moving target was much harder to isolate and Marcel believed that escape was easiest when the mind of the security forces was focused on the scene of the outrage.

Just when each man was able to lie on a hotel bed and feel at ease after three days hard travelling, he received an order to travel immediately to Rome. A flagrant violation of security, it was impossible to reconcile with the way Marcel normally arranged events. It was a command nonetheless, and had to be obeyed. Dutifully, each man arrived in Rome at different times, from their different destinations, despite their desperate need for sleep.

When the last man had arrived, Marcel explained why he had breached security and contacted them so soon after the destruction of the museum.

The eight men gathered in the Caesar Suite of the Hotel Mondiale, in Rome's northern outskirts, were surrounded by a day's worth of coffee cups, dried sandwiches and bottles of Perrier water.

The terrorist attack had done more, much more, than destroy the museum, Marcel told them. It had mobilised the entire Israeli nation. Many were behind the Prime Minister. Some were demanding his removal. The country was riven by factions. Although the next event in the terror campaign was not due until August, the Imam had decreed that it should be brought forward to take advantage of the confusion. The Holy One had ordered it be undertaken immediately to capitalise on the mood of violence and demands for revenge which were spreading through the body of the population.

There were howls of protest from the seven others. They cited the danger of doing something so soon. They warned of the paranoia of the Israeli police. They demanded that other people be involved. But Marcel insisted that these very circumstances made the next bombing even more propitious … dangerous, certainly … but its success would totally demoralise the entire Jewish population. At the same time it would boost Arab morale.

'Brothers, there is no one here I would replace. Your skills are honed to a fine point. You will do what I order.'

They immediately agreed. No one in his right mind would argue against Marcel. Evening was drawing near, and each man would soon be leaving. Marcel had timed his charade to minimise discussion of the plans by the terrorists.

'Brothers,' he said, taking seven brown envelopes from his jacket pocket. 'We are going to destroy the Knesset, the Israeli parliament.' There were whistles of surprise. 'Here are the individual plans for your arrival ports and for your escapes as well as details of the target. Open the envelopes now and commit the details to memory. Then give the information back to me and I will destroy it. Each of you has a different function. We will meet again next week in this same room.'

The men were surprised. Why no discussion of the plans? They took the envelopes and opened them. Each smiled broadly as the details became known.

'This is the work of a genius,' said Saud ibn Masse, one of the few people in the group who knew Marcel personally as well as professionally. Marcel nodded in gratitude.

'I cannot accept praise for the idea. It is the work of the Imam, but I will not let him down in its execution,' said Marcel. 'When you have all finished, give back the papers to me.'

When they had been returned, Marcel gathered them together. Each man stood, kissed Marcel, and left the room at irregular intervals.

When he was alone, Marcel allowed himself the luxury of relaxation. Unlike the Moslems, he was allowed to enjoy a beer. Normally, he did not drink. It clouded the mind and made reactions slow. But patience was now required to allow the traitor to do his work.

As he sat, he breathed deeply. An overwhelming urge to wash his face came over him. One of the seven brothers who had kissed him was a Judas. He had left his stain, his impurity, on Marcel's cheek.

Going into the bathroom to shower, Marcel wondered how quickly the dog would run to the Russian Embassy for his thirty pieces of silver. When he did, he would reveal himself. Each of the envelopes contained minor differences in detail. When the traitor's message was intercepted by the Imam, the difference would expose the traitor.

Marcel had a hot shower to wash away the tensions of the day. As he stood in the stream of water, his mind played with the different ways in which he could dispose of the turncoat. Sexual pleasure stirred in his groin.

Dressed only in a bathtowel, he entered the loungeroom, and

was surprised by a soft knock on the door. Grabbing a gun, he stood by the wall beside the door, and called: 'Yes?'

A muffled voice from the other side said: 'Brother, it's Saud. May I come in?'

Marcel smiled. Saud. It was good that he had returned. He had worked with Saud for fifteen years. They were closer than friends. He opened the door, and the stocky, elegant, beautiful form of his long-time lover stood there.

Saud smiled and walked into the room: 'Are you angry with me for returning?'

'I knew you would come back,' said Marcel as he held the man's hand and closed the door.

'You looked strained tonight, Marcel. As though the world was troubling you.'

'I feel easier now you are here, my love.'

♟♟♟

Marshal Petrovsky drummed his fingers on the antique table as he listened to Bukharin's report. Colonel Scherensky feared that the force would drive his fingers through the wood.

'And so I made the decision to terminate them both,' said Bukharin.

'And the photo?' asked the marshal.

'It is still unrecovered, excellency, but because of the actions of the Arabs the conclusion to the Jericho Plan has come much sooner than we thought. Therefore, regardless of what might be concluded from their deaths, I judged it essential that the Australians get no closer to proving our asset's identity,' Bukharin insisted.

'But you assured me that they would get no closer. You advised me not to terminate them in Israel and now you have attempted ... and failed ... to terminate them in Warsaw. What in the name of hell is going on, Bukharin? Are you totally incompetent? Must I remove you from heading this operation?'

'Marshal,' Colonel Scherensky interrupted, 'the problem does not lie with either the general or myself. The problem lies with inadequate attention to detail by the agents who sanitised Ben Ari's past. Nobody believed the Australians would come this close. We have no idea what the old rabbi in Jerusalem told them. All we know is that they decided to go to Poland. They were closer and closer and we had to take action.'

Marshal Petrovsky looked with hostility at the younger man. 'When I require your gratuitous input, Scherensky, I'll ask for it. In the meantime, I want these two people terminated immediately.'

CHAPTER TWENTY

For the first time in days, President Jack Harrison felt good. Really good. He was back in the driving seat. Up until now he had been a passenger, swerving all over the place in a vehicle driven by a crazy Israeli who didn't know where he was going. But now he was going to take control and it was Ben Ari's turn to be the passenger.

In the Rose Garden of the White House, surrounded by high walls to block the telephoto lenses of reporters, and under a canopy of inaudible white noise to prevent their conversation being recorded, sat eight men.

Jack Harrison had invited the Secretary General of the United Nations, Ratu Sir Sidomante Bara; the United Nations ambassadors of Britain, France, the Republic of Russia and Saudi Arabia; as well as John Dewhurst and the head of the Joint Chiefs of Staff, Colin Manners.

All listened carefully to the President and his Secretary of State. The plan they had concocted was clever and stood a strong chance of working. Initially the group had been sceptical, reminding the President that similar plans had failed in Bosnia-Herzegovina and in Iraq. United Nations sanctions only worked in countries where the rule of law prevailed. And in Israel, the law was determined by the Ruling Council. But the President insisted that his plan would work. Although the majority of Israelis supported the Ruling Council, America doubted that the support would remain for very long. Israel was isolated. A tiny country could not stand up for long against the condemnation of the world.

In American and United Nations eyes, Ben Ari and the other members of his triumvirate were hanging on by the skin of their teeth. President Harrison had read the CIA Station Chief's assessment from Tel Aviv, but against the advice of John

Dewhurst, had largely discounted it. The CIA head in Israel claimed that opinion in Israel was strongly divided. But while there were external threats against the country, either from terrorists or the Arabs, or the United Nations, the majority of the people would be more likely to support a strong military government than to allow the country to fall into political anarchy.

Harrison had read similar assessments before and they had been hopelessly inaccurate in virtually every troublespot throughout the world. CNN and the BBC knew more about politics than the Ivy League spooks drawing untold amounts of money. Even the GCHQ in Cheltenham seemed to assess foreign intelligence and signals more quickly and more accurately than the button-down-collar limpwrists in Langley.

'So,' said the Secretary General. 'Do you think it can be pulled off?'

Harrison put down his cup of coffee. 'Mr Secretary, I'm sure it can. Look, we've got economic and financial sanctions against a country with a tiny money base and a small infrastructure. They can't last on their own for more than a couple of months. Then we've got Syria and Jordan moving divisions up to the border. Without the information from our AWACs, Israel's virtually blind. They can only rely on their ground-based radar.'

The other men gathered around the table nodded in agreement. Each had a vested interest, but tried to seem as though he was committed to a common consensus that would be to the benefit of the entire world community.

The Saudi Ambassador felt an inner glow. The British Ambassador was composing how best to explain the situation to his minister. He thought of a neat comparison between Harrison and John Wayne. That would cause amusement in Downing Street and Whitehall. And the French Ambassador glanced at John Dewhurst and saw a man divided between duty on the surface and deep despair. The Russian, cosmopolitan, elegant and enjoying his camaraderie with the American, said: 'I agree, Mr President. It's a good plan. The Israelis struggled against British colonialism in the 1948 Mandate ...'

The British Ambassador winced.

'… and as soon as the United Nations votes for a peace-keeping force on the border, the whole country will rally against the government. They'll never stand for blue helmets on their borders. They're too independent, too democratic. They'd rather depose the militarists who've brought them to this stage, than have foreign troops on their soil.'

John Dewhurst lifted his head in order to say something, but the weight of the combined opinion seemed to overwhelm him. He looked back down onto the ground. If Jack Harrison saw the movement, he appeared not to take notice of it.

Harrison continued. 'Mr Secretary, would you lobby the Lebanese, the Syrians, the Jordanians and the Egyptians? Tell them the US is sponsoring a resolution to impose a peace-keeping force on the Israeli side of the Syrian border? The Security Council will agree. If the General Assembly votes in favour, we'll move two aircraft carriers to the eastern Mediterranean and station a division in Turkey in readiness. Just the threat of such intervention to enforce the UN resolution will topple Ben Ari and his cronies like a pack of cards.'

While the ambassadors and the Secretary General nodded in agreement, John Dewhurst was already working on his resignation speech.

An hour later, away from the vulture eyes of the White House press corps, the ambassadors' cars drove from the basement garage to a little-known entryway on Lexington, and then to their various embassies or offices.

Only Dewhurst remained in the private apartments of the President, in a rare moment when Jack Harrison had no appointments. Dewhurst was beyond diplomacy as he fought the contempt rising in his craw.

'Jack, what you're planning is perhaps the single most divisive action of your presidency. Sponsoring UN sanctions against Israel is one thing. But sponsoring a peace-keeping force will strike a blow at the heart of every American Jew. You'll lose massive amounts of support.'

Harrison shrugged his shoulders. 'I doubt whether it'll come to the use of troops. Frankly, just the shock of UN soldiers on Israeli soil will bring back so many memories of Suez and the days of war there'll be a revolt against Ben Ari. Once he's out of the way, Israel will press for a resumption of the peace talks and we'll all be back to square one. Just imagine if we were negotiating with Mordecai Avit. Now there's a guy I can go fishing with. Have faith, John. Have some faith.'

Jack Harrison disappeared down one of the quiet carpeted corridors of the East Wing as John Dewhurst stood, restraining his fury. Backing his president in front of the United Nations delegation had been necessary but what angered him most was having the buffoon tell him to have faith. Didn't the idiot see where this was going to lead? It wasn't only going to divide Israel. It would also polarise America. When he had taught obdurate opinionated graduate students in Harvard, John Dewhurst had felt contempt for their closed minds. Jack Harrison was one of his failures.

♜♜♜

For a month the world's quest for peace was in a tailspin. Raphael Ben Ari was featured on the front covers of *Time* and *Newsweek*. Both articles were contemptuous. It had been a month of increasing international tension and a plummeting mood of depression in the Western world. There had been a few occasions in the history of the world when a mood of hope spread around the planet. The period between the collapse of Communism and the prospect of peace in the Middle East promised to be such a one, despite short term and vicious internecine warfare in Europe and a rise in racism in Germany and France. But Ben Ari put paid to the hopes of millions.

The desire that peace could become a reality teetered on the edge of a precipice. International terrorism had again reared its head like a ravenous bear waking from hibernation.

Four elderly men sat like trolls in a luxurious Moscow apartment and reminisced about old times. Retired Marshal of the

Army Genardy Arkyovich Petrovsky delicately sniffed the huge balloon of Napoleon Courvoisier brandy, allowing its anaesthetising, acrid perfume to fill his nose. He loved the burning sensation at the back of his throat as he sipped it. Most of all, he relished the way in which the initial shock to the senses was metamorphosed into a pleasant, suffusive warmth which eased his old bones.

Opposite him sat the ageing remnants of Mother Russia, men who had changed their politics as easily as the government changed its policies. The Minister for Industry, the Minister for Posts and Telecommunications, and the Minister of Finance. All three were members of what *Pravda* called 'the old guard'. They had been included in President Abayev's cabinet because of their loyalty to Gorbachev in the early days of *perestroika*. And because of their wealth of experience. But Abayev was a pragmatic politician. These men were really in his government because each held the loyalty of vast sections of the Russian Republic.

'So Genardy Arkyovich,' said the Industry Minister, 'things are coming to a pretty head, aren't they? What a disgrace. Whoever would have thought that Israel would have become a rogue nation like Iraq and Libya?'

All four men roared with laughter. Petrovsky viewed them with a mixture of warmth and wariness. While they were within his sphere of operation they were amenable and friendly. But cross them and they would instantly expose him to the cold winds of Siberia without giving it a moment's thought.

Their inclusion in the ruling cabinet had been made to ensure its unity. But old Russia was very different from the rest of Abayev's cabinet, which was composed of experts in their field, or intellectuals co-opted from universities. These three remaining warhorses were tolerated, but were never allowed to be party to serious decisions. By encouraging regional harmony for the government, they enjoyed an unprecedented lifestyle. They took with one hand, and kept with the other. They owed their positions in Russian society to Abayev, but their hearts lay elsewhere. Their loyalty to the principles of Gorbachev was a function of the old days; the days before the food riots, the break-away of the republics, the emergency relief from the US and NATO. Their shame was seeing once mighty Russia prostrating itself like some Third World whore before the United Nations, begging for food and shelter for its citizens. None of the old guard could have imagined that their support of Gorbachev would result in what Russia had become today. And when it did, they became bitter opponents of Gorbachev and his politics … but not bitter enough to join the incompetent imbeciles who tried to oust him. They read the mood of the people and abstained, but they were bitter enough to harbour a deep resentment and an uncompromising desire for a return to the old days. Their resentment intensified with the patronising Abayev.

Then Marshal Petrovsky had approached each of his old friends with a sophisticated plan to draw the Russian people together and make the Russian nation proud once again. By creating a global role for itself, Russia would again be a force in the world. The men had greedily jumped at the opportunity. They were surprised and delighted at the initial meeting at Petrovsky's apartment to find that each was a member of a cabal, a co-conspirator. They were even more surprised that Petrovsky had concocted such a brilliant and devious plot. But what surprised them most of all was that a plan created by Petrovsky in the days of Stalin would only now be coming to fruition. They expressed doubts as to its viability. But Petrovsky had been persuasive, explaining to them that dramatic changes in circumstances in the Middle East, involving the elevation of Raphael Ben Ari to the Prime Ministership of Israel, formed the cornerstone of converting the plan into a reality.

For the past two years Petrovsky had been working with the troika to prepare the ground for a *rapprochement* with Israel as soon as the Israeli Prime Minister asked Abayev for aid.

For Abayev and his band of intellectuals, the approach from Ben Ari would come out of the blue. It had been planned to be a complete surprise. But for two years the three ministers had done a great deal of groundwork and lobbying amongst members of the Ministry. When approached, Abayev would be sure to give his approval. First, they had pointed out to their colleagues and the government *apparatchiks* the way in which the Arab world had turned from Russia to befriend the United States. Then they ensured everyone realised the extent to which Israel, a strong, advanced country within a Third World environment, had become isolated. With Petrovsky's guidance, they had undertaken their tasks subtly, cautiously, dropping hints here and suggestions there, all the while putting the greater interests of Mother Russia in the forefront of their remarks.

Tonight's gathering was more in the way of a celebration than anything else. Despite its informality, the usual precautions had been taken. The three ministers had given their wives and staff excuses about private discussions with foreign diplomats; their drivers had been dismissed early. Each had driven himself by a circuitous route to Petrovsky's apartment. Each had parked his car in a side street and waited for ten minutes before leaving the car to ensure that he was not followed.

During the evening, Petrovsky had expounded on the success of the plan to date and the fact that a bunch of barbaric Arabs had, without realising it, accomplished what Petrovsky could not have done for another six months. They had unified vast sections of the public of Israel behind Ben Ari, while at the same time creating a militant opposition and grounds for the continuation of martial law.

By eleven-thirty, all four were hopelessly drunk. The following day would see a cabinet meeting to discuss the latest depressing industrial output figures, so each of the men bade Petrovsky goodnight and staggered to his car.

Boris Krychkov's Zil limousine was parked four streets away. When he left the portico of the apartment building, the cool air hit him like a gloved fist. He propped himself against the wall to stop himself from falling over.

Giggling, he lurched down the wide pavement and fought to remember where he had left his car. As Krychkov finally turned into the street where it was parked, a police car accelerated and drew up noiselessly just feet away. Krychkov's mind, normally suspicious to the point of paranoia, failed to make the connection as the nearside doors of the car opened and two men in police uniforms jumped out.

'Excuse me, friend,' said one, 'you're weaving all over the pavement like a whore on heat. You don't intending driving this car, do you?'

Krychkov tried to stop his body weaving, but all he could manage was an inane giggle.

'Come with me, please, friend. I am taking you into custody for being drunk and incapable on a public street, contrary to Article 26 of the Russian Penal Code. Get into the car, hand over your keys and my colleague will follow us to the police station.'

Clarity was beginning to dawn on Krychkov. The joke was rapidly wearing thin.

'You stupid moron. Don't you recognise me? I'm the Minister for Industry, Boris Krychkov. You can't arrest me.'

The policeman smiled apologetically, then punched Krychkov sharply in the solar plexus. He doubled over in agony and clawed the air for breath. Like an expert pickpocket, the policeman searched the minister's pockets and gave the keys for the Zil to his colleague. He bundled the minister into the back of the car and told the driver to proceed.

Krychkov's body fought for breath, but his mind began to operate. Sluggishly at first, he emerged from his drunken mists. He started to protest, using his most authoritarian manner, threatening reprimands, dismissals, even summary arrests. But the policeman drove on impassively. After a further minute of ministerial abuse, one of the policemen turned to his captive. 'Sorry, minister,' he said, 'but I have my orders.'

A fear seeped through the old man's body. Orders? Whose orders? Then he began to observe where they were going. The route the car was taking was directly towards the Kremlin, not Central Police Headquarters. Krychkov suddenly felt sick.

Ten minutes later he was sitting alone in a gilded antechamber adjacent to the cabinet room where the Governing Council of the Praesidium of the Supreme Soviet had met in private session. His head was still spinning, but he was sufficiently conscious to know of the danger he was in.

Krychkov was shocked as the door was thrown open. In walked President Abayev, followed by the poet Ivan Yeszersky, his colleague who dabbled as Minister for Agriculture. Krychkov stood up and began to protest to Abayev about his treatment. 'Mr President, I have been defiled tonight by ...'

'Shut up, you snivelling traitor.'

Krychkov stopped talking and sat down, wide-eyed in shock, and waited for the inevitable. Was it worth denying? Could he do a deal? Would he be sent to a *gulag*? Surely not. He was too old.

Abayev and Yeszersky sat beside each other at the opposite end of the table. Surprisingly, it was Yeszersky who did most of the talking. But this poet was not an important figure in government. Krychkov was much more senior. Why was this intellectual, this academic buffoon, this professor of literature, involved?

'For the past two years, you, plus two colleagues, have conspired with retired Marshal Petrovsky to pervert and prostitute the foreign policies of the Republic of Russia. The four of you have incited senior Russian and Ukrainian military officers to act traitorously, contrary to their oaths of allegiance.'

Krychkov's mouth opened and closed like a fish on a river bank. No sound emerged.

'Your every movement, meeting and conversation has been recorded by the police,' Yeszersky told him, 'and you have been arrested because your treachery is close to completion. Will you at least admit your complicity, or must it be dragged out of you in the shame of a public trial, which will destroy your family as well as yourself?'

Krychkov was so terrified that he nearly lost control of his bladder. He remained silent, not knowing what to say. To deny it would be a waste of time; to admit it could mean a prison sentence.

President Abayev waited a moment, then shook his head in disgust. 'You haven't even got the guts to confess.'

The President stood up, and turned to Yeszersky. 'Shoot him. Right now. Take him into the cells below, and put a bullet through his cowardly brain.' Turning, he walked towards the door.

Krychkov's bladder burst. 'No!', he screamed as he pissed into his trousers. 'You can't. You can't just kill me. It's not like the old days. You're not Stalin!'

The pathetic old man's mouth gaped open in stupor as he fought for words.

Yeszersky stood up, and followed his President to the door.

Abayev turned to Krychkov. 'Stay there,' he said. 'The guard will be in to get you soon to take you to your execution. Then we'll feed your rotten carcass to the lions in Moscow zoo.'

Krychkov looked imploringly at the two men. 'Please, don't go. Don't leave me. You can't shoot me. You just can't. It's illegal. It's inhuman. I'll tell you anything. What do you want to know? I know all the details …'

Abayev turned and shouted at the decaying old man. 'It's too late. We know everything already.'

Krychkov shook his head vehemently. 'No! Not everything. I'll tell you what we've planned tonight. Who's involved. I'll tell you everything.'

But the two men simply walked through the door. Even when it was shut tight, Krychkov's wailing could clearly be heard.

President Abayev and Ivan Yeszersky smiled at each other. 'Soon we'll have all the details we need,' said Abayev.

'Yes, but can he be turned? Do you think he'll want to work for us?'

Abayev smiled. He had been completely taken aback by the

plotting of the three cabinet ministers with Petrovsky. But when Yeszersky told him, he had reacted immediately to see what was behind it all. Yeszersky had suggested calling them all together and confronting them with the allegations, but Abayev had come up with a more devious scheme. It appeared to be working.

'My friend,' said Abayev, 'as a poet you are a genius, but you know little about the workings of the political mind. That snivelling hulk in there can be moulded like bread dough. By tomorrow morning, he'll be the most loyal, the most patriotic Russian in Moscow. He'll beg you to give him the opportunity to inform on Petrovsky. Right now, he's just a piece of dogshit. Your job over the next day or two is to give him back his self-respect, so that his greatest objective in life is to overthrow Petrovsky and expose his plot. You've actually got to rebuild him.'

Yeszersky smiled. The President was right. Yeszersky knew little of the political mind. He had merely brought his intellect to bear on solving Russia's problems. He never thought he would have to deal with matters like this. Again, Yeszerski was amazed by Abayev's perception. Abayev had suggested the set-up and charade. The threat of immediate death had also been his idea. Neither would have occurred to the poetic mind. Yet Russian literature was replete with such scenes. Politics! The art of making fiction into fact. Would he ever get used to it? Probably not.

Slowly, Yeszersky turned back towards the black oak door. He took a deep breath before going inside. He had never had to rebuild a man before. In fact, he had never had to break one down.

♜♜♜

Miriam was still sedated twenty hours after the devastating explosion which had killed a hapless waiter, four passers-by and two motorists. She always thought of herself as stoic, yet she had been so traumatised by the bombing that sleep was only a reality after 20 milligrams of diazepam. Now she slept deeply, drugged unconscious in a hospital bed.

Paul stroked her hand as she lay cold and impassive between the starched white sheets. Her face was covered with red stains from the mercurochrome used after the tiny fragments of glass had been extracted. She looked as if a child had scribbled on her face. The doctors told Paul that she would remain in the hospital for at least two days, until they were satisfied her mind was under control.

Paul had not suffered the same degree of damage; nor had Rabbi Miklos, who left the hospital only hours after being treated in casualty. Before he left, the rabbi came to the ward where Miriam was sleeping and said a *barucha* over her prostrate form; then he accompanied a sergeant to the police station, to make a full report.

Kissing her gently on the forehead, Paul turned and left the ward, followed by a police officer who drove him to the Central Police Station four blocks away.

He was interrogated with that gentle consideration which is reserved by police forces around the world for victims of a terrorist outrage. But considerate as he was, the inspector who listened to the statement showed his frustration at the paucity of details. The police had interviewed over twenty witnesses. None was able to cast any light as to why a bomb was planted in an ordinary cafe in a quiet suburb of metropolitan Warsaw.

Since Poland had left the Communist bloc years earlier, and trod the capitalist road, there had been no incidents of civil unrest. Until now. The city was a haven of peace, if not prosperity. What had happened at lunchtime the previous day was inexplicable, senseless. Terrorists usually telegraph their atrocities but there were none of the usual warnings or demands. Even twenty-two hours after the murderous incident, no one had claimed responsibility.

Paul's statement to the police was similar to Rabbi Miklos'. He confirmed the details. He and his Jewish-Australian girlfriend visited the old rabbi to find details of her grandfather.

They went to the cafe to have a thank you drink with the rabbi. Then ... boom ... the bomb went off.

The inspector thanked Paul. When he left the interrogation room, he told the young sergeant to check the man's passport details with Interpol and the Australian Embassy.

The inspector was mystified. Doubtless he would eventually find out why the bombing had occurred; but in the meantime, his superintendent had received a call from the country's President, demanding a quick resolution and speedy arrests. The inspector already had three or four old-guard dyed-in-the-wool Communists in mind. He would arrest them publicly and incarcerate them for a couple of days. That would take the heat off until the real perpetrators could be caught. The news media were buzzing like flies around the police station and the hospital but the inspector had issued strict instructions to keep them at bay.

Paul was escorted out of the police station by a back door and got into a police car. He asked to be taken back to the hospital so he could visit Miriam. Then he would book air tickets to get them both out of the country. He'd had enough! The story wasn't worth the risk of being killed. No story was. He would phone Jack Muir, tell him what had happened and organise tickets back to Australia. He felt a responsibility for Miriam and that put a different complexion upon his professionalism.

As he got out of the police car and walked towards the front door of the hospital, a young woman approached him and, in faltering English, said: 'You are Mr Sinclair?' Paul was surprised. How did she know his name? Who was she?

'Yes,' he said suspiciously.

'I am ask you please do not visit Miss Davis. She is all right. Please get to taxi and go back to Hotel Victoria where you stay. Change clothes completely, then leave hotel by back service entrance and go to public phone box. Then telephone this number. Instructions will be given.'

She thrust a small piece of paper into his hand and walked

quickly away. He wanted to call after her but the men in the police car were looking at him, wondering whether to assist. He walked into the hospital foyer and waited for the police car to disappear. Then he got a taxi back to the hotel. As the taxi weaved its way through lunchtime traffic, Paul opened the note. All it contained was a telephone number. The shock of being confronted by the young woman made him feel nervous. He desperately wanted to take Miriam back home to the relative safety of Australia, to leave the hellish maelstrom which they had entered. Two minutes ago, he would have, but the reporter in him smelled a lead and a good reporter follows through every lead. That was Max Mandle's credo, a holy writ, the eleventh commandment emblazoned on walls in every newsroom of every paper he owned throughout the world.

Max Mandle! There was a name he hadn't thought about for days. Was Max Mandle doing this to them? Was he working with Mossad to ensure that the photos were found and destroyed? Was he trying to kill both Miriam and himself to protect Ben Ari? But that was senseless. Mandle couldn't be involved. Or could he?

Paul felt secure that nobody would find the photo. The copy was safely hidden inside his wallet, and the original in a bank deposit box he knew could never be found ... not unless Mandle and Mossad organised a robbery of the vault of Westpac's head office.

The taxi screeched to a halt outside the Hotel Victoria, and Paul went up to his room. Instinct told him that it had been searched by experts. Nothing seemed to have been moved; nothing appeared out of place; everything seemed exactly as it had been left the previous morning when they had gone to visit the rabbi ... yet there was a presence in the room. Someone had been inside. Paul could sense that whoever it was had opened drawers and rifled through bags. With trepidation, Paul opened the suitcase to see if his personal effects had been tampered with. Then he went through drawers and personal papers. Everything seemed to be in order, but he knew his privacy had been violated.

Following instructions, Paul changed his clothes, left the hotel by the service entrance and found a public phone on a corner four blocks from the Victoria. With heart pounding, he rang the number he had been given. It was answered instantly. There was no greeting.

'Listen to me very carefully,' a voice told him. 'Your life is in great danger. Walk away from the Hotel Victoria, turn right past the large department store, and two blocks further on, near the Lot Airline office, you will see a travel agency. It is on a corner of a narrow laneway. There you will see another telephone booth. Phone this number again for further instructions.'

The line disconnected before Paul could ask any questions. His skin prickled with fear. He had three options. One was to collect Miriam and flee the country, though how far he would get was a moot point. The second was to go to the police and demand protection, though he was sure he would be disbelieved, and anyway, who could he speak to that was not involved in the plot? And the third option was to obey the instructions—to go along with the scheme. There had been many opportunities to harm both Miriam and himself straight after the bomb blast … in the hospital, the police station, the hotel room. Logic demanded that he do as he was instructed, to follow the lead through, as Mandle would have said. He shuddered, thinking of Mandle. But the emotional side of his mind told him to flee. Why was he getting involved in other people's battles? He wasn't even Jewish!

Eight minutes later, he opened the door to the telephone booth and dialled the number. Unlike the first occasion, it did not answer straight away; in fact it did not answer at all. Paul was mystified. He dialled the number again, but the same thing happened. What the hell was going on? He knew that he had obeyed the instructions accurately. Could it be some sort of a hoax? Was he in the process of being set up?

Paul left the booth, and started to walk back to the hotel. An Opel drew up and a massive, Asiatic-Slavic man dressed in a 1950s double-breasted suit stepped out of the front passenger's seat.

'Mr Sinclair. Get into car please, now! Quickly. Do not argue. You are in danger.'

Paul was terrified, his body breaking into a sweat, his scalp tingling in fear. But he wasn't going to get into the car. Not for any reason. He shook his head, turned and started to walk in the other direction but the Slav's massive hand gripped him by the arm with great strength and pulled him back towards the car.

'Now listen here you …' But before he could continue, the man said, 'Mr Sinclair, if I wanted to kill you, I could have done it ten times in past five minutes. You have friend who wants to meet you and help you and Miss Davis. Please get into car, and off street. Now!'

Paul half fell into the car and the huge Slav sat beside him. His mind was reeling in terror. But to show terror would be to show weakness. Attack was the best defence.

'What the hell's going on? Who are you, and who is this friend? Is this anything to do with the bombing? Is Miriam all right? Is she in danger at the hospital?'

The Slav stared ahead, refusing to communicate. The car was driven by another robotic individual in what appeared to be a circuitous route around the city. After ten minutes, the two men broke the silence in the car by exchanging a terse sentence in Polish. The Slav turned to Paul and told him: 'We are not followed.'

The car was then driven out of the centre of Warsaw into an industrial suburb, where it entered a carpark. It descended three levels until it came to a screeching halt. The Slav opened his door and walked around to help Paul out. He escorted him to a Fiat, in which a young woman, the one who had approached him at the hospital and given him the note, was sitting in the driver's seat. Paul got into the back seat and the car shot off up the ramp to the carpark exit.

The girl picked up a mobile phone—the first Paul had seen

since leaving Australia—and dialled a number. She held a brief conversation and then turned to Paul, who sat quietly, not knowing what to do or say.

'You are Mr Sinclair. I am Gosia. I take you to your friend.'

'I don't suppose you'll tell me who this friend of mine is, will you?'

Gosia laughed but said nothing.

'I thought not,' said Paul, who stared out of the car window at the suburbs speeding by.

After ten minutes, having passed through one drab featureless district after another, each containing barrack after barrack of grey monotonous housing blocks, the car left the city suburbs and entered a more rural setting. They drove through parkland and a countryside offering colours, hues and gentleness. Very different from the angular starkness of Warsaw's suburbs.

A side road led to a boulevard of majestic poplar trees. Finally, the car arrived at an old mansion, a nineteenth-century extravaganza which looked incongruous in rural Poland. It was the sort of eclectic house Liverpool shipping millionaires built for themselves in Victorian times as a reflection of their success—heavy, solid, ornate and respectable.

Gosia drove up the driveway and parked outside the front portico. A young athletic-looking man wearing a sporty blue blazer and grey tailored slacks emerged from the shadow of the doorway and opened Paul's door. Impassive, he indicated for Paul to go through into the house.

The interior was a dramatic contrast to the outside. It was a cosmopolitan delight. Thick pile Axminster carpet, *fin de siècle* paintings, religious tapestries in thick gilt frames, Regency writing bureaux, nineteenth-century credenzas … the house was a tribute to the taste and wealth of a collector of *objets d'art*. In Poland, with its bankrupt economy, it was unnerving.

'My dear Mr Sinclair. Please come in. May I organise a cup of tea or coffee for you?'

An old man, speaking perfect English with a strong Eastern European accent, appeared in the hall vestibule, beaming with recognition, greeting Paul like a long-lost friend. Paul simply stood and stared.

'Do come through into the library. My name is … John Smith, I think you Australians say when you want not to be identified. As opposed to John Doe in America.'

Paul stood granite-faced, his indication that he was unimpressed by the cordiality. But he was in a state of utter confusion.

The old man smiled and led him into the magnificent library, where each wall was covered with a lifetime's reading of magnificently bound books. There were four leather armchairs scattered for convenience around the room and two oak coffee tables, inlaid with ornate filigrees of brass. On one of the coffee tables was a Polish newspaper, folded back to reveal a half-completed crossword.

When the two were seated, and the old man had poured tea, Paul burst out: 'Look, I've just been abducted by your henchmen and forced …'

The old man held up his hand. 'Please don't insult my colleagues. An attempt was made on your life yesterday. It took me completely by surprise. I didn't expect them to do anything so overt. Only a miracle saved you and Miss Davis. She is currently being guarded by one of my "henchmen" as you put it, to ensure that no further harm comes to her.'

'Them? Who do you mean by them?'

The old man ignored Paul's question. 'Your decision to leave Jerusalem and come here was stupid. You do not have the resources, or the background, to understand the danger in which you find yourself. You are mixing with forces of incalculable strength. I am willing to help you return in one piece to Australia, on the condition that you tell me everything you know. If not, I will simply have you delivered back to your hotel to fend for yourself.'

'How dare you talk to me like that? Look, Mr Smith or whatever your name is, I'm an Australian citizen holidaying in Poland. If I go to my embassy, you will be in serious trouble …'

The old man smiled and shook his head.

'Mr Sinclair, you are a senior reporter with Max Mandle's *National* newspaper in Australia. You are the lover of Miriam Davis, a junior partner in the Sydney law firm of Boyd, Royal and Trimmett. Her grandfather was recently killed and your apartment was searched. You came to Jerusalem a week after the death of her grandfather, and there you stayed in the King David Hotel. In the room one floor below yours, an extensive and very expensive surveillance operation was established and your every move was monitored. After Miss Davis had seen the curator of the Institute of the Diaspora, he was murdered; after you had seen Rabbi Yossi Gartenbaum in Mea Shearim, he too was murdered. Both murders were arranged to look like death by natural causes.'

Paul's mouth fell open. He only just managed to put down the cup without spilling anything.

'On arrival in Warsaw, you were shadowed everywhere and a surveillance operation has been established in the Hotel Victoria. Your visit to the Organisation of Polish Martyrs was known about in advance and I assume that, yesterday morning, the people of whom I speak made the decision to eliminate you and the Davis girl, as well as the rabbi, before you could do any further harm. Now, before you use any more heroic language about what you're going to do to me, why don't you simply accept that you've stumbled into a snake-pit, and I'm here with a rope to pull you out?'

Paul sat stunned. He couldn't say anything. His mind was lurching from one fact to another, but no intelligible thought was forming.

The old man smiled. 'Another cup of tea, perhaps?'

'Who are you?' gasped Paul

'Mr Sinclair, you are a guest in my house, so please do me the honour of answering me first. Who are *you*?,' asked the old man. 'Why are espionage services so interested in a reporter and a lawyer from Australia? What information have you got that makes this espionage service kill whoever you come into contact with? Perhaps if you tell me all the details, I can piece it together and solve the puzzle.'

Paul's mind had slowed its spinning.

'Look, I have absolutely no idea why these things have been happening to me. I don't know what's going on. Why not tell me who you are, and then I'll feel more comfortable with you.'

The old man rose from the armchair and walked over to the window. He delighted in the permanency of the tall trees.

'You know, Mr Sinclair, you may deal with me in many ways, but never treat me like a fool. You don't have so much time up your sleeves that you can waste precious moments denying the information you possess. You have stumbled on something of immeasurable importance to certain powerful parties. My belief is that it is connected with the girl Davis' grandfather, though my enquiries have failed to determine anything of interest about him. You can help me, or deny me that help. If you deny me, then I'll simply throw you back into the snake-pit. Your continued good health will be of no further interest to me.'

Paul's earlier option of returning to Australia had been taken away from him. The nightmare that he had stepped into was too threatening for him to fully comprehend. Being shadowed halfway around the world by some dark malevolent force was too alien, too dangerous, too much outside his experience. It slowly dawned on him how naive he had been.

But could he trust the old man? He didn't know him or his organisation from a bar of soap. Then again, how could he not trust him? He decided to test the water.

'One thing I can tell you …'

The old man looked round in interest.

'The Israeli secret service, Mossad, have been trailing us. It was they who killed Miriam's grandfather.'

A smile broke on the old man's face. Then he let out a strangled laugh.

'You really are a very stupid man,' he said, and walked out of the library, leaving Paul alone.

Deep in the Kremlin, buried out of the view of ordinary Russians who were struggling daily with the problems of existence, is a fully equipped ultra-modern hospital that would be the envy of any Western country.

Installed on the orders of Leonid Brezhnev when his diabetes and congestive heart condition began to interfere with his ability to conduct the affairs of state, the facility was further expanded by Yuri Andropov, who was even frailer than Brezhnev when he came to power. On the ascension of Konstantine Chernenko, the only man more dead than alive ever to lead the Soviet Union, the facility was upgraded to include sophisticated technology more commonplace in hospitals like America's Bethesda or the Mayo Clinic.

The facility was used these days not only by Russia's ruling elite, but by the hundreds of office and administrative staff who worked in the vast secretariat within the Kremlin. It was used for routine medical investigations as well as for emergencies. And it was because of an emergency that it would be used again.

When Minister Yeszersky re-entered the conference room to begin the painful process of extracting information from Boris Krychkov, he was relieved to know the facility was there. Yeszersky was shocked to see the metamorphosis. When Krychkov had first entered the conference room he had been scared and drunk. Now he was no longer drunk but the man facing Yeszersky was teetering on the brink of collapse.

Krychkov sat in a bundle at the end of the table, his body convulsed by shakes. Saliva was dribbling from his mouth. He was repetitively mumbling words which Yeszersky could not comprehend.

'Krychkov, I am ordered to take you to the cells for immediate execution, but I'm sure that if you cooperate and give me whatever information you have, the President can be persuaded to be lenient and to commute the sentence. It is even possible that I can persuade him to save both you and Russia the embarrassment of public exposure and allow you to live out the rest of your life in your dacha.'

Yeszersky looked carefully at Krychkov for a reaction. Had he been too quick to offer clemency? Should he have allowed the old man to sweat in a cell overnight? If only he was more experienced at interrogation …

But Krychkov showed no reaction; he didn't even appear to have heard what Yeszersky had said. He just continued to mumble and shake. Yeszersky began to worry about his health. A shock so severe could damage the body of an elderly man. The poet strained to listen.

'No … Fool. And why … there was strength … cabbage one day, gone … like … it all goes … borscht next …'

His words were meaningless, the ramblings of a mind in shock. Yeszersky determined not to listen to any more, but to phone for a doctor to administer some palliative. The interrogation could continue tomorrow morning after the old fool had slept it off. Then suddenly the old man shouted:

'Stalin! You old bastard! Still you pace the corridors. Still you tread on the Russian people. Damn you. Damn you to hell. Damn the Jericho Plan. Damn you and your blasted Jericho Plan. May you rot in the endless wastes of Siberia!'

The old man stood. His face and body were a shambles, his eyes red and watering, his nose leaking green slime; his trousers were drenched with urine. He pitched forward, retching yellow-grey bile onto the table, his body shaking with convulsions.

Yeszersky was horrified and grabbed a telephone. 'Get a doctor up here immediately!' he barked at the telephone operator.

He knew that he should go over and loosen the old man's clothing, but he was so repelled, so disgusted by the fluids pouring out of every uncontrolled orifice, that he held back in horror.

Still, Krychkov shouted, twitching face-down on the table. 'Stalin! I see you. I know you. You can't hurt me. I know the plan. You think you're clever. Damn the Jericho Plan. You hear that, Stalin? You hear that Josef Dzugashvili? You hear that, you priest! You thing. Damn you and damn your Jericho Plan.'

The shouting ended and Krychkov began crying, his frame racked with a mixture of fear, grief and shame. As he lay sprawled on the table, the door to the conference room flew open. A doctor marched in, followed by two orderlies wheeling in a crash trolley. With no respect for rank or status, the doctor pushed Yeszersky out of the way, and walked over to his patient, giving orders as he walked.

The two orderlies stripped off layers of clothing and transferred the prostrate form onto the trolley. His mouth and nose were cleared of any obstruction and an oxygen mask was placed over his face. He was wheeled out of the door, to descend into the care and concern of those whose job it was to repair the excesses of the men who ran the country. There were no judgments, no moralising statements, as the doctor followed the trolley, gave a curt nod to Minister Yeszersky, and closed the door.

Only the snot and vomit and saliva marks on the table, and the stench of urine in the room gave witness to the destruction of a man's essence.

Two hours later, Krychkov's condition had been stabilised. He was sleeping comfortably, overseen by an orderly who was monitoring his vital signs. At three in the morning, the doctor retired to his cot to sleep the rest of the night away. The second duty orderly was off in another part of the building, doing a biochemical analysis of the Minister of Defence's blood.

Oleg Resniko had worked as a medical orderly from the time he joined the KGB twenty-two years ago, in the clinic which had been established to tender to the medical needs of senior KGB men in Headquarters on Dzerzinsky Square. With the destruction of the KGB, its equipment and personnel were transferred to the Kremlin. Oleg enjoyed the easy-going relationship he had had with some of the most powerful men in the land. He had seen them without their uniforms and that made them more human, less frightening.

His personal favourite had been Marshal Petrovsky, who often allowed Oleg and his wife access to the restricted shops where senior party men and women did their shopping ... where luxury consumer goods including toiletries, cosmetics, clothes, records, and electrical equipment could be purchased for a song. By re-selling them, he had augmented his salary and achieved a superior lifestyle. In return, he had told Petrovsky about the health of the Marshal's colleagues. Now that he was attached to the Kremlin, he regularly informed the Marshal about the welfare of the nation's leaders.

Even though it was three in the morning, Oleg knew that Marshal Petrovsky would want to know immediately about the health of the Minister for Industry.

The telephone rang twice. Petrovsky was immediately alert. 'Marshal, it's Oleg in the Kremlin clinic. You may be interested to learn that Minister Krychkov has been brought to us semi-comatose.'

Petrovsky's skin prickled. He asked Oleg under what circumstances the minister had been brought into the clinic. Where had the minister been? Who had he seen prior to entering the clinic? Had he spoken to anyone, and if so, what was the conversation? In what condition was the minister when the doctor had examined him?

Oleg was only able to answer a few of the questions, but Petrovsky heard enough to be deeply concerned.

'Tell me, Oleg, how is your pretty wife? Is she still after that astrakhan coat that she so admired?'

Oleg smiled. 'How may I help your excellency?'

'You can assist me with a medical query. If you had to ensure a natural-looking end to a problem, are there substances that you could use ... say something like insulin?'

'I would say that 10,000 international units of insulin would ensure that tomorrow, our glorious Mother Russia would be in urgent need of a new Minister for Industry.'

'Goodnight, Oleg.'

'Goodnight, Marshal.'

CHAPTER TWENTY-ONE

Marshal Petrovsky sat in his deep armchair, nursing a glass of brandy and brushing away a few crumbs of toast which had fallen on his white shirt as he ate the Beluga caviar.

Opposite him was Colonel-General Bukharin, wearing tailored fawn slacks and a short-sleeved brown and yellow plaid shirt. The Marshal noticed with satisfaction that the younger man's body was superbly fit; when he had first known him, it had been in the heavy, unflattering fabric of a military uniform.

'When will the broadcast take place?'

Bukharin looked at his watch. 'In just under an hour.'

The old man nodded. Then he smiled. 'I'd love to be in the Oval Office when that boorish Texan first hears that his lapdog has turned around and bitten him.'

'More to the point, sir, is the reaction of John Dewhurst. I would imagine that he has been warning the President not to push the Jews too far. He must have been predicting that Israel would seek some form of *rapprochement* with the Soviet Union … I'm sorry, the Russian Republic'

Petrovsky smiled at the mistake. Not even the intervening years had changed the pattern of old habits. 'Why would Dewhurst suspect? More likely, he'd suppose that Israel would turn to the uncommitted Europeans, like Italy or Greece. Even France.' Petrovsky let out a laugh.

The two men finished their brandy and Bukharin poured each of them another.

'Marshal, I am not given to unnecessary words of praise, but your handling of this game plan has been nothing short of brilliant. When you first included me in the Jericho Plan, I had severe reservations about it, but …'

'And you, my dear Mikhail Alexandrovich, have been a key instrument in its success, despite that unfortunate business with the Australians.' Petrovsky looked at him sternly. Bukharin chose not to meet his eyes. 'We have had some luck because of the Arabs, but that merely contracted your timescale. All the recent events, all the computer strategies, have been yours. Despite hiccups along the way, you have rewarded my confidence.' The old man took another sip of his brandy. 'Have the Australians surfaced yet?'

'No, Genardy Arkyovich. Our agents in Warsaw have lost all trace of the man. The girl of course is still in hospital, but heavily guarded. Anyway, since we failed to terminate them another attempt would seem unwise.'

'Is it even necessary? I'm rapidly coming to the opinion that by the time they put two and two together, it will be too late.'

'I agree.'

Both men settled back in the warmth of mutual respect, and sipped their brandy. Bukharin could see the future clearly. It was the past that still held small mysteries for him.

'Is it permissible to ask the Marshal a certain question?'

Petrovsky looked at the younger man and nodded. He was holding back very few secrets and was prepared to be a little more forthcoming.

'There seems to have been an extraordinarily long time gap between the creation of the Jericho Plan and its fulfilment. Have you been developing the idea all this while? Or …'

'Or has luck played a part in it? Of course it has played a part. Napoleon used to choose his generals on the basis of how lucky they were. Luck always plays a role in these things. An event here, a circumstance there. But things develop their own momentum, Bukharin, and that's what happened with Jericho.'

Petrovsky sniffed again at his brandy and threw some more to the back of his throat. How odd it was that twists and turns of events sometimes made even the most deeply buried ideas suddenly blossom. Twenty years ago, he had written off the Jericho Plan as another idea which had not come to fulfilment. But Ben Ari had astounded him by remaining faithful to the principles of Communism long after everybody else had written it off as yesterday's credo. The inconspicuous, unassuming little Jew had grown taller than all the other assets in Petrovsky's pantheon of spies. There were two others who had risen alongside Ben Ari, yet not to his level. The two, one a Russian, the other a Pole, had trailed behind Ben Ari as he made his way through the tortuous pathways of the Israeli secret service and then into politics. It had suited Petrovsky to have back-up in Israel. If Ben Ari ever caused problems for him he would be removed and one of the others elevated.

In time, he would possibly answer Bukharin's question. For the time being, he preferred to keep the knowledge to himself, as he had done for half his lifetime. The Jericho Plan had begun as a private conspiracy shortly after the end of the Great Patriotic War. A conspiracy between Josef Stalin and himself. He was then a young rising luminary in the NKVD. At Yalta, in February 1945, it was Petrovsky's strategic genius which showed Stalin how to play Roosevelt and Churchill at their own game. They had given Stalin control over all Eastern Europe in return for a promise to keep Communism out of Italy and Greece and Soviet ships out of the Mediterranean. But Petrovsky never once meant Stalin to abide by the decision, especially as they had enormous numbers of covert assets all over the world. When the war was over, Stalin had pumped millions of roubles into their assets in America, England and other parts of the world, but it was the Soviet Union's budding relationships in the Middle East which were of greatest interest to Petrovsky. Using unlimited capital assigned secretly for the purpose, Petrovsky had established special security and communication systems. Dead-letter couriers and signals personnel were appointed. Dispatch routes and instant response mechanisms created. An entire infrastructure was built. And Genardy Arkyovich Petrovsky was able to use all of these massive resources to aid the little Polish Jew who called himself Ben Ari to climb the ladder of success in Israel. First his role as an operative in Mossad. Then in politics. Money was available to buy what others had to earn, and over the entire period, every conceivable link to Ben Ari's past was discovered and eliminated. All to ensure the survival and success of the Jericho Plan.

Petrovsky allowed himself a smile. Bukharin realised that no answer would be forthcoming and asked a less crucial question. 'How well do you know Ben Ari?'

'Never met him,' said Petrovsky and threw his head back in a roar of laughter.

Bukharin was staggered. 'But ... but ... I assumed.'

'And he's never met me. Only knows me by name if at all. He's got no idea I'm behind this. No idea whatsoever.'

'But how has he kept so loyal all these years?' asked Bukharin.

Petrovsky nodded. 'I understand your question, Bukharin. It's something that you will understand better when you are much older. Faith to a cause is the province of the very young and the very old.'

Bukharin continued: 'Men like Philby, Burgess, those other Englishmen were petit-bourgeois adventurers, small-minded ideologues. These I can understand. Their treason of their country was an intellectual exercise, a particularly middle-class British phenomenon. But Ben Ari has been first and foremost an Israeli for the past fifty years. All his adult life has been spent growing into the role of Prime Minister.'

The Marshal chortled and sipped more vodka: 'And you think that a Jew may be less of a Communist than an Englishman? May I remind you that Communism, like Christianity, owes its origin to a Jew.'

'But with respect, sir, there surely has to be a difference in the mind between an Communist who retains his ideology, and a man who attains ultimate power in his own country. Where we have had sleepers in place, the most difficult task has been to ensure they remain loyal after years of their adoptive lifestyle. But a man like Ben Ari is a different proposition. To have kept him in place and to have maintained his loyalty over nearly half a century is nothing short of astounding. How did you do it, Genardy Arkyovich?'

The Marshal smiled to himself and drained his glass of brandy.

'When you know that, Mikhail Alexandrovich, you will be wearing the uniform of a Marshal of the Army.'

The old man allowed himself a grin, then a chuckle, and then he looked up towards the ceiling and roared a belly laugh.

Bukharin, also affected by the brandy, looked at the usually sombre old man racked by laughter. He too roared a full-throated laugh. It was fortunate that at that moment, no one could hear them, not even the two teams of men from the Russian Secret Service, stationed in vantage points around Petrovsky's apartment keeping note of the comings and goings.

♜♜♜

Although it was just a short walk from his air-conditioned car to the television studio, the burning heat produced sweat droplets on the balding forehead of the Prime Minister, Raphael Ben Ari. As he strode towards the double glass doors, Brett Oxenford, the station manager, came out to meet him. A Chicagoan who had been resident in Tel Aviv for five years, Brett escorted him into the Green Room. The producer and the director were already there, along with a number of assistants. They didn't need to be there until the broadcast started, but everyone in the station sensed that history was about to be made.

It was six in the evening, but as was always the case, the bar was open and a waitress offered Ben Ari a glass of Chivas Regal. All were eager to meet the prime minister, and find out why he had asked for facilities to broadcast a message to the Israeli people.

The last time the Prime Minister had requisitioned airtime had been some days earlier, when he had announced a state of martial law to an angry and polarised people. A large section of the population bitterly resented the restrictions on their traditional liberties, but a majority had swung behind Ben Ari following the latest terrorist outrage.

The destruction of the Holocaust Museum and the death of the guards had achieved what no one around the world had believed possible—mass support by large sections of the population for the Ruling Council. The massive popular street demonstrations against America enabled Raphael Ben Ari to claim that he now enjoyed an unofficial mandate.

The diminutive Prime Minister stood in the centre of a ring of people, looking up at them and talking casually about the international situation. Subtle questions about the subject matter of his speech were met by smiles.

'You will know when you will know,' was all he would say.

'What about a teleprompt? Surely you'll want to read from your prepared script,' said the production assistant.

'You worry about your job. Let me worry about mine.'

At a cue from the floor manager, the director led the Prime Minister down to make-up. Within ten minutes, he was being led into Studio B, to be seated at a desk. Three cameras faced him; the backdrop which the director had chosen was a plain wash of lemon, which would blend well with Raphael Ben Ari's dark grey jacket and white open-necked shirt, the uniform of Israeli politicians.

Before the broadcast began, the director would edit on shots of the Knesset and the Jerusalem skyline before titles rolled up to reveal the Prime Minister. He would then use the three cameras to cut from medium close ups to ultra-tight shots on his face. Speeches were by their nature boring, but his product was entertainment, and his job was to ensure that the speech was as lively and aesthetically pleasing as possible.

At exactly six-thirty, the announcer explained the interruption to scheduled programs and cued in Raphael Ben Ari.

'Fellow citizens of Israel, good evening. The past few days have been amongst the most shocking, the most traumatic that we have experienced as a people in our half century of nationhood. Even in times of war, when our very survival was threatened, when our enemies had their weapons at our throats, we have always been one people, with one common purpose, and one destiny.'

The director settled back in his position next to the camera.

The Prime Minister continued to speak directly into the camera.

'Since I opted out of the so-called peace process, a process which would not have guaranteed us any long term security, I have been vilified throughout the world. I was prepared for that, and accepted its personal consequences. But what I was not prepared for, and what I cannot and will not accept, is the blackmail, bullying and strong-arm tactics being used by European countries and the United States against you, the Israeli people.

'Our overseas bank accounts have been frozen as though we were common criminals instead of a sovereign nation; our diplomats have been called to account by formerly friendly governments; our ability to trade has been severely compromised with restrictions, embargoes, and the curtailment of credit. There is even a move sponsored by America to impose a United Nations peace-keeping force on our soil, as though we were a renegade nation. Yet when Arab nations like Libya and Syria acted as hosts for terrorists, were they held to account? Why is there one rule for Israel; another for the rest of the world?'

The Prime Minister looked down at his notes. The director was amazed that he still acted like a schoolmaster lecturing to children, despite years of coaching by media experts.

'In other words, we are being unfairly pressured into accepting a Western/Arab solution to the problems of the region, rather than being allowed to follow our own agenda to the process of peace.

'Much of the impetus for the actions against us has been directed by the President of the United States, Jack Harrison, and his Secretary of State, John Dewhurst. I have no personal quarrel with these two men. They are both decent, honourable people. But they are not Israelis. They only have the good of America in their minds; to further that path, they have recently signed agreements with Arab nations who are currently our enemies. So I am left to wonder, "Why should we Israelis tread the path laid down by America?" The more you ask yourself this question, the more you may come to the same conclusion that I have.'

The director and producer looked at each other. Something dramatic was about to happen. This was quality television.

'The origin of most of our population is not in the West, but in the East ... in Russia, Poland, Hungary, Lithuania, Latvia ... in those great monuments to the might of the Jewish people before the creation of the State of Israel. Although many of you or your parents or grandparents left your homes because of pogroms or persecution, times have changed ... Eastern Europe has changed.

'The old borders and the old hatreds have gone forever. The Soviet Union is no more. In its place is a new republic, a young and innocent republic, unstained by the bloodshed of the past, eager to acquire new friends and relationships around the world. And it is about this that I want to talk to you tonight ...'

♜♜♜

'He said *what?!*'

'Mr President, Prime Minister Ben Ari has just announced to the Israeli people that he will be going to see President Abayev of Russia to discuss matters of mutual national interest; that he's going to offer military facilities in Israel to the Russians; that he's going to offer naval, rest and recreational facilities to Russian warships and their crews ...'

'Which means that he's going over to the Russian camp.'

'Well, Mr President, we've effectively driven him there by ostracising him, signing treaties with his enemies, and ...'

'Don't you fucking moralise with me, John. And don't say you've been warning me. Right now, I don't need your holier-than-thou Harvard attitude. I need a cool head to help me think this through. Jesus, I didn't imagine for one goddam minute that they'd go this far. I was just putting pressure on them to see sense, to come back to the fucking negotiating table.' The President stared into the distance. 'They must have got wind of the deal in the UN. But the Russians were involved in that. What's going on?'

John Dewhurst looked at Harrison with a mixture of pity and contempt.

'I think this has come as much out of the blue for the Russians as it has for us. As of this morning, President Abayev was agreeing to a military task force from the UN. Ben Ari has to be the most unpredictable leader since Idi Amin.'

The President stood and walked from behind his desk to join the others in the room. 'The Russians! That defies all logic … for the past twenty years Ben Ari has been the world's leading anti-Communist; he's been slating the Reds to Kingdom Come, calling them terrorists and loony tunes. Mossad was the first to tell the CIA every twist and turn the KGB were making in Syria and Iraq and in the Gulf. Jesus! What does he think he's playing at?'

'Maybe he's playing the world as he sees it today, Jack. Maybe he's just ahead of the game …'

Jack Harrison, President of the United States of America, looked at his Secretary of State and nodded.

♜♜♜

President Mikhail Abayev, the third democratically elected leader of the Russian Republic, looked at his junior Minister of Agriculture, Ivan Yeszersky, and nodded. Yeszersky couldn't believe what he had just been told.

'But how could he tell his people before he's made any approach to us? He's risking personal disaster. What happens when we reject him? There'll be a coup. No leader can take that sort of rejection and survive. What remains of the Opposition from the old Knesset will crucify him. The man's crazy.'

President Abayev looked at his brilliant friend and briefly considered the difference between the academic and the political mind … between the mind steeped in Tolstoy, Dostoyevsky, Gogol and Turgenev, and the mind steeped in tortuous international relations.

He smiled and looked down at the papers on his desk. Yeszersky's brow creased with a frown.

'You knew, didn't you?'

Abayev looked up, and nodded. 'Last night, Ministers Princhkov and Zaskoy came in to see me. The Israeli Ambassador had told them that Prime Minister Ben Ari would like to speak to me. They put up a very persuasive case for negotiating a treaty of concord between our two countries.

'You would no doubt be aware that the Israelis are advanced in desalination, agriculture, metals technology and information transfer … all areas in which we are currently suffering from a lack of expertise; areas, my dear Ivan Semyonovich, that can benefit our agricultural and industrial output and gain us invaluable foreign currency in the long run. We can learn a lot from them …'

'And what do they expect in return from us?'

'Merely to send some advisers to assist in … .'

'Advisers! Mikhail … are you out of your mind? Like the Americans sent advisers to Vietnam and Cambodia? Like we sent advisers to Afghanistan? Haven't we got enough problems at home without committing our resources and efforts to playing an international role? The saints preserve us, we were even going to support the imposition of a peace-keeping force between Syria and Israel!'

The President began to interrupt, but Yeszersky talked him down. 'And what will the Americans say? You can't expect them to sit on their haunches and do nothing. If they see Russian troops active in the Gulf area, or the Eastern Mediterranean, they'll withdraw the aid and economic support that has kept us alive these past years. They've already got fifty thousand men stationed in Saudi Arabia. They'll move in their Fifth Fleet. They'll take it as a huge provocation. Do you want an increase in international tension when all our energy should be directed towards solving our most pressing problems at home?'

Yeszersky sat back, drained. He had never spoken to the President like this before. Since Mikhail Abayev had called him to the Kremlin to discuss his transfer from Moscow University's Department of Russian Literature to work within the cabinet, their relationship had been one of respectful friendship, with Yeszersky learning much from the canny politician.

Now, Yeszersky saw his leader as just another opportunist politician, more intent on ends than the morality of the means. As though a small light was turned on in a dark room, he slowly began to perceive a connection between events

'And since when do you trust Princhkov and Zaskoy? You know damn well that they've been working behind your back with Petrovsky. If Boris Krychkov hadn't died yesterday ... And we don't yet know what the Jericho Plan is. Don't you think that you should find out what's going on here before you start committing the Republic to a new path of international relations?'

It never ceased to amaze Abayev how much Russia had changed in the few short years since the death of Brezhnev. If a junior minister for agriculture had spoken to any past president in the way that Abayev had just been treated, he would have been taken out and shot. There were many advantages to a democratic republic. A disadvantage was not being able to shoot critics.

Still, he owed his friend an explanation: '*Tovarich*, understand one thing. Any actions I may take will be in the interests of Russia. When you were in Moscow University you had the luxury of standing on your principles. You could set the standards which others had to follow. In politics, you simply don't have that luxury. The Jews were our enemies one day; the Arabs our friends. Now the Jews are our friends and the Arabs are our enemies. Same difference ...'

'Mikhail,' Yeszersky interrupted, 'you can't just abandon your principles. They're not chaffs of wheat, blowing in the wind of the steppes.'

Abayev listened with a mixture of pleasure and annoyance. He couldn't stand Yeszersky's high moral attitude, but he expressed his indignation more articulately than most of the others in his cabinet.

Yeszersky continued: 'After seventy years of repressive, unrelenting Communism our government has given the people their first whiff of freedom. We've spent years undoing the shackles which Stalin and Krushchev and the others chained us in. To do it, we've had to look at who we really are, and see ourselves for the first time as a country which needs to compete openly and honestly with every other country in the world. We've had to admit our weaknesses. To overcome them, we've had to pull away from foreign commitments and adventures and our support for our former puppets around the world.'

Abayev wondered when the lecture was going to finish. He had important work to do.

'Now, just because Ben Ari comes to us begging for friendship, you lie down like a bitch in heat and let him ...' Yeszersky searched for an image. 'And what of the Jericho Plan? You don't even know what it is. For all we know, this approach could be part of it. Why did the Israeli Ambassador approach Princhkov and Zaskoy, rather than the Foreign Ministry, or you directly?'

'Ivan, my friend,' said the President of the Russian Republic, 'how are the agricultural production figures for last month? Are we going to have enough cabbages when winter is upon us?'

The interview was over.

♜♜♜

The Imam shook his head in amazement. This was unexpected. Again he glanced at the transcript of the speech made just hours earlier by Raphael Ben Ari. The Jews were seeking a political relationship with the Russian devils. They were inviting the Communists to station troops in their land to counterbalance the growing influence of the Americans in Arabia. They were offering airbase facilities, port, docking and repair facilities for the Russian navy, and exchanges of army personnel—euphemistically called joint training exercises.

The statement made it clear that the Russians had not yet agreed to the offer. Raphael Ben Ari would be seeking talks with Abayev to sound him out on the deal. This was not the way it was meant to be. The Imam had sought divine guidance. He knew, with the absolute certainty of the inspired, that Allah had ordained a jihad between the Israelis and the frontline Arab states. At the swift conclusion of that war the Imam would march into Jerusalem brandishing a sword, in the footsteps of the Ayyubid, Saladin, like the conquering prophet Mohammed.

Yet the Russians now figured in the balance. They had not been factored in by the Imam. He had not even considered them in his reckoning. This man, this evil, this walking devil, this Israeli, Ben Ari, had upset the equation. That was something which the Imam would never forgive. He would pay, and pay dearly with his life.

The Imam screwed up the transcription and tossed it furiously at the wall.

♜♜♜

Marcel Dupain knew that he should not watch. It was beneath his dignity. He was sullied by their crudeness. Yet he was fascinated by the depths to which ordinary people will descend for what the American artist Andy Warhol had once described as a telling aspect of the human condition. Everyone will be famous for fifteen minutes. Well, Italian television certainly ensured that every Italian had the opportunity to be famous— if only by making a fool of himself in asinine talent shows. And on the other channels, garrulous, gullible, talentless housewives, unable even to warble or screech, attempted to be famous by taking their clothes off and acting like sluts.

A noise from the bedroom distracted his viewing. The sliding door separating the lounge from the bedroom was not soundproof. Marcel could hear a low, guttural moaning. In the ten minutes he had been sitting naked watching television, he had forgotten about the bedroom. Now he rose and walked towards the partition, sliding it open to reveal a young black-haired boy lying spreadeagled on a plastic sheet.

The boy was returning to consciousness. His naked body leaked excrement onto the sheet, its pungent stench filling the room, and making Marcel feel like gagging. The hair on the boy's head was damp, matted to his high brown forehead; his young body was devoid of hair, except for a mass of curly pubic hair, a birdsnest, with the head of a tiny penis peeking through. The boy moaned again, his head moving from side to side on the pillow as he fought to regain consciousness. The effort was too great. He lapsed back into sleep, freed from the pain which had made him faint.

Marcel looked at the boy with contempt. He moved over to the side of the bed, grabbed the boy by his pubic hair and tugged, lifting his body off the bed. The boy was dragged back into wakefulness. The excruciation, the torment made him scream. Furious, Marcel slapped the boy in the face. 'Shut up, you Italian moron,' he hissed.

The child tried to focus his eyes on Marcel. He began to shake his head: *'Per favore signore la smetta. O Mio Dio …'*

Seeing the child's growing hysteria, Marcel felt a shock of pleasure run through his body. Just moments before his penis had been flaccid. Now it started to grow again, his stomach muscles constricting in anticipation of the pleasure he was about to experience.

The boy had lapsed into unconsciousness with his arms tied to the bedhead. Now he struggled to pull them free. His body was rigid with fear from the experience of the violation an hour earlier. Marcel slapped the boy's face hard with the back of his hand, nearly dislocating his jaw. It was a warning. Unless he cooperated in every way, and allowed his body to be totally at Marcel's disposal, then he would be further tortured.

The boy's lip split and started to ooze blood. Marcel untied one of the straps restraining his hands and turned the child's body so he was lying sideways. Then he reached down to the foot of the bed and picked up a large battery, with two copper wires attached to its terminals.

The boy looked around to see what he was doing. When he saw what Marcel was planning, his body arched and his eyes stared open, the pupils distended in shock. *'Non, non signore, non per favore ...'*

'Shut up, you street slime,' Marcel commanded, but the boy continued to scream. Marcel again hit him across the ear, knocking the boy's head back onto the pillow.

The child's body slumped and seemed to give in. It was the last, the final insult. He could fight no more. Whatever Marcel would do to him now, he would have to allow. He had lost the strength, the will, the ability to resist. All he could do was to bury his head deeply into the pillow and whimper.

Marcel reached over and slid his fingers into a tub of lubricating jelly on the bedside table, which he smeared onto the head of his erect penis. He slid it easily into the boy's rectum ... the pain made the child arch his back again, which gave Marcel even greater depth and added to his pleasure. The tight, wet warmth of the boy's anus all but made Marcel explode in his third orgasm of the night. He gripped the shaft of his penis hard to stop himself from coming. There was one more experience to be had before he threw the thing on the bed back into the street. One further final pleasure which he had planned days ago, on the flight between Greece and Israel, after he had disposed of the fat insult, Aristo Haggopian.

When the desire to orgasm began to subside he again pushed his penis deeper into the boy's rectum, thrusting further with every angry beat. Marcel was able to control himself long enough to connect one wire of the battery to the end of the boy's penis, and the other to the child's scrotum.

A final surge of strength, a denial of the pain, made the boy take his head from out of the pillow and look down towards his penis. He saw the wires and looked up at Marcel, hatred burning in his eyes. *'Bastard!'* he said before strength drained away again and his head sank back, into the pillow.

Marcel smiled. Now it was doubly pleasurable. Pushing the switch, the current surged through the wires, sending an excruciating pain into the boy's penis. He screamed and clawed at the air, his rectum contracting like a vice around Marcel's penis. Marcel could control himself no longer. He screamed in the fulfilment, the pleasure, the wash of his explosion. Again and again, Marcel's penis thrust and thrust, tearing the delicate skin in the child's anus until it bled dark red blood which mingled with his watery excrement. They remained there, man and boy, crying together in pleasure and pain, each one's body exhausted, drained, ended.

Marcel extracted his penis, and a stream of semen and shit drained from the immobile, whimpering boy.

Marcel walked unsteadily to the toilet and washed his whole pubic area carefully. Then modestly wrapping a towel around his torso, he went into the loungeroom and helped himself to a diet soda. His mood of relaxation was interrupted by the stupid boy's whimpering. There were many advantages to having a young boy. They were firm and tight and always terrified. But that only satisfied one part of his needs. The other part, the more sensuous part was the act of seduction. He didn't seduce little boys. He only paid for them. Later that night, Marcel promised himself a real treat. What his body craved, what his mind needed, was a strong, sweet-smelling, virile Italian Caesar, one of the young gods who strutted their wares in the Via Padrone. When one led the life of an itinerant, one could not spend the time developing relationships and Marcel didn't even mind paying for his pleasures, provided the Caesar played hard to get.

He walked out of the bathroom and saw that the ridiculous television show had come to an end. The mid-evening news was on. Heading the news was an item concerning Israel. Marcel strained to understand it. The background pictures indicated that the Prime Minister, Ben Ari, was about to travel to Moscow. Marcel frowned. That was unusual. If Marcel was right in his interpretation of the excited Italian newsreader, Raphael Ben Ari was going to offer the Russians access to Israeli air bases, ports, military establishments. In effect, the Jews would be entering into the sort of client relationship that Syria and Iraq had enjoyed with the Soviet Union until recently.

Marcel was stunned. For him, it was the most dangerous news imaginable. The Russians held extensive details of terrorist groups throughout the world … names, locations, descriptions, records, histories, codes, safe houses, everything. It had been a miracle that so few details had been released to the West by the new Russian leaders. But now Israel was befriending them! If these details should fall into Israeli hands, into the hands of Mossad!

As he was thinking, there was a gentle, almost apologetic rap on the door. Marcel grabbed his gun and, standing to the right of the door, out of the line of possible fire, he called out 'Pronto'.

'Sir. Is me,' came a whispered voice. 'I come collect grandson. You are finished with him, yes?'

Marcel concealed the gun behind his back and opened the door. Standing there was a man in his sixties, scrawny, unshaven, smelling of the streets. He walked in and beamed a smile at Marcel, his yellow and brown teeth stained by food and nicotine.

'Is boy was good, sir?'

'Boy was good,' said Marcel. 'Take him and go quickly. I have left money for you by the bed.'

The man hesitated. 'Sir, boy is only grandson. He I love very very much. Price you pay … is not much for virgin. Boy was virgin till today. I think you pay more. Yes!' The man opened his jacket to reveal a black-handled stiletto, tucked into his trousers. He moved his hand swiftly down and grabbed its handle. In response, Marcel pulled the gun from behind his back and stuck the barrel up the man's left nostril.

'Listen to me, you piece of stinking Italian horseshit. If you're still here in the next ten seconds, I'll blow your face away. And take your "grandson" with you. He was useless, anyway. He's had more men than a sixty-year-old whore. Now take him and go, and if you ever dare show your face in this hotel again, I'll kill you, and your little money-making machine in there.'

The Italian did not understand the words, but fully understood their intent. He rushed terrified into the bedroom to pick up and dress the little orphan he had rescued from the streets of Naples five years before.

As the elderly man and the partly dressed child left the hotel room, Marcel felt a wave of nausea sweep over him. His confrontation with the Italian had been expected, but was distressing. How could an adult, *in loco parentis*, allow a child to be used in that way? Marcel was amazed at the cruelty, the inhumanity, of some human beings.

♜♜♜

'Shut up! Quiet! They're crossing over to America …'

No matter how much he insisted on silence in his own home, Mordecai Avit was unable to restore order. The lounge room was capable of holding twenty, perhaps twenty-five people at the most, but Shoshanna Avit had given up counting when the fortieth person arrived at the Avits' small home in Rechov HaZicharon just minutes after the Prime Minister's broadcast.

The first had been Motu Jacobs, a middle-aged radical whose fervour for Israeli politics was diminished after spending twenty years weaving his way through the mazes of the political process. Shoshanna opened the door, and Motu barged past, pecking her on the cheek as he broadcast his indignation. 'Did you hear what that bastard has done? He's invited in the Russians without consulting me or Mordecai or anyone. We've got to do something. This is going to lead to civil war.'

The next to arrive had been Avi Hershkovitz, speaker of the Knesset. Since the declaration of martial law he was a man without his usual political power. 'This is it!' he said as he strode into the house, steaming with ire and indignation 'This is too much. Now he's gone too far. Martial law he could justify on the grounds of public order. Changing the foreign policy of an elected government without the franchise of the people is treason. For this, he deserves to be overthrown.'

After Avi Hershkovitz came Rabbi Baruch Close, leader of the religious faction and an immigrant from New Jersey. In short order afterwards came other members of Avit's party, then friends, comrades, allies, opponents, members of the press corps, all gathering around the voice of reason. In the lounge room, Shoshanna gave up on the idea of serving everyone but hung around to see what would happen. Tonight would be pivotal to the future of Israel, and she wanted to be part of it.

When the lounge room was filled past its capacity, Mordecai shouted above the hubbub to be heard: 'Will you all please, please be quiet. There's something on the television which we must hear.'

At last the room descended into silence and Mordecai turned the volume of the television higher.

It was tuned to CNN. The anchorman in Atlanta was saying: 'And for the latest from the White House, we cross live to Christina Cassubin ... Christina, I understand that the President has just given the first American response to the Israeli Prime Minister's amazing statement of half an hour ago.'

'That's right, Jerry, and to stress how seriously the White House is taking the dramatic change in policy by its long-time ally, it was the President himself who appeared before the White House Press Corps and not the official State Department spokeswoman. Here's what President Harrison had to say just a few moments ago ...'

The picture changed from the correspondent speaking live on the lawns of the White House to the briefing room in the press compound on the second floor of the building. President Harrison stood behind a cluster of microphones, answering one of a dozen questions which had been shouted at him since he stepped onto the lectern. The film started when he was in mid-sentence:

'... more disappointed than shocked. We've been anticipating for some time that the Israeli government would be seeking closer ties with the Russians, since the Israelis have effectively become *persona non grata* with the Western community ...'

'Mr President,' a reporter shouted, 'wasn't Russia supporting a peace-keeping force?'

The President ignored him, but listened to another reporter.

'Mr President, do you accept any responsibility for having driven them over to the Russians by your hard-line stance?'

'I accept no responsibility at all. Don't forget that it was Prime Minister Ben Ari who insulted every Arab leader, and one hundred million Arabs, with a scurrilous, racist attack at the peace conference that Secretary Dewhurst had spent years negotiating and setting up. It was Ben Ari who declared a state of martial law and made virtually every Israeli a prisoner in his own nation. If the Israeli people want to return to a relationship with the West, they will be welcomed with open arms. But to do that, they may very well have to think who they want to lead them back here …'

'Mr President, are you advocating that the Israelis overthrow their Ruling Council by force?'

'I would never advocate the use of force. But let's look at the reality of the situation. In the past month, Israel has been ostracised by the its former friends in the West, and has earned the enmity and hostility of an entire world … or almost the entire world. I forgot their new-found friendship with the government of Russia.'

The loungeroom in Mordecai Avit's house erupted into bedlam as irate Israeli politicians shouted their views.

'Even the Americans say we should overthrow the madman.'

'For God's sake, we can't sit idly by and tolerate this.'

'How do we get rid of this … this … Herod?'

Mordecai held his hands above his head for silence. Shoshanna bent down and turned off the television in anticipation of her husband's speech. He moved over to one of the chairs and stood on it to be visible to everyone in the room. His head nearly touched the ceiling.

'Friends, in every society, there comes a time when the political process becomes corrupted; when the law becomes a perverted instrument of an ambitious few who prostitute power to their own nefarious ends; when the people must take the law into their own hands for the moral health of the majority.

We are at such a transitional point. I am in no doubt that the good of our country lies in wresting control of the political process from the hands of a crazed few. This decision tonight, this change in the foreign policy of the country without consulting the electorate, is an act of treason, an act of despotism. It is unconstitutional, undemocratic, and immoral …'

The people in the room nodded in agreement. But as Mordecai spoke, the distant wailing of sirens could be heard. As it grew closer and more distinct, people in the room grew increasingly distracted. An undercurrent of murmur passed through the group.

Tyres screeched to a halt outside the house, car doors banged and footsteps could be heard running over the gravel on the pavement towards the front door. People in the room looked at each other in consternation. No one spoke. Orders barked outside became louder and louder as men ran imperiously towards the front door.

Those old enough to remember the raids of the SS Blackshirts in pre-war Nazi Germany felt a cold shudder in their spines.

Danny Navar switched off the television set in his office and sat back stunned. All his adult life he had worked for Mossad. When he left the army he could have gone into his father's business but instead he decided to accept the offer and become a member of the world's most sophisticated secret service organisation.

To fight the enemy! To protect Israel! And the enemy? The Arabs … sure. But also Russia. Things had been easier these past years since the collapse of the USSR. All he had to contend with was the Arabs. But that didn't make Russia a friend.

How in God's name could that idiot Ben Ari have decided to seek help from Russia? Had he no sense of history? No understanding of the blackness in the Russian soul, the hatred of the Russians towards the Jews. And what was all that crap, that self-serving bullshit about the origin of the Israeli population not being in the West but the East? And that bullshit about Russia and Poland and Latvia being great monuments to the might of the Jewish people? Had he forgotten the pogroms? The six million killed? Where had they come from? Not America or England. It was the Eastern Europeans. The Russians and Poles and Germans that killed the Jews for the last thousand years.

Danny slammed his pen down on the desk despondently. Was it worth going on? He opened his desk drawer to take out a bottle of whisky and saw the fat file of things he still had to do by the end of the week.

There was something in the file. What was it? He took it out and flicked through the miscellaneous documents, testaments to Israel's current state of paranoia. Yes! There it was. That fax sent by the Australian girl. A photograph of Ben Ari as a young Pole. A Communist? Leading pogroms? No, nobody in his right name would think that Ben Ari … But there again, Ben Ari had just told the nation that he was going to Russia … No! It couldn't be …

♜♜♜

Paul looked out of the dining room window at the aspen, oak and elm trees in the wide expanse of garden. The lush European trees stood solid and timeless, sentinels of Europe's history. So unlike those of Australian gardens, where the spindly trees struggled out of the dry scrub.

At the extremity of the garden, he could see the high security fence, with a safety zone of six feet on either side. He had not noticed it when Gosia had driven him to the mansion the previous morning.

He had been a 'guest' at the house for nearly thirty-six hours, free to go at any time. But his elderly host had made it quite clear that the moment Paul was delivered back to his hotel, he would lose the protection which was offered.

He still had no idea who the old man was, or who or what

he represented. Yet he had been treated with courtesy and consideration, despite Paul's aggression towards everyone within the house. He had shouted, demanded, argued and become taciturn in order to find out who his host was and what he wanted. But with a stoicism bordering on the heroic, all the people in the household merely smiled and nodded, as though they understood no English.

Paul had been taken to see Miriam late the previous afternoon. He was left alone in the room with her for over an hour. She was still drugged and had smiled a lot. They had talked about little of importance. Before returning to the house, he and Gosia had driven in a more leisurely way around Warsaw, followed at all times by a Lada containing four of the old man's heavily built colleagues.

Yet in all the time he had spent with his host, he had only once been asked to supply information. The old man seemed to have lost all interest in Paul when he mentioned Mossad's involvement.

Dusk was falling outside and Paul's attention reverted to the ornate dining room in which he had just eaten a delicious meal. It was some sort of beef stew with dumplings, and thick crusty bread with lashings of butter. A 1978 Côte de Rhone had complemented the food perfectly. At the table had been the old man, Gosia, and three others who Paul now knew as part of the old man's entourage. They were Valeriy, Roman, and Valdek.

After the meal, Gosia and Paul were left alone. In the subdued lighting of the dining room, he noticed for the first time how attractive she was. Delicate cheekbones, eyes black as jet, raven hair cascading down her shoulders. She was sensuous while being innocent, something which Paul found erotic. Gosia knew that she was being scrutinised, and blushed. Paul found her modesty even more attractive, but before he had a chance to ask her any personal questions, the dining room door opened. Valdek, standing at the threshold, said in appalling English: 'Now my boss said to come see television. Umm! Is Israeli talk.'

Paul and Gosia walked across the hall into the study where the old man, Valeriy and Roman were watching the television.

The picture was of the Israeli Prime Minister speaking earnestly in Hebrew to the Israeli people. His words were translated instantly into Polish by a voice-over. Paul was lost in both languages, but the old man explained what was going on: 'It seems that Mr Ben Ari has had enough of American pressure politics, and has decided to seek an intimate relationship with the Russian Republic.'

Paul showed no surprise, which in itself surprised the old man.

'Doesn't that strike you as unusual?' the old man asked.

Paul sat down on a leather sofa and shook his head. 'Not when you know something of Ben Ari's background.'

It seemed as good a time as any to tell the old man more of what he knew. So far he had only mentioned Mossad's involvement. Perhaps if he told the old man and his colleagues a bit more, he would be given information in exchange. It was worth a try. After all, he had been shown real courtesy this last day and a half. His captor could have disposed of him at any time, or set him loose in Warsaw to be murdered by whoever had planted the bomb in the cafe. Yet he had done none of these things. Rather than try to bully Paul into telling him what he knew, the old man was content to wait until Paul was ready to share his knowledge.

'Do you know something of Ben Ari's background?' asked the old man.

'Yes! Miriam's grandfather came from the same village. Apparently, Ben Ari was a rabid Communist, who organised pogroms against the other Jews in his village.'

The old man's television viewing was at an end. He turned around to Paul and willed him to continue.

'Over many years, Ben Ari has tried to bury his background, and we … Miriam and I … have recently been trying to uncover it … to prove that he's a mass murderer. I made the mistake of telling Max Mandle. He's a close friend of Ben Ari.

He told Ben Ari, and that's why Mossad is after us. They've killed Miriam's grandfather, searched my apartment, and according to you killed Rabbi Gartenbaum and the old man at the Institute of the Diaspora. That's why I know it's Mossad. I know you disbelieved me, laughed at me, but now do you understand?'

The old man smiled and nodded to Valdek to turn off the television. A further nod indicated to his colleagues that he wanted to be alone with Paul.

'Mr Sinclair, why don't you tell me more about Miriam's grandfather, and exactly what he told you. Perhaps I could organise a cup of coffee while you think back on all the details.'

He walked towards the window, then stopped and turned to Paul. 'You know, it occurs to me that your young friend Miriam would be feeling much better by now. I think it would be appropriate to have her brought here. She can assist us in learning more about her grandfather. Anyway, I'm sure you would agree that she's far safer here than in the hospital, or the hotel.'

CHAPTER TWENTY-TWO

The black Volga hardly seemed to slow as it entered the middle of the city at the height of Moscow's evening rush hour. Despite his exhaustion, the passenger managed a thin smile. So different from Berlin. With fewer and fewer cars in private hands and gasoline still a luxury, peak hour meant only a small increase in the pulse rate of the city. The car drove around the massive stone walls of the Kremlin, until it reached the outskirts of the city where the traffic thinned even more. It sat confidently on the road and when the driver was certain that the traffic police had been left behind, he drove quickly to the Pasternak Woods south-east of the capital.

The driver and his passenger remained silent. It was neither a sign of disrespect nor a measure of security. Andrei Alexandrovich Yezhov was exhausted. He had been awake the whole night debriefing the young Australian journalist and his mistress. It had been gruelling and frustrating. The girl had exhibited the usual paranoia and spent the first hour of the interrogation issuing a list of demands. Australian and American women were so demonstrative. The more courteous he was to her the more irritable she became. She had called him patronising. He felt insulted. He didn't understand today's young women. But he didn't understand women at all. That was why he had never married.

In the end with Miriam, he relied on the tactic of dismissal. When she refused point-blank to cooperate, he walked out of the library leaving the door open and retired to his room, where he put on headphones to listen to their conversation.

He enjoyed listening to people's innermost secrets. Only when one knew the essence of an enemy could one hope to control him. The girl ranted and raved at first, using bluster to cover her fear. During her conversation with Paul, she had

418

talked of a dybbuk, some sort of demon or devil trying to grasp her ankles and pull her down. Yezhov found it odd that a young educated woman would talk in these terms. Yet his experience with Jews was limited. If the Russian peasant was naive and superstitious, how much more so were those Jews who still seemed to live in the eighteenth century?

It had taken Paul fifteen minutes to persuade Miriam to cooperate. After that, Yezhov used the tactic of concession, by feeding them tidbits of information, little more than gossip they could have picked up from taxi-drivers. Having scored a victory in her eyes, the girl became a fountain of information, telling Yezhov all she could remember. At the time he thought it odd. He would have expected a lawyer to be more guarded. But with the shock of the bombing and the news that the people she had contacted in Israel had died, her fear had opened her mouth.

In certain essential matters concerning her grandfather's home town, she knew next to nothing. The process of extracting the details of the old Jew's life before he emigrated to Australia had been difficult and exacting. The woman divulged most of the major facts, but missing were the small, seemingly insignificant details—inferences, innuendos, inflexions—about which her knowledge was vague. Yezhov knew from his decades of debriefings that these could be as vital in defining the truth as the major details.

The young man and woman had fallen into bed exhausted at 5.00 a.m. Yezhov didn't have that luxury. Luckily, the older he got, the less sleep he seemed to need. He wondered if Petrovsky was also something of a night owl.

Yezhov didn't know when they would wake up. He didn't care. A twenty-four hour guard was protecting them. That was the end of his responsibilities.

He would be glad when they returned to Australia. He detested it when he was forced to work with outsiders. They were unpredictable. Their actions were capricious. They were more difficult to control. They didn't know the rules. Which was why he had discounted most of the theories that the young couple had come up with. Yezhov was dealing with the real world, not the phantoms of their overactive imaginations. Mossad? Max Mandle? Dybbuks? Mere shadow boxing. The real spectre was Petrovsky. And a recidivist bunch of KGB hardliners, men and women who hadn't yet come to terms with the status quo. Still acting as though they were warriors in a Cold War.

What the hell did the old Jew's information mean? Why kill people to hide it? So Ben Ari was a Communist in his youth. So what? Many young idealistic men and women were attracted to what Communism once had to offer. But if he was Petrovsky's mole! Then it all fitted together. Ben Ari's smooth rise to the top; the Cyprus peace conference; the imposition of martial law; the approach to Russia. Pure Petrovsky. Grudgingly, the old man smiled. If the implications weren't so serious ... but the implications were breathtaking. Petrovsky was rising to the top again, like a snake sloughing off its old skin.

What Yezhov had to do, and do immediately, was to convert the Australians' theories into hard fact. Then give the evidence to Yeszersky so he could confront the Russian leadership before it was too late, before Petrovsky was again the puppeteer. And Yezhov wouldn't be there as a counterbalance. Now he was an outsider.

Yezhov had revealed next to nothing to the Australians. The less they knew, the better. And better they did not die. The boy was of no interest to Yezhov. A typical reporter. Full of bravado, airing knowledge when he knew little. And the girl was also full of bravura. She had a natural aggression and suspicion, typical of female lawyers, but she was so totally out of her depth that her bravado was simply a front for her insecurity.

The old Jew's allegations about Ben Ari leading pogroms in pre-war Poland might or might not be true—it was a matter of little concern to Yezhov. But for Ben Ari to be a long-term Communist mole, a sleeper ... That was something of which Yezhov had no inkling. If it were true then his old nemesis,

Petrovsky, had pulled off the coup to end all coups. Professional respect enabled Yezhov to admire the covert masterstroke, though it was not sufficient to challenge the detestation he felt for the man. The two men had known each other for decades, their careers in the NKVD and its subsequent manifestations largely mirroring each other's.

Both at different times were Head of the First Chief Directorate in charge of Foreign Intelligence. Both had been head of the Fifth Directorate in charge of Ideology and Dissidents. And both were put out to graze at the end of their careers. When he settled in Berlin to make some money for his retirement, Yezhov considered that the last man about whom he would have to worry was Genardy Arkyovich Petrovsky.

As the car drove out of Moscow and entered its wooded outskirts, Yezhov began to relax. Here there was virtually no chance of detection. The road narrowed from four lanes to two as it neared the deepening woods, drear with tangled overgrowth. Yezhov's exhaustion dulled his mind. Events were happening too fast. They were becoming increasingly menacing. He cursed himself for leaving Moscow without tidying up the loose ends of his life. He should have acted against Petrovsky before he retired. The opportunity had been there when Petrovsky went to live in his dacha on the Black Sea. He was unprotected. The wet division would have done the job elegantly, even painlessly, but Yezhov made the mistake of allowing the old Marshal a retirement. Now he had risen like an ageing phoenix from the cold embers of an unremitting war, an old warrior who refused to fade away, playing out a battle that had long since been lost.

Yezhov shuddered at the thought that his *bête noire*, Marshal of the Army Genardy Arkyovich Petrovsky was rearing his old head again. Yezhov had contacted Ivan Yeszersky to seek an urgent appointment when he discovered the dangerous new information about Ben Ari. To his surprise, Yeszersky asked to meet in his dacha in the Pasternak Woods, a dozen miles from the outskirts of Moscow, rather than in the Kremlin.

The car's headlights made the trees dance in a spectral jig as it weaved along the narrow roads which took it deeper and deeper towards the Poet's Lake. Yezhov remembered the last time he had taken this drive. The woods were known then as the Stalin Forest; it was in the black days of the cold war … 1951 or '52 … he couldn't remember. He had been summoned to speak to Stalin about the development of SIGINT.

Today, he was driving there because of a renegade Polish Jew and an out-of-control Communist reactionary. Poles! Why did they always seem to form a part of the political machinations of Russian life? Even Dzerzinsky's chief lieutenants half a century before were known as the 'Polish faction', and look at the problems they caused in the early days of the Revolution.

The car turned into a side road of the Pasternak Woods, which led to a series of villas by the lakeside. Pasternak, the poet of light. Lara's poems. Poems of soft and sensual beauty. He thought back to their song. A madrigal to the Russian people. To their open hearts and buried souls. The trees grew still thicker and more enclosing, cutting what poor light remained into horizontal shafts. A darkening, lowering light. The paradox of Pasternak. Surrounded by the solid authoritarianism of censorship until he could say no more. Until his light was extinguished. And in Pasternak's woods, Yezhov was surrounded by the solid phalanx of trees, like a regiment of censors.

Through the trees, the dachas loomed heavy and foreboding. Symbols of privilege. He first visited the Pasternak Woods to spend time with Yeszersky's father, Mikhail Vladimir. What a man. Handsome, elegant. A real ladies' man. When they went drinking together, dressed in their uniforms, Mikhail as an army officer, he as a member of the elite NKVD, they had made the girls' heads swim. What a life. The power, the privilege. And the joy of seeing young Ivan Semyonovich Yeszersky grow from a straggly youth into a brilliant young man.

Both he and the Yeszerskys had been in positions of privilege. But neither had abused the trust of, and the hardships suffered by, the Russian people. Not for them the outrageous escapades, the imperious use of power or misspent holidays. Yezhov smiled as he thought back to those days. He was a dedicated Communist, but that didn't mean he couldn't enjoy himself. There had been many women, but they had been free of the coercion imposed by his colleagues. Coercion had brought him into conflict with the hierarchy. It had been a weekend party at Yeszersky's dacha on the lake. In the middle of the night, Yezhov and Yeszersky had woken to the sounds of a woman sobbing on the shores of the lake. She was naked. Her face was bruised. Yezhov wrapped her in a blanket. After hot chocolate and a vodka she told them about the party. She and two other typists from the Authors' Union had come to a dacha as weekend guests of two senior party men. When they arrived, there were seven other men, NKVD, GRU, who knows? They were raped repeatedly. The girl managed to escape. Yeszersky insisted he call the authorities. His wife begged him not to. Young Ivan Semyonovich reacted angrily to his mother's cowardice. Yezhov was ambivalent, but Yeszersky's morality was outraged and they called the Militia. The men were arrested. Beria intervened, but Stalin overruled him and the rapists were sentenced to harsh terms of imprisonment. The typist ended up beyond the Urals and Yezhov was a pariah for years afterwards. From the moment it was reported to Petrovsky that Yezhov had called the Militia, he made it his goal to destroy Yezhov's career. Only constant vigilance and outmanoeuvring had frustrated Petrovsky's scheming. Despite him and his connections, Yezhov's talents were rewarded by increasingly important posts in the KGB hierarchy. But always there was the spectre of Petrovsky in his background. Somewhat akin to the way the Jewess had described the ... what was its name?—the dybbuk ... in her private conversation with the Australian reporter.

Yezhov looked out of the car's window at the dachas which had once been the weekend playgrounds of Stalin, Beria and the other grey men of the Cold War. Stalin also had another dacha at Semyonovskoye, a hundred kilometres south of

Moscow, which he used for official gatherings, but the one near here was his private lair, where he would stalk those whom his tortured mind believed plotted against him. Much like Hitler's lair at Berchtesgaden, granite-hewn, paramount and unforgiving.

As the car drove down the minister's driveway, Yezhov again wondered why they should be meeting here. Only a couple of days before, Yeszersky had been open, ebullient and interested in the tidbits of information Yezhov gave him; now he was guarded, secretive and worried. The Volga drew up to the front door of the dacha. Standing there was Ivan Yeszersky, palely loitering.

♜♜♜

Paul and Miriam sat mournful and quiet in the seats of the bay window, looking out over the luxuriant gardens. Below them was the glass roof of the conservatory. Miriam could see luscious bunches of grapes, hanging like pendulous breasts, between the yellowing leaves.

They had woken with a start to the sounds of the morning, birds chirping, dogs barking, a person vacuuming, people talking. Both felt drugged from lack of sleep.

As they sat, Miriam still looking like a wounded soldier with the mercurochrome colouring her skin, they tried to recall the way in which the conversation had moved. It was like a delicate tracery, weaving in one direction and then another. The movements were subtle, indistinct. Only in retrospect did they realise how many areas they had covered. Only in retrospect did they realise that, despite an entire night's discussion, they still were no more knowledgeable about their situation than when they arrived.

Paul looked at Miriam as she stared out of the window, her eyes fixed on a distant spot. He was concerned that the shock of the bomb might have wounded her mentally as well as physically. This morning, she was quite withdrawn. Last night, and into the early hours, she had been loquacious. At first, she had been suspicious and cautious, but when their interrogator told her how much he already knew and drew some conclusions tied in to current Middle East politics, Miriam opened up.

Paul had been surprised. After his initial flurry of information, he had held back, waiting for a quid pro quo. But Miriam felt no such caution. As soon as their host convinced her that he posed no threat to either of them, she had told him almost everything. All about life with her grandparents; what her *zeida* had to say about Ben Ari; as much as she knew about her grandparents' village and much more. But when she came to the day of the pogroms, Paul willed her to keep quiet about the photograph. Something—a look? a feeling?—stopped her from mentioning it. She was the lawyer, still playing the trump card close to her chest. Did the old man notice or suspect that they were still holding something back? If he did, he was far too shrewd to press them.

'Miriam, last night … You seemed to be willing to tell the old guy more than I thought you would have done.'

She turned slowly from the window towards him, as though trying to focus her mind and her eyes. In a dry, emotionless voice, she said: 'Really?'

'Yes. I'm not saying you've done any harm. It's just that I don't understand why you seemed to be so … well … talkative.'

She looked at him more clearly, able to focus herself on his presence.

'Oh!' It was all she felt like saying.

'I thought lawyers were trained to be cautious in what they said. I think I probably gave him too much information myself.'

'You could be right.' She still sounded flat, drained. 'Who knows? I feel so out of my depth here, it's as if none of the old rules apply any more.'

She stood and went to the dresser to comb her hair. At least she could look more confident than she felt.

'We're both out of our depth,' Paul said, choosing his words carefully, 'but ever since we left Australia, you've been acting …

oddly.' It was such a stupid, meaningless word, he hated himself for saying it. But it masked his real feelings, his fears.

Miriam turned and frowned: 'Oddly?'

Paul began to feel trapped, as though he had unlocked Pandora's box and demons were about to be set loose.

'Perhaps "oddly" is the wrong word. Just not as you were in Sydney. It's too easy to blame the circumstances. It's as though something deeply hidden in you, something you've always managed to control, has suddenly sprung up. It's also come between us and I'm not equipped to fight it. I don't know what it is, but it frightens the life out of me.'

She could have become angry. In Israel, possibly even in Australia, she would have. But after the bombing, after finding that she was responsible for the deaths of two sweet old men, she felt raw.

'Paul. I have changed. I know it. And it's got to do with coming to Europe. God, this is hard to explain.'

'Then don't bother. Leave it. Let it rest until you feel better.'

'No,' she said. 'It has to be said. This … feeling began to clarify while I was lying in the hospital bed. You know, they pump you full of Valium, but you wake up with such vivid images of what you've been dreaming. Sometimes, I'd lie there awake for hours, pretending to be asleep, just thinking.'

'Thinking about what?'

She hesitated before answering, unsure whether to let him into her mind. 'Thinking about who I am, and where I've come from. And where I'm going.'

Paul nodded. He knew where he was going, and couldn't wait to get out. He felt overwhelmed and was biding his time before being let out of the country to return to Australia, to the terra firma of his own security. Back to the life over which he had control.

So how much worse for Miriam, who had not before now known a rough or tumble greater than a squabble over a contract, or a scrap with a client?

'And what conclusion did you come to?' he asked.

Miriam smiled as she slowly brushed her hair. Sitting in front of a hinged mirror on an ornate dressing table, she seemed to belong to an earlier century, so very different from the Miriam he knew in Sydney who tugged a brush through her hair on the way to the front door with a cup of black coffee in the other hand, barking instructions as she disappeared.

'I don't know whether I came to a specific conclusion. I think it's more a definition of feelings, sort of a clarification. I feel different in Europe. It didn't press home so much when I was in Israel, because that was Jewish. But as I started to fly closer to Europe, to Poland, I felt this sense of menace. As though …'

She stopped brushing her hair.

'As though what?'

'As though I was being brought here by some malevolent force. All my life I've been told about the old country. But never with pleasure. Never with the sort of yearnings that you see in films, or read about. It's hard for you to understand because so much of Jewish history has been moving under compulsion from one country to another. Every couple of generations, we seem to be made refugees, uprooted from our homes and our possessions, and forced to start again somewhere else. Just because we're Jews.'

'But why should that affect you? Your home is in one of the safest countries on earth.'

'Yes, I know. That's why I'm surprised. But there's something about Poland, or Europe. So much suffering, so much misery. Everything here seems to harbour forces which I fear. In the trees, in the buildings, in the alleyways. Even in the faces of people. I look at people and I wonder "Did your parents do harm to my family? Were they involved in their misery?"'

'Don't you think you're being a bit paranoid?'

'Maybe. But that's why I opened up to the old man. Why I told him so much. It was because I came to trust him. After a while, I could see that he wasn't a part of the evil.'

She turned back to the mirror and silently continued to brush her hair.

Paul walked the few steps over to Miriam and put his arms around her. They embraced. As she nuzzled her head into his neck he felt her body torn by sobs. He held her tightly as she silently wept.

Through the sobs, she struggled to force out words which she had been repressing for a lifetime.

'I'm so scared,' she said.

He held her even closer, tighter. She felt more secure in his arms. Paul wanted to offer words of comfort, but he resisted. This was her time, her soliloquy. The ancient burden weighing her down was shifting. He opted for silence. He couldn't control the weight of her burden. If it teetered and fell, he was powerless to stop it.

'So scared,' she gasped. 'It's as though I'm all alone in the half light, wrestling with shadows. Sometimes an anger wells up inside me. The same sort of anger a woman feels when men stare at her, sizing her up. Not for her mind, or her abilities, but just for her body.'

She sobbed. Paul found it hard to understand her.

'Sometimes, I just want to stare back at them, or I fantasise about following them and going into their bedrooms at night when they're asleep and picking up a chair and waking them and saying, "Here, this is for you!" and smashing it down on them so they bleed.'

She held on to him tightly, her sobbing showing no signs of abating.

'Oh God. What's wrong with me?'

Paul answered by stroking her hair.

'Why am I so scared? I've lost control of myself and of my surroundings. Just like my grandparents lost control of theirs. As though huge forces are at work, and I can't stop them trying to destroy me.'

At last, Paul responded. 'We're leaving here as soon as possible. I'm going to get you out of this.'

She looked up at him, her cheeks tear-stained, her eyes puffy.

'And where can I go? Where's safe for me? They'll always

find me. I'm a Jew. I've got no country, no security. There are too many of them and too few of us.'

'I'm here, darling,' he said, kissing her on the forehead. 'You've got me.'

She looked at him closely, peering as though seeing his face clearly for the first time. Then she shook her head slowly from side to side.

'But where will you be when the dybbuk grabs me, and pulls me down?'

Paul tried to understand, but the gap between them had widened. He didn't know its depth. He couldn't judge its limits. But he knew with a depressing certainty that from then on, he and Miriam stood on either side of an abyss.

There was a gentle knock on the door. Valdek stood there, asking whether they would like breakfast. Miriam kept her face hidden in Paul's chest.

'You go downstairs. I can't appear in public with red eyes. I'll be down in a minute.'

When she joined him downstairs, they ate hot nutty rolls, conserves and drank the thick black coffee of the Poles.

'I'll tell you one thing,' said Paul when Valdek was out of earshot, 'the guy was bloody good. I've been cross-examined by QCs on a few occasions, but even the best of them don't have a fraction of his abilities. He was so subtle, so devious, I didn't realise how much I'd told him until it was too late.'

Miriam nodded. Her opinion of QCs was low, thinking them little better than expensive actors with a law degree, but she didn't want to interrupt Paul with her private prejudices.

'I've dealt with some hard bastards, but he's the most skilful I've ever known. No, not hard!' he corrected himself. 'He never raised his voice, never got angry. All he did was smile and encourage us to help him with the information, as though it was all to our advantage.'

Miriam nodded. Even she had been surprised by the way his gentlemanly, courteous ways had lulled her into giving him details about her family life that she had half forgotten.

'He did tell us stuff,' said Paul 'but it was all general, vague, meaningless. In the end, it didn't add up to a lick of shit.'

'Do you reckon it could be the KGB?'

'The KGB disappeared years ago. It was disbanded by Yeltsin.'

'Then who could it be? More to the point, what the hell can we do about it? I don't feel completely safe in this house, but I feel a hell of a lot more vulnerable walking around the streets of Warsaw. Paul, I want to go back to Australia the quickest way possible.'

He looked at her, feeling a protectiveness which he was ill-equipped to exercise. They were assured they were not prisoners in the house, so after breakfast, Paul told Valdek that he and Miriam wanted to return to their hotel to pack, and fly out to Australia as soon as possible. Valdek simply nodded. His instructions were to protect them until they left Poland. After that, he didn't care.

Two hours later, they arrived back at the Hotel Victoria, Valdek and Valeriy guarding them every moment until they could safely be put on a plane to the Far East. The idea of staying in the country mansion until the flight didn't appeal to Miriam. She felt frightened by its isolation, despite Paul's re-assurances. Valdek was also pleased that they were moving back to Warsaw. He did not want the safe house to be further compromised by them staying a long time. Miriam felt more comfortable being in public than hiding like squirrels in the country. Hiding places could be discovered.

When Valdek was taking them back to their hotel, he told them to be very careful, as the room would be bugged. He assured them that they were in no great danger. Since the bungled assassination attempt, the chances of another one being carried out was remote. Gosia began trying to book seats for a flight out of Poland for the two of them.

When they had been back in their room for only a few hours, the telephone rang.

'Mr Sinclair. Is Archimovski from Australian Embassy. Is

430

message for you from Foreign Office in Canberra. Can you come to Australian Embassy, third floor, and collect message. Please. Is very important.'

'Can it wait till after lunch?'

'No, is very important now. Will not take long. Thank you.'

The phone went dead.

They told Valdek, who said he would go and pick it up for them, but they assured him that they would feel safer if they all stayed together. Valdek at first refused to allow them out of the hotel, but Miriam smiled sweetly and said, 'Valdek, we're going. Regardless of what you say.'

Shrugging his shoulders, Valdek followed, grateful that Polish women were not like her.

Half an hour later, Paul and Miriam entered the front door of the Australian Embassy and told the guard on the door that they had an appointment with a Mr Archimovski on the third floor. The guard looked puzzled, and asked them to go to the information desk. Before they reached it, a young man, thin and scrawny, with a wispy beard, wearing a battered hat and an old black suit approached them. He had been sitting in the reception area, reading a newspaper. Miriam froze. Valdek pushed forward to interpose himself between them and the young man.

'Please, I do not harm you. I am Moshe Ahronovitski, pupil of Rabbi Miklos. He asks how are you, and sends his respects.'

Paul and Miriam relaxed, but Valdek was still suspicious. He was ready to break the boy's thin bones at the first hint of trouble, even though the young man, presumably a Bible scholar, looked nothing like an assassin.

'Why did the rabbi send for us to come here?' asked Paul. 'Why not meet us in a cafe or a museum or something?'

The young man smiled conspiratorially.

'After bomb, we think your hotel looked at … how you say …'

'Under surveillance?' suggested Miriam. The young man nodded in gratitude.

'Rabbi says to get you here, where is private, and tell you information. Polish government cannot spy on embassy very easily. You are Australian, so we make you come here. Is natural.'

The young rabbinic student motioned towards Valdek, who had been standing with them since they entered the embassy. The student became stiff and surly.

'Is it safe to talk in front of this person?' he asked.

'This is a friend of ours, who is protecting us.'

The young man looked at him suspiciously, but continued: 'Rabbi Miklos say that you must leave Poland straight away. He says to go, but not home. First you go to Moscow, see rabbi's friend. Then all become more clear. Say friend in Moscow has friends who will help you.'

The young man was struggling to communicate the message. Miriam urged him on, smiling and nodding in encouragement.

'He says he has a friend in Moscow who has access to KGB files. May be help to you in finding what you want to know. Rabbi says many Communist people from Poland leave before the start of the Great Patriotic War to go to Russia, and maybe some people from Rawicz go there. Rabbi Miklos phoned his friend in Moscow from very safe telephone line. Friend in Moscow say he want to help you. He can open files from old days, days of Stalin maybe, so can find out maybe what you want.'

Paul interrupted. 'Would you thank Rabbi Miklos very much for trying to help us, but we believe that we're in too much danger, and we want to get back home to Australia as soon as possible …'

Miriam shot an angry look at Paul. 'Who is this friend of Rabbi Miklos that is willing to help us?'

The young man smiled. He knew something of enormous importance, and was about to experience the palpable pleasure of imparting a secret: 'Is Chief Rabbi from Moscow.'

'The Chief Rabbi?' Miriam said, in surprise.

From the depths of depression, attacked from all fronts, wallowing in pity and self-doubt, Miriam's dulled sensibilities were instantly transformed. She might not be the same woman who left Australia determined to find out whether her grandfather had been killed, but she still felt the need to right the wrong done to her family. Not only was her grandfather a victim, but she too had become one.

The prospect of flying to Moscow to meet with the Chief Rabbi frightened her, but she was so close to exposing the evil, she knew the next step was inevitable. She looked at Paul and recognised a man whose mind was caught up in the excitement of an exposé. He would want to go to Moscow to unravel the knot in which they had become enmeshed, but this was new territory for her. She was so far from her comfort zone of corporate law in Sydney that there was no one to rely on other than herself. Not even Paul. Yet was she alone? Other members of her faith were working to help her. Unlike Jews throughout history who had been the chaff in the threshing mill of alien forces, she would not allow herself to be victimised. A Jew today was different from a Jew a generation ago. Hitler had seen to that.

God, she loved being Jewish. Where else, how else, could one experience the unity of a global family? The fears and doubts of the past days receded as her anger at being a victim swelled up and cried out for justice and retribution.

♜♜♜

'Don't you see,' Yeszersky said to his old friend, 'now that Abayev is being counselled by old-guard bastards like Princhkov and Zaskoy, he's effectively being counselled by Marshal Petrovsky. Surely you must appreciate how dangerous that is.'

'Of course,' Yezhov said. He smiled benevolently at his younger colleague. '*Tovarich*, nobody is underestimating the danger Petrovsky poses to the Republic. But he is operating in a very different environment from previously. Our President can no longer act in an isolation. He's got a council to temper his decisions. And he can't just rampage around the world.

Yesterday, we were a superpower, and could make unilateral decisions. We had a dictator at the helm. Today, we've lost the ability to act like a puppeteer and so has he.' He took another drink. 'Just because Abayev makes a decision without consulting you or his other colleagues doesn't mean that America or even the Russian people will sit still and allow it to happen!'

Yeszersky shook his head. 'But what of Princhkov and Zaskoy? Last week, I was the President's confidant. He sought my advice, my friendship. You of all people must have realised that my role as Agriculture Minister was largely titular. Together, we helped to shape the moral and philosophical direction of the country. Yet now he is making decisions without consultation …'

The minister glumly stirred his coffee, as though the whirlpool which he created in the cup could somehow spirit away his concerns.

'Is your problem that you were not consulted, or that your President is now being influenced by Petrovsky?'

'It's probably a little bit of both, to be honest. But putting my pride to one side for the moment, you seem to be minimising the danger that the moves over the past day or two have caused. It was you, after all, who first warned me of this cabal.'

'No, I'm not minimising the danger. Not at all. But I'm trying to come to terms with the overall picture. Since debriefing the young Australian couple, much has been clarified.'

'What did they tell you?'

'He and the woman were off on some wild goose chase about Ben Ari. They seem to think that he was a mass murderer. Whether he was, or not, doesn't matter. Regardless of how many he did or didn't murder, he couldn't begin to equal the record of Stalin or Beria.'

'Ben Ari? A mass murderer? What in God's name are you talking about?'

'The young man claims that Ben Ari was taken up by the Communist movement, spirited away to Russia and indoctrinated as a member of the Comintern. Then he appears to have been turned loose on his village like some mafioso. A few years later he appears in Palestine kicking the British in the balls by becoming a terrorist. And in the fullness of time, becomes a top operative of Mossad, goes into politics and ultimately becomes Prime Minister.'

'Are you mad?'

Ignoring him, Yezhov continued: 'Now, putting two and two together, we have the young man's allegations about Ben Ari's Communist leanings, we have Petrovsky launching a covert operation in Moscow and Jerusalem, we have Ben Ari scuttling the reunification of Jerusalem, which was the best chance for peace in half a century, and now we have him begging Russia for support. Wouldn't you agree that Russia is being compromised?'

The minister was stunned by the allegations made against Ben Ari, and mechanically nodded in agreement. 'And Princhkov and Zaskoy?' he asked.

'Thick as thieves with Petrovsky. They're old style Marxists in the Brezhnev model, totally out of place in a modern intellectual government like yours. Abayev kept them because of the influence they still wielded in their homelands, and because they were more of a danger outside government than in it.'

'And Petrovsky? What will his next action be now?'

'That, my friend, is the sixty-four million rouble question. If Abayev agrees to support Israel, then I have no doubt Petrovsky will already be putting some deeper plan into effect to increase our influence in the area. On the other hand, if the President disagrees, Petrovsky will have some plan to twist his arm. Don't sound surprised, old friend. Yeltsin used exactly the same coercion on Gorbachev to get him to sign away the power of the Soviet Union.'

'A coup d'état?' asked Yeszerski.

'No. Nothing so crude. The Russian people wouldn't stand for it. They're living hand to mouth, but their freedom is just as important to them today as it was when the Union dissolved.

Petrovsky will have some more subtle plan for influencing our illustrious President to agree to a trade and military agreement with Israel. And the agreement, I would imagine, would only be the first stage of the plan. After he's bedded that down, there'll be other developments.'

'Is this what the Jericho Plan is all about?'

Yezhov shrugged his shoulders. 'Doubtless. But we have to have proof before we can make Abayev listen. That's why it's imperative that you and I start a thorough surveillance operation on Petrovsky immediately. I don't know the full details, of course, but I would imagine that the Jericho Plan was something that Petrovsky put up to Stalin.'

'Stalin? Good God!' said Yeszersky. 'You're joking, surely.'

'If I'm right, the walls of Israel are about to come tumbling down and Russia is about to march in. It's precisely the sort of thing that Stalin did in Europe. Why not the eastern Mediterranean?'

The minister toyed with the name: 'Jericho … Jericho … the walls came tumbling down. The walls of Israel? But we've been Israel's enemy since the nation was created. Let's face it, Israel's nuclear program wasn't there just to destroy Arab capitalists. It was there as a threat to send nuclear bombs and rockets against us as well. For forty years, our relationship has been with Syria, Iraq and the others. Why does Petrovsky think he can change that sort of history?'

Yezhov shrugged. 'I haven't got all the answers yet. What is essential is that we find out the full details of the Jericho Plan. Only then will we be able to offer a convincing case to Abayev that he should be very cautious about treading this dangerous path.'

'Abayev must know by now. If he doesn't, my faith in him has been sorely shaken. You know, *tovarich*, from the little I gathered listening to that drunken imbecile Boris Krychkov before he died, the Jericho Plan was an operation which had its origin after the Great Patriotic War.'

'Yes, that would seem to fit the scenario of Ben Ari's activities before the war if what the Australian couple said is true. Obviously, there was a sanitising operation carried out.'

Both men settled back to ponder the implications of all they had discussed.

'Tell me,' Yezhov asked, 'how are your contacts in the Ministry of Records? How do you feel about delving through some dusty NKVD archives?'

The minister took a sip of vodka and smiled.

Paul and Miriam had just finished their evening meal in the Cafe Chopin, an attractive, intimate trattoria in the heart of Warsaw's Old City. Valdek had chosen the cafe because it was at street level, had a rear exit, and he could observe whoever walked in and out of its doors. He would allow no surprise bombings while he was in charge of his two clients. Not that any attack was probable after the failed attempt. The couple would undoubtedly be executed in Australia, but that was their problem. His responsibilities ended at the airport.

Valdek listened with disinterest to their conversation. Paul had suggested she leave Poland immediately but she was obviously unhappy at the suggestion.

'Please don't patronise me, Paul. I'm not leaving Poland until I've been to Rawicz. That's it, period. Any further discussion is a waste of time.'

He looked at her unhappy face and risked one more attempt at reason. 'Look, we've got two options. Either we fly back to Sydney or we fly to Moscow. But tomorrow we've got to get out of this place. Going to some village in the middle of nowhere is just inviting risk. Don't you realise that?'

She took a deep breath. Valdek didn't know whether she was restraining anger or struggling to make a decision. 'Paul, it's not "some" village. It's where my family came from. If I decide to go to where my grandparents and my father were born, then that's my business, and mine alone. You can come or you can stay, but I'm going. Okay?'

'Miriam, five hours ago, you were shit-scared and couldn't

wait to get out of here. Now you want to traipse halfway across Poland on some pilgrimage to kiss the soil that your family came to hate so much they couldn't wait to leave. Don't you think that borders on the macabre?'

Valdek looked at Miriam again in the restrained light of the cafe. She was quite attractive. Valdek usually preferred the finer features of Polish women to those of Western origin … now he thought that he might have underestimated their beauty. Then he remembered that she was a Jewess. She was of Semitic origin. He quickly lost interest and returned to his food.

'You have no right to comment on my family and its reasons for leaving Poland.'

'Oh, for Christ's sake, I'm not talking about events that happened a lifetime ago. I'm talking about the here and now, and the danger of going to Rawicz.'

Miriam shrugged. She had said enough. Further discussion was pointless.

Silence descended on the table. Valdek continued to eat while Miriam played around with her food, eventually pushing the plate disinterestedly into the middle of the table. Paul also lost interest in his meal, and nursed a glass of a rough claret, the best that the Polish restaurant could offer.

The silence around the table allowed Miriam time to reflect. When was the last time she had had true European food in a restaurant? It was in Sydney with her grandfather on his birthday. A wave of sadness swept over her and she could feel the warm saltiness of tears welling up in her eyes. She turned away and looked at the other diners in the restaurant so that she didn't show her emotions to the two men. She noticed a Polish man at a nearby table. He was heavy-set, wearing a battered homburg hat and a thick coat indoors, despite the heat. He was eating a large bowl of soup. It spilt and sprayed on the tablecloth in exactly the same way as her *zeida*'s soup had spilt just a few short weeks before.

After a strained couple of minutes, Paul broke the ice.

'If you're so determined, and if you can persuade Valdek, do you want me to come to Rawicz with you? It'll be much easier for him to mind us if we're together.'

'I'd prefer you to come, but it's really not necessary. For me, it's a pilgrimage.' Her words rang false. It seemed the closer they came to Miriam's roots, the less of a place he held in her life. Paul was left in no doubt that she wanted to make the pilgrimage alone.

The following morning, Miriam, Paul and Valdek stole silently out of their room, crept down to the back door of the hotel and picked up Valdek's Opel from the garage. He was going against his orders but the Jewess had given him no option. She told him the previous night that she was going to Rawicz, even if she had to get there by public transport. He reckoned that the easiest and safest way was to take her.

Valdek was five kilometres south of the Hotel Victoria before he breathed a sigh of relief and said to Paul and Miriam, 'We not being followed. Is not worry.'

It was a four-hour drive from the southern suburbs of Warsaw to Rawicz. The town now boasted a population of 100,000; in the days when Miriam's grandfather lived there, there were only 50,000, with one thousand five hundred Jews living in the *shtetl* of Chelmnitz. Although the town's population had doubled since the war, its Jewish population had dropped to zero.

The road south-west towards Lodz took them through low undulating hills, enabling Miriam to glimpse brooding villages in the distance. Occasionally, on the horizon, there was a group of chimneys belching black smoke into the leaden sky. It was a vivid reminder that Eastern Europe's industrial output was antediluvian by Western standards. Such things as smoke emission standards and anti-pollution measures were the province of an affluent Western world which could afford a conscience. Despite the demise of stifling Communism, it would take decades to bring Eastern Europe into the modern post-industrial world.

They drove through Lodz and took the road towards Kalisz. Every thirty minutes, the speeding car would slow down to pass through yet another village. Monuments were everywhere in the rich agricultural landscape. In fields. In the centre of the village. In the cornices of churches.

'Who are all these monuments to?' Miriam asked.

Valdek shrugged his shoulders. 'Some to soldier. Some to poet. Some to battle.' He thought for a while. 'Some to musician and composer. We Poles love to celebrate music.'

They had been travelling for nearly two hours. The coldness in the car was becoming more oppressive, except to Valdek who enjoyed the scenery. Paul tried on several occasions to patch up the situation, not only in words, but also by gentle actions. He had been attentive, offered solace as they drew nearer to Miriam's origins, entertained her and tried to anticipate her needs; but to no avail. All he managed to do was to drive the wedge between them even deeper. It was a hopeless, thankless task and Paul decided on silence instead.

Miriam hoped that her own silence was not taken by Paul as hostility. She could think of little to say. She was encased by her thoughts and as she travelled closer to her origins her mind grew more attentive to the weight of past times.

Valdek merely drove down the road, following his instincts. If the crazy pair wanted to behave like small, spoilt children, that was up to them. His job was to ensure that they left Warsaw safely to return to their home country.

Before reaching Kalisz, the road divided and Valdek took the route west towards the German border. In the fields, looking like characters from a Tolstoy novel, men and women were wielding pitchforks and bundling the first harvest into gigantic haystacks. What would have been a scene of quaint, historic interest in the West—an activity created for tourists in some rural theme park—was the hard, exacting reality of daily existence for these Polish farmers.

Another hour's drive and the scenery transformed itself from rural to urban. An instinct told Miriam that she was approaching the home where her grandparents, and their parents before them, had lived their lives.

A feeling of *déjà vu* came over her, sweeping her mind empty of the here and the now. It transposed her to a time and place which was part of her being and her history, but alien to her present.

Miriam didn't believe in anything like metempsychosis. She was an adherent to the rigid finality of death, but driving along the paths and laneways of her grandparents' world, the world where her own seed had its genesis, she was no longer so certain. Was there a transmigration of the soul? Could she have received the spirit of her grandfather when he died? Had she, had any part of her, in a past existence, shared these fields with her grandfather? Had she walked by his side, holding his hand, talking to him in Yiddish and Polish, discussing the Torah and the Prophets, and the mystery of the Cabbala? Had she been here before?

She looked deeply into the furrows in the fields. 'Yes, this is you,' she thought. 'This is your inheritance, your past, your future.' She felt despair. Miriam studied every blade of grass and every hedgerow like a painter absorbing the essence of a subject, to etch their characteristics into her memory before she was forced to transfer herself back into the tainted present.

'Now we enter Rawicz. Where we go? You tell, I drive,' said Valdek.

Miriam cleared her throat of its emotion. 'I think that we should go to the Town Hall first, to see the records; then I'd like to drive to where the *shtetl* is, was, to have a look.'

Miriam turned to look at Paul, regretting her coldness. She felt like a petulant child, cold one minute, conciliatory the next. The dybbuks were close to the surface.

Miriam felt ashamed at the way she treated him. He was a good man. A generous man. But he was not like her. Paul could not feel with the same feelings. He was from a different world. A world of the present and the future. She owed her present to the past. The lease she held on the future was inscribed in these fields. She was the future of her faith. How could she dissipate the trust of her ancestors by marrying out of the faith? Most of all, she wanted to be alone.

As the car slowed on its approach to Rawicz, Paul squeezed her hand and smiled. No words were necessary. He knew that Miriam's cauldron of emotions was beginning to settle and she was now living with her realities.

♜♜♜

The best time to observe someone is in the middle of the day, in the mass of a crowd. With petrol so expensive, Muscovites rarely used cars. The streets were constantly crowded during the day. Unlike other Russian capitals, Moscow's citizens always wore a hurried air, a feeling of expectancy. A Muscovite was easy to distinguish from a citizen of St Petersburg or Kiev. Muscovites were seemingly indifferent to everything going on around them except those things conected with their innermost thoughts. Though hospitable and easy-going, they will complain to anyone who listens about the incompetence of the government, the food shortages, the new Red Mafia, or anything which takes their fancy. But being so busy they would not stop to wonder why a handful of men were concentrating their efforts on the apartment of an Old Red Warrior.

Half an hour after most Muscovites left their offices and shops for lunch, a van drove around to the back of Marshal Petrovsky's apartment building on Tvezskaya Prospekt and parked. Two men dressed in grey overalls got out. Using the ladder which the van carried, they climbed to the first floor fire escape. From there, they mounted landing after landing until they reached the roof, eight storeys above the street.

The Marshal's apartment was on the top floor. It was a simple task to trace the cable coaxial cable wire from the antenna to the air vent which gave it entry to his rooms.

The two men expertly spliced the coaxial cable lengthwise and connected the inner and outer wires to a small video cassette player. When the Marshal tuned in to watch his favourite show that night, the television would behave normally. When

442

the time was right, one of the technicians would patch through the recorder; then the television would show whatever picture was on the tape.

At the same time as the cable was being doctored, two other technicians were opening the telephone motherboard in the sub-exchange three streets away from the Marshal's apartment. They found the switches to the Marshal's home and began preparations to splice them to a nearby van. Inside was a listening post, complete with digital read-out interfaces which would instantly tell the surveillance team which number was being telephoned.

When all the arrangements were in place, the four technicians retreated to their van to play cards and wait until later that evening, when the Marshal returned home from his club. As he settled down for the evening—hopefully to switch on the night-time news, the technicians could go to work.

Luck was on their side. At six o'clock, Checkpoint 1, stationed across the road from the entrance to the Marshal's apartment, reported that the subject had just entered his lounge-room.

Checkpoint 3 on the roof tensed himself for action. That was the problem with surveillance; you became tense and alert at the very beginning, but if nothing happened for a couple of hours—which was very possible—you lost your edge and could easily miss the opportunity.

The Marshal was obviously keen to see what was happening in the world. After going to the toilet, he switched on the television. Checkpoint 3 warned Checkpoint 5 that within the next five minutes, he would begin operations. At any time after that, the Marshal would use his phone.

Checkpoint 3 allowed the Marshal to settle down to watching the television news in peace. When he was as sure as he could be that the Marshal was relaxed and involved, he pressed the control button, disconnecting the signal. Instantly, the picture on the Marshal's television disappeared, replaced by loud, irritating static. Just as quickly, the technician pressed the 'play' button on the VCR, and a pre-recorded melee of pictures rolled onto the screen.

Petrovsky went over to the machine and tried to fix the vertical hold. No matter what he did, he couldn't slow the picture down.

After a few moments, he phoned the television repair man. At the Marshal's level of importance within the Moscow community, a special coterie of technicians was available at all hours of the day or night. He picked up the phone, and dialled the number in his address book. Instantly, the number was recorded on the digital readout in the van at Checkpoint 5. The technician read it, switched the line to the phone within the van, and checked the number which the Marshal was dialling. Using a reverse telephone book, which gave numbers, rather than names as the primary reference, the technician saw that the number was for a nearby television repair shop.

The technician in the van answered the telephone with the name: 'Novgorod Repairs, good evening.'

'This is Marshal Petrovsky at apartment 85, 10, Tvezskaya Prospekt. My television is playing up. Can you send somebody round right away?'

'Excellency, could you tell me what is wrong?' asked the technician in the van.

The Marshal explained that the picture was rolling and the vertical control switch would not control it.

'We will be there first thing tomorrow morning, excellency. Around eight.'

'Not tomorrow morning, I want it fixed now. Send somebody round, please.'

'But your excellency, I was just going home …'

'I don't give a damn about your private life. Get round here right away.'

Cowed into submissiveness, after a suitable pause the technician said: 'Yes, Marshal. Right away.'

He put the phone down, switched back the Marshal's line

so that it would make and accept normal calls once again, and winked at his companion.

Fifteen minutes later, the Marshal's doorbell rang. The technician stood there, looking submissive and embarrassed.

'Sir, I apologise for my rudeness before. It has been one of those days.'

'We all have bad days. Could you please fix the television quickly. I have guests coming shortly.'

The technician was shown where the set was, and switched it on. Instantly, the picture rolled, and the technician disconnected the front control panel. He took out a small Philips head screwdriver and pretended to twirl some screws. With his back to the Marshal, he cautiously picked up the infra-red hand control unit, used to change the channels and the volume, and opened it. Inside, he placed a radio transmitter with a range of 100 metres. The transmitter was tiny enough to be mistaken for one of the components of the remote control's internal circuitry.

The transmission frequency of the implant would be masked by the infra-red frequency of the hand-held unit, so it would be difficult to detect its presence if Petrovsky's apartment was swept for bugs. Ten metres away, on the roof, the signals would be picked up, filtered of extraneous noise, amplified and transmitted by microwave to a listening post which was in the process of being set up in an apartment block just over a mile away in line of sight. No conversation held in the loungeroom would be private.

Finally, after a further half hour of fiddling, the technician pretended that he had repaired the set and explained to the Marshal what had gone wrong. He stood, wrote out a bill and asked the Marshal for immediate payment.

When he was back in his van, he phoned the operation's controller.

The technician had worked for Yezhov many times in the past, and it was a privilege for him to be working for the canny old devil again. Unlike many senior officers of the former KGB,

Yezhov had always treated the KGB's Technical Directorate with respect. During his tenure of control, he ensured that as much money was spent on training and purchasing the latest innovations as was necessary to match the CIA and Mossad.

'Has the job been completed?' asked Yezhov

'Would you expect the answer to be no?' said the technician.

Yezhov smiled. 'Thank you, old friend. Tomorrow, shall we have dinner together?'

'The pleasure would be mine,' the technician replied. Putting the phone down, he turned up the volume to listen to whatever was going on in the Marshal's apartment. To his intense pleasure, the Marshal had turned on his CD player and both men, separated by nearly a mile, listened to the swelling chords of Rachmaninov's Piano Concerto No. 3.

CHAPTER TWENTY-THREE

The streets of Tel Aviv, Jerusalem and Haifa were thronged with people who had no way of venting their emotions other than by joining with a million others in despair at their betrayal. News broadcasts showed the anger and shame on their faces. A people who had awoken to the reality of deceit. In the old days, the days of the Prophets, Jeremiah was there to speak on their behalf. But who was for the people of Israel if their leaders were selling their conscience? And those who dared to oppose were being imprisoned. Were Isaiah or Ezekiel or Nehemiah imprisoned for standing up to the tyrants?

The crowds flowed onto the streets to protest against their rulers' actions, to denounce America for allowing it to happen and to vent their frustration against Russia. Citizens who met spontaneously in cafes and squares, defying the ban on meetings, joined up into groups; groups joined together to form gatherings; gatherings quickly became crowds and when the crowds coalesced in the centre of the cities, they became vast, organic, swelling masses, gigantic amoebae, the same as those which flowed through the streets and alleyways of Peking or New Delhi, cities whose mass anger or mass grief was ever-present. When a crowd came to a halt outside a building—an embassy, a government department—someone would spontaneously stand up and ask: 'How can we allow this to happen? How can America tolerate this? How can it abandon us to the cold isolation of being an international pariah?' But the sirens in the background and the chanting of the crowd drowned out much of the rhetoric.

Closeted in his suite of offices within the Knesset building, watching a bank of television screens relaying pictures from the centres of the major towns, Raphael Ben Ari, Yitzhak Stein, and Zalman Gershowitz were fascinated. For the first time that any of them could remember, Jews, Christians and Druze had congregated. They were divided and unified by common anger. Half the population was furious with the East, half with the West, and most were furious with the troika ruling their lives. They marched to protest against a decision which had been made without their consent. The only significant section of the population absent were the Arabs, who were simply bemused by the train of events. They sat content in their houses and coffee shops as Israel tore itself apart. Tomorrow they would have a new ruler. Ottoman Turk, British, French, Jew … it made little difference. Soon maybe they would be lucky enough to be ruled again by an Arab government. *In'sh'allah*.

During the past two weeks, there had been a dramatic upsurge in the activities of Hamas which had spilled over from the Occupied Territories into Israeli cities. Random knifings, car bombs and button bombs in gutters had done more than kill and maim a handful of Jews. It had dispirited the entire Israeli population and stretched the capacity of the police and defence forces to the very limit. Hundreds of Hamas members had been arrested and imprisoned under emergency laws and were currently awaiting investigation, while the wheels of Israel's police turned slowly. The government would not make the mistake again of deporting four hundred Hamas members into a no-man's-land between Israel and Lebanon.

But internal and external pressures were not the only problems that the Jews of Israel began to worry about. A gnawing fear was developing. Israelis were starting to talk about the prospect of a fourth temple. The first was destroyed in 537 BC by Nebuchadnezzar; the second by the Roman Emperor Titus in AD 70. The creation of the third Jewish temple was the building of modern Israel by Zionists in the twentieth century. But the fear was that the state was being destroyed by Ben Ari, who was building a fourth temple, a Communist one, without asking the people. Russian Jewish émigrés, especially, were terrified, with good reason. Their Judaism had been virtually destroyed by the Russian Communists. Would they try to do the same here?

Ben Ari looked at his colleagues, and smiled at their consternation. 'Second thoughts?' he asked.

Zalman looked at him quizzically. 'Can you look at these pictures, and not have second thoughts? Do you, do any of us, know for certain what we've done?'

'Zalman, *chav'air*, everything is going to plan. We knew that there would be mass uprisings. This was predicted,' said Ben Ari. 'And we also know how long it will last. Provided we don't over-react and let the police or military loose, things will quieten down by the end of the week. Once people wake up and see that the sun's still shining and they've still got money in the bank, they'll quickly get over it. Especially when the Russians come in small numbers at first.'

Yitzhak turned to his old friend in surprise. Hearing mention of the Russians, spoken so openly after all those years of secrecy, would take some getting used to. The three men had come to Israel at the same time, Zalman from the Pale of Settlement in Russia, Raphael and Yitzhak from Poland. They were comrades in the Stern Gang, the Irgun and in Israeli life after the British left. But one other thing made the men close colleagues, closer than anybody realised. Each was recruited as a youth, and indoctrinated over a two year period at his most impressionable age. The only person in Israel who knew about the deep relationship between the three was their control. For the past ten years, since taking over from the elderly officer who had installed the three after the war, the ex-KGB colonel had nurtured their progress. He guided them, funded their lifestyles, arranged the deaths of opponents and secured their paths of ascension. When Ben Ari had been a senior operative in Mossad he had passed invaluable information to Moscow and vice versa. Now Moscow had assisted him to the very top of the political ladder, and Raphael had pulled his two comrades up with him.

Being the man he was, hard, dedicated, unidirectional, he rose to the top in the different organisations he joined. But having a paymaster like the KGB, with its endless supply of money and ability to take care of those nagging obstacles which block the progress of politicians in democracies, certainly helped. The KGB was expert at creating scandals which destroyed those in its path. Ambitious politicians found themselves inextricably enmeshed in financial and sexual webs which caused their downfall. In the 1950s, the KGB deliberately sacrificed one of their better spies in Israel to bring down four senior Mossad and Shin Bet men who were blocking Ben Ari's path to the top. It was one of Marshal Petrovsky's more daring gambles, but the master player in Moscow was still smiling when the dust settled, and Ben Ari's place as a top Mossad operative was secured. The other masterstroke was exposing the activities in 1985 of Israel's nuclear spy in America, Jonathan Pollard, which poisoned the Israeli–American relationship and allowed Petrovsky to reinvigorate the near-dormant Jericho Plan. Ben Ari was in the perfect position to conduct the game plan created by Petrovsky forty years earlier. It had all knitted together like a glorious patchwork quilt. None of this detracted from Ben Ari's skill as a tactician and political strategist—but without Petrovsky's guiding hand the diminutive Pole would have been prey to the vagaries of Israeli political life, in which nothing was predictable.

Yitzhak and Zalman had also been successful, but they were not in the same league and had settled for a more comfortable, less ideologically pure life.

'The key,' said Yitzhak, 'is that there are so few Jews of Russian descent in the army. They don't have the same hatred of the Communists as older civilians. It's the newly arrived Russians in the civilian crowd which will cause us the headaches, or the *alter-kackers* of our generation. Thank God they don't have power or guns. The thing to do is let them have their say, allow them to let off steam, but keep an eye on them.'

'Any news from our friends about the next phase of the operation?' asked Zalman.

Ben Ari turned and glared at his colleague. It was a stupid

breach of security, even in private. Zalman shifted uncomfortably in his chair as Ben Ari stared at him. 'I have many friends,' said Ben Ari, 'who are actively helping me. You worry about your job. Let me worry about mine!'

The moment was relieved by a knock on the door. A man with greying hair but a young face walked in, wearing the chevrons of a general of the Israeli Army. In the casual manner of the Israeli military, he nodded to the three members of the Council and took a seat. Formality was out of place anywhere in Israel, but that did not imply lack of respect or ability. And the three members of the Council had enormous regard for the competence of the young head of the Israeli Defence Force.

General Dov Baer was a Sabra and a man who held the loyalty of all branches of the IDF. Israel's youngest tank commander during the Yom Kippur War in 1973, he led his brigade back from the brink of defeat to a stunning victory. It was a simple stroke of strategic genius. While feigning withdrawal and allowing the Syrian tank squadrons to follow him down from the Golan Heights for the kill below the city of Kuneitra, he used hidden and uncommitted tanks to surround the enemy. Then, for the *coup de grâce*, he turned his tanks around to face the oncoming Syrians. With massive air cover, he destroyed the encircled enemy divisions. It was a manoeuvre the Romans had perfected with devastating effect two thousand years earlier, and General Baer had learnt the lesson well.

After his successes, he was put in charge of the planning of the 1976 rescue of an El Al jet which terrorists had hijacked to Entebbe Airport in Uganda, during which his closest friend had died. The tragic death of one of Israel's best and brightest tempered the steel from which he was made. Dov Baer became a fatalist.

His subsequent rise to the top of the military was rapid, and following the declaration of martial law, he was commissioned by the Ruling Council both to control the external defences of Israel against certain incursion and attack, and to ensure good order.

Dov Baer hated his assignment, just like he hated being part of the Israeli force in 1973 that had destroyed the city of Kuneitra, demolishing the homes of 60,000 inhabitants as a sign of vengeance and anger. He had always looked on himself as a defender of his homeland. He wore his uniform with pride, whether he was on the streets of Haifa or wandering the corridors of the Pentagon. But now he found himself an enforcer of law and order against a population which looked on him as a part of the dictatorship. He was the man who directed the police and the military to quell riots, break up meetings and arrest people who had only ever known freedom.

'So Dov, how's it going?' said Ben Ari

Dov declined to answer. Shrugging his shoulders in the taciturn manner of the Sabra, he nodded towards the screens.

'Does it worry you?' asked Yitzhak.

Dov breathed in deeply. He thought for a moment, and said: 'Keeping control of the crowds doesn't worry me. We've got good contingency plans. What concerns me is the long-term effect of your actions … Oh! I don't mean inviting the Russians. Frankly, it doesn't matter who we side with today. Tomorrow, we're on our own.'

Zalman agreed: 'Remember the way de Gaulle refused to deliver planes and gunboats that we'd already paid for. We had to steal them in the dead of night.'

'Maybe,' Yitzhak interrupted, 'but they also helped us build our nuclear capability. The French weren't always bastards.'

General Baer nodded: 'No, they weren't. What matters is that the country is being split. And that does worry me. It worries me a lot.'

Raphael Ben Ari considered his commander's thoughts. 'But don't you see this as merely an outgrowth of modern Zionism?' he asked.

Dov frowned and shook his head. 'What do you mean?'

'Look, there's always been an ambivalence in being an Israeli. Israel isn't like Northern Ireland, or modern Russia. They see their version of religion or nationalism as the one true answer. In Israel there's been a real dichotomy since 1948. Part of us wants to be like every other nation, to be a member of the international community, standing on a moral high ground and having the ethical answers to the divisive questions. We're inspired by God and the Bible; but another part of us wants us to be a conqueror, an avenger, to stand righteously and be the David slaying Goliath.'

'But don't you see?' said Dov. 'That's precisely the point. We justified what we did in the occupied territories as our struggle for the right to live within secure borders. What we're doing today is against our own people. How can that be right?'

'When one is in a state of martial law, rights sometimes have to be subjugated to the good of law and order,' said Zalman.

'Isn't that what Hitler would have said?'

Ben Ari stiffened at the impertinence. 'I believe an apology would be in order, general.'

The younger man shrugged his shoulders. 'And if I apologise, does that make it right? Can you sit there and tell me what I've said is wrong? *Chaverim*, you haven't been out into the streets. You don't know the mood of the people. It's not my job to argue the political case. It's your decision who you make friendships and alliances with.'

'Yes, general,' said Yitzhak, 'it's our decision. Your job is to carry out our instructions. If you don't think you're capable, you're free to resign your commission.'

'I'm no politician, thank God. Just a simple soldier. But it is my job to judge the mood of the people, and to determine when to use my forces to maintain or restore public order. Right now, the crowds could turn nasty. It'll be like the Intifada transferred from Gaza to Tel Aviv.'

The three men looked at their younger, earnest colleague. He was more concerned than they were about the next few days. Their analysis of the situation and how it would develop was based on advice from Colonel-General Bukharin. As the man least in the public eye, Zalman had met several times with his Russian control and relayed Bukharin's analysis of the local and international reactions to Ben Ari's actions. The general's computer models were brilliant, analysing every possible contingency. But General Baer was not privy to any such computer models and was forced to accept the analysis of the ruling troika, who had not felt the reaction on the street.

'Dov, why do you feel that what we're doing is so different from what Churchill did in England during the Second World War, or what any other leaders have done in times of emergency?' asked Yitzhak.

Dov shook his head. 'Look, when we began to return to Palestine at the end of the last century, we fought for the right to be a free people. It's even in our anthem … *le'heyot am hofshee, b'aretz'anu* … to be a free people in our own land … But then we became Israel and developed the mentality to be colonisers ourselves … over the West Bank in '67, over Sinai, over the Golan, over East Jerusalem.'

Ben Ari angrily disagreed: 'How can you compare that situation to this …?'

But the general overruled him: 'Oh! I know all the justifications … we did it for our security … . for peace … we were attacked first … the Palestinians posed a threat. But in the process of changing from a winning army to being colonisers, we've made compromises and sacrificed a lot of our morality.'

All three members of the ruling troika were furious at the impertinence of the history lesson, but Dov didn't seem to care.

'As a people,' he continued, 'we've accepted the loss of individual freedoms in the name of security. In the past, we've even surrendered to the might of the religious faction, both here and from New York. And now we've destroyed any semblance to moral authority in the eyes of the world by declaring a state of martial law …'

That was all that Ben Ari could take: 'How dare you talk this way to me? Since the day you were born, you've lived free from the domination of the British, the Arabs, from any colonialists. We've given your generation rights and privileges which were unknown to me and my generation, growing up under the threat of Nazism and Fascism.'

Ben Ari stood and walked over to the general. He stood close to the younger man's chair as though about to throw a punch. Dov Baer did not flinch.

'And how dare you tell me how Israel should stand up in the eyes of the world as the moral standard bearer? Do you think Russia or America or Japan or Germany gives a damn about the eyes of the world when they make a decision about their future? They do what's right for them. They don't think "is this a morally, ethically right decision?" They don't give a damn about what the world thinks. Why should we be any different?'

His anger was spent once he had made his point, but he still needed to re-establish his authority over the younger man. 'We, the Ruling Council of the State of Israel, have taken a decision to invite a small delegation of the Russian Armed Forces to use our facilities, and to train jointly with us. Your job, General Baer, is to ensure that our orders are carried out, and that public order is maintained!'

Again, Dov Baer shrugged his shoulders, stood, and walked towards the door. When he reached it, he turned and asked: 'And do we shoot Jewish troublemakers, or just break their arms like we used to do to the Arabs in the Occupied Territories?'

Before any of the three could react to the barb, he left the room.

'This cannot be allowed to continue,' said Zalman. 'Soon we'll have an army revolt on our hands.'

'And why do you believe that General Baer will spread his insubordination?' asked Ben Ari. 'Just because he airs his criticism to us, doesn't mean he'll do it to others. He's just a typical *kibbutznik*. Says what he thinks, but acts for the communal good.'

'So you don't think there'll be any repercussions? Or that Dov's attitude will spread?'

Raphael Ben Ari shook his head. 'The IDF has a 100 per cent record of doing what it's told. They'll do it this time. They'll do it because they've been ordered to do it.'

The other two men nodded in agreement, and turned to watch the television screens. By now, the crowds in the city centres had swelled so that the television cameras seemed to pan from horizon to horizon in order to capture their magnitude. As men and women stood on plinths and the tops of cars to address the crowds, the cameras panned in on them. Some were unknowns, men or women whose morality was simply outraged; others were immediately recognisable either as politicians or intellectuals. Their words were shouted to the audience or called over a make-shift public address system. They weren't easily audible on television, but their faces were testiment to their anger and shame.

♜♜♜

'Jack? It's Paul.'

'Paul, thank God you've phoned. I've been worried sick about you. Hang on, I'll put you through to Mandle. He wants to talk to you straight away …'

'No,' shouted Paul. 'I don't want to talk to Mandle …' But it was too late. He was forced to listen to the telephone's background music as Muir transferred the call upstairs. Paul considered putting down the phone.

'Sinclair? Is that you? What the fuck's going on? Where are you? Why haven't you been in touch since the stories about the Jerusalem riots? I've got your expenses from Israel. What are you trying to do, ruin me?'

'Mr Mandle.'

'Sinclair? Why are you whispering?'

'I'm not whispering. It's a bad line. I'm calling from a public telephone in the Polish countryside, and we've come …'

'The Polish countryside? What are you doing there? A couple of days ago you were in Israel. Why have you gone to Poland? Are you getting closer to finding out about our friend? What the hell kind of a trip is this, anyway? Are you taking me for some sort of a ride? Do you know how much this is costing me?'

It was like interrupting a politician making a campaign speech. 'Mr Mandle, I don't have much time, and I don't trust the security of the telephone system. Miriam and I have been …'

'What do you mean "security system"? What security system?'

'Mr Mandle, will you just listen for a moment?' Paul said harshly, the distance giving him an unexpected courage. 'I'll phone again later and explain things in greater detail, but Miriam and I have been involved in a bombing and we're in the protection of someone who's looking after our interests. I can't go into too much detail right now. The reason I'm calling is to let you know that we're about to fly off to Moscow. We have a contact there who we think can help us. That should peg our "friend" once and for all. Could you arrange for your people in Moscow to be on hand if I need some back-up? I don't know the system over there.'

'Moscow! Are you crazy? I've got a dozen top reporters flying there already to cover the Ben Ari story. I don't want you or the girl to fuck things up. Listen, Sinclair, enough's enough! I want you back in Australia immediately …'

'Sorry, boss, but no way. I don't give a shit what your other reporters are doing. There's a story behind the story, and I want to find out what's going on.'

'Now listen to me, you upstart. You're out of your league. I'm ordering you back home … Sinclair? Sinclair?'

But the line was dead. Paul hoped Mandle would accept the explanation of an antiquated Polish telephone network. If he didn't … well, being fired wouldn't be that bad. Not if he got the story of the decade and turned it into the world's best-selling book.

♜♜♜

It was now 10 p.m. in Cairo, but the city still suffered the enervating heat of the day. The place merely got darker, not cooler or quieter. The fumes from the traffic, the omnipresent angry cacophony of sound which came from car horns—there to release drivers' frustrations rather than give warning of an impending accident—and the shouts of street traders made Cairo a confusion of the ancient and the modern, the rich and the poor.

The air was suffocating with dust, the stench of petrol and the maddening insistence of flies. Even the birds had deserted the city long ago for the less noisy and polluted environments on the outskirts.

In the cafes and sitting at tables and chairs on the footpaths, a million Egyptians sat and played *sheshbesh*, drinking thick Arabic coffee. They whiled away the time until exhaustion enabled them to sleep in the humidity and heat. In the clubs, music wailed through loudspeakers. The heaving bosoms of the singers, clad in metallic harnesses, undulated as though on pulleys. The sound of violins, guitars and flutes was the currency of the air. Customers raised their voices above the ululations of cabaret artists who dutifully persisted despite being unappreciated and ignored. In the more fashionable hotels, the thick walls acted as sentinels, barring the city noises from the wealthy patrons. The air-conditioning cooled the air, isolating those inside in a refined and spacious environment, completely disassociated from the reality of the outside world.

Saud Ibn Masse, moustachioed and arrogant, sat in a thick padded armchair in the Hotel Saddat. Once the headquarters of the conquering British army, the hotel had opened its reserved private halls and corridors to the wealthy Cairo public following the overthrow of King Farouk. Now it was one of the major focuses of the city's cultural and social elite. Everybody who was anybody was seen at least three times a week in its lobby. Like the restaurants of Hollywood, it was a magnet for stars and those aspiring to be stars; for business leaders, army generals, diplomats and the upwardly social.

The only thing more impressive than being seen taking coffee at night in the Hotel Saddat was *not* being seen in the Hotel Saddat. Egyptians of the very upper echelons—government

ministers, megastars of television and film, business leaders—
didn't need to go into the Hotel Saddat. They paraded at private functions, meeting with others who belonged to the same
stratospheric level.

Saud Ibn Masse did not move in such circles. Nor did he
usually associate with the parasites who normally infested the
Saddat. He would not have been recognised by any of the
Hotel Saddat's usual patrons. As a terrorist and a leader of the
Cairo-based Arabic Democratic Freedom Fighters, he had deliberately kept a low profile these past twenty years. He could
have been anything he wanted, a politician, a senior army man,
even a leading businessman in the Cairo community, but
twenty years earlier, after the humiliation of the Arabs in the
early 1970s, Saud became a freedom fighter, taking up the Arab
cause with a vengeance. At the time he left Cairo University's
Department of Engineering to follow a career as an army officer, he was a patriot. But his patriotism turned to shame
when, in 1973, the Egyptian army refused to answer the call
for a jihad and advance the cause of Pan-Arab unity by fighting
with its brother nations in the Yom Kippur War. That decision
encouraged Saud to seek a deeper understanding of the Arab
cause in general, and the Palestinian cause in particular. Within
a year he was a militant fighter for Arab solidarity against the
Israeli enemy.

His stance was considered to be anti-governmental and Saud
was dismissed from the army. The subsequent years saw him
hone his skills as one of the major terrorist freedom fighters in
the Middle East, working in Israel, Egypt, Iran, Iraq and Syria,
as well as all over Europe. His training under Russian auspices
indoctrinated him in the value of Communism as a means of
righting the wrongs of the world, and his loyalties now lay as
much with Marxist ideology as with Pan-Arab pride.

Saud sat in the lobby of the hotel for an hour, sipping coffee
and waiting for his messenger to return. Out of the corner of
his eye, he saw a young man dressed in a traditional Arab
galabaya, different from the European suits and dresses of the

cosmopolitan hotel patrons. The boy walked over towards him. He sat down and nodded to Saud.

'Did things go as planned?'

'Yes, *effendi*. The message was delivered.'

Saud nodded. 'You're a good boy. The same financial arrangements as before. Collect it from me tomorrow afternoon.'

The young man, a caretaker in the embassy, who was sleeping with a Russian encryption clerk, nodded and walked towards the door of the hotel.

Saud was pleased that his third message to General Bukharin had been safely transmitted. He had contacted the general a month earlier when he was whisked from inactivity by his old friend, Marcel Dupain, to become a key member of the terrorist group. He and Marcel had worked together many times in the past. He understood Marcel. But Marcel was a loner. When they came together, they enjoyed each other's bodies but each respected the other's right to lead an independent existence.

The activities being planned against Israel after the destruction of the peace conference were wonderful. He had not known until it was too late about the downing of the Magnum jet, but gave as many details as possible to Bukharin after the event. Then he had been included in the raid which destroyed the Museum of the Holocaust and was pleased to be able to give the general details in advance. Now he had told the general about his briefing the previous day in Rome.

What an extraordinary plan it was! The audacity, the size and the scope of what Marcel Dupain planned defied belief. To blow up the Knesset building itself when it was in full session and with every leading Israeli politician present was the most brilliant act of terrorism since Guy Fawkes. No one terrorist alone could do it. The security in the building was simply overwhelming, but ten visitors, each entering the public gallery of the building at different times, and each carrying a small component of the bomb, could do it and get away with it.

Marcel's briefing document showed him how. All they

needed was a simple battery, radio, a timer and Semtex … that was all.

Of course, everyone entering the building was thoroughly searched, and put through a metal detector. But their chance of picking up the small individual components of a bomb was remote. The micro-components were made of plastic. Semtex was invisible to X-rays and would be vacuum-sealed in plastic to fool sniffer dogs. And the battery was a special cadmium mercury affair, lightweight and potent.

Saud was to walk into the building wearing a Timex watch whose insides would become part of the sophisticated timing device. Micro-electronics had transformed the early clumsy terrorist weaponry into minute, deadly and almost undetectable nightmares. Marcel would carry in a kilo of Semtex, strapped inside a jockstrap on the inside of his underpants. It wouldn't show up in a metal detector and being a dense material, it had very little bulk.

Two other terrorists would each carry a kilo of Semtex in the same way, making a bomb big enough to collapse pillars in the building and bring the roof crashing down on the politicians.

Other terrorists would carry in the wiring wrapped around the inside of their belts. More would bring in other components.

At different pre-arranged times, they would stand up from their seats in the public gallery. One by one they would go to the toilet. The bomb maker would take a permanent stall in the toilet. As the components were slipped under the wall of his compartment, he would assemble it.

No two terrorists would leave the public gallery at the same time. Each would wait until the other returned before standing and going to the toilet with his particular component.

Marcel estimated it would take an hour for the bomb to be constructed. No security guard would have been alerted. The bomb maker would walk out with the small but deadly bomb strapped underneath his clothes, waiting for the right opportunity to prime the timing device. Marcel had not given details of where the bomb was to be placed, and how the escapes would take place from the building. He had only told each terrorist which component he would be carrying. Saud was given the privilege of carrying the cadmium mercury battery and the Timex watch. It was a brilliant and audacious plan, and Saud felt no compunction in telling the Russians about it immediately. It could be something on which they, too, might want to capitalise. After all, General Bukharin was paying him very well and would certainly not stand in the way of the terrorists' action. Their actions were in his interests.

Saud was content that the information was being transmitted at that very moment to his Russian general. But Bukharin never received it. Instead of being transmitted, the Imam's man in the Russian Embassy in Cairo, a devout Moslem, converted when he was on duty in Afghanistan, read it carefully and checked its details against the information which he had been given the previous day. Each terrorist would carry a specific piece of equipment. Saud revealed his identity as a traitor when he told Bukharin that it was a cadmium mercury battery. No one else had that information. The message was destroyed and the name of the traitor sent to Baghdad, then to Rome, where Marcel Dupain waited.

The telephone rang. Marcel snatched it from its cradle. The indistinct voice of the old Imam said: 'Your traitor is Saud.' Marcel replaced the telephone, feeling sick to his stomach.

He would never have suspected Saud in a million years. It was just too elementary. Saud, the loyal Egyptian ... Saud. The man who had worked with Marcel for the past fifteen years. The man whose body he had enjoyed. He had hoped beyond hope that it wasn't Saud. That another of the terrorists was using the Egyptian embassy as a double blind, a secondary transmission point to hide his geographic location. For Saud to use the Russian Embassy in his home town was madness, an unforgivable breach of elementary security which would cost him his life. And the life of the boy who helped him.

As Saud left the Hotel Saddat, followed by two men walking

a dozen yards behind, he turned right towards Boulevard Nasser, where his car was parked. His mind was lost in the heady details of the Jews' forthcoming Armageddon. This ultimate victory; this rare, bold, imaginative ... but his mind ceased thinking about Jerusalem as a searing pain in his thigh made him wince. When he looked down, he was horrified to see a hypodermic syringe sticking out of his trousers. He looked up into the grinning face of his nemesis.

Saud tried to understand what was happening, but a gentle warmth suffused him and lulled him into a sense of well-being, just before he collapsed into the outstretched arms of his assailant.

Twenty minutes later, the two men had driven the unconscious body south-east into the Muqattem Hills, towards the tens of thousands of flyblown, fetid hovels, each looking like a tiny pustule which had erupted out of the decaying skin of the city. They had always been the slums of Cairo, but since the devastating earthquake at the end of 1992, they had become even worse. The concrete and cement hovels had been levelled by the devastation and now people were living in cardboard and plywood shanties, while the city authorities tried to cope with the enormity of homeless millions. Water, electricity and gas were only just being restored to shells of houses that in richer societies would have been condemned as uninhabitable. The impoverished denizens who lived here barely existed. The hovels at the foot of the hills were like an accusation against the mansions of Cairo's wealthy at the crest of the hills, which had been the first to receive government assistance following the earthquake.

The two assassins pulled Saud roughly out of the car. They were unconcerned that their actions might be noticed. There were no police here to question their activities or to maintain a standard of social behaviour. Here, life and death, right and wrong, good and bad were the assets of Allah and the powerful, not the wretched. Here, luck meant that you awoke in the morning. Survival was a lottery.

As they dumped Saud's unconscious body unceremoniously on the bed, they looked at each other and smiled. They were instructed to kill him slowly, using the techniques perfected by the uneducated in their resentment of the privileged. They had already worked out their game plan. When he woke, they would torture him back into unconsciousness; when he woke again, then they would allow him to glimpse the possibility of an escape, provided he emptied his bank account and gave them his money; then they would slowly dismember him, until he died from pain, shock, or loss of blood.

The vultures in the nearby desert would happily take care of the problem of disposal. None of this concerned Marcel in his Rome hotel. All he wanted to do was to eliminate the traitor and carry on with his real work. He took a long hot shower and scrubbed his face until it was as raw as meat.

♜♜♜

Half a hemisphere away, in the cooler, civilised atmosphere of Moscow, Colonel-General Bukharin waited impatiently for the latest news about the next terrorist manoeuvre. Matters were at such a delicate stage right now that the last thing he wanted was an unexpected firecracker exploding in the powderkeg he was controlling.

The Arabs had been a welcome, if unauthorised, addition to his plans. Miraculously, their bumbling, fanatical activities accelerated the process which led to an inevitable dialogue between Russia and Israel. In fact, their terrorist outrages gave considerable amusement to Bukharin, Petrovsky and the others; somewhat like watching a horse bucking in a field. But events had now reached a point where their antics had to be controlled, where caution, subtlety and a mature guiding hand were required. He did not need undisciplined fanaticism. His contact in Egypt had come good recently, and Bukharin was anxious to hear of the latest plan created in the mind of Marcel Dupain. Provided it did not dramatically disadvantage Bukharin's scenario, he would probably allow it to happen; but if it cut across any path about to be trodden by the leaders of Israel or Russia, Bukharin would be forced to dispose of Mr Dupain and the rest of his band of maniacs. He would only know that when his Egypt station contacted his SIGINT division in the industrial section south of Moscow.

CHAPTER TWENTY-FOUR

When the city of Rawicz underwent the transition from nine-teenth-century ruralism to late twentieth-century urbanism, its architects failed the citizenry. Other towns and villages which were destroyed by Adolf Hitler's armies were rebuilt after the war to look similar to the way they were before. Not so, Rawicz. Although some buildings were similar, the architects of the western Polish town were content to erect mundane buildings to house local officials and to construct square-shoul-dered barrack blocks to accommodate residents. An eighteenth-century market square boasting a Baroque town hall, the work of Italian architect Pompeo Ferrari, was the only building of distinction in the entire town.

For twenty generations Miriam's ancestors had known Rawicz as a charming collection of peasant huts, servicing the food needs of western Poland. For centuries the economy of the city was based upon growing potatoes, cabbages, corn and wheat. Events of history had bypassed Rawicz. It was not on any main road and had been ignored by successive waves of conquerors until the arrival of Adolf Hitler.

But it was not only the modern architects who had let the citizens of Rawicz down. During the 500 years that the Jews lived in Rawicz the city fathers had also failed in their civic responsibilities. Until the twentieth century the town was an economic backwater. Only with the advent of centralised eco-nomics did the government in Warsaw think of Rawicz as any-thing other than a source of crops.

In the last part of the twentieth century, Rawicz became a medium-sized urban settlement, devoid of any Jewish influence but replete with the trappings of towns around the world. It had its police, fire, medical and civil service elites, its leading business people, a sprinkling of artists, writers and intellectuals, and a large retired community. There was an industrial work-force in a grey barrack settlement outside the city to service the factories which had grown up where Miriam's grandparents once trod through undulating fields of corn, rye and wheat.

In the Baroque town hall where Miriam's grandfather once begged for a licence to collect coal from a nearby village, Valdek stood beside Paul and Miriam in front of an obdurate records clerk. Miriam wondered how her grandparents had coped with this level of stubbornness. Her rising anger was not being communicated by Valdek, whose translation of her requests was by word, not by emotion.

'But surely, *surely*, you must have some records left going back before the Second World War,' she shouted at the un-comprehending clerk. 'There's got to be something left, for God's sake.'

Miriam waited for Valdek to translate. But as he had done for the past thirty minutes, the clerk just shook his head and addressed his remarks to the Pole.

Valdek turned to Miriam and Paul and translated as best he could. 'He say again, no records before Great Patriotic War. Stalin's people come after war ... poof! ... to all records. Like Stalin's people did to all towns here.'

The clerk spoke to Valdek, his voice rising with anger. Valdek said, 'He say, he not waste no more time with you. You want to find record of Jews, you go see rabbi in Warsaw. He no deal with Jews. Jews bring trouble to Poland.'

The clerk became more passionate and turned to vent the full force of his anti-Semitism, which Valdek translated simultaneously. 'He say, Jew cause Hitler to come into Poland. He say, Jew should be kicked out here and everywhere else, and go to Israel. He not want to talk with you no more.'

Miriam's face turned bright red in anger. She turned to Valdek and hissed: 'Tell him he can go fuck himself'.

Valdek smiled at her and told the clerk what the young woman said. The clerk hissed a reply, turned and walked back into the anonymity of his office.

Valdek said: 'He say he rather fuck you'. He led the way from the town hall. Paul and Miriam followed behind, Paul angry that Miriam's intemperance had alienated the clerk, and Miriam justified in her belief that all Poles were anti-Semites.

As they returned to the car, Valdek asked: 'You want see where Jew village was? I take you now if you like.'

Paul looked at Miriam and was about to advise her against going there. Looking at the countryside on the way into Rawicz, he doubted whether much would have been left of a *shtetl.* To go to an empty, desolate area which once had throbbed with Jewish colour and culture could only add to her distress. 'Yes,' she said, 'I want to see where my grandparents lived. Is it possible to drive there?'

Valdek shrugged, more out of boredom than ignorance. 'I ask.'

He disappeared back into the town hall and emerged a couple of moments later.

'Clerk. He laugh. He give direction but say is only fields and houses. He say is good now for Polish people, not for Jews.'

Paul walked over to Miriam and put his arm around her shoulders. 'Are you sure you want to go there? I think it's going to be very upsetting for you.'

Miriam eased herself gently away from him. 'I think it's important that I go. I can't travel all the way here without at least seeing where my grandparents lived. Where my father was born.'

They got back into the car and Valdek drove through the crowded marketplace where local residents had set up stalls selling fresh vegetables, summer fruits, tinned goods and handcrafts. If it had been in England or in an outback Australian town, Miriam would have been fascinated. Here, she felt the menace of oppression. These were the people whose ancestors had tormented her family. She searched their faces for signs of recognition.

The car drove slowly through the centre of the town and picked up speed as it reached the outskirts. Valdek came to a large sign pointing towards Poniec and Krobia to the left, and Gora to the right. A little more than two minutes later, Miriam saw a collection of houses on the horizon, an estate whose style dated it back to the 1950s. One storey, red-tiled roofs, grey dispiriting walls. The area was devoid of trees and the houses so crowded together that none could boast a garden.

Her palms began to sweat as she neared the area. She felt abused at the realisation that her heritage had been mown into the ground. The estate, the children playing happily in the streets, the women hanging washing in the confined spaces around the house … all were trampling down the earth which held her origins, walking on her history.

Miriam was overcome with a monumental sadness as the car drove towards the housing estate. By the side of the road was a sign in Polish, identifying the community. She didn't ask Valdek to translate it. She knew it would bear no resemblance to her grandparents' *shtetl* of Chelmnitz but would be called something Communist and alien like 'People's Housing Block No. 52'. At the point of telling Valdek to turn the car around and drive away, he turned and said: 'Here is Jewish quarter. Is no Jew left. What you want I do? You want to walk?'

'Yes, I want to walk.'

'Shall I come with you?' asked Paul.

'No, just give me some time on my own. Please. I won't be long, I promise.'

She got out of the car, closed the door quietly and walked down the main street. In the middle of the day the village was full of women, who stopped what they were doing to look at her. Strangers were rare in Rawicz; unknown in this housing estate. But Miriam didn't care. She walked through the streets with a strange sense of confidence, looking directly into people's eyes. She wanted to shout out, 'This is my village, not yours.' Where once her ancestors had cringed in fear and suspicion when strangers entered their *shtetl*, now it was the turn of these Polish people. It was Miriam's turn to be intimidating. She was the one with power. She was the one who held authority.

Miriam walked slowly, purposefully, looking unflinchingly at the women who stared back at her. She walked in the middle of the main street. There were no cars to endanger her. Her confidence increased.

She wondered where her grandparents' home had once been. Where was the butcher shop that her great-grandfather had owned? Where was the house of the *shammus*? Or the home of the rabbi? And where among these boring and anonymous buildings was the synagogue where men had argued and debated, day in, day out, about God's law and the Hebrew Torah?

Miriam walked until she reached the top of the hill. She knew a hundred women had come out of their homes to stare at her and wonder who she was and what authority she held. She turned and looked back over the roofs of the houses. Miriam was surprised how small the village was and wondered whether the people in this modern monstrosity were forced to live within the same borders in which her ancestors had been confined. No! They were Poles. They were free.

Miriam was surprised by her calmness and confidence. Her fear on entering the village had changed to indifference. She felt strangely quiet and at ease. Different from how she thought she would feel. As she turned back away from the village towards the countryside, the ground sloped downwards and the houses seemed to peter out. To the left was a series of rolling hills, reaching far out into the distance. To the right the land gently descended to a copse of trees and beyond that to a river. Miriam's throat suddenly dried and the fear which she first felt on entering the village returned to her.

Was this the river beside which her *bubba* and *zeida* had picnicked that last day? The day on which Ben Ari had led a pogrom against the village. Was the copse of trees in the valley the one behind which her grandfather had hidden and photographed Ben Ari as he rode towards the village to view his handiwork? It was a short walk to the river. The same river that her grandfather had extolled when telling her of the beauty of his home. How long ago was that? Four weeks? One short month in which the quiet order of her life had been disrupted irreparably by incalculable forces. In which her grandfather had died, her relationship with Paul had probably come to an end and in which all the fears of her childhood had bubbled to the surface.

Miriam wanted to walk down to the river, to touch the trees, to drink the water, but held back. She was afraid of stepping off the harsh concrete of the road into the black yielding earth of the country. Afraid that, as she walked down towards the river, she would tread on the bones and bodies of her ancestors or sink into the same ground which had sucked down her forefathers. She was afraid that some demon, some dybbuk, would reach up, grab her by the ankles and pull her below the surface, stifling her and suffocating her forever.

She stood stock still, paralysed, unable to move, until her leaden body turned around and she walked slowly, painfully, down the hill and back towards the car. And as she walked, she held her head low to avoid the stares of the villagers.

♜♜♜

'No!'

'But Max, I insist that …'

'No!'

'Max, I don't think it's a question of yes or no. As editor of *The National*, I'm telling you what I'm going to do next, not asking your permission.' Jack Muir was breathing heavily, his face florid.

Max Mandle smiled and stood up from the huge desk which curved in graceful lines around his portly frame. He looked menacingly at Jack Muir. Then he smiled thinly in appreciation of the man's courage. He would make his editor regret his misunderstanding of power; not now, but later.

'Jack, when you own *The National* you can say these sorts of things. Until then, please allow me the right to make my own decisions. Paul Sinclair does not go to Moscow, and there's an end to it.'

Muir stared down at his feet, wondering whether now was as good a time as any to climb the long stairs to the gallows of unemployment. He decided that it was not. The work situation for journalists in general, and editors in particular, was far from good. However irritating Mandle was, his long trips to Australia were growing fewer as his global debt escalated. Jack knew that he had more autonomy than most other editors around the world, whoever their boss was.

'Max, of course you have the right to say what goes on in your paper. But as editor, surely I have the right to decide what's in the paper's best interests. I'm sure you're only trying to protect him, but he's a reporter, for God's sake, not a tourist. Other reporters put themselves in danger every day. Why not Paul? He's good, very good, and right now he's got a ringside seat at this meeting between the Israelis and the Russians. And while he's there, he could uncover a story that'll scoop all the others.'

Mandle started to interrupt, but Muir was in full flight. 'Let's face it, you'd insist that one of my reporters went storming into the front line of a war zone or undercover on some drugs story wouldn't you?' Mandle was being lectured and didn't enjoy it, but Muir didn't give him a chance to say anything. 'Well, I can't see the difference between those situations and the one that Paul finds himself in.'

'Jack, stop badgering me and listen for a minute,' Mandle said. 'Good editors know how to listen. It's not that I don't want him to get into a dangerous situation; he takes his risks just like all my other reporters. You seem to forget that there are at least a dozen reporters from my other newspapers in Moscow to cover this meeting. And they've been briefed by me as to how to cover it. The world's against Israel. I want to present a more balanced view. Anyway, it's not like we're unprotected as a media organisation. But surely you must realise that what Sinclair's doing is different. Suddenly he rings me out of the blue and tells me that he's heading off to Moscow to do God knows what in a country that's falling apart at the seams. You've got no idea what's happening right now in Moscow. For all you know, there could be gangs of ex-KGB or Red Army or terrorist lunatics roaming the streets, just looking to pick off somebody that's asking embarrassing questions.'

Muir shook his head in disbelief. 'Max, surely you more than anybody knows what's going on in Moscow. It isn't some frontier town. There are dangers there, sure, but when you told me that he and his girlfriend …'

'I'd forgotten he'd got a girl with him. What's her name … Marilyn?'

'Miriam. All they're going to do is to go see somebody in the Jewish community. There's no big deal. He isn't trying to break down the front door of the Kremlin. I wouldn't worry about Paul if I were you. He's got enough intelligence to know how to look after himself.'

Mandle nursed the remnants of his whisky and soda. Even if he had wanted to argue further, he couldn't think of anything else to say. It was an unusual position for him to be in.

♜♕♜

Ivan Yeszersky paced the floor of his dacha.

'I just don't understand why we can't march in there. I know that the KGB still has residual force, but for Christ's sake, Andrei Alexandrovich, PhD students in America have had access to these records for the past couple of years. Why can't I just go in and politely ask some *apparatchik* to show me the files?'

'*Tovarich*, the minute you go barging in there with your booming voice and size fourteen shoes, everybody from Petrovsky to the woman cleaning the toilets in St Petersberg Central Station will know what you're up to. I'd have thought with your sense of literary subtlety you would have been more attuned to the need for caution.'

Yezhov nursed the remnants of his vodka and stared at his shoes. Yeszersky's inexperience in dealing with the complexities of the situation was beginning to show, as was his drunken state. Yezhov was also drunk, but he handled his liquor better. He continued to address the minister's wandering form.

'My dear Ivan Semyonovich, granted it's not like the old days. But there are enough Old Guard loyalists and Revisionists who would willingly flock to Petrovsky's side if they saw him as a rallying point.'

The minister laughed, startling his elderly *babushka*. The old retainer's drooping eyes were not yet fully closed, just in case her excellencies wanted more vodka. 'You know, old friend, you would have made a brilliant conspiracy theorist in the US. You're the kind that sincerely believes that aliens are controlling the decisions of the President of America, or that Jack Kennedy was killed by the industrial–military complex.'

Yezhov giggled. 'You know what they say. Even paranoids have real enemies. Well, even conspiracy theorists are some-times right.'

Yeszersky continued. 'Look, the KGB is still there, but it's got no balls. It's anti-Semitism, anti-republicanism, anti- this and anti- that, are all a function of the past. Andrei Alexandrovich, the KGB is dying. Soon, thank God, even the Old Guard remnants will be dead and buried.'

'But like Dracula and Jesus Christ, they'll be resurrected. That's why we have to be so careful. You were blithely ignorant of its activities, even though you are a minister in the government. We can't just barge in without them realising what we're doing. It's why Petrovsky's so dangerous and we have to stop the old bastard.' He laughed at his slurred words.

Yeszersky shook his head in confusion. 'No, they're not important any more. This is just the final death croak from the throat of Petrovsky and a few old bastards like him.'

'If they're dying, then how do you explain what Petrovsky's managed to do?'

The rest of his sentence was mumbled into his vodka. Both men had spent the whole night drinking in front of a fire in the minister's dacha. Even though it was midsummer, the night was cold. The old *babushka* got up and tended the pine log fire. She had worked for the minister for five years. She was deaf and dumb to the intrigues of political life.

Both men settled back in their comfortable armchairs in front of the fire. Ivan Semyonovich Yeszersky began to giggle in a manner uncharacteristic of Russia's finest living poet. 'You know, I should write a novella about the death of the KGB. I could compare it to Kafka's giant cockroach. Sort of metamorphosis in reverse. One day it woke up and found that what used to be a cockroach had suddenly, overnight, changed into some hideous collection of human beings.' He stared at his glass and continued giggling.

'How are we going to get into the KGB files? Come on, old friend, seriously! This bastard Petrovsky is striding around Russia, making revolutions, overthrowing governments, trying to kill Australian Jews, God knows what the poisonous bastard is up to. How are we going to prove what the Jericho Plan is all about? And do we care?' Yeszersky slurred the last few words.

'It's not going to be a problem getting into the files,' said Yezhov. 'The problem is finding the information we want. Virtually anybody can look at the records these days. But something like the Jericho Plan would be so deeply buried, finding it would be more luck than skill. Before Krychkov died …'

'Murdered,' said Yeszersky.

Yezhov looked at him in surprise. 'Murdered? You think he was murdered? He was an old man, scared shitless.'

'Murdered,' repeated Yeszersky, nodding confidently at his glass.

'Before that idiot Krychkov was murdered, he said that this Jericho crap was all a Stalinist plot. Doesn't that tell you how devious Petrovsky is?'

'By God,' said the minister, 'that was half a century and half a world ago. Stalin has no influence today, except in the minds of novelists and historians. What in God's name could a Stalinist plot have to do with you and me?'

He swirled the remainder of his vodka in his glass, and smiled. The old spy took a deep breath to clear his mind before he answered: 'Friend, just because Stalin is all dry bones, it doesn't mean that his influence has gone. Bastards like Petrovsky and Krychkov and a thousand others would love to regain the sort of power they had under Stalin. It's just like that old bastard to have put something into place fifty years ago and for it still to be alive and well today.'

Yeszersky poured himself another vodka. The second bottle that night, it was half empty.

Yezhov continued, 'I've still got deep moles in America and Canada waiting for a password to activate them. What they don't realise is that I've forgotten the passwords,' and he lapsed into a helpless gale of laughter.

Yeszersky was caught up in the infection and both men sat laughing at the absurdity. 'Poor bastards,' Yezhov said when he composed himself. 'Just waiting there like sheep dogs for me to send them the word, and then they'll blow up the Pentagon or the White House. They don't realise that the gunpowder's all wet and that I've forgotten their names and addresses.'

Yeszersky stood up and stretched his legs. He wandered around the room trying to shake off the fuzziness that he felt. He hadn't been this drunk in ages. As he walked, Yezhov continued, 'Why do you think it's any different with Petrovsky and his damned Jericho Plan? For all we know, somebody could have activated it accidentally. We have to find out who and why.'

Yeszersky grunted. 'That's not hard. I know what you said about me barging in, but for God's sake, Andrei Alexandrovich, I'm a minister and I can do anything! There can't be more than a thousand civil servants left in the whole of Moscow. Not now the mafia controls things. There'll be no one to stop us.'

He raised his arm, as though carrying a sword. 'We'll march in there like Ivan the Terrible and drag out the files,' he shouted. 'No bloody civil servant will stop us. They're all out starting their own businesses, anyway—the machinery of government has ground to a halt, now we're all capitalists.'

Both men stared into the fire as a stream of incandescent gas escaped from a knot in the pinewood. It flared momentarily, before disappearing into the ether. Yeszersky sat down again and began to giggle. The old retainer looked at the two drunks and wondered what their heads would be like in the morning.

♜♜♜

Ten hours after he was due to report, Colonel-General Mikhail Bukharin was certain that something serious had happened to Saud Ibn Masse. His biggest fear was that Saud, his only contact in the group, had been uncovered and terminated. So much that the terrorists did was uncontrolled and uncontrollable. But that was the very nature of the Arabs. Wild! Unorganised! Passionate! Look at the dramatic rise in the activities of Hamas over the past few weeks. Madmen! Blowing up bombs in the middle of cities, killing and maiming without thought. Violent, vicious people, like the Slavs and the Croats and the Serbs and all the other lunatics who were driven by passion, rather than intellect.

The possibility of anything the Arabs did affecting his carefully wrought latticework of intrigue was slim, but Bukharin still felt uneasy. All the elements were in place. He sat back in his leatherette armchair and swivelled round to gaze out of the window at the suburban rooftops that surrounded him. His unimpressive building was Moscow's first attempt at an office park, built to herald its tentative move into capitalism. The buildings had been hurriedly constructed by a mafia-controlled building firm and had revealed their lack of care and use of poor quality materials within the first year.

As he looked at the barren roofs, he thought back over the past month. Petrovsky had switched on the light in his dark cellar of a life. A life without purpose. Where nothing was built and where the hopes and promises of yesterday had been dashed.

Everything had been good before Gorbachev and his reckless experiments with the biggest and proudest country on earth.

Not perfect, but good. Sure, some reforms were necessary, but Yeltsin and his successors had stuffed up the works with their asinine shock treatment. And he had been forced to sit meekly by as a two-bit clerk behind a desk, watching his country being destroyed. Until Petrovsky's invitation. He had relished writing his resignation from the army more than any other document he could remember. At last his self-respect had returned.

Petrovsky had only invited him on board at the last minute when events were reaching a climax. Until then, the old marshal had not been ready. But Bukharin didn't feel he had been overlooked. The timing was perfect.

They had been busy, these last four weeks. He had taken over a sophisticated team of signals, intelligence and political specialists at the last minute. Now it was now time for the *coup de grâce*, and Bukharin had been selected to deliver it. Years, decades of planning, all coming together in a matter of days. And Petrovsky had asked him to control matters. The computer models were inexact, the cleansing of Ben Ari's past had weak points, and the political situation was fraught with complications. But it was all coming together.

How proud his father would have been. Bukharin closed his eyes, and pictured his father as a young man, when Bukharin was a lad. His father rose to the rank of major because he showed the same characteristics of attention to detail that his son now exhibited. He should have risen to be a general but for that tragic incident in 1951 in the dacha in the Stalin Woods. He only survived two years of Siberian imprisonment before being killed by criminals. Ironically, it was Petrovsky's enemies, he had recently discovered, who had brought his father down.

When he was still a boy, his father would take him on fishing expeditions to a tributary of the Moskva River, and while waiting for the fish to bite, his father would quiz him on the heroes of the Soviet Union. Young Mikhail had to get every detail right, or he would be forced to start again from the beginning. His room always had to be spotless, his blanket folded back on his bed, with crisp knife-like military creases. His pyjamas had to be folded under his pillow so that not even a hint of fabric showed. In matters of discipline, his father was very stern, and yet the gentle side of him also shone, especially when the two spent much of their time in front of the fire on cold winter nights, playing chess, reading, or cleaning weapons for the following day's hunt. His upbringing gave Mikhail a reference point to life as an adult. Although his father had been dead many years, and he was much more lenient towards his own children, Bukharin's life was still led by the example forged in the furnace of his own strict upbringing.

It was this very upbringing, this attention to the minutiae of a plan, which made Bukharin a success as a KGB officer. And it made him uncomfortable today. He sat back and drew a long breath, while surveying the trappings of his current station in life. Five years ago he had a chauffeur-driven car, a seven-room apartment and a small but functional office in KGB headquarters in Dzerzinsky Square. But his station in life had plummeted. Only over the past month, since he had been taken under Marshal Petrovsky's wing, had the personal trappings of his rank begun to re-establish themselves ... not overtly, but he had more money, some small luxuries and a few privileges. Today he was enjoying the freedom of working in a recently constructed factory building in the southern industrial suburbs of Moscow. Petrovsky's elite group of SIGINT tacticians, strategists and manipulators, with ears around the world, were his to control. Bukharin again felt that he was at the centre of power. Power had never been a life-force for him, as it was for so many senior KGB men, but he admitted that he enjoyed its benefits.

Slowly he breathed out the tensions of the ten-hour wait for his Arab mole. Then he picked up the secure phone to speak directly to Petrovsky and share his concerns.

♟♟♟

The drone of the El Al 747 was less audible in the upstairs lounge than it was at the rear of the plane, where advisers and a few journalists congregated. Up in the first-class cabin, as the plane flew over the Mediterranean, before heading north-east towards Moscow, Raphael Ben Ari sat with Yitzhak Stein and a few senior bureaucrats who worked for the Ruling Council and observed the painful beauty of the night-time sky.

Thoughtfully, the captain turned out the cabin lights so that his passengers could see the crescent of land which was their country. Looking backwards as the plane flew over the Mediterranean coast of Israel, high above Tel Aviv, it was possible to see the entirety of their nation, a nation clinging with bloodied fingers to the continent from which it had been created. Surrounded on all sides by intransigence and hostility, Israel gripped tightly to its position as the interface between the Western and the Arabic world.

Decades before, there was a plan to relocate the Jewish people, not in Palestine, but in Africa. It had been a fanciful notion at best, and a total misunderstanding of the Jewish soul at worst. It was possible that Israel in Africa could have saved thousands of young valiant lives and overcome the anguish and torment of three generations of parents. But the Israeli will triumphed. The Israeli soul was pacified. And Israel spent fifty years establishing its right to existence.

Now there was a new direction being forged by its leaders. Ben Ari and Stein, two former freedom fighters who now ruled through force rather than law, were travelling to Moscow to form a treaty with President Abayev and to invite the participation of his new republic in the lifeblood of Israel's existence. Goodbye America; goodbye England and France. Goodbye those former allies who had been content to sell Israel and its people for the transient benefits of their own peace of mind ... and welcome Russia, a new republic with new leaders, facing new challenges in a world which was undergoing a metamorphosis of relationships, values and understandings.

Down below, in the belly of the plane, carefully chosen journalists and government advisers were standing around the drinks trolleys, talking about the future. Up above, in the peace and harmony of the magic carpet, the two old men were sipping whiskies and soda and ruminating. Like two grand masters playing chess with the pawns ten thousand feet below them, they discussed the consequences of their actions.

'Do you think there'll be a military guard, and all the pomp and ceremony?' asked Yitzhak Stein.

'I think Abayev would want to keep this fairly low-key. He'll probably be alone, or have along his Foreign Minister and a couple of others at the most. Then we'll go straight to the Kremlin. This whole thing has been so hastily arranged they probably haven't even had time to put together anything official like dinners or receptions. I must say I'm glad. The last thing I want to do is to sit at a head table with Abayev while half the Praesidium is staring daggers at me. This is the sort of thing that I would prefer to have conducted in private. But you know our advice. Do this part fairly openly and signal to the West quite clearly what our intentions are.'

'What's the latest on Jack Harrison?'

'I think he's all talk and indignation at this stage. His plan to rally the UN to enforce their sanctions looks like it's floundering. Dewhurst got a solid rebuff from the British. And Germany refused because it doesn't want to get involved in the area. Pity. I'd like our boys to kick the shit out of the Nazis.'

'So the Yanks are pretty much on their own in this manic determination to keep us under their control.'

'Yes. Everyone's condemning us but no one will do a thing. You know Harrison can't bring himself to hate me. I suspect he just finds me an irritation. The one who really hates me is Dewhurst, but he's got no real power any more. Harrison's suggested to our ambassador in Washington that we can kiss goodbye to US aid and any transfer of funds from the Jewish community, but most of our money has dried up and we're living on credit as it is. That will sort itself out as soon as we get an injection from Abayev.'

'But what happens if he refuses to help us? I mean, it's one thing for him to station people on our territory, but unless he comes good with US dollars we're in serious trouble.'

'*Chaver*, let me assure you that the pressure right now is mounting so strenuously on Abayev to open up the coffers that by the time we land he will have a cheque book in his hand. Russia needs our technology and it also needs a morale boost. He will be forced to pay any price to get them.'

The two old men settled back with their feet up to sleep for a few precious hours before landing early the next morning at Moscow's Sheremetevo Airport.

♜♜♜

Marcel Dupain's criterion for judging people was whether or not they were useful to him. He didn't care what nationality or ethnic group they belonged to. If they were useless, they were expendable. If they were useful, he would court them and extract whatever they had to offer.

Marcel shared the same dispassion towards races as did his father before him. Having been a child of the French Foreign Legion for the first formative years of his life, Marcel's credo was the credo of the Legion: 'THE LEGION IS OUR FATHERLAND'.

Entering the Al Kasim mosque held the same emotions for Marcel as entering a supermarket. His visit was purely functional. It didn't matter to him whether he was dealing with Arabs, Jews or Christians. He had an embarrassing duty to perform, that of informing the Imam of the events of the previous day.

Seated in his office, the Imam waited for Marcel to show the signs of respect which his office demanded. He was not surprised when Marcel came straight to the point.

'You were right. I was wrong. There was a traitor. I have known him for fifteen years. I didn't realise that he was double-dealing, but he has been dealt with and will not trouble us any further.'

The Imam nodded and remained silent. Marcel knew that this was the old man's way of extracting a more subservient apology. But Marcel merely remained quiet and stared at the old man. After an uncomfortable silence, the Imam was forced to speak.

'Now you must go to Moscow.'

'Moscow? What for?'

'Your negligence has caused word of our activities to spread. You must eliminate the traitor's contacts.'

Marcel snorted in anger and dismissed the old man's foolishness. 'Holy One, why does it matter that anyone in Moscow knows about us?'

'The newspapers trumpet the goings on in Moscow and Israel,' the Imam answered in his calculating voice. 'We are exposed.'

Marcel laughed. 'Moscow is a spent force. I can't see that Ben Ari's visit there is going to do our cause any harm. The fact that the Prime Minister of Israel is forming an agreement with the government of Moscow has no short-term implication for us. Long-term, I must agree there are serious dangers. The Israelis will undoubtedly want details of who was once funded by the KGB. But in terms of what we are doing, there is no immediate danger.'

The Imam looked at him dispassionately, in contrast to the words he used. 'Idiot! Any information about our plans which filters back to Israel through this new relationship between the Jews and the Russians could be devastating to our strategy.'

Marcel tried to assure the old cleric that things were not as bad as he was painting. 'The traitor was killed before the message got through. On top of which Ben Ari is on his way there right now. My presence would simply tip off the security people. It would be a dreadful and unnecessary risk.'

The Imam spat on the ground, in contempt. Had it been anyone else Marcel would have killed him instantly. But then Marcel would not have left the mosque alive. The Imam continued to speak as though addressing a simpleton: 'You were chosen because the plastic surgery made you invisible to the eyes of the security forces. For no other reason. Had it not been for that we would have used a Freedom Fighter for Allah, one of the brotherhood. You and people like you are *moharabeen*. You have no value in the eyes of Islam. But we have paid you well.'

Marcel's eyes hid the hatred which welled up within him. He was tempted to kill the old man for the insult he had suffered. But he would only trade one life for his own. Better to deal with the old man later. Assassinate him. No, bomb the mosque. That was better still.

'You won't be uncovered when you are in Moscow,' the Imam said. 'You may simply go there as a French or Arabic businessman. And with the Jew, Ben Ari, being there, the attention of the police and security forces will be diverted for his protection.'

Marcel shook his head. 'But you don't understand. Who received the information? It could have been anybody.'

'You think that we are fools, without the sophistication of modern technology. The message initially was received in Signals Intelligence in Moscow. An Islamic brother from Afghanistan who works there traced its final destination to a building complex in the south of the city. You should have no trouble in tracking it down and eliminating all those who now know.'

'But if it's gone through Signals Intelligence then everyone must know about it. Do you want me to eliminate the whole of Moscow?'

The Imam breathed in asthmatically. 'Sarcasm is the refuge of fools. The message would have been meaningless to most people in Moscow Signals Intelligence.'

'But you can't just mount an operation like this overnight. I'd be exposing myself to all manner of risk.' Marcel was using every device he could muster, short of storming out of the mosque, to avoid going to Moscow. It was madness, folly. He was sure the old man was on the verge of issuing a fatwa against him—and had to avoid that happening at all costs.

The Imam scowled at the infidel's cowardice. It was beyond both his understanding and comprehension how non-Moslems could live in the modern world. A Moslem man would have been ecstatic at the thought of dying for the cause of Allah; it would have been the apotheosis of his life and guarantee him entry into Paradise; yet this infidel, this mercenary, was more concerned with saving his own skin than earning the rewards of eternal joy.

'Our Islamic brothers in Moscow will assist you.'

The Imam nodded at one of the mullahs sitting beside him. The cleric took a briefcase from under the table and passed it over to Marcel.

'Perhaps this will make your journey more comfortable.'

Marcel opened the case. Inside were bundles upon bundles of US dollars, German marks and Swiss francs. He had no idea how much was in the satchel but it was enough to make him comfortable for many years. With that sort of persuasion, Marcel found it difficult to argue.

'Why are you getting me to do this? Why not merely get your Islamic brethren in Moscow to eliminate those who saw the message?'

The Imam gazed at the man through rheumy eyes. 'They are guest workers,' he replied wearily. 'Honest men. And only animals foul their own dens.'

♜♜♜

Like iron filings attracted to a magnet, the crowd coalesced in front of the familiar ten foot high fencing which surrounded the front gardens and porticos of the White House.

They had come from colleges, schools, synagogues, Beth Israel halls, B'nai B'rith buildings. As they travelled by car or bus they constructed instant placards as their medium of protest. They read

No nukes for Syria

Harrison, don't ditch your friends in the midEast!

Syria sponsors terrorism. Israel sponsors morality

485

Short-term thinking is long-term danger! Don't give Syria nuclear weapons.

The placards were too small to be read by the President and wouldn't have bothered him anyway. His fury at Ben Ari's flying visit and Israel's rejection of its longstanding ties needed to be dealt with. The President had to show America's anger. He couldn't get the wimps in the UN to back him, so he was doing things his way.

For the second time in a decade, the geopolitical map of the world was being overturned. Gorbachev cut the umbilical cord of the Soviet satellite nations in the 1980s; now Ben Ari's recent *volte face* at the peace conference and his sudden courting of Russia was about to rewrite history yet again. The West had only recently accepted the newly independent countries in their own right, rather than as puppets of the USSR. Peace had seemed a very real prospect. Now it appeared that the world was heading into another period of protracted realignment, where old friends became new enemies, and old enemies were seduced into an intimacy for which neither side was prepared. A new Cold War.

As people drew closer to the White House and began the by-now mandatory mantra of shouted protests '… No nukes for Syria …' the President turned away from the window to discuss the Syrian treaty with his closest adviser. Jack Harrison wasn't particularly interested in the vocal minority. He was more concerned with what Vice-President Spiro Agnew had once dubbed 'the silent majority'.

Most Americans and indeed Western world opinion had turned completely against Israel and its courting of Russia. Most people, the President believed, saw it as nothing more than political prostitution for short-term gain. An injudicious relationship in which expediency triumphed over rationality. The majority of Americans were either apathetic to Jews and Arabs or distrustful of them. The mood in the country favoured

America pursuing its own interests rather than maintaining a moral relationship with the persecuted Jews. David had become Goliath with the successes of the Jewish nation over the Arabs in four wars. Now David was showing his true biblical colours by his underhanded and peremptory adultery with his old enemy. As David cast Uriah into the wilderness in order to seduce Bathsheba, so David today was seducing Russia and casting America into the Middle East wilderness.

Well, so be it! If that was the way the Jews wanted it, then Jack Harrison was more than happy to accommodate them. Step One was to condemn Israel and to warn it against its reckless adventure. Step Two was to negotiate privately with Syria to fund a nuclear program in order to give the Syrian people cheap electricity. Step Three was to counteract the Jewish lobby in Congress. He could postpone this last step since, day-by-day, the Jewish lobby was increasingly isolated and finding it more difficult to make a case. And Step Four was to announce publicly to America and the world that what would have been unthinkable two years ago—giving Syria a nuclear facility—was now a top priority in America's Middle Eastern policy. Let's face it, he thought, the French had given Israel and Iraq nuclear power. Why shouldn't the US give Syria some?

President Harrison sat slouched back in his chair with his feet up on his desk. His back was to the bulletproof windows, and so the only person that could see the placards peeking over the high security fence was John Dewhurst. Harrison had anticipated that Dewhurst would resign when instructed to negotiate a nuclear power facility with the Syrians. But he had not. Obviously Dewhurst was much angrier and disappointed with his former friends than Harrison expected. A man who was once a voice of moderation and even-handedness within the cabinet was now a militant advocate of retribution. This pleased Harrison, who was spared the need to fire him and risk weakening the presidency.

'How are we going to deal with security?' asked the President.

'The International Atomic Energy Authority has got rigid guidelines and inspection facilities …'

'No, John, I don't mean in Syria. I know that's taken care of. I mean here. The Jewish lobby is getting into full flight. Now they're ostracised, they'll likely become militant. You know, the Jews have always been model citizens. But push them too far and God knows what could happen.'

'I don't follow you,' said Dewhurst.

'John, up till now the Arabs have been the terrorists. Even in America, the bastards bombed the World Trade Center. They did it because they've always been the dispossessed people. They've blown shit out of planes and trains and automobiles. But now the boot's on the other foot and ain't nothing stoppin' the Jews becoming the terrorists. Let's face it, boy. Go back fifty years and they were the bad guys in Palestine. They gave the Brits the run around.'

'And you think they could do that here?'

'I'm not saying they could but I'm certainly not saying they couldn't. And I'm not just talking about this country. Once we start putting nuclear stuff into Syria they'll try to bomb the shit out of it, like they bombed Iraq back in the '80s. Should we be responsible for protecting Syria?'

'I think that's the last thing that we should be doing, Mr President. Our gesture of giving Syria a nuclear facility simply shows the Israelis that all previous ties are broken and all bets are off. They have lain down with the wolves and now they'll have to suffer the consequences. If the Israelis bomb the facility that we build, then that's not our fault.'

'That's a bit crass, isn't it? Don't you think we have some duty to protect the Syrians' installation?'

'Jack, you know as well as I do that this is just a political manoeuvre on our part to tell the Israelis that they've made the biggest mistake of their lives.'

President Harrison stood up from his chair, turned his back on Dewhurst and looked out of the window. He saw the protesters, but didn't make any comment.

'And what if our guys get hurt? We're going to have advisers over there. Engineers. Security people building the place, working side by side with the Syrians. What happens if one of them gets killed or injured?'

'Mr President, a couple of hundred Marines were killed trying to keep peace in Lebanon and the people accepted it as a fact of life. I don't think we should react too strongly if somebody is hurt. We'll give them an honour guard when they're buried, and we might even use Arlington, but that's as far as I think we should go.'

Harrison smiled at the change that had come over his Secretary of State. The rarefied academic world of Harvard was a long way away from the real world in which Professor John Dewhurst now lived.

'Should we use AWACs to give early warning?'

'Sure,' said Dewhurst. 'We told the Israelis when the Arabs were on the move. Now we just do the same for the other side.'

John Dewhurst stood up and stretched his back. He had been sitting talking to the President for the better part of an hour and was desperate to go to the toilet. But experience told him that leaving the Oval Office even for a minute would be a mistake. When he did it in the past it had taken him days to get the President's mind back on to the topic of conversation. He walked over to the drinks cabinet and put his cold cup of coffee back on the tray.

'You know, Jack, I find it uncomfortable after all these years to have changed camps but it wasn't us that did it. We gave Ben Ari a platform. He could be at peace right now. Instead look at what he's done. He's screwing the ass off the Russians like some twenty-dollar hooker.'

Harrison smiled. It wasn't in John Dewhurst's nature to speak like this and it was all the funnier when he did.

'Nobody can blame your presidency, me, the Arabs, or even the Russians, for what Ben Ari's done. Why, even his own foreign minister …'

'Are you sure about that?' Harrison cut in.

'Sure about what?'

'Are you sure that the Russians had nothing to do with it?'

Dewhurst reacted in surprise. 'Oh, come on, Jack. Russia is in such a state of turmoil at the moment, it has no influence in the Mid East. You're looking at a random act by a renegade Ben Ari. He's gone over the top.'

Jack Harrison turned, and his full imposing frame faced John Dewhurst, legs apart, hands behind his back as though waiting for a fight to start.

'I'm not so sure about that, John. Ben Ari caught me and everybody else by surprise. It was the most unpredictable, extraordinary and unnecessary change of direction that I've ever experienced. It has to rank with Hitler lying his balls off to Chamberlain, telling him he had no further territorial claims in Europe. I can't believe that he'd have done that without some plan. He's such a wily old bastard. Christ boy, he knew what he was doing, and I'll bet you a dime to a dollar that Abayev is in on it somehow.'

'Jack, neither the NSA, nor the CIA, nor any of our Eastern European embassies knew what was going to happen until the last minute. Nobody knew, Jack. Nobody! This was all in Ben Ari's twisted mind. It wasn't planned. Don't forget, I was in Akrotiri. I saw him. He could hardly breathe when he was addressing the meeting. There was hatred in his eyes. An unyielding hatred. Don't let conspiracy theories get in the way of reality.'

'I'm no conspiracy theorist, John, but I'm telling you that there's more to this than meets the eye, and don't go quoting the CIA and its prediction power to me. Look at the fuck-up they made when the Iraqis moved into Kuwait. CNN knew before we did.'

'But surely we would have known something …'

'My guts tell me that there's something wrong. That Russia's behind all this. Israel's too small to be manipulating countries like Russia and America. It's all too convenient. Too neat. I've got no proof, but somebody in Russia, maybe Abayev, maybe somebody else, knows more than we do. Ben Ari's being manipulated whether he knows it or not … And so are we.'

CHAPTER TWENTY-FIVE

It stood like a fortress against the blue-black sky above Moscow. The Hotel Dvor was a thousand-room monolith, as different from a Hilton, a Sheraton or a Hyatt as was a ziggurat from a mud hut. Paul and Miriam spent their working lives in huge buildings, but the Hotel Dvor was on a scale so much bigger and more imposing than these, that they felt belittled. Nor had they been prepared for its size as their taxi had driven them in from the airport.

Leaving Poland, they did not have time to wonder about what Moscow would be like. It was just another city. But on the plane, when the tensions evaporated, they studied the guidebooks they had bought at the airport and marvelled at its beauty. The full-page colour photos of the wonders of the city—the domes of Saint Basil the Blessed, the classical splendour of the Bolshoi—gave their spirits a lift.

When the flight landed, and the taxi sped through the dreary outer suburbs, they held each other's hands, strangers in a strange land, but as it entered the inner circles of Moscow, they separated to opposite sides of the cab, staring out of the windows like children looking at a parade.

The guidebook had portrayed the centre of Moscow as the big heart of a big city, but even its elevated phrases had failed to convey the sense of size, of magnificence. The capitalist West had spent most of the twentieth century painting Russia as a godforsaken and backward country of Stalinist grey. But as they approached its centre, nothing could have been further from the truth. Despite its poverty, the long queues, the filth in the streets, Moscow vibrated with life and verve, a vital, energetic city of grandiose buildings and imposing vistas. Here was a city wearing the confident laurels of a thousand years of civilisation, despite the temporary backstep of its experiment with Communism.

They were transfixed by the width and size of its streets, and the geometry of its construction. Stalin had once called the streets of Moscow the roads into the future, anticipating, like the Romans and Napoleon before him, that good roads were the skeleton of a country's economy. And the roads and the buildings had survived, in spite of Stalin and all those who followed him. So had the grand residences which sat imperiously beside modern houses, old money next to modern capitalism.

Sensing their wonder, the taxi driver deviated slightly and took them to the Hotel Dvor by way of Pushkin Square, then traversing the city to show them the Old Arbat, with its hippies, punks and Hell's Angels, anachronisms in an ancient place. In painful English their driver said that he wanted to show them the best part of Moscow.

Driving to Kalinin Prospekt, he took them slowly through Red Square and past the Kremlin, circling the vast, triangular walls until he reached the north bank of the Moskva River. Miriam's misgivings on landing in Russia disappeared as soon as she entered this fantasy-land at Moscow's core. She had never seen anything so magical, so wondrous as what Muscovites call 'the eighth wonder of the world'. The Kremlin's 500-year-old red-brick walls were a mile and a half long, and with its four huge gates and nineteen towers, rose up to sixty-five feet in height in places. It was the ultimate fortress, impregnable, yet it enjoyed a lightness of feeling, a delicacy of construction.

Miriam turned to Paul to give expression to her wonder, but saw that he too was lost in wonder and admiration. The taxi driver smiled to himself. It happened every time he took tourists here for the first time.

As he dropped them off outside the Hotel Dvor, the impression of Moscow's heart was still imprinted on their minds. The size of the Dvor did nothing to dispel their amazement.

Although it had been a relatively short flight, they were both tired from their departure from Warsaw. It had been fraught with tension, especially the subterfuge necessary to escape from a vigilant Valdek.

Now they picked up the one and only bag they had managed to take with them and trudged wearily down the long red carpet towards the stairs leading up to the hotel foyer. Inside the hotel, they stepped into a bygone era. Its black mahogany staircases, ornate chandeliers, marble floors, leather club armchairs and heavy red drape curtains made the entrance seem like an exclusive men's club in Victorian England. Gladstone, Disraeli or the Duke of Wellington would have felt comfortable here. It was not a Hilton lobby, instantly identifiable no matter which city you were in. The Dvor was a symbol of solidity in an age of plastic replicas.

The arrangements to stay in the Hotel Dvor had been made from Moscow airport. It was all done in a hurry. They had managed to escape from the protective clutches of Valdek in Warsaw. He had underestimated their deviousness, and fooling him was simpler than they thought it would be. Paul had packed their passports and some essentials for them in an overnight bag telling Valdek that it contained some things they needed for the journey. When they were driving back to their hotel through central Warsaw, Miriam asked Valdek to stop the car and get her some headache medicine from a pharmacy. The moment he was out of the car, Paul jumped into the front seat, and drove off, ditching the car ten blocks away, and the couple made their way by taxi to the airport.

In the Hotel Dvor, they began to feel free from the horrors of Poland. They walked over to the registration area, a tall mahogany and leather facade. Not one of the dozen or so porters, dressed in the pre-Tsarist elegance of frockcoats, chevrons and cummerbunds, offered them assistance with their bag. Rather they viewed them with a studied disinterest as they talked in huddles, reading papers or standing around gazing at the passing parade of Muscovites. Conrad Hilton would have been apoplectic at the sight.

After they booked in, the clerk managed to persuade a desultory porter to help them up to their room. He grudgingly carried their valise to the entrance and dumped it unceremoniously in the corridor. Nodding curtly, he turned and walked away. Like his colleagues in the reception area, he judged from their dishevelled appearance that the young couple were probably student tourists, without the money to tip. Not like the Japanese who often tipped heavily in US dollars.

Paul and Miriam surveyed the room in dismay. If the lobby was ornate and extravagant, the double room on the sixth floor of the Hotel Dvor suffered from post-Gorbachev utilitarianism. The once burgundy carpet was now orange-red in patches, grey elsewhere. Corners of the wallpaper arched back on itself where it touched the ceiling and even down some of the seams. The sink in the room wore a mosaic of brown spidery cracks throughout the bowl, due to the disintegration of its porcelain over generations of residents.

Miriam forced herself to smile at Paul as she walked across the room towards the only other door, which led to the bathroom. When she made the booking on arrival at Moscow airport she specified that their room must contain modern plumbing. Yes, the offended Intourist official told her, every four-star hotel in Moscow has the latest in Western plumbing.

When she opened the door, she saw with disgust that it was like the rooms she used to stay in when she was on holiday as a child. The tawdry hotels with fly-blown wallpaper she was forced to stay in when other friends' parents were able to afford five-star luxury. In her later childhood, when her parents' fortunes improved, they stayed at better places but she never lost her disgust with cheap accommodation.

It was hardly a room ... she had stood in larger cupboards. To the left, immediately behind the door was an old-fashioned toilet, with a stained yellow porcelain bowl and cracked bakelite seat. To its immediate right were a dark yellow shower curtain and the shower whose head was caked brown from the sediment of constantly dripping water, and the neglect of the hotel's cleaners.

She turned to Paul. 'You're going to hate me, but I can't stay here. For God's sake, let's upgrade to a suite or something?'

Paul nodded in agreement. It was too much like an outback country motel. 'Okay. Let's not even unpack,' he said in a joke, pointing to the single valise dwarfed by the double bed. Miriam didn't smile. 'You rest here for a couple of minutes and I'll go downstairs and make a few demands.'

'Don't be too demanding. The guy behind the desk could be KGB,' she smiled, trying to make the best of her tired joke.

In the ten minutes since they had checked in, the lobby had become like a railway station. Crowds of recent arrivals clustered around the statue-like martinets at the reception desk, trying to make themselves understood; a Tower of Babel in the land of the deaf. The two clerks were looking impassively as a crowd of Japanese businessmen tried to convince them of the existence of their bookings. Paul hung around in the background, waiting for somebody to acknowledge him but he realised he would be given no attention until the Japanese businessmen had been satisfied. It would be pointless trying to find anyone else to help him, so he decided to while away some time in the bar.

He walked through the lobby, past the grille of the lift cage, groaning noisily from floor to floor, towards a gaudy neon sign of a dancing cocktail glass. He entered the bar and sat down on one of the high stools, waiting for the bedlam outside to settle.

Hotels offered a closeness not often found in restaurants, offices or other such places. Deals, assignations, seductions ... all were the stuff of the lobbies, foyers and bars of hotels. Paul could happily spend hours sitting as an observer in a busy international hotel foyer, fantasising about the people who sat in corners whispering into companions' ears or writing messages to be posted into guests' pigeon holes.

As Paul's drink arrived, so did a tall, languidly beautiful girl with deep-set black eyes and a pert and sensuous mouth. Her presence was telegraphed moments before her arrival by the waft of an expensive perfume. As he smelt the perfume, he looked up and saw her sashay towards him in the mirror behind the bar. It was so unexpected he continued to stare at her reflection, even after she had sat down on the stool next to his. She was wearing a cocktail dress. Her hair was cropped short and clinging to the line of her cheeks. She moved her stool closer to Paul, turned to him and smiled. In a smooth contralto voice, she called the barman over and asked for a drink. He poured her a vodka.

Paul's hormone level rose just sitting beside her. Everything about her was conducive to sexuality. Her short black silk dress, conservatively gathered at the neck, her long legs encased in black stockings, her crucifix pivoting acrobatically between her breasts. He had an overpowering urge to turn and look at her. He kept staring straight ahead at the barman.

'Hello. I am Natalie. I am whore. I sell to you body for $US 100. I use condom but give you good time. I no do drugs. You buy?'

Paul turned to her and swallowed at the same time. 'Thanks for the offer, Natalie, but I'm with a lady.'

'Is no matter. I fuck lady as well as man. Is cost double. You buy?'

'I'm afraid not, but thanks again.'

'Is no problem,' said Natalie, standing up and walking back towards her table.

Paul noticed that there were at last four or five other whores in the bar. He swallowed his whisky and soda, took several deep breaths to the amusement of the barman, and went out into the reception area to rejoin the fray.

It took Paul and Miriam two more hours to be relocated into a larger and more modern suite; two hours accompanied by aggression, studied looks, and disparagement. Eventually, they were given an acceptable three-room suite on the tenth floor. It was called the Presidential Suite by the hotel management and they were curtly informed that they would be charged accordingly. Paul was not concerned. Max Mandle was picking up the charges. He couldn't see Mandle discomforting himself in anything but a suite of rooms like these.

Exhausted, they went to bed and lay in each other's arms.

'Guess what happened to me downstairs,' said Paul.

Miriam didn't answer.

'I was approached by a prostitute in the bar.'

'Was she attractive?'

'Why is that the first thing that springs to your mind? Surely you should be outraged that a respectable, almost-married man like me is approached by some hooker. What have her looks got to do with it?'

'Well, if she's an old slag, then I wouldn't be worried about your fidelity. I assume she was a bit like that, otherwise you wouldn't have told me.'

Paul grinned. 'Quite the contrary. She was very beautiful. Tall, expensively dressed. She came right to the point.'

'Did you fancy her?'

'Only superficially. She was great looking, but not as attractive as you are … to me.

There was a long silence between them as they lay in the dark. Paul turned around in the bed so that his body flowed around hers, forming a question mark.

After a few minutes of lying comfortably together, Miriam turned around and faced Paul. Their knees, arms and chests were touching. In the darkness there was anonymity. Each lost identity. They were just two anonymous people drawn together by the hostility of an outside world. Paul ran his arms over Miriam's back and pulled her even closer towards him. She was exhausted, but craved him. His strength was sensuous and gentle, a blend of a husband and a lover. Miriam eased herself into him, as more of their bodies touched. She felt his penis growing against her thigh. Paul kissed her gently on her mouth, her neck, and gently opened her nightdress until he could cup her breasts in his hands. As he kissed her nipples, she kissed his forehead. He lay her gently on her back and positioned himself until he was inside.

He lasted no more than a minute. As he came, he cried out like a hungry baby and Miriam held him closer, enfolding him tightly in her arms. His need satisfied, his body relaxed. Miriam's still strained to climax, and she rubbed herself against him until she too arched her back and breathed out loudly in her orgasm. She sobbed from the exhaustion and the tension, from the deaths and the outrages, from loneliness and from a life which had lost its security. She cried for long moments, even as he held her tightly.

Still joined together, they fell within seconds into a deep sleep.

♜♜♜

Since the election of President Abayev, Moscow had become a centre of international trade and commerce. Moscow's Sheremetevo airport accepted flights from all over the world throughout every day and night. It was very different from the days of Leonid Brezhnev, when the airport mainly served the capital cities of the various Soviet republics and was virtually unused during the night.

Russia was being propped up by billions of dollars worth of loans from the World Bank and the United States—loans needed to purchase the expertise and equipment to build a secondary and tertiary industrial base. Flights of relief aid were landing daily from New York, Berlin and Tokyo.

This left Russia stable but still desperately poor. International traders from Japan to America arrived daily to supply the Abayev Government with everything it needed from agriculture to computers, running up massive debts to be paid off when productivity improved. Despite the modernisation of its industry, the people still suffered massive deprivation.

The Middle East Airlines flight 84 from Beirut via Vienna to Moscow was one of six 747s to land at Sheremetevo airport between 8 and 11 p.m. Eighteen hundred passengers, accompanied by 4,000 pieces of luggage, forced their way into the bottleneck of the battleship-grey arrival and customs area only to be greeted by Moscow's world famous apathetic bureaucracy.

Twenty customs officials processed the passengers in a cursory manner. Marcel Dupain, travelling under the alias of Helmut Schlessermann, a German importer/exporter, found it a relatively easy task to present his passport and to slip through the net.

Schlessermann was one of twenty aliases, false identities and false passports that Marcel Dupain possessed. Every identity from each of the twenty countries was backed up by documentation, including contacts at accommodation addresses who would verify his identity if requested. He had incurred considerable expense during the last two years in inserting his post-plastic surgery face into all his passports. The expense had been worthwhile and his forger in Lebanon had done him a remarkable deal.

Marcel had only twice been to Moscow. Both occasions had been to meet KGB paymasters who were financing a particular terrorist deal.

The taxi driver took him by the most direct route to the centre. He was surprised how much Moscow had changed. Last time he was there it had been a blaze of lights. Now, he felt it was threatening. Even the Arbat, with its confusion of lights and movement, failed to excite him.

As the driver came closer to the Kremlin, Marcel settled back in the seat. All the way from the airport he had anticipated that the driver would take him on a circuitous route to increase the mileage but it had not happened. And anyway, Marcel would have said nothing. He would even have given the man a moderate tip. Taxi drivers, policemen, and interfering old women were notorious for remembering those trivial bits of detail which later led to identification.

But the taxi drove Marcel directly into the centre of town, where he got out, paid the fare, picked up his bag and wandered through the city streets until he was sure that the cab was well out of sight. He then hailed another taxi, close to one of the approaches to Red Square, and directed him to the northern Moscow suburb where his Islamic brethren were waiting for him.

The apartment was north of Sokolniki Park, in one of Moscow's typically nondescript barrack block suburbs, a grey, flat edifice trumpeting the triumphs of Stalinism over private enterprise. Originally, it was built as home to the workers in nearby factories. More recently it had become home to thousands of migrant workers from the Third World. Like slaves, they were imported by Russia's capitalist elite to labour in the new private-enterprise system. Many had migrated east out of Germany when the neo-Nazis openly attacked their hostels. Now, like the inhabitants of thousands of other apartment blocks throughout Moscow, they were living either by their wits or as wards of the state's burgeoning welfare system … another import of capitalism.

Marcel told the taxi to drop him off at an apartment block four streets away from his proper destination. When the taxi was well out of sight, he emerged from the entryway of the building and slowly walked to the address he had been given. From a quick look at the directory board, Marcel estimated that there were ten apartments per floor for the six floors. Apartment 56 would therefore be on the top floor and entry could only be through the stairwell. This would make escape near to impossible in the event of a raid—a prospect which did not please Marcel one little bit.

He stood outside the building for ten minutes. Even though he couldn't understand the Cyrillic characters of the noticeboard, a simple computation told him that the apartment on the extreme left-hand side facing the street was the one he required.

Marcel waited in darkness, invisible from the street, and gazed silently at the lights in the apartment. It was late. There were almost no other lights visible in the building. Everybody had gone to bed. Everybody except those in the Islamic brothers' apartment. Its lights were blazing for all to see, acting as a magnet for police and passers-by. If this was an indication of their understanding of security, Marcel feared very seriously for his own safety.

He waited a further ten minutes to make absolutely certain that the building was not a trap before silently crossing the street and climbing five flights of steps. Softly rapping on the door, he waited breathless for the response from the brothers inside.

♜♜♜

'Colonel Lubin. How very nice to see you again!'

Lubin looked up and grinned at Yezhov. 'So, Andrei Alexandrovich, today you come to us in sunshine, rather than in the dark.'

His first visit to Minister Yeszersky's office had been a furtive night-time meeting. Today it was open, honest.

'You're here to see Minister Yeszersky?'

The old man nodded and the two walked across the courtyard of the Kremlin towards one of the smaller entrances of the palace. Lubin, now more familiar with his visitor, chatted amiably about the way in which Russia seemed to have changed its direction over the last few days.

'I know that change is supposed to be invigorating, but I'm just an old-fashioned military man. I guard whoever happens to be leading the country at the time. Left, right, centre, in the end it all makes very little difference, does it?'

Like Russians before him throughout the ages, serfs quietly accepted their lot under the divine rights of their rulers. The Bolsheviks' Revolution was simply an aberration in a thousand-year history of slavery.

The old man smiled. He found it difficult to argue. Looking back at his seventy-five years, he wondered how much beneficial change political revolution really brought the world. After all the idealists and placard-wavers, all the rhetoric and the invective, all the revolutions and wars and uprisings … was the world really a better place for it, or were they the same things called by different names? His own country, an amalgam of disparate peoples, had been encircled and cemented to the body of Russia by Stalin's glue of fear and power, and yet in the end each went its separate way to determine its own identity.

In America, the Democrats led the people in one direction, the Republicans in another, but who held the real power in America? It was the capitalists, the industrialists, the owners of property and producers of goods. Even Europe's recent experiment with unification dissolved into a farce of internecine hatred. Nations still clung to rigid identities, demarcated by artificial boundaries; despite 100 million people dying in the European wars of this century, there was still as much suspicion, hatred and animosity between people as ever ... so what did change and revolution do? Did it lead to a permanent state of peace for humanity? No, all it led to was racial sterility, to absolutism and religious fundamentalism.

Would Abayev's treaty with Israel and the re-establishment of a foothold in the Middle East do anything for the long-term good of the Russian people? Would it lead to anything different from the way in which Brezhnev, Kosygin, Andropov and Chernenko had courted the Arabs? Yezhov frankly doubted it. More likely , the Russian people would still be bound together, at the end of the day, oxen under the yoke of Tsarism, be it the tsar of imperialism, the tsar of Communism or this latest one, the tsar of capitalism.

Yezhov turned to Colonel Lubin as they walked through the entranceway towards the lift, and smiled. If anybody personified Russia, it was Colonel Lubin. He was the steppes of Russia, bountiful and peaceful, unchanging, but dangerous to those who crossed them without realising their awesome extent.

'Colonel, I'm always worried about commenting on other peoples' political ideas, but in this case I find it difficult to argue with you. In the long run, I agree. I don't think it matters a single damn.'

Once settled in Minister Yeszerski's office, Andrei Alexandrovich Yezhov realised that something had altered his friend's pessimism from the previous night. There was mischief written in the minister's expression.

'Dear friend,' he said, 'how would you like some good news for a change?'

'Any news at this stage would improve the way I am currently feeling.'

'Is that a reflection on last night's indulgences, or your curiosity to know what's going on?'

'It could be both. But tell me your news.'

'When I was at Moscow University, one of my dearest friends was Paval Pyotor Sakharovsky. Paval is the son of the late Alexander Mikhailovich Sakharovsky, who I'm sure you remember was once the Head of the First Chief Directorate of the KGB. Pavel's father joined the NKVD in 1939 when he was a man of thirty, and served for many years in Rumania. He was instrumental in turning the Finnish politician, Kekkonen, who became one of our highest ranking assets.'

Yezhov dismissed the history lesson with a wave of his hand.

'Anyway, the point is this. Because of his father's reputation, Professor Sakharovsky was asked by Yeltsin to become the chief archivist of the KGB, and to build up a documented history of it since its first days as the Cheka. It's a monumental task. What I didn't realise was that Paval has been engaged on it full-time for the last six years.'

Yezhov nodded. 'I've often wondered why only the top echelons of the KGB were put on trial. I assume this friend of yours is holding back information?'

'No, he's not the type. Straight as an arrow. I reckon he's been quiet about things because he doesn't think it wise to broadcast too widely what he's doing. He's about to report on their activities. If his report is accepted by the government and published, it will do to the KGB what the Senate did to the CIA in the late 1980s … blow the lid off.'

Yezhov laughed out loud. 'Do you seriously think it will? There's already been a vast amount published in the West from KGB files.'

'You can scoff, but don't underestimate the climate of revisionism. Every day there are public meetings of dyed-in-the-wool hardliners telling the people that capitalism is the road to ruin, and that under the Communists, everybody had bread in their mouths'

'In many ways, they're right.'

'It's one thing for revisionists to weep about the old days,' said Yeszersky. 'But the spectre that's terrifying me is that the climate will lead to the resurgence of the KGB.'

'With Petrovsky at its head,' said Yezhov.

'Do you think it will happen?' asked the younger man.

'If this damned Jericho nonsense isn't exposed, it very well could.'

'That's why I've asked Sakharovsky to come and meet with us,' said Yeszersky.

Almost on cue, there was a knock at the door. Without waiting for the minister to give permission to enter, the door was opened by two large men who stood in the doorway filling its entire frame. Unsmiling, they scanned the office, then stood aside to permit the diminutive Paval Pyotor Sakharovsky to enter. On seeing the minister, he walked over to the desk and the two men embraced each other. The man had 'Academician' written all over him. His crumpled charcoal suit gave him the look of an ordinary Muscovite, while his tie and shirt didn't match. His skin had a grey pallor and was mottled with liver spots. But there was life in his eyes and an enthusiasm. Yeszersky introduced the two men.

'Of course I can assist you,' said Paval in a nervous high-pitched voice after the two men explained to him the role of Petrovsky and the mystery of the Jericho Plan. 'But I can't understand why you need my help. The files are open to anybody with a bona fide need to research. As a minister your request would be given to me and I'd authorise it immediately.'

'Paval, my friend,' said Yeszersky, 'we can get into the files without any problem. But we need an agile mind like yours to find material that I'm sure is well hidden. Listen to what we've got to tell you, and you'll understand why.'

Sakharovsky listened patiently, nodding at times, expressing shock and disapproval at other parts of the saga. Then it was his turn to contribute.

'People used to go to Stalin all the time with hare-brained schemes. One was to build a huge nuclear power plant in the frozen tundra and use its heat to melt the ice and create an irrigation system, to open up new food production areas in Siberia. He actually commissioned a study to determine its feasibility but of course the danger of radioactive water put a stop to that.

'This Jericho Plan, it sounds terribly biblical. It would certainly tie in with what's happening with our relationships with Israel. But as for the details, there are millions and millions of files and I only have limited resources.'

'How many are still unopened?' Yeszersky asked.

Sakharovsky didn't have to think. 'The majority. You know, after the KGB was disbanded, historians raided the file rooms like pirates. They found some treasure, explaining a lot about the Stalin years. Then the data they discovered became repetitive … arrests here, executions there … a litany of tens of millions of dead people, so they lost interest. Me? I'm an archivist. I love classifying things, so I continue.'

'I can't believe that historians aren't still poring over those records,' said Yeszersky.

Sakharovsky smiled. 'There is another reason. The files are so cryptic. They're not obvious. You actually have to tie lots of things into each other in order to understand what's going on. Most historians don't seem to like that. They like to pick up things, read them and understand them straight away. It's a specialist task for archivists … people like me.'

'What about Stalin's personal files?' asked Yezhov.

'They're the worst,' said Sakharovsky. 'You almost have to learn a new lexicon.' Sakharovsky looked at the old man and wondered how much to tell him. His credential of being the minister's friend was impressive, but the archivist had learned the value of caution in the years he had been investigating the KGB.

'Stalin's files have been studied extensively, but there are still many rooms in his library of collected papers which remain largely undisturbed. Not only is the stuff cryptic, but we're also suffering from a dramatic lack of funds and equipment for the research.'

Yezhov had heard the story so often about academic research in Russia. The greatest minds were constrained by the greatest poverty.

'Has anybody thought of confronting Petrovsky and asking him what the Jericho Plan is all about?' asked Sakharovsky.

'Of course. That would have been the simplest thing to do. But once he's denied it, he'll just stonewall,' said Yeszersky. 'Don't forget that he is still powerful. Having masterminded this adventure in the Middle East proves that he's much more potent than we thought. And of course we have no idea who else in the government is involved. We do know that the late Boris Krychkov and two of his colleagues were under Petrovsky's influence. In fact, by the way he has suddenly done a *volte face* and capitulated to revisionist forces, I wouldn't be surprised if Abayev himself was involved.'

Sakharovsky stared silently at the floor. Yezhov wondered what to say next. Yeszersky reflected.

'Explain to me your motivation,' Sakharovsky said.

Yeszersky shook his head. 'I don't follow.'

'Why are you doing this?'

'Why? Shouldn't that be obvious?'

'Not to me,' said the archivist. 'Let's say you do discover some Stalinist plot, and let's also say that Petrovsky is behind it and that it's currently going on. What difference does it make?'

Both men wondered where the archivist was heading.

'You're not going to be able to change things. Abayev will do what he considers best for Russia, and he's answerable to cabinet, like any true democrat. What's in this for you two?'

Yezhov smiled at the academic's perception. His thoughts were an amplification of those voiced by Colonel Lubin just half an hour earlier. 'Professor, one of the reasons that the CIA has become such a tame instrument of the American government is because it is now closely scrutinised by the Senate. The days of subculture, of intrigue, spy networks and undercover deals have gone.'

Yezhov paused and poured himself another coffee. 'Today, however flawed, we have a struggling democracy in Russia trying to compete with those in the rest of the world. If we allow ourselves to be manipulated by the likes of the old guard again, then we'll just end up behind the same ghetto walls built by Lenin and Stalin. Our only chance is to do what we have been doing for the last several years … to be open and honest, admit our mistakes and deal honestly and openly with other countries.'

'That sounds too high-minded for me, Andrei Alexandrovich. I'm only an archivist. I don't predict the future. I only record the obscenities of the past. So, we want to find out about Stalin in the 1940s. Gentlemen, will you join me in visiting the archives?'

♜♜♜

As Yeszersky, Yezhov and Sakharovsky drove in the small, noisy and crowded Lada towards Lubyanka Square—the minister having considered it less public to go by an ordinary car than in a Zil—Paul and Miriam were travelling towards Petrovo in the north-west of the city to visit the home of Moscow's Chief Rabbi.

In the far outer suburbs of Moscow, land congestion was not as severe as it was in the centre, and some private houses had been built in the days of Brezhnev. Rabbi Mironov occupied one of them. Had it been in London, New York or Sydney, it would have been considered a home suitable for a middle-ranking public servant. Part wood, part cinder-brick, its outside was dominated by a protective boundary of fir trees, giving it a sense of privacy which had only recently become acceptable in Russia. When it was first built, it had been one of the utilitarian residences built for the new affluent elite of post-war Communism. Today, it was the meeting point for senators, congressmen, prime ministers, presidents and rabbinic leaders from around the world, whose concern was still for the plight of Russia's multitude of Jews. The tap had been turned on by Gorbachev, enabling Soviet Jewry to leave the country for re-settlement in Israel, but it had been turned off by Abayev, who had seen the policy drain the resources of universities and scientific, academic and intellectual institutions.

Although tiny in number, the place of Jews in Russia's intellectual life since the end of the Stalin era had become increasingly imposing. Anti-Semitism had been endemic in Russia since the days of Catherine the Great, but despite the obstacles placed in their paths, many Jews had risen to the highest levels of Russia's intellectual life. Although anti-Semitic from birth, Russia's leaders never could escape the fact, like anti-semitic Christians, that the founders of their faith, and many who gave early support, had been Jewish. And some of the most faithful Communists around the world, especially those who led the Polish Communist Party before the Second World War, were Jews.

As Paul and Miriam drove up in their taxi, she moved closer towards him. 'I hope to God this isn't another waste of time,' she whispered. Since arriving in Moscow the previous night, the strains which had been a part of their relationship had eased. Paul, especially, felt that they were treading a new and more hopeful path.

Rabbi Mironov came out of the house to greet them. A short, rotund man with a huge grey beard, he was one of those jovial characters who grace the pages of the works of Dickens. He would have been out of place, though, in the Gothic fiction of Tolstoy, Turgenev or Dostoyevsky.

'Yes. Yes. Come in. Come in. Hello. I am Rabbi Mironov.

I am welcome you. Please, please, children, come in, come in. Yes. You will have tea? I learn English good from world service of BBC. Is good, no?'

Paul and Miriam told him that his English was good, no!, and he led them into the loungeroom of his immaculately kept house. It had a very different atmosphere from Rabbi Yossi Gartenbaum's home in Jerusalem but showed a close relationship with Judaism, with the occasional painting of rabbis praying at the Wailing Wall in Jerusalem, or a biblical prophet staring towards the sky. On the credenza in the loungeroom was a *menorah*. Other religious objects included a silver salver with gold goblets and an ornately carved cup on the top of which was a type of pepper shaker containing the spices used for the conclusion of the Sabbath service. On the lintel of each door was a *mezuzah*. As the rabbi entered the lounge, he stood on tiptoe to touch it with his fingers, kiss it and intone a breathless prayer.

They sat in the leather armchairs, which were studded with brass pins and covered by fussy lace protectors. The potbellied stove in the corner of the room belched out an unwelcome heat despite the warmth of the outside air. Miriam grimaced at the staleness of the atmosphere. The room stank of old cigarettes, though a cursory glance failed to find the ashtrays. The rabbi sat opposite them, and before either could say anything, asked: 'Excuse me, children, but you smoke?'

Both shook their heads. The rabbi nodded philosophically: 'So, sometimes I am lucky and visitor brings Marlboro and Camel and sometimes cigar. Then two weeks is heaven. So, child, tell me what you want.'

Miriam told him of her quest. At first, the rabbi could not believe the story about Ben Ari. He shook his head vigorously.

'No,' he said. 'No. This is not possible. No, I'm sorry. I know the Prime Minister. He is good man. He has done much to help us since Abayev stopped Jews from leaving Russia. He is not a murderer. Your grandfather, child, is mistaken. Your photograph is wrong. It is of wrong man. I'm sorry to say this.

I have written to Prime Minister Ben Ari and he has been very helpful to me, and to my people. He is not a killer. You're wrong. I am sorry.'

'But rabbi, explain to me why it is that since we've been investigating Ben Ari the people around us have been dying. First, my grandfather. Then Paul's flat was searched. And not only that, but the curator of the Museum of the Diaspora, then Rabbi Gartenbaum.'

She stopped as the Russian rabbi reeled back in shock. 'Rabbi Gartenbaum is dead?' he asked in a whisper.

Miriam nodded. 'Yes, I am so sorry to have to be the one to tell you. It was just after my visit to him.'

The rabbi stared at the floor in distress. Silently, he mumbled a prayer. Paul and Miriam remained silent in respect for the rabbi's distress. Miriam grew concerned and turned to face Paul.

'Oh God, I didn't think. Maybe we shouldn't have come here. Maybe we're putting Rabbi Mironov in danger.'

Paul was about to respond when the rabbi said: 'All Russia is danger for Jew. Some Jews are too big for danger. Little Jew they can make disappear, but big Jew like me cause too much difficulty.'

Paul pulled his wallet from his jacket pocket and extracted a photograph. It was of an elderly man, his father. Carefully using his fingernail, he prised another photograph from the back of the first.

The rabbi looked at him with curiosity, wondering what he was doing. He gave the picture of Ben Ari to Rabbi Mironov.

'We're not a couple of crazies, rabbi, but we're convinced that people around us have been killed by this man's accomplices. Can you see the birthmark? That shot was taken when he was leading a pogrom against his own village. And not only that, we were nearly assassinated in Poland … Surely you must see that something is going on. Miriam and I were advised— no—we were told by some mysterious Russian man to go back to Australia.'

'Russian man. What Russian man?'

'We don't know, rabbi, but he made it very clear to us that our lives were in danger because we were asking embarrassing questions. Don't you see that something terrible is happening. It all centres around Prime Minister Ben Ari.'

The old man shook his head and stroked his beard. 'Nothing you have told me says Ben Ari is behind this. Everything could be old guard KGB or CIA or somebody, but not Ben Ari. Nothing you say is to me, Ben Ari.'

'But rabbi,' stressed Paul, 'if we can just look back into the early days of Ben Ari's life, using some of your contacts to get into old files, we can prove one way or the other if he was involved. We hope to God you're right, but the last two weeks have convinced us that he's behind what's been happening to us.'

The rabbi silently looked at the two young people opposite him. He knew that Paul was non-Jewish, but that didn't appear to prejudice him. Unlike Rabbi Gartenbaum in Jerusalem, intermarriage of Russian Jews to non-Jews was a daily fact of life, something he coped with emotionally as well as religiously. But it was usually a one-way passage, the Jew all but invariably assimilating into Russian life. He wondered when Miriam would lose her identity.

'Ben Ari was Polish-born. But you are right. Many Jews in Poland were Communists. In early days before Great Patriotic War. Files may be in archives, some KGB some MVD, others, who knows? Yes, this I will do. You are right. We must find out what is the story.'

Miriam looked with fondness at the rabbi, and then at Paul. He was not a part of her religion, and she was sorry. At that moment, she felt more in common with a Russian stranger than with a man who had shared so much of her life for the last five years.

'Many years ago, we have a man who is secret Jewish. Join KGB, and becomes records clerk. Rabbi Miklos of Poland know this. This is why he send you. He has helped us many time. We get Jew with KGB file out of Russia to Rabbi Miklos, then to Israel. This man is still working in KGB headquarters in files. Many times he help us alter files or remove them when my people are investigated. We will see this man this afternoon. I will take you there and together we will see Ben Ari not in files. Now children, you will have more tea. Then I will telephone this man, and we will go. Yes'.

♜♜♜

The Gorbachev Hall of the Palace of the Kremlin was packed to capacity with journalists, photographers, cameramen and sound recordists, all surrounded by Russian Foreign Ministry officials and their Israeli counterparts, each looking uncomfortable in the others' presence.

At the front of the hall, raised on a dais from which presidents and prime ministers had announced statements to the world for the past thirty years, was a table which had once belonged to Tsar Nicholas I. It was covered with green baize. On the table were two carafes of water covered by glasses and a cluster of microphones. In the old days, the backdrop to the room had been an enormous profile of Lenin staring intently into the future of Soviet Russia. Today, the backdrop against which world leaders faced the press was more prosaic, a blank wall covered with green velvet curtains.

The room fell into an anticipatory hush as President Abayev and Prime Minister Raphael Ben Ari walked in from the wings of the room and sat down. Each man carried a sheaf of papers which he laid carefully on the table, nervously shuffling them to square off their edges, as though it would make any difference to the assembled journalists.

Raphael Ben Ari cleared his throat and looked apprehensively at the President. It was his press conference. His right to open the proceedings. In his thick Russian accent, carried by a deep baritone voice, President Abayev informed the world of the results of his meeting with the Israeli.

'Ladies and gentlemen,' he said, 'I am delighted to tell you that Prime Minister Ben Ari of the Republic of Israel and I have just concluded and signed a Deed of Intent which opens a new era of understanding, harmony and cooperation between the people of the Russian Republic and the people of Israel. My aides are currently distributing to you the terms of the Deed. In a month's time I will be visiting Israel in order to sign a Treaty of Friendship and Cooperation to formalise our relationship.

'You will see from the Deed being given to you that Israel has asked me to supply them with 1,500 advisers in order to assist Prime Minister Ben Ari's country in the management of its agricultural, industrial and technological infrastructure. In return, Israel will be providing the Republic of Russia with certain repair, maintenance, rest and recreation facilities for our fleet of ships which will now have a permanent and safe harbour in the Mediterranean, as and when needed, as well as an exchange of advice on desalination and hydroponics—areas in which Israel leads the world. Israel's current needs for large scale financial assistance have also been discussed, following the criminal freezing of its bank accounts throughout the world. I am pleased to say that the Bank of Moscow will match, dollar for dollar, any money held in escrow by American or European banks. As soon as the overseas banks in question are allowed by their governments to free up Israel's funds, Israel will repay our loan by transferring their dollar values back to the Bank of Moscow. As soon as this happens, further facilities for future loans will be negotiated with the government of Israel so that it will never again be held to ransom by adventurists and speculators.'

Having finished his statement, there was a cacophony of shouts from the journalists, but ignoring them, the President turned to Ben Ari.

'Perhaps you would like to comment further,' Abayev said.

The room fell silent as Raphael Ben Ari spoke.

'I would merely like to amplify a few of President Abayev's words. For many years, Russia and Israel were silent enemies.

In the days of Mrs Golda Meir, who was Israel's first Minister appointed to be the Ambassador in Moscow, the hostilities and tensions began to thaw and a dialogue was established. That dialogue reached fulfilment under President Gorbachev, and his liberalising of Russian Jewish emigration.'

Abayev shifted uncomfortably in his seat, hoping his visitor would have the grace not to comment on his policy towards emigration of Russian Jews.

The Prime Minister continued: 'Israel is a sovereign nation and the actions of President Harrison of the United States and other leaders, in trying to force us into a disadvantagous alliance with our Arab neighbours, has done much to speed up the relationship which for years we have intended to enter into with the people of Russia.'

There was a buzz of noise throughout the room. No one had any idea that the Israelis and the Russians had been talking about a relationship for years. That was something every journalist had missed.

'This may surprise you, as for many years I have been critical of Russia. Yes, indeed, we were going to sign a treaty with President Abayev … not this year, not next year, but maybe in a few years' time. The criticisms I had were in relation to Moscow's alliances with our Arab neighbours, which we perceived as being to our disadvantage. Our Arab neighbours have, I believe, shown their true sentiments by turning to America against their long-term ally. We have not severed our links with America; they have severed their links with us! No matter who our friends used to be, they could no longer be considered friends if they tried to force us into a position of disadvantage. I have the assurance of President Abayev that no pressure will be brought to bear on Israel to sign a treaty with the Arabs which is in any way disadvantageous to our security or viability as a nation. Further, President Abayev will now use his best endeavours to search for a peaceful solution to the Arab–Israeli impasse, and we will work painstakingly towards that end.'

Ben Ari cleared his throat and took a sip of water before

concluding the press conference. 'Ladies and gentlemen of the world's media. It is my wish that within the space of one year, I may be able to invite you to a Peace Conference to debate the internationalisation of Jerusalem to be hosted under the auspices of the Republic of Russia, here in Moscow.'

As soon as the Prime Minister of Israel finished his speech, one hundred journalists stood up from their chairs, arms waving in the air, and shouting, 'Mr President' ... 'Mr Prime Minister'.

The melee was on, broadcast live around the world by television. Sitting at home not two miles from the Kremlin, Marshal Petrovsky looked at the television screen, a smile slowly spreading on his face.

CHAPTER TWENTY-SIX

Marcel Dupain sat for an interminable time in a car in a southern industrial Moscow suburb with three Arabs as they talked about him in the most disparaging terms. It made Marcel's mind flash back to those hideous days in Algeria when his despised status caused him to be ridiculed by his mother's family and friends. Only his mother had treated him with regard and kindness. Only she.

The Islamic brethren in the car did not realise that he spoke fluent Arabic. When he arrived at their apartment he pretended not to speak their language. That way, he could tell what was in their minds. Thinking he was just a French mercenary, sent to deal with some Russian or other, they spent the whole of that morning in the steamy atmosphere of the car telling each other childish, humourless and viciously racist jokes about him, Europeans in general and the French in particular. Marcel would kill them all before he returned to Europe, but that satisfaction would have to wait, just as the death of the Imam would have to wait until a more convenient time. For the moment, he was content to be the butt of their puerile humour. To stop himself from listening, he pictured their agony as he slowly murdered all three of them. He smiled at them. That increased their ridicule.

For much of his youth he had been the butt of ridicule. He would no longer permit it. As a boy he had been sodomised by his father's comrades in the French Foreign Legion. He was a part of the troop; he was the Legion mascot, like a goat or a donkey, and was ridiculed for it. But he enjoyed the feeling of belonging. Yet he did not hate the French or the Germans or the Spaniards or the other nationalities in the Legion.

Nor did he hate Arabs, even though his mother's relatives and friends had rejected him, treating him like a half-caste, a stranger. And their rejection had not only been of him; it extended to his mother, who was a Legionnaire's whore.

He should have hated Arabs but he didn't. He just hated mankind.

His society and sexuality were violent. His greatest pleasure came from humiliating, and if possible, dehumanising men, women and children. Bombing airports or terrorising civilians made him feel strong, superior. He didn't care whom he terrorised, black, white, yellow; he didn't hold any particular racial hatred of one group or nation above another. When he killed the Arabs, there would be no aspect of racial hatred in it. Just an end to their ridicule.

They had been watching the squat three-storey building at No. 27 Gagarin Prospekt in Birvuleva for three hours. The journey to the industrial suburb had taken over two hours; they left the apartment as the sun rose, and drove on the circular outer roads of Moscow to avoid the city centre. The journey began in contempt and blossomed into hatred when the car parked. They sat interminably, smelling each other's breaths and bodies, waiting for arrivals at the office block.

The car was carefully positioned behind a screen of trees around a corner and on the opposite side of the road. The building under observation was barely visible. Only the most observant of security staff would have realised what the four men inside were watching. The Arabs had wanted to keep moving the car, thinking that would avoid suspicion. Marcel spoke in French and convinced them that a static, concealed car blends into the surroundings and has less chance of being spotted than a car which makes regular sorties past a building.

From the easy way in which people arrived and entered, security was obviously minimal. This surprised Marcel. Perhaps the security of the building was that its purpose was a closely-guarded secret. Or perhaps, like the CIA building at Langley, entry was easy into reception and public areas, but highly restricted where sensitive work was carried out.

Early in the morning, shortly after 8 o'clock, five people

arrived by foot. Moments later, four or five others left the building, the night shift returning to their homes. Abdul, one of the Islamic brothers, busily photographed the men who came and went using a telephoto lens.

At 9 o'clock a green Moskvich of indeterminate age drove up to the building and turned into the adjoining carpark. A middle-aged man wearing what passed for a smart Western business suit got out. The driver of the car waved him goodbye, reversed through a brown cloud of exhaust fumes back onto the road, and then sped off. Gamal, the oldest of the brethren, gasped as the car neared the corner and slowed before driving off: 'I know the driver!'

Abdul quickly snapped off three or four frames before the car disappeared down the road.

Marcel turned around and asked in Arabic: 'Who is it?'

The three Arabs in the car failed to realise that Marcel had just spoken Arabic, rather than in French. He wondered when their ape-like brains would comprehend.

'His name escapes me. God, what was his name? He taught me. I know him. Let me think where, and then I'll get his name.' Gamal banged his forehead with his fist. 'Where? Where? Where?'

All the men in the car remained silent, waiting on Gamal. Marcel used a technique that he had tried many times before, with considerable success.

'Listen to me, my brother ...'

'You!' Abdul squawked: 'You speak Arabic!'

'It is of no consequence. I speak the Mother of All Languages as well as French. Now brother, you must stop racking your brain and let me help you. You must associate this man's face with where you have been and what you have done in all your adult life. Put him in the context of everything you have experienced, one thing at a time. Now, think of your home town in Iraq. Think of the markets and the streets in the middle of the city. Was it there? Do you see his face there?'

Gamal shook his head.

'Now, think of Baghdad. Does his face remind you of any-where in Baghdad; something to do with the military or a terrorist cell where you trained?'

Gamal shook his head again. 'Where else have you been since you left Baghdad? Think carefully, my brother. Have you been to other European cities?'

As though coming out of a trance, Gamal shouted, 'I have it.' He slapped his head with his fist. 'I'm so stupid sometimes. He taught me at Patrice Lumumba University. When I was with Abu Nidal. He is an expert on signals intelligence and planning strategies. His name is … God almighty! What's his name? … He taught me twice … Colonel … Colonel … No, general! That's it. He is a general.'

The moments passed in agony. Gamal shouted out, 'Buk-harin! That's it. Colonel-General Bukharin. Colonel-General Mikhail Bukharin. He was with the KGB. Such a mind! Their top strategist. He was the London resident in the middle '80s. He ran agents from the Libyan People's Embassy, the Egyptian Embassy … he even got that Jew to photograph the inside of the Israelis' nuclear plant, the one at Dimona. Then they brought him back to teach in the university when things began to go wrong. How could I have forgotten his name?'

Abdul nodded appreciatively to his brother. 'Well, if he is here, then this is definitely a KGB operation.'

'Then, why is it being run out of the backwaters of Moscow?' asked Marcel.

'They are all discredited. Where else can they go?'

Marcel shook his head. 'No, there are no more KGB oper-ations. Not ones that the government knows about. But if you are right it's quite likely that he was the one responsible for turning the Egyptian rat.'

'Why in the name of the Prophet would the KGB run an illegal operation?' asked Abdul. As an afterthought, he said: 'And why did you not tell us you spoke Arabic? What games are you playing with us?'

Marcel smiled but remained silent.

In the silence, Marcel worked out the danger of dissident elements of the former KGB receiving information from the traitor in Egypt. Was this why Ben Ari was in Moscow? Had Abayev fooled the world?

Either way, the people inside the building had received information from Saud Ibn Masse. They had first-hand information about the terrorist cell and its past activities. They even knew plans which had been in the pipeline for forthcoming events. One thing Marcel was sure about … they knew nothing about the forthcoming attack on the Knesset. Saud Ibn Masse and his little helper had been killed and the information suppressed before it could be transmitted.

The four men observed the building for a further two hours until General Bukharin's car appeared once again. Marcel flexed his muscles, and put into effect an idea which he had conceived the previous night, lying in bed while listening to the brethren ridiculing him under their breath.

As the Moskvich turned into the building's carpark, Marcel got out of the brethren's car.

'Where are you going?' called Abdul, but Marcel slammed the door. In full and public view he wandered slowly around the corner and over to the building's carpark. The red stop lights of Colonel-General Bukharin's car turned off as the general took his foot off the brake, opened the door, and climbed out of the car. Marcel quickened his step in order to catch the man while he was still near to his car. Although his heart was beating fast, he controlled his emotions to show no outward signs of concern.

'Excuse me,' he called to the general. 'I'm sorry to bother you but my Russian is not very good. I'm a Frenchman doing business in an office near here, and I'm lost.'

Bukharin beamed a smile. He knew immediately that the story was false. No one but Russians came around this area.

'I'll speak slowly,' said the general. 'How may I help you?'

'You'll think me an idiot,' said Marcel. 'I'm visiting the district with a friend and he dropped me off and told me to meet him back at our hotel, but I've got completely lost. Are we far from a bus terminus or station, or something?'

'We're miles away from one, but I'll get a street map out of my car and point you in the right direction.'

'That's very kind of you.'

The general bent over and reached into the glove box of his car to retrieve a gun, intending to kill this man instantly and ask questions later. But he never got the chance. He did not hear the spit of the silencer as the bullet ripped through his skull and blew the front of his face away. As he slumped forward over the front seats, Marcel put the gun back into his pocket, lifted Bukharin's dead torso, and crumpled it unceremoniously into the well of the passenger's seat. Blood pumped from the massive hole which was his skull, on to the floor of the car. He closed the door and walked slowly back across the road to where the three Arabs were sitting. 'Drive your car into the carpark and we'll load his with the explosives,' he ordered them.

Without questioning, the Arabs drove into the carpark and parked beside Bukharin's car. Taking out an attache case full of Semtex, and two full jerrycans of petrol, they placed them on the back seat and taped them together. Marcel felt repelled by the stench of blood, but searched the general's pockets for keys and turned on the engine as silently as he could. He cautiously reversed out of the car park, and stopped opposite the communications building, looking with complete disinterest at the swelling puddle of blood and brains beside him as gravity emptied the general's body fluids through the gaping hole that once was his face.

Marcel looked up at the building to estimate how much damage the Semtex would do. The windows were small and covered in a fine mesh, behind which were iron bars. Good! That would concentrate the explosion indoors. He manoeuvred the car until it was directly in line with the front doors of the building, and put the gear stick into neutral. He grunted. This type of car bomb was much easier carried out with automatic cars. Damn the Russians and their lousy old-fashioned vehicles.

Marcel opened the briefcase and primed the Semtex, then he took the activator out of the briefcase and held it in his sweaty hand. He picked up the general's heavy briefcase and placed it on the accelerator. The car's engine screamed in a neutral agony. Pulling against the resistence of the road, Marcel managed to twist the wheels so that as closely as possible they were aimed for the glass front doors of the building. He got out of the car, then, when he was certain that everything was working, he put his foot on the clutch and placed the car into first gear. Bukharin's briefcase pushed the accelerator onto the floor and the Moskvich shot forward. Marcel dived out of the driver's seat onto the roadway, bruising his shoulder as he hit the ground. The car tyres screamed on the surface, puffing smoke, as the old car raced across the road. Colonel-General Bukharin's Moskvich headed directly for the glass doors, to the astonishment of the people who had rushed to the windows to find out what was making all the noise.

Marcel stood up to ensure that the car still travelled in the right direction. He saw a man running towards the door as though to warn the driver, but the car mounted the pavement with a bump and continued its drive towards the front doors of the communications building. The steering wheel twisted slightly, but not enough for the car to be diverted. It smashed through the doors with a huge crash of breaking glass and hit the stairwell to the left of the entryway where it roared in mechanical fury. Inside the building, Marcel could hear shouting and screaming. Through the dust and confusion, he saw men and women running around inside. People in the upper stories disappeared from the windows to go downstairs and see what was wrong. Everybody would be gathered together for Marcel's little surprise. He closed his eyes as he thought delicious thoughts of the crowd of people gathered round the car, like excited children around a Christmas tree. Smiling to himself, he slowly ambled to the other side of the road, where he pressed the button on the hand-held device whose infra-red signal activated the large parcel of Semtex. The explosion was so vast that the brilliant white and yellow tongues of flame burst out of the door like a hideous giant jellyfish, and then through successive windows as the blast wound its way through the building, first sucking the air out of people's mouths and then engulfing them in a searing torch of fire.

The flames were followed seconds later by an almighty roar which deafened Marcel. But it was not until the concussion wave hit him that he realised he had forgotten the first rule of the bomber. To hide behind a solid object. Sitting on the grass, he smiled at every glorious, hideous moment of the explosion, and thought with pleasure of the people inside who were dying in agony. He was their executioner. He had not given them life, but he had taken it away. He had made them terrified. He had made them despair and in their despair he ended their hopes. Never again would their lips kiss others' lips or their hands hold others' hands. He was the power and the glory. They suffered an agony created by him. He began to feel an erection growing.

As he stood and marvelled at his power as the building roared aloud in flame and smoke, he was happy. He was as happy as he had been those early years when he was a little boy in the Foreign Legion. When he was a part of the Legion. And the Legion was a part of him. '*Legio Patria Nostra*'. He began to walk towards the opposite side of the road, softly whistling the anthem of the Legion, and as he did so, his step slowed to the bold, swaggering march of the Legionnaires as they walked into and out of battles.

Lost in his glory, Marcel didn't notice the Arabs, whose car screamed to a halt in front of him. He was surprised to feel a searing pain in his chest and it was only then that he saw the spit of flame from the gun in Abdul's hand.

The light left his eyes as the building opposite disappeared in smoke and flames.

An hour later, while the Moscow police were still attempting to uncover the identity of the dead man outside the gutted building, which was a mass of smoke, flame and torn humanity, the Imam of Baghdad put down the telephone and smiled in satisfaction. His order to kill the infidel had been made on purely pragmatic grounds. Any man who held a traitor close to his bosom without realising it was a fool. Allah did not smile kindly on fools. Now, the Imam's plans could proceed without the fear of exposure. But that still left the Zionist dog in the land of the Godless ones. Israel's Prime Minister was signing an alliance. Soon he would be back, and his people would overthrow him ... even before the Russians were able to take up position.

The man was a fool. To form an alliance with the Russians! His time was limited. Already reports were flooding in to the Imam's office, telling of massive discontent on the streets of Israel. Soon the Imam would contact his brothers, the Syrians and the Jordanians ... maybe even the Egyptians ... and tell them to strike at the festering, rotten heart of Israel while it was in chaos. And then the Imam would be able to walk into the mosque of al Aksar on the most holy Mount where the blessed Prophet had ascended to Heaven. It would be the most glorious moment of his life, and a turning point in the history of Islam. Again, the Islamic crescent would fly over Palestine, undoing the wrong done to the Arabic people when the British and French arrogantly carved lines in the sand.

Paul and Miriam looked conspicuous walking down the Norodny Boulevard in central Moscow towards the home of Rabbi Mironov's covert agent inside the archives of the KGB. The three were an incongruous sight. Miriam and Paul dressed in smart Western clothes, walking among Russian men and women whose clothes bore all the hallmarks of post-war European utilitarianism. And as though Paul and Miriam didn't stand out from the crowd, Rabbi Mironov, short, roly-poly and congenial, was talking animatedly to them both, his hands darting backwards and forwards like a snake's tongue.

They would have been conspicuous if any secret service organisation had been watching, but Paul and Miriam had tried to be careful since leaving Poland. They paid cash wherever they went, so nothing was traceable through credit cards. Paul was starting to think like one of the characters in his book, two steps ahead of the KGB or the CIA.

'Here is building. Now we see,' said Rabbi Mironov.

Sitting down in the archivist's apartment, Rabbi Mironov spent tedious minutes explaining his relationship. 'I introduce to you real name Dov Levkovitch. In Russia, he is known as Aleksei Borisovich Karpov. From now we call him Aleksei, so as we don't confuse nothing with nothing.

'Aleksei is Jew. Parents become baptised Christians in Stalin's day but Aleksei comes to me and says "Rabbi, I want to be Jew". They don't know he is Jew and even today is best for him not to be one. Next year, maybe year after, Aleksei goes to Israel to live but that is later. Today we ask Aleksei to help us with Ben Ari.'

Aleksei turned to Paul and Miriam. 'Ben Ari? The Prime Minister? What is this all about?' His English was far better than the rabbi's.

Paul explained the entire story. It seemed the more he repeated it, the more it became a reality in his mind. 'We want to determine from KGB records whether the story is true. We know that many KGB records have been published in the West. Is it possible to uncover this particular file, do you think?'

'And if I can?' asked Aleksei.

'Then the man will be exposed through my newspapers. I work for Max Mandle and every newspaper throughout the world controlled by him will carry the story, along with this photograph.'

Paul took the picture out of his wallet and again peeled it from the back of his father's photograph before giving it to Aleksei.

'He'll be discredited and hounded from office, and this whole fiasco of martial law in Israel and relationships with Russia will be at an end.'

Aleksei studied the photo and nodded. 'Could be. Who knows? Stalin brought many people from the Polish Communists to Moscow long before the war. Most of them were Jews. Stalin and the rest of them hated the Jews, although he needed them because they were pro-Soviet and anti-Hitler. But Stalin wasn't only operating in Poland. Soviet intelligence in those days was very weak in general, especially within Germany. We had a very poor wartime network gathering information.'

'Poland was of special interest, though, wasn't it?' asked Miriam.

'In some ways. In other ways, not. All over Europe we were desperate to know what Hitler was up to. A man called Leopold Trepper, a Polish Jew, worked for the Comintern and was recruited to the Fourth Department of the NKVD in 1936. With another Jew, Leon Grossvogel they built a brilliant espionage network composed of Jews who hated Nazi anti-Semitism and were happy to work against Hitler. Alexander Rado was an outstanding Hungarian who was recruited by the Fourth Department. He worked out of Geneva. There are many stories like that, but I must say I have never heard of Ben Ari being involved.'

'But that's not to say he wasn't. I mean, the entire operation was top secret.' Miriam looked at Paul for support.

'I've certainly never heard any stories about Jews being involved in organising pogroms. Sure, there was the ONR before the war, who were viciously anti-Semitic, but the state officially condemned it. There's no doubt that after 1935, the public as well as the state became more and more anti-Semitic. Still I don't know of any Jewish involvement. Jews were excluded from universities and there were certainly pogroms in small towns, but the government denounced the violence and encouraged Jewish emigration. I mean, there was a strong Yiddish community in Poland before the war, unlike in Russia, where Stalin virtually destroyed the culture.'

Paul felt it necessary to interrupt. 'Perhaps the reason you haven't heard anything is that Ben Ari's real name used to be Wladyslaw Mikolajczyk.'

Miriam looked at him in appreciation. It was so obvious, she could have kicked herself for forgetting it. He had only taken the name 'Ben Ari' on arrival in Israel. He would have been known by his Polish name in the records.

Aleksei shook his head. 'Still, it doesn't remind me of anyone. But there are thousands … millions … of names in NKVD and KGB files. I'll take you down to my office and together we will look.'

Miriam was stunned. 'You mean, we're going into the KGB?'

'There's no KGB any longer. All that is left in the head-quarters are historians and archivists like me. People who were non-operational, who are building up a body of evidence in case there are any war crimes trials.'

'War crimes trials of the KGB?' Paul asked. He was staggered.

'Sure. Have you forgotten who was responsible for the mas-sacre in the Katyn woods? The Russians blamed the Nazis for the killing of fifteen thousand Polish officers, but it was the NKVD that did it. And who do you think carried out Stalin's edicts or Beria's or Krushchev's?'

'But these must be old men by now.'

Miriam turned on him angrily. 'So what? Age doesn't wipe out the enormity of the crime. War criminals must be brought to account, no matter how old they are.'

'Maybe so,' said Aleksei, 'but the current rulers think that it isn't in our interests to raise old ghosts. Still, the archives are there and the documentation, in case the KGB tries to revive itself and poses a threat to the government.'

'Anyway, we've spoken enough,' Aleksei said. 'Why don't we go down to KGB headquarters, and look up … what's his name?'

'Wladyslaw Mikolajczyk,' said Miriam.

Professor Sakharovsky grew in stature and dimension as he flipped through the hundreds of brown index cards he had retrieved from a wall full of drawers. This was his domain, his palace, and he was the ruler. As the chief archivist he had the ability to look into each and every file which Stalin and Beria and Krushchev and Brezhnev and all the other megalomaniacs had built on the tens of millions of hapless Russian citizens who had been unlucky enough to have been born when they were. His domain gave him no real power but an intense satisfaction. In these files, ordinary people whose lives had been relegated to being ciphers came alive again in his mind. These files gave back dignity to people who had been treated like the excrement of the diseased body of the USSR. Each one of the millions upon millions of card index files was a man or woman, boy or girl, a human being who had been born, had loved and been loved in return ... and whose existence had been obliterated purposelessly by madmen. These files were records of the victims of Russia's power-mad rulers; victims of suspicious neighbours, malicious children or paranoid state police.

Ivan Semyonovich Yeszerski and Andrei Alexandrovich Yezhov waited patiently. They knew that it could take hours, indeed days, to search through this mass of detail. What the CIA did in seconds with supercomputers at Langley took Russians days using a large labour force. Whole departments in universities or other institutes functioned on the sort of old-fashioned PCs on which schoolchildren in the West did their homework. And the scarce resources of the Russian government certainly did not stretch to computerising the dusty archives of a bygone era. So Paval Pyotor Sakharovsky was forced to do what a chief archivist in the West would have considered beneath his dignity.

The field at least was a narrow one—the Jericho Plot, or the Jericho Plan, whatever the dead Minister Krychkov had called it, shouldn't be too difficult to discover, if indeed there was such a file. And after an hour or so of searching, Sakharovsky turned to his colleagues and shook his head sadly. 'Nothing.

Nothing at all under Plans, or Plots or Jericho or Jordan, Stalin or anything. I think we'll have to search through the various years and try to track it back through minutes of conversations between Petrovsky and Stalin. Though God knows what year. I know that there were lots of covert things happening between Russia and the Middle East before the war. Some Jews were sent to Palestine to act as a fifth column. But as to this Jericho Plan, if it's got anything to do with Petrovsky, it's likely to be midway through the war or shortly after it. I think it's safe if we look for files of discussions between Stalin and Petrovsky between, say, 1942 and 1948.'

Yezhov let out a soft whistle. 'You're talking about thousands of documents. I know Petrovsky. He was the most meticulous man I've ever worked with.'

The academician smiled and nodded. 'Nobody said this was going to be easy. But don't worry. We're looking for a particular needle in this haystack, so for the time being we'll ignore everything that doesn't seem to relate. We wouldn't be looking for records of the cabinet discussions. I can't imagine it having been discussed there, so we'll go straight to his private papers.'

Yeszersky groaned: 'That could take hours and we need to know immediately. With Ben Ari in the country signing agreements, we haven't got much time.'

'Hours? It could take months,' Sakharovsky said. Then he grinned at Yeszersky sheepishly. 'Out of interest, Ivan Semyonovich, how long does it take you to compose one of your poems?'

The minister accepted the chiding, and allowed the archivist to continue.

'If it is in secret memos, then one of the war-time *apparatchiks* would have written something about it. If so, then unless they called it by a different name, it would be recorded under these files. I think it's going to take a lot more searching than I realised.'

Like neophytes, they obediently followed Sakharovsky to another section of the archives in the fifth basement floor of the building under Dzerzinsky Square. The room was a claustro-phobic's nightmare. It had a low ceiling and was illuminated by row upon row of bare strips of neon lights, casting a white shroud over the ranks of filing cabinets. They could have been a roomful of Egyptian mummies, undiscovered sarcophagi standing un-disturbed for millennia until the insistence of the modern world broke in on them. The three men walked respectfully through the echoing silence until they came to a room whose door was marked 'Records of Josef Stalin'. Inside the room were further banks upon banks of filing drawers, some large, containing whole files, some small containing card indexes and cross-references.

Like an experienced mountaineer searching for a grip on a cliff face, Sakharovsky knew exactly where to lay his hand. He had lived in this and similar rooms every working day for the past five years. He walked over to a large dusty cabinet set four rows back from the front section and, muttering to himself as though in silent prayer to whatever God it was that held sway over the files, his face lightened as he opened the drawer and started to search through a mass of old and yellowing manila folders. He pulled out a huge bundle, placed them on the table, returned to the drawer and pulled out more, until eventually the table was full. Some he gave to Yezhov, some to Yeszersky and the rest he kept for himself.

'These are the private files which Stalin kept on all matters for 1942. Let's look through these, especially any reference to Petrovsky. Then we'll look at all the other years to 1948.'

'Petrovsky?' asked the minister. 'But he would have been hardly more than a boy in 1942. He would still have been in his twenties. How could he have had any influence over a man like Stalin?'

'Good question,' said the archivist.

'May I answer?' said Yezhov.

The archivist deferred with a nod of his head.

'The source of all Petrovsky's power was his relationship as a young man with Stalin. Stalin somehow spotted him before the war and catapulted him up the ranks.'

'Why?'

'I don't know. But when I was a young man in the NKVD, Petrovsky's name was always whispered in hushed terms. He had Stalin's ear. He was his secretary or something.'

'Correct,' said Sakharovsky curtly. 'But we've got work to do. We're looking for any reference at all to Jericho, Palestine, Middle East … anything like that.'

Four hours later no record or detail of the Jericho Plan had been discovered. They put back the files for the year 1942 and removed those for 1943. After another hour Yezhov found a number of references to the Mediterranean but nothing which identified Palestine or any scheme or plan. The faded yellow pages of smudged type contained details of decisions, conversations, discussions which Stalin had held with members of his cabinet, visiting dignitaries, military men, diplomats and spies, all faithfully recorded by Petrovsky, whose presence was felt throughout every page like an *éminence grise*.

The pace was too slow, so rather than examine each page in detail they checked the heading and discarded what didn't interest them. Two hours later, they had reached the post-war years.

By now all three men were hungry and discouraged and Yezhov was about to suggest that they break for food—he didn't know whether to suggest lunch or dinner. He had completely lost track of time when Yeszersky said, 'Paval. Come. Look at this.'

Yezhov pricked up his ears and Paval came to lean over his friend's shoulder. The three silently read the memo.

'You've found it. You clever bugger. Look at this.'

Minutes of Discussion held 7.30 a.m., July 15, 1947.
Present—J. Stalin
     G.A. Petrovsky
G.A. Petrovsky showed Supreme Commander of Forces and Father of Russia a discussion paper concerning current disposition of Communist Polish Jewish assets who were relocated before war

for covert work within Palestine and possible use as source to benefit future Middle East involvement by CCCP. G.A. Petrovsky informed J. Stalin of value of Jews in Palestine working as fifth column in preparation for UN vote. J. Stalin genuinely gratified and congratulatory. Suggested discussion with Constantine Fyodor Vezhnov and Viktor Poremsky before proceeding further. J. Stalin instructed G. A. Petrovsky to draw up initial plans for total Russification following CCCP backing for creation of State of Israel at expiration of British Mandate. Redefinition of Europe successfully under way. Middle East now to be accorded top priority. Imperative keep identity of all assets involved in covert operation under closest guard. J. Stalin insisted that further check is made to ensure that all details of Wladyslaw Mikolajczyk, in particular, have been fully obliterated, especially connection with place of birth. Newly chosen Hebrew name 'R. Ben Ari' meaning 'Son of Lion' to be used all future contact. Funds to be sent to asset in Jerusalem by way of Bank of Lausanne in Switzerland. All records and traces of asset have been destroyed. Work of Polish Communist sympathisers said to be 'excellent' by J. Stalin. Our agents in Palestine to ensure elimination of all Rawicz residents who have settled there from 1930 onwards as well as elimination of records wherever possible. File confidential memo only. No copies to be taken. Access J. Stalin and G.A. Petrovsky only.

'Russification of Palestine!' said Yezhov.

Sakharovsky shook his head. 'I've always known we had field agents in Palestine but didn't realise why. Not fully. Until now.'

'This memo shows Polish assets being sent into Palestine before the war as some form of undercover agents on a covert mission,' said Yezhov. 'Of course, it was widely known but nobody thought it was part of a plan to make Israel into a Russian client.'

'Of course nobody knew. It was at the very highest level. Stalin and Petrovsky only,' said Yeszersky. 'Now think about the name that's been bandied around these past few days. Before he died Krychkov referred to it, remember. Jericho Plan. What happened at Jericho in the days of the Bible?'

'The walls came tumbling down,' said Sakharovsky.

'The walls came tumbling down,' Yeszersky repeated. 'That's what it's all about.'

Yezhov nodded and smiled. 'My God!' Yeszersky shouted. 'What an unbelievable concept. How absolutely Machiavellian. That evil old bastard ...'

'And fifty years later, it's about to happen,' said Yezhov.

'But why now?' asked Yeszersky. 'Why suddenly today? That old bastard's had decades to pull this off.'

Yezhov smiled at his poet friend, until late in life a man uncontaminated by the cesspool of intrigue.

'Because, old friend, Ben Ari has only recently become Prime Minister of Israel.'

CHAPTER TWENTY-SEVEN

The walls were sweating inside the airless room. Every now and then, a bead of water would trickle down, as though the apartment itself was crying. And the smells! Both inside and outside. Heavy, oily smells. Smells of burning cabbage stuck to the bottom of a frying pan; or of borscht bubbling away, the acrid perfume of purple beetroots seeping through tightly sealed doors. The smells of stale old tobacco and clammy underarms.

They suffered in the name of secrecy. Bolted windows and doors ensured that no one outside could surreptitiously listen in to the conversation. The shades were also shut tight, another obeisance to a paranoia which still dominated the Russian psyche. Miriam held an ageing manila folder to her breasts, as though it were a holy relic, but the atmosphere won out and she used it to fan herself.

She broke the silence: 'I know what you've said, but I just can't believe how easy it was to find.' She was seated in one of the understuffed armchairs in Aleksei's apartment in central Moscow. She could feel every one of the slats and springs which held it together. 'I just think it extraordinary, somehow, that it was … bingo … just there.'

'Bingo?' queried Rabbi Mironov.

Paul smiled. 'Doesn't matter, rabbi.'

Aleksei looked again at the attractive girl and admired the flow of her beautiful neck. He fantasised about the hidden curves of her breasts, modestly shrouded by her expensive jacket. Perhaps this was the sort of woman he would meet in Israel. Or maybe he should migrate to Australia? Who knows?

'Yes, it was surprising. I thought, with the huge volume of files, we would have much greater difficulty. Don't forget that since *perestroika* and the disbanding of the KGB, their files have been picked over by historians looking for hidden answers. I guess we were just lucky.'

'But just to be able to walk in,' Paul said, 'and tell the guard that we were your long lost cousins from St Petersburg. Really!'

'No, sir, that aspect is not surprising really,' Aleksei said. 'Even a few years ago, these files would have been absolutely top secret. Today, under President Abayev, we have little to hide and we historians and archivists are encouraged to search.'

Paul shook his head. 'But why wasn't this file discovered years ago? Think of what it means. Of what's happened today because of it. It's so important'.

Aleksei reached over and gently retrieved the file from Miriam. He held up the dossier containing details about Wladyslaw Mikolajczyk. 'People are interested,' he said, 'but only to find answers to their personal grief and misery. Some time ago, there was talk of a War Trials Commission, but it becomes less likely as time goes by.'

'How did you know where to look?' Paul asked. 'It didn't take you more than a couple of hours.'

'In Stalin's personal papers, I checked files on pre-war Poland. Following certain references concerning pre-war Jews in Communist Party, and because we knew proper name of Mr Ben Ari was Wladyslaw Mikolajczyk, it wasn't all that hard.'

Miriam was still amazed. 'Well you may think it's easy, but I've never seen so many files. And what about all the nightmare stories about the government's ability to bury people and their families? It's a wonder we were able to find one man's files amongst all those millions.'

'Your grandfather was one of the few people left on earth that knew Ben Ari's Polish name,' Paul reminded her. 'Anyone looking for Ben Ari would have missed it.'

When the archivist discovered the file he had hurried his guests out of the building, into the comparative safety of his apartment. No one yet had looked properly inside the dossier.

Aleksei opened it, and said to them: 'Perhaps if I read the Russian, I will translate into English. Rabbi, for you I will read the Russian first, and then the English.'

The group fell silent. It was the culmination of a long and painful search. The denouement that Paul and Miriam had worked so hard to achieve.

The congregation sat, heads lowered, eyes to the floor, listening to the sins of the fathers. Like a priest intoning a lesson, Aleksei began to read.

'What do you mean, it's not here?'

The junior archivist wilted as Minister Ivan Semyonovich Yeszersky gave him a look normally reserved for recidivist agricultural workers demanding a return to the good old days of collective farming. It was not every day that a cabinet minister visited the archives. It was certainly a rare occurrence that the junior clerk got bawled out by somebody of his rank. Struggling for words, he looked again at the three imposing men. He only knew the chief archivist Sakharovsky. 'But sir,' he stammered, 'I'm sorry. I have no idea where the file is. There is no record of it having been taken and … I just don't know. I'm sorry. I'm really sorry. I don't even know if there is such a file.'

'We can assure you that there is,' Yezhov said softly. 'We have been to the alphabetical list kept of Communist Poles, brought over to Russia for Comintern training, and the file that we seek is missing. And there is clear evidence that it has been recently removed.'

'Is there any other area in this filing system where the file of Wladyslaw Mikolajczyk could have been placed?' the minister demanded.

The clerk shook his head. 'Sir, these files …' he waved his hands across the vast basement, '… it would take months, years, to find it, if it had been misplaced.'

'Well, who's been in here recently—say within the past couple of weeks—and had a look at the files?' Yeszersky asked.

'Only researchers and historians. Also Archivist Aleksei Dmitri Karpov came in today on his day off with some relatives.'

'His day off?'

'Yes sir. He wanted to show his visitors around the building. I didn't think anything of it. We often have visitors these days.'

Sakharovsky brought the full weight of his authority down upon the young clerk. 'Visitors? Who were these visitors? Who gave them permission to enter these archives without a permit from me?'

'I don't know who they were, sir. They weren't introduced. One of them was a short fat man with a big grey beard. He looked like a Lithuanian or a Latvian or something ...'

'Or a Jew?' asked Yezhov.

The clerk became excited. 'Yes, sir. Yes, that's it. He was a Jew, no question. And the other two were younger. They were dressed very well. A man and a woman.'

'Were they dressed like foreigners?' The clerk gulped and nodded. 'And did these people talk to you?'

'No, excellency. Archivist Karpov did all the talking. He said that they were cousins from ... St Petersburg, I think, and said he was going to show them over his area of interest. That was all.'

'My friend,' Yezhov said in a much more mellow tone, 'what is Archivist Karpov's address?'

The heat in the apartment was overpowering by the time the young man came to the end of the file. It was a long file, filled with official correspondence, memos, receipts and innumerable cryptic references which no one understood. They were exhausted. And the weight of the atmosphere did nothing to help. They sat back in their chairs, the rabbi's feet hardly touching the floor. Miriam sniffed. A chill was coming on. Nobody wanted to be the first to speak. All were lost in a trance. A nightmare which had come true. The Apocalypse charging mercilessly towards them. It was the middle of the day, but they felt as though they were awakening into a dawn with no light, no warmth—just an awful comprehension, a confirmation of fear.

'I just can't believe it,' Miriam said. 'It's so much worse than I feared. Its hideous. It proves that the man's venal, awful. We have to confront Ben Ari with it to hear what he's got to say before we plaster this all over the newspapers.'

'The dossier doesn't contain everything your grandfather said,' Paul commented. 'There's not a word in here about the pogroms. Surely if he had been involved in planning pogroms it would have been on his file.'

Paul, the observer. Paul, the only one not involved by accident of birth.

Aleksei emerged from his stupor, listened to what the non-Jew had to say and shook his head. 'Maybe. Maybe not. It's difficult to know. Everything else is here. His indoctrination. His record in classes. His associations with other Polish Jews. His achievements. The amount of money given to him to go to Palestine. Who he went with, who his associates were. How the NKVD eliminated opposition to assist him. How it supplied him with secret information so he could show himself to be a good agent. How it developed a network of double agents in Israel which he ran.' The archivist shook his head at the complexity of the plan; at how so much had been done so secretly.

'It's all here,' Paul said once more, tapping the file. 'If he was involved in the pogroms, I think it would have been listed, mentioned somewhere. It's quite possible that he had nothing to do with them. That everything else that your grandfather said was true, but in this one area he was in error.'

Miriam shook her head. 'More likely, if everything Zeida said was true, then so was the fact that Ben Ari was involved in organising pogroms.'

'And just as likely would be pact with Adolf Hitler,' said Rabbi Mironov quietly.

'What?' exclaimed Miriam. Paul stared at the rabbi intently.

'Child. Is history. Stalin make pact with Hitler before Great Patriotic War. Stern Gang, of which Ben Ari was top man, tried to make pact with Hitler. Often I have wondered why. Official reason … something to do with securing homeland for European Jews. But now I think real reason is that Stalin signed treaty with Hitler to keep Russia out of war. Maybe in treaty, Stalin promised Hitler that he could make Palestine Communist state, and then Jews in Palestine will fight against English and on side of Nazis. Maybe Ben Ari and other Communists in Israel try to make this happen. Now it begins to make sense.'

The enormity of Jews forming an agreement with Hitler was more than Miriam could stomach. She averted her gaze from those around her and stared at the floor, fighting back tears of despair. Her training as a lawyer, in which the burden of proof was paramount, was being sorely tested in her disgust.

Rabbi Mironov shook his head. 'If this is case, I think I understand. Is better for Jews to be in Palestine than Europe; but still I cannot believe that Ben Ari leads pogrom and kills Jews. No. You were right about him being Russian spy. This I must agree with. Even forming pact with Hitler to fight English I understand. But a Jew making pogroms, making to kill family and friends. Never has this happened. Not in two thousand years since time Romans kicked out Children of Israel from Judea. No, this is not true. Your *zeida* makes mistake. Sorry for that. But is mistake.'

Paul cut in before Miriam had a chance to respond. Whether the story about the pogroms was true or not, the fact that an Israeli leader tried to make a pact with Hitler defied understanding. 'I think I have to agree with the rabbi, Miriam. Surely it's logical that if Ben Ari did these hideous things, it would have been part of his record. It talks about him going back to Poland to his village, spending a year there. And then returning to Russia before going to Palestine. I can't believe that a record this complete would have omitted something as important as that.'

Miriam stood and walked to the sideboard. The others

looked at her. She picked up a family photograph and studied it carefully. She replaced it, and picked up one of a pair of silver candlesticks, holding them closely so that she could read the inscription. It was written in Cyrillic letters, but she peered carefully, as though understanding every word. Paul watched her movements. She appeared to be dazed, acting without thinking. When she saw the look of concern on his face, she smiled reassuringly.

There was a loud rap on the front door of the apartment. Aleksei jumped in shock. Miriam turned to him and gave him the same reassuring smile she had given to Paul a moment earlier. It didn't help. Both Aleksei and the rabbi looked like trapped animals and Paul was affected by their fear. Calmly, as though in another world, Miriam began to walk to the door. Aleksei jumped up to stop her.

There was another knock, this one louder and more insistent. Aleksei looked helplessly at the rabbi. He did not want to admit his terror. He didn't need to. Guiding Miriam back to her chair, he left to admit the visitors. Rabbi Mironov and Paul listened apprehensively to the conversation outside, which was conducted in muffled Russian. Miriam looked numbly at the walls.

Aleksei walked back into the room, his face white as a ghost, followed by two men; one tall, imposing, a man of power and position, self-assured and commanding; the other shorter, older. Paul and Miriam immediately recognised him as the old man who had interrogated them in Warsaw.

They stood up as the newcomers walked into the room. The old man spoke first, showing no surprise. 'Well, how nice to see you again Mr Sinclair, and you Miss Davis. Congratulations on fooling Valdek. It was resourceful of you, but I was disappointed you didn't fly back to Australia. He was very annoyed.'

If Aleksei and the rabbi were intimidated, Paul showed no such signs to the new arrivals. 'I told you in Warsaw that I intended to find out the truth about Raphael Ben Ari. You wouldn't help me, so I've used Miriam's contacts in the Jewish community to open some doors.'

The moment he said it, Paul realised that he had divulged Aleksei's secret. He could sense Aleksei shrinking from him and wondered what effect his stupidity in exposing the man's Judaism would have on his future.

The tall powerfully built man spoke in English. 'I don't know who you two are. But I am a minister in the Russian government. And this man,' he said, pointing to Aleksei, 'has taken an official file contrary to Moscow Criminal Code 1983. If he gives the file back now I will take no more action.'

'Just a minute,' said Miriam. She had recovered from her earlier trance and seemed not to be intimidated by officialdom, even if it was exercised by a Russian minister. 'This file is public property since the disbandment of the KGB. It is open to scrutiny by bona fide researchers, which is precisely what my Australian friend and I are. If it has been taken wrongly, we will write a letter of apology to the relevant authority, but I should point out that most of the files are already on public view, so your bullying, minister, is falling on deaf ears.'

Rabbi Mironov and Archivist Aleksei looked at her in astonishment. She was the new breed of woman, daughter of a new world they did not yet comprehend.

Yeszersky also turned and appeared to notice her properly for the first time. He bowed courteously and smiled. 'Madam, in Moscow, citizens tend to capitulate in the face of the government. You, I understand, are from Australia. You are like Americans. You don't respect the rank of cabinet minister.'

'Quite the contrary, minister. Of course I respect you. But it's obvious that we know the contents of these files. Rather than take them away, why don't we discuss what we know, share information and work out a plan of action?'

'How much do you know?' asked Yezhov.

Paul smiled 'Oh no, Mr ...' He realised that he still didn't know the old man's name.

'Yezhov,' he said, bowing slightly in studied formality. 'Andrei Alexandrovich Yezhov.'

Paul bowed back, a ridiculous pantomime following the

strains of the last few moments. 'Well, Mr Yezhov. I've fallen for that trick before. None of us is going to say one single thing until you first tell us just what the hell it is that *you* know and what you're doing here.'

Impressed by the confidence of his response, Miriam took a step and stood closer to him.

Yezhov smiled courteously. The art of diplomacy lay in knowing when to reveal information, as well as how much to give away. 'I think, ladies and gentlemen, if we all sit down, perhaps open a few windows, we can sort this thing out.'

Like an automaton, Aleksei did as he was instructed and a cooling breeze blew into the room.

Yezhov continued. 'I think it fair to say, Mr Sinclair, that we are all at approximately the same position of knowledge. Therefore, further discussion would be of mutual benefit. You are, of course, aware that Raphael Ben Ari, who is presently signing a treaty with our esteemed President, was a Polish Communist, born Wladyslaw Mikolajczyk. We know this, because we have just this morning examined Stalin's private files giving us his Polish name. I wish you had told me what it was in Warsaw. It would have saved me so much time.'

'You didn't ask,' Miriam said.

Yezhov bowed his head in self-deprecation. 'Anyway, you took Mikolajczyk's personal files this morning and you must now know that he was taken from his parents at the age of fifteen and educated in the Communist Youth in Stalinist philosophy until he was seventeen, when he returned as a Komsomol officer to his native village …'

'… where he organised pogroms against his own people,' added Miriam.

'Mr Sinclair told me that in Poland but I don't know there's any evidence that he was personally responsible. It's possible, of course, but there's nothing to suggest it, unless it's contained in his files. The Jewish Stalinists in Eastern Europe didn't organise pogroms. They were Zionists. They merely acted as left-wing infiltrators fighting Fascism. I ignored what you told me in Warsaw because I thought you were being hysterical.'

Miriam refrained from commenting.

'What makes you think that he was involved in pogroms?' Yezhov asked.

'We have a photo which shows him leading a group of men against his own village. It's not proof, but it would hold up very well in a court of law.'

'Photo? Where is this photo?' demanded Yeszersky.

Paul looked at Miriam questioningly. She nodded, satisfied that despite his naivety in Poland, he had held two vital pieces of information back from Yezhov—Ben Ari's real name and this photo. He stood and took his wallet out of his back pocket. 'I've been carrying it with me all the way around the world, waiting for the opportunity to confront Ben Ari with it.'

'Did you have this with you in my house in Poland?'

Paul nodded. The old man grinned. 'Interesting. We searched your effects and found no photograph.'

Paul was delighted. 'I glued it to the back of a photograph of my father with artists' paste. It's sticky but non-permanent.'

As Paul fingered through the credit cards to find where he had hidden the photograph, Yeszersky shook his head. 'You won't get near Ben Ari,' he told them. 'This is something which must be done on a government-to-government basis. He won't see you. Show me the photograph and I'll take it to him.'

'No way I'm letting this out of my possession,' said Paul. 'Miriam's grandfather died because of this picture, and the man responsible is going to pay.'

'Young man,' Yezhov interrupted, 'this isn't some western movie, with goodies and badies. Minister Yeszersky is one of Russia's most honourable men. But more to the point, he is a minister. Ben Ari is a prime minister on an official visit. Kings talk with kings, princes with princes. You stand no chance of being given an audience by Ben Ari. Yeszersky here stands at least some.'

Paul glanced at Miriam. She looked angry but Paul realised that the old man was right. Hesitantly, Paul took the photograph out of his wallet and prised it free. He delicately rubbed the surface to remove the glue. It was probably the last time that Paul would need to hide it. He handed it over to Minister Yeszersky. Yezhov stood and walked behind his friend, so he could look at the photo over the minister's shoulder.

Yezhov's face lost its normal impassive look as he viewed the image. His eyes widened. He recoiled.

But the reaction was very different from Yeszersky's. 'It's a photograph of a young man on horseback. So what?'

'But look at the face!' Miriam insisted.

The minister peered closely and noted the birthmark. Even so, he was not impressed. 'So it's probably Ben Ari as a boy. So what?'

'Can't you see the value of this evidence?' Miriam said angrily. 'It shows that he was there, for Christ's sake. He was on a horse leading an attack against his people ... my people ... my grandparents and my family. Can't you see that?' Her voice was raised in pitch as she fought to control her emotions.

'Madam,' said Yeszersky, looking at Miriam with contempt, 'in Russia, we don't jump to these sorts of conclusions. This isn't the time of Stalin with puppet judges. We would require proof before we could accuse Ben Ari of what you're saying. '

Yezhov also turned on Miriam. He spoke for the first time since seeing the photo. 'Miss Davis,' he said, 'I'm somewhat surprised that you of all people can ask us to accept this as proof. Certainly, it's Ben Ari and it opens some very interesting possibilities for future discussion, but all it shows is him in a village on horseback.'

'But look at the background,' said Paul. 'Can't you see the smoke in the village? Ben Ari's leading Cossacks or something against a Jewish *shtetl*.'

Yeszersky burst out laughing: 'Cossacks? Why not Georgians? Or Estonians or Kazaks or Mongols ... or anyone of a dozen different races? Are you serious? What would a Cossack be doing in Poland? Especially before the war?'

Paul flushed at the ridicule. 'I may have been wrong about

the nationality, minister, but instead of laughing, if you look between the houses you can see small images of people who look like Cossacks on horseback. It isn't proof, but it's a strong pointer, isn't it?'

The minister looked more closely.

'And I reckon that's the reason that Miriam's grandfather was killed. They tried to get this photo back.'

'Well,' said Yeszersky, 'to me it's not proof. But for other reasons, I will try to see Prime Minister Ben Ari tonight, and this photo is something I will discuss with him.'

'Aren't we all forgetting something?' Miriam asked. 'All these murders; Ben Ari's visit to Moscow; the disruption of the conference to bring peace to Jerusalem. It's all happened. Whatever Ben Ari has been planning all these years is already under way. We're probably too late to stop it.'

Yezhov smiled. 'Things are in progress, my dear, but it may not be too late. Right now, information is the key to power. Let me continue with my analysis of Ben Ari's file. After he returned from Poland he was financed to go to Palestine along with hundreds of other refugees from Nazi Europe, and there he continued to be financed through his activities as an anti-British terrorist in the Stern Gang. In 1951 he was asked by David ben Gurion to be one of a handful of men to participate in the new Israeli secret service, Mossad. Along with Isser Harel he recruited other young men and women and was responsible for uncovering a large number of Soviet agents operating in Israel. Information supplied to him by his MGB control. Then he entered politics and recently became Prime Minister.'

Yeszersky turned in surprise to Yezhov. 'How in the hell did you know all that about the spies? You haven't seen the file yet. That's why we came.'

'I assume that's what the file says.'

'Well, the file only goes up to 1952 but it certainly accords with everything you said up until then,' Miriam conceded.

'What I've said about his later career is an assumption, of course, although it would be recorded somewhere. And if my guess is correct, those files won't be hidden in a public place. In fact, they would be known only to one man.'

'But what's the purpose of all this?' Miriam asked. 'I mean, why did Stalin finance a Communist Pole in Israel? Why trust a Jew when he was so anti-Semitic?'

'Because, my dear, of a scheme called the Jericho Plan. Russia has always wanted a year-round warm-water port for its ships. If you have a look at a map you'll see why. The Baltic ports can't guarantee to be open all the year round. And Vladivostok is thousands of miles from Europe. Stalin once conceived of a plan to buy a corridor of land from Turkey on either side of the Bosporus, but that was just too foolish. Then a certain Marshal Petrovsky …'

The rabbi gasped. Yezhov continued: 'A certain Marshal Petrovsky submitted to Stalin a plan to Russify Palestine when the British pulled out. He had been quietly putting assets in place since before the war. Stalin jumped at it.'

'How in God's name can you know these things?' Yeszersky said.

'I have worked with Petrovsky all my life. I know him and the way he thinks. It's just the type of thing he would have planned. Imagine how it would have benefited Stalin. His new navy could compete in the Mediterranean and the Atlantic on equal footing with the Americans and the British. Of course, it was in complete defiance to the deal Stalin had made at Yalta. He made fools of his allies by taking half of Europe. Having access to the Mediterranean would have given him equal prominence in the Western hemisphere. That's why he was one of the first to vote for the creation of the State of Israel in 1948.'

'Now Israel is giving all those facilities to Russia,' said Paul. 'Stalin's concept is exactly, to the word, what President Abayev announced yesterday.'

Yezhov smiled. 'Now you know the Jericho Plan.'

'It's horrible, evil,' said Miriam, shaking her head at the enormity of the subterfuge.

Rabbi Mironov spoke for the first time since Yezhov and

Yeszersky had entered the room. He breathed deeply, as though intoning some mystic incantation, and muttered words in Russian which neither Paul nor Miriam understood.

Yezhov translated: 'And it came to pass that the people shouted with a great shout, and the walls of Jericho fell down flat, so that the people went up into the city and they took the city.'

'Joshua, Chapter 6, Verse 20,' the rabbi said. But he was not content to stop there. 'Also Joshua. Another verse about Ben Ari. "And Joshua the son of Nun sent out of Shittim two men as spies secretly, saying, 'Go view the land, even Jericho'." Book of Joshua, Chapter 2. Ben Ari is bad man. Very bad man, I think.'

There was a long-drawn-out silence. 'I think it's about time I spoke to Ben Ari,' said Yeszersky. 'I think if he knows what we know, we might be able to save Russia some considerable embarrassment.'

'I don't understand,' said Miriam. 'Russia stands to gain enormously out of this. Why are you trying to stop it? Why do you care about Ben Ari? It's to Russia's advantage, isn't it?'

The minister considered her comments before answering. 'When the Russian people have no bread or meat on their tables, why are we wasting billions of roubles on a foreign adventure? Russian leaders now have the duty to care for the Russian people, not to build up again to an arms race or make agreements like this with foreigners. First we must help ourselves. With this treaty, we are helping the old guard to return.'

Paul began to speak, but then held back. The minister looked at him quizzically, wondering what the young man was going to say. Finally, Paul formulated his thoughts. 'Minister, I think it's important that I come with you. As a journalist, and as somebody close to this whole dismal matter, I want to talk to Ben Ari myself. Would you allow me to join you?'

The minister shook his head. 'Some things are person-to-person. Some things are government-to-government. First I will go and speak to Ben Ari. I'll talk to him, tell him he is an evil man, confront him and tell him about the photo. It'll come as a shock. He may agree to meet you. But Ben Ari will not speak to me if you're there. Do you understand?'

The two men left. Paul, Miriam and the two Russians sat silently for a long time. Miriam got up and walked to the windows to breathe fresh air.

Later that night, Paul telephoned Jack Muir but again Jack put him straight through to Max Mandle.

'Mr Mandle, I've got a story which I'm going to send you tomorrow. I can't go into details over the phone but you have to believe that tomorrow morning I'm going to fax you a story that will make the front page of every newspaper of yours around the world.'

There was a silence. 'Have you got the facts, Sinclair?'

'Mr Mandle, I'm doing everything in my power to meet this very important friend of yours in Moscow tonight. A Russian cabinet minister is going to try to set up an appointment. This story is bigger than the one I told you about in Sydney. It's a quantum leap bigger …'

'Cut the hyperbole, Sinclair. Just tell me what you've got.'

'Sorry. There's no way I'll tell you over an open line. Miriam and I have been subjected to assassination attempts, and …'

'What? Are you serious?'

'In Warsaw …'

'You were there?' interrupted Mandle. 'We carried the story but there was no mention about you or the girl being involved. Jesus fucking Christ, man, why didn't you send us an eye-witness story?'

'Miriam was in hospital. I didn't even think of the newspaper. But why didn't you know that we were there? It doesn't make sense. Unless …'

'Unless what?'

'There's an old man who claims he's looking after our interests. Yezhov. He used to be with the KGB but I think he's retired now. I don't know much about him.'

'KGB? Bombing? What the hell are you talking about, Sinclair? Look, I want you and your girl out of there. This is beyond journalism. I'm not going to have your lives on my conscience. I want you out of there now. I want you to get a plane and …'

'Mr Mandle, when you read my story, you'll realise why I have to stay on.'

'I want those details now. You hear me? What evidence have you got about …?'

Paul took a deep breath, and hung up. He reckoned that nobody hung up on Mandle and survived. He'd done it twice.

Yeszersky had never met Raphael Ben Ari. He had seen pictures of him on television but it wasn't until they were alone in the room that he realised how imposing he was. The Russian Goliath towered over the Israeli David, but Ben Ari's essence made him potent beyond his stature. Years of public life had given Yeszersky the confidence of authority, but in the fussily decorated hotel room it was he who felt subservient.

Yeszersky managed to force an unscheduled meeting on Ben Ari by hinting at a private matter of grave importance which needed to be dealt with immediately. The Israeli agreed, perhaps a little too readily, and asked Yeszersky to come to his hotel suite that night. When Yeszersky arrived he was met at the door by Ben Ari. As agreed, no one else was present.

'Minister, please come in and sit down. I've heard much about you from President Abayev. Now, tell me, what's so important that you had to see me under these circumstances?'

'Prime Minister, I am a Russian minister, and loyal to my people. Loyal to them before the government. So the information which I've recently come upon is of deep concern to me. It may be in the interests of those people in control of Russia at the moment but it is not in the interests of the Russian people.'

Ben Ari nodded briefly, willing the minister to continue. His face showed no emotion, of concern or distress.

'I have been given information about you being an agent for the NKVD and later for the KGB. I know of your friendship with Marshal Petrovsky.'

Ben Ari interrupted. 'Petrovsky? I've never met him. I know of him, of course, but I assure you we've never met.'

The Russian would not allow himself to be sidetracked. 'I know you have introduced the Russian army to Israel and that your people are against this move. I suspect you are trying to make Stalin's Jericho Plan come into effect today.'

He paused, looking at Ben Ari for some reaction, but he was disappointed. Ben Ari's eyes did not even flicker, his mouth did not curl in anger, his face was unchanged.

'I am disgusted with you and what you have done,' Yeszersky continued, 'and I will make everything I know public unless you reject this treaty with Russia and go back to Israel, and never return to this country again.'

Yeszersky had played most of the cards in his deck. He had one other ace to play, but not yet. Now he must wait for Ben Ari's reaction. If he had miscalculated, his career would be at an end; but his career was probably at an end anyway.

Ben Ari sat quietly looking at Minister Yeszersky. The only perceptible movement was a minute nod of the head. It could have been an agreement, a resignation to the facts or the nervous movements of an old man's body. A smile appeared on the Prime Minister's face. He stood up and walked over to the drinks cabinet beside the lounge suite and poured a Chivas Regal for himself. Perhaps deliberately, perhaps in forgetfulness, he failed to offer Yeszersky a drink.

'You've been a very busy man,' said the Prime Minister. 'I could of course deny the whole thing, throw you out on your ear and make you a laughing stock throughout Russia. After all, since I announced I was seeking an accommodation with Russia, my critics have been condemning me as a Communist lackey. Your allegations don't surprise me. Tell me, what proof do you have?'

'Please be assured I'm not so stupid that I've come here with-out any proof. The information I've been given comes from a very reliable source. I've got all the proof I need.'

The Prime Minister sipped his whisky. His self-confidence terrified Yeszersky. The man had formidable courage.

'Aren't you just a little bit afraid of the danger you place yourself in by trying to expose me? Even if you do have evi-dence, my denial will carry much more weight than your allegations.'

'Do you think I am stupid … Wladyslaw Mikolajczyk?'

Yeszersky had played his ace. The very mention of the name was proof positive. It was a name which the Prime Minister had not been called for fifty years; a name which was last used by his mother and father, his sisters and brothers, his rabbi, *Melamud*, and the people on his *shtetl* in Poland. It was a name he had buried half a century earlier, along with his heritage.

He clutched at the arm of a chair and sat down heavily.

'Who else knows?'

'Enough people to guarantee my safety.'

Ben Ari nodded silently, allowing the words to sink in. 'Allow me to consider your proposal overnight. If I am still in Russia tomorrow night you will know I have rejected it. If I leave in the morning, I will say that irreparable damage has been done to the treaty. You will know you have succeeded in your wishes to see the end of me.'

Yeszersky nodded and stood up. He had no intention of shaking the man's hand but couldn't resist letting loose a part-ing shot. 'I just don't understand how you, as a Jew, could have organised pogroms against your own people.'

Ben Ari's face registered further shock. 'Pogroms? What are you talking about? I have never organised a pogrom. Are you crazy?'

'I've seen a photograph of you on a horse, looking and smil-ing at the people who were killing the Jews in your village.'

Ben Ari slumped back into his chair. 'I swear before God I've no idea what you're talking about.'

'The picture shows you clearly. In the background is a village on fire. There are horsemen riding through the village, killing people. Like the Cossacks did in pogroms in the Jewish Pale of Settlement.'

Ben Ari frowned, narrowing his eyes as if to peer through the veils which covered half a century. Slowly the picture became clear.

'Are you mad? These were my people. You're talking about Chelmnitz. This is before the war. I remember the day. I could never forget it.'

Yeszersky stopped and turned to face the Israeli. Had he been wrong about this?

'I had ridden along the river back to the village with some Komsomol comrades. As we got to the brow of the hill I saw that there were horsemen in the village, on the rampage. I turned to my comrades and told them that we had to fight. They didn't want to. They were too scared. But I forced them. We drew our weapons, swords and guns, and went into the madness. We didn't try to kill Jews, you fool! We tried to stop the Fascists. I myself was wounded, as were two of my comrades. My horse stumbled and I fell to the ground. When I woke up, the village was in ruins. There were dead and dying lying all around me. I did what I could but it was useless. My family was murdered. So were my friends.'

The Prime Minister fidgeted in his chair, moved by emotion, the pain of memory. 'I'd only just come back from Russia. I was a Komsomol officer, proud of what Stalin had achieved. I wanted to help my people fight Fascism and expansionism. How could you think that I could have done such a thing? My God, is that what you think? How could you ever accuse me of murdering my family and my friends?'

Yeszersky flushed in embarrassment. In his heart he knew that he had made a hideous mistake. That this damned photo had led everyone down the wrong track, especially the pathetic boy and girl from Australia.

Ben Ari looked flustered and bewildered. Yeszersky hesitated before speaking.

'Prime Minister, if you take my advice it is important for you to tell this to a young Australian reporter and his girlfriend. They have the photo and will use it as evidence against you. It's necessary for you to confront them. I think you are a man who made a very bad error in trying to make Israel a Communist country. However, I am sorry I have accused you of leading a pogrom. I know Russia's history and I know something of the history of Poland. Our endemic anti-Semitism created these things. I believe you were fighting the Fascists. I'm sorry it's turned out like this, but the real issue is the Jericho Plan. It is an obscenity in today's world.'

But Ben Ari was distracted. 'Minister, I respect your candour, but it is my right to follow my own political path. However, you must believe me when I say that my views have never led me to harm the Jews. I must speak to these people and stop them claiming that I am a murderer.'

Yeszersky nodded. 'The boy's name is Paul Sinclair …'

'And the girl's name is Miriam Davis,' said Ben Ari.

Yeszersky was stunned. How did he know? The Russian grasped for the door handle, and tried to leave the room. How in God's name did he know?

'I'll phone them,' Ben Ari said.

Yeszersky left the hotel suite in a state of utter confusion. There were forces beyond his control in operation. He hated the intrigues and shadows into which his life had fallen. There was no question that now Abayev would ask him to resign. And he would do so willingly. How happy he would be to return to Moscow University and bury himself in the genius of those literary giants upon whose shoulders he stood.

But if Ben Ari did not return to Israel, what was Yeszersky to do then? The Russian people must be told. He must betray his friend, his mentor, Mikhail Abayev. Then there would be no returning to Moscow University. He would be a man disgraced, a man without friends, position or protection. What were they called in the West? … Whistleblowers, that's it. In America they even paid whistleblowers. But that was America.

In Russia there was an old saying: 'The people are happiest when they know the least.'

Should he say anything? Would it make a jot of difference? What did it matter to an Uzbek or a Mongol or a Kazakhstani that Russia and Israel had formed a treaty? Their lives wouldn't change. They would still struggle to survive.

He emerged onto the street desperate to share his fears about Ben Ari with his old friend Yezhov. As a man who had spent his life manipulating others Yezhov would have a better idea of what the hell was going on.

An hour later, Yeszersky and Yezhov were sitting in the minister's office, trying to understand where they had gone wrong. How had Ben Ari known about Paul Sinclair and Miriam Davis? It didn't add up.

There was the dulled sound of marching feet in the carpeted corridor outside, and an officious knock on the door. Yezhov and Yeszersky looked at each other, but before the minister had a chance to speak, the door was flung open, and standing there was Colonel Lubin. Behind him in the corridor were stern-faced guards. Colonel Lubin, followed by four soldiers, walked into the office uninvited. On the few previous occasions that Yezhov had visited the Kremlin, Colonel Lubin's impassive face had recently begun to smile. The smile had gone.

'Comrade Yezhov, Comrade Yeszersky, it is my painful duty to arrest you for treason in the name of the President and the people of the Republic of Russia. I am ordered to remove you and order you to accompany me to the Kremlin cells, where you will be dealt with by people other than me, thank God.'

Yeszersky's chest swelled with anger. He started to rise out of his chair, but Yezhov held his arm in restraint. 'Not now, dear friend. Don't blame Colonel Lubin for a decision of President Abayev.'

'May I at least phone my wife and children and say goodbye …?'

Colonel Lubin avoided the minister's eyes. 'I regret to inform you that your family are not there …'

'You bastards,' said Yeszersky.

Slowly the two men stood, and were marched out of the office, sandwiched between the guards. It was a scene which hadn't been played out in Russia for nearly half a century, and if anybody had been there to witness it, it would have brought back memories of the days when Josef Stalin lifted his finger and a thousand people fell down dead.

Yezhov marched beside Colonel Lubin towards the stairs in the sombre building.

'So, colonel,' said Yezhov, 'this is an order which you have decided to obey.' Lubin marched ahead, jaw clenched, staring with shame at the ground.

CHAPTER TWENTY-EIGHT

Paul put his hand over the telephone mouthpice and smiled at Miriam's anxious face. 'Told you it'd be okay. He wants to speak to you.' He handed the telephone to her.

Cautiously she took it and said, 'Hello …'

'Miriam? This is Raphael Ben Ari. How are you?'

Miriam was disarmed. 'Fine, thank you,' she mumbled.

'My dear, Ivan Yeszersky has just this minute left my hotel suite. He told me your *zeida*'s story. Oh! my darling. Your poor *zeida*. Some of what he said was right. But some was so very, very wrong. Sure, I was a little *mumzer* back then. I was an idealist, a wild young hothead. And yes, I did join the Communist Party, something I've been regretting since the day I set foot in *Eretz Yisroel*. But Miriam, pogroms? Me? Surely in your heart of hearts, you can't believe that.'

Miriam stammed, ' I … but Zeida … he told me …'

'Miriam, listen to me. In the morning, I'll send over my driver to bring you and Paul to see me. I owe you an explanation. You deserve to be told what really happened after everything you've been through. Please. Indulge an old man. A *landsman* of your *zeida*'s. Please have a cup of coffee with me.'

'Yes, yes I'd like to.' Miriam put the phone down. It was Paul's turn to look quizzical. Miriam smiled at him. Her face showed the first signs of relaxation in weeks.

'So?' asked Paul.

'Oh, Paul. It was just like talking to Zeida.'

After an early breakfast, they waited for the car, wavering between confidence and doubt. Miriam's sense of ease after last night's phone call had evaporated with the reality of the morning. The knock on the door came when Miriam was in a trough of apprehension.

'It's all right. Come on, it's almost over.'

Paul walked to the door and opened it. Standing there was a man who simply said, 'Mr Sinclair?'

'Yes.'

'I am Dmitri. I was told to take you and the lady to Prime Minister Ben Ari.'

Paul turned to Miriam and smiled reassuringly but saw the look of consternation on her face. 'Darling, trust me, this is going to be all right. If you don't want to come, you stay here and I'll go on my own.'

'No, I've got to face this. I should come.' She was still plagued by doubt.

The three walked towards the waiting Zil limousine. A man in a charcoal grey suit sat in the front passenger seat. He opened his door as they emerged from the hotel and stood on the pavement to greet them.

'Mr Sinclair, Miss Davis, good morning. I'm sorry it's so early but the Prime Minister has a very busy schedule today. My name is Aaron. I'm Mr Ben Ari's aide.'

Paul shook hands but Miriam held back. Aaron opened the back door to usher them into the car.

'How far away is the hotel in which Ben Ari is staying?' Miriam asked.

'Prime Minister Ben Ari thought that this should remain a highly confidential discussion,' said Aaron. 'He suspects his hotel room is not sufficiently secure and has asked if he can talk to you in a house just outside of Moscow in the Pasternak Woods. It's a short drive from here, maybe thirty minutes.'

Miriam froze. 'Why … what's the reason for this?'

Dmitri turned to her with a reassuring smile. 'Miriam, please, you must understand, Moscow is full of ears. Especially at the moment. This house has been used by the Prime Minister for private meetings in the past few days. It was checked by Mossad only this morning.'

'I don't give a damn. I'm not driving into any woods to meet Ben Ari.'

Aaron shook his head. 'I promise it is completely safe.'

'I don't care about your promises. I'm not driving out of Moscow to meet him and that's final.'

Paul turned on her. 'Miriam, the house was checked out by Mossad this morning, for God's sake.'

'Paul, we only have his word for that,' she said.

Dmitri and Aaron looked at her in surprise. 'Miriam, if you feel unsure of yourself, please stay here. There's no need for you to come.'

Paul walked over and put his arm around her shoulder. 'Why don't you wait here, Miriam. I don't want you to come if you think it's a risk.'

As the four of them stood on the pavement, Miriam turned to Paul in sorrow. 'We're dealing with ... well, you *know* what we're dealing with.' She pointed to the network of small scars on her arms and face. 'Look at these. Do you think these are just my imagination?'

'But Miriam, last night after you spoke to Ben Ari, you were ...'

'That was last night,' she interrupted.

'If you don't want to go, don't. But I'm going and that's final,' Paul said.

Paul got into the back seat of the car. Dmitri looked at Miriam and smiled. He walked around the front of the Zil and got into the driver's seat. Aaron got into the front seat, leaving her alone on the pavement. Standing there on her own with three men looking at her from the car, Miriam felt alienated and alone. The car didn't drive away, it waited for her to make up her mind. More than anything, she hated being pressured. In anger, she opened the door, got into the back seat and slammed the door shut.

She turned to Paul. 'I think you're the most naive man I've ever known,' she hissed.

'You've got to stop thinking everyone's your enemy. You're becoming paranoid, Miriam. You're acting like a victim.'

'I am a victim. I've been a victim all my life.' She stared at him. 'And now, so are you.' But Paul didn't respond. Miriam turned away to look at the Moscow streets.

The grandiose centre of Moscow silently gave way to prosaic suburbs which gave way to greener and greener landscapes. The car drove along a narrow country lane and then turned into a smaller one. In the distance, Miriam could see dark, sombre houses. The car drove deeper into the woods. Left, left again, then right and finally left onto a narrow track. The trees grew denser, more menacing. They stopped at the foot of a gentle ridge. She looked questioningly at Aaron.

'Where are we?' she asked.

'Because we don't want to attract attention, the car will be parked here. Mr Ben Ari is ready to meet you. He spent the night in a dacha. It's just over the brow of that hill. It'll only take you a few minutes to get there. And there are a few rules. Please don't record anything on a tape recorder or make notes of conversations. Do you agree?'

Paul nodded. 'Yes, that's fine.'

They got out of the car and walked up the small hill, across the crackling bracken, leaves and twigs in the dense forest. Miriam felt estranged from Paul as well as her surroundings.

The leaden green-grey light of the forest contrasted with the softness and warmth of the daylight in the outside world. There was no birdsong. Miriam felt a sharp pain in her ankle and looked down to see that her foot had become trapped in a knot of roots. Bits of bracken were sticking to her stockings. She bent down and freed herself. As she walked further, her feet sank into the spongy earth.

They reached the top of the incline and Miriam was seized once more by an acute feeling of vertigo. She clutched at Paul to prevent herself from falling. Paul turned and put his arm around her. He looked for the pathway to the house. There was no pathway. There was no house. Just acres and acres of the intense claustrophobic forest.

He looked around and glanced down to the foot of the hill. Miriam did not notice, but held tightly to him, trying to control her giddiness. Paul saw a large oblong hole in the ground, whose recently turned earth glistened with dampness. Miriam followed his eyes and gasped. Her mind flashed to nightmare scenes of open graves in which Jews were thrown in the concentration camps of Nazi Germany. Her knees weakened as she clutched Paul's arm tighter for its security. The more she stared downwards, the more the ground appeared alive, as though the floor of the forest was a morass, moving and writhing. Full of darkness and despair. She tried to clear her mind, but the ground beneath her feet wouldn't stay still. She swayed and gasped as the bracken and undergrowth took on the appearance of a huge nest of snakes slithering towards her; or of demons, inching forward to grab her ankles and pull her beneath the ground.

Paul's mouth opened as though he were about to say something, but no sound came out. He shook his head. He understood what was going on only too well. And yet he was mystified. What was happening? Where was Ben Ari?

The noise of crackling twigs behind and below them made them both turn around. Dmitri stood ten feet behind them, levelling an assault rifle. Before Paul could open his mouth to ask what was going on, Dmitri cocked the Kalashnikov, the bolt sliding with murderous precision.

It was like being in a dream which suddenly turned into a nightmare. As Miriam saw the gun, her mind flashed to other scenes from her past. Times when she was in danger in her youth. When she fell from the roof of the garage at her grandfather's house; when she was attacked late one night walking through the streets of Sydney; when a boyfriend turned violent and tried to rape her. Warm urine filled the inside of her pants and ran down her leg. She was too terrified to move. Her knees would have buckled had she not been clutching onto Paul. Standing in front of her was her dybbuk. Her devil. He was below her, waiting to drag her into the earth, to suffocate her.

'Now you will both take off your clothes, please, and throw them down to me,' Dmitri's voice was soft, gentle.

A thought ran through Miriam's mind, so stupid that for the few remaining moments of her life she wondered how she could have thought it. Her underwear was wet. She couldn't die with dirty knickers.

Paul's throat dried up. His shock at seeing the gun and the graves had overwhelmed him. He forced himself, in a voice deeper than his own, to say, 'Now, listen you ...'

The driver let loose a short burst of automatic fire which whistled between their heads, so close they could feel the concussion waves.

Dmitri was unmoved by their fear. It was as though he was uninvolved with the action. The drama was Paul and Miriam's. Not his. He was the one with power. 'Now you will take off your clothes, please,' he repeated, still in a gentle manner.

Miriam became light-headed. So this was the dybbuk from the old country her grandfather had always warned her of. He didn't have horns or a tail. Just a gun in his hands.

She slowly began to undress, her wet skirt clinging to her stockings. As she slid them down, she prayed that no-one would see the urine on her legs. She unbuttoned her jacket. She behaved mechanically, obeying his commands.

Paul was still immobile. His eyes were wide, wild, staring at the man and shaking his head in incomprehension. Miriam found her voice and began to whimper. 'No,' she said. 'Please God, no. Don't let this happen. Please don't do this to us. Please.'

Like her Jewish forebears in the camps fifty years earlier, she numbly obeyed the obscene commands to disrobe before the final act of barbarity.

Paul slowly began to move. In his novel, his hero would have done something, but the author just couldn't think what to do. He wanted to protect himself but he was rooted to the spot. All he could do was move his arms. His legs were as heavy as lead. He prayed that the earth would open up and remove him from this horror.

He slowly unbuttoned his jacket and removed his tie. Miriam

turned around to him. Her face was flushed red with embarrassment. Her wet knickers. Everyone would see her wet knickers. She began to giggle at the absurdity, then to laugh hysterically until Dmitri let out a further burst of bullets. Miriam screamed. 'It's like Auschwitz,' she said. 'It's like Treblinka. Oh God. He's stripping us before he sends us into the gas chambers. Oh God! What are we going to do? He's going to kill us.' She fell to her knees but Paul put his arms around her trembling body and lifted her up. She was shaking violently now. There were no tears. Her body was too numbed to cry … it convulsed in waves of fearful hysteria. She shook her head and screamed, 'No!'

A flock of blackbirds wheeled into the air with the screaming and the gunfire, crowing in disdain.

But Dmitri just stood there impassively. 'Now you will take off your clothes, please.' He let off another burst of automatic fire. This one ripped into the ground in front of their feet.

Its violence shook them out of their hysteria. Mechanically, with the resignation of those who know they are about to die, they slowly took off the rest of their clothes. Miriam and Paul stood there in their underwear. The driver could not help but admire Miriam's beauty. 'And these too,' he said, pointing the barrel of the Kalashnikov towards their underwear.

Modestly, Miriam turned towards Paul as she removed her bra and pants. She looked at her lover. Naked, standing terrified in the bracken and dead undergrowth of the forest, they held each other closely, delicately. A man and a woman in a life-giving embrace. Two young people who would never know the joys of family life, of children, of old age, of security.

Miriam nuzzled her head into the nape of Paul's neck. She had forgotten the anger and the quarrels. All she could remember was his warmth and softness. The bullets of the Kalashnikov ripped through their bodies. Their pink flesh sprouted jets of blood as the force of the bullets lifted them off their feet and deposited them into the cold earth.

Their dead bodies rolled down the gentle hill and fell headlong into the double grave. Aaron joined the gunman. He was carrying a bottle. They walked down to the dead couple. The smell of death and explosives hung in the pure air of the forest. They kicked the bodies into position, one beside the other, until they lay deep in their earth coffin.

Carefully, so as not to injure himself, Aaron withdrew the glass stopper from the sulphuric acid, and poured the contents over Miriam and Paul's faces and fingertips. By nightfall, any resemblance to human beings would be removed, their skin and cartilage turned to a blackened pulp. With the butt of the Kalashnikov, Dmitri smashed Paul's mouth, then Miriam's. What had once been attractive faces now looked like obscene gargoyles, lying white and shocked, gaping at the trees. It took no more than ten minutes to cover the grave with earth and to sprinkle twigs and leaves and bracken over it. Passers-by would walk happily over the buried bodies without realising the horror beneath the ground.

Carefully they gathered Paul and Miriam's clothes, and with an expert precision, Aaron rifled through Paul's jacket to find the picture. It wasn't in his pockets, so he opened the man's wallet, removed two hundred dollars and the picture. He put the picture in his pocket to give to his boss when he reported back to him later that night. The money he would share with his colleague.

Marshal Petrovsky would be particularly happy with the turn of events. Paul's and Miriam's behaviour had been so eccentric in the past month that friends would not even wonder what had happened to them until several weeks had passed.

As Dmitri and Aaron drove back to Moscow, they talked amiably about soccer and the price of vodka. It never occurred to either that, because she had no relations left in the world, there would be no one to say a mourner's *kaddish* for Miriam.

CHAPTER TWENTY-NINE

Max Mandle sat at his opulent desk, scratching in between his big toe and its smaller companion. Athlete's foot was the bane of his life. No matter how much cream he applied, the painful reddening never seemed to be cured. He was disturbed by the telephone, which he picked up in anger.

'Yes?' he snarled. It was his apologetic secretary. 'I'm sorry, sir, but it's Prime Minister Ben Ari calling you from Moscow.'

'Put him on … Raphael, how are you?'

The reply came back seconds later, distant and echoing.

'My dear friend. I'm well, how are you?'

'Fine, fine. Tell me, how are things in Russia?'

'More to the point, how is the world taking our decision to sign a treaty with the enemy?'

Mandle grinned. The two men were old friends but even so, the undiplomatic conversation was silly over an open phone line. 'I think the world will accept it soon enough. The way we're playing it here is that you've made a pragmatic move. That because of the Americans, it was one of the few moves left open to you.'

Raphael Ben Ari appreciated the assistance. 'Oh, by the way, I sorted out that little problem that you told me of. Many thanks for your help.'

'Not a worry. Glad I could be of assistance.'

Mandle grimaced. What a shame two nice young people had to die. He never, for one minute, thought they'd get that close. But Ben Ari had handled it well. He felt relaxed talking to Ben Ari, a world away from his own financial problems. Somehow the troubles of the world were easier to deal with than satisfying the demands of bankers. He joked with his old friend. 'Now you're in Russia, any chance you could stop off in Poland and say hello to the old country?'

'I think that would be a little bit divisive.'

Ben Ari had reverted to being a politician. Mandle did not expect the change, especially from a man he had known most of his life.

'You must excuse me now, Max. President Abayev and I still have to confirm details from yesterday. I wanted to thank you for your help and tell you that everything has been tidied up.'

'Let's meet next month in Jerusalem,' said Mandle.

'*L'shana haba b'Yerushalyim,*' said Ben Ari, and hung up.

Mandle shook his head in confusion. It was an odd thing to say. They were the final few words of the Passover service, recited by Jews throughout the world to commemorate the exodus of the children of Israel from the bondage of being slaves in Egypt. It had been a paean of the desire by the Jews in the Diaspora since time immemorial. It had been recited by husbands to wives, fathers to children, for a time longer than the collective memory of the race. Yet for all that, for all its importance as a symbol between one Jew and another, it was a very odd thing for his friend to have said and he frowned as he returned the phone to its cradle.

He regretted the necessity of killing his reporter and the girl. Sinclair was brilliant to have got as close to his comrade as he had. What a reporter! But the photo … that was a massive breach in security, for which heads would roll. For fifty years, it hadn't surfaced, so its safe recovery after so long was a matter of fortune rather than skill.

Max looked at his watch and decided to call it a day. It had been a long, hard one, full of drama and business complications. What he looked forward to was the pleasure of a long bath, a well cooked meal and perhaps the company of a young secretary, which one of his *apparatchiks* no doubt could organise.

Four hours later, Mandle was preparing to climb into bed after satisfying every need his body had. His chef had excelled himself and the young woman—obviously an experienced whore—

had worked long and hard to assist him with his erection …
something he found increasingly difficult to maintain as the
stresses and strains of business drained his libido.

His silk pyjamas felt deliciously cool in the centrally-heated
apartment which overlooked the grandiose sweep of Sydney
Harbour, the Opera House, and the famous coat-hanger
Bridge.

He had just picked up a novel and settled down when the
intercom buzzed. In annoyance, he got out of bed and grabbed
it.

'Yes,' he said, abruptly.

'Sorry to disturb you, Mr Mandle. I've got an urgent letter
from Mr Jack Muir. I have to give it to you straight away.'

Mandle grumbled and pressed the intercom, telling the messenger to come up to the penthouse. Irritated that his office
would disturb him, he put on his dressing gown. Not even his
nights were sacrosanct. He was used to working fifteen hour
days—he had done so since he was a boy—but with his position in life, his evenings should have been respected by his staff.

A minute later there was a knock on the front door. Mandle
padded through the corridors of his apartment and opened it
in annoyance. Standing there was a middle-aged man dressed
in a business suit. He was clearly not a messenger.

'Hello, Max,' said the stranger. He was a man of medium
height, thin shoulders. Average.

A pain gripped Mandle's chest and made him feel giddy. He
knew who this man must be. It was the cold, confident look
in his eye, so different from the subservience of those with
whom he came into daily contact.

'Can I come in?'

Mandle struggled to speak. It was his nemesis. He knew it.
It was as if he was looking at death itself. He tried to shut the
door quickly, but the man's reflexes were like sprung steel. He
whipped his foot into the crack and shouldered himself past
Mandle.

'Get out, or I'll call my staff …'

'Max, don't be so silly. You're alone here.'

'What do you want? Who sent you? Mossad? The CIA? Who?'

'Max,' said the visitor, 'I'm a businessman. You wouldn't expect me to give confidential information like that away, would you? Who would ever trust me in the future if I did? Now come on, don't make this more difficult for yourself than it has to be. Your papers carry stories about burglaries and break-ins and murders every day. You should know the rules.'

The man forced himself into the loungeroom. Mandle backed away from him, his jaw slack in fear. There was a gun in the drawer next to his bed.

'Just go into your bedroom for a minute, will you Max? There's something I've got to get. Then we'll go back into the loungeroom and have a quick chat. I don't like doing this sort of thing without talking first. Some people do, mind you. But I find it, I don't know, a bit heartless.'

Mandle found the strength to speak. 'Who sent you?' he repeated. Could he get to the gun before this maniac? 'Tell me please, who sent you?' The gunman indicated for Max to stop talking and walk into the bedroom. The intruder immediately went to the drawer nearest the window, opened it and withdrew the gun.

'It's interesting, isn't it,' he said when they had returned to the loungeroom. 'Here I was, getting ready to take my wife to the ballet, and I get this urgent job. Not your average one, mind you, but with full details of your apartment, your security. Someone's planned this carefully, Max. Very professional, I call it.'

Mandle looked at the man in sheer terror. All his escape routes had been closed off. The gunman stood and walked over to Max, pointing the gun at his head.

'Do you like ballet, Max? We were going to see "Swan Lake". I love it myself. It's very graceful but there's lots of strength required.'

Mandle stared with incomprehension at the lunatic sitting opposite him. Ballet?

'Still, can't sit here gossiping all night, pleasant as it is. I promised the wife I'd meet her on the forecourt of the Opera House. Goodbye Max.'

Putting the gun to Mandle's head, he shot him once through the brain. He put Mandle's hand on the gun's handle, finger over the trigger and laid out it to mimic suicide. The assassin left the apartment, checking every detail, and as he entered the lift he took off his rubber gloves. He wondered what the next edition of the paper would say about its owner's suicide.

'Funny,' thought the killer, 'they never seem to cry out, or fight, or say anything. They just seem to sit there.'

♜♜♜

Marshal Petrovsky sat alone in his Moscow apartment deeply absorbed in his thoughts. Even the music playing on the CD did not connect with his consciousness.

In his hand was a glass of brandy. It was one of his greatest pleasures. He would have liked to be sexual again, but it took too much time and effort. And it would divert him from the more important things at hand. Things which he only had a limited time left to complete. Sex created more problems than it solved. He had had enough sex in his life. Now he was content with the quiet comfort of old friends and good brandy.

In many ways, it was better that Bukharin had been killed. It saved the old man the unpleasant task of arranging it himself. Nor was he particularly concerned about the dozen other men and women who had perished in the inferno which followed the massive car bomb. Some of them, certainly the most senior, were scheduled to die anyway. A long-term operation like the Jericho Plan required maximum security and couldn't be compromised by too many loose tongues. If it meant that a few people had to go for the good of the many, then so be it.

Best of all, that meddling fool Yezhov and the poet Yeszersky were locked away from activities. Yezhov would die, of course. Yeszersky? Well, maybe Petrovsky could re-introduce some of the old psychiatric hospitals. A couple of months of injections and he wouldn't do too much talking. Nor write more poetry. But that was a minor loss. There was too much poetry. Not enough action. Then he would be returned to his wife and family, maybe to do some sightseeing in their new home in the frozen north. Petrovsky smiled. He grudgingly admired Yezhov. Placing that bug in the TV tuner had been inspired. Pity Yezhov had to die. Still, couldn't be sentimental.

And then there were the Arabs. Why had they blown up the communications centre? They were like loose cannons on the deck of a ship. Petrovsky would never be able to understand them. Their fanaticism had been of unexpected assistance, so why look a gift horse in the mouth, as they say.

Once more the Arabs had miraculously, accidentally, facilitated the smooth running of the operation. He neither knew nor cared what their objectives were. Now that Abayev and Ben Ari had signed the concordat and Russian experts were preparing to relocate into Israel, the Jericho Plan was at an end. Clean, clear and precise. Just the way Josef Stalin liked things. The rest would follow smoothly as Israel became more and more dependent upon Russia's might.

Marshal Petrovsky lifted his glass and toasted his long-dead mentor.

Had it been a mistake to terminate Mandle?

For fifty years since his training as a Komsomol youth, Max Mandle had been of enormous assistance. As Petrovsky was private, Mandle was public. He had slowly built his empire, constantly railing in his newspapers on three continents against the evils of Communism. Keeping the Cold War going just as effectively as Joe McCarthy in America. But his recent stupidity in business dealings was making too many people look too deeply into his affairs. With the information that he knew about Ben Ari, the danger of his knowledge far outweighed his future usefulness. It would be just like a Jew to sell the information to get himself out of trouble, thought Petrovsky. The final straw, the reason he had to die, was because he contacted Ben Ari and told him what that boy and girl were up to. How stupid. What a breach of security. He should have told his KGB control. Let the professionals handle it. But no! The Jews conspired together. Well, not any longer.

Petrovsky thought back over all the details to ensure that no outstanding matters were overlooked. He hated loose ends. That damned memo Yezhov found had come as a surprise. He'd thought that every conceivable file had been removed immediately after Stalin died. He'd clearly instructed the two operatives what files to take. Obviously those idiots … what were their names? … had failed to follow his orders. Still, it was too late now, no matter what was discovered. The clock had been put back. Things were as they should be.

Satisfied, he relaxed back into his armchair, a smile on his face. He had an orderly mind. Now the Russian presence was re-established in the Middle East, he could turn his attention to reclaiming the Kurile Islands which had recently been handed back to Japan. Then he would send a few divisions to Georgia to defend the Russian minorities, and perhaps send in some ex-KGB troops to protect dispossessed Russians in the Baltic States.

Marshal Petrovsky looked at the telephone, impatient for President Abayev to call.

EPILOGUE

Twelve months after Prime Minister Ben Ari returned from Moscow, events in Israel had settled back to normal. Russian advisers quietly worked side-by-side with Israeli scientists, technologists, nuclear power specialists, and armed forces personnel.

Only in certain areas was there remaining friction. One was within the ranks of the Israeli secret service organisation, Mossad, where Russian technicians were favoured by the Israeli military government over its own nationals. This was because the Russians fed the Israelis with the latest mapping data from their Voyuz satellite systems, giving up-to-the-second reconnaisance on the disposition of American and Arab forces' ground and air movements.

Danny Navar sat in his musty office, smelling the black smoke from the cheap Russian cigarette that was constantly dangling from the lips of the GRU lieutenant to whom he was answerable. In fairness, the man had tried to befriend him, offering him vodka every five minutes, and inviting him and his wife over to the Russian compound for drinks. But Danny was always busy with other social arrangements.

The lieutenant got up, grunted, and announced he was going to the toilet. As he did whenever he was alone, Danny opened the bottom drawer of his filing cupboard, and pulled out a worn, dog-eared manila folder, labled the *meshuggeneh* file. He rifled through the countless pages, until he came to one which he knew by heart. Miriam Davis had sent it twelve months ago, almost to the day. Miriam Davis. Danny wondered who she was. What she looked like. What had become of her. And why the hell, when something could have been done about it, she hadn't gone to the newspapers with that photograph. Then maybe none of this would have happened.

⚔⚔⚔

It was twelve months to the day since Paul Sinclair had been reported missing by Jack Muir. The Moscow police were diligent in their attempts to find him and Miriam Davis, but they were unable to trace their movements after they left the Hotel Dvor, accompanied by two unidentified men, entered a black limousine, probably a Zil, and drove northwards out of the city.

No one had seen or heard from either Paul or Miriam since. It was fair to assume that after twelve agonising months they were now certainly dead.

In that time, the world had become a cold and inhospitable place, and the disappearance of the two Australians in Russia had faded from public view.

Paul's relatives had been contacted, and his apartment cleared by a cousin, who put all Paul's effects into storage, pending a coroner's inquest and certification of death. This finality could take another year. Nonetheless, Jack managed to obtain a court order to view Paul's safe deposit box in Westpac's George Street branch.

The ex-editor of the now defunct *National* stood in the safe deposit cellar with an officer of the court, a solicitor for the bank and the bank manager. Officiously the manager of the safe deposit room signed the bank's receipt of the letter of consent and handed it to the bank's solicitors. He then turned and walked towards a metal cage, which he opened by pressing a series of numbers on a computer pad. Jack fancifully thought that there might be a creak as the door opened, reminiscent of dark woods, graves and Dracula coming back to life. But the door, like everything else in the bank, was well-oiled.

Less than a minute later, the manager came back with a small brown box. With a key from his desk, he opened it gingerly, as though it might contain high explosives. The box contained hardly anything … just a will, shares in publicly listed companies, a gold ring and a photo.

The photo was sepia brown.

Jack knew from his dead friend just how important it was.

ACKNOWLEDGMENTS

In this book, I have occasionally positioned real people in fictional situations, and fictional people in real situations, both geographical and historical. Wherever this has happened, the accuracy of certain historical or geographical facts may have suffered—I ask the reader to be lenient. Naturally, I am responsible for all the fiction which appears. The experts I list below only commented upon the facts. I have approached many people for their help in putting this book together. Everyone has given of their time and effort selflessly, but among those who have aided me, I would particularly like to thank the following people.

Selwa Anthony, my literary manager and good friend.

Nikki Christer, my publisher, without her encouragement this book would never have found its way into print.

Carl Harrison-Ford, my editor, whose keen eye and perception I will always treasure.

Garth Nix, my in-house editor at HarperCollins, whose intelligent and imaginative comments, along with his technical knowledge, proved invaluable.

Angelo Loukakis and **Terry Kitson** of HarperCollins, whose support and advice were always first-rate.

Daniel Nevo, whose knowledge of Israel and its customs is encyclopaedic.

Piotr Longchamps de Berier, who guided me through the tortuous pathways of Polish history, geography and pronunciation.

Dr Michael Dodd, who assisted me with certain aspects of medicine, as they relate to some fictional episodes.

Professor Aubrey Newman, of the Holocaust Studies Department of Leicester University, England.

Robin Walsh of Macquarie University, Sydney, who assisted me in tracking down arcane sources and whose superb ability to fight his way through the jungle of a university library is second to none.

Jenny Roberts, whose good nature and eye for detail were invaluable when I lost the thread.

Dr Peter Veitch, Dr Tony Wicks and Dr Roger Neuberg, in the United Kingdom, for their assistance in keeping this novel alive.

Shirley Weiss and **Sigrid Freeman** for their assistance in idiomatic Yiddish.

Linda and **Jack Berman** for their support and forbearance.

But especially to **Georgina**, my daughter, who painstakingly read every word and advised me on the latest aspects of Israeli culture.

As always, to **Eva, Jonathan, Raphael** and my mother for their patience during the long, lonely hours spent in writing this book.

ABOUT THE AUTHOR

Alan Gold was born in Leicester, England, in 1945. His first career was as a journalist, working all over Europe, in France, Germany, Italy, Spain and the United Kingdom.

Shortly after the Six Day War, Alan moved to Israel to work as a correspondent for an international news agency. Later, he lived on a kibbutz in the Carmel Mountains, before moving to Tel Aviv and Jerusalem, where he worked as a feature writer.

In 1970, he met his Czech-born wife, Eva, and travelled to her home in Australia to marry. After working for some years as a stockbroker, Alan founded an industry award-winning marketing consultancy, which he has been running for the past fifteen years.

He now divides his time between his marketing consultancy and writing. He is currently at work on another thriller.